The Murder Book

the murder book

jonathan kellerman

headline

First published in 2002
by HEADLINE BOOK PUBLISHING

10 9 8 7 6 5 4 3 2 1

ISBN 0 7472 6701 4 (hardback)
ISBN 0 7472 6986 6 (trade paperback)

Typeset in Plantin by
Letterpart Limited, Reigate, Surrey

Printed and bound in Great Britain by
Mackays of Chatham plc, Chatham, Kent

HEADLINE BOOK PUBLISHING
A division of Hodder Headline
338 Euston Road
London NW1 3BH

www.headline.co.uk
www.hodderheadline.com.

To Faye

the murder book

one

The day I got the murder book, I was still thinking about Paris. Red wine, bare trees, gray river, city of love. Everything that happened there. Now, this.

Robin and I flew in to Charles de Gaulle airport on a murky Monday in January. The trip had been my idea of a surprise. I'd pulled it together in one manic night, booking tickets on Air France and a room at a small hotel on the outskirts of the Eighth *arrondissement*, packing a suitcase for two, speeding the 125 freeway miles to San Diego. Showing up at Robin's room at the Del Coronado just before midnight with a dozen coral roses and a *voilà!* grin.

She came to the door wearing a white T-shirt and a hip-riding red sarong, auburn curls loose, chocolate eyes tired, no makeup. We embraced, then she pulled away and looked down at the suitcase. When I showed her the tickets, she turned her back and shielded me from her tears. Outside her window the night-black ocean rolled, but this was no holiday on the beach. She'd left L.A. because I'd lied to her and put myself in danger. Listening to her cry now, I wondered if the damage was irreparable.

I asked what was wrong. As if I had nothing to do with it.

She said, 'I'm just . . . surprised.'

We ordered room-service sandwiches, she closed the drapes, we made love.

'Paris,' she said, slipping into a hotel bathrobe. 'I can't believe you did all this.' She sat down, brushed her hair, then stood. Approached the bed, stood over me, touched me. She let the robe slither from her body, straddled me, shut her eyes, lowered a breast

1

to my mouth. When she came the second time, she rolled away, went silent.

I played with her hair and, as she fell asleep, the corners of her mouth lifted. Mona Lisa smile. In a couple of days, we'd be queuing up as robotically as any other tourists, straining for a glimpse of the real thing.

She'd fled to San Diego because a high school chum lived there – a thrice-married oral surgeon named Debra Dyer, whose current love interest was a banker from Mexico City. ('So many white teeth, Alex!') Francisco had suggested a day of shlock-shopping in Tijuana followed by an indeterminate stay at a leased beach house in Cabo San Lucas. Robin, feeling like a fifth wheel, had begged off, and called me, asking if I'd join her.

She'd been nervous about it. Apologizing for abandoning me. I didn't see it that way, at all. Figured her for the injured party.

I'd gotten myself in a bad situation because of poor planning. Blood had spilled and someone had died. Rationalizing the whole thing wasn't that tough: innocent lives had been at stake, the good guys had won, I'd ended up on my feet. But as Robin roared away in her truck, I faced the truth:

My misadventures had little to do with noble intentions, lots to do with a personality flaw.

A long time ago, I'd chosen clinical psychology, the most sedentary of professions, telling myself that healing emotional wounds was how I wanted to spend the rest of my life. But it had been years since I'd conducted any long-term therapy. Not because, as I'd once let myself believe, I'd burned out on human misery. I had no problem with misery. My other life force-fed me *gobs* of misery.

The truth was cold: once upon a time I *had* been drawn to the humanity and the challenge of the talking cure, but sitting in the office, dividing hour after hour by three quarters, ingesting other people's problems, had come to *bore* me.

In a sense, becoming a therapist had been a strange choice. I'd been a wild boy – poor sleeper, restless, overactive, high pain threshold, inclined to risk-taking and injuries. I quieted down a bit when I discovered books but found the classroom a jail and raced through school in order to escape. After graduating high school at sixteen, I bought an old car with summer-job cash, ignored my mother's tears and my father's scowling vote of no-confidence, and left the plains of Missouri. Ostensibly for college, but really for the threat and promise of California.

Molting like a snake. Needing something *new*.

Novelty had always been my drug. I craved insomnia and menace punctuated by long stretches of solitude, puzzles that hurt my head, infusions of bad company and the delicious repellence of meeting up with the slimy things that coiled under psychic rocks. A racing heart jolted me happy. The kick start of adrenaline punching my chest made me feel alive.

When life slowed down for too long, I grew hollow.

But for circumstance, I might've dealt with it by jumping out of airplanes or scaling bare rocks. Or worse.

Years ago, I'd met a homicide detective and that changed everything.

Robin had put up with it for a long time. Now she'd had enough and, sooner rather than later, I'd have to make some kind of decision.

She loved me. I know she did.

Maybe that's why she made it easy for me.

two

I n Paris, clichés are just fine.

You leave your hotel, step out into the winter drizzle, walk aimlessly until you find yourself at a café near the Jardin des Tuileries where you order overpriced baguettes and grainy, French-press coffee, then move on to the Louvre, where even during the off-season the lines prove daunting. So you cross the Seine on the Pont Royal, ignoring the motor din that washes the bridge, study the murk of the water below, try the Musée d'Orsay and murder your feet for a couple of hours, sucking in the fruits of genius. Then, deeper into the grubby side streets of the Left Bank, where you press yourself into the all-in-black throng, and laugh inwardly at an imagined wheezy accordion soundtrack overpowering the burping motor scooters and the whining Renaults.

It was early afternoon, near a shop in St Germain, when it happened.

Robin and I had stepped into a dark, narrow men's haberdashery with a window full of aggressive neckties and slouching mannequins with pickpocket eyes. The rain had been coming in fitful bursts all day. The umbrella we'd cadged from the hotel concierge wasn't generous enough to shelter both of us and we each ended up more than half-wet. Robin didn't seem to mind. Her curls were beaded with droplets and her cheeks were flushed. She'd been quiet since we'd boarded the plane in L.A., sleeping for most of the flight, refusing dinner. This morning, we'd woken up late and barely talked. During the walk across the river, she seemed distracted – staring off at nothing in particular, holding my hand, then dropping it, then grabbing again and squeezing hard, as if scrambling to cover for some infraction. I put it down to jet lag.

The St Germain stroll led us past a private school where beautiful, chittering adolescents spilled out onto the sidewalk, then a bookstore where I'd intended to browse until Robin pulled me into the clothing store, saying, 'These are good silks, Alex. You could use something new.'

The store peddled menswear, but smelled like a nail salon. The shop girl was a skinny thing with hacked-up hair the color of eggplant rind and the anxiety of a new hire. Robin took a while thumbing through the goods, finally found me a very blue shirt and an extravagant red-and-gold tie of heavy weave, got my nod, asked the girl to wrap it up. Aubergine Tresses scurried to a back room and returned with a stout, cardiganed woman in her sixties who sized me up, took the shirt, and returned moments later brandishing a steaming iron in one hand and the garment in the other – newly pressed, on a hanger, shielded by a clear plastic bag.

'Talk about service,' I said, as we returned to the street. 'Hungry?'

'No, not yet.'

'You didn't touch breakfast.'

Shrug.

The stout woman had followed us out and was standing in the doorway of the shop. She looked up at the sky dubiously. Checked her watch. Seconds later, thunder clapped. Flashing us a satisfied smile, she went back inside.

The rain was harder, colder. I tried to draw Robin under the umbrella but she resisted, remained out in the open, raised her face and caught the spray full force. A man scrambling for cover turned to stare.

I reached for her again. She continued to balk, licked moisture from her lips. Smiled faintly, as if enjoying a private joke. For a moment I thought she'd share it. Instead, she pointed to a brasserie two doors up the street and ran in ahead of me.

'Bonnie Raitt,' I repeated.

We were at a tiny table tucked in a corner of the clammy brasserie. The restaurant floor was a grubby mesh of white tile and the walls were cloudy mirrors and oft-painted brown woodwork. A clinically depressed waiter brought us our salads and wine as if

5

service was harsh penance. Rain washed the front window and turned the city to gelatin.

'Bonnie,' she said. 'Jackson Brown, Bruce Hornsby, Shawn Colvin, maybe others.'

'Three-month tour.'

'At least three months,' she said, still avoiding my eyes. 'If it goes international, it could stretch longer.'

'World hunger,' I said. 'Good cause.'

'Famine and child welfare,' she said.

'Nothing nobler.'

She turned to me. Her eyes were dry and defiant.

'So,' I said. 'You're an equipment manager, now. No more guitar-making?'

'There'll be luthiery involved. I'll be overseeing and repairing all the gear.'

I'll, not *I'd*. *One-vote election, nothing tentative.*

'When exactly did you get the offer?' I said.

'Two weeks ago.'

'I see.'

'I know I should've said something. It wasn't – it dropped in my lap. Remember when I was at Gold-Tone Studios and they needed those vintage archtops for that retro Elvis video? The tour manager happened to be in the next booth, watching some mixing, and ended up talking.'

'Sociable fellow.'

'Sociable woman,' she said. 'She had her dog with her – an English bulldog, a female. Spike started playing with her and we started talking.'

'Animal magnetism,' I said. 'Is the tour dog-friendly, or do I keep Spike?'

'I'd like to take him along.'

'I'm sure that'll thrill him no end. When do you leave?'

'In a week.'

'A week.' My eyes hurt. 'Lots of packing ahead.'

She lifted her fork and pronged dead lettuce leaves. 'I can call it off—'

'No,' I said.

'I wouldn't have even considered it, Alex, not for the money—'

'Good money?'

She named the figure.

'Very good money,' I said.

'Listen to what I'm saying, Alex: that doesn't matter. If you're going to hate me, it can be undone.'

'I don't hate you, and you don't want it undone. Maybe you accepted the offer because I made you unhappy, but now that you've committed yourself, you're seeing all kinds of positives.'

I craved argument but she didn't answer. The restaurant was filling, drenched Parisians seeking shelter from the downpour.

'Two weeks ago,' I said, 'I was running around with Milo on Lauren Teague's murder. Hiding what I was doing from you. I was stupid to think this trip would make a difference.'

She pushed salad around. The room had grown hotter, smaller; scowling people crowded tiny tables, others stood huddled at the doorway. The waiter began to approach. Robin repelled him with a glare.

She said, 'I've felt so alone. For a while. You were gone all the time. Putting yourself in *situations*. I didn't bring up the tour, because I knew you couldn't – shouldn't be distracted.'

She rolled the side of a small fist along the table rim. 'I guess I've always felt that what you do is important and that what I do is . . . just craft.' I started to speak but she shook her head. 'But this last time, Alex. Meeting with that woman, seducing her. Planning a damned *date* in order to – your intentions were good, but it still came down to seduction. Using yourself as a . . .'

'Whore?' I said. Thinking suddenly about Lauren Teague. A girl I'd known a long time ago, from my quiet job. She'd sold her body, ended up head-shot and dumped in an alley . . .

'I was going to say "lure." Despite all we've had together – this supposed enlightened *relationship* we've got, you go about your own business . . . Alex, basically you've built this whole other life from which I'm excluded. From which I *want* to be excluded.'

She reached for her wineglass, sipped, made a face.

'Bad vintage?'

'Fine vintage. I'm sorry, baby, I guess it just comes down to timing. Getting the offer exactly when I was so down.' She grabbed my hand, squeezed hard. 'You love me, but you left me, Alex. It made me realize how alone I'd been for so long. We both were. The difference is, you enjoy going it alone – you get high on solitude and danger. So when Trish and I started talking and she told me she'd heard about my work – my reputation – and all of a sudden I realized I *had* a reputation, and here was someone offering me great money and the chance for something of my own, I said yes. Just blurted it out. And then driving home, I panicked, and said, *What did you just* do? And told myself I'd have to renege and wondered how I'd do it without looking like an idiot. But then I got home and the house was empty and all of a sudden I didn't *want* to renege. I went out to my studio and cried. I still might've changed my mind. I probably *would've*. But then you arranged that date with that tramp and . . . it felt completely right. It still does.'

She looked out the rain-clouded window. 'Such a beautiful city. I never want to see it again.'

The weather remained gray and wet and we kept to our room. Being together was agonizing: suppressed tears, edgy silences, too-polite chit-chat, listening to the rain tormenting the dormer windows. When Robin suggested we return early to L.A., I told her I'd try to change her ticket but I'd be staying for a while. That hurt her but it also relieved her and the next day when the cab showed up to take her to the airport, I carried her bags, held her elbow as she got into the taxi, paid the driver in advance.

'How long will you be staying?' she said.

'Don't know.' My teeth ached.

'Will you be back before I leave?'

'Sure.'

'Please be, Alex.'

'I will.'

Then: the kiss, the smile, trembling hands concealed.

As the taxi drove away I strained for a look at the back of her head – a tremor, a slump, any sign of conflict, regret, grief.

Impossible to tell.

Everything moved too fast.

three

The break came on a Sunday – some young smiley-faced, ponytailed guy I wanted to punch, arriving with a large van and two paunchy roadies wearing black *Kill Famine Tour* T-shirts. Ponytail had a Milk-Bone for Spike, high fives for me. Spike ate out of his hand. How had the bastard known to bring the treat?

'Hi, I'm Sheridan,' he said. 'The tour coordinator.' He wore a white shirt, blue jeans, brown boots, had a narrow body and a clean, smooth face full of optimism.

'Thought that was Trish.'

'Trish is the overall tour manager. My boss.' He glanced at the house. 'Must be nice, living up here.'

'Uh-huh.'

'So you're a psychologist.'

'Uh-huh.'

'I was a psych major in college. Studied psychoacoustics at UC Davis. Used to be a sound engineer.'

How nice for you. 'Hmm.'

'Robin's going to be part of something important.'

'Hey,' I said.

Robin came down the front stairs with Spike on a leash. She wore a pink T-shirt and faded jeans and tennis shoes and big hoop earrings, began directing the roadies as they loaded her valises and her toolboxes into the van. Spike looked stoned. Like most dogs, his emotional barometer is finely tuned and for the last few days he'd been uncommonly compliant. I went over and stooped to pat his knobby French bulldog head, then I kissed Robin, and recited, 'Have fun,' and turned my back and trudged up to the house.

She stood there, alongside Sheridan. Waved.

9

Standing at the door, I pretended not to notice, then decided to wave.

Sheridan got behind the wheel of the van and everyone piled in behind him.

They rumbled away.

Finally.

Now, for the hard part.

I started off determined to maintain my dignity. That lasted about an hour and for the next three days I turned off the phone, didn't check with my service or open the curtains or shave or collect the mail. I did read the paper because news coverage is heavily biased toward the hopeless. But other people's misfortunes failed to cheer me and the words danced by, as foreign as hieroglyphics. The little I ate, I didn't taste. I'm no problem drinker but Chivas became a friend. Dehydration took its toll; my hair got dry and my eyes creaked and my joints stiffened. The house, always too big, expanded to monstrous proportions. The air curdled.

On Wednesday, I went down to the pond and fed the koi because why should they suffer? That got me into a scut-work frenzy, scouring and dusting and sweeping and straightening. On Thursday I finally collected my messages. Robin had called every day, left numbers in Santa Barbara and Oakland. By Tuesday, she sounded anxious, by Wednesday, confused and annoyed and talking fast: the bus was headed for Portland. Everything was fine, Spike was fine, she was working hard, people were being great. *Iloveyouhopeyou'reokay.*

She called twice on Thursday, wondered out loud if I'd gone off on a trip of my own. Left a cell-phone number.

I punched buttons. Got: *Your call cannot be completed.*

Just after 1 P.M. I put on shorts and a workout shirt and sneakers, began stomping up Beverly Glen facing the traffic, easing into a clumsy jog when I felt loose enough, ending up running harder and faster and more punishingly than I'd done for years.

When I got home, my body burned and I could barely breathe. The mailbox down at the bridle path that leads up to the front gate was stuffed with paper and the postman had left several packages on the ground. I scooped it all up, dumped the batch on the dining-room table, thought about more Scotch, drank a half-gallon of water instead, returned to the mail and began sorting listlessly.

Bills, ads, solicitations from real estate brokers, a few worthy causes, lots of dubious ones. The packages were a psychology book I'd ordered a while back, a free sample of toothpaste guaranteed to heal my gums and feed my smile, and an eight-by-twelve rectangle wrapped in coarse blue paper with DR A. DELAWARE and my address typed on a white label.

No return information. Downtown postmark, no stamps, just a meter. The blue paper, a heavy linen rag so substantial it felt like cloth, had been folded neatly and sealed tightly with clear tape. Slitting the folds revealed another snug layer of wrapping – pink butcher paper that I peeled away.

Inside was a three-ring binder. Blue, pebble-grain leather – substantial morocco, thumbed, grayed and glossy in spots.

Stick-on gold letters were centered precisely on the front cover.

THE MURDER BOOK

I flipped the cover to a blank, black frontispiece. The next page was also black paper, encased in a stiff plastic jacket.

But not blank. Mounted with black, adhesive corner pockets was a photograph: sepia-toned, faded, with margins the color of too-whitened coffee.

Medium shot of a man's body lying on a metal table. Glass-doored cabinets in the background.

Both feet were severed at the ankles, placed just under ragged tibial stumps, like a puzzle in partial reassembly. No left arm on the corpse. The right was a mangled lump. Same for the torso above the nipples. The head was wrapped in cloth.

A typed caption on the bottom margin read: **East L.A., nr Alameda Blvd. Pushed under a train by common-law wife.**

The facing page featured a shot of similar vintage: two sprawled gape-mouthed bodies – men – lying on a wooden plank floor, angled at forty degrees from each other. Dark stains spread beneath the corpses, tinted deep brown by age. Both victims wore baggy pants with generous cuffs, plaid shirts, lace-up work boots. Extravagant holes dotted the soles of the man on the left. A shot glass lay on its side near the elbow of the second, clear liquid pooling near the rim.

Hollywood, Vermont Ave. Both shot by 'friend' in dispute over money.

I turned the page to a photo that appeared less antique – black-and-white images on glossy paper, close-up of a couple in a car. The woman's position concealed her face: stretched across the man's chest and sheathed by a mass of platinum blond curls. Polka-dot dress, short sleeves, soft arms. Her companion's head rested against the top of the car seat, stared up at the dome light. A black blood-stream trickled from his mouth, separated into rivulets when it reached his lapel, dribbled down his necktie. Skinny necktie, dark with a pattern of tumbling dice. That and the width of the lapel said the fifties.

Silver Lake, near the reservoir, adulterers, he shot her, then put the gun in his mouth.

Page 4: pale, naked flesh atop the rumpled covers of a Murphy bed. The thin mattress took up most of the floor space of a dim, wretched closet of a room. Undergarments lay crumpled at the foot. A young face stiffened by rigor, lividity pools at the shins, black-thatched crotch advertised by splayed legs, panty hose gathered to midcalf. I knew sexual positioning when I saw it so the caption was no surprise.

Wilshire, Kenmore St. Rape-murder. Seventeen-year-old Mexican girl, strangled by boyfriend.

Page 5: **Central, Pico near Grand, 89 y.o. lady crossing street, purse snatch turned to head-injury homicide.**

Page 6: **Southwest, Slauson Ave. Negro gambler beaten to death over craps game.**

The first color photo showed up on page ten: red blood on sand-colored linoleum, the green-gray pallor that marked escape of the soul. A fat, middle-aged man sat slumped amid piles of cigarettes and candy, his sky-blue shirt smeared purple. Propped near his left hand was a sawed-off baseball bat with a leather thong threaded through the handle.

Wilshire, Washington Blvd near La Brea, liquor store owner shot in holdup. Tried to fight back.

I flipped faster.

Venice, Ozone Avenue, woman artist attacked by neighbor's dog. Three years of arguments.

. . . Bank robbery, Jefferson and Figueroa. Teller resisted, shot six times.

. . . Strong-arm street robbery, Broadway and Fifth. One bullet to the head. Suspect stuck around, discovered still going through victim's pockets.

. . . Echo Park, woman stabbed by husband in kitchen. Bad soup.

Page after page of the same cruel artistry and matter-of-fact prose.

Why had this been sent to me?

That brought to mind an old cartoon: *Why not?*

I thumbed through the rest of the album, not focusing on the images, just searching for some personal message.

Finding only the inert flesh of strangers.

Forty-three deaths, in all.

At the rear, a black end page with another centered legend, similar stick-on gold letters:

THE END

four

I hadn't talked to my best friend in a while, and that was fine with me.

After giving the DA my statement on Lauren Teague's murder, I'd had my fill of the criminal justice system, was happy to stay out of the loop until trial time. A wealthy defendant and a squadron of paid dissemblers meant that would be years away, not months. Milo had remained chained to the details, so I had a good excuse for keeping my distance: the guy was swamped, give him space.

The real reason was, I didn't feel like talking to him, or anyone. For years, I'd preached the benefits of self-expression but *my* tonic since childhood had been isolation. The pattern had been set early by all those bowel-churning nights huddled in the basement, hands over ears, humming 'Yankee Doodle' in order to block out the paternal rage thundering from above.

When things got rough, I curled like a mollusk into a gray pocket of solitary confinement.

Now I had forty-three death shots on my dining-room table. Death was Milo's raw material.

I called the West L.A. detectives' room.

'Sturgis.'

'Delaware.'

'Alex. What's up?'

'I got something I thought you should see. Photo album full of what look like crime-scene photos.'

'Photos or copies?'

'Photos.'

'How many?'

14

'Forty-three.'

'You actually counted,' he said. 'Forty-three from the same case?'

'Forty-three different cases. They look to be arranged chrono-logically.'

'You "got" them? How?'

'Courtesy the US Postal Service, first-class, downtown cancella-tion.'

'No idea who might've favored you with this.'

'I must have a secret admirer.'

'Crime-scene shots,' he said.

'Or someone takes very nasty vacations and decided to keep a scrapbook.' The call-waiting signal clicked. Usually I ignore the intrusion, but maybe it was Robin from Portland. 'Hold for a sec.' *Click.*

'*Hello*, sir,' said a cheerful female voice. 'Are you the person who pays the phone bill in the house?'

'No, I'm the sex toy,' I said, and reconnected to Milo. Dial tone. Maybe he'd gotten an emergency call. I punched his desk number, got the West L.A. civilian receptionist, didn't bother to leave a message.

The doorbell rang twenty minutes later. I hadn't changed out of my running clothes, hadn't made coffee or checked the fridge – the first place Milo heads. Looking at portraits of violent death would make most people lose their appetites, but he's been doing his job for a long time, takes comfort food to a whole new level.

I opened the door, and said, 'That was quick.'

'It was lunchtime, anyway.' He walked past me to where the blue leather binder sat in full view, but made no move to pick it up, just stood there, thumbs hooked in his belt loops, big belly heaving from the run up to the terrace.

Green eyes shifted from the book to me. 'You sick or something?'

I shook my head.

'So what's this, a new look?' A sausage finger aimed at my stubbled face.

'Maintaining a leisurely shaving schedule,' I said.

He sniffed, took in the room. 'No one chewing at my cuffs. El Poocho out back with Robin?'

15

'Nope.'

'She's here, right?' he said. 'Her truck's out front.'

'You must be a detective,' I said. 'Unfortunately, false leads abound. She's out.' I pointed to the book. 'Check that out while I forage in the larder. If I can find anything that hasn't petrified, I'll fix you a sandwich—'

'No thanks.'

'Something to drink?'

'Nothing.' He didn't budge.

'What's the problem?' I said.

'How do I put this delicately,' he said. 'Okay: you look like shit, this place smells like an old-age home, Robin's truck is here but she isn't and my bringing her up makes your eyes drop to the floor like a suspect. What the hell's going on, Alex?'

'I look like shit?'

'To euphemize.'

'Oh, well,' I said. 'Better cancel the photo shoot with *In Style*. And speaking of photography . . .' I held the book out to him.

'Changing the subject,' he said, squinting down at me from his six-three vantage. 'What do they call that in psychologist school?'

'Changing the subject.'

He shook his head, kept his expression mild, folded his arms across his chest. But for spring-loaded tension around the eyes and mouth, he looked at peace. Pallid, acne-pitted face a bit leaner than usual, beer gut light-years from flat but definitely less bulge.

Dieting? On the wagon, yet again?

He'd dressed with uncommon color harmony: cheap but clean navy blazer, cotton khakis, white shirt with just a touch of fray at the neckline, navy tie, brand-new beige desert boots with pink rubber soles that squeaked as he shifted his weight and continued to study me. Brand-new haircut, too. The usual motif – clipped fuzzy at the sides and back, the top left long and shaggy, multiple cowlicks sprouting at the crown. A black forelock hooked over his pockmarked forehead. The hair from his temples to the bottoms of too-long sideburns had denatured to snow-white. The contrast with the black hair on top was unseemly – Mr Skunk, he'd taken to calling himself.

'Spiffed and freshly barbered,' I said. 'Is this some new-leaf

16

thing? Should I not attempt to feed you? Either way, take the damn book.'

'Robin—'

'Later.' I thrust the blue album at him.

He kept his arms folded. 'Just put it back down on the table.' Pulling out a pair of surgical gloves from the sets, he encased his hands in latex, studied the blue leather cover, opened the book, read the frontispiece, moved on to the first photo.

'Old,' he murmured. 'The tint and the clothes. Probably someone's creepy collection from the attic.'

'Department shots?'

'Probably.'

'A home collection pilfered from the evidence room?'

'Cases get filed away, someone gets itchy-fingered, who's gonna notice if one shot per file gets lifted.'

'A cop?'

'A cop or a civilian ghoul. Lots of people have access, Alex. Some of them like the job because they dig blood.'

' "The murder book," ' I said. 'Same title as an official case file.'

'Same color, too. Whoever sent this knows procedure.'

'Evoking procedure . . . why send it to me?'

He didn't answer.

I said, 'It's not all antique. Keep going.'

He studied several more photos, flipped back to the initial shot, then forward to where he'd left off. Resuming his inspection, picking up speed and skimming the horror, just as I had. Then he stopped. Stared at a photo toward the back of the book. Chunky knuckles swelled the gloves as he gripped the album.

'When exactly did you get this?'

'Today's mail.'

He reached for the wrapping paper, took in the address, verified the postmark. Turned back to the album.

'What is it?' I said.

He placed the book on the table, open to the page that had stopped him. Resting his palms on either side of the album, he sat there. Ground his teeth. Laughed. The sound could have paralyzed prey.

Photograph Number 40.

A body in a ditch, muddy water pooled in the trough. Rusty blood on beige dirt. Off to the right side of the frame, dry weeds bristled. White-ink arrows were aimed at the subject, but the subject was obvious.

A young woman, maybe a teenager. Very thin – concave belly, washboard ribcage, fragile shoulders, spindly arms and legs. Slash and puncture wounds meshed her abdomen and neck. Curious black polka dots, too. Both breasts were gone, replaced by purplish discs the shape of marquis diamonds. Her angular face had been posed in profile, gazing to the right. Above her brow, where the hair should have been, floated a ruby cloud.

Purple ligature marks banded both wrists and ankles. More black dots speckled both legs – punctuation marks ringed with rosy haloes – inflammation.

Cigarette burns.

Long white legs had been drawn up in a parody of sexual welcome.

I'd skimmed right past this one.

Central, Beaudry Ave, body dump above 101 freeway on-ramp. Sex murder, scalped and strangled and slashed and burned. NS.

' "NS," ' I said. 'No Solve?'

Milo said, 'There was nothing else besides the book and wrapping? No note?'

'Nope. Just this.'

He checked the blue wrapping again, did the same for the pink butcher paper, returned to the brutalized girl. Sat there for a long time until, finally, he freed one hand and rubbed his face as if washing without water. Old nervous habit. Sometimes it helps cue me in to his mood, sometimes I barely notice it.

He repeated the gesture. Squeezed the bridge of his nose. Rubbed yet again. Twisted his mouth and didn't relax it and stared some more.

'My, my,' he said.

Several moments later: 'Yeah, that would be my guess. No Solve.'

' "NS" wasn't appended to any of the other photos,' I said.

No answer.

'Meaning this is what we're supposed to look at?' I said.

No answer.

'Who was she?' I said.

His lips slackened and he looked up at me and showed me some teeth. Not a smile, not even close to a smile. This was the expression a bear might take on when it spots a free meal.

He picked up the blue book. It vibrated. Shaking hands. I'd never seen that happen before. Emitting another terrible laugh, he repositioned the binder flat on the table. Squared the corners. Got up and walked into the living room. Facing the fireplace, he lifted a poker and tapped the granite hearth very softly.

I took a closer look at the mutilated girl.

His head shook violently. 'What do you wanna fill your head with that for?'

'What about *your* head?' I said.

'Mine's already polluted.'

Mine, too. 'Who was she, Milo?'

He put the poker back. Paced the room.

'Who was she?' he said. 'Someone turned into nothing.'

five

The first seven killings weren't as bad as he'd thought.

Not bad at all, compared to what he'd seen in Vietnam.

The department had assigned him to Central Division, not far – geographically or culturally – from Rampart, where he'd paid a year of uniform dues, followed by eight months with Newton Bunco.

Managing to talk his way out of the initial Newton assignment: Vice. Wouldn't *that* have been a yuk-fest. Ha ha ha. The sound of one voice laughing.

He was twenty-seven years old, already fighting the battle of the bulge, brand-new to Homicide and not sure if he had the stomach for it. For any kind of police work. But, at this point – after Southeast Asia, what else was there?

A freshly minted Detective One, managing to hold on to his secret, though he knew there'd been talk.

No one confronting him directly, but he had ears.

Something different about him – like he thinks he's better than anyone.

Drinks, but doesn't talk.

Doesn't shoot the shit.

Came to Hank Swangle's bachelor party but when they brought the groupie in and the gang bang started, where the fuck was he?

Free blow job and he splits.

Doesn't chase pussy, period.

Weird.

His test scores and solve-rates and persistence got him to Central Homicide, where they paired him with a rail-thin forty-eight-year-old D-II named Pierce Schwinn, who looked sixty and fancied himself a philosopher. Mostly, he and Schwinn worked nights, because Schwinn thrived in the dark: bright lights gave the guy

20

migraines, and he complained of chronic insomnia. No big mystery there, the guy popped decongestants like candy for a perpetually stuffed nose and downed a dozen cups of coffee per shift.

Schwinn loved driving around, spent very little time at his desk, which was a pleasant switch from the butt-numbing routine Milo had experienced at Bunco. But the downside was Schwinn had no attention span for white-collar work, couldn't wait to shove all the paperwork at his new junior partner.

Milo spent hours being a goddamned secretary, figured the best thing was to keep his mouth shut and listen, Schwinn had been around, must have something to offer. In the car, Schwinn alternated between taciturn and gabby. When he did talk, his tone got hyper and preachy – always making a *point*. Guy reminded him of one of his grad school professors at Indiana U. Herbert Milrad, inherited wealth, specialist on Byron. Lockjaw elocution, obese pear of a physique, violent mood swings. Milrad had figured Milo out by the middle of the first semester and tried to take advantage of it. Milo, still far from clear about his sexuality, had declined with tact. Also, he found Milrad physically repugnant.

Not a pretty scene, the Grand Rejection, and Milo knew Milrad would torment him. He was finished with academia, any idea of a PhD. He finished the goddamned MA thesis by flogging the life out of poor Walt Whitman's words, escaped with a bare pass. Bored to tears, anyway, by the bullshit that passed for literary analysis, he left IU, lost his student deferment, answered a want ad at the campus student employment center, and took a job as a groundsman at the Muscatatuck National Wildlife Refuge, waiting for Selective Service to call. Five weeks later, the letter arrived.

By year's end, he was a medic wading through rice paddies, cradling young boys' heads and watching the departure of the barely formed souls, cupping steaming viscera in his hands – intestines were the big challenge, the way they slipped through his fingers like raw sausage. Blood browning and swirling as it hit the muddy water.

He made it home alive, found civilian life and his parents and brothers unbearable, struck out on a road trip, spent a while in San Francisco, learned a few things about his sexuality. Found SF claustrophobic and self-consciously hip, bought an old Fiat, and drove down the coast to L.A., where he stayed because the smog and the ugliness were reassuring. He knocked around for a while on temp jobs, before deciding police work might be interesting and why the hell not?

Then there he was, three years later. Seven P.M. call, as he and Schwinn sat in the unmarked in the parking lot of a Taco Tio on Temple Street, eating green chili burritos, Schwinn in one of his quiet moods, eyes jumpy as he gorged himself with no apparent pleasure.

When the radio squawked, Milo talked to the dispatcher, took down the details, said, 'Guess we'd better shove off.'

Schwinn said, 'Let's eat first. No one's coming back to life.'

Homicide number eight.

The first seven had been no big deal, gross-out-wise. Nothing whodunit about them, either. Like nearly every Central case, the victims were all black or Mexican and the same for the victimizers. When he and Pierce showed, the only other white faces at the scene would be uniforms and techs.

Black/brown cases meant tragedy that never hit the papers, charges that mostly got filed and plea-bargained, or, if the bad guy ended up with a really stupid public defender, a long stay in county lockup, then a quick trial and sentencing to the max allowable.

The first two calls had been your basic bar shootings, juicehead perpetrators drunk enough to stick around when the uniforms arrived – literally holding the smoking guns, putting up no resistance.

Milo watched Schwinn deal with fools, caught on to what would turn out to be Schwinn's routine: first, he'd mumbled an unintelligible Miranda to an uncomprehending perp. Then he'd pressured the idiot for a confession right there at the scene. Making sure Milo had his pen and his pad out, was getting everything down.

'Good boy,' he'd say afterward to the suspect, as if the asshole had passed a test. Over-the-shoulder aside to Milo: 'How's your typing?'

Then back to the station, where Milo would pound the keys and Schwinn would disappear.

Cases Three, Four, and Five had been domestics. Dangerous for the responding blues, but laid out neatly for the Ds. Three low-impulse husbands, two shootings, one stabbing. Talk to the family and the neighbors, find out where the bad guys were 'hiding' – usually within walking distance – call for backup, pick 'em up, Schwinn mumbles Miranda . . .

Killing Six was a two-man holdup at one of the discount jewelry outlets on Broadway – cheap silver chains and dirty diamond chips in cheesy ten-karat settings. The robbery had been premeditated, but the 187 was a fluke that went down when one of the stickup morons' guns went off by accident, the bullet zipping straight into the forehead of the store clerk's eighteen-year-old son. Big, handsome kid named Kyle Rodriguez, star football player at El Monte High, just happened to be visiting Dad, bringing the good news of an athletic scholarship to Arizona State.

Schwinn seemed bored with that one, too, but he did show his stuff. In a manner of speaking. Telling Milo to check out former employees, ten to one that's the way it would shake out. Dropping Milo off at the station and heading off for a doctor appointment, then calling in sick for the rest of the week. Milo did three days of legwork, assembled a list, zeroed in on a janitor who'd been fired from the jewelry store a month ago for suspected pilferage. Turned the guy up in an SRO hotel on Central, still rooming with the brother-in-law who'd been his partner in crime. Both bad guys were incarcerated and Pierce Schwinn showed up looking pink and healthy, and saying, 'Yeah, there was no other possibility – did you finish the report?'

That one stuck in Milo's head for a while: Kyle Rodriguez's beefy bronze corpse slumped over the jewelry case. The image kept him up for more than a few nights. Nothing philosophical or theological, just general edginess. He'd seen plenty of young, healthy guys die a lot more painfully than Kyle, had long ago given up on making sense out of things.

He spent his insomnia driving around in the old Fiat. Up and down Sunset from Western to La Cienega, then back again. Finally veering south onto Santa Monica Boulevard.

As if that hadn't been his intention all along.

Playing a game with himself, like a dieter circling a piece of cake.

He'd never been much for willpower.

For three consecutive nights, he cruised Boystown. Showered and shaved and cologned, wearing a clean white T-shirt and military-pressed jeans and white tennies. Wishing he was cuter and thinner, but figuring he wasn't that bad if he squinted and kept his gut sucked in and kept his nerves under control by rubbing his face. The first night, a sheriff's patrol car nosed into the traffic at Fairfax and stayed two car lengths behind his Fiat, setting off paranoia alarms. He obeyed all the traffic rules, drove back to his crappy little apartment on Alexandria, drank beer until he felt ready to burst, watched bad TV, and made do with imagination. The second night, no sheriffs, but he just lacked the energy to bond and ended up driving all the way to the beach and back, nearly falling asleep at the wheel.

Night three, he found himself a stool in a bar near Larabee, sweating too damn much, knowing he was even tenser than he felt because his neck hurt like hell and his teeth throbbed like they were going to crumble. Finally, just before 4 A.M., before sunlight would be cruel to his complexion, he picked up a guy, a young black guy, around his own age. Well-dressed, well-spoken, education grad student at UCLA. Just about the same place as Milo, sexual-honesty wise.

The two of them were jumpy and awkward in the guy's own crappy little grad student studio apartment on Selma south of Hollywood. The guy attending UCLA but living with junkies and hippies east of Vine because he couldn't afford the Westside. Polite chitchat, then . . . it was over in seconds. Both of them knowing there would be no repeat performance. The guy telling Milo his name was Steve Jackson but when he went into the bathroom, Milo spotted a date book embossed WES, found an address sticker inside the front cover. Wesley E. Smith, the Selma address.

Intimacy.

A sad case, Kyle Rodriguez, but he got over it by the time Case Seven rolled around.

A street slashing, good old Central Avenue, again. Knife fight, lots of blood all over the sidewalk, but only one db, a thirtyish Mexican guy in work clothes, with the homemade haircut and cheap shoes of a recently arrived illegal. Two dozen witnesses in a nearby *cantina* spoke no English and claimed blindness. This one wasn't even detective work. Solved courtesy of the blues – patrol car spotted a lurching perp ten blocks away, bleeding profusely from his own wounds. The uniforms cuffed him as he howled in agony, sat him down on the curb, called Schwinn and Milo, *then* phoned for the ambulance that transported the wretch to the jail ward at County Hospital.

By the time the detectives got there, the idiot was being loaded onto a gurney, had lost so much blood it was touch-and-go. He ended up surviving but gave up most of his colon and a bedside statement, pled guilty from a wheelchair, got sent back to the jail ward till someone figured out what to do with him.

Now, Number Eight. Schwinn just kept munching the burrito.

Finally, he wiped his mouth. 'Beaudry, top of the freeway, huh? Wanna drive?' Getting out and heading for the passenger side before Milo could answer.

Milo said, 'Either way,' just to hear the sound of his own voice.

Even away from the wheel, Schwinn went through his jumpy predrive ritual. Ratcheting the seat back noisily, then returning it to where it had been. Checking the knot of his tie in the rearview, poking around at the corner of his lipless mouth. Making sure no cherry-colored residue of decongestant syrup remained.

Forty-eight years old but his hair was dead white and skimpy, thinning to skin at the crown. Five-ten and Milo figured him for no more than 140, most of it gristle. He had a lantern jaw, that stingy little paper cut of a mouth, deep seams scoring his rawboned face, and heavy bags under intelligent, suspicious eyes. The package shouted dust bowl. Schwinn had been born in Tulsa, labeled himself Ultra-Okie to Milo minutes after they'd met.

Then he'd paused and looked the young detective in the eye. Expecting Milo to say something about his own heritage.

How about Black Irish Indiana Fag?

Milo said, 'Like the Steinbeck book.'

'Yeah,' said Schwinn, disappointed. '*Grapes of Wrath*. Ever read it?'

'Sure.'

'I didn't.' Defiant tone. 'Why the fuck should I? Everything in there I already learned from my daddy's stories.' Schwinn's mouth formed a poor excuse for a smile. 'I hate books. Hate TV and stupid-ass radio, too.' Pausing, as if laying down a gauntlet.

Milo kept quiet.

Schwinn frowned. 'Hate sports, too – what's the point of all that?'

'Yeah, it can get excessive.'

'You've got the size. Play sports in college?'

'High school football,' said Milo.

'Not good enough for college?'

'Not nearly.'

'You read much?'

'A bit,' said Milo. Why did that sound confessional?

'Me too.' Schwinn put his palms together. Aimed those accusatory eyes at Milo. Leaving Milo no choice.

'You hate books but you read.'

'Magazines,' said Schwinn, triumphantly. 'Magazines cut to the chase – take your *Reader's Digest,* collects all the bullshit and condenses it to where you don't need a shave by the time you finish. The other one I like is *Smithsonian.*'

Now there was a surprise.

'*Smithsonian,*' said Milo.

'Never heard of it?' said Schwinn, as if relishing a secret. 'The museum, in Washington, they put out a magazine. My wife went and subscribed to it and I was ready to kick her butt – just what we needed, more paper cluttering up the house. But it's not half-bad. They've got all sorts of stuff in there. I feel educated when I close the covers, know what I mean?'

'Sure.'

'Now *you,*' said Schwinn, 'they tell me you *are* educated.' Making it sound like a criminal charge. 'Got yourself a master's degree, is that right?'

Milo nodded.

'From where?'

'Indiana U. But school isn't necessarily education.'

'Yeah, but sometimes it is – what'd you study at Indiana *Yooo?*'

'English.'

Schwinn laughed. 'God loves me, sent me a partner who can spell. Anyway, give me magazines and burn all the books as far as I'm concerned. I like science. Sometimes when I'm at the morgue I look at medical books – forensic medicine, abnormal psychology, even anthropology 'cause they're learning to do stuff with bones.' His own bony finger wagged. 'Let me tell you something, boy-o: one day, science is gonna be a big damn deal in our business. One day, to be doing our job a guy's gonna have to be a scientist – show up at a crime scene, scrape the db, carry a little microscope, learn the biochemical makeup of every damn scrote the vic hung out with for the last ten years.'

'Transfer evidence?' Milo said. 'You think it'll get that good?'

'Sure, yeah,' Schwinn said, impatiently. 'Right now transfer evidence is for the most part useless bullshit, but wait and see.'

They had been driving around Central on their first day as partners. Aimlessly, Milo thought. He kept waiting for Schwinn to point out known felons, hot spots, whatever, but the guy seemed unaware of his surroundings, all he wanted to do was talk. Later, Milo would learn that Schwinn had plenty to offer. Solid detective logic and basic advice. ('Carry your own camera, gloves, and fingerprint powder. Take care of your own self, don't depend on anyone.') But right now, this first day, riding around – everything – seemed pointless.

'Transfer,' said Schwinn. 'All we can transfer now is ABO blood type. What a crock. Big deal, a million scrotes are type O, most of the rest are A, so what does *that* do? That and hair, sometimes they take hair, put it in little plastic envelopes, but what the fuck can they do with it, you always get some Hebe lawyer proving hair don't mean shit. No, I'm talking serious science, something nuclear, like the way they date fossils. Carbon dating. One day, we'll be anthropologists. Too bad you don't have a master's degree in anthropology . . . can you type okay?'

A few miles later. Milo was taking in the neighborhood on his own, studying faces, places, when Schwinn proclaimed: 'English won't do you a damn bit of good, boy-o, 'cause our customers don't talkie mucho *English*. Not the Mexes, not the niggers, either – not unless you want to call that jive they give you English.'

Milo kept his mouth shut.

'Screw English,' said Schwinn. '*Fuck* English in the ass with a hydrochloric acid dildo. The wave of the future is science.'

They hadn't been told much about the Beaudry call. Female

Caucasian db, discovered by a trash-picker sifting through the brush that crested the freeway on-ramp.

Rain had fallen the previous night and the dirt upon which the corpse had been placed was poor-drainage clay that retained an inch of grimy water in the ruts.

Despite a nice soft muddy area, no tire tracks, no footprints. The ragpicker was an old black guy named Elmer Jacquette, tall, emaciated, stooped, with Parkinsonian tremors in his hands that fit with his agitation as he retold the story to anyone who'd listen.

'And there it was, right out there, Lord Jesus . . .'

No one was listening anymore. Uniforms and crime-scene personnel and the coroner's man were busy doing their jobs. Lots of other people stood around, making small talk. Flashing vehicles blocked Beaudry all the way back to Temple as a bored-looking patrolman detoured would-be freeway speeders.

Not too many cars out: 9 P.M. Well past rush hour. Rigor had come and gone, as had the beginnings of putrefaction. The coroner was guestimating a half day to a day since death, but no way to know how long the body had been lying there or what temperature it had been stored at. The logical guess was that the killer had driven up last night, after dark, placed the corpse, zipped right onto the 101, and sped off happy.

No passing motorist had seen it, because when you were in a hurry, why would you study the dirt above the on-ramp? You never get to know a city unless you walk. Which is why so few people know L.A., thought Milo. After living here for two years, he still felt like a stranger.

Elmer Jacquette walked all the time, because he had no car. Covered the area from his East Hollywood flop to the western borders of downtown, poking around for cans, bottles, discards he tried to peddle to thrift shops in return for soup kitchen vouchers. One time, he'd found a working watch – gold, he thought, turned out to be plated but he got ten bucks for it, anyway, at a pawnshop on South Vermont.

He'd seen the body right away – how could you not from up close, all pale in the moonlight, the sour smell, the way the poor girl's legs had been bent and spread – and his gorge had risen immediately and soon his franks-and-beans dinner was coming back the wrong way.

Jacquette had the good sense to run a good fifteen feet from the body before vomiting. When the uniforms arrived, he pointed out the emetic mound, apologizing. Not wanting to annoy anyone. He was sixty-eight years old, hadn't served state time since fifteen years ago, wasn't going to annoy the police, no way.

Yessir, nossir.

They'd kept him around, waiting for the detectives to arrive. Now, the men in suits were finally here and Jacquette stood over by one of the police cars as someone pointed him out and they approached him, stepping into the glare of those harsh lights the cops had put all over the place.

Two suits. A skinny white-haired redneck type in an old-fashioned gray sharkskin suit and a dark-haired, pasty-faced heavyset kid whose green jacket and brown pants and ugly red-brown tie made Elmer wonder if nowadays *cops* were shopping at thrift shops.

They stopped at the body first. The old one took one look, wrinkled his nose, got an annoyed look on his face. Like he'd been interrupted in the middle of doing something important.

The fat kid was something else. Barely glanced at the body before whipping his head away. Bad skin, that one, and he'd gone white as a sheet, started rubbing his face with one hand, over and over.

Tightening up that big heavy body of his like *he* was ready to lose his lunch.

Elmer wondered how long the kid had been on the job, if he'd actually blow chunks. If the kid did heave, would he be smart enough to avoid the body, like Elmer had?

'Cause this kid didn't look like no veteran.

six

This was worse than Asia.

No matter how brutal it got, war was impersonal, human chess pieces moving around the board, you fired at shadows, strafed huts you pretended were empty, lived every day hoping you wouldn't be the pawn that flipped. Reduce someone to The Enemy, and you could blow off his legs or slice open his belly or napalm his kids without knowing his name. As bad as war got, there was always the chance for making nice sometime in the future – look at Germany and the rest of Europe. To his father, an Omaha Beach alumnus, buddying up to the krauts was an abomination. Dad curled his lip every time he saw a 'hippie-faggot in one of those Hitler beetle-cars.' But Milo knew enough history to understand that peace was as inevitable as war and that as unlikely as it seemed, one day Americans might be vacationing in Hanoi.

War wounds had a chance of healing *because* they weren't personal. Not that the memory of guts slipping through his hands would fade, but maybe, somewhere off in the future . . .

But *this*. This was nothing *but* personal. Reduction of human form to meat and juice and refuse. Creating the antiperson.

He took a deep breath and buttoned his jacket and managed another look at the corpse. How old could she be, seventeen, eighteen? The hands, about the only parts of her not bloody, were smooth, pale, free of blemish. Long, tapering fingers, pink-polished nails. From what he could tell – and it was hard to tell anything because of the damage – she'd had delicate features, might've been pretty.

No blood on the hands. No defense wounds . . .

The girl was frozen in time, a heap of ruin. Aborted – like a shiny little wristwatch, stomped on, the crystal shattered.

Manipulated after death, too. The killer spreading her legs, tenting them, pointing the feet at a slight outward angle.

Leaving her out in the open, horrible statuary.

Overkill, the assistant coroner had pronounced, as if you needed a medical degree for *that.*

Schwinn had told Milo to count wounds, but the task wasn't that simple. The slashes and cuts were straightforward, but did he count the ligature burns around both wrists and ankles as wounds? And what about the deep, angry red trench around her neck? Schwinn had gone off to get his Instamatic – always a shutterbug – and Milo didn't want to ask him – loathed coming across uncertain, the rookie he was.

He decided to include the ligatures in a separate column, continued making hash marks. Reviewed his count of the knife wounds. Both premortem and after death, the coroner was guessing. One, two, three, four . . . he confirmed fifty-six, began his tally of the cigarette burns.

Inflammation around the singed circles said the burns had been inflicted before death.

Very little spent blood at the scene. She'd been killed somewhere else, left here.

But lots of dried blood atop the head, forming a blackening cap that kept attracting the flies.

The finishing touch: scalping her. Should that be counted as one giant wound, or did he need to peer under the blood, see how many times the killer had hacked away the skin?

A cloud of night gnats circled above the body, and Milo scatted it away, noted 'removal of cranial skin,' as a separate item. Drawing the body and topping it with the cap, his lousy rendering making the blood look like a beanie, so inadequately offensive. He frowned, closed his pad, stepped back. Studied the body from a new perspective. Fought back yet another wave of nausea.

The old black guy who'd found her had heaved his cookies. From the moment Milo had seen the girl, he'd struggled not to do the same. Tightening his bowels and his gut, trying to come up with a mantra that would do the trick.

You're no virgin, you've seen worse.

31

Thinking of the worst: *melon-sized holes in chests, hearts bursting –
that kid, that Indian kid from New Mexico – Bradley Two Wolves –
who'd stepped on a mine and lost everything below the navel but was still
talking as Milo pretended to do something for him. Looking up at Milo
with soft brown eyes –* alive *eyes, dear God – talking calmly, having a
goddamn conversation with nothing left and everything leaking out.
That was worse, right? Having to talk back to the upper half of Bradley
Two Wolves, chitchatting about Bradley's pretty little girlfriend in
Galisteo, Bradley's dreams – once he got back to the States, he was gonna
marry Tina, get a job with Tina's dad putting up adobe fences, have a
bunch of kids. Kids. With nothing below the—* Milo smiled down at
Bradley and Bradley smiled back and died.

That had been worse. And back then Milo had managed to keep
his cool, keep the conversation going. Cleaning up afterward,
loading half-of-Bradley in a body bag that was much too roomy.
Writing out Bradley's death tag for the flight surgeon to sign. For
the next few weeks, Milo had smoked a lot of dope, sniffed some
heroin, done an R and R in Bangkok, where he tried some opium.
He'd even hazarded an attempt at a skinny Bangkok whore. That
hadn't gone so great, but bottom line: he'd *maintained.*

You can handle this, stupid.

Breathe slowly, don't give Schwinn something else to lecture about—

Schwinn was back now, clicking away with his Instamatic. The
LAPD photographer had spotted the little black plastic box,
caressed his Nikon, smirked. Schwinn was oblivious to the contempt, in his own little world, crouching on all sides of the body.
Getting close to the body, closer than Milo had hazarded, not even
bothering to shoo the gnats swarming his white hair.

'So what do you think, boy-o?'

'About . . . ?' said Milo.

Click click click. 'The bad guy – what's your gut telling you about
him?'

'Maniac.'

'Think so?' Schwinn said, almost absently. 'Howling-lunatic-
drooling-crazyman?' He moved away from Milo, kneeled right next
to the flayed skull. Close enough to kiss the mangled flesh. Smiled.
'Look at this – just bone and a few blood vessels, sliced at the
back . . . a few tears, some serrations . . . real sharp blade.' *Click*

32

click. 'A maniac . . . some shout-at-the-moon Apache warrior? *You,* naughty squaw, *me* scalpum?'

Milo battled another abdominal heave.

Schwinn got to his feet, dangled the camera from its little black string, fiddled with his tie. His Oakie hatchet face bore a satisfied look. Cool as ice. How often had *he* seen this? How often did this kind of thing come up in Homicide? The first seven – even Kyle Rodriguez – had been tolerable compared to this . . .

Schwinn pointed at the girl's propped-up legs. 'See the way he posed her? He's talking to us, boy-o. Talking through her, putting words in her mouth. What's he want her to say, boy-o?'

Milo shook his head.

Schwinn sighed. 'He wants her to say, "Fuck me." To the whole world – "C'mon over, whole damn world, and fuck me silly, anyone wants to do anything to me, they can 'cause I got no power." He's using her like . . . a puppet – you know how kids move puppets around, get puppets to say things they're too scared to say for themselves? This guy's like that, only he likes big puppets.'

'He's scared?' said Milo doubtfully.

'What the fuck do *you* think?' said Schwinn. 'We're talking about a coward, can't talk to women, get laid in any normal way. Which isn't to say he's a wimpy type. He could be macho. He's sure nervy enough, taking the time for that.' Backward glance at the legs. 'Posing her right out in the open, risking being seen. I mean, think about it: you had your fun with the body, needed to get rid of the body, you're carrying it around in your car, want to dump it, where would you go?'

'Somewhere remote.'

'Yeah, 'cause you're not a nervy killer, to you it would just be dumping. Not our boy. On the one hand, he's smart. Doing it right by the freeway – once he's finished, he can get back on, no one's conspicuous on the 101. He does it after dark, checks to make sure no one's watching, pulls over, arranges her, then zoom zoom zoom. It's a decent plan. It could work nice, especially this late, rush hour's over. But taking the time to *stop* is still a risk, just to play puppet. So this wasn't about dumping. This was showing off – having his cake and eating it twice. He ain't stupid or crazy.'

'Playing a game,' said Milo, because that sounded agreeable.

33

Thinking about chess, but unable to really reconcile this with any game.

' "*Look at me,*" ' said Schwinn. 'That's what he's telling us. "Look what I can do." It's not enough he overpowered her and fucked the hell out of her – hundred to one we'll find a mess of semen up her twat, her ass. What he wants now is to share her with the world. I control her, everyone hop on board.'

'Gang bang,' said Milo, hoarsely, flashing back to Hank Swangle's party at Newton Division. The Newton groupie, a heavy, blonde bank clerk, prim and upright during the day, a whole other life when it came to cops. Pillowy, drunk, and glazed when collegial hands had shoved Milo into the room with her. The groupie reaching out to Milo, lipstick smeared, mouthing, 'Next.' Like a take-a-number line in a bakery. He'd muttered some excuse, hurried out . . . why the hell was he thinking of that, now? And now the nausea was returning – his hands throbbed, he was clenching them.

Schwinn was staring at him.

He forced himself to release the fingers, kept his voice level. 'So he's more rational than a maniac. But we are talking someone mentally abnormal, right? Someone normal wouldn't do this.' Hearing the stupidity of each word as it tumbled out.

Schwinn smiled again. 'Normal. Whatever the hell that means.' He turned his back on Milo, walked away without a word, swinging his camera. Stood off by himself next to the coroner's van, leaving Milo with his bad sketches and compulsive hash marks.

Whatever the hell that means.

A knowing smile. Loose talk about Milo's sexuality wafting from Rampart and Newton to Central? Was that why the guy was so hostile?

Milo's hands were clenching again. He'd started to think of himself as maybe fitting in, handling the first seven 187s okay, getting into the 187 groove and thinking he might stick with Homicide, murder would turn out to be something he could finally live with.

Now he cursed the world, got close to the girl. Closer even than Schwinn. Taking in the sights, the smell, every wound – drinking in the horror, telling himself *shut up, idiot, who the hell are you to complain, look at her.*

But the rage intensified, flowed over him, and suddenly he felt hard, cruel, vengeful, analytic.

Seized by a rush of *appetite*.

Trying to make sense of this. Needing to.

He smelled the girl's rot. Wanted, suddenly, to enter her hell.

It was nearly eleven by the time he and Schwinn were back in the unmarked.

'You drive again,' said Schwinn. No sign of any hostility, no more possible doubles entendres, and Milo started to think he'd been paranoid about the normalcy comment. Just Schwinn flapping his lips, because the guy was like that.

He started up the engine. 'Where to?'

'Anywhere. Tell you what, take the freeway for a couple exits, then turn around, go back downtown. I need to think.'

Milo complied. Cruising down the ramp, as the killer had done. Schwinn stretched and yawned, sniffed and produced his bottle of decongestant and took a long red swallow. Then he leaned over and switched off the radio, closed his eyes, fooled with the corners of his lips. This was going to be one of those silent stretches.

It lasted until Milo was back on city streets, driving up Temple, passing the Music Center and the dirt lots that surrounded it. Lots of empty space as the rich folk planned additional shrines to culture. Talking urban renewal – pretending anyone would ever bother with this poor excuse for a downtown, pretending it wasn't a cement grid of government buildings where bureaucrats worked the day shift and couldn't wait to get the hell out of there and everything got cold and black at night.

'So what's next?' said Schwinn. 'On the girl. What do you think?'

'Find out who she was?'

'Shouldn't be too hard, those smooth nails, nice straight teeth. If she was a street slut, her comedown was recent. Someone'll miss her.'

'Should we start with Missing Persons?' said Milo.

'*You'll* start with Missing Persons. Start calling tomorrow morning 'cause MP doesn't staff heavy at night, good luck trying to get those guys off their asses at this hour.'

'But if she was reported missing, getting the info tonight would give us a head start—'

'On what? This is no race, boy-o. If our bad boy's out of town, he's long gone, anyway. If not, a few hours won't make a damn bit of difference.'

'Still, her parents have got to be worried—'

'Fine, amigo,' said Schwinn. 'Be a social worker. I'm going home.'

No anger, just that know-it-all smugness.

'Want me to head back to the station?' said Milo.

'Yeah, yeah. No, forget that. Pull over – *now*, boy-o. Over *there*, yeah yeah yeah stop next to that *bus* bench.'

The bench was a few yards up, on the north side of Temple. Milo was in the left-hand lane and had to turn sharply not to overshoot. He edged to the curb, looked around to see what had changed Schwinn's mind.

Dark, empty block, no one around – no, there *was* someone. A figure emerging from the shadows. Walking west. Walking quickly.

'A source?' said Milo, as the shape took form. Female form.

Schwinn tightened his tie knot. 'Stay put and keep the engine going.' He got out of the car, quickly, got to the sidewalk just in time to meet the woman. Her arrival was heralded by spike heels snapping on the pavement.

A tall woman – black, Milo saw, as she shifted into the streetlight. Tall and busty. Maybe forty. Wearing a blue leather mini and a baby blue halter top. Jumbo pile of henna-colored waves atop her head, what looked to be ten pounds of hair.

Schwinn, standing facing her, looking even skinnier than usual. Legs slightly spread. Smiling.

The woman smiled back. Offered both cheeks to Schwinn. One of those Italian movie greetings.

A few moments of conversation, too low for Milo to make out, then both of them got in the backseat of the unmarked.

'This is Tonya,' said Schwinn. 'She's a good pal of the department. Tonya, meet my brand-new partner, Milo. He's got a master's degree.'

'Ooh,' said Tonya. 'Are you masterful, honey?'

'Nice to meet you, ma'am.'

Tonya laughed.

'Start driving,' said Schwinn.

'Master's degree,' said Tonya, as they pulled away.

At Fifth Street, Schwinn said, 'Turn left. Drive into the alley behind those buildings.'

'Masturbator's degree?' said Tonya.

'Speaking of which,' said Schwinn. 'My darling dear.'

'Ooh, I love when you talk that way, Mr S.'

Milo reduced his speed.

Schwinn said, 'Don't do that, just drive regular – turn again and make a right – go east. Alameda, where the factories are.'

'Industrial revolution,' said Tonya, and Milo heard something else: the rustle of clothing, the *sprick* of a zipper undone. He hazarded one look in the rearview, saw Schwinn's head, resting against the back of the seat. Eyes closed. Peaceful smile. Ten pounds of henna bobbing.

A moment later: 'Oh, yes, Miss T. I missed you, did you know that?'

'Did you, baby? Aw, you're just saying that.'

'Oh, no, it's true.'

'*Is* it, baby?'

'You bet. Miss me, too?'

'You know I do, Mr S.'

'Every day, Miss T?'

'Every day, Mr S – c'mon, baby, move a little, help me with this.'

'Happy to help,' said Schwinn. 'Protect and serve.'

Milo forced his eyes straight ahead.

No sound in the car but heavy breathing.

'Yeah, yeah,' Schwinn was saying now. His voice weak. Milo thought: This is what it takes to knock off the asshole's smugness.

'Oh yeah, just like that, my darling . . . dear. Oh, yes, you're . . . a . . . specialist. A . . . scientist, yes, yes.'

seven

Schwinn told Milo to drop Tonya off on Eighth near Witmer, down the block from the Ranch Depot Steak House.

'Get yourself a hunk of beef, darling.' Slipping her some bills. 'Get yourself a lovely T-bone with one of those giant baked potatoes.'

'Mr S,' came the protest. 'I can't go in there dressed like this, they won't serve me.'

'With this they will.' Another handful of paper pressed into her hand. 'You show this to Calvin up front, tell him I sent you – you have any problem, you let me know.'

'You're sure?'

'You know I am.'

The rear door opened, and Tonya got out. The smell of sex hung in the car. Now the night filtered in, cool, fossil-fuel bitter.

'Thank you, Mr S.' She extended her hand. Schwinn held on to it.

'One more thing, darling. Hear of any rough johns working the Temple-Beaudry area?'

'How rough?'

'Ropes, knives, cigarette burns.'

'Ooh,' said the hooker, with pain in her voice. 'No, Mr S, there's always lowlife, but I heard nothing like that.'

Pecks on cheeks. Tonya clicked her way toward the restaurant, and Schwinn got back in front. 'Back to the station, boy-o.'

Closing his eyes. Self-satisfied. At Olive Street, he said: 'That's a very intelligent nigger, boy-o. Given the opportunity a free, white woman woulda had, she woulda made something of herself. What's that about?'

38

'What do you mean?'

'The way we treat niggers. Make sense to you?'

'No,' said Milo. Thinking: What the hell is this *lunatic* about?

Then: Why hadn't Schwinn offered the hooker to *him*?

Because Schwinn and Tonya had something special? Or because he *knew*?

'What it says,' offered Schwinn. 'The way we treat niggers, is that sometimes smart doesn't count.'

Milo dropped him off at the Central Division parking lot, watched him get into his Ford Fairlane and drive off to Simi Valley, to the wife who liked books.

Alone, at last.

For the first time since the Beaudry call, he was breathing normally.

He entered the station, climbed the stairs, hurried to the scarred metal desk they'd shoved into a corner of the Homicide room for him. The next three hours were spent phoning Missing Persons bureaus at every station and when that didn't pay off, he extended the search to various sheriffs' substations and departments of neighboring cities. Every office kept its own files, no one coordinated, each folder had to be pulled by hand, and MP skeleton crews were reluctant to extend themselves, even on a 187. Even when he pressed, emphasized the whodunit aspect, the ugliness, he got resistance. Finally, he hit upon something that pried cooperation and curses on the other end: the likelihood of news coverage. Cops were afraid of bad press. By 3 A.M., he'd come up with seven white girls in the right age range.

So what did he do, now? Get on the horn and wake up worried parents?

Pardon me, Mrs Jones, but did your daughter Amy ever show up? Because we've still got her listing as missing and are wondering if a sackful of tissue and viscera cooling off in a coroner's drawer just might be her?

The only way to do it was preliminary phone contact followed by face-to-face interviews. Tomorrow, at a decent hour. Unless Schwinn had other ideas. Something else to correct him about.

He transcribed all the data from his pad onto report sheets, filled out the right forms, redrew the outline of the girl's body, summarized the MP calls, created a neat little pile of effort. Striding across the room to a bank of file cabinets, he opened a top drawer and pulled out one of several blue binders stored in a loose heap. Recycled binders: when cases were closed, the pages were removed and stapled, placed in a manila folder, and shipped over to the evidence room at Parker Center.

This particular blue book had seen better times: frayed around the edges with a brown stain on the front cover vaguely reminiscent of a wilting rose – some D's greasy lunch. Milo affixed a stick-ummed label to the cover.

Wrote nothing. Nothing to write.

He sat there thinking about the mutilated girl. Wondered what her name was and couldn't bring himself to substitute *Jane Doe*.

First thing tomorrow, he'd check out those seven girls, maybe get lucky and end up with a name.

A title for a brand-new murder book.

Bad dreams kept him up all night, and he was back at his desk by 6:45 A.M., the only detective in the room, which was just fine; he didn't even mind getting the coffee going.

By 7:20, he was calling families. MP number one was Sarah Jane Causlett, female cauc, eighteen, five-six, 121, last seen in Hollywood, buying dinner at the Oki-burger at Hollywood and Selma.

Ring, ring ring. 'Mrs Causlett? Good morning, hope I'm not calling too early . . .'

By 9 A.M., he was finished. Three of the seven girls had returned home, and two others weren't missing at all, just players in divorce dramas who'd escaped to be with noncustodial parents. That left two sets of distraught parents, Mr and Mrs Estes in Mar Vista, Mr and Mrs Jacobs in Mid-City. Lots of anxiety, Milo withheld facts, steeled himself for the face-to-face.

By 9:30 a few detectives had arrived, but not Schwinn, so Milo placed a scrawled note on Schwinn's desk, left the station.

By 1 P.M., he was back where he started. A recent picture of Misty Estes showed her to be substantially obese with short curly hair. West L.A. Missing Persons had misrecorded her stats: 107

pounds instead of 187. Oops, sorry. Milo left the tearful mother and hypertensive father standing in the doorway of their GI Bill bungalow.

Jessica Jacobs was approximately the right size, but definitely not the girl on Beaudry: she had the lightest of blue eyes, and the victim's had been deep brown. Another clerical screwup, no one bothering to note eye color in the Wilshire Division MP file.

He left the Jacobs house sweating and tired, found a pay phone outside a liquor store at Third and Wilton, got Schwinn on the line, and gave a lack-of-progress report.

'Morning, boy-o,' said Schwinn. 'Haul yourself over here, there might be something.'

'What?'

'Come on back.'

When he got to the Homicide room, half the desks were full, and Schwinn was balancing on two legs of his chair, wearing a nice-looking navy suit, shiny white-on-white shirt, gold tie, gold tie tack shaped like a tiny fist. Leaning back precariously as he chomped a burrito the size of a newborn baby.

'Welcome home, prodigious son.'

'Yeah.'

'You look like shit.'

'Thanks.'

'Don't mention it.' Schwinn gave one of his corkscrew smiles. 'So you learned about our excellent record-keeping. Cops are the worst, boy-o. Hate to write and always make a mess out of it. We're talking barely literate.'

Milo wondered about the extent of Schwinn's own education. The topic had never come up. The whole time they'd worked together, Schwinn had parceled out very few personal details.

'Clerical screwups are the fucking rule, boy-o. MP files are the worst, because MP knows it's a penny ante outfit, most of the time the kid comes home, no one bothers to let them know.'

'File it, forget it,' said Milo, hoping agreement would shut him up.

'File it, *fuck* it. That's why I was in no big hurry to chase MP.'

'You know best,' said Milo.

41

Schwinn's eyes got hard. Milo said, 'So what's interesting?'

'*Maybe* interesting,' Schwinn corrected. 'A source of mine picked up some rumors. Party on the Westside two days before the murder. Friday night, Upper Stone Canyon – Bel Air.'

'Rich kids.'

'Filthy rich kids, probably using Daddy and Mommy's house. My source says there were kids from all over showing up, getting stoned, making noise. The source also knows a guy, has a daughter, went out with her friends, spent some time at the party, and never came home.'

Maybe interesting.

Schwinn grinned and bit off a wad of burrito. Milo had figured the guy for a late-sleeping pension-sniffing goldbrick and turned out the sonofabitch had been working overtime, doing a solo act, and *producing*. The two of them were partners in name only.

He said, 'The father didn't report it to MP?'

Schwinn shrugged. 'The father's a little bit . . . marginal.'

'Lowlife?'

'Marginal,' Schwinn repeated. Irritated, as if Milo was a poor student, kept getting it wrong. 'Also, the girl's done this before – goes out partying, doesn't come home for a few days.'

'If the girl's done it before, why would this be different?'

'Maybe it's not. But the girl fits stat-wise: sixteen, around five-seven, skinny, with dark hair, brown eyes, nice tight little body.'

An appreciative tone had crept into Schwinn's voice. Milo pictured him with the source – some street lech, the source laying it on lasciviously. Hookers, pimps, perverts, Schwinn probably had a whole stable of lowlifes he could count on for info. And Milo had a master's degree . . .

'She's supposed to be cute,' Schwinn went on. 'No virgin, a wild kid. Also, at least one time before, she got herself in trouble. Hitchhiking on Sunset, got picked up by some scrote who raped her, tied her up, left her in an alley downtown. A juicehead found her, lucky for her he was just a bum, not a perve fixing to get himself some sloppy seconds. The girl never reported it officially, just told a friend, and the story made the rounds on the street.'

'Sixteen years old, tied and raped and she doesn't report it?'

'Like I said, no virgin.' Schwinn's hatchet jaw pulsed, and his

Okie squint aimed at the ceiling. Milo knew he was holding back something.

'Is the source reliable?'

'Usually.'

'Who?'

Schwinn's headshake was peevish. 'Let's concentrate on the main thing: we got a girl who fits our vic's stats.'

'Sixteen,' said Milo, bothered.

Schwinn shrugged. 'From what I've read – psychology articles – the human rope gets kinked up pretty early.' He leaned back and took another big bite of burrito, wiped salsa verde from his mouth with the back of his hand, then gave the hand a lick. 'You think that's true, boy-o? Think maybe she didn't report it 'cause she liked it?'

Milo covered his anger with a shrug of his own. 'So what's next? Talk to the father?'

Schwinn righted his chair, swabbed his chin, this time with a paper napkin, stood abruptly, and walked out of the room, leaving Milo to follow.

Partners.

Outside, near the unmarked, Schwinn turned to him, smiling. 'So tell me, how'd you sleep last night?'

Schwinn recited the address on Edgemont, and Milo started up the car.

'Hollywood, boy-o. A real-life Hollywood girl.'

Over the course of the twenty-minute ride, he laid out a few more details for Milo: the girl's name was Janie Ingalls. A sophomore at Hollywood High, living with her father in a third-floor walk-up in a long-faded neighborhood, just north of Santa Monica Boulevard. Bowie Ingalls was a drunk who might or might not be home. Society was going to hell in a handbasket; even white folk were living like pigs.

The building was a clumsy pink thing with undersized windows and lumpy stucco. Twelve units was Milo's guess: four flats to a floor, probably divided by a narrow central corridor.

He parked, but Schwinn made no attempt to get out, so the two of them just sat there, the engine running.

43

'Turn it off,' said Schwinn.

Milo twisted the key and listened to street sounds. Distant traffic from Santa Monica, a few bird trills, someone unseen playing a power mower. The street was poorly kept, litter sludging the gutters. He said, 'Besides being a juicehead, how's the father marginal?'

'One of those walking-around guys,' said Schwinn. 'Name of Bowie Ingalls, does a little of this, little of that. Rumor has it he ran slips for a nigger bookie downtown – how's that for a white man's career? A few years ago, he was working as a messenger at Paramount Studios, telling people he was in the movie biz. He plays the horses, has a chicken-shit sheet, mostly drunk and disorderly, unpaid traffic tickets. Two years ago he got pulled in for receiving stolen property but never got charged. Small-time, all around.'

Details. Schwinn had found the time to pull Bowie Ingalls's record.

'Guy like that, and he's raising a kid,' said Milo.

'Yeah, it's a cruel world, isn't it? Janie's mother was a stripper and a hype, ran off with some hippie musician when the kid was a baby, overdosed in Frisco.'

'Sounds like you've learned a lot.'

'That what you think?' Schwinn's voice got flinty, and his eyes were hard, again. Figuring Milo was being sarcastic? Milo wasn't sure he hadn't *meant* to be sarcastic.

'I've got a lot to learn,' he said. 'Wasting my time with those MP clowns. Meanwhile you're getting all this—'

'Don't lick my ass, son,' said Schwinn, and suddenly the hatchet face was inches from Milo's and Milo could smell the Aqua Velva and the salsa verde. 'I didn't *do* dick, and I don't *know* dick. And you did way *less* than dick.'

'Hey, sorry if—'

'*Fuck* sorry, pal. You think this is some *game*? Like getting a master's degree, hand in your homework, and lick the teacher's ass and get your little ass-licking *grade*? You think *that's* what this is about?'

Talking way too fast for normal. What the hell had set him off?

Milo kept silent. Schwinn laughed bitterly, moved away, sat back so heavily against the seat that Milo's heavy body rocked. 'Let me

44

tell you, boy-o, that other shit we've been shoveling since I let you ride with me – niggers and pachucos offing each other and waiting around for us to pick 'em up and if we don't, no one gives a shit – you think that's what the 187 universe is all about?'

Milo's face was hot from jawline to scalp. He kept his mouth shut.

'This . . .' said Schwinn, pulling a letter-sized, baby blue envelope from an inside suit pocket and removing a stack of color photos. Twenty-four-hour photo lab logo. The Instamatic shots he'd snapped at Beaudry.

He fanned them out on his skinny lap, faceup, like fortune-teller's cards. Close-ups of the dead girl's bloody, scalped head. Intimate portraits of the lifeless face, splayed legs . . .

'*This*,' he said, 'is why we get paid. The other stuff *clerks* could handle.'

The first seven murders had gotten Milo to think of himself as a clerk with a badge. He didn't dare agree. Agreement seemed to infuriate the sonofa—

'You thought you were gonna get some fun for yourself when you signed up to be a Big Bad Homicide Hero,' said Schwinn. 'Right?' Talking even faster, but managing to snap off each word. 'Or maybe you heard that bullshit about Homicide being for intellectuals and you've got that master's degree and you thought hey, that's me! So tell me, this look *intellectual* to you?' Tapping a photo. 'You think this can be figured out using brains?'

Shaking his head and looking as if he'd tasted something putrid, Schwinn hooked a fingernail under a corner of a photo and flicked. *Plink, plink.*

Milo said, 'Look, I'm just—'

'Do you have any idea how often something like this actually gets closed? Those clowns in the Academy probably told you Homicide has a seventy, eighty percent solve rate, right? Well, that's *horseshit*. That's the stupid stuff – which should be a hundred percent it's so stupid, so big fucking deal, eighty percent. *Shit.*' He turned and spit out the window. Shifted back to Milo. 'With *this*' – *plink, plink* – 'you're lucky to close four outta ten. Meaning most of the time you lose and the guy gets to do it again and he's saying "Fuck you" to *you* just like he is to *her*.'

45

Schwinn freed his fingernail and began tapping the snapshot, blunt-edged index finger landing repetitively on the dead girl's crotch.

Milo realized he was holding his breath, had been doing it since Schwinn launched the tirade. His skin remained saturated with heat, and he wiped his face with one hand.

Schwinn smiled. 'I'm pissing you off. Or maybe I'm scaring you. You do that – with the hand – when you're pissed off or scared.'

'What's the point, Pierce?'

'The point is you said I learned a lot, and I didn't learn dick.'

'I was just—'

'Don't *just* anything,' said Schwinn. 'There's no room for just, there's no room for bullshit. I don't need the brass sending me some . . . fly-by-night master's deg—'

'Fuck that,' said Milo, letting out breath and rage. 'I've been—'

'You've been watching me, checking me out, from the minute you started—'

'I've been hoping to learn something.'

'For what?' said Schwinn. 'So you can add up the brownie points, then move on to an ass-warming job with the brass. Boy-o, I know what you're about—'

Milo felt himself using his bulk. Moving closer to Schwinn, looming over the skinny man, his index finger pointing like a gun. 'You don't know shi—'

Schwinn didn't yield. 'I know assholes with master's degrees don't stick with *this*.' *Tap tap.* 'I *know* I don't wanna waste my time working a whodunit with a suck-up intellectual who all he wants to do is climb the ladder. You got ambition, find yourself some suck-up job like Daryl Gates did, driving Chief Parker's car, one day that clown'll probably end up chief.' *Taptaptap.* '*This* ain't career-building, muchacho. This is a *whodunit*. Get it? *This* likes to munch on your insides, then shit you out in pellets.'

'You're wrong,' said Milo. 'About me.'

'Am I?' Knowing smile.

Ah, thought Milo. *Here it comes. The crux.*

But Schwinn just sat there, grinning, tapping the photo.

Long silence. Then suddenly, as if someone had pulled the plug on him, the guy slumped heavily, looking defeated. 'You have no *idea* what you're up against.' He slipped the photos back in the envelope.

Milo thought: *If you hate the job, retire, asshole. Grab your pension two years early and waste the rest of your life growing tomatoes in some loser trailer park.*

Long, turgid moments passed.

Milo said, 'Big whodunit, and we're sitting here?'

'What's the alternative, Sherlock?' said Schwinn, hooking a thumb at the pink building. 'We go in there and talk to this asshole and maybe his daughter's the one who got turned into shit, or she's not. One way, we've crawled an inch on a hundred-mile hike, the other way, we haven't even started. Either way we got nothing to be proud of.'

eight

Just as quickly as his moods had shifted, Schwinn bounded out of the car.

The guy was unstable, no question about it, Milo thought as he followed.

The front door was unlocked. Twelve mailboxes to the right. The layout was precisely as Milo had envisioned.

Screw you, expert.

Box Eleven was labeled *Ingalls* in smudged red ballpoint. They climbed the stairs, and Schwinn was out of breath by the time they reached the third floor. Tightening his tie knot, he pounded the door, and it opened a few seconds later.

The man who answered was bleary-eyed and skinny-fat.

All sharp bones and stick limbs and saggy sallow skin but with a melon gut. He wore a dirty yellow tank top and blue swim shorts. No hips or butt, and the shorts bagged under the swell of his pot. Not an ounce of extra flesh anywhere but his belly. But what he carried there was grotesque and Milo thought, *Pregnant.*

'Bowie Ingalls?' said Schwinn.

Two-second delay, then a small, squirrelly nod. Beery sweat poured out of the guy, and the sour smell wafted into the hallway.

Schwinn hadn't recited any physical stats on Ingalls – hadn't said anything at all by way of preparation. To Milo, Ingalls appeared in his midforties, with thick, wavy coarse black hair worn past his shoulders – too long and luxuriant for a guy his age – and five days of gray stubble that did nothing to mask his weak features. Where his eyes weren't pink they were jaundiced and unfocused. Deep brown irises, just like those of the dead girl.

Ingalls studied their badges. The guy's timing was off, like a clock with damaged works. He flinched, then grinned, said, 'Whus up?' The words wheezed out on a cloud of hops and malt that mixed with the odors already saturated into the building's walls: mold and kerosene, the incongruous blessing of savory home cooking.

'Can we come in?' said Schwinn.

Ingalls had opened the door halfway. Behind him was dirt-colored furniture, heaps of rumpled clothes, takeout Chinese cartons, Bud empties.

Lots of empties, some crushed, some intact. Even at a good clip, the number of cans added up to more than one day of serious drinking.

A multiday bender. Unless the guy had company. Even *with* company, a focused juice-a-thon.

Guy's daughter goes missing for four days, he doesn't report it, holes up instead, sucking suds. Milo found himself entertaining the worst-case scenario: Daddy did it. Began scanning Ingalls's sallow face for anxiety, guilt, scratches, maybe that explained the delays . . .

But all he saw was confusion. Ingalls stood there, caught up in a booze-flummox.

'Sir,' said Schwinn, using the word as an insult, the way only cops can, 'can we come in?'

'Uh – yeah, sure – whu for?'

'Whu *for* your daughter.'

Ingalls's eyes drooped. Not anxiety. Resignation. As in, *here we go again*. Preparing himself for a lecture on child-rearing.

'Whu, she cut school again? They call in the cops for that now?' Schwinn smiled and moved to enter the apartment and Ingalls stepped aside, nearly stumbling. When the three of them were on the other side of the door, Schwinn closed it. He and Milo began the instinctive visual scan.

Off-white walls, brown deepening to black in the cracks and the corners. The entire front space was maybe fifteen feet square, a living room–dining area–kitchen combo, the kitchen counters crowded with more takeout boxes, used paper plates, empty soup cans. Two miserly windows on the facing wall were shuttered by yellow plastic blinds. A scabrous brown-gray sofa and a red plastic chair were both heaped with unwashed clothes and crumpled paper. Next to the chair, a stack of records tilted precariously. The Mothers of Invention's *Freak Out* on top, a fifteen-year-old LP. Nearby was a cheap phonograph half-covered by a snot green bathrobe. An open doorway led to a dead-end wall.

A full view of the front room revealed even more beer cans.

'Where does Janie go to school, sir?' said Schwinn.

'Hollywood High. What kinda hassle she get herself into now?' Bowie Ingalls scratched an armpit and drew himself up to his full height. Trying to produce some fatherly indignation.

'When's the last time you saw her, sir?'

'Um . . . she was – she slept over a friend's.'

'When, sir?' said Schwinn, still taking in the room. Cool, all business. No one watching him do the detective thing would've imagined his lunatic tirade five minutes ago.

Milo stood to the side, worked on his cool. His mind wanted to work, but his body wasn't giving up the anger planted by Schwinn's outburst; heart still racing, face still hot. Despite the importance of the task at hand, he kept entertaining himself with images of Schwinn falling on his ass – hoist on his own petard, the self-righteous fucker – busted *in flagrante* with Tonya or some other 'source.' That brought a smile to Milo's brain. Then a question arose: if Schwinn didn't trust him, why had he risked doing Tonya right in front of him? Maybe the guy was just nuts . . . he shook all that off and returned to Bowie Ingalls's face. Still no fear, just maddening dullness.

'Um . . . Friday night,' Ingalls said, as if guessing. 'You can sit down if you want.'

There was only one place to sit in the damned sty. A man-sized clearing among the garbage on the couch. Ingalls's dozing spot. Appetizing.

'No, thanks,' said Schwinn. He had his pad out now. Milo waited a few moments before producing his. Not wanting to be part of some Ike-and-Mike vaudeville routine. 'So Janie slept at a friend's Friday night.'

'Yeah. Friday.'

'Four days ago.' Schwinn's gold Parker ballpoint was out, and he scrawled.

'Yeah. She does it all the time.'

'Sleeps over at friends'?'

'She's sixteen,' said Ingalls, whining a bit.

'What's the friend's name? The one from Friday night.'

Ingalls's tongue rolled around his left cheek. 'Linda . . . no – Melinda.'

'Last name?'

Blank stare.

'You don't know Melinda's last name?'

'Don't like the little slut,' said Ingalls. 'Bad influence. Don't like her coming around.'

'Melinda's a bad influence on Janie?'

'Yeah. You know.'

'Gets Janie in trouble,' said Schwinn.

'You know,' said Ingalls. 'Kids. Doing stuff.'

Milo wondered what could possibly offend a scrote like Ingalls.

Schwinn said, 'Stuff.'

'Yeah.'

'Such as?'

'You know,' Ingalls insisted. 'Cutting school, running around.'

'Dope?'

'I dunno about that.'

'Hmm,' said Schwinn, writing. 'So Melinda's a bad influence on Janie but you let Janie sleep over Melinda's house.'

'*Let?*' said Ingalls, coughing. 'You got kids?'

'Haven't been blessed.'

'Figures you ask me that. Nowadays, kids don't get *let* anything. They do whatever the hell they want to. Can't even get her to tell me where she's going. Or to stay in school. I tried dropping her off, personally, but she just went in, waited till I was gone, and left. That's why I figured this was about school. What is it about, anyway? She in trouble?'

'You've had trouble with Janie before?'

'No,' said Ingalls. 'Not really. Like I said, just school and running around. Being gone for a few days. But she always comes back. Let me tell you, man, you can't control 'em. Once the hippies got in and took over the city, forget it. Her mother was a hippie back in the hippie days. Hippie junkie slut, ran out on us, left me with Janie.'

51

'Janie into drugs?'

'Not around here,' said Ingalls. 'She knows better than that.' He blinked several times, grimaced, trying to clear his head and not succeeding. 'What's this about? What'd she do?'

Ignoring the question, Schwinn kept writing. Then: 'Hollywood High . . . what year's she in?'

'Second year.'

'Sophomore.'

Another delayed-reaction nod from Ingalls. How many of the cans had been consumed this morning?

'Sophomore.' Schwinn copied that down. 'When's her birthday?'

'Um . . . March,' said Ingalls. 'March . . . um . . . ten.'

'She was sixteen last March ten.'

'Yeah.'

Sixteen-and-a-half-year-old sophomore, thought Milo. A year behind. Borderline intelligence? Some kind of learning problem? Yet another factor that had propelled her toward victimhood? If she was the one . . .

He glanced at Schwinn but Schwinn was still writing and Milo hazarded a question of his own: 'School's hard for Janie, huh?'

Schwinn's eyebrows rose for a second, but he kept making notes.

'She hates it,' said Ingalls. 'Can barely read. That's why she hated to—' The bloodshot eyes filled with fear. 'What's going on? What'd she do?'

Focused on Milo, now. Looking to Milo for an answer, but that was one ad lib Milo wasn't going to risk, and Ingalls shifted his attention back to Schwinn. 'C'mon, what's going on, man? What'd she do?'

'Maybe nothing,' said Schwinn, producing the blue envelope. 'Maybe something was done to her.'

He fanned out the snaps again, stretching his arm and offering Ingalls the display.

'Huh?' said Ingalls, not moving. Then: 'No.'

Calmly, no inflection. Milo thought: Okay, it wasn't her, false lead, good for him, bad for us, they'd accomplished nothing, Schwinn was right. As usual. The pompous bastard, he'd be gloating, the remainder of the shift would be unbearable—

But Schwinn continued to hold the pictures steady, and Bowie

Ingalls continued to stare at them.

'No,' Ingalls repeated. He made a grab for the pictures, not a serious attempt, just a pathetic stab. Schwinn held firm, and Ingalls stepped away from the horror, pressing his hands to the sides of his head. Stamping his foot hard enough to make the floor quake.

Suddenly, he grabbed his melon-belly, bent over as if seized by cramps. Stamped again, howled, '*No!*'

Kept howling.

Schwinn let him rant for a while, then eased him over to the clearing on the couch, and told Milo, 'Get him some fortification.'

Milo found an unopened Bud, popped the top, held it to Ingalls's lips, but Ingalls shook his head. 'No, no, no. Get that the fuck away from me.'

The guy lives in a booze-haze but won't medicate himself when he sinks to the bottom. Milo supposed that passed for dignity.

He and Schwinn stood there for what seemed to be an eternity. Schwinn serene – used to this. Enjoying it?

Finally, Ingalls looked up. 'Where?' he said. 'Who?'

Schwinn gave him the basic details, talking quietly. Ingalls moaned through the entire recitation.

'Janie, Janie—'

'What can you tell us that would help us?' said Schwinn.

'Nothing. What could I tell . . . ?' Ingalls shuddered. Shivered. Crossed skinny arms over his chest. 'That – who would – oh, God . . . *Janie* . . .'

'Tell us something,' pressed Schwinn. 'Anything. Help us.'

'What . . . I don't know . . . She didn't – since she was fourteen, she's basically been gone, using this place as a crash pad but always gone, telling me to fuck off, mind my own business. Half the time, she ain't here, see what I'm sayin'?'

'Sleeping at friends' houses,' said Schwinn. 'Melinda, other friends.'

'Whatever . . . oh God, I can't believe this . . .' Tears filled Ingalls's eyes, and Schwinn was there with a snow-white hankie. PS monogram in gold thread on a corner. The guy talked despair and pessimism, but offered his own starched linen to a drunk, for the sake of the job.

'Help me,' he whispered to Ingalls. 'For Janie.'

'I would . . . I don't know – she . . . I . . . we didn't talk. Not since . . . she used to be my kid, but then she didn't want to be my kid, telling me to fuck off all the time. I'm not saying I was any big deal as a daddy, but still, without me, Janie would've . . . she turned thirteen and all of a sudden she didn't appreciate anything. Started going out all hours, the school didn't give a shit. Janie never went, no one from the school ever called me, not one time.'

'You call them?'

Ingalls shook his head. 'What's the point? Talking to people who don't give a shit. I'da called, they'da probably sent cops over and busted me for something, child neglect, whatever. I was busy, man. Working – I used to work at Paramount Studios.'

'Oh, yeah?' said Schwinn.

'Yeah. Publicity department. Information transfer.'

'Janie interested in the movies?'

'Nah,' said Ingalls. 'Anything I was into she *wasn't* into.'

'What was she into?'

'Nothing. Running around.'

'This friend, Melinda. If Janie never told you where she was going, how do you know she was with Melinda Friday night?'

'Because I seen her with Melinda on Friday.'

'What time?'

'Around six. I was sleeping, and Janie busts in to get some clothes, I wake up, by the time I'm sitting up, she's heading out the door, and I look out there.' He jabbed a thumb at the shuttered windows. 'I seen her walking away with Melinda.'

'Walking which way?'

'That way.' Hooking his finger north. Toward Sunset, maybe Hollywood Boulevard, if the girls had kept going.

'Anyone else with them?'

'No, just the two of them.'

'Walking, not driving,' said Schwinn.

'Janie didn't have no license. I got one car, and it barely drives. No way was I gonna – she didn't care, anyway. Got around by hitching. I told her about that – I used to hitch, back when you could do it, but now, with all the – you think that's what happened? She hitched and some . . . oh, God . . .'

Unaware of Janie's downtown rape? If so, the guy was being truthful about one thing: Janie had been lost to him for a long time.

'Some what?' said Schwinn.

'Some – you know,' moaned Ingalls. 'Getting picked up – some stranger.'

The death snaps were back in the envelope, but Schwinn had kept the envelope in full view. Now he waved it inches from Ingalls's face. 'I'd say, sir, that only a stranger would do something like this. Unless you have some other idea?'

'Me? No,' said Ingalls. 'She was like her mother. Didn't talk – gimme that beer.'

When the can was empty, Schwinn waved the envelope again. 'Let's get back to Friday. Janie came home to get clothes. What was she wearing?'

Ingalls thought. 'Jeans and a T-shirt – red T-shirt . . . and those crazy black shoes with those heels – platform heels. She was *carrying* her party clothes.'

'Party clothes.'

'When I woke up and saw her going out the door, I could see part of what she had in the bag.'

'What kind of bag?'

'Shopping bag. White – Zody's, probably, 'cause that's where she shops. She always stuffed her party stuff inside shopping bags.'

'What did you see in the bag?'

'Red halter the size of a Band-Aid. I always told her it was hooker shit, she should throw it out, used to threaten her I'd throw it out.'

'But you didn't.'

'No,' said Ingalls. 'What woulda been the point?'

'A red halter,' said Schwinn. 'What else?'

'That's all I saw. Probably a skirt, one of those microminis, that's all she buys. The shoes she already had on.'

'Black with big heels.'

'Shiny black,' said Ingalls. 'Patent leather. Those crazy heels, I kept telling her she'd fall and break her neck.'

'Party outfit,' said Schwinn, copying.

Red-and-black party outfit, thought Milo. Remembering

something that had gone round in high school, boys sitting around pontificating, pointing with glee: red and black on Fridays meant a girl put out all the way. Him, laughing along, pretending to care . . .

Bowie Ingalls said, 'Except for the jeans and T-shirts, that's all she buys. Party stuff.'

'Speaking of which,' said Schwinn, 'let's take a look at her closet.'

The rest of the apartment was two cell-sized bedrooms separated by a windowless bathroom stale with flatulence.

Schwinn and Milo glanced into Bowie Ingalls's sleep chamber as they passed. A queen-size mattress took up most of the floor. Unwashed sheets were pulled half-off, and they puddled on cheap carpeting. A tiny TV threatened to topple from a pressed-wood bureau. More Bud empties.

Janie's room was even smaller, with barely enough space for a single mattress and a nightstand of the same synthetic wood. Cutouts from teen magazines were taped to the walls, mounted at careless angles. A single, muddy-looking stuffed koala slumped on the nightstand, next to a soft pack of Kents and a half-empty box of Luden's cough drops. The room was so cramped that the mattress prevented the closet door from opening all the way, and Schwinn had to contort to get a look inside.

He winced, stepped out, and told Milo, 'You do it.'

Milo's size made the task excruciating, but he obeyed.

Zody's was a cut-rate barn. Even at their prices, Janie Ingalls hadn't assembled much of a wardrobe. On the dusty floor sat one pair of tennis shoes, size 8, next to red Thom McAn platform sandals and white plastic boots with see-through plastic soles. Two pairs of size S jeans were carelessly hung in the closet, one faded denim with holes that could've been genuine wear or contrivance, the other denim patchwork, both made in Taiwan. Four ribbed, snug-fit T-shirts with bias-cut sleeves, a floral cotton blouse with moth wounds pocking the breast pocket, three shiny, polyester halter tops not much bigger than the hankie Schwinn had offered to Ingalls – peacock blue, black, pearlescent white. A red sweatshirt emblazoned *Hollywood* in puffy gold letters, a black plastic shortie jacket pretending to be leather, cracking like an old lady's face.

On the top shelf were bikini underpants, bras, panty hose, more dust. Everything stank of tobacco. Only a few pockets to search. Other than grit and lint and a Doublemint wrapper, Milo found nothing. Such a *blank* existence – not unlike his own apartment, he hadn't bothered to furnish much since arriving in L.A., had never been sure he'd be staying.

He searched the rest of the room. The magazine posters were the closest thing to personal possessions. No diary or date book or photographs of friends. If Janie had ever called this dump home, she'd changed her mind sometime ago. He wondered if she had some other place of refuge – a crash pad, a sanctuary, somewhere she *kept* stuff.

He checked under the bed, found dirt. When he extricated himself, his neck hurt and his shoulders throbbed.

Schwinn and Ingalls were back in the front room, and Milo stopped to check out the bathroom, compressing his nostrils to block out the stench, examining the medicine cabinet. All over-the-counter stuff – painkillers, laxatives, diarrhea remedies, antacids – a host of antacids. Something eating at Bowie Ingalls's gut? Guilt or just alcohol?

Milo found himself craving a drink.

When he joined Schwinn and Ingalls, Ingalls was slumped on the couch, looking disoriented, saying, 'What do I do now?'

Schwinn stood away from the guy, detached. No more use for Ingalls. 'There'll be some procedures to go through – identification, filling out forms. Identification can wait till after the autopsy. We may have more questions for you.'

Ingalls looked up. 'About what?'

Schwinn handed Ingalls his card. 'If you think of anything, give a call.'

'I already told you everything.'

Milo said, 'Was there anywhere else Janie mighta crashed?'

'Like what?'

'Like a crash pad. Somewhere kids go.'

'I dunno where kids go. Dunno where my own kid goes, so how would I know?'

'Okay, thanks. Sorry for your loss, Mr Ingalls.'

Schwinn motioned Milo to the door, but when they got there, he turned back to Ingalls. 'One more thing: what does Melinda look like?'

Basic question, thought Milo, but he hadn't thought to ask it. Schwinn had, but he orchestrated it, time everything. The guy was nuts but miles ahead of him.

'Short, big tits – built big – kinda fat. Blond hair, real long, straight.'

'Voluptuous,' said Schwinn, enjoying the word.

'Whatever.'

'And she's Janie's age?'

'Maybe a little older,' said Ingalls.

'A sophomore, too?'

'I dunno what she is.'

'Bad influence,' said Schwinn.

'Yeah.'

'Do you have a picture of Janie? Something we could show around?'

'I'd have to have one, wouldn't I?' said Bowie, making it sound like the answer to an oral exam. Pulling himself to his feet, he stumbled to his bedroom, returned moments later with a three-by-five snap.

A dark-haired child around ten years old, wearing a sleeveless dress and staring at a five-foot-tall Mickey Mouse. Mickey giving that idiot grin, the kid unimpressed – scared, actually. No way to connect this child to the outrage on Beaudry.

'Disneyland,' said Ingalls.

'You took Janie there?' said Milo, trying to imagine that.

'Nah, it was a school trip. They got a group discount.'

Schwinn returned the photo to Ingalls. 'I was thinking in terms of something more recent.'

'I should have something,' said Ingalls, 'but hell if I can find anything – if I do, I'll call you.'

'I noticed,' said Milo, 'that there was no diary in Janie's room.'

'You say so.'

'You never saw a diary or a date book – a photo album?'

Ingalls shook his head. 'I stayed out of Janie's stuff, but she wouldn't have any of that. Janie didn't like to write. Writing was hard for her. Her mother was like that, too: never really learned to read. I tried to teach Janie. The school didn't do shit.'

Papa Juicehead huddled with Janie, tutoring. Hard to picture.

Schwinn frowned – he'd lost patience with Milo's line of

questioning and gave the doorknob a sharp twist. 'Afternoon, Mr Ingalls.'

As the door closed, Ingalls cried out: 'She was my kid.'

'What a stupid asshole,' said Schwinn, as they headed to Hollywood High. 'Stupid parents, stupid kid. Genes. That's what you were getting at, right, with those questions about school?'

'I was thinking learning problems coulda made her an easier victim,' said Milo.

Schwinn grumbled, 'Anyone can be a victim.'

The school was an ugly pile of gray-brown stucco that filled a block on the north side of Sunset just west of Highland. As impersonal as an airport, and Milo felt the curse of futility the moment his feet touched down on the campus. He and Schwinn walked past what seemed to be thousands of kids – every one of them bored, spaced, surly. Smiles and laughter were aberrations, and any eye contact directed at the detectives was hostile.

They asked directions of a teacher, got the same icy reception, not much better at the principal's office. As Schwinn talked to a secretary, Milo studied girls walking through the sweaty corridor. Tight or minimal clothes and hooker makeup seemed to be the mode, all those freshly developed bodies promising something they might not be able to deliver, and he wondered how many potential Janies were out there.

The principal was at a meeting downtown, and the secretary routed them to the vice principal for operations, who sent them farther down the line to the guidance office. The counselor they spoke to was a pretty young woman named Ellen Sato, tiny, Eurasian, with long, side-winged, blond-tipped hair. The news of Janie's murder made her face crumple, and Schwinn took advantage of it by pressing her with questions.

Useless. She'd never heard of Janie, finally admitted she'd been on the job for less than a month. Schwinn kept pushing and she disappeared for a while, then returned with bad news: no *Ingalls, J.* files on record for any guidance sessions or disciplinary actions.

The girl was a habitual truant, but hadn't entered the system. Bowie Ingalls had been right about one thing: no one cared.

The poor kid had never had any moorings, thought Milo, remembering his own brush with truancy: back when his family still lived in Gary and his father was working steel, making good money, feeling like a breadwinner. Milo was nine, had been plagued by terrible dreams since the summer – visions of men. One dreary Monday, he got off the school bus and instead of entering the school grounds just kept walking aimlessly, placing one foot in front of the other. Ending up at a park, where he sat on a bench like a tired old man. All day. A friend of his mother spotted him, reported him. Mom had been perplexed; Dad, always action-oriented, knew just what to do. Out came the strap. Ten pounds of oily iron-worker's belt. Milo hadn't sat comfortably for a long, long time.

Yet another reason to hate the old man. Still, he'd never repeated the offense, ended up graduating with good grades. Despite the dreams. And all that followed. Certain his father would've killed him if he knew what was *really* going on.

So he made plans at age nine: *You need to get away from these people.*

Now he mused: *Maybe I was the lucky one.*

'Okay,' Schwinn was telling Ellen Sato, 'so you people don't know much about her—'

The young woman was on the verge of tears. 'I'm sorry, sir, but as I said, I just . . . what happened to her?'

'Someone killed her,' said Schwinn. 'We're looking for a friend of hers, probably a student here, also. Melinda, sixteen or seventeen. Long blond hair. Vo*lup*tuous.' Cupping his hands in front of his own, scrawny chest.

Sato's ivory skin pinkened. 'Melinda's a common name—'

'How about a look at your student roster?'

'The roster . . .' Sato's graceful hands fluttered. 'I could find a yearbook for you.'

'You have no student roster?'

'I – I know we have class lists, but they're over in V.P. Sullivan's office and there are forms to be filled out. Okay, sure, I'll go look. In the meantime, I know where the yearbooks are. Right here.' Pointing to a closet.

'Great,' said Schwinn, without graciousness.

'Poor Janie,' said Sato. 'Who would do such a thing?'

'Someone *evil*, ma'am. Anyone come to mind?'
'Oh, heavens no – I wasn't . . . let me go get that list.'

The two detectives sat on a bench in the counseling office waiting room, flipping through the yearbooks, ignoring the scornful eyes of the students who came and went. Copying down the names of every Caucasian Melinda, freshmen included, because who knew how accurate Bowie Ingalls was about age. Not limiting the count to blondes, either, because hair dye was a teenage-girl staple.

Milo said, 'What about light-skinned Mexicans?'

'Nah,' said Schwinn. 'If she was a greaser, Ingalls would've mentioned it.'

'Why?'

'Because he doesn't like her, would've loved to add another bad point to the list.'

Milo returned to checking out young white faces.

The end product: eighteen possibles.

Schwinn regarded the list and scowled. 'Names but no numbers. We'll still need a fucking roster to track her down.'

Talking low but his tone was unmistakable and the receptionist a few feet away looked over and frowned.

'Howdy,' said Schwinn, raising his voice and grinning at the woman furiously. She flinched and returned to her typewriter.

Milo looked up Janie Ingalls's freshman photo. No list of extra-curricular activities. Huge, dark hair teased with abandon over a pretty oval face turned ghostly by slathers of makeup and ghoulish eye shadow. The image before him was neither the ten-year-old hanging with Mickey nor the corpse atop the freeway ramp. So many identities for a sixteen-year-old kid. He asked the receptionist to make a photocopy, and she agreed, grudgingly. Staring first at the picture.

'Know her, ma'am?' Milo asked her as pleasantly as possible.

'No. Here you go. It didn't come out too good. Our machine needs adjusting.'

Ellen Sato returned, freshly made-up, weak-eyed, forcing a smile. 'How'd we do?'

Schwinn bounded up quickly, was in her face, bullying her with body language, beaming that same hostile grin. 'Oh, just great, ma'am.' He brandished the list of eighteen names. 'Now how about introducing us to these lovely ladies?'

Rounding up the Melindas took another forty minutes. Twelve out of eighteen girls were in attendance that day, and they marched in looking supremely bored. Only a couple were vaguely aware of Janie Ingalls's existence, none admitted to being a close friend or knowing anyone who was, none seemed to be holding back.

Not much curiosity, either, about why they'd been called in to talk to cops. As if a police presence was the usual thing at Hollywood High. Or they just didn't care.

One thing *was* clear: Janie hadn't made her mark on campus. The girl who was the most forthcoming ended up in Milo's queue. Barely blond, not-at-all voluptuous Melinda Kantor. 'Oh yeah, her. She's a stoner, right?'

'Is she?' he said.

The girl shrugged. She had a long, pretty face, a bit equine. Two-inch nails glossed aqua, no bra.

Milo said, 'Does she hang around with other stoners?'

'Uh-uh, she's not a social stoner – more like a loner stoner.'

'A loner stoner.'

'Yeah.'

'Which means . . .'

The girl shot him a *you-are-a-prime-lame-o* look. 'She run away or something?'

'Something like that.'

'Well,' said Melinda Kantor, 'maybe she's over on the Boulevard.'

'Hollywood Boulevard?'

The resultant smirk said, *Another stupid question,* and Milo knew he was losing her. 'The boulevard's where the loner stoners go.'

Now Melinda Kantor was regarding him as if he were braindead. 'I was just making a *suggestion.* What'd she do?'

'Maybe nothing.'

'Yeah, right,' said the girl. 'Weird.'

'What is?'

'Usually they send over narcs who are young and cute.'

Ellen Sato produced addresses and phone numbers for the six

absent Melindas, and Milo and Schwinn spent the rest of the day paying house calls.

The first four girls lived in smallish but tidy single homes on Hollywood's border with the Los Feliz district and were out sick. Melindas Adams, Greenberg, Jordan were in bed with the flu, Melinda Hohlmeister had been felled by an asthma attack. All four mothers were in attendance, all were freaked out by the drop-in, but each allowed the detectives access. The previous generation still respected – or feared – authority.

Melinda Adams was a tiny, platinum-haired, fourteen-year-old freshman who looked eleven and had a little kid's demeanor to match. Melinda Jordan was a skinny fifteen-year-old brunette with a frighteningly runny nose and vengeful acne. Greenberg was blond and long-haired and somewhat chesty. Both she and her mother had thick, almost impenetrable accents – recent immigrants from Israel. Science and math books were spread over her bed. When the detectives had stepped in, she'd been underlining text in yellow marker, had no idea who Janie Ingalls was. Melinda Hohlmeister was a shy, chubby, stuttering, homely kid with short, corn-colored ringlets, a straight A average, and an audible wheeze.

No response to Janie's name from any of them.

No answer at Melinda Van Epps's big white contemporary house up in the hills. A woman next door picking flowers volunteered that the family was in Europe, had been gone for two weeks. The father was an executive with Standard Oil, the Van Eppses took all five kids out of school all the time for travel, provided tutors, lovely people.

No reply, either, at Melinda Waters's shabby bungalow on North Gower. Schwinn knocked hard because the bell was taped over and labeled 'Broken.'

'Okay, leave a note,' he told Milo. 'It'll probably be bullshit, too.' Just as Milo was slipping the *please-call-us* memo and his card through the mail slot, the door swung open.

The woman who stood there could have been Bowie Ingalls's spiritual sister. Fortyish, thin but flabby, wearing a faded brown housedress. She had a mustard complexion, wore her peroxided hair pinned back carelessly. Confused blue eyes, no makeup, cracked lips. That furtive look.

'Mrs Waters?' said Milo.

'I'm Eileen.' Cigarette voice. 'What is it?'

Schwinn showed her the badge. 'We'd like to talk to Melinda.'

Eileen Waters's head retracted, as if he'd slapped her. 'About what?'

'Her friend, Janie Ingalls.'

'Oh. Her,' said Waters. 'What'd she do?'

'Someone killed her,' said Schwinn. 'Did a right sloppy job of it. Where's Melinda?'

Eileen Waters's parched lips parted, revealing uneven teeth coated with yellow scum. She'd relied upon suspiciousness as a substitute for dignity and now, losing both, she slumped against the doorjamb. 'Oh my God.'

'Where's Melinda?' demanded Schwinn.

Waters shook her head, lowered it. 'Oh God, oh God.'

Schwinn took her arm. His voice remained firm. 'Where's Melinda?'

More headshakes, and when Eileen Waters spoke again her voice was that of another woman: timid, chastened. Reduced.

She began crying. Finally stopped. 'Melinda never came home, I haven't seen her since *Friday*.'

nine

The Waters household was a step up from Bowie Ingalls's flop, furnished with old, ungainly furniture that might've been hand-me-downs from some upright Midwestern homestead. Browning doilies on the arms of overstuffed chairs said someone had once cared. Ashtrays were everywhere, filled with gray dust and butts, and the air felt sooty. No beer empties, but Milo noticed a quarter-full bottle of Dewars on a kitchen counter next to a jam jar packed with something purple. Every drape was drawn, plunging the house into perpetual evening. The sun could be punishing when your body subsisted on ethanol.

Either Schwinn had developed an instant dislike for Eileen Waters or his bad mood had intensified or he had a genuine reason for riding her hard. He sat her down on a sofa, and began peppering her with questions.

She did nothing to defend herself other than chain-smoke Parliaments, was easy with the confessions:

Melinda was wild, had been wild for a long time, had fought off any attempts at discipline. Yes, she used drugs – marijuana, for sure. Eileen had found roaches in her pockets, wasn't sure about anything harder, but wasn't denying the possibility.

'What about Janie Ingalls?' asked Schwinn.

'You kidding? She's probably the one introduced Melinda to dope.'

'Why's that?'

'That kid was stoned all the time.'

'How old's Melinda?'

'Seventeen.'

'What year in school?'

65

'Eleventh grade – I know Janie's in tenth but just because Melinda's older doesn't mean she was the instigator. Janie was street-smart. I'm sure Janie's the one got Melinda into grass . . . Lord, where could she *be*?'

Milo thought back to his search of Janie's room: no evidence of dope, not even rolling paper or a pipe.

'Melinda and Janie were a perfect pair,' Waters was saying. 'Neither of them gave a damn about school, they cut all the time.'

'What'd you do about it?'

The woman laughed. 'Right.' Then the fear came back. 'Melinda will come back, she always does.'

'In what way was Janie streetwise?' said Schwinn.

'You know,' said Waters. 'You can just tell. Like she'd been around.'

'Sexually?'

'I assume. Melinda was basically a good girl.'

'Janie spend much time here?'

'No. Mostly she'd pick up Melinda, and they'd be off.'

'That the case last Friday?'

'Dunno.'

'What do you mean?'

'I was out shopping. Came home, and Melinda was gone. I could tell she'd been here because she left her underwear on the floor and some food out in the kitchen.'

'Food for one?'

Waters thought. 'One Popsicle wrapper and a Pepsi can – I guess.'

'So the last time you saw Melinda was Friday morning, but you don't know if Janie came by to pick her up.'

Waters nodded. 'She claimed she was going to school, but I don't think so. She had a bag full of clothes, and when I said, "What's all that?" she said she was going to some party that night, might not be coming home. We got into a hassle about that, but what could I do? I wanted to know where the party was but all she told me was it was fancy, on the Westside.'

'Where on the Westside?'

'I just told you, she wouldn't say.' The woman's face twitched. 'Fancy party. Rich kids. She said that a bunch of times. Told me I had nothing to worry about.'

She looked to Schwinn, then Milo, for reassurance, got two stone faces.

'Fancy Westside party,' said Schwinn. 'So maybe Beverly Hills – or Bel Air.'

'I guess . . . I asked her how she was getting all the way over there, she said she'd find a way. I told her not to hitch, and she said she wouldn't.'

'You don't like her hitching.'

'Would you? Standing there on Sunset, thumbing, any kind of pervert . . .' She stopped, went rigid. 'Where was – where'd you find Janie?'

'Near downtown.'

Waters relaxed. 'So there you go, the complete opposite direction. Melinda wasn't with her. Melinda was over on the Westside.'

Schwinn's slit eyes made the merest turn toward Milo. Bowie Ingalls had seen Melinda pick up Janie on Friday, watched the two girls walking north toward Thumb Alley. But no reason to get into that, now.

'Melinda'll come back,' said Waters. 'Sometimes she does that. Stays away. She always comes back.'

'Sometimes,' said Schwinn. 'Like once a week?'

'No, nothing like that – just once in a while.'

'And how long does she stay away?'

'A night,' said Waters, sagging and trying to calm herself with a twenty-second pull on her cigarette. Her hand shook. Confronting the fact that this was Melinda's longest absence.

Then she perked up. 'One time she stayed away two days. Went up to see her father. He's in the Navy, used to live in Oxnard.'

'Where's he live now?'

'Turkey. He's at a naval base there. Shipped out two months ago.'

'How'd Melinda get to Oxnard?'

Eileen Waters chewed her lip. 'Hitched. I'm not going to tell him. Even if I could reach him in Turkey, he'd just start in with the accusations . . . and that bitch of his.'

'Second wife?' said Schwinn.

'His whore,' spat Waters. 'Melinda hated her. Melinda will come home.'

Further questioning was futile. The woman knew nothing more

about the 'fancy Westside party,' kept harping on the downtown murder site as clear proof Melinda hadn't been with Janie. They pried a photo of Melinda out of her. Unlike Bowie Ingalls, she'd maintained an album, and though Melinda's teen years were given short shrift, the detectives had a page of snaps from which to choose.

Bowie Ingalls hadn't been fair to Melinda Waters. Nothing chubby about the girl's figure, she was beautifully curvy with high, round breasts and a tiny waist. Straight blond hair hung to her rear. Kiss-me lips formed a heartbreaking smile.

'Looks like Marilyn, doesn't she?' said her mother. 'Maybe one day she'll be a movie star.'

Driving back to the station, Milo said, 'How long before her body shows up?'

'Who the fuck knows?' said Schwinn, studying Melinda's picture. 'From the looks of this, maybe Janie was the appetizer and this one was the main dish. Look at those tits. That'd give him something to play with for a while. Yeah, I can see him holding on to this one for a while.'

He pocketed the photo.

Milo envisioned a torture chamber. The blond girl nude, shackled . . . 'So what do we do about finding her?'

'Nothing,' said Schwinn. 'If she's already dead, we have to wait till she shows up. If he's still got her, he's not gonna tell us.'

'What about that Westside party?'

'What about it?'

'We could put the word out with West L.A., the sheriffs, Beverly Hills PD. Sometimes parties get wild, the blues go out on a nuisance call.'

'So what?' said Schwinn. 'We show up at some rich asshole's door, say, "Excuse me, are you cutting up this kid?" ' He sniffed, coughed, produced his bottle of decongestant, and swigged. 'Shit, Waters's dump was dusty. All-American mom, another poor excuse for an adult. Who knows if there even *was* a party.'

'Why wouldn't there be?'

'Because kids lie to their parents.' Schwinn swiveled toward Milo. 'What's with all these fucking questions? You thinking of going to law school?'

Milo held his tongue, and the rest of the ride was their usual joyfest. A block from the station, Schwinn said, 'You wanna go snooping for Westside nuisance calls, be my guest, but I think Blondie was lying to Mommy like she always did because a fancy Westside party was exactly the kind of thing that would calm the old lady down. Hundred to one Blondie and Janie were fixing to thumb the Strip, score some dope, maybe trade blow jobs for it, or whatever. They got into the wrong set of wheels and ended up downtown. Janie was too stupid to learn from her past experience – or like I said, maybe she liked being tied up. She was a stoner. Both of them probably were.'

'Your source mentioned a Westside party.'

'Street talk's like watermelon, you got to pick around the seeds. The main thing is Janie was *found* downtown. And chances are Melinda's somewhere around there, too, if a scrote got her and finished with her. For all we know, he kept her in the trunk while he was setting up Janie on Beaudry. Got back on the freeway, he could be in Nevada by now.'

He shook his head. 'Stupid kids. Two of them thought they had the world in their sweet little hands, and the world upped and bit 'em.'

Back at the station, Schwinn collected his things from his desk and walked off without a word to Milo. Not even bothering to sign out. No one noticed: none of the detectives paid much attention to Schwinn, period.

An outcast, Milo realized. *Did they stick me with him by coincidence?*

Pushing all that aside, he played phone poker until well after dark. Contacting every police entity west of Hollywood Division in search of 415 party calls. Throwing in rent-a-cop outfits, too: The Bel Air Patrol, and other private firms that covered Beverlywood, Cheviot Hills, Pacific Palisades. The privates turned out to be the worst to deal with – no one was willing to talk without supervisory clearance and Milo had to leave his name and badge number, wait for callbacks that probably wouldn't happen.

He kept going, casting his net to Santa Monica and beyond, even including the southern edge of Ventura County, because Melinda

Waters had once hitched PCH to Oxnard to see her father. And kids flocked to the beach for parties – he'd spent many a sleepless night driving up and down the coast highway, spotting bonfires that sparked the tide, the faint silhouettes of couples. Wondering what it would be like to have someone.

Four hours of work resulted in two measly hits – either L.A. had turned sleepy, or no one was complaining about noise anymore.

Two big zeros: an eye surgeon's fiftieth birthday party on Roxbury Drive in Beverly Hills had evoked a Friday midnight complaint from a cranky neighbor.

'Kids? No, don't think so,' laughed the BH desk officer. 'We're talking black tie, all that good stuff. Lester Lanin's orchestra playing swing and still someone bitched. There's always some killjoy, right?'

The second call was a Santa Monica item: a bar mitzvah on Fifth Street north of Montana had been closed down just after 2 A.M., after rambunctious thirteen-year-olds began setting off firecrackers.

Milo put the phone down and stretched. His ears burned and his neck felt like dry ice. Schwinn's voice was an obnoxious mantra in his head as he left the station just before 1 A.M.

Told you so, asshole. Told you so, asshole.

He drove to a bar – a straight one on Eighth Street, not far from the Ambassador Hotel. He'd passed it several times, a shabby-looking place on the ground floor of an old brick apartment building that had seen better days. The few patrons drinking this late were past their prime, too, and his entrance lowered the median age by a few decades. Mel Tormé on tape loop, scary-looking toothpicked shrimp and bowls full of cracker medley decorated the cloudy bar top. Milo downed a few shots and beers, kept his head down, left, and drove north to Santa Monica Boulevard, cruising Boystown for a while, but didn't even wrestle with temptation: tonight the male hookers looked predatory, and he realized he wanted to be with no one, not even himself. When he reached his apartment, images of Melinda Waters's torment had returned to plague him, and he pulled down a bottle of Jim Beam from a kitchenette cupboard. Tired but wired. Removing his clothes was an ordeal, and the sight of his pitiful, white body made him close his eyes.

He lay in bed, wishing the darkness was more complete. Wishing for a brain valve that would choke off the pictures. Alcohol lullabies finally eased him, stumbling, to sleep.

The next morning, he drove to a newsstand and picked up the morning's *Times* and *Herald-Examiner.* No reporter had called him or Schwinn on the Ingalls murder, but something that ugly was sure to be covered.

But it wasn't, not a line of print.

That made no sense. Reporters were tuned in to the police band, covered the morgue, too.

He sped to the station, checked his own box and Schwinn's for journalistic queries. Found only a single phone slip with his name at the top. Officer Del Monte from the Bel Air Patrol, no message. He dialed the number, talked to a few flat, bored voices before finally reaching Del Monte.

'Oh, yeah. You're the one called about parties.' The guy had a crisp, clipped voice, and Milo knew he was talking to an ex–military man. Middle-aged voice. Korea, not VN.

'That's right. Thanks for calling back. What've you got?'

'Two on Friday, both times kids being jerks. The first was a sweet sixteen on Stradella, all-girls' sleepover that some punks tried to crash. Not local boys. Black kids and Mexicans. The girls' parents called us, and we ejected them.'

'Where were the crashers from?'

'They claimed Beverly Hills.' Del Monte laughed. 'Right.'

'They give you any trouble?'

'Not up front. They made like they were leaving Bel Air – we followed them to Sunset, then hung back and watched. Idiots crossed over near UCLA, then tried to come back a few minutes later and head over to the other party.' Del Monte chuckled, again. 'No luck, Pachuco. Our people were already there on a neighbor complaint. We ejected them before they even got out of the car.'

'Where was the second party?'

'That was the live one, big-time noise. Upper Stone Canyon Drive way above the hotel.'

The locale Schwinn's source had mentioned. 'Whose house?'

'Empty house,' said Del Monte. 'The family bought a bigger one but didn't get around to selling the first one and the parents took a vacation, left the kiddies behind and, big surprise, the kiddies decided to use the empty house for fun 'n' games, invited the entire damn city. Must've been two, three hundred kids all over the place, cars – Porsches and other good wheels, and plenty of outside wheels. By the time we showed up, it was a scene. It's a big property, coupla acres, no real close-by neighbors, but by now the closest neighbors were fed up.'

'By now?' said Milo. 'This wasn't the first time?'

Silence. 'We've had a few other calls there. Tried to contact the parents, no luck, they're always out of town.'

'Spoiled brats.'

Del Monte laughed. 'You didn't hear that from me. Anyway, what's up with all this?'

'Tracing a 187 victim's whereabouts.'

Silence. 'Homicide? Nah, no way. This was just kids partying and playing music too loud.'

'I'm sure you're right,' said Milo. 'But I've got rumors that my db might've attended a party on the Westside, so I've gotta ask. What's the name of the family that owns the house?'

Longer silence. 'Listen,' said Del Monte. 'These people – you do me wrong, I could be parking cars. And believe me, no one saw anything worse than drinking and screwing around – a few joints, big deal, right? Anyway, we closed it down.'

'I'm just going through the routine, Officer,' said Milo. 'Your name won't come up. But if I don't check it out, *I'll* be parking cars. Who owns the house and what's the address?'

'A rumor?' said Del Monte. 'There had to be tons of parties Friday night.'

'Any party we hear about, we look into. That's why yours won't stick out.'

'Okay . . . the family's named Cossack.' Del Monte uttered it weightily, as if that was supposed to mean something.

'Cossack,' said Milo, keeping his tone ambiguous.

'As in office buildings, shopping malls – Garvey Cossack. Big downtown developer, part of that bunch wanted to bring another football team to L.A.'

'Yeah, sure,' lied Milo. His interest in sports had peaked with Pop Warner baseball. 'Cossack on Stone Canyon. What's the address?'

Del Monte sighed and read off the numbers.

'How many kids in the family?' said Milo.

'Three – two boys and a girl. Didn't see the daughter there, but she could've been.'

'You know the kids personally?'

'Nah, just by sight.'

'So the boys threw the party,' said Milo. 'Names?'

'The big one's Garvey Junior and the younger one's Bob but they call him Bobo.'

'How old?'

'Junior's probably twenty-one, twenty-two, Bobo's maybe a year younger.'

More than kids, thought Milo.

'They gave us no trouble,' said Del Monte. 'They're just a couple guys like to have fun.'

'And the girl?'

'Her I didn't see.'

Milo thought he picked up something new in Del Monte's voice. 'Name?'

'Caroline.'

'Age?'

'Younger – maybe seventeen. It was really no big deal, everyone dispersed. My message said you're Central. Where was your db found?'

Milo told him.

'There you go,' said Del Monte. 'Fifteen miles from Bel Air. You're wasting your time.'

'Probably. Three hundred partying kids just caved when you showed up?'

'We've got experience with that kind of thing.'

'What's the technique?' said Milo.

'Use sensitivity,' said the rent-a-cop. 'Don't treat 'em like you would a punk from Watts or East L.A. 'cause these kids are accustomed to a certain style.'

'Which is?'

'Being treated like they're important. If that doesn't work, threaten to call the parents.'

'And if that doesn't work?'

'That usually works. Gotta go, nice talking to you.'

'I appreciate the time, Officer. Listen, if I came by and showed a photo around, would there be a chance anyone would recognize a face?'

'Whose face?'

'The vic's.'

'No way. Like I said, it was a swarm. After a while they all start to look alike.'

'Rich kids?'

'Any kids.'

It was nearly 10 A.M., and Schwinn still hadn't shown up. Figuring sooner rather than later was the best time to spring Janie's photo on Del Monte and his patrol buddies, Milo threw on his jacket and left the station.

Del Monte had been decent enough to call and look where it got him.

No good deed goes unpunished.

It took nearly forty minutes to reach Bel Air. The patrol office was a white, tile-roofed bungalow tucked behind the west gate. Lots of architectural detail inside and out – Milo would've been happy to make it his house. He'd heard that the gates and the private-cop scrutiny had been instituted by Howard Hughes when he lived in Bel Air because the billionaire didn't trust LAPD.

The rich taking care of their own. Just like the party on Stone Canyon: ticked-off neighbors, but everything kept private, no nuisance call had reached the West L.A. station.

Del Monte was at the front desk, and when Milo came in, his dark, round face turned sour. Milo apologized and whipped out a crime-scene snap he'd taken from the pile Schwinn had left in his desk. The least horrifying of the collection – side view of Janie's face, just the hint of ligature ring around the neck. Del Monte's response was a cursory head flick. Two other guards were drinking coffee, and they gave the picture more careful study, then shook their heads. Milo would have liked to show Melinda Waters's photo, but Schwinn had pocketed it.

He left the patrol office and drove to the party house on Stone Canyon Drive. Huge, redbrick, three-story, six-column colonial. Black double doors, black shutters, mullioned windows, multiple gables. Milo's guess was twenty, twenty-five rooms.

The Cossack family had moved to something more generous.

A huge dry lawn and flaking paint on some of the shutters said the maintenance schedule had slackened since the house had emptied. Shredded hedges and scraps of paper confettiing the brick walkway were the only evidence of revelry gone too far. Milo parked, got out, picked up one of the shreds, hoping for some writing, but it was soft and absorbent and blank – heavy-duty paper towel. The gate to the backyard was bolted and opaque. He peered over, saw a big blue egg of a pool, rolling greenery, lots of brick patio, blue jays pecking. Behind one of the hedges, the glint of glass – cans and bottles.

The nearest neighbor was to the south, well separated from the colonial by the broad lawns of both houses. A much smaller, meticulously maintained one-story ranch emblazoned with flower beds and fronted by dwarf junipers trimmed Japanese-style. The northern border of the Cossack property was marked by a ten-foot stone wall that went on for a good thousand feet up Stone Canyon. Probably some multiacre estate, a humongous chateau pushed back too far from the street to be visible.

Milo walked across the dry lawn and the colonial's empty driveway, up to the ranch house's front door. Teak door, with a shiny brass knocker shaped like a swan. Off to the right a small cement Shinto shrine presided over a tiny, babbling stream.

A very tall woman in her late sixties answered his ring. Stout and regal with puffy, rouged cheeks, she wore her silver hair tied back in a bun so tight it looked painful, had sheathed her impressive frame in a cream kimono hand-painted with herons and butterflies. In one liver-spotted hand was an ivory-handled brush with pointed bristles tipped with black ink. Even in black satin flat slippers she was nearly eye level with Milo. Heels would have made her a giantess.

'Ye-es?' Watchful eyes, deliberate contralto.

75

Out came the badge. 'Detective Sturgis, Mrs . . .'

'Schwartzman. What brings a detective to Bel Air?'

'Well, ma'am, last Friday your neighbors had a party—'

'A party,' she said, as if the description was absurd. She aimed the brush at the empty colonial. 'More like rooting at the trough. The aptly named Cossacks.'

'Aptly named?'

'Barbarians,' said Mrs Schwartzman. 'A scourge.'

'You've had problems with them before.'

'They lived there for less than two years, let the place go to seed. That's their pattern, apparently. Move in, degrade, move out.'

'To something bigger.'

'But of *course*. Bigger is better, right? They're vulgarians. No surprise, given what the father does.'

'What does he do?'

'He destroys period architecture and substitutes grotesquerie. Packing cartons pretending to be office buildings, those drive-in monstrosities – strip malls. And *she* . . . desperately blonde, the sweaty anxiety of an *arriviste*. Both of them gone all the time. No supervision for those brats.'

'Mrs Schwart—'

'If you'd care to be precise, it's Dr Schwartzman.'

'Pardon me, Doctor—'

'I'm an endocrinologist – retired. My husband is Professor Arnold Schwartzman, the orthopedic surgeon. We've lived here twenty-eight years, had wonderful neighbors for twenty-six – the Cantwells, he was in metals, she was the loveliest person. The two of them passed on within months of one another. The house went into probate, and *they* bought it.'

'Who lives on the other side?' said Milo, indicating the stone walls.

'Officially, Gerhard Loetz.'

Milo shot her a puzzled look.

'German industrialist.' As if everyone should know. 'Baron Loetz has homes all over the world. Palaces, I've been told. He's rarely here. Which is fine with me, keeps the neighborhood quiet. Baron Loetz's property extends to the mountains, the deer come down to graze. We get all sorts of wildlife in the canyon. We love it.

Everything was perfect until *they* moved in. Why are you asking all these questions?'

'A girl went missing,' said Milo. 'There's a rumor she attended a party on the Westside Friday night.'

Dr Schwartzman shook her head. 'Well, I wouldn't know about that. Didn't get a close look at those hoodlums, didn't want to. Never left the house. Afraid to, if you'd like to know. I was alone, Professor Schwartzman was in Chicago, lecturing. Usually, that doesn't bother me, we have an alarm, used to have an Akita.' The hand around the brush tightened. Man-sized knuckles bulged. 'But Friday night was alarming. So *many* of them, running in and out, screaming like banshees. As usual, I called the patrol, had them stay until the last barbarian left. Even so, I was nervous. What if they came back?'

'But they didn't.'

'No.'

'So you never got close enough to see any of the kids.'

'That's correct.'

Milo considered showing her the death photo anyway. Decided against it. Maybe the story hadn't hit the papers because someone upstairs wanted it that way. Dr Schwartzman's hostility to the Cossacks might very well fuel another rumor. Working alone like this, he didn't want to screw up big-time.

'The patrol,' he said, 'not the police— '

'That's what we do in Bel Air, Detective. We pay the patrol, so they respond. Your department, on the other hand – there seems to be a belief among law enforcement types that the problems of the . . . fortunate are trivial. I learned that the hard way, when Sumi – my doggie – was murdered.'

'When was this?'

'Last summer. Someone poisoned him. I found him right there.' Indicating the front lawn. 'They unlatched the gate and fed him meat laced with rat poison. That time, I did call your department, and they finally sent someone out. A detective. Allegedly.'

'Do you remember his name?'

Dr Schwartzman gave a violent headshake. 'Why would I? He barely gave me the time of day, clearly didn't take me seriously. Didn't even bother to go over there, just referred it to Animal

Control, and all *they* offered to do was dispose of Sumi's body, thank you very much for nothing.'

'They?' said Milo.

Schwartzman's brush pointed at the party house.

'You suspect one of the Cossacks poisoned Sumi?'

'I don't suspect, I know,' said Schwartzman. 'But I can't prove it. The daughter. She's mad, quite definitely. Walks around talking to herself, a bizarre look in her eyes, all hunched over. Wears the same clothes for days on end. And she brings black boys home – clearly not right. Sumi despised her. Dogs have a nose for madness. Anytime that crazy girl walked by, poor Sumi would fly into a rage, throw himself against the gate, it was all I could do to calm him down. And let me tell you, Detective, the only time he responded that way was to stranger intrusion. Protective, Akitas are, that's the whole point of an Akita. But sweet and smart – he loved the Cantwells, even grew accustomed to the gardeners and the mailman. But never to that girl. He knew when someone was wrong. Simply despised her. I'm sure she poisoned him. The day I found his poor body, I spied her. Watching me through a second-story window. That pair of mad eyes. Staring. I stared right back and waved my fist, and you'd better believe that drapery snapped back into place. *She* knew that *I* knew. But soon after, she came out and walked past me – right past me, staring. She's a frightening thing, that girl. Hopefully that party was the last time we'll see them around here.'

'She was at the party?' said Milo.

Dr Schwartzman crossed her arms across her bosom. 'Have you been listening to me, young man? I told you, I didn't get close enough to check.'

'Sorry,' said Milo. 'How old is she?'

'Seventeen or eighteen.'

'Younger than her brothers.'

'*Those* two,' said Schwartzman. 'So *arrogant.*'

'Ever have any problems with the brothers other than parties?'

'All the time. Their attitude.'

'Attitude?'

'Entitled,' said Schwartzman. 'Smug. Just thinking about them makes me angry, and anger is bad for my health, so I'm going to resume my calligraphy. Good day.'

Before Milo could utter another syllable, the door slammed shut and he was staring at teak. No sense pushing it; *Frau Doktor* Schwartzman could probably beat him in an arm wrestle. He returned to the car, sat there wondering if anything she'd said mattered.

The Cossack brothers had a bad attitude. Like every other rich kid in L.A.

The sister, on the other hand, sounded anything but typical – if Schwartzman could be believed. And if Schwartzman's suspicion about her dog was right, Sister Cossack's quirkiness was something to worry about.

Seventeen years old made Caroline Cossack an age peer of Janie Ingalls and Melinda Waters. A rich girl with a wild side and access to the right toys might very well have attracted two street kids.

Taking black boys home. Racism aside, that spelled rebel. Someone willing to push the envelope.

Dope, a couple of party girls venturing from Hollywood into uncharted territory . . . still, it came down to nothing more than rumor, and he had nowhere to take it.

He stared at the empty party house, took in Bel Air silence, shabby grace, a lifestyle he'd never attain. Feeling out of his element, every inch the ignorant rookie.

And now he had to report back to Schwinn.

This is a whodunit. This likes to munch on your insides, then shit you out in pellets . . .

The bastard's reproachful voice had crept into his head and camped there, obnoxious but authoritative.

While Milo'd spun his wheels, Schwinn had come up with the single useful lead on the Ingalls case: the tip that had led them straight to Janie's father.

A source he wouldn't identify. Not even bothering to be coy, coming right out and accusing Milo of spying for the brass.

Because he knew he was under suspicion? Maybe *that's* why the other Ds seemed to shun the guy. Whatever was going on, Milo'd been shoved square in the middle of it . . . he had to push all that aside and concentrate on the *job*. But the job – going

79

nowhere – made him feel inadequate.

Poor Janie. And Melinda Waters – what was the chance *she* was alive? What would *she* look like when they finally found her?

It was nearly noon and he couldn't remember the last time he'd eaten. But he could find no reason to stop for grease. Had no appetite for anything.

ten

He arrived back at the station wondering if Schwinn had returned and hoping he hadn't. Before he made it to the stairwell, the desk sergeant said, 'Someone's waiting for you,' without looking up.

'Who?'

'Go see for yourself. Interview Five.'

Something in the guy's voice pinged Milo's gut. 'Interview Five?'

'Uh-huh.' The blue kept his head down, busy with paperwork.

An interrogation room. Someone being questioned – a suspect for Ingalls in custody so soon? Had Schwinn pulled off another solo end run?

'I wouldn't keep them waiting,' said the sergeant, writing something down, still avoiding eye contact.

Milo peered over the counter, saw a crossword puzzle book. 'Them.'

No answer.

Milo hurried down the too-bright corridor that housed the interview rooms and knocked on Five. A voice, not Schwinn's, said, 'Come in.'

He opened the door and came face to face with two tall men in their thirties. Both were broad-shouldered and good-looking, in well-cut charcoal suits, starched white shirts, and blue silk ties.

Corporate Bobbsey twins – except one guy was white – Swedish pink, actually, with a crew cut the color of cornflakes – and the other was black as the night.

Together they nearly spanned the width of the tiny, stale room, a two-man offensive line. Black had opened the door. He had a smooth, round head topped by a razor-trimmed cap of ebony fuzz and glowing, hairless, blue-tinged skin. The clear, hard eyes of a drill instructor. His unsmiling mouth was a fissure in a tar pit.

Pinkie hung toward the rear of the tiny room, but he was the first to speak.

'Detective Sturgis. Have a seat.' Reedy voice, Northern inflection – Wisconsin or Minnesota. He pointed to the room's solitary chair, a folding metal affair on the near side of the interrogation table, facing the one-way mirror. The mirror, not even close to subterfuge, every suspect knew he was being observed, the only question was by whom? And now Milo was wondering the same thing.

'Detective,' said the black man. Offering him the *suspect* chair.

On the table was a big, ugly Satchell-Carlson reel-to-reel tape recorder, the same gray as the twins' suits. Everything color-coordinated – like some psychology experiment and guess who was the guinea pig . . .

'What's going on?' he said, remaining in the doorway.

'Come in and we'll tell you,' said Pinkie.

'How about a proper introduction?' said Milo. 'As in who are you and what's this all about?' Surprising himself with his assertiveness.

The suits weren't surprised. Both looked pleased, as if Milo had confirmed their expectation.

'Please come in,' said Black, putting some steel into 'please.' He came closer, stepped within inches of Milo's nose, and Milo caught a whiff of expensive aftershave, something with citrus in it. The guy was taller than Milo – six-four or -five – and Pinkie looked every bit as big. Size was one of the few advantages Milo figured God had given him; for the most part, he'd used it to avoid confrontation. But between these guys and the Wagnerian Dr Schwartzman it had been a bad day for exploiting body type.

'Detective,' said Black. His face was strangely inanimate – an African war mask. And those eyes. The guy had presence; he was used to being in charge. That was curious. Since the Watts riots, there'd been some race progress in the department, but for the most part it was lip service. Blacks and Mexicans were despised by the brass, shunted to dead-end patrol jobs in the highest-crime segments of Newton, Southwest, and Central, with scant chance for advancement. But this guy – his suit looked like mohair blend, the stitching on the lapels hand-sewn – what kind of dues had he paid and who the hell was he?

He stepped aside and, as Milo entered the room, nodded approvingly. 'In terms of an introduction, I'm Detective Broussard and this is Detective Poulsenn.'

'Internal Affairs,' said Poulsenn.

Broussard smiled. 'In terms of why we want you here, it would be better if you sat down.'

Milo settled on the folding chair.

Poulsenn remained in the far corner of the interrogation room, but cramped quarters placed him close enough for Milo to count the pores in his nose. If he'd had any. Like Broussard, his complexion glowed like a poster for clean living. Broussard positioned himself to Milo's right, angled so Milo had to crane to see his lips move.

'How do you like Central Division, Detective?'

'I like it fine.' Milo chose not to strain to meet Broussard's eyes, kept his attention on Poulsenn but stayed inert and silent.

'Enjoying homicide work?' said Broussard.

'Yes, sir.'

'What about homicide work do you like, specifically?'

'Solving problems,' said Milo. 'Righting wrongs.'

'Righting wrongs,' said Broussard, as if impressed by the originality of the response. 'So homicide can be righted.'

'Not in the strict sense.' This was starting to feel like one of those stupid grad school seminars. Professor Milrad taking out his frustration on hapless students.

Poulsenn checked his fingernails. Broussard said, 'Are you saying you enjoy trying to achieve justice?'

'Exactly—'

'Justice,' said Poulsenn, 'is the point of all police work.'

'Yes, it is,' said Broussard. 'Sometimes, though, justice gets lost in the shuffle.'

Slipping a question mark into the last few words. Milo didn't bite, and Broussard went on: 'A shame when that happens, isn't it, Detective Sturgis?'

Poulsenn inched closer. Both IA men stared down at Milo.

He said, 'I'm not getting the point of—'

'You were in Vietnam,' said Broussard.

'Yes—'

'You were a medic, saw lots of action.'

'Yes.'

'And before that you earned a master's degree.'

'Yes.'

'Indiana University. American literature.'

'Correct. Is there some—'

'Your partner, Detective Schwinn, never went to college,' said Broussard. 'In fact, he never finished high school, got grandfathered in back when that was acceptable. Did you know that?'

'No—'

'Nor did Detective Schwinn serve in any branch of the military. Too young for Korea, too old for 'Nam. Have you found that a problem?'

'A problem?'

'In terms of commonality. Developing rapport with Detective Schwinn.'

'No, I . . .' Milo shut his mouth.

'You . . . ?' said Broussard.

'Nothing.'

'You were about to say something, Detective.'

'Not really.'

'Oh, yes you were,' said Broussard, suddenly cheerful. Milo craned, involuntarily. Saw his purplish, bowed lips hooked up at the corners. But Broussard's mouth locked shut, no teeth. 'You were definitely going to say something, Detective.'

'I . . .'

'Let's recap, Detective, to refresh your memory. I asked you if Detective Schwinn's lack of higher education and military service had posed a problem for you in terms of rapport and you said, "No, I . . .". It was fairly obvious that you changed your mind about saying what you were going to say.'

'There's no problem between Detective Schwinn and myself. That's all I was going to say. We get along fine.'

'Do you?' said Poulsenn.

'Yes.'

Broussard said, 'So Detective Schwinn agrees with your point of view.'

'About what?'

'About justice.'

'I – you'd have to ask him.'

'You've never discussed weighty issues with Detective Schwinn?'

'No, as a matter of fact, we concentrate on our cases—'

'You're telling us that Detective Schwinn has never verbalized any feelings about the job to you? About righting wrongs? Achieving justice? His attitude toward police work?'

'Well,' said Milo, 'I can't really pinpoint—'

Poulsenn stepped forward and pushed the RECORD button on the Satchell-Carlson. Kept going and ended up inches from Milo's left side. Now both IA men were flanking him. Boxing him in.

Broussard, 'Are you aware of any improper behavior on the part of Detective Schwinn?'

'No—'

'Consider your words before you speak, Detective Sturgis. This is an official department inquiry.'

'Into Detective Schwinn's behavior or mine?'

'Is there a reason to look into *your* behavior, Detective Sturgis?'

'No, but I didn't know there was any reason to look into Detective Schwinn's behavior.'

'You didn't?' said Poulsenn. To Broussard: 'His position seems to be that he's unaware.'

Broussard clicked his tongue. Switched off the recorder, pulled something out of a jacket pocket. A sheaf of papers that he waved. Milo was craning hard now, saw the front sheet, the familiar layout of a photocopied mug shot.

Female arrestee, dead-eyed and dark-skinned. Mexican or a light-skinned black. Numbers hanging on her chest.

Broussard peeled off the sheet, held it in front of Milo's eyes.

Darla Washington, DOB 5-14-54, HT 5-06 WT 134.

Instinctively, Milo's eyes dropped to the penal code violation: **653.2**

Loitering for the purpose of prostitution . . .

'Have you ever met this woman?' said Broussard.

'Never.'

'Not in the company of Detective Schwinn or anyone else?'

'Never.'

'It wouldn't be in the company of anyone else,' said Poulsenn, cheerfully.

Nothing happened for a full minute. The IA men letting that last bit of dialogue sink in. Letting Milo know that they knew he was the least likely man in the room to engage a female hooker?

Or was *he* being paranoid? This was about Schwinn, not him. *Right?*

He said, 'Never saw her anywhere.'

Broussard placed Darla Washington's sheet at the bottom of the stack, flashed the next page.

LaTawna Hodgkins.

P.C. 653.2.

'What about this woman?'

'Never saw her.'

This time, Broussard didn't push, just moved to the next page. The game went on for a while, a collection of bored/stoned/sad-eyed streetwalkers, all black. Donna Lee Bumpers, Royanne Chambers, Quitha Martha Masterson, DeShawna Devine Smith.

Broussard shuffled the 653.2 deck like a Vegas pro. Poulsenn smiled and watched. Milo kept outwardly cool but his bowels were churning. Knowing exactly where this was going.

She was the eighth card dealt.

Different hair than last night's red extravagance – a bleached blond mushroom cloud that made her look ridiculous. But the face was the same.

Schwinn's backseat tumble.

Tonya Marie Stumpf. The Teutonic surname seemed incongruous, where had *that* come from—

The mug shot danced in front of him for a long time, and he realized he hadn't responded to Broussard's, 'And this woman?'

Broussard said, 'Detective Sturgis?'

Milo's throat tightened and his face burned and he had trouble breathing. Like one of those anaphylactic reactions he'd seen as a medic. Perfectly healthy guys surviving firefights only to keel over from eating peanuts.

He felt as if *he'd* been force-fed something toxic . . .

'Detective Sturgis,' Broussard repeated, nothing friendly in his tone.

'Yes, sir?'

'This woman. Have you seen her before?'

They'd been watching the unmarked, surveilling Schwinn and *him* – for how long? Had they been spying the Beaudry murder site? Snooped during the entire time he and Schwinn had been riding together?

So Schwinn's paranoia *had* been well justified. And yet, he'd picked up Tonya Stumpf and had her do him in the backseat, the stupid, no-impulse-control sonofa—

'Detective Sturgis,' Broussard demanded. 'We need an answer.'

A whir from the table distracted Milo. Tape reels, revolving slowly. When had the machine been switched on again?

Milo broke out in a full-body sweat. Recalling Schwinn's tirade in front of Bowie Ingalls's building, the sudden, vicious distrust, convinced Milo was a plant, and now . . .

Told you so.

'Detective,' said Broussard. 'Answer the question. *Now.*'

'Yes,' said Milo.

'Yes, what?'

'I've seen her.'

'Yes, you have, son,' said Broussard, crouching low, exuding citrus and success.

Son. The asshole was only a few years older than Milo, but it was clear who had the power.

'You definitely *have* seen her.'

They kept him in there for another hour and a half, taping his statement then replaying it, over and over. Explaining that they wanted to make sure everything had copied accurately, but Milo knew the real reason: wanting him to hear the fear and evasiveness in his own voice in order to instill self-loathing, soften him up for whatever they had in store.

He copped only to the basic details of Tonya's pickup – stuff they knew already – and resisted the pressure to elaborate. The room grew hot and rancid with fear as they changed the subject from Tonya to Schwinn's comportment, in general. Picking at him like

87

gnats, wanting to hear about Schwinn's political views, racial attitudes, his opinions about law enforcement. Prodding, pushing, cajoling, threatening Milo subtly and not so subtly, until he felt as alive as chuck steak.

They returned to probing sexual details. He maintained his denial of witnessing any actual sexual encounters between Schwinn and Tonya or anyone else. Which was technically correct, he'd kept his eyes on the road, had harbored no desire to rearview-peep the blow job.

When they asked about the conversation between Schwinn and Tonya, he gave them some bullshit story about not hearing because it had all been whispers.

'Whispers,' said Broussard. 'You didn't think that was unusual? Detective Schwinn whispering to a known prostitute in the backseat of your department-issue vehicle?'

'I figured it for work talk. She was an informant, and Schwinn was pressing her for info.'

Waiting for the obvious next question: 'Info on what?' But it never came.

No questions at all about Janie Ingalls's murder or any other case he and Schwinn had worked.

'You thought she was an informant,' said Poulsenn.

'That's what Detective Schwinn said.'

'Then why the whispering?' said Broussard. 'You're Detective Schwinn's alleged partner. Why would he keep secrets from you?'

Because he knew this would happen, asshole. Milo shrugged. 'Maybe there was nothing to tell.'

'Nothing to tell?'

'Not every snitch has something to offer,' said Milo.

Broussard waved that off. 'How long were Schwinn and Tonya Stumpf in the backseat of the car as *you* drove?'

'Not long – maybe a few minutes.'

'Quantify that.'

Knowing the car had probably been observed, Milo kept it close to the truth. 'Ten, maybe fifteen minutes.'

'After which Tonya Stumpf was dropped off.'

'Correct.'

'Where?'

'Eighth Street near Witmer.'

'After she left the unmarked, where did she go?'

He named the Ranch Depot Steak House, but didn't mention Schwinn's funding of Tonya's dinner.

'Did money exchange hands?' said Poulsenn.

Not knowing how much they'd seen, he chanced a lie. 'No.'

Long silence.

'During the entire time,' Broussard finally said, 'you were driving.'

'Correct.'

'When Detective Schwinn asked you to stop to pick up Tonya Stumpf, you weren't at all concerned about being an accessory to prostitution?'

'I never saw any evidence of prosti—'

Broussard's hand slashed air. 'Did Tonya Stumpf's mouth make contact with Detective Schwinn's penis?'

'Not that I—'

'If you were driving, never looked back, as you claim, how can you be so sure?'

'You asked me if I saw something. I didn't.'

'I asked you if oral-genital contact occurred.'

'Not that I saw.'

'So Tonya Stumpf's mouth might have made contact with Detective Schwinn's penis without your seeing it?'

'All I can say is what I saw.'

'Did Detective Schwinn's penis make contact with Tonya Stumpf's vagina or Tonya Stumpf's *anus*?'

'I never saw that.' Was the bastard emphasizing *anus* because . . . ?

'Did Tonya Stumpf engage in physical intimacy of any sort with Detective Schwinn?'

'I never saw that,' Milo repeated, wondering if they'd used some sort of night scope, had everything on film and he was burnt toast—

'Mouth on penis,' said Poulsenn. 'Yes or no?'

'No.'

'Penis on or in vagina.'

'No.'

'Penis on or in *anus*.'

89

Same emphasis. Definitely not coincidence. 'No,' said Milo, 'and I think I'd better talk to a Protective League representative.'

'Do you?' said Broussard.

'Yes, this is obviously—'

'You could do that, Detective Sturgis. If you think you really need representation. But why would you think that?'

Milo didn't answer.

'Do you have something to worry about, Detective?' said Broussard.

'I didn't until you guys hauled me in—'

'We didn't haul you, we invited you.'

'Oh,' said Milo. 'My mistake.'

Broussard touched the tape recorder, as if threatening to switch it on again. Leaned in so close Milo could count the stitches on his lapel. No pores. Not a single damn pore, the bastard was carved of ebony. 'Detective Sturgis, you're not implying coercion, are you?'

'No—'

'Tell us about your relationship with Detective Schwinn.'

Milo said, 'We're partners, not buddies. Our time together is spent on work. We've cleared seven homicides in three months – one hundred percent of our calls. Recently, we picked up an eighth one, a serious whodunit that's gonna require—'

'Detective,' said Broussard. Louder. Cutting off that avenue of conversation. 'Have you ever witnessed Detective Schwinn receiving money from anyone during work hours?'

No desire to talk about Janie Ingalls.

Caught up in his headhunter ritual, one that wouldn't – couldn't – be stopped – until it played itself out. Or something else: an *active* disinterest in Janie Ingalls?

Milo said, 'No.'

'Not with Tonya Stumpf?'

'No.'

'Or anyone else?' barked Broussard.

'No,' said Milo. 'Never, not once.'

Broussard lowered his face and stared into Milo's eyes. Milo felt his breath, warm, steady, minty – now suddenly sour, as if bile had surged up his gullet. So the guy had body processes after all.

'Not once,' he repeated.

★　★　★

They let him go as abruptly as they'd hauled him in, no parting words, both IA men turning their backs on him. He left the station directly, didn't go upstairs to his desk or bother to check his messages.

The next morning a departmental notice appeared in his home mailbox. Plain white envelope, no postmark, hand-delivered.

Immediate transfer to the West L.A. station, some gobbledygook about manpower allocation. A typed addendum said he'd already been assigned a locker there and listed the number. The contents of his desk and his personal effects had been moved from Central.

His outstanding cases had been transferred to other detectives.

He phoned Central, tried to find out who'd caught Janie Ingalls's murder, got a lot of runaround, finally learned that the case had left the station and gone to Metro Homicide – Parker Center's high-profile boys.

Kicked upstairs.

Metro loved publicity, and Milo figured finally Janie would hit the news.

But she didn't.

He phoned Metro, left half a dozen messages, wanting to give them the information he hadn't had time to chart in the Ingalls murder book. The Cossack party, Melinda Waters's disappearance, Dr Schwartzman's suspicions about Caroline Cossack.

No one returned his calls.

At West L.A., his new lieutenant was piggish and hostile, and Milo's assignment to a partner was delayed – more department gibberish. A huge pile of stale 187s and a few new ones – idiot cases, luckily – landed on his desk. He rode alone, walked through the job like a robot, disoriented by his new surroundings. West L.A. had the lowest crime stats in the city, and he found himself missing the rhythm of the bloody streets.

He made no effort to make friends, avoided socializing after hours. Not that invitations came his way. The Westside's Ds were even colder than his Central colleagues, and he wondered how much of it could be blamed on his pairing with Schwinn, maybe picking up a snitch jacket. Or had the rumors followed him here, too?

Fag cop. Fag *snitch* cop? A few weeks in, a cop named Wes Baker tried to be social – telling Milo he'd heard Milo had a master's, it was about time someone with brains went into police work. Baker figured himself for an intellectual, played chess, lived in an apartment full of books and used big words when small ones would've sufficed. Milo saw him as a pretentious jerk, but allowed Baker to rope him in on double dates with his girlfriend and her stewardess pals. Then one night Baker drove by and spotted him standing on a West Hollywood street corner, waiting for the light to change. The only men out walking were seeking other men, and Baker's silent stare told Milo plenty.

Shortly after, someone broke into Milo's locker and left a stash of sadomasochistic gay porn.

A week after that, Delano Hardy – the station's only black D – was assigned to be his partner. The first few weeks of their rides were tight-lipped, worse than with Schwinn, almost unbearably tense. Del was a religious Baptist who'd run afoul of the brass by criticizing the department's racial policies, but he had no use for sexual nonconformity. News of the porn stash had gotten round; ice-eyes seemed to follow Milo around.

Then things eased. Del turned out to be psychologically flexible – a meticulous straight-arrow with good instincts and an obsession with doing the job. The two of them began working as a team, solved case after case, forged a bond based on success and the avoidance of certain topics. Within six months, they were in the groove, putting away bad guys with no sweat. *Neither* of them invited to station house barbecues, bar crawls. Cop-groupie gang bangs.

When the work day was over, Del returned to a Leimert Park tract home and his upright, uptight wife who still didn't know about Milo, and Milo skulked back to his lonely-guy pad. But for the Ingalls case, he had a near-perfect solve rate.

But for the Ingalls case . . .

He never saw Pierce Schwinn again, heard a rumor the guy had taken early retirement. A few months later he called Parker Center Personnel, lied, managed to learn that Schwinn had left with no record of disciplinary action.

So maybe it had nothing to do with Schwinn, after all, and

everything to do with Janie Ingalls. Emboldened, he phoned Metro again, fishing for news on the case. Again, no callback. He tried Records, just in case someone had closed it, was informed they had no listing of the case as solved, no sighting of Melinda Waters.

One hot July morning, he woke up dreaming about Janie's corpse, drove over to Hollywood, and cruised by Bowie Ingalls's flop on Edgemont. The pink building was gone, razed to the dirt, the soil chewed out for a subterranean parking lot, the beginnings of framework set in place. The skeleton of a much larger apartment building.

He drove to Gower and headed a mile north. Eileen Waters's shabby little house was still standing but Waters was gone and two slender, effeminate young men – antiques dealers – were living there. Within moments, both were flirting outrageously with Milo, and that scared him. He'd put on all the cop macho, and still they could tell . . .

The pretty-boys were renting, the house had been vacant when they'd moved in, neither had any idea where the previous tenant had gone.

'I'll tell you one thing,' said one of the lads. 'She was a smoker. The place reeked.'

'Disgusting,' agreed his roomie. 'We cleaned up everything, went neo-Biedermeier. You wouldn't recognize it.' Grinning conspiratorially. 'So tell us. What did she *do*?'

eleven

Milo finished the story and walked into my kitchen.

The beeline to the fridge, finally.

I watched him open the freezer compartment where the bottle of Stolichnaya sat. The vodka had been a gift from him to Robin and me, though I rarely touched anything other than Scotch or beer and Robin drank wine.

Robin . . .

I watched him fill half a glass, splash in some grapefruit juice for color. He drained the glass, poured a refill, returned to the dining-room table.

'That's it,' he said.

I said, 'A black detective named Broussard. As in . . .'

'Yup.'

'Ah.'

Tossing back the second vodka, he returned to the kitchen, fixed a third glass, more booze, no juice. I thought of saying something – sometimes he wants me to play that role. Remembered how much Chivas I'd downed since Robin's departure and held my tongue.

This time, when he returned, he sat down heavily, wrapped thick hands around the glass, and swirled, creating a tiny vodka whirlpool.

'John G. Broussard,' I said.

'None other.'

'The way he and the other guy leaned on you. Sounds Kafkaesque.'

He smiled. 'Today I woke up as a cockroach? Yeah, good old John G. had a knack for that kind of thing from way back. Served the lad well, hasn't it?'

John Gerald Broussard had been L.A.'s chief of police for a little over two years. Handpicked by the outgoing mayor, in what many claimed was an obvious pander aimed at neutralizing critics of LAPD's racial problems, Broussard had a military bearing and a staggeringly imperious personality. The City Council distrusted him, and most of his own officers – even black cops – despised him because of his headhunter background. Broussard's open disdain for anyone who questioned his decisions, his apparent disinterest in the details of street policing, and his obsession with interdepartmental discipline helped complete the picture. Broussard seemed to revel in his lack of popularity. At his swearing-in ceremony, decked out as usual in full dress uniform and a chestful of ribbon candy, the new chief laid out his number one priority: zero tolerance for any infractions by police officers. The following day, Broussard dissolved a beloved system of community-police liaison outposts in high-crime neighborhoods, claiming they did nothing to reduce felonies and that excessive fraternization with citizens 'deprofessionalized' the department.

'Spotless John Broussard,' I said. 'And maybe he helped bury the Ingalls case. Any idea why?'

He didn't answer, drank some more, glanced again at the murder book.

'Looks like it was really sent to you,' I said.

Still no reply. I let a few more moments pass. 'Did anything ever develop on Ingalls?'

He shook his head.

'Melinda Waters never showed up?'

'I wouldn't know if she did,' he said. 'Once I got to West L.A., I didn't pursue it. For all I know, she got married, had kids, is living in a nice little house with a big-screen TV.'

Talking too fast, too loud. I knew confession when I heard it.

He ran a finger under his collar. His forehead was shiny, and the stress cracks around his mouth and eyes had deepened.

He finished the third vodka, stood, and aimed his bulk back at the kitchen.

'Thirsty,' I said.

He froze, wheeled. Glared. 'Look who's talking. Your eyes. You gonna tell me you've been dry?'

'This morning I have been,' I said.

'Congratulations. Where's Robin?' he demanded. 'What the hell's going on with you two?'

'Well,' I said, 'my mail's been interesting.'

'Yeah, yeah. Where is she, Alex?'

Words filled my head but logjammed somewhere in my throat. My breath got short. We stared at each other.

He laughed first. 'Show you mine if you show me yours?'

I told him the basics.

'So it was an opportunity for her,' he said. 'She'll get it out of her system, and come back.'

'Maybe,' I said.

'It happened before, Alex.'

Thanks for the memory, pal. I said, 'This time I can't help thinking it's more. She kept the offer from me for two weeks.'

'You were busy,' he said.

'I don't think that's it. The way she looked at me in Paris. The way she left. The fault line might have shifted too much.'

'C'mon,' he said, 'how about some optimism? You're always preaching to me about that.'

'I don't preach. I suggest.'

'Then I *suggest* you shave and scrape the crud from your eyes and get into clean clothes, stop ignoring her calls, and try to work things out, for God's sake. You guys are like . . .'

'Like what?'

'I was gonna say an old married couple.'

'But we're not,' I said. 'Married. All these years together and neither of us took the initiative to make it legal. What does that say?'

'You didn't need the paperwork. Believe me, I know all about that.'

He and Rick had been together even longer than Robin and I.

'Would you if you could?' I said.

'Probably,' he said. 'Maybe. What's the big issue between you guys, anyway?'

'It's complicated,' I said. 'And I haven't been avoiding her. We just keep missing each other.'

'Try harder.'

'She's on the road, Milo.'

'Try harder, anyway, goddammit.'

'What's *with* you?' I said.

'Acute *disillusionment*. On top of all the chronic disillusionment the job deals me.' He clapped a hand on my shoulder. 'I need some things in my life to be constant, pal. As in you guys. I want Robin and you to be okay for *my* peace of mind, okay? Is that too much to ask? Yeah, yeah, it's self-centered, but tough shit.'

What can you say to that?

I sat there, and he swiped at his brow. More sweat leaked through. He looked thoroughly miserable. Crazily enough, I felt guilty.

'We'll work it out,' I heard myself saying. 'Now tell me why you looked like death when you saw Janie Ingalls's photo?'

'Low blood sugar,' he said. 'No time for breakfast.'

'Ah,' I said. 'Hence the vodka.'

He shrugged. 'I thought it was out of my head, but maybe I figure I should've pursued it.'

'Maybe "NS" means someone else thinks you should pursue it now. Do any of the other photos in the book mean anything to you?'

'Nope.'

I looked at the gloves he'd discarded. 'Going to run prints?'

'Maybe,' he said. Then he grimaced.

'What?'

'Ghost of failures past.'

He poured a fourth glass, mostly juice, maybe an ounce of vodka.

I said, 'Any guesses who sent it?'

'Sounds like you've got one.'

'Your ex-partner, Schwinn. He had a fondness for photography. And access to old police files.'

'Why the hell would he be contacting me now? He couldn't stand me. Didn't give a damn about the Ingalls case or any other.'

'Maybe time has mellowed him. He worked Homicide for twenty years before you came on. Meaning he'd have been on the job during much of the period covered by the photos. The ones that preceded his watch, he swiped. He bent the rules, so lifting a few crime-scene photos wouldn't have been much of an ethical stretch. The book could be part of a collection he assembled over the years. He called it the murder book and bound it in blue, to be cute.'

'But why send it to me *via* you? Why now? What's his damn point?'

'Is Janie's picture one Schwinn could've snapped himself?'

Peeling on a new pair of gloves, he flipped back to the death shot.

'Nah, this is professionally developed, better quality than what he'd have gotten with that Instamatic.'

'Maybe he had the film reprocessed. Or if he's still a photography bug, he's got himself a home darkroom.'

'Schwinn,' he said. 'Screw all this hypothesizing, Alex. The guy didn't trust me when we worked together. Why would he be contacting me?'

'What if he learned something twenty years ago that he's finally ready to share? Such as the source that directed him to Bowie Ingalls and the party. Maybe he feels guilty about holding back, has the urge to come clean. By now, he'd be close to seventy, could be sick or dying. Or just introspective – age can do that. He knows *he's* in no position to do anything about the case but figures you might be.'

He thought about that. Degloved again, stood, stared at the fridge but didn't move. 'We can spin theories all day, but the book could've been sent by anyone.'

'Could it?' I said. 'Janie's murder never hit the news, so it had to be someone with inside information. And Schwinn's belief in science becoming a major investigative tool might play into it. That day has arrived, right? DNA testing, all that other good stuff. If semen and blood samples were saved—'

'I don't even know if there *was* any semen in her, Alex. Schwinn figured it for a sex thing, but neither of us ever saw the autopsy results. Once they closed us down, I never saw a scrap of official paper.' A big fist slammed the table, and the murder book jumped. 'This is total bullshit.'

I kept my mouth shut.

He began pacing the dining room. 'Bastard – I have a good mind to go face to face with him. If it was him – so why was it sent to you?'

'Covering tracks,' I said. 'Schwinn knew we worked together – another indication of an interest in police affairs.'

'Or just someone who reads the paper, Alex. Our names were paired on the Teague case.'

'And you came out of that one smelling sweet, big solve. Schwinn may not have liked you or respected or trusted you, but maybe he's followed your career and changed his mind.'

'Give me a break.' He picked up his glass. A thread of vodka had settled on the bottom, an icy ribbon of alcohol. 'All this hypothesizing, my head feels like it's gonna split open. Sometimes I wonder what exactly it is that forms the basis for our friendship.'

'That's easy,' I said. 'Common pathology.'

'What pathology?'

'Mutual inability to let go. Schwinn – or whoever sent the murder book – knows it.'

'Yeah, well screw him. I'm not biting.'

'Your decision.'

'Damn right.'

'Ah,' I said.

'I hate when you do that,' he said.

'Do what?'

'Say "Ah." Like a fucking dentist.'

'Ah.'

His arm drew back and a big-fisted hand shot toward my jaw. He tapped gently, mouthed, 'Pow.'

I hooked a thumb at the blue album. 'So what do you want me to do, toss it?'

'Don't do anything.' He got to his feet. 'I'm feeling a little . . . gonna take a nap. The spare bedroom fixed up?'

'As always. Pleasant dreams.'

'Thank you, Norman Bates.' He stomped toward the rear of the house, was gone for maybe ten minutes before returning tieless, shirt untucked. Looking as if he'd crammed a night's worth of nightmares into six hundred seconds.

'What I'm gonna do—' he said. '—*all* I'm gonna do, is make a basic attempt to find Schwinn. As in make a call. If I find him and it turns out he did send the book, he and I will have a little chat, believe me. If it wasn't him, we forget the whole thing.'

'Sounds like a plan.'

'What? You don't like it?'

'It's fine with me,' I said.

'Good. 'Cause that's it.'

'Great.'

Regloving, he picked up the murder book, headed for the front door, said, 'Sayonara. It's almost been fun.' As he stepped outside, he said: 'Be there for Robin's call. Deal with it, Alex.'

'Sure.'

'I don't like when you get agreeable.'

'Then screw you.'

He grinned. 'Ah.'

I sat there a long time, feeling low. Wondering if Robin would call from Eugene. Figuring if she didn't within a couple of hours, I'd go somewhere, anywhere.

I fell asleep at the dining-room table. The phone woke me two hours later.

'Alex.'

'Hi.'

'I finally got you,' she said. 'I've tried so many times.'

'Been out. Sorry.'

'Out of town?'

'Just errands. How's it going?'

'Fine. Great – the tour. We've been getting excellent publicity. Sellout crowds.'

'How's Oregon?'

'Green, pretty. Mostly I've seen soundstages.'

'How's Spike?'

'He's good . . . adapting . . . I miss you.'

'Miss you, too.'

'Alex?'

'Uh-huh?'

'What's – are you okay?'

'Sure . . . so tell me, are sex, drugs, and rock 'n' roll what they're cracked up to be?'

'It's not like that,' she said.

'Which part? The sex or the drugs?'

Silence. 'I'm working really hard,' she said. 'Everyone is. The logistics are incredible, putting everything together.'

'Exciting.'

'It's satisfying.'

'I'd hope so,' I said.

Longer silence. 'I feel,' she said, 'that you're very far away from me. And please don't be literal.'

'As opposed to metaphorical?'

'You're angry.'

'I'm not, I love you.'

'I really *do* miss you, Alex.'

'Nothing's stopping you from coming home anytime,' I said.

'It's not that simple.'

'Why not?' I said. 'What, it's turned into a heavy metal tour, shackles and chains?'

'Please don't be like this, Alex.'

'Like what?'

'Sarcastic – veiled. I know you're mad at me, and that's probably the real reason you didn't call me back right away, but—'

'You leave, and I'm the bad guy?' I said. 'Yes, the real reason we missed each other was I was in no shape to talk to anyone. Not anger, I just got . . . hollow. After that I did try to call but like you said, you're busy. I'm not angry, I'm . . . do what you need to do.'

'Do you want me to quit?'

'No, you'd never forgive me for that.'

'I want to stay.'

'Then stay.'

'Oh, Alex . . .'

'I'll try to be Mr Cheerful,' I said.

'No, I don't want that.'

'Probably couldn't pull it off anyway. Never been much of a performer – guess I wouldn't fit in with your new buddies.'

'Alex, please . . . oh, *damn* – hold on! They're calling me, some sort of crisis – dammit, I don't want to sign off like this—'

'Do what you need to do,' I said.

'I'll call you later – I love you, Alex.'

'Love you too.'

Click.

Good work, Delaware. For this we sent you to therapist school?

I shut my eyes, struggled to empty my head, then filled it with mental snapshots.

Finally, I found the image I wanted and wedged it behind my eyes.

Janie Ingalls's brutalized body.

A dead girl, granting me momentary grace, as I lost myself in her imagined agony.

twelve

One thing about sensory deprivation: it does tend to freshen up your perceptions. And a plan – any plan – opens the door to self-importance.

When I left the house, the sun kissed me like a lover, and the trees were greener under a benevolent sun that reminded me why people kept moving to California. I collected the day's mail – junk junk junk – then walked around to the rear garden and stopped at the pond. The koi were a sinuous brocade, hyperactive, clamoring at the rock border, brought to the surface by my footsteps.

Ten very hungry fish. I made them happy. Then I drove to school.

I used my crosstown med school faculty card to get a parking spot on the U's north campus, walked to the Research Library, sat myself down in front of a computer, began with the in-house data banks, then logged onto the Internet and made my way through half a dozen search engines.

Janie or *Jane Ingalls* pulled up the Ingalls-Dudenhoffer family tree website from Hannibal, Missouri. Great-great-great-grandmother Jane Martha Ingalls would be 237 years old next week.

Bowie Ingalls connected me to a David Bowie fan club in Manchester, England, and to a University of Oklahoma history professor's site on Jim Bowie.

Several *Melinda Waters* hits popped up but none seemed remotely relevant: a physicist by that name worked at Lawrence Livermore Laboratory, nineteen-year-old Melinda Sue Waters was hawking nude pictures of herself from a small town in Arkansas, and Melinda Waters, Attorney-at-Law ('*Specializing in Bankruptcy and*

Evictions!) advertised her services on a legal bulletin board out of Santa Fe, New Mexico.

No crime stories or death notices on either girl. Perhaps Janie's friend had indeed surfaced, as Milo had suggested, and slipped back into society unnoticed.

I tried her mother's name – Eileen – with no success.

Next search: Tonya Marie Stumpf. Nothing on Pierce Schwinn's backseat playmate. No surprise there, I hadn't expected an aging hooker to have her own website.

No data on Pierce Schwinn, either. His surname pulled up several Schwinn bicycle items and one news piece that caught my eye because it was relatively local: a Ventura weekly's account of a horse show last year. One of the winners was a woman named Marge Schwinn, who raised Arabians in a place called Oak View. I looked up the town. Seventy miles north of L.A., near Ojai. Exactly the kind of semirural escape that might attract an ex-cop. I wrote down her name.

Logging the activities of the Cossack family kept me busy for a long time, as I caught dozens of articles in the *L.A. Times* and the *Daily News* that stretched back to the sixties.

The boys' father, Garvey Cossack, Senior, had received intermittent coverage for tearing down buildings and putting up shopping centers, working the zoning board for variances, mixing with politicians at fundraisers. Cossack Development had contributed to the United Way and to all the right diseases, but I found no records of donations to the Police Benevolent Society or any links to John G. Broussard or the LAPD.

A twenty-five-year-old social-page picture showed Cossack Senior to be a short, bald, rotund man, with huge black-framed eyeglasses, a tiny dyspeptic mouth, and a fondness for oversize pocket squares. His wife, Ilse, was taller than he by half a head, with dishwater hair worn too long for her middle-aged face, hollow cheeks, tense hands, and barbiturate eyes. Other than chairmanship of a Wilshire Country Club charity debutante ball, she'd stayed out of the limelight. I checked the list of young women presented at the ball. No mention of Caroline Cossack, the girl who never changed her clothes and might've poisoned a dog.

Garvey, Jr, and Bob Cossack began making the papers by their midtwenties – just a few years after the Ingalls murder. Senior had keeled over on the seventh hole of the Wilshire Country Club golf course, and the reins of Cossack Development passed to the sons. They'd diversified almost immediately, continuing ongoing construction projects but also bankrolling a slew of independent foreign films, none of which made money.

Calendar shots showed the Cossack brothers attending premieres, sunning in Cannes, venturing to Park City for the Sundance Festival, eating hip-for-a-nanosecond cuisine, hanging out with starlets and fashion photographers, addicted heirs, people famous for being famous, the usual assortment of Hollywood leeches.

Garvey Cossack, Jr, seemed to love the camera – his face was always closest to the lens. But if he thought himself photogenic, that was more than a bit of delusion. The visage he flaunted was squat, porcine, topped by thinning, curly, light brown hair and anchored by a squishy dinner roll of a neck that propped up the sphere of cranium like an adipose brace. Younger brother Bob ('Bobo' because as a kid he'd loved the wrestler Bobo Brazil) was also coarse-featured, but thinner than his brother, with long, dark hair combed straight back from a low, square brow and a Frank Zappa mustache that diminished his chin. Both brothers favored the black suit-and-T-shirt combo, but it came across as costumery. Nothing fit Garvey right, and Bobo looked as if he'd shoplifted his threads. These countenances were meant for the back room, not the klieg lights.

The Cossack brothers' big-screen adventures appeared to last for three years, then they shifted gears and began making noises about bringing a football team to the Coliseum. Resurrecting one of their father's unfulfilled dreams. Assembling a 'consortium' of financial types, the brothers submitted a proposal to the city council that ended up being denounced by the more populist members as a scheme to lock in taxpayer financing of their for-profit plan.

The sports venture fizzled as had the movie game, and for a couple years, the Cossacks were out of print. Then Garvey Cossack resurfaced with plans for a federally funded community redevelopment project in the San Fernando Valley, and Bobo garnered attention for attempting to demolish a Hollywood bowling alley that the locals wanted preserved as a landmark in order to put up a giant strip mall.

Their mother's obituary was dated three years ago. Ilse Cossack had died '. . . *after a long battle with Alzheimer's disease . . . private services, in lieu of flowers, donations to. . .* '

Still no mention of Sister Caroline.

I began scanning the Web and the periodicals files for accounts of sexual homicides taking place within five years of Janie Ingalls's murder, found nothing dramatically similar. Interesting, because sexual sadists don't quit voluntarily, so maybe Janie's murderer was dead or imprisoned. If so, would Milo ever get the answers he wanted?

I went downstairs to the Public Affairs Room, got my hands on every back issue of the *FBI Law Enforcement Journal* I could find, along with stacks of forensic magazines and crime periodicals. Because the savagery of what had been done to Janie was notable and perhaps the wound pattern – scalping in particular – had repeated itself.

But if it had, I couldn't find the evidence. The FBI magazine had veered away from VICAP alerts and detailed crime studies to bland cop-speak articles geared for public relations, and the only case report involving removal of cranial skin cropped up in a wire service piece on crime in Brazil: a German-born doctor, son of a Nazi immigrant, had murdered several prostitutes and kept their scalps as trophies. The man was in his late twenties – a toddler at the time of the Ingalls case. Everyone starts off as a cute little baby.

Maybe Janie's murderer had continued to pursue his grisly interests without leaving any bodies behind.

But that didn't make sense. He'd flaunted Janie's corpse twenty years ago and was likely to get more, not less, brazen.

When I got home, my message machine registered zero calls. I phoned Milo's house and Rick Silverman answered, sounding sleepy. He's an ER surgeon. No matter when I call, I seem to be waking him up.

'Alex. How's it going?' He sounded casual. So Milo hadn't told him about Robin.

'Fine, and with you?'

'I'm working, they're paying me, I'm not complaining.'

'You're the only doctor who isn't.'

He laughed. 'Actually, I'm bitching plenty, but too much of that and you get bored with yourself. I keep telling myself it's a good thing I'm salaried, don't have to deal with the HMOs directly. Maybe one day Milo'll pay all the bills.'

'That'll be the year he heads to Paris for the big couture shows.'

He laughed again but I was thinking: *Paris? Where did that come from, Professor Freud?*

'So you're busy,' I said.

'Just came off an eighteen-hour fun-fest. Multicar collision. Daddy and Mommy having a spat in front, two kids in the back, three and five, no car seats, no belts. Daddy and Mommy survived. She may even walk again – enough of this or I'll have to pay you. The big guy's not in. Breezed by for dinner, then left.'

'He say where he was going?'

'Nope. We had Chinese takeout and I nearly fell asleep in my moo goo. When I woke, he'd tucked me in and left a note saying he might be busy for a while. He did seem a little edgy. Is there something I should know about? You two into something new?'

'No,' I said. 'Everything's old.'

I tried reading, watching TV, listening to music, meditating – what a joke *that* was, all I could focus on was bad stuff. By 10 P.M. I was ready to claw the plaster from the walls and wondering when Robin would call again.

At this hour, the Eugene concert would be in full force and she'd be backstage, wonderfully harried. *Needed.* All those guitar-strumming, save-the-world sonofabitch—

Rrrrring.

My 'hello' was breathless. 'What, you in the middle of working out?' said Milo.

'I'm in the middle of nothing. What's up?'

'I can't locate Schwinn, but I might've found his old lady.'

'First name Marge? Mecca Ranch in Oak View?' I said.

His exhalation was a protracted hiss. 'Well, well, well, someone's been a busy worker bee.'

'More like a drone. How'd you find her?'

'Exemplary detective work,' he said. 'I got hold of Schwinn's retirement file – a naughty thing, so this stays between you and me.'

'His pension checks went to the ranch?'

'For the first fifteen years after he left, they went to an address in Simi Valley. Then he switched to a post-office box in Oxnard for two years, *then* the ranch. He's not listed in any DMV files, but the address cross-referenced to Marge Schwinn. I just called her, got a machine, left a message.'

'No DMV listing for him,' I said. 'Think he's dead?'

'Or he doesn't drive anymore.'

'An ex-cop who doesn't drive?'

'Yeah,' he said. 'True.'

'Suburban life in Simi followed by a two-year POB interlude before the ranch. That could be divorce, intervening lonely bachelor-hood, remarriage.'

'Or widowhood. His first wife was named Dorothy and she stopped being a beneficiary when he moved to Oxnard. Two years later, Marge came on.' He paused. 'Dorothy . . . I think he mentioned her name. It's getting hard to tell what I remember and what's wishful thinking. Anyway, that's it, for now.'

I recounted my time in the library, what I'd learned about the Cossacks.

'Rich kids stay rich,' he said. 'Big surprise. I also looked for Melinda Waters. She's on no state files, and neither is her mother, Eileen. That may not mean much if she got married and/or Mom got remarried and they both changed their names. I wish I knew the name of Melinda's Navy dad, but I never learned it. The guy had shipped out to Turkey, good luck tracing that. I did locate Bowie Ingalls, and he's definitely dead. Nineteen years dead.'

'A year after Janie,' I said. 'What happened?'

'Single-motorist vehicular accident up in the hills. Ingalls plowed into a tree and went through the windshield. Blood alcohol four times the legal limit, dozen Bud empties in the car.'

'Up in the hills where?'

'Bel Air. Near the reservoir. Why?'

'Not that far from the party house.'

'So maybe he was reminiscing,' he said. 'The facts still say drunk driver. The whole Cossack angle was pure supposition. For all I know, Janie and Melinda went to a whole other party. Or Schwinn was right and there was no Westside link at all, they got picked up by a psychopath and slaughtered nearer to the dump site. I'm tired, Alex. Gonna head home.'

'What's the plan with Marge Schwinn?'

'She's got my message.'

'And if she doesn't return it?'

'I'll try again.'

'If Schwinn is dead, maybe Marge sent the murder book,' I said. 'She could've come across it in his effects, along with a reference to you and me—'

'Anything's possible, my friend.'

'If you do reach her, mind if I tag along?'

'Who says I'm visiting her?'

I didn't answer. He said, 'What, you've got nothing better to do?'

'Not a thing.'

He humphed.

'Robin called,' I said. 'We talked.'

'Good,' he said, putting a question mark on the end of it.

I swerved back into safe territory: 'By the way, did you have time to run the prints on the murder book?'

'Just one set that I can see.'

'Mine.'

'Well,' he said, 'I'm no ace powder man, but I *have* printed you, and those whorls look familiar.'

'So whoever sent it wiped it clean,' I said. 'Interesting. Either way.'

He knew exactly what I meant: a careful cop, or a fastidious, taunting killer.

'Whatever,' he said. 'Nighty-night.'

'Have some sweet dreams, yourself.'

'Oh, sure. Here come the sugarplum fairies.'

thirteen

I didn't expect to hear from him anytime soon, but the following morning at eleven, he showed up at my front door, wearing a navy windbreaker over a plaid shirt and baggy jeans. Below the jacket, his gun bulged his waistline, but otherwise he looked like a guy with a day off. I was still in my robe. No call, so far, from Robin.

'Ready for fresh air?' he said. 'Horse manure? All of the above?'

'The second Mrs Schwinn got back to you.'

'The second Mrs Schwinn didn't, but I figured what the hell, Ojai's pretty this time of year.'

A reflexive 'Ah' rose in my throat and stuck there. 'I'll get dressed.'

'That would be best.'

He said, 'The Seville's nice on long drives,' and I obliged. The moment I started the engine, he threw back his head, shut his eyes, covered them with a handkerchief, let his mouth drop open. For the next hour, he dozed in the passenger seat, opening his eyes periodically to gaze out the window and appraise the world with distrust and wonder, the way kids and cops do.

I didn't feel conversational, either, and I played music for company. Some old Oscar Aleman cuts from the Buenos Aires days, Aleman wailing away on a diamond-bright, nickel-silver National guitar. The route to Oak View was north on the 405, transfer to the 101 toward Ventura, then an exit on Highway 33. Ten more miles on two lanes that sliced through pink-gray mountains but rose barely above sea level took us toward Ojai. Ocean moisture hung in the air and the sky was cottony white above the horizon, then slate-colored strata where the sun should have been.

The stifled light brought out the greens, turned the world nuclear-blast emerald.

It had been a few years since I'd been here – chasing down a psychopath bent on revenge and meeting up with an impressive man named Wilbert Harrison. I had no idea if Harrison still lived in Ojai. A psychiatrist and a philosopher, he'd taken a reflective view of life, and given the violence I'd introduced him to, I could see him moving on.

The first few miles of Highway 33 were insulted by slag fields, oil rigs, rows of metallic coils that crowned the cable-and-pylon salad of an electrical plant like so much oversize *fusilli*. Soon after that everything turned woodsy and Ojai-heterogenous: cute little cabins graced by meticulous stone walls and shadowed by live oaks and pines, cute little shops selling homemade candles and fragrances. Massage clinics, yoga institutes, schools that would teach you how to draw, paint, sculpt, find inner peace, if only you'd let them into your consciousness. Mixed in with all that was the other side of small-town life: rusty mobile homes behind barbed-wire fencing, bait-and-tackle sheds, trucks on blocks, dusty homesteads with one or two hollow-bellied horses nosing the dirt, crude placards advertising beef jerky and homemade chili, boarding stables, modest shrines to the conventional God. And everywhere the hawks, huge, relaxed, confident, circling in lazy predatory arcs.

Mecca Ranch was on the west side of 33, announced by nailed-on iron letters in a pine slab, the sign bordered by cactus and some sort of wild grass. A left turn up a barely paved road lined with scraggly birds of paradise in poor flower, took us five hundred yards into low, gentle hills that topped off at a couple of acres of gravel-colored mesa. Off to the right was a corral fashioned from iron posts and wooden crossbeams, more than big enough for the five brown horses grazing. Sleek, well-nourished steeds. They paid us no attention. Directly behind the enclosure were several unhitched horse trailers and a bunk of paddocks. Up at road's end, the birds of paradise were planted more closely together and better tended, and the orange-and-blue blossoms led the eye to a small, flat-roofed salmon-colored house with teal green wood trim. Parked in front were a ten-year-old brown Jeep Wagoneer and a Dodge pickup of the same color and vintage. A transitory shadow washed over the corral – a hawk orbiting so low I could see the surgical curve of its beak.

I turned off the engine, got out, filled my nose with the bite of pine and that curious maple-syrup-and-rot tang of dried equine dung. Dead silence. I could see Pierce Schwinn thinking this would be heaven. But if he was like Milo and so many other people hooked on noise and evil, how long would that have lasted?

Milo slammed the passenger door hard, as if offering fair warning. But no one came out to greet us, and no face appeared in the house's undraped front windows.

We walked to the front door. Milo's bell-push set off fifteen seconds of chimes – some tune I couldn't identify, but it brought back memories of Missouri department store elevators.

Now, sound from the corral: one horse whinnying. Still no human response. The hawk had flown off.

I studied the animals. Well-muscled mahogany creatures, two stallions, three mares, manes glossy and combed. Over the corral arced a semicircle of iron soldered with vaguely Moorish lettering. *Mecca.* A triangle of blue had broken through the cottony sky. The foothills ringing the ranch were green-topped, gentle, a nurturant border. It was hard to imagine the murder book emanating from this quiet place.

Milo rang again, and a female voice called out, 'One minute!' Moments later the door opened.

The woman who stood there was petite and strong-shouldered, anywhere from fifty to sixty. She wore a royal blue and yellow checked shirt tucked into tight jeans that showed off a flat tummy, tight waist, boyish hips. Creased but clean work boots peeked out from under the jeans. White hair that retained some of its blond origins was tied back in a short ponytail – a merest upward twist of free locks. Her features were strong in a way that made them attractive in later life, but as a girl she'd probably been plain. Her eyes were a mottle of green and brown, lacking too much of the former to be called hazel. She'd plucked her eyebrows into spidery commas but wore no makeup. Her skin was testament to everything the sun could do to skin: puckered, cracked, corrugated, coarse to the point of woodiness. A few scary-looking dark patches danced under the eyes and crowned her chin. When she smiled, her teeth were the milky white pearls of a healthy virgin.

'Mrs Schwinn?' said Milo, reaching for the badge.

Before he got it out of his pocket, the woman said, 'I'm Marge, and I know who you are, Detective. I got your messages.' No apology for not returning the calls. Once the smile faded, not much in the way of any emotion, and I wondered if that contributed to even-tempered horses.

'I know the cop look,' she explained.

'What look is that, ma'am?'

'Fear mixed with anger. Always expecting the worst. Sometimes, Pierce and I would be riding, and there'd be a sound, a scurrying in the brush, and he'd get the look. So . . . you were his last partner. He talked about you.' She glanced at me. The past tense hung heavy.

She bit her lip. 'Pierce is dead. Died last year.'

'I'm sorry.'

'So am I. I miss him terribly.'

'When did—'

'He fell off a horse seven months ago. One of my tamest, Akhbar. Pierce was no cowboy, he never rode until he met me. That's why I gave him Akhbar as a regular mount, and they bonded. But something must've spooked Akhbar. I found him down near Lake Casitas, on his side, with two broken legs. Pierce was a few yards away, head split on a rock, no pulse. Akhbar had to be put down.'

'I'm so sorry, ma'am.'

'Yeah. I'm dealing with it okay. It's the goneness that hits you. One day someone's here and then . . .' Marge Schwinn snapped her fingers, looked Milo up and down. 'Basically, you're what I expected, given the passage of time. You're not here to tell me something bad about Pierce, are you?'

'No, ma'am, why would I—'

'Call me Marge. Pierce loved being a detective, but he had bitter feelings about the department. Said they'd been out to get him for years because he was an individualist. I've got his pension coming in, don't want funny business, don't want to have to hire a lawyer. That's why I didn't call you back. I wasn't sure what you were up to.'

Her expression said she still wondered.

Milo said, 'It's absolutely nothing about Pierce's pension, and I'm not here as a representative of the department. Just working a case.'

'A case you worked with Pierce?'

'A case I was supposed to work with Pierce, till he retired.'

'Retired,' said Marge. 'That's one way to put it . . . well, that's nice. Pierce would've liked that, you seeking his opinion after all these years. He said you were smart. Come in, coffee's still warm. Tell me about your days with Pierce. Tell me good things.'

The house was spare and low-ceilinged, walls alternating between rough pine paneling and sand-colored grass cloth, a series of tight, dim rooms furnished with well-worn, severe, tweedy fifties furniture for which some twenty-year-old starlet would gladly overpay at the latest La Brea junktique.

The living room opened to a rear kitchen, and we sat down opposite a blond, kidney-shaped coffee table as Marge Schwinn filled mugs with chicory-scented coffee. Western prints hung on the grass cloth, along with equestrian portraits. A corner trophy hutch was full of gold and silk. In the opposite corner was an old Magnavox console TV with Bakelite dials and a bulging, greenish screen. Atop the set was a single framed photo – a man and a woman, too far away to make out the details. The kitchen window framed a panoramic mountain view but the rest of the place was oriented toward the corral. The horses hadn't moved much.

Marge finished pouring and sat in a straight-backed chair that conformed to her perfect posture. Young body, old face. The tops of her hands were a giant freckle interrupted by spots of unblemished dermis, callused, wormed with veins.

'Pierce thought a lot of you,' she told Milo.

Milo got rid of the surprised look almost immediately, but she saw it and smiled.

'Yes, I know. He told me he gave you all sorts of grief. His last years on the force were a rough time in Pierce's life, Detective Sturgis.' She lowered her eyes for a moment. No more smile. 'Did you know that when you rode with Pierce he was a drug addict?'

Milo blinked. Crossed his legs. 'I remember that he used to take cold remedies – decongestants.'

'That's right,' said Marge. 'But not for his sinuses, for the high. The decongestants were what he did openly. On the sly, he was fooling around with amphetamines – speed. He started doing it to stay awake on the job, to be able to get back home to Simi Valley without falling asleep at the wheel. That's where he lived with his first wife. He got hooked bad. Did you know Dorothy?'

Milo shook his head.

'Nice woman, according to Pierce. She's dead, too. Heart attack soon after Pierce retired. She was a chain smoker and very overweight. That's how Pierce first got his hands on speed – Dorothy had lots of prescriptions for diet pills, and he started borrowing. It got the better of him, the way it always does. He told me he'd turned really nasty, suspicious, had mood swings, couldn't sleep. Said he took it out on his partners, especially you. He felt bad about that, said you were a smart kid. He figured you'd go far . . .'

She trailed off.

Milo tugged at the zipper of his windbreaker. 'Did Pierce talk much about his work, ma'am?'

'He didn't talk about specific cases, if that's what you mean. Just how rotten the department was. *I* think his work poisoned him as much as the speed. When I met him, he'd touched bottom. It was right after Dorothy's death, and Pierce had stopped paying rent on the Simi house – they never bought, just rented. He was living in a filthy motel in Oxnard and earning minimum wage sweeping the floors at Randall's Western Wear. That's where I first saw him. I was doing a show in Ventura, came in to Randall's to look at boots, collided with Pierce when he took out the trash. He knocked me on my rear, we both ended up laughing about it. I liked his laugh. And he made me curious. Someone that age, doing that job. Usually it's young Mexicans. Next time I came in, we talked some more. There was something about him – strong, no wasted words. I'm a gabby type, as you can see. Comes from living alone most of my life, talking to the horses. Talking to myself so as not to go nuts. This land was my grandfather's. I inherited it from my parents. I was the youngest, stayed home to take care of Mom and Dad, never strayed very far. The horses pretend they're listening to me. That's what I liked about Pierce, he was a good listener. Soon, I was making up reasons to drive down to Oxnard.' She smiled. 'Bought a lot of boots and jeans. And he never knocked me down again.'

She reached for her coffee. 'We knew each other a full year before we finally agreed to get married. We did it because we're old-fashioned, no way would either of us live together without paper. But most of what we had was friendship. He was my best friend.'

Milo nodded. 'When did Pierce get off speed?'

'He was already getting off when I met him. That's why he moved into that fleabag. Punishing himself. He had some savings and his pension, but was living like he was a broke bum. Because that's how he thought of himself. By the time we started going out, he was off dope completely. But he was sure it did damage to him. "Swiss-cheese brain," he used to call it. Said if they ever x-rayed his head, they'd find holes big enough to stick a finger through. Mostly, it was his balance and his memory – he had to write things down or they were gone. I told him that was just age, but he wasn't convinced. When he told me he wanted to learn how to ride, I worried. Here he was, not a young man, no experience, not the best balance. But Pierce managed to stay in the saddle until . . . The horses loved him, he had a calming influence on them. Maybe because of all he'd been through, getting himself clean. Maybe he ended up at a higher level than if he hadn't suffered. You'll probably find this hard to believe, Detective Sturgis, but during his time with me, Pierce was a blessedly serene man.'

She got up, retrieved the picture atop the TV, held it out to us. Snapshot of Schwinn and her, leaning against the posts of the corral out front. I had only Milo's rawbone Oakie description to fuel my expectation of the former detective and had expected a grizzled old cop. The *look*. The man in the photo had long, white hair that snaked past his shoulders and a snowy beard that reached nearly to his navel. He wore a peanut-butter-colored buckskin jacket, denim shirt, blue jeans, a turquoise bracelet, one turquoise earring.

Old-time trapper or geriatric hippie, hand in hand with a sun-punished woman who barely reached his shoulder. I saw Milo's eyes widen.

'He was my Flower Power Grandpa,' said Marge. 'Different from when you knew him, huh?'

'A bit,' said Milo.

She placed the picture in her lap. 'So what kind of advice did you hope to get from him on this case of yours?'

'I was just wondering if Pierce had any general recollections.'

'Something that old and now you're working it again? Who got killed?'

'A girl named Janie Ingalls. Pierce ever mention that name?'

'No,' she said. 'Like I said, he didn't talk about his work.'

'Did Pierce leave any papers behind?'

'What kind of papers?'

'Anything to do with his work – newspaper clippings, photos, police mementos?'

'No,' she said. 'When he moved out of his Simi house, he got rid of everything. Didn't even own a car. When we went out, I had to pick *him* up.'

'Back when I knew him,' said Milo, 'he was a photography buff. He ever get back into that?'

'Yes, he did, as a matter of fact. He enjoyed taking walks in the hills and capturing nature, bought himself a cheap little camera. When I saw how much he liked it, I bought him a Nikon for his sixty-eighth birthday. His pictures were pretty. Want to see them?'

She took us to the house's single bedroom, a tidy, pine-paneled space filled by a queen bed covered with a batik spread and flanked by two mismatched nightstands. Framed photos blanketed the walls. Hills, valleys, trees, arroyos dry and flowing, sunrises, sunsets, the kiss of winter snow. Crisp colors, good composition. But nothing higher than vegetable on the evolutionary scale, not even a bird in the sky.

'Nice,' said Milo. 'Did Pierce have his own darkroom?'

'We converted a half bath. Wasn't he talented?'

'He was, ma'am. When I knew Pierce, he liked to read about science.'

'Did he? Well, I never saw that. Mostly he'd turned meditative. Could just sit in the living room and stare out at the view for hours. Except for the times when he got the cop look or had those dreams, he was at peace. Ninety-nine percent of the time he was at peace.'

'During the one percent,' I said, 'did he ever say what was bothering him?'

'No, sir.'

'During the last month or so before his accident, how was his mood?'

'Fine,' she said. Her face clouded. 'Oh no, don't go thinking *that*. It was an accident. Pierce wasn't a strong rider, and he was sixty-eight years old. I shouldn't have let him ride that long by himself, even on Akhbar.'

'That long?' said Milo.

'He was gone half a day. Usually, he only rode for an hour or so. He had his Nikon with him, said he wanted to catch some afternoon sun.'

'Taking pictures.'

'He never got to. The roll inside his camera was blank. He must've fallen right at the beginning and lain there for a while. I should've gone looking sooner. The doctor assured me that kind of head wound would have taken him right away. At least he didn't suffer.'

'Hit his head on a rock,' said Milo.

She shook her head. 'I don't want to talk about this anymore.'

'Sorry, ma'am.' Milo stepped closer to the photos on the wall. 'These really *are* good, ma'am. Did Pierce keep any albums of his slides or proofs?'

Marge stepped around the bed to the left-hand nightstand. Atop the table were a woman's watch and an empty glass. Sliding open a drawer, she removed two albums and placed them on the bed.

A pair of blue leather books. Fine morocco, a size and style I recognized.

No labeling. Marge opened one, began turning pages. Photographs encased in stiff plastic jackets, held in place by black adhesive corner pockets.

Green grass, gray rock, brown dirt, blue sky. Pages of Pierce Schwinn's fantasy of an inanimate world.

Milo and I made admiring noises. The second book held more of the same. He ran a finger down its spine. 'Nice leather.'

'I bought them for him.'

'Where?' said Milo. 'Love to have one for myself.'

'O'Neill & Chapin, right down the road – over by the Celestial Café. They cater to artists, carry quality things. These are originally from England, but they're discontinued. I bought the last three.'

'Where's the third?'

'Pierce never got to it – you know, why don't I give it to you? I have no need for it and just thinking about Pierce's unfinished business makes me want to cry. And Pierce would've liked that – your having it. He thought a lot of you.'

'Really, ma'am—'

'No, I insist,' said Marge. Crossing the room and stepping into a walk-in closet, she emerged a moment later, empty-handed. 'I could swear I saw it up here, but that was a while back. Maybe it's somewhere else . . . maybe Pierce took it over to the darkroom. Let's check.'

The converted bathroom was at the end of the hall, five-by-five, windowless, acrid with chemicals, a narrow, wooden file cabinet next to the sink. Marge slid open drawers, revealed boxes of photographic paper, assorted bottles, but no blue leather album. No slides or proofs, either.

I said, 'Looks like Pierce mounted everything he had.'

'I guess,' she said. 'But that third book – so expensive, it's a shame to let it go to waste . . . it's got to be here, somewhere. Tell you what, if it shows up, I'll send it to you. What's your address?'

Milo handed her a card.

'Homicide,' she said. 'That word just jumps out at you. I never thought much about Pierce's life before me. Didn't want to picture him spending so much time with the dead – no offense.'

'It's not a job for everyone, ma'am.'

'Pierce – he was outwardly strong, but inside, he was sensitive. Had a need for beauty.'

'Looks like he found it,' said Milo. 'Looks like he found real happiness.'

Marge's eyes moistened. 'You're nice to say so. Well, it's been good meeting you. Coupla good listeners.' She smiled. 'Must be a cop thing.'

We followed her to the front door, where Milo said, 'Did Pierce ever have any visitors?'

'Not a one, Detective. The two of us hardly ever left the ranch, except to buy provisions, and that was maybe once a month for bulk

119

shopping in Oxnard or Ventura. Once in a while we'd go into Santa Barbara for a movie or to a play at the Ojai Theater, but we never socialized. Tell the truth, we were both darned *anti*social. Evenings we'd sit and look up at the sky. That was more than enough for us.'

The three of us walked to the Seville. Marge looked toward the horses, and said, 'Hold on, guys, groom time's coming.'

Milo said, 'Thanks for your time, Mrs Schwinn.'

'Mrs Schwinn,' said Marge. 'Never thought I'd be Mrs Anybody, but I do like the sound of that. I guess I can be Mrs Schwinn forever, can't I?'

When we got in, she leaned into the passenger window. 'You would've liked the Pierce I knew, Detective. He didn't judge anyone.'

Touching Milo's hand briefly, she turned on her heel and hurried toward the corral.

fourteen

Back on Highway 33, I said, 'So now we know where the book came from.'

Milo said, 'Guy pierces his ear, turns into Mr Serene.'

'It's California.'

' "He didn't judge." You know what she meant by that, don't you? Schwinn decided my being gay was acceptable. Gee, I feel so validated.'

'When you rode together, was he homophobic?'

'Nothing overt, just general nastiness. But what man of that generation likes queers? I was always on edge with him. With everyone.'

'Fun times,' I said.

'Oh yeah, whoopsie-doo. I always felt he didn't trust me. Finally, he came out and said so but wouldn't explain why. Knowing what we know now, maybe it was speed-paranoia, but I don't think so.'

'Think the department knew about his addiction?'

'They didn't bring it up when they interrogated me, just concentrated on his whoring.'

'What I find interesting is that they eased him out with full pension rather than bring him up on charges,' I said. 'Maybe because going public about a doping, whoring cop might have brought other doping, whoring cops to light. Or, it had something to do with handling the Ingalls case.'

Several miles passed before he spoke again. 'A speed freak. Asshole was a jumpy insomniac, skinny as a razor, gulped coffee and cough syrup like a vampire chugs blood. Add paranoia and the sudden mood swings, and it's Narco 101, I shoulda seen it.'

'You were concentrating on the job, not his bad habits. Anyway, turns out whatever personal feelings he had toward you, he respected your skills. That's why he had someone send you the book.'

'*Someone,*' he snarled. 'He dies seven months ago, and the book arrives now. Think that someone could be good old Marge?'

'She seemed to be dealing straight with us, but who knows? She's lived alone for most of her life, could've developed some survival instincts.'

'If it was her, what are we dealing with? Schwinn's last wish to wifey-poo? And that doesn't explain why you were the go-between.'

'Same reason,' I said. 'Schwinn covering his tracks. He pierced his ear but held on to a cop's survival instinct.'

'Paranoid to the end.'

'Paranoia can be useful,' I said. 'Schwinn had built a new life for himself, finally had something to lose.'

He thought about that. 'Okay, put aside who sent the damn thing and shift to the big question: Why? Schwinn held something back about Janie for twenty years and started feeling guilty all of a sudden?'

'For most of those twenty years, he had other things on his mind. Bitterness toward the department, widowhood, serious addiction. Sinking to the bottom, like Marge said. He got old, kicked his habit, and bought himself a bunch of new distractions: remarriage, easing into a new life. Learning to sit still and stare at the stars. Finally had time to introspect. I had a patient once, a dutiful daughter taking care of her terminally ill mother. A week before the mother passed on, she motioned the daughter over and confessed to stabbing the woman's father with a butcher knife as he lay sleeping. My patient had been nine at the time, all these years, she and the rest of the family had been living with the myth of the bogeyman – some nocturnal slasher. Her life had been a mass of fear and now she learned the truth from an eighty-four-year-old murderer.'

'What, Schwinn knew he was gonna die? The guy fell off a horse.'

'All I'm saying is old age and introspection can be an interesting combination. Maybe Schwinn started reflecting about unfinished business. Decided to communicate with you about Janie, but still wanted to hedge his bets. So he used me as a conduit. If I didn't pass the book on to you, he'd have fulfilled his moral obligation. If I gave it to you and you traced it to him, he'd deal with that. But if you threatened him in any way, he could always deny.'

'He puts together a whole bloody scrapbook just to remind me about Janie?'

'The book probably started out as a twisted hobby – exorcising his demons. It's no coincidence his later photos had no people in them. He'd seen people at the worst.'

We rode in silence.

'He sounds like a complicated man,' I said.

'He was a freak, Alex. Pilfered death shots from the evidence room and cataloged them for personal enjoyment. For all I know he got a sexual kick out of the book, then he grew old and couldn't get it up anymore and decided to share.' He frowned. 'I don't think Marge knew about the murder book. He wouldn'ta wanted her to think of him as a freak. That means someone else sent it to you, Alex. She made like the two of them had built this little domestic cocoon, but I think she was *real* wrong.'

'Another woman,' I said.

'Why not? Someone he visited when he wanted out from hilltop nirvana. This is a guy who tumbled with whores in the backseat while on duty. I don't have that much faith in transformation.'

'If there was another woman,' I said, 'she might live far from Ojai. This is a small town, too hard to be discreet. That would explain the L.A. postmark.'

'Bastard.' He cursed under his breath. 'I never liked the guy, and now he's yanking my chain from the grave. Let's say he did have some big moral epiphany about Janie. What does the book communicate? Where am I supposed to take it? Screw this, I don't have to play this game.'

We didn't talk until I was back on the freeway. At Camarillo, I shifted to the fast lane, pushed the Seville to eighty. He mumbled, 'Pedal to the metal . . . bastard starts feeling righteous, and I've got to jump like a trained flea.'

'You don't have to do anything,' I said.

'Damn right, I'm an *Amurrican*. Entitled to life, liberty and the pursuit of unhappiness.'

We crossed the L.A. county line by midafternoon, stopped at a coffee shop in Tarzana for burgers, got back on Ventura Boulevard, hooked a right at the newsstand at Van Nuys, continued to Valley Vista, and on to Beverly Glen. Along the way, I had Milo call my service on his cell phone. Robin hadn't called.

When we reached my house, Milo was still in no mood to talk, but I said, 'Caroline Cossack sticks in my mind.'

'Why?'

'A girl poisoning a dog is more than a prank. Her brothers are all over the papers, but she doesn't get a word of newsprint. Her mother ran a debutante ball, but Caroline wasn't listed as one of the debs. She wasn't even included in her mother's funeral. If you hadn't told me the poisoning story, I'd never know she existed. It's as if the family spit her out. Maybe for good reason.'

'The neighbor – that cranky old lady doc, Schwartzman – might've been overly imaginative. She had no use for any of the Cossacks.'

'But her most serious suspicions were of Caroline.'

He made no move to exit the car. I said, 'A girl using poison makes sense. Poisoning doesn't require physical confrontation, so a disproportionate number of poisoners are female. I don't have to tell you psychopathic killers often start with animals, but they're usually males who dig blood. For a girl that young to act out so violently would be a serious red flag. I'm wondering if Caroline's been confined all these years. Maybe because of something a lot worse than killing a dog.'

'Or she died.'

'Find the death certificate.'

He knuckled his eyes, looked up at my house. 'Poison's sneaky. What was done to Janie was blatant – the way the body was dumped in an open spot. No way did a girl do that.'

'I'm not saying Caroline murdered Janie by herself, but she might've been part of it – might've served as a lure for whoever did the cutting. Plenty of killers have used young women as bait – Paul Bernardo, Charlie Manson, Gerald Gallegos, Christopher Wilding. Caroline would've been the perfect lure for Janie and Melinda – a girl their age, outwardly inoffensive. And rich. Caroline could've stood by and watched as someone else did the wet work or participated the way the Manson girls did. Maybe it was a group thing, just like the Mansons, party scene gone bad.

Females are affiliative – even female killers. Group settings lower their inhibitions.'

'Sugar and spice,' he said. 'And the family found out, put the screws on with the department to hush up the case, locked Crazy Caroline away somewhere . . . the ghoul in the attic.'

'Big family money can furnish a really nice attic.'

He accompanied me inside, where I went through the mail and he got on the phone with County Records and Social Security. No death certificate on Caroline Cossack; nor had she received a social security number or a driver's license.

Melinda Waters had received a card at age fifteen, but she'd never driven in California or worked or contributed payroll tax. Which made sense if she'd died young. But no certificate on her, either.

'Disappeared,' I said. 'Melinda probably died the same night Janie did, and Caroline's either very well hidden or she expired, too, and the family hushed it up.'

'Hidden as in hospitalized?'

'Or just watched carefully. Rich kid like that, she'd have a trust fund, could be living in some Mediterranean villa with twenty-four-hour supervision.'

He began pacing. 'Little Miss Nowhere . . . but at some point, when she was a kid, she had to have an identity. Be interesting to pinpoint when exactly she lost it.'

'School records,' I said. 'Living in Bel Air would've meant Palisades or University High if the Cossacks chose public school. Beverly, if they played fast and loose with residency forms. On the private side, there'd be Harvard-Westlake – which was Westlake School for Girls, back then – or Marlborough, Buckley, John Thomas Dye, Crossroads.'

He flipped open his pad, scrawled notes.

'Or,' I added, 'a school for troubled kids.'

'Any particular place come to mind?'

'I was in practice back then, can recall three very high-priced spreads. One was in West L.A., the others were in Santa Monica and the Valley – North Hollywood.'

'Names?'

I recited, and he got back on the phone. Santa Monica Prep was defunct, but Achievement House in Cheviot Hills and Valley Educational Academy in North Hollywood were still in business. He reached both schools but hung up frowning.

'No one'll give me the time of day. Confidentiality and all that.'

'Schools don't enjoy confidentiality privileges,' I said.

'You ever deal with either of the places, professionally?'

'I visited Achievement House, once,' I said. 'The parents of a boy I was seeing kept holding the place over the kid's head as a threat. "If you don't shape up, we'll send you to Achievement House." That seemed to scare him, so I dropped by to see what spooked him. Talked to a social worker, got the five-minute tour. Converted apartment building near Motor and Palms. What stuck in my mind was how small it was – maybe twenty-five, thirty kids boarding in, meaning it had to cost a fortune. No snake pit that I could see. Later, I talked to my patient and turns out what he was worried about was stigmatization. Being thought of as a "weirdo-geek-loser." '

'Achievement House had a bad reputation?'

'In his mind, any special placement had a bad reputation.'

'Did he get sent there?'

'No, he ran away, wasn't seen for years.'

'Oh,' he said.

I smiled. 'Don't you mean *"Ah"*?'

He laughed. Got himself grapefruit juice, opened the freezer and stared at the vodka bottle but changed his mind. 'Ran away. Your version of loose ends.'

'Loose ends were a big part of my life, back then,' I said. 'The price of an interesting job. As it turns out, this particular kid made it okay.'

'He stayed in touch?'

'He called after his second child was born. Ostensibly to ask about how to handle sibling jealousy. He ended up apologizing for being a surly teen. I told him he had nothing to be sorry about. Because I'd finally learned the whole story from his mother. His older brother had been molesting him since he was five.'

His face got hard. 'Family values.' He paced some more, finished his juice, washed the glass, got back on the phone. Contacting Palisades and University and Beverly Hills High Schools, then the

private institutions. Putting on the charm, claiming to be conducting an alumnus search for *Who's Who.*

No one had Caroline Cossack on their files. 'Little Miss
Nowhere.' He'd talked about washing his hands of the Ingalls
case, but his face was flushed, and hunter's tension bunched his
shoulders.

'I didn't tell you,' he said, 'but yesterday I went over to Parker
Center and searched for Janie's case file. Disappeared. Nothing at
the Metro office or in evidence or the coroner's, not even a
cold-case classification or a notice that the file had been moved
somewhere else. There is absolutely no paper *anywhere* that says the
case was ever opened in the first place. I know it was because I
opened it. Schwinn used to shove all the paperwork at me. I filled
out the right forms, transcribed my street notes, created the murder
book.'

'No coroner's records, so much for science,' I said. 'When's the
last time you saw the file?'

'The morning before my interrogation by Broussard and that
Swede. After they worked me over, I was so shaken up I didn't
return to my desk, just split the station. The next day, the transfer
notice was in my box, and my desk had been cleared.'

He tilted back in his chair, stretched his legs, seemed suddenly
relaxed. 'You know, my friend, I've been working too damn hard.
Maybe *that's* what I can learn from old Mr Serene. Stop and sniff
the manure.'

A smile, abrupt and broad, did something unsettling to his
mouth. He rotated his head for several turns, as if working kinks
out of his neck. Brushed black strands of hair out of his face.
Sprang to his feet.

'See you. Thanks for your time.'

'Where are you headed?' I said.

'Into a life of meditative leisure. Got lots of vacation time stored
up. Seems a good time to cash in.'

fifteen

Leisure was the last thing I needed. The moment the door closed, I reached for the phone.

Larry Daschoff and I have known each other since grad school. After our internships, I took a professorship at the med school crosstown and worked the cancer wards at Western Pediatric Medical Center, and he went straight into private practice. I stayed single and he married his high school sweetheart, sired six kids, made a good living, converted his square-meal-in-a-round-can defensive-guard physique to middle-aged fat, watched his wife go back to law school, took up golf. Now, he was a young grandfather, living on investment income, wintering in Palm Desert.

I reached him at his condo there. It had been some time since we'd spoken, and I asked him about the wife and kids.

'Everyone's great.'

'Especially the Ultimate Grandchild.'

'Well, as long as you asked, yes, Samuel Jason Daschoff is clearly the messenger of the Second Coming – another Jewish savior. Little guy just turned two and has evolved from sweetness and light to age-appropriate obnoxiousness. Let me tell you, Alex, there's no revenge sweeter than watching your own kids contend with the crap they shoveled at you.'

'I'll bet,' I said, wondering if I'd ever know.

'So,' said Larry, 'how've you been doing?'

'Keeping busy. I'm actually calling you about a case.'

'I figured as much.'

'Oh?'

'You were always task-oriented, Alex.'

'You're saying I can't be purely sociable?'

'Like I can be purely skinny. What kind of case, therapy or the bad stuff you do with the constabulary?'

'The bad stuff.'

'Still subjecting yourself to that.'

'Still.'

'I guess I can understand the motivation,' he said. 'It's a helluva lot more exciting than breathing in angst all day, and you were never one to sit still. So how can I help you?'

I described Caroline Cossack, without mentioning names. Asked him to guess where a teen that troubled might've been schooled twenty years back.

'Dosing Rover with cyanide?' he said. 'Impolite. How come she didn't end up in trouble?'

'Maybe family connections,' I said, as I realized incarceration would be an excellent reason not to have a social security card, and neither Milo nor I had thought of checking prison records. Both of us thrown off kilter.

'A *rich*, not-nice kid,' said Larry. 'Well, back then there was no real place for a run-of-the-mill dangerous delinquent other than the state hospital system – Camarillo. But I suppose a rich family could've placed her somewhere cushy.'

'I was thinking Achievement House or Valley Educational, or their out-of-state counterparts.'

'Definitely not Valley Educational, Alex. I consulted there, and they stayed away from delinquents, concentrated on learning probs. Even back then they were getting fifteen-grand tuition, had a two-year waiting list, so they could afford to be picky. Unless the family covered up the extent of the girl's pathology, but that kind of violent tendency would be hard to suppress for very long. As far as Achievement House, I never had any direct experience with them, but I know someone who did. Right around that time period, too, now that I think about it – nineteen, twenty years ago. Not a pretty situation.'

'For the students?'

'For the someone I know. Remember when I used to do mentoring for the department – undergrads considering psych as a career? One of my mentorees was a freshman girl, precocious, barely seventeen. She got herself a volunteer placement at Achievement House.'

'What problems did she have there?'

'The director got . . . overtly Freudian with her.'

'Sexual harassment?'

'Back then it was just called mashing and groping. Despite her age, the girl was a clearheaded feminist way ahead of her time, complained to the board of directors, who promptly gave her the boot. She talked to me about pursuing it – she was really trauma-tized – and I offered to back her up if she wanted to take it further, but in the end she decided not to. She knew it was his word against hers, he was the respected health administrator, and she was a good-looking teenager who wore her skirts too short. I supported the decision. What would she have gained other than a mess?'

'Was there ever any suggestion the director was molesting students?'

'Not that I heard.'

'Remember his name?'

'Alex, I really don't want my mentoree drawn into it.'

'I promise she won't be.'

'Larner. Michael Larner.'

'Psychologist or psychiatrist?'

'Business type – administrator.'

'Are you still in touch with the mentoree?'

'Occasionally. Mostly for cross-referrals. She stayed on track, graduated summa, got her PhD at Penn, did a fellowship at Michigan, moved back here. She's got a nice Westside practice.'

'Is there any way to ask her if she'd talk to me?'

Silence. 'You think this is important.'

'Honestly, I don't know, Larry. If asking her will put you in a difficult position, forget it.'

'Let me think about it,' he said. 'I'll let you know.'

'That would be great.'

'Great?' he said.

'Extremely helpful.'

'You know,' he said, 'right as we speak, I've got my feet up and my belt loosened and I'm looking out at miles of clean white sand. Just finished a plate of *chile rellenos con mucha cerveza*. Just let out a sonic-boom belch and no one's around to give me a funny look. To me, *that's* great.'

I heard from him an hour later. 'Her name's Allison Gwynn, and you can call her. But she definitely doesn't want to get involved in any police business.'

'No problem,' I said.

'So,' he said. 'How's everything else?'

'Everything's fine.'

'We should get together for dinner. With the women. Next time we come into town.'

'Good idea,' I said. 'Call me, Larry. Thanks.'

'Everything's really okay?'

'Sure. Why do you ask?'

'Don't know . . . you sound a bit . . . tentative. But maybe it's just that I haven't talked to you in a while.'

I called Dr Allison Gwynn at her Santa Monica exchange.

A *you-have-reached-the-office* tape answered, but when I mentioned my name, a soft-around-the-edges female voice broke in.

'This is Allison. It's funny, Larry calling out of the blue and asking if I'd talk to you. I've been reading some articles on pain control, and a couple were yours. I do some work at St Agnes Hospice.'

'Those articles are ancient history.'

'Not really,' she said. 'People and their pain don't change that much, most of what you said still holds true. Anyway, Larry says you want to know about Achievement House. It's been a long time – nearly twenty years – since I had anything to do with that place.'

'That's exactly the time period I'm interested in.'

'What do you need to know?'

I gave her the same anonymous description of Caroline Cossack.

'I see,' she said. 'Larry assures me you'll be discreet.'

'Absolutely.'

'That's essential, Dr Delaware. Look, I can't talk now, have a patient in two minutes and after that I'm running a group at the hospice. This evening, I'll be teaching, but in between I will be eating dinner – fiveish, or so. If you want to stop by, that's fine. I usually go to Café Maurice on Broadway near Sixth, because it's close to St Agnes.'

'I'll be there,' I said. 'I really appreciate it.'

'No problem,' she said. 'I hope.'

I endured the afternoon by running too fast for too long. Trudged up my front steps winded and dehydrated and checked the phone machine. Two hang-ups and a canned solicitation for discount home loans. I pressed *69 and traced the hang-ups to a harried woman in East L.A. who spoke only Spanish and had dialed a very wrong number, and a Montana Avenue boutique wondering if Robin Castagna would be interested in some new silk fashions from India.

'I guess I should've left a message,' said the nasal girl on the other end, 'but the owner likes us to make personal contact. So do you think Robin might be interested? According to our records, she bought a bunch of cool stuff last year.'

'When I talk to her, I'll ask her.'

'Oh, okay . . . you could come in yourself, you know. Do like a *gift* thing? If she doesn't like it, we'll give her full store credit on return. Women love to be surprised.'

'Do they?'

'Oh, sure. Totally.'

'I'll bear that in mind.'

'You really should. Women *love* when guys like surprise them.'

'Like a trip to Paris,' I said.

'Paris?' She laughed. 'You can surprise *me* with that – don't tell Robin I said that, okay?'

At 4 P.M., I stepped out the kitchen door to the rear patio, crossed the garden to Robin's studio, unlocked the cool vaulted room, and walked around smelling wood dust and lacquer and Chanel No. 19 and listening to the echos of my footsteps. She'd swept the floor clean, packed her tools, put everything in its place.

Afternoon sun streamed through the windows. Beautiful space in perfect order. It felt like a crypt.

I returned to the house and skimmed the morning paper. The world hadn't changed much; why did I feel so altered? At four-thirty, I showered, got dressed in a blue blazer, white shirt, clean blue jeans, brown suede loafers. At ten after five, I walked into Café Maurice.

The restaurant was compact and dark, with a copper-topped bar and a half-dozen tables set with white linen. The walls were raised walnut panels, the ceiling repoussé tin. Inoffensive music on low volume competed with low conversation among three white-aproned waiters old enough to be my father. I couldn't help but think of the Left Bank bistro where Robin had told me of her plans.

I buttoned my jacket and allowed my eyes to acclimate. The sole patron was a dark-haired woman at a center table peering into a glass of burgundy. She wore a form-fitted, whiskey-colored tweed jacket over a cream silk blouse, a long, oatmeal-colored skirt with a slit up the side, beige calfskin boots with substantial heels. A big leather bag sat on the chair next to her. She looked up as I approached and gave a tentative smile.

'Dr Gwynn? Alex Delaware.'

'Allison.' She placed her bag on the floor and held out a slender white hand. We shook, and I sat.

She was a long-stemmed beauty out of John Singer Sargent. Ivory face, soft but assertive cheekbones highlighted with blush, a wide strong mouth shaded coral. Huge, judiciously lined deep blue eyes under strong, arching brows studied me. Warm scrutiny, no intrusiveness; her patients would appreciate that. Her hair was a sheet of true black that hung midway down her back. Circling one wrist was a diamond tennis bracelet; the other sported a gold watch. Baroque pearls dotted each earlobe, and a gold link cameo necklace rested on her breastbone.

Her hand returned to her wineglass. Good manicure, French-tipped nails left just long enough to avoid frivolousness. I knew she was thirty-six or -seven but despite the tailored clothes, the baubles, the cosmetics, she looked ten years younger.

'Thanks for your time,' I said.

'I wasn't sure if you were a punctual person,' she said, 'so I ordered for myself. I only have an hour till class.' Same gentle voice as over the phone. She waved, and one of the ancient waiters tore himself away from the staff confab, brought a menu, and hovered.

'What do you recommend?' I asked.

'The *entrecôte* is great. I like it rare and bloody, but they've got a pretty good selection of more virtuous stuff if you're not into red meat.'

The waiter tapped his foot. 'What're you drinking, sir? We've got a good selection of microbrews.' I'd expected a Gallic accent, but his drawl was pure California – surfer boy grown old – and I found myself musing about a future where grandmothers would be named Amber and Heather and Tawny and Misty.

'Grolsch,' I said. 'And I'll have the *entrecôte*, medium rare.'

He left and Allison Gwynn smoothed already-smooth hair and twirled her wineglass. She avoided my eyes.

'What kind of work do you do at St Agnes?' I said.

'You know the place.'

'I know of it.'

'Just some volunteer work,' she said. 'Mostly helping the staff cope. Do you still work in oncology?'

'No, not for a while.'

She nodded. 'It can be tough.' She drank some wine.

'Where do you teach?' I said.

'The U, adult extension. This quarter I'm doing Personality Theory and Human Relations.'

'All that and a practice. Sounds like a busy schedule,' I said.

'I'm a workaholic,' she said, with sudden cheer. 'Hyperactivity channeled in a socially appropriate manner.'

My beer arrived. We both drank. I was about to get down to substance when she said, 'The girl you described. Would that be Caroline Cossack?'

I put down my mug. 'You knew Caroline?'

'So it *was* her.'

'How did you know?'

'From your description.'

'She stood out?'

'Oh, yes.'

'What can you tell me about her?'

'Not much, I'm afraid. She stood out because of how they labeled her. There was a pink tab on her chart, the only one I'd seen. And I'd seen most of the charts, was a gofer that summer, running errands, picking up and delivering files. They used a color-coding system to alert the staff if a kid had a medical problem. Yellow for juvenile diabetes, blue for asthma, that kind of thing. Caroline Cossack's tab was pink and when I asked someone what that meant, they said it was a behavioral warning. High risk for acting out. That and your saying it might be a police case helped me put it together.'

'So Caroline was high risk for violence.'

'Someone thought so, back then.'

'What specifically were they worried about?' I said.

'I don't know. She never did anything wrong during the month I was there.'

'But she was the only one labeled like that.'

'Yes,' she said. 'There weren't a lot of kids, period. Maybe thirty. Back then Achievement House was exactly what it is today: a repository for rich kids who fail to perform to their parents' expectations. Chronically truant, drug-abusing, noncompliant, children of the dream.'

I thought: Take away the dream and you had Janie and Melinda.

'But,' she went on, 'they were basically harmless kids. Other than the obvious sneaky doping and drinking, nothing seriously antisocial went on that I saw.'

'Harmless kids locked up,' I said.

'It wasn't that draconian,' she said. 'More carrot than stick. High-priced baby-sitting. They locked the doors at night, but it didn't feel like a prison.'

'What else can you tell me about Caroline?'

'She didn't seem scary, at all. I recall her as quiet and passive. That's why the behavioral warning surprised me.'

She licked her lips, moved her wineglass aside. 'That's really all I can tell you. I was a student volunteer, fresh out of high school, didn't ask questions.' Her face tilted to the left. The enormous blue eyes didn't blink. 'Bringing up that place is . . . not the most fun thing I've done all week. Larry told you about my experience there with Larner.'

I nodded.

'If the same thing happened today,' she said, 'you can bet I'd be a lot more proactive. Probably page Gloria Allred, close that place down, and walk away with a settlement. But I'm not blaming myself for how I handled it. So . . . have you worked with the police for a while?'

'A few years.'

'Do you find it difficult?'

'Difficult in what way?' I said.

'All the authoritarian personalities, for starts.'

'Mostly, I deal with one detective,' I said. 'He's a good friend.'

'Oh,' she said. 'So you find it fulfilling.'

'It can be.'

'What aspect?'

'Trying to explain the unexplainable.'

One of her hands covered the other. Jewelry everywhere else, but no rings on her fingers. Why had I noticed that?

I said, 'If you don't mind, I have a few more questions about Caroline.'

She grinned. 'Go ahead.'

'Did you have much personal contact with her?'

'Nothing direct, but I was allowed to sit in on some therapy groups, and she was in one of them. General purpose rap session. The leader tried to draw her out, but Caroline never talked, would just stare at the floor and pretend not to hear. I could tell she was taking it in, though. When she got upset, her facial muscles twitched.'

'What upset her?'

'Any personal probing.'

'What was she like physically?' I said.

'All this interest twenty years later?' she said. 'You can't tell me what she did?'

'She may have done nothing,' I said. 'Sorry to be evasive, but this is all very preliminary.' Unofficial, too. 'A lot of my work is random archaeology.'

Both her hands cupped her wineglass. 'No gory details? Aw, shucks.' She laughed, showed perfect teeth. 'I'm not sure I'd really want to know, anyway. Okay, Caroline, physically . . . this is all through the perspective of my seventeen-year-old eyes. She was short, kind of mousy . . . a little chubby – unkempt. Stringy hair . . . mousy brown, she wore it to here.' She leveled a hand at her own shoulder. 'It always looked unwashed. She had acne . . .

what else? She had a defeated posture, as if something heavy sat on her shoulders. The kids were allowed to dress any way they wanted, but Caroline always wore the same shapeless dresses – old lady's housedresses. I wonder where she found them.'

'Dressing down,' I said. 'She sounds depressed.'

'Definitely.'

'Did she hang around with the other kids?'

'No, she was a loner. Shleppy, withdrawn. I guess today I'd look at her and be thinking schizoid.'

'But they saw her as potentially aggressive.'

'They did.'

'How'd she spend her time?'

'Mostly she sat in her room by herself, dragged herself to meals, returned alone. When I'd pass her in the hall, I'd smile and say hello. But I kept my distance because of the pink tab. A couple of times I think she nodded back, but mostly she shuffled on, keeping her eyes down.'

'Was she medicated?'

'I never read her chart. Now that I think about it, it's possible.'

'The group leader who tried to draw her out. Do you remember a name?'

'Jody Lavery,' she said. 'She was a clinical social worker – very nice to me when I had my problem with Larner. Years later I ran into her at a convention, and we ended up becoming friends, did some cross-referring. But forget about talking to her. She died two years ago. And she and I never talked about Caroline. Caroline was more of a nonentity than an entity. If not for the pink tab, I probably wouldn't have paid her any attention at all. In fact, the only—'

'Sir, madam,' said the waiter. Our dishes were set in place, and we cut into our steaks.

'Excellent,' I said, after the first bite.

'Glad you like it.' She speared a french fry.

'You were about to say something.'

'Was I?'

'You were talking about Caroline not being memorable. Then you said "In fact, the only—" '

'Hmm – oh yes, I was saying the only person I ever saw her talk to was one of the maintenance men. Willie something . . . a black guy . . . Willie Burns. I remember his name because it was the same as Robert Burns and I recall thinking there was nothing Scottish about him.'

'He paid special attention to Caroline?'

'I suppose you could say that. Once or twice I came across him and Caroline chatting in the hall, and they moved apart very quickly and Willie resumed working. And one time I did see Willie coming out of Caroline's room, carrying a mop and broom. When he saw me, he said she'd been sick, he was cleaning up. Volunteering an explanation. It was kind of furtive. Whatever the situation, Burns didn't stick around long. One week, he was there, then he was gone and Caroline went back to being alone.'

'A week,' I said.

'It seemed like a short period.'

'Do you remember what month this was?'

'Had to be August. I was only there during August.'

Janie Ingalls had been murdered in early June.

'How old was Willie Burns?'

'Not much older than Caroline – maybe twenty, twenty-one. I thought it was nice, someone paying attention to her. Do you know something about him?'

I shook my head. 'You didn't read the chart, but did you ever hear why Caroline was sent to Achievement House?'

'I assumed the same reason every other kid was: unable to jump high hurdles. I know that world, Alex. Grew up in Beverly Hills, my dad was an assistant attorney general. I thought I wanted something simple, would never return to California.'

'Larry said you went to Penn for grad school.'

'Went to Penn and loved it. Then I spent a couple of years at Ann Arbor, came back to Penn and took an assistant professorship. If it had been up to me, I'd have stayed back East. But I married a Wharton guy and he got a fantastic job offer at Union Oil here in L.A. and all of a sudden we were living in a condo on the Wilshire Corridor and I was cramming for the California boards.'

'Sounds like things have worked out,' I said.

She'd speared steak on her fork and dipped it in béarnaise. The meat remained suspended for a moment, then she placed the fork down on her plate. 'Life *was* rolling along quite nicely, then three summers ago, my father woke up at 4 A.M. with chest pains and my mom called us in a panic. Grant – my husband – and I rushed over and the three of us took Dad to the hospital and while they were working him up, Grant wandered off. I was so caught up supporting Mom and waiting for the verdict on Dad that I didn't pay much attention. Finally, just as they told us Dad was fine – gastric reflux – and we could take him home, Grant showed up and from the look on his face, I knew something was wrong. We didn't talk until after we dropped Mom and Dad off. Then he told me he hadn't been feeling well for a while – bad stomachaches. He'd figured it was job stress, kept thinking the pain would go away, was eating antacids like candy, hadn't wanted to alarm me. But then the pain got unbearable. So while we were at the hospital, he got hold of a doctor he knew – a Penn golfing buddy – and had x rays taken. And they found spots all over. A rare bile-duct tumor that had spread. Five weeks later, I was the mourning widow, living back with Mom and Dad.'

'I'm sorry.'

She nudged her plate away. 'It's rude of me to unload like this.' Another tentative smile. 'I'll blame it on your being too good a listener.'

Without thinking, I reached out and patted her hand. She squeezed my fingers, then spider-walked away, took hold of her wineglass, drank while staring past me.

I took a healthy swallow of beer.

'Want to hear something funny?' she said. 'Tonight I'm lecturing about post-traumatic stress. Listen, Alex, it's been nice meeting you, and good luck with whatever you're trying to do, but I've really got to run.'

She summoned the waiter, and, over her objections, I paid the check. She removed a gold compact and lipstick from her bag, freshened her mouth, touched a long, black eyelash, checked her face in the mirror. We got up from the table. I'd figured her for tall, but in three-inch heels she wasn't more than five-five. Another little looker. Just like Robin.

We left the restaurant together. Her car was a ten-year-old black Jaguar XJS convertible that she stepped into with agility and revved hard. I watched her drive away. Her eyes stayed fixed on the road.

sixteen

Two new names:
Michael Larner.
Willie Burns.

Perhaps both were irrelevant, but I drove south into Cheviot Hills, located Achievement House on a cul-de-sac just east of Motor and south of Palms, idled the Seville across the street.

The building was an undistinguished two-story box next to an open parking lot, pale blue in the moonlight, surrounded by white iron fencing. The front façade was windowless. Glass doors blocked entry to what was probably an interior courtyard. Half a dozen cars sat in the lot under high-voltage lighting, but the building was dark and there was no signage I could see from this distance. Wondering if I had the right location, I got out and crossed the street and peered through the fence slats.

Tiny white numbers verified the address. Tiny white letters, nearly invisible in the darkness spelled out:

Achievement House
Private Property

I squinted to get a look at what was behind the glass doors, but the courtyard – if that's what it was – was unlit, and all I made out was reflection. The street was far from quiet; traffic from Motor intruded in bursts, and the more distant rumble of the freeway thrummed nonstop. I got back in the car, drove to the U, returned to the Research Library, got my itchy hands on that old friend, the periodicals index.

Nothing on Willie Burns, which was no surprise. How many

janitors made the news? But Michael Larner's name popped up twelve times during the past two decades.

Two citations were dated from Larner's tenure as director of Achievement House: coverage of fund-raising events, no photos, no quotes. Then nothing for the next three years, until Larner popped up as official spokesman for Maxwell Films, demeaning the character of an actress sued by the film company for breach of contract. No follow-up on how that case resolved, and a year later Larner had made another occupational change: an 'independent producer' inking a deal with the very same actress for a sci-fi epic – a movie I'd never heard of.

The Industry. Given Larner's sexual aggressiveness, it was either that or politics.

The next four citations caught my eye because of Larner's *new* affiliation: director of operations for Cossack Development.

These were brief items from the business section of the *Times*. Larner's job seemed to be lobbying council members for Garvey and Bob's development deals.

Caroline Cossack shunted to Achievement House soon after Janie Ingalls's murder. Not the kind of kid Achievement House accepted but a few years later the director was working for the Cossack family.

I'd be brightening Milo's evening.

I got home and checked my phone machine. Still nothing from Robin.

Not like her.

Then I thought: *Everything's new, the rules have changed.*

I realized I'd never gotten an itinerary of the tour. I hadn't asked, and Robin hadn't offered. No one's fault, both of us caught up, everything moving so fast. The two of us tripping through the calisthenics of separation.

I went into my office, booted up the computer, found the Kill Famine Tour's homepage. PR shots and cheerful hype, links to mail-order CD purchases, photo-streams of previous concerts. Finally, times and dates and venues. Eugene, Seattle, Vancouver, Denver, Albuquerque . . . everything subject to change.

I phoned the Vancouver arena. Got voice mail and entered a

pushbutton maze to learn *Our offices are closed . . . open tomorrow at 10 A.M.*

Left out in the cold.

I'd never set out to exclude Robin from my life. Or had I? During all the time we'd spent together I'd kept my work to myself – kept her at arm's length. Claiming confidentiality even when it didn't apply. Telling myself it was for her good, she was an artist, gifted, sensitive, needed to be protected from the ugliness. Sometimes she'd learned what I'd been up to the hard way.

The night I'd blown it, she'd left the house for a recording studio, full of trust. The moment she was gone, I left for a meeting with a beautiful, crazy, dangerous young woman.

I'd screwed up royally, but hadn't my intentions been noble? Blah blah blah.

Two tickets to Paris; pathetic. A sudden rush of memories took hold. Exactly what I'd worked hard at forgetting.

The other time we'd separated.

Ten years ago, nothing to do with my bad behavior. That had been all Robin, needing to find her own way, forge her own identity.

Lord, rephrased that way it sounded like a pop-psych cliché, and she deserved better.

I loved her, she loved me. So why wasn't she calling?

Grow up, pal, it's only been two days and you weren't exactly Mr Charming the last time she tried.

Had I failed some kind of test by letting her go too easily?

Ten years ago she'd come back but not before . . .

Don't get into that.

But at that moment, I wanted nothing but punishment. Opened the box, let loose the furies.

The first time, she'd stayed away for a long time and eventually I'd found another woman. Then that had ended well before Robin returned.

When we reunited, Robin had seemed a bit more fragile, but otherwise everything seemed to be fine. Then one day, she broke down and confessed. She'd found someone, too. A guy, just a guy, a stupid guy, she'd been stupid.

Really stupid, Alex.

I'd held her, comforted her. Then she told me. Pregnancy, abortion. She'd never told the guy – Dennis, I'd blocked out his name – goddamn Dennis had gotten her pregnant, and she'd left him, gone through the ordeal alone.

I kept holding her, said the right things, what a sensitive guy, the essence of understanding. But a nagging little voice in my head refused to let go of the obvious:

All those years together, she and I had waltzed around the topic of marriage and kids. Had been *careful*.

A few months away from me, and another man's seed had found its way—

Had I ever really forgiven her?

Did she wonder about that, too? What was she thinking about, right now?

Where the hell *was* she?

I picked up the phone, wondered who to call, swept the damn thing off the desk and onto the floor – screw you, Mr Bell.

My face was hot and my bones twitched and I began pacing, the way Milo does. Not limiting myself to one room, racing around the entire house, unable to burn off the pain.

Home smothering home.

I headed for the front door, threw it open, threw myself into the night.

I walked the glen, north, up into the hills. Did it the stupid way – with the traffic to my back, undeterred by the rush of approaching engines, the flash-freeze of headlights.

Drivers sped by honking. Someone yelled, *'Idiot!'*

That felt right.

It took miles before I was able to conjure up Janie Ingalls's corpse and relax.

When I got back to the house, the front door was ajar – I'd neglected to shut it – and leaves had blown into the entry. I got down on my knees, picked up every speck, returned to my office. The phone remained on the floor. The answering machine had tumbled, too, and lay there, unplugged.

But the machine in the bedroom was blinking.

One message.

I ignored it, went to the kitchen, got the vodka out of the freezer. Used the bottle to cool my hands and my face. Put it back.

I watched TV for hours, ingested hollow laughter, tortured dialogue, commercials for herbal sexual potency remedies and miracle chemicals that attacked the most hideous of stains.

Shortly after midnight, I punched the bedroom machine's PLAY button.

'Alex? . . . I guess you're not in . . . we were supposed to fly to Canada, but we've been held over in Seattle – doing an extra show . . . there were some equipment modifications that needed to be done before the concert, so I was tied up . . . I guess you're out again . . . anyway, I'm at the Four Seasons in Seattle. They gave me a nice room . . . it's raining. Alex, I hope you're okay. I'm sure you are. Bye, honey.'

Bye, honey.

No *I love you.*

She always said *I love you.*

seventeen

At 1 A.M., I called the Four Seasons in Seattle. The operator said, 'It's past the time where we put calls through, sir.'

'She'll talk to me.'

'Are you her husband?'

'Her boyfriend.'

'Well . . . actually, it looks like you're going to have to leave a message. I've got her as out of her room, her voice mail's engaged, here you go.'

She put me through. I hung up, trudged to bed, fell into something that might've been called sleep had it been restful, found myself sitting up at 6:30 A.M. dry-mouthed and seeing double.

At seven, I phoned Milo. His voice was fuzzy, as if filtered through a hay bale.

'Yo, General Delaware,' he said, 'isn't it a little early for my field report?'

I told him what I'd learned about Caroline Cossack and Michael Larner.

'Jesus, I haven't even brushed my teeth . . . okay, let me digest this. You figure this Larner did a favor for the Cossacks by stashing Caroline and they paid him back – what – fifteen years later? Not exactly immediate gratification.'

'There could've been other rewards along the way. Both Larner and the Cossacks were involved in independent film production.'

'You find any film link between them?'

'No, but—'

'No matter, I'll buy a relationship between Larner and Caroline's family. She was a screwy kid, and Larner ran a place for screwy kids. It says nothing about what got her in there in the first place.'

'The behavioral warning on her chart says plenty. My source says Caroline was the only one tagged. Anyway, do what you want with it.'

'Sure, thanks. You all right?'

Everyone kept asking me the same damn question. I forced amiability into my voice. 'I'm fine.'

'You sound like me in the morning.'

'You rarely hear me this early.'

'That must be it. Behavioral warning, huh? But your source didn't know why.'

'The assumption was some kind of antisocial or aggressive behavior. Add to that Dr Schwartzman's dead Akita, and a picture starts forming. A rich kid doing very bad things would explain a cover-up.'

'Your basic disturbed loner,' he said. 'What would we homicide folk do without them?'

'Something else,' I said. 'I was thinking maybe the reason Caroline never got a social security card was because eventually she did act out and ended up in—'

'Lockup. Yeah, I thought of that right after we talked. Stupid of me not to jump on that sooner. But, sorry, she's not in any state penitentiary in the lower forty-eight, Hawaii or Alaska. I suppose it's possible she's stashed at some Federal pen, or maybe you were right about them shipping her to some nice little villa in Ibiza, sun-splashed exterior, padded walls. Know of anyone who'll fund a fact-finding Mediterranean tour for a deserving detective?'

'Fill out a form and submit it to John G. Broussard.'

'Hey, gosharoo, why didn't *I* think of that? Alex, thanks for your time.'

'But . . .'

'The whole thing is still dead-ending, just like twenty years ago. I've got no files, no notes to fall back on, can't even locate Melinda Waters's mother. And I was thinking about something: I gave Eileen Waters my card. If Melinda never returned home, wouldn't she have called me back?'

'Maybe she did, and you never got the message. You were in West L.A. by then.'

147

'I got other calls,' he said. 'Bullshit stuff. Central forwarded them to me.'

'Exactly.'

Silence. 'Maybe. In any event, I can't see anywhere to take it.'

'One more thing,' I said. I told him about Willie Burns, expected him to blow it off.

He said, 'Willie Burns. Would he be around . . . forty by now?'

'Twenty or twenty-one then, so yeah.'

'I knew a Willie Burns. He had a baby face,' he said. 'Woulda been . . . twenty-three back then.' His voice had changed. Softer, lower. Focused.

'Who is he?' I said.

'Maybe no one,' he said. 'Let me get back to you.'

He phoned two hours later sounding tight and distracted, as if someone was hovering nearby.

'Where are you?' I said.

'At my desk.'

'Thought you were taking vacation time.'

'There's paper to clear.'

'Who's Willie Burns?' I said.

'Let's chat in person,' he said. 'Do you have time? Sure you do, you're living the merry bachelor life. Meet me out in front of the station, let's say half an hour.'

He was standing near the curb and hopped into the Seville before the car had come to a full stop.

'Where to?' I said.

'Anywhere.'

I continued up Butler, took a random turn, and cruised the modest residential streets that surround the West L.A. station. When I'd put half a mile between us and his desk, he said, 'There is definitely a God and He's jerking my chain. Payment for old sins.'

'What sins?'

'The worst one: failure.'

'Willie Burns is another cold one?'

'Willie Burns is an old *perp* on a cold one. Wilbert Lorenzo Burns, DOB forty-three and a half years ago, suspicion of homicide; I picked it up right after I transferred. And guess what,

148

another file seems to have gone missing. But I did manage to find one of Burns's old probation officers, and he came up with some old paper and there it was: Achievement House. Willie'd finagled a summer placement there, lasted less than a month, and was booted for absenteeism.'

'A homicide suspect and he's working with problem teens?'

'Back then he was just a junkie and a dealer.'

'Same question.'

'Guess Willie never told him about his background.'

'Who'd he kill?'

'Bail bondsman name of Boris Nemerov. Ran his business right here in West L.A. Big, tough guy, but he sometimes had a soft heart for cons because he himself had spent some time in a Siberian gulag. You know how bail bonds work?'

'The accused puts up a percentage of the bail and leaves collateral. If he skips trial, the bondsman pays the court and confiscates the collateral.'

'Basically,' he said, 'except generally the bondsman doesn't actually pay the initial bail with his own money. He buys a policy from an insurance company for two to six percent of the total bail. To cover the premiums and make a profit, he collects a fee from the perp – usually ten percent, nonrefundable. If the perp goes fugitive, the insurance company shells out to the court and has the right to collect the collateral. Which is usually a piece of property – Grandma letting her beloved felon offspring tie up the cute little bungalow where she's lived for two hundred years. But seizing the cottage from poor old Grandma takes time and money and gets bad press and what do insurance companies want with low-rent real estate? So they'd always rather have the perp in hand. That's why they send out bounty hunters. Who take *their* cut.'

'Trickle-down economics,' I said. 'Crime's good for the GDP.'

'Boris Nemerov made out okay as a bondsman. Treated people like human beings and had a low skip rate. But he sometimes took risks – forgoing collateral, discounting his ten percent. He'd done that for Willie Burns because Burns was a habitual client who'd never let him down before. Last time Burns presented himself to Nemerov, he had no collateral.'

'What was the charge?'

'Dope. As usual. This was after he was fired at Achievement House and didn't show up at his probation appointment. Up till then, Burns had been nonviolent, as far as I could tell. His juvey record began at age nine and it was sealed. His adult crime career commenced the moment he was old enough to be considered an adult: one week after his eighteenth birthday. Petty theft, drugs, more drugs. Yet more drugs. A whole bunch of plea bargains put him back on the street, then he finally had to stand trial and got probation. The last bust was more serious. Burns was caught trying to peddle heroin to some junkies on the Venice walkway. The junkie he picked was an undercover officer and the arrest came during one of those times when the department claimed to be fighting The War On Drugs. All of a sudden, Burns faced a ten-year sentence and the court imposed a fifty-thousand-dollar bond. Burns went to Boris Nemerov, as usual, and Nemerov posted for him and accepted Burns's promise to work off the five grand. But this time, Burns skipped. Nemerov called around, trying to locate Burns's family, friends, got zilch. The address Burns had listed was a parking lot in Watts. Nemerov started to get irritated.'

'Started?' I said. 'Patient fellow.'

'Cold winters on the steppes can teach you patience. Eventually, Nemerov put the bounty hunters on Burns's trail, but they got nowhere. Then out of the blue, Nemerov got a call from Burns. Guy claimed to want to give himself up but was scared the hunters were gonna shoot him in his tracks. Nemerov tried to put his mind at ease, but Burns was freaking out. Paranoid. Said people were after him. Nemerov agreed to pick up Burns personally. East of Robertson, near the 10 East overpass. Nemerov set out late at night in this big old gold Lincoln he used to tool around in, never came home. Mrs Nemerov went crazy, Missing Persons prioritized it because Boris was well-known at the station. Two days later, the Lincoln was found in an alley behind an apartment on Guthrie, not far from the meeting place. Those days, the neighborhood was serious gang territory.'

'Meeting Burns alone there didn't worry Nemerov?'

'Boris was self-confident. Big, jolly type. Probably thought he'd seen the worst and survived. The Lincoln was stripped and gutted and covered with branches – someone had made a half-baked attempt to conceal it. Boris was in the trunk, bound and gagged, three holes in the back of his head.'

'Execution,' I said.

'No good deed goes unpunished. Del Hardy and I got the case and worked it all the way to nowhere.'

'You would think something like that would make the papers. Burns's name pulled up zilch.'

'That I can explain. Nemerov's family wanted it kept quiet, and we obliged. They didn't want Boris's lapse in judgment made public – bad for business. And they had quite a few favors to pull in – reporters' kids who'd been bailed out. Cops' kids, too. Del and I were ordered to do our job but to do it very quietly.'

'Did that hamstring you?'

'Not really. Finding Burns wasn't going to be accomplished by feeding the press. The Nemerovs were decent folk – first everything they'd gone through in Russia and now this. We didn't want to upset them, everyone felt bad about the whole thing. The business almost went under, anyway. The insurance companies weren't pleased, wanted to sever all ties. Nemerov's widow and son agreed to eat all fifty grand of Burns's forfeited bail and begged for a chance to prove themselves. They managed to hold on to most of their policies. Eventually, they got their heads above water. They're still in business – same place, right around the corner from the station. Nowadays they're known for never giving an inch.'

'And Willie Burns's trail went cold,' I said.

'I dogged him for years, Alex. Anytime I had a lull, I checked on the asshole. I was sure he'd turn up eventually because a junkie's unlikely to change his ways. My bet was he'd end up incarcerated or dead.'

'Maybe he did end up dead,' I said. 'The Nemerov family had access to professional searchers. Even good folk can develop a thirst for revenge.'

'My gut says no, but if that's what happened, it's a definite dead end. I'm starting to feel like I'm back in junior high, staring at tests I flunked.'

'Maybe it's only one big test,' I said. 'Maybe Willie Burns knew Caroline before she was sent to Achievement House – one of the black guys Dr Schwartzman saw Caroline hanging with. Burns's

151

murdering Nemerov could've been nothing new for him, because he'd killed before. At a party in Bel Air.'

'Burns's record was nonviolent, Alex.'

'Till it wasn't,' I said. 'What if the nonviolent crimes were the ones he never got caught for. Was he only into heroin?'

'No, poly-drug addict. Heroin, acid, pills, meth. Since the age of ten.'

'Ups and downs,' I said. 'Unpredictable behavior. Put someone like that in contact with an unbalanced kid like Caroline, stick both of them at a dope party where two not-too-bright street girls show up, and who knows what might happen? Caroline's family suspected – or knew she'd been part of something bad and sent her to Achievement House. Willie split back to the streets but found his way over to Achievement House to visit Caroline. Stupid move, but junkies are impulsive. And no one caught on. He worked there for a month, was fired because of absenteeism.'

He drummed his fingers on his knees. 'Burns and Caroline as a killing couple.'

'With or without additional friends. Burns participating in a murder could also explain his skipping out on Nemerov. The city was clamping down on dope dealers, and he knew he was likely to serve time. That would've made him a captive audience if Janie Ingalls's murder came to light.'

'Then why'd he call Nemerov and offer to turn himself in?'

'To accomplish exactly what he did: ambush Nemerov, rob him, take his car – it was stripped. For all we know, Burns fenced the stereo and the phone. And that half-baked attempt at hiding it is pure hype. Also, Caroline's disappearance could be Willie taking no chances. Figuring she was high risk to talk.'

'If Burns or anyone else disappeared Caroline, you don't think her family would've reacted? Leaned on the department to solve it?'

'Maybe not. Caroline had been an embarrassment to them all through childhood – the weird sib – and if they knew she'd been an accomplice to murder, they'd have wanted to keep it quiet. It's consistent with sequestering her at Achievement House.'

'With a pink tab,' he said.

'Burns found her anyway. Maybe *she* contacted *him*. For all we know, she was with him when he ambushed Boris Nemerov. When exactly was Nemerov executed?'

'December, right before Christmas. I remember Mrs Nemerov talking about it. How they were Russian Orthodox, celebrated in January, there'd be nothing to celebrate.'

'Caroline was at Achievement House in August,' I said. 'Four months later, she could've been out of there. Willie could've broken her out. Perhaps they were planning to cut town all along, and that's why Burns was trying to sell dope in Venice.'

'My, my, so many possibilities,' he said. 'Ah.'

He had me drive in the direction of the station, then turn onto Purdue and park in front of an old redbrick building just south of Santa Monica Boulevard.

The entrance to Kwik 'n' Ready Bail Bonds was a glass-fronted storefront heralded by neon above the door and gold leaf on the glass. Unlike Achievement House, this placed welcomed attention.

I pointed to the *No Stopping, Tow Away* warning.

Milo said, 'I'll watch out for the parking Nazis. Failing that, I'll go your bail.'

The front office was a stuffy sliver of fluorescence with a high counter and walls paneled in something mustard-colored that bore no biological link to trees. A knobless door was cut into the rear paneling. A single Maxfield Parrish print – purple mountains' majesty – hung to the left of the doorway. Behind the counter, a round-faced man in his late thirties sat on an old oak swivel chair and ate a big wet sandwich wrapped in wax paper. A coffeemaker and a computer sat to his left. Cabbage and slabs of meat and something red protruded from the sandwich. The man's short-sleeved white shirt was clean but his chin was moist, and as the door closed behind us he swiped at himself with a paper napkin and aimed cautious gray eyes at us. Then he grinned.

'Detective Sturgis.' He hauled a thick body out of the chair and a pink forearm shot across the counter. An anchor tattoo blued the smooth flesh. His brown hair was cropped to the skull and his face was a potpie that had been nibbled at the edges.

'Georgie,' said Milo. 'How's everything?'

'People are very bad, so everything's very good,' said Georgie. He glanced at me. 'He doesn't look like a business opportunity for me.'

'No business today,' said Milo. 'This is Dr Delaware. He consults for the department. Doctor, George Nemerov.'

'A doctor for the cops,' said Georgie, pumping my hand. 'What do you specialize in, sexually transmitted diseases or insanity?'

'Good guess, Georgie. He's a shrink.'

Nemerov chuckled. 'People are nuts, so everything's good for *you*, Doctor. If you knew more about this business, you'd try to lock me up, too.' Heavy eyelids drooped, and the gray eyes narrowed. But the rest of the soft, doughy face remained placid. 'So what's up, Detective Milo?'

'This and that, Georgie. Eating your spinach?'

'Hate that stuff,' said Nemerov, patting his anchor tattoo. To me: 'When I was a kid, I was a big cartoon fan, Popeye the Sailor. One night, when I was a high school punk, me and some friends were over at the Pike in Long Beach and I got this shit put on me. My mother almost skinned me alive.'

'How is your mom?' said Milo.

'Good as can be expected,' said Nemerov. 'Next month she's seventy-three.'

'Give her my best.'

'Will do, Milo. She always liked you. So . . . why you here?' Nemerov's smile was angelic.

'I've been looking into some old files, and your dad's case came up.'

'Oh, yeah?' said Nemerov. 'Came up how?'

'Willie Burns's name surfaced with regard to another 187.'

'That so?' Nemerov shifted his weight. His smile had died. 'Well, that wouldn't surprise me. The guy was lowlife scum. You telling me he's been spotted around?'

'No,' said Milo. 'The other case is also old and cold. Actually went down before your dad.'

'And this never came to light when you guys were looking for that murderous fuck?'

'No, Georgie. Burns isn't officially a suspect on the other one. His name just came up, that's all.'

'I see,' Georgie said. 'Actually, I don't.' He rolled a wrist, and muscles bulged in his forearm. 'What, things are so relaxed around the corner that they've got you chasing ghosts?'

'Sorry to bring up old crap, Georgie.'

'Whatever, Milo, we all got our jobs. Back then I was a kid, first-year college, Cal State Northridge, I was going to become a lawyer. Instead, I got this.' Pudgy hands spread.

Milo said, 'I just wanted to verify that you guys never caught any wind of Burns.'

Nemerov's eyes were ash-colored slits. 'You don't think I'd tell you if we did?'

'I'm sure you would, but—'

'We go by the law, Milo. Making our living depends on it.'

'I know you do, Georgie. Sorry—'

Georgie picked up his sandwich. 'So who else did Burns off?'

Milo shook his head. 'Too early to let that out. When you guys were looking for him did you uncover any known associates?'

'Nah,' said Nemerov. 'Guy was a fucking loner. A dope-head and a bum and a scumbag. Today, those Legal Aid assholes would call him a poor, poor pitiful homeless citizen and try to get you and me to pay his rent.' His mouth twisted. 'A bum. My dad always treated him with respect and that's how the fuck repaid him.'

'It stinks,' said Milo.

'It stinks bad. Even after all this time.'

'Your dad was a good guy, Georgie.'

Nemerov's gray slits aimed at me. 'My dad could read people like a book, Doctor. Better than a shrink.'

I nodded, thinking: Boris Nemerov had misread Willie Burns in the worst possible way.

Georgie rested one beefy arm on the countertop and favored me with a warm gust of garlic and brine and mustard.

'He could read 'em, my dad could, but he was too damn good, too damn soft. My mom tortured herself for not stopping him from going to meet the fuck that night. I told her she couldn'ta done nothing – Dad got an idea in his head, you couldn't stop him. That's what kept him alive with the communists. Heart of gold, head like a rock. Burns, the fuck, was a loser and a liar but he'd always made his court dates before so why wouldn't my dad see the best in him?'

'Absolutely,' said Milo.

'Ah,' said Nemerov.

The door in the rear panel was pushed open and seven hundred pounds of humanity emerged and filled the office. Two men, each close to six-six, wearing black turtlenecks, black cargo pants, black revolvers in black nylon holsters. The larger one – a fine distinction – was Samoan, with long hair tied up in a sumo knot and a wispy mustache-goatee combo. His companion wore a red crew cut and had a fine-featured, baby-smooth face.

Georgie Nemerov said, 'Hey.'

Both monsters studied us.

'Hey,' said Sumo.

Red grunted.

'Boys, this is Detective Milo Sturgis, an old friend from around the corner. He investigated the scumfuck who murdered my dad. And this is a shrink the department uses because we all know cops are crazy, right?'

Slow nods from the behemoths.

Georgie said, 'These are two of my prime finders, Milo. This here's Stevie, but we call him Yokuzuna, 'cause he used to wrestle in Japan. And the little guy's Red Yaakov, from the Holy Land. So what's new, boys?'

'We got something for you,' said Stevie. 'Out back, in the van.'

'The 459?'

Stevie the Samoan smiled. 'The 459 and guess what? A bonus. We're leaving the 459's crib – idiot's right there in bed, like he doesn't believe anyone's gonna come looking for him and in two secs we've got him braceleted, are taking him out to the car and a window shade in the next-door house moves and some other guy's staring out at us. And Yaakov says, waitaminute, ain't that the 460 we been looking for since the Democratic convention?'

Yaakov said, 'Det stoopid guy Garcia, broke dose windows and reeped off all dot stereo.'

'Raul Garcia?' said Georgie. He broke into a grin. 'No kidding.'

'Yeah, him,' said Stevie. 'So we go in and get him, too. Both of them are out there in back, squirming in the van. Turns out they played craps together – neighborly spirit and all that. They actually asked us to loosen the bracelets so they could play in the van.'

Georgie high-fived both giants. 'Two for one, beautiful. Okay, let me process the papers, then you can take both geniuses over to the jail. I'm proud of you boys. Come back at five and pick up your checks.'

Stevie and Yaakov saluted and left the way they'd come in.

'Thank God,' said Georgie, 'that criminals are retarded.' He returned to his chair and picked up his sandwich.

Milo said, 'Thanks for your time.'

The sandwich arced toward Nemerov's mouth, then paused inches from its destination. 'You actually going to be looking for Burns again?'

'Should I?' said Milo. 'I figure if he was findable, you guys woulda brought him in a long time ago.'

'You got that,' said Georgie.

Knots formed along Milo's jawline as he sauntered closer to the counter. 'You think he's dead, Georgie?'

Nemerov's eyes shifted to the left. 'That would be nice, but why would I think that?'

'Because you never found him.'

'Could be, Milo. 'Cause we're good at what we do. Maybe when it first happened we weren't. Like I said, I was a college kid, what did I know? And Mom was all torn up, you remember how the insurance companies were jerking us around – one day we're doing the funeral, the next day we're fighting to stay out of bankruptcy. So maybe Burns didn't get looked for like he should. But later I sent guys out for him, we've still got him on our list – look, I'll show you.'

He got up, pushed the paneled door hard, was gone for a few moments, came back with a piece of paper that he dropped on the counter.

Wilbert Lorenzo Burns's wanted sheet. Mug shot in full face and profile, the usual necklace of numbers. Medium-dark face, well-formed features that were soft and boyish – what would have been a pleasant face but for the hype eyes. Burns's long hair protruded in wooly tufts, as if it had been yanked. His statistics put him at six-two, one-sixty, with knife-scars on both forearms and the back of the neck, no tattoos. Wanted for PCs 11375, 836.6., 187.

Possession with intent to sell, escape after remand or arrest, homicide.

'I think of him from time to time,' said Georgie, between bites of wet sandwich. 'Probably he is dead. He was a hype, what's those fuckheads' life expectancies, anyway? But you learn different, call me.'

eighteen

As we left the bail bond office, a meter reader's go-cart pulled up behind the Seville. Milo said, 'Let's get going,' and we ran for the car. The reader got out with his little computerized instrument of evil, but I peeled away before he could punch buttons.

'Close call,' said Milo.

'Thought you had clout,' I said.

'Clout's an ephemeral thing.'

I turned the corner, headed back to the station.

He said, 'So what do you think?'

'About what?'

'Georgie's demeanor.'

'I don't know Georgie.'

'Even so.'

'He seemed to get edgy when you brought up Burns.'

'He did, at that. Normally, he's even-tempered, you never hear him swear. This time he was tossing out the f-word.'

'Maybe recalling his father's murder got him worked up.'

'Maybe.'

'You're wondering if he did take care of Burns. But you're unlikely to ever know.'

'Thought you were supposed to make people feel better.'

'Purification through insight,' I said, pulling up near the Westside staff parking lot and letting the Seville idle. Milo remained in place, long legs drawn up high, hands flat on the seat.

'Screw Schwinn,' he finally said.

'That would be easy,' I said. 'If it was really about Schwinn.'

He glared at me. 'More purification?'

'What are friends for?'

159

A few minutes later: 'Why the murder book? If he really wanted to help, all he had to do was call and give me the facts.'

'Maybe there's more to the book than just Janie's photo.'

'Such as?'

'I don't know, but it's worth a second look.'

He didn't answer. Made no effort to leave the car.

'So,' I said.

'So . . . I was thinking of a visit to Achievement House, maybe pick up on the latest trends in special education.'

'You're still on it.'

'I don't know what I am.'

I took Pico east to Motor, sped past Rancho Park and into Cheviot Hills. In the daylight, Achievement House didn't look any more impressive. The light stucco I'd seen last night was baby blue. A few more cars occupied the lot, and a dozen or so adolescents hung in loose groups. When we pulled up to the curb, they paid scant notice. The kids were a varied bunch ranging from black-lipped Goths to preppy chirpers who could've been extras on the *Ozzie and Harriet* set.

Milo rang the bell on the gate, and we were buzzed in without inquiry. Another buzz got us through the door. The lobby smelled of room freshener and corn chips. A reception desk to the right and an office door marked ADMINISTRATION were separated by a hallway that emptied to a softly lit waiting room where no one waited. Cream walls hung with chrome-framed floral prints, plum-colored carpeting, neatly arranged magazines on teak tables, off-white, overstuffed chairs. Glass panes in the rear double doors provided a view of more corridor and bursts of gawky adolescent movement.

The receptionist was a young Indian woman in a peach sari, surprised, but untroubled, by Milo's badge.

'And this is about?' she said, pleasantly.

'An inquiry,' said Milo, with downright good cheer. During the ride he'd been tense and silent, but all that was gone now. He'd combed his hair, tightened his tie, was coming across like a man with something to look forward to.

'An inquiry?' she said.

'A look at some student records, ma'am.'

'I'll get you Ms Baldassar. She's our director.'

She left, returned, said, 'This way,' and showed us to the door across the hall. We entered a front office and a secretary ushered us through a door to a tidy space where an ash blonde woman in her forties sat behind a desk and stubbed out a cigarette.

Milo offered the badge, and the blonde said, 'Marlene Baldassar.' Thin, tan, and intensely freckled, she had hollow cheeks, golden brown eyes, and a knife-point chin. Her navy blue A-line dress was piped with white and bagged on her bony frame. The ash hair was blunt-cut to mid-neck, bangs feathered to fringe. She wore a gold wedding band and an oversize black plastic diver's watch. Tortoise-framed glasses hung on a chain. The big glass ashtray on her desk was half-filled with lipstick-tipped butts. The rim read *Mirage Hotel, Las Vegas*. The rest of the desk was taken up with books, papers, framed photos. And a shiny silver harmonica.

She saw me looking at the instrument, picked it up with two fingers, tooted twice, put it down, smiling. 'Tension reliever. I'm trying to quit smoking. And obviously not doing very well.'

'Old habits,' I said.

'Very old. And yes, I *have* tried the patch. All of them. My DNA's probably saturated with nicotine.' She ran a finger along the edge of the harmonica. 'So, what's this Shoba tells me about a police inquiry? Has one of our alumni gotten into trouble?'

'You don't seem surprised by that possibility,' said Milo.

'I've worked with kids for going on twenty years. Very little surprises me.'

'Twenty years here, ma'am?'

'Three here, seventeen with the county – Juvenile Hall, community mental health centers, gang-violence prevention programs.'

'Welcome change?' I said.

'For the most part,' she said. 'But county work could even be fun. Lots of futility, but when you do come across a gem in the trash pile, it's exciting. Working here's extremely predictable. By and large, the kids are a decent bunch. Spoiled but decent. We specialize in serious learning disabilities – chronic school failure, severe dyslexia, kids who just can't get it together educationally. Our goal's specific: try to get them to a point so that when they get hold of their trust funds they can read the small print. So if your *inquiry* is about one of my current charges, I'd be surprised. We steer away from high-risk antisocials, too much maintenance.'

Milo said, 'Are the kids confined twenty-four hours a day?'

'Heavens no,' she said. 'This isn't prison. They go home on weekends, earn passes. So what do you need to know and about whom?'

'Actually,' said Milo, 'this is more of a historical venture. Someone who was here twenty years ago.'

Marlene Baldassar sat back, fooled with her eyeglasses. 'Sorry, I'm not free to talk about alumni. An emergent situation with a current student would be something else – someone in the here and now posing a danger to themselves and/or others. The law would require me to work with you on that.'

'Schools have no confidentiality, ma'am.'

'But psychotherapists do, Detective, and many of our files contain psychotherapeutic records. I'd love to help, but—'

'What about personnel records?' said Milo. 'We're also looking into someone who worked here. There'd be no protection of any sort, there.'

Baldassar fiddled with her glasses. 'I suppose that's true, but . . . twenty years ago? I'm not sure we even have records going back that far.'

'One way to find out, ma'am.'

'What's this person's name?'

'Wilbert Lorenzo Burns.'

No recognition on the freckled face. Baldassar got on the phone, asked a few questions, said, 'Wait right here,' and returned a few moments later with a scrap of pink paper.

'Burns, Wilburt L.,' she said, handing it to Milo. 'This is all we've got. Mr Burns's notice of termination. He lasted three weeks. August third through the twenty-fourth. Was terminated for absenteeism. See for yourself.'

Milo read the scrap and handed it back.

'What did Mr Burns do?'

'There's a fugitive warrant out on him. Mostly he was a narcotics violator. Kind of alarming that when he worked here he was on probation for a drug conviction. About to face trial for selling heroin.'

Baldassar frowned. 'Wonderful. Well, that wouldn't happen today.'

'You vet your employees carefully?'

'A pusher wouldn't get by me.'

'Guess the former director wasn't that picky,' said Milo. 'Do you know him – Michael Larner?'

'The only one I know is my immediate predecessor. Dr Evelyn Luria. Lovely woman. She retired and moved to Italy – she's at least eighty. I was told that she was brought in to beef up clinical services. I was brought in to organize things.' She poked the harmonica. 'You're not implying this Burns was dealing to the kids here.'

'Do the kids here have drug problems?'

'Detective, please,' said Baldassar. 'They're teenagers with poor self-esteem and plenty of disposable income. You don't need a PhD to figure it out. But believe me, I don't allow any species of felon to pass through our gates. As far as what happened twenty years ago . . .'

She picked up the harmonica, put it down. 'If that's all . . .'

'Actually,' said Milo, 'the investigation's not just about Willie Burns. It's about a student Burns was friendly with. A girl named Caroline Cossack.'

Baldassar stared. Then she snorted – I suppose it was laughter, but she looked anything but happy. She said, 'Let's go outside. I want to smoke, but I don't want to poison anyone else.'

She took us through the glass-paned double doors, past ten rooms, some of which had been left open. We walked by carelessly made beds, piles of stuffed animals, movie and rock star posters, boom boxes, guitars, books stacked in little wooden desks. A few teens were stretched across beds listening to music through earphones, one boy did push-ups, a girl read a magazine – brow knitted, lips moving laboriously.

We followed Marlene Baldassar under a rear staircase, where she pushed a door marked EXIT and let us pass through to an alley behind the building. Two dumpsters were pushed against a cinder-block wall. Nearby stood a chesty girl with her elbows to the block, hips thrust at a tall, buzz-cut boy wearing low pants that puddled around his unlaced sneakers. He looked like a scarecrow about to come apart. Moved in for a kiss but stopped as the girl said something, turned and frowned.

Baldassar said, 'Hi, guys.' Expressionless, the couple ambled off and disappeared around a corner.

'Somethingus interruptus,' said Baldassar. 'I almost feel guilty.'

Power lines were strung ten feet above the wall, and I could hear them buzzing. A pigeon soared overhead. Baldassar lit up, dragged hungrily, smoked down a half inch of her cigarette.

'Is there any chance we can talk confidentially?' she said.

'I'd like to promise you that,' said Milo. 'But if you've got knowledge of a crime—'

'No, it's nothing like that. And I never met the Cossack girl, though I do know that she was once a resident. But in terms of her family . . . let's just say they're not very popular around here.'

'Why's that, ma'am?'

Baldassar smoked and shook her head. 'I suppose if you dug around enough, you'd find out, anyway.'

'Where should I be digging?'

'What, I should do your job for you?'

'I'll take anything I can get, ma'am,' said Milo.

She smiled. 'County records. I'll tell you what I know, but I can't have any of it traced back to me, okay?'

'Okay.'

'I'm trusting you, Detective.'

'Thank you, ma'am.'

'And no more ma'ams please,' she said. 'I'm starting to feel like I'm in some old *Dragnet* script.'

'Fair enough, Ms—'

Baldassar cut him off with a wave of her cigarette. 'To make a long story exquisitely short, several years ago, seventeen or eighteen years ago, Achievement House ran into some severe financial problems due to bad investments. The board was comprised of stuffy old farts who were conservative with their personal fortunes but turned out to be a good deal more adventurous with Achievement House's endowment. Remember all that junk-bond foolishness? The board hired a money manager who traded Achievement House's blue chips for a whole slew of what ended up as worthless paper. At the time, the interest rates were enticing, and the income allowed the school to run at such a high paper profit that the board was starting to think Achievement House would pay for itself. Then everything crashed. And to make matters worse, the manager had taken out a second mortgage and bought additional bonds on margin. When everything hit the fan, Achievement House was way in the hole and facing foreclosure on the property.'

'The rich old farts would've let that happen?'

'The rich old farts served on the board in order to feel noble and to get their names in the social pages during gala season. To make matters worse, there'd been a bit of unpleasantness with the director – your Mr Larner. I know all this from Evelyn Luria. She briefed me before she left for Europe, but wouldn't give me details. But she did hint that it had been something of a sexual nature. Something that might've gotten the board members the worst type of publicity.'

'So the school was in danger of closing down, and the board wouldn't go to bat.'

'God, I hope this doesn't blow up, after all these years. I was looking at this job as a way to relax.'

'Nothing will get traced to you, Ms. Baldassar. Now tell me why the Cossacks aren't popular.'

'Because they came to the rescue – white knights – and then turned into something quite different.'

'Caroline's father?'

'Caroline's father and brothers. The three of them had some kind of real estate business and they stepped in and renegotiated with the bank and got a better rate for the mortgage, then had Achievement House's deed signed over to them. For a while, they made payments, no questions asked. Then a couple of years later, they announced they were evicting the school because the land was too valuable for a nonprofit – they'd been buying up lots, had plans to develop the entire block.'

She dropped her cigarette, ground it out with the toe of her pump.

'Achievement House is still here,' said Milo. 'What happened?'

'Threats, accusations, lawyers. The board and the Cossacks finally reached an agreement, but it meant dipping into some deep pockets in order to pay the Cossacks off. From what I was told, the outrage was compounded by the fact that Caroline Cossack's stay here had been a favor to the family. She didn't qualify.'

'Why not?'

'She was a psychiatric case – severe behavior problems, not learning disabilities.'

'Custodial care?' I said.

'Yes, the rules were bent for her. Then, for her family to do *that*.'

Milo said, 'Do you have any records on Caroline?'

Baldassar hesitated. 'Let me check – wait out here, please.'

She reentered the building. I said, 'I wonder if Michael Larner had something to do with the Cossacks trying to evict the school. After the board fired him, he wouldn't have been fond of the institution.'

Milo kicked one of the dumpsters. Another pigeon flew overhead. Then three more. 'Airborne rats,' he muttered. Barely audible, but the vibrations must have reached the birds, and they scattered.

Marlene Baldassar returned, another cigarette in one hand, a pink index card in another.

'No chart. All I found was this, listing the dates of her stay.'

Milo took the card. 'Admitted 9 August, discharged 22 December. But it doesn't say where she went.'

'No, it doesn't,' said Baldassar.

'You don't hold on to old charts?'

'We do. It should be here.' She studied Milo's face. 'You're not shocked.'

'Like you, I'm pretty much beyond being shockable, Ms Baldassar. And I'm going to ask you to return the favor: keep this visit confidential. For everyone's sake.'

'No problem with that,' said Baldassar. She took a deep drag, blew a smoke ring. 'Here I thought it was going to be a lazy day, and it turned out to be heavy-duty déjà vu. Gentlemen, you brought back memories of my days with the county.'

'How so?' I said.

'Problems that can't be solved with phonics and a credit card.'

nineteen

'Interesting time line,' I said, as we headed for the car under the now-watchful eyes of the kids in the parking lot. 'Janie Ingalls is murdered in early June. Two months later, Caroline gets checked into Achievement House and Willie shows up and works there for three weeks. Willie's fired, then he's busted for dope, gets Boris Nemerov to bail him out. When was Nemerov ambushed?'

'23 December,' said Milo.

'The day after Caroline leaves Achievement House – voluntarily or otherwise. Maybe Willie took his girlfriend out, then took care of her. Or Cossack family money found both of them a nice safe place to hide out. And one more thing: Georgie could've gotten nervous when you brought up Burns not because his men finished off his dad's killer but because they didn't. Were paid off not to.'

'He accepted money to let his dad's murderer off the hook? Uh-uh, not Georgie.'

'He and his mother were in severe financial straits. Maybe it took more than twenty-hour days and clever negotiating to keep the business going.'

'No, I can't see it,' he said. 'Georgie's always been a straight-ahead guy.'

'You'd know.'

'Yeah, I'm a font of knowledge. C'mon, let's go over to my place, have another look at that damn book.'

Rick and Milo lived in a small, well-kept bungalow in West Hollywood, on a quiet, elm-darkened street further shadowed by Design Center's alarming blue bulk. Rick's white Porsche was gone and the blinds were drawn. A few years ago, L.A. suffered through a drought and Rick had the lawn dug up and replaced with pea gravel and gray-leafed desert plants. This year, L.A. had plenty of water but the xeriscape remained in place, bursts of tiny yellow blossoms punctuating the pallid vegetation.

I said, 'The cactus are thriving.'

Milo said, 'Great. Especially when I come home in the dark and snag my pants.'

'Nothing like seeing the bright side.'

'That's my core philosophy,' he said. 'The glass is either half-empty or broken.'

He unlocked the front door, disarmed the alarm, picked up the mail that had fallen through the slot and tossed it on a table without breaking stride. The kitchen often lures him in his own digs, too, but this time he walked through it into the service porch nook that serves as his office: a cramped, dim space, sandwiched between the washer-dryer and the freezer and smelling of detergent. He'd set it up with a hideous metal desk painted school-bus yellow, a folding chair, and a painted wooden shark-face lamp from Bali. The blue book sat in an oversize Ziploc bag, on the top shelf of a miniature bookcase bolted above the desk.

He gloved up, unbagged the book, flipped to Janie Ingalls's photo, and studied the death shot. 'Any sudden insights?'

'Let's see what follows.'

Only three more pages after Janie. A trio of crime-scene photos, all of the victims, young men. One black youth, two Hispanics, each sprawled on blood-splotched pavement. White lights on the corpses and dark periphery said nighttime death. A shiny revolver lay near the right hand of the final victim.

The first photo was labeled 'Gang drive-by, Brooks St, Venice. One dead, two wounded.'

Next: 'Gang drive-by, Commonwealth and Fifth, Rampart.'

Finally: 'Gang drive-by, Central Ave.'

'Three of a kind,' I said. 'That's kind of interesting.'

'Why?'

'Until now there was variety.'

Milo said, 'Gang stuff . . . business as usual. Maybe Schwinn ran out of interesting pictures – if these took place after Janie, when he was already out of the department, he coulda had trouble getting hold of crime-scene shots. God only knows how he managed to get these.' He closed the book. 'You see any way drive-bys could be connected to Janie? I sure don't.'

'Mind if I take another look?'

'Take as many looks as you want.' He produced another pair of gloves from a desk drawer, and I slipped them on. As I turned to the first photo, he stepped around the washer-dryer and into the kitchen. I heard the fridge door creak open.

'Want something to drink?'

'No, thanks.'

Heavy footsteps. A cabinet opened. Glass touched tile. 'I'm gonna go check the mail.'

I took my time with the crime-scene shots. Thinking about Schwinn, addicted to speed and divesting himself of worldly goods even as he held on to his purloined photos. Moving on to a life of serenity but assembling this leather-bound monstrosity in secrecy. As I turned pages – now-familiar pages – and images began to blur, I tore myself away from speculation and tried to focus on each brutal death.

The first go-round, I came up with nothing, but on the second circuit something made me pause.

The two photos that *preceded* Janie's death shot.

The second page back was a full-color medium-range shot of a thin, rangy black man whose skin had begun to fade to postmortem gray. His long body lay on brown dirt, and one arm curled toward his face, protectively. Gaping mouth, half-open, lifeless eyes, splayed limbs.

No blood. No visible wounds.

Drug OD, possible 187 hotshot.

The next page faced Janie's. I'd avoided it because it was one of the most repellent images in the book.

The camera had focused on a heap of mangled flesh, beyond recognition as human.

Hairless legs and a battered, concave pelvic section suggested a woman. The caption precluded the need for deduction.

Female Mental Case, fell or thrown in front of double tractor trailer.

I flipped back to the skinny black man.

Returned to the beginning of the murder book and double-checked.

Then I went to get Milo.

He was in the living room, studying his gas bill, a shot glass of something amber in his paw. 'Finished?'

I said, 'Come look at this.'

He tossed back the rest of his drink, held on to the glass, and followed me.

I showed him the pictures preceding Janie. He said, 'What's your point?'

'Two points,' I said. 'First of all, content: right before Janie are a black drug-using male and a white woman with mental problems. Sound familiar? Second, context: these two deviate *stylistically* from every other photo in the book. Forty-one photos, including Janie's, list the location and the police division where the murder took place. These are the only two that don't. If Schwinn lifted the photos from police files, he had access to the data. Yet he left the locales out. Are you willing to consider a bit of psychological interpretation?'

'Schwinn being symbolic?' he said. 'These two represent Willie Burns and Caroline Cossack?'

'They're missing information because they represent the *missing* Willie Burns and the *missing* Caroline Cossack. Schwinn designated no locations because Burns's and Cossack's whereabouts remain unknown. Then he followed up with Janie's picture and wrote NS for No Solve. Right *after* Janie, he placed three drive-bys, grouped together. I don't think that's a coincidence, either. He knew how you'd see them: business as usual, just like you said. He's outlining a process here: a missing black man and mentally ill white woman are connected to Janie, whose murder is never solved. On the contrary: she's abandoned, and then it's business as usual. He's describing the cover-up.'

He pulled at his lower lip. 'Games . . . pretty subtle.'

'You said Schwinn was a devious sort,' I said. 'Suspicious, verging on paranoid. LAPD dumped him, but he continued to think like a rogue cop, played games to the end, in order to cover his rear. He decided to communicate with you, but set it up so that only you would get it. That way, if the book went astray, or was ever traced back to him, he could disclaim ownership. He took pains to make sure it *wasn't* traced to him – no fingerprints. Only you were likely to recall his photography hobby and make the connection. He might have planned to send you the book himself, but changed his mind and chose someone else as a go-between, as another layer of security.'

He studied the dead black man. Paged to the truck-crash nightmare, then Janie. Repeated the process.

'Willie and Caroline's surrogates . . . too weird.'

I pointed to the black man's corpse. 'How old does he look to you?'

He squinted at the ashen face. 'Forties.'

'If Willie Burns were alive today, he'd be forty-three. That means Schwinn saw the dead man as a surrogate for Willie *in the here and now*. Both the pictures are faded, probably decades old. But Schwinn oriented them toward the present. Meaning he finished the book fairly recently, wanted to focus *you* on the present.'

He rolled the empty shot glass between his palms. 'Bastard was a good detective. If the department got rid of him because someone was worried about what he knew about Janie, that means they didn't worry about me.'

'You were a rookie—'

'I was the dumb shit they figured would just follow orders. And guess what?' He laughed.

'It's likely when Schwinn learned he'd been forced out and you hadn't, it confirmed his suspicions of you. Maybe he figured you'd played a role in his dismissal. That's why he didn't tell you what he'd learned about Janie for years.'

'And then he changed his mind.'

'He came to admire you. Told Marge.'

'Mr Serenity,' he said. 'So he enlists his girlfriend or some old cop washout to serve as go-between. Why'd whoever it was wait until seven months after Schwinn died?'

I had no answer for that. Milo tried to pace, but the confined quarters of the laundry area made it a two-step exercise.

He said, 'Then the guy falls off a horse.'

'A horse so gentle Marge felt comfortable with Schwinn riding up into the hills alone. But Akhbar got spooked, anyway. Marge said by "something." Maybe it was some*one*.'

He stared past me, reentered the kitchen, washed out the shot glass, returned, and glared at the book. 'Nothing says Schwinn's death wasn't an accident.'

'Nothing at all.'

He pressed his hands flat against the wall as if straining to push it down.

'Bastards,' he said.

'Who?'

'Everyone.'

We sat down in his living room, each of us thinking in silence, neither of us coming up with anything. If he felt as weary as I did, he needed a break.

The phone rang. He snatched up the receiver. 'This is him . . . what? Who – yes . . . one week. Yeah . . . I did . . . that's right. What's that? Yeah, I just told you that, anything else? Okay, then. Hey, listen, why don't you give me your name and number and I'll—'

The other party cut him off. He held the phone at arm's length, began gnawing his upper lip.

'Who was that?' I said.

'Some guy claiming to be from Department Personnel downtown, wanting to verify that I was indeed taking vacation time and how long did I plan to be away. I told him I'd filled out the forms.'

'*Claiming* to be from Personnel?'

'I've never known the department to make calls like that, and he hung up when I asked his name. Also, he didn't sound like a department clerk.'

'How so?'

'He sounded like he gave a damn.'

twenty

He slipped the murder book back into the plastic bag, and said, 'This goes in the safe.'

'Didn't know you had a safe,' I said.

'For all my Cartier and Tiffany. Wait here.'

He disappeared and I stood there, humbled once more by the truism I'd learned a thousand patients ago: Everyone has secrets. At the core, we're alone.

That made me think of Robin. Where was she? What was she doing? With whom?

Milo returned, minus his necktie. 'Hungry?'

'Not really.'

'Good, let's eat.'

He locked up and we got back in the car. I said, 'That call from Personnel. Maybe procedures have tightened up with John Broussard in charge. Isn't troop discipline his pet issue?'

'Yeah. How about Hot Dog Heaven?'

I drove to San Vicente just north of Beverly and parked at the curb. Hot Dog Heaven was built around a giant hot dog, yet another testament to L.A.'s literal thinking. The fast-food joint became a landmark when the pony ride that had occupied the corner of La Cienega and Beverly for decades was replaced by the neon-and-concrete assault known as the Beverly Center. Too bad Philip K. Dick had committed suicide. A few years later and he'd have seen *Blade Runner* spring to life. Or maybe he'd known what was coming.

Back during pony-ride days, the dirt track had been a favorite weekend visitation hangout for divorced dads and their kids. Hot Dog Heaven had thrived peddling nitrites to lonely men who smoked and hung around the low-slung corral, watching their progeny go round and round. Where did displaced dads go now? Not the mall. The last thing kids at the mall wanted was proximity to their parents.

Milo ordered two jumbo chili cheese dogs with extra onions, and I got a knockwurst. We filled out the bill with two large Cokes and sat down to eat as traffic roared by. It was late for lunch and early for dinner and only two other tables were occupied, an old woman reading the paper and a tall, long-haired youth in hospital blues – probably a Cedars-Sinai intern.

Milo wolfed the first chili dog without the aid of respiration. After tweezing every scrap of cheese from the wax paper with his fingers, he gulped Coke and got to work on the second. He finished that one, too, sprang up, and bought a third. My wurst tasted fine, but it was all I could do to feign hunger.

He was counting his change when a bronze Jeep Cherokee parked in front of my Seville and a man got out and walked past me toward the counter. Black suit, pearl shirt, soot-colored tie. Smiling. That's what made me notice him. A big, wide, toothy grin, as if he'd just received terrific news. I watched him stride quickly to the counter and come to a stop just behind Milo, where he waited, bouncing on his heels. His black suede loafers were lifted by two-inch heels. Without them he was an easy six feet. He stood close to Milo, kept bouncing. Milo didn't seem to notice. Something made me put down the wurst and keep my eyes on both of them.

Smiley was thirty or so, with dark hair gelled and combed back, curling over his collar. Big-jawed face, prominent nose, golden tan. The suit was well cut – Italian or pretending to be, and it looked brand-new, as did the suede shoes. The gray shirt was satin-finish silk, the tie a bulky knit. Dressed for an audition as a game show host?

He edged even closer to Milo. Said something. Milo turned and answered.

Smiley nodded.

Milo picked up his food and returned to the table.

'Friendly sort?' I said.

'Who?'

'The guy behind you. He's been smiling since he left that Jeep.'

'So?'

'So what's to smile about?'

Milo allowed his own mouth to curl upward. But he let his eyes drift back to the counter, where the smiling man was now conversing with the counter girl. 'Anything other than that bother you about him?'

'He was standing close enough to you to smell your cologne.'

'If I wore any,' he said, but he continued to watch the goings-on at the counter. Finally sat back and sank his teeth into the third chili dog. 'Nothing like health food.' He regarded my half-finished wurst. 'What's with the anorexia?'

'Just out of curiosity, what did he say to you up there?'

'Oh, boy . . .' He shook his head. 'He wanted to know what was good, okay? I told him I liked anything with chili. Heavy-duty intrigue.'

I smiled. 'Or flirting.'

'Me?'

'Him.'

'Oh, sure, strangers always come up and hit on me. The old fatal charm and all that.'

But he hazarded another glance at the counter, where Smiley was still gabbing with the girl as he paid for his dog. Plain, no chili. He sat down at the table closest to ours, unfolded a napkin over his lap, flipped his hair, beamed at Milo, said, 'Chickened out on the chili.'

'Your loss.'

Smiley laughed. Tugged at his lapel. Took a bite. A dainty little bite that didn't alter the shape of the hot dog.

I mumbled, 'Fatal charm.'

Milo said, 'Enough,' and wiped his face.

Smiley continued to nibble without making much progress. Dabbed his chin. Showed off his dental work. Made several attempts at catching Milo's eye. Milo moved his bulk around, stared at the ground.

Smiley said, 'These really *are* a mouthful.'

I fought back laughter.

Milo nudged my arm. 'Let's go.'

175

We stood. Smiley said, 'Have a nice day.'

He got to his feet as we reached the car and jogged toward us, sandwich in one hand, the other waving.

'What the hell,' said Milo, and his hand sidled under his coat.

Smiley reached into his own jacket and all at once Milo had interposed himself between the stranger and me. A flesh barrier, immense; tension seemed to enlarge him. Then he relaxed. Smiley was still waving, but the something in his hand was small and white. A business card.

'Sorry for being so forward, but I . . . here's my number. Call me if you'd like.'

'Why would I do that?' said Milo.

Smiley's lips drew back, and his grin morphed into something hungry and unsettling. 'Because you never know.'

He dangled the card.

Milo stood there.

Smiley said, 'Oh, well,' and placed the card on the hood of the Seville. His new face was serious, vulpine, purposeful. He trotted away from us, tossed the uneaten hot dog in the trash, got into the Jeep, and sped away as Milo hustled to copy down his license plate. He picked the card off the hood, read it and handed it to me.

Off-white vellum with a faintly greasy feel, engraved letters.

Paris M. Bartlett
Health Facilitator

Below that, a cell phone number.

' "Because you never know," ' said Milo. 'Health facilitator. Do I look sick?'

'Other than stains on your shirt you look perfectly put-together.'

'Health facilitator,' he repeated. 'Sounds like something from the AIDS industry.' He pulled out his cell phone and jabbed in Paris Bartlett's number. Frowned again. 'No longer in service. What the hell . . .'

'Time to DMV the plates?' I said.

'DMVing is illegal when I'm on vacation. Using departmental resources for personal reasons, big no-no.'

'John G. would disapprove mightily.'

'Mightily.' He made the call to State Motor Vehicles, recited the plate, waited a while, wrote something down. 'The plates belong to a two-year-old Jeep, so that's kosher. Registered to the Playa del Sol Corporation. The address is right here in West Hollywood. I recognize it. Parking lot of the Healthy Foods market on Santa Monica. There's a post–office box outlet there. I know because I used to rent there myself.'

'When?'

'Long time ago.'

A safe. A POB. All the new things I was learning about my friend.

'Dead number, shadow address,' I said. 'Playa del Sol could be nothing more than a cardboard box in someone's apartment, but it does have the ring of a real estate outfit.'

'As in the Cossacks.' He studied the card. 'That and the call about my vacation time. Right after we talk to Marlene Baldassar. Maybe she *can't* be trusted.'

Or maybe he hadn't covered his trail. I said, 'It could be just a pickup attempt.' But I knew that was wrong. Paris Bartlett had bounded out of his car with clear intention.

He slipped the card in his pocket. 'Alex, I grew up in a big family, never got much attention, never developed a taste for it. I need some alone time.'

I drove him back to his place, and he hurtled out of the Seville, mumbled something that might've been 'Thanks,' slammed the door, and loped toward his front door.

I made it to my own front door thirty-five minutes later, told myself I'd be able to walk right past the phone. But the red blinking 1 on the answering machine snagged me, and I stabbed the message button.

Robin's voice: 'Looks like I missed you again, Alex. There's another change in schedule, we're adding an extra day in Vancouver, maybe the same in Denver. It's crazy around here, I'll be in and out.' Two-second delay, then several decibels lower: 'I love you.'

Obligatory add-on? Unlike Pierce Schwinn, I didn't need drugs to prime the paranoia pump.

I phoned the Four Seasons Seattle again and asked for Ms Castagna's room. This time if they gave me voice mail, I'd leave a message.

But a man answered. Young, one of those laughing voices. Familiar.

Sheridan. He of the ponytail, the cheerful outlook, and the Milk-Bone for Spike.

'Robin? Oh, hi. Yeah, sure.'

Seconds later: 'This is Robin.'

'And this is Alex.'

'Oh . . . hi. Finally.'

'Finally?'

'Finally we connect. Is everything okay?'

'Everything's peachy,' I said. 'Am I interrupting something?'

'What – oh, Sheridan? No, we were just finishing up a meeting. A bunch of us.'

'Busy busy.'

'I've got time now. So how *are* you? Busy yourself?'

This was too much like small talk, and it depressed me. 'Muddling along. How's Spike?'

'Thriving. There's a bunch of other dogs along for the ride, so there's a nice kennel space. Spike's getting pretty sociable. There's an eighty-pound shepherd bitch who seems to have caught his fancy.'

'Does the kennel space include a ladder for him to reach her?'

She laughed, but sounded tired. 'So . . .'

I said, 'So are you getting in any social time?'

'I'm working, Alex. We're putting in twelve-, thirteen-hour days.'

'Sounds tough. I miss you.'

'Miss you, too. We both knew this would be difficult.'

'Then we were both right.'

'Honey – hold on, Alex . . . someone just stuck their head in.' Her voice got muffled and distant; hand over the phone. '*I'll see what I can do, give me a little time on it, okay? When's sound-check? That soon? Okay, sure.*' Back to me: 'As you can see I haven't had much solitude.'

'I've had plenty.'

'I'm jealous.'

'Are you?'

'Yes,' she said. 'We both like our solitude, right?'

'You can have yours back anytime.'

'I can't exactly walk out on everyone.'

'No,' I said. 'As Richard Nixon said, that would be wrong.'

'I mean I – if there was some easy – if that would really make you happy, I'd do it.'

'It would ruin your reputation.'

'It sure wouldn't help it.'

'You're committed,' I said. 'Don't worry about it.' *Why the hell is Sheridan so happy?*

'Alex, when I do get a minute to breathe, I think of you, wonder if I did the right thing. Then I plan all the things I'm going to tell you, but then when we finally talk . . . it doesn't seem to go the way I'd planned.'

'Absence makes the heart cranky?'

'Not my heart.'

'Guess it's me, then,' I said. 'Guess I don't do well with separation. Never got used to it.'

'Used to it?' she said. 'Your parents?'

My parents were the last thing I'd been thinking of. Now bad old memories ignited: the wasting away of the two people who'd brought me into this world, bedside vigils, a pair of funerals in as many years.

'Alex?'

'No,' I said. 'I was just talking generally.'

'You sound upset,' she said. 'I didn't mean to—'

'You didn't do anything.'

'What did you mean by that? Never getting used to separation?'

'Random blather,' I said.

'Are you saying that even when we were together you felt abandoned? That I neglected you? Because I—'

'No,' I said. 'You've always been there for me.' *Except for the other time you left.*

Except for finding another man and— 'It really was blather, Rob. Put it down to missing you.'

'Alex, if this is really bad for you, I'll come *home*.'

'No,' I said. 'I'm a big boy. It wouldn't be good for you. For either of us.'

And I've got things on my *plate. Little odd jobs, the kind you hate.*
'That's true,' she said. 'But just say the word.'
'The word is I love you.'
'That's three words.'
'Picky picky.'
She laughed. Finally. I uttered a few pleasantries, and she did the same. When we hung up she sounded okay, and I figured I faked it pretty well.

Milo claimed to want 'alone time,' but I figured he'd be nosing around on the fringes of the LAPD bureaucracy.

If the call from Personnel and/or the encounter with the toothy Paris Bartlett did have something to do with his raking up the Ingalls case, that meant he – *we* – had been tagged, were being watched.

Marlene Baldassar as the source didn't sit right with me, and I thought about the trail we might've left.

My solo activities had consisted of the call to Larry Daschoff, dinner with Allison Gwynn, computer work at the Research Library. None of that was likely to attract attention.

Together, Milo and I had interviewed Marge Schwinn and Baldassar and Georgie Nemerov. I supposed either woman could've reported the conversation, but neither had been hostile, and I couldn't see why they'd have bothered.

Nemerov, on the other hand, had grown antsy when talking about his father's murder and Willie Burns's skip. Nemerov's bail bond business gave him close ties to the department. If John G. Broussard had been part of a fix, the department would care.

A third possibility was Milo's solo work on Janie Ingalls had attracted attention. As far as I knew that had been limited to phone work and unearthing old files. But he'd worked at the West L.A. station, sneaked around Parker Center.

Thinking he'd been discreet but he could've invited scrutiny – from clerks, other cops, anyone in a position to witness him nosing. John G. Broussard had sent a clear directive to tighten up discipline among the rank and file. The new chief had also waged war on the blue code of silence – talk about irony. Maybe cops informing on cops was the new LAPD Zeitgeist.

The more I thought about that, the more it made sense: Milo was a pro, but he'd taken too much for granted.

Procedurally, he'd been outed.

That made me think about his continuing vulnerability. Twenty years in the department with one of the highest solve rates in Homicide, but that wasn't enough, would never be enough.

For two decades he'd functioned as a gay man in a paramilitary organization that would never be free of gut-level bias and still hadn't acknowledged the existence of homosexual cops. I knew – everyone knew – that scores of gay officers patrolled the streets, but not a single one had gone public. Neither had Milo, in a strict sense, but after those first brutal years of self-torment he had stopped hiding.

Department statisticians were happy to file his solves in the Assets column but the brass continued to retard his progress and made periodic attempts to get rid of him. Milo had collected secrets of his own along the way, finally managed to leverage his way to relative job security and seniority. He'd turned down the offer to take the lieutenant's exam twice because he knew the department's real intention was to shunt him to some desk job where they could pretend he didn't exist, while boring him to the point of voluntary retirement. Instead, he'd stayed on the detective track, had taken it as far as it would go: to Detective-III.

Maybe Pierce Schwinn had followed all that, come to respect Milo for holding his own. Offered Milo a perverse gift.

Normally, nothing heated Milo's blood like a good cold case. But this was a rethaw from his own past, and perhaps he'd gotten careless and turned himself into prey.

I thought of how Paris Bartlett had targeted Milo, ignored me.

Meaning I had room to move.

The timing was perfect, the logic exquisite: what were friends for?

twenty-one

Alone, at his crappy little piss-colored desk, the washer churning the clothes he'd just loaded for background noise, Milo felt better.

Free of *Alex*, he felt better.

Because Alex's mind could be a scary thing – cerebral flypaper; stuff flew in but never left. His friend was capable of sitting quietly for long stretches when you'd think he was listening – actively listening the way they'd taught him in shrink school – then he'd let loose a burst of associations and hypotheses and apparently unrelated trivialities that turned out too often to be right-on.

Houses of cards that, more often than not, withstood the wind. Milo, on the receiving end of the nonstop volleys, felt like a wobbly sparring partner.

Not that Alex pushed. He just kept *supposing. Suggesting.* Another shrink tactic. Try ignoring any of it.

Milo had never met anyone smarter or more decent than Alex, but hanging with the guy could be draining. How many nights' sleep had he lost because one of his friend's *suggestions* had hooked a barb in his brain?

But for all his bloodhound instincts, Alex was a civilian and out of his element. And he'd failed to mature in one regard: had never developed a proper sense of threat.

In the beginning, Milo had attributed it to the carelessness of an overenthusiastic amateur. It hadn't taken long to learn the truth: Alex got off on danger.

Robin understood that, and it scared her. Over the years she'd confided her fears to Milo – more nuance than complaint. And when the three of them were together and Alex and Milo lapsed

182

into the wrong type of conversation and her face changed, Milo caught it quickly and changed the subject. Strangely enough, Alex, for all his perceptiveness, sometimes missed it.

Alex had to realize how Robin felt, yet he made no effort to change. And Robin put up with it. Love is blind and deaf and dumb . . . maybe she'd simply made a commitment and was smart enough to know it was damn near impossible to change anyone.

But now, she'd gone on that tour. And taken the dog. For some reason that felt wrong – the damn pooch. Alex was claiming to be okay, but that first day Milo'd dropped in, he'd looked really bad, and even now, he was different . . . distracted.

Something was off.

Or maybe not.

He'd poked a bit at Alex's resistance. Playing shrink to the shrink, and why the hell shouldn't he? How could you have a real friendship when the therapy went only one way? But no luck. Alex talked the talk – openness, communication, blah blah blah, but in his own articulate, empathetic, ever-so-disgustingly *civilized* way, the guy was pain-in-the-ass, dead-end *immovable*.

Now that he thought about it, had Alex *ever* been deterred? Milo couldn't remember a single instance.

Alex did exactly what Alex wanted to do.

And Robin . . . Milo'd offered his smoothest reassurances. And he supposed he'd done a decent job of keeping Alex out of harm's way. But there were limits.

Everyone stood alone.

He got up, poured himself a vodka and pink-grapefruit juice, rationalizing that the vitamin C counteracted the oxidation, but wondering how closely his liver resembled that medical journal photo Rick had shown him last month.

Erosion of hepatic tissue and replacement with fatty globules due to advanced cirrhosis.

Rick never pushed either, but Milo knew he wasn't happy with the fresh bottle of Stoli in the freezer.

Switch channels: back to Alex.

Other people's problems were so much more engaging.

He walked half a mile to a Budget Rent-a-Car on La Cienega and got himself a fresh blue Taurus. Driving east on Santa Monica, he crossed into Beverly Hills, then West Hollywood. Not much traffic past Doheny Drive, but at the West Hollywood border the boulevard had been narrowed to one lane in either direction and the few cars in sight were crawling.

West Hollywood, The City That Never Stopped Decorating, had been digging up the streets for years, plunging businesses into bankruptcy and accomplishing little Milo could see other than a yawning stretch of dirt piles and ditches. Last year, the ribbon had been cut on a spanking new West Hollywood fire station. One of those architectural fancies – peaks and troughs and gimcracks and weird-shaped windows. Cute, except the doors had proved too narrow for the fire engines to squeeze through, and the poles didn't allow the firefighters to slide down. This year, West Hollywood had embarked on a sister-city deal with Havana. Milo doubted Fidel would approve of Boystown nightlife.

Among the few businesses the roadwork couldn't kill were the all-night markets and the gay bars. A guy had to eat and a guy had to party. Milo and Rick stayed in most nights – how long had it been since he'd cruised?

And now, here he was.

He found himself smiling, but it felt like someone else's mirth.

Because what the hell was there to be happy about? Pierce Schwinn and/or a confederate had manipulated him into warming up Ingalls, he'd accomplished nothing but had managed to screw up royally.

Attracting attention.

Playa del Sol. That toothy putz Paris Bartlett. First thing he did after ditching Alex was to check city records for a business registration on Playa. Nothing. Then he ran Bartlett through every database he could think of. Like that could be a real name.

Taking a giant risk because what he'd told Alex had been true: as a civilian he was forbidden to use departmental resources, he was treading felonious water. He'd put up a firewall by using the ID numbers of other cops for the requests. Half a dozen IDs of cops he didn't care for, jumping around different divisions. His version of identity theft; he'd been collecting data for years, stashing loose bits of paper in his home safe because you never knew when your back was gonna be against the wall. But if someone tried hard enough, the calls could be traced back to him.

Clever boy, but the search had been futile: no such person as Paris Bartlett.

Which he supposed he'd known right away – apart from the moniker having a phony ring, Bartlett, all hair and teeth and eagerness, had had that *actor* thing going on. In L.A. that didn't necessarily mean a SAG card and a portfolio full of headshots. LAPD liked guys who were good at pretending, too. Channeled them into undercover work. Nowadays, that meant mostly Narcotics, occasionally Vice when the word came down to run yet another week or two of hooker rousts for public relations.

Years ago undercover had meant another Vice game, a regularly scheduled weekend production: Friday and Saturday night operations put together with military lust. Staking out targets and delineating the enemy and moving in for the attack.

Bust the queers.

Not naked aggression, the way it had been back before Christopher Street, when gay bars were ripe for routine, big-time head-breaking. Most of that ended by the early seventies, but Milo had caught the tail end of the department's fag-bashing fervor: LAPD masked the raids as drug busts, as if hetero clubs weren't fueled by the same dope. During his first month at West L.A. he'd been assigned to a Saturday night bivouac against a private club on Sepulveda near Venice. Out-of-the-way dive in a former auto-painting barn where a hundred or so well-heeled men, believing themselves to be secure, went to talk and dance and smoke grass and gobble Quaaludes and enjoy the bathroom stalls. LAPD had a different notion of security. The way the supervisor – a hypermacho D II named Reisan who Milo was certain was tucked deeply in the closet – laid out the plan, you'da thought it was a swoop on some Cong hamlet. Squinty eyes, military lingo, triangulated diagrams scrawled on the board, give me a break.

Milo sat through the orientation, struggling not to succumb to a full-body sweat. Reisan going on about coming down hard on resisters, don't be shy about using your batons. Then, leering, and warning the troops not to kiss anyone because you didn't know where those lips had been. Looking straight at Milo when he'd cracked wise, Milo laughing along with the others and wondering: *Why the hell is he doing that?* Fighting to convince himself he'd imagined it.

The day of the raid, he called in sick with the flu, stayed in bed for three days. Perfectly healthy, but he worked hard at degrading himself by not sleeping or eating, just sucking on gin and vodka and rye and peach brandy and whatever else he found in the cupboard. Figuring if the department checked on him, he'd look like death warmed over.

VN combat vet, now a real-life working detective, but he was still thinking like a truant high school kid.

Over the three days, he lost eight pounds, and when he stood his legs shook and his kidneys ached and he wondered if that yellow tinge in his eyes was real or just bad lighting – his place was a dingy hovel, the few windows it offered looked out to airshafts, and no matter how many bulbs he used, he could never get the illumination above tomb-strength.

The first time in three days that he tried food – a barely warmed can of Hearty Man chili – what he didn't heave whooshed out the other end. He smelled like a goat pen, his hair felt brittle, and his fingernails were getting soft. For a full week later, his ears rang and his back hurt and he drank gallons of water a day just in case he'd damaged something. The day he returned to the station, a transfer slip – Vice to Auto Theft, signed by Reisan – was in his box. That seemed a fine state of affairs. Two days later, someone slipped a note through the door of his locker.

How's your bunghole, faggot?

He pulled into the Healthy Foods lot, stayed in the Taurus, scanned the parking lot for anything out of the ordinary. During the drive from his house to the station, then from Budget to the market, he'd been on alert for a tail. Hadn't picked up any, but this wasn't the movies, and the hard truth was, in a city built around the combustion engine, you could never be sure.

He watched shoppers enter the market, finally satisfied himself that he hadn't been followed, and crossed over to the row of small stores – rehabbed shacks, really – that sat across from Healthy

Foods. Locksmith, dry cleaners, cobbler, West Hollywood Easy Mail Center.

He flashed his badge to the Pakistani behind the mail-drop counter – pile up those violations, Sturgis – and inquired about the box number listed on the Jeep's registration. The clerk was sullen, but he thumbed through his circular Rolodex and shook his head.

'No Playa del Sol.' Behind him was the wall of brass boxes. A sign advertised FedEx, UPS, rubber stamps, *While-U-Wait* gift-wrapping. Milo spotted no ribbons or happy-face wrapping paper. This was all about secrets.

'When did they stop renting?' he said.

'Had to be at least a year ago.'

'How do you know?'

'Because the current tenant has been renting for thirteen months.'

Tenant. Milo pictured some leprechaun setting up house in the mailbox. Tiny stove, refrigerator, Murphy bed, thumbnail-sized cable TV blaring *The Pot of Gold Network*.

'Who's the current tenant?' he said.

'You know I can't tell you that, sirrr.'

'Aw, shucks,' said Milo, producing a twenty-dollar bill. Keep those felonies coming . . .

The Pakistani stared at the bill as Milo placed it on the counter, closed his hand over Andrew Jackson's gaunt visage. Then he turned his back on Milo and began fiddling with one of the empty mailboxes and Milo reached over and took hold of the Rolodex and read the card.

Mr and Mrs Irwin Block

Address on Cynthia Street. Just a few blocks away.

'Know these people?' said Milo.

'Old people,' said the Pakistani, still showing his back. 'She comes in every week, but they don't get anything.'

'Nothing?'

'Once in a while, junk.'

'Then why do they need a POB?'

The clerk faced him and smiled. 'Everyone needs one – tell all your friends.' He reached for the Rolodex, but Milo held on to it, thumbing back from *Bl* to *Ba*. No Bartlett. Then up to *P*. No Playa del Sol.

The Pakistani said, 'Stop, please. What if someone comes in?'

Milo released the Rolodex, and the clerk placed it under the counter.

'How long have you been working here?'

'Oh,' said the clerk, as if the question was profound. 'Ten months.'

'So you've never dealt with anyone from Playa del Sol.'

'That is true.'

'Who worked here before you?'

'My cousin.'

'Where is he?'

'Kashmir.'

Milo glared at him.

'It's true,' said the man. 'He had enough of this place.'

'West Hollywood?'

'America. The morals.'

No curiosity about why Milo wanted to know about Playa del Sol. Given the guy's line of work, Milo supposed he'd learned not to be curious.

Milo thanked him, and the clerk rubbed his index finger with his thumb. 'You could show your thanks in another way.'

'Okay,' said Milo, making a very low bow. 'Thank you *very much*.'

As he left, he heard the man utter something in a language he didn't understand.

He drove to the Cynthia Street apartment of Mr and Mrs Irwin Block, pretended to be a census taker, and enjoyed an affable five-minute chat with the possibly hundred-year-old Selma Block, a blue-caftaned, champagne-haired pixie of a woman so bent and tiny she might very well have fit into one of the mailboxes. Behind her sat Mr Block on a green-and-gold sofa, a mute, static, vacant-eyed apparition of similar antiquity whose sole claim to physiologic viability was the occasional moist and startling throat clear.

Five minutes taught Milo more about the Blocks than he'd wanted to know. Both had worked in the Industry – Selma as a costume mistress for several major studios, Irwin as an accountant

for MGM. Three children lived back East. One was an orthodon-
tist, the middle one had gone into 'the financial world and became a
Republican, and our daughter weaves and sews hand-fashioned—'

'Is this the only address you keep, ma'am?' said Milo, pretending
to write everything down but doodling curlicues. No chance of Mrs
B spotting the ruse. The top of her head was well below the pad.

'Oh, no, dear. We keep a post-office box over by the Healthy
Foods.'

'Why's that, ma'am?'

'Because we like to eat healthy.'

'Why the post-office box, ma'am?'

Selma Block's tiny claw took hold of Milo's sleeve, and he felt as
if a cat was using his arm for a spring post.

'Politics, dear. Political mailers.'

'Oh,' said Milo.

'What party do you belong to, dear?'

'I'm an independent.'

'Well, dear, we like the Green Party – rather subversive, you
know.' The claw dug in deeper.

'You keep the box for Green Party mailers?'

'Oh, yes,' said Selma Block. 'You're too young, but we remember
the way it used to be.'

'The way it used to be when?'

'The old days. Those House UnAmerican fascists. That louse
McCarthy.'

Refusing the invitation to stay for tea and cookies, he extricated
himself from Mrs Block and drove around aimlessly, trying to figure
out his next move.

Playa del Sol. Alex was right, it did have that real estate ring, so
maybe the Cossacks did have their hand in this – assisted by LAPD.

The fix. Again.

Early on, he'd looked up Cossack Development's address, found
it on Wilshire in Mid-City, but he hadn't retained the numbers in
his head – those days were gone – so he called Information and
fixed the placement between Fairfax and La Brea.

The sky was dark and traffic had started to thin and he made it
over in less than a quarter-hour.

★ ★ ★

The Cossack brothers had headquartered themselves in a three-story pink granite, ziggurat-dominated complex that occupied a full city block just east of the County Art Museum. Years ago, this had been junk real estate – the fringes of the pathetically misnamed Miracle Mile. Back in the forties, The Mile's construction had been an historic first: a commercial strip with feeble street appeal but entry through the rear parking lots – yet another symptom of L.A.'s postwar infatuation with The Car. Twenty years later, westward flight had left the central city area a sump of poorly maintained buildings and low-rent businesses, and the only miracle was that any part of The Mile survived.

Now, the current cycle: urban renewal. County Art – not much in the way of a museum, but the courtyard did offer free concerts and L.A. didn't expect much – had spawned other museums – tributes to dolls, folk art, and most effectively, The Car. Big, glossy office structures had followed. If the Cossacks had gotten in early and owned the land under the pink granite thing, they'd made out well.

He parked on a side street, climbed wide, slick granite steps past a huge, shallow black pool filled with still water and dotted with pennies, and entered the lobby. Guard desk to the right, but no guard. Half the lights were off and the cavernous space echoed. The complex was divided into east and west wings. Most of the tenants were financial and showbiz outfits. Cossack Development took up the third floor of the east wing.

He rode the elevator, stepped into an unfurnished, white-carpeted, white-walled space. One big abstract lithograph greeted him – yellow and white and amorphous, maybe some genius's notion of a soft-boiled egg – then, to the left, double white doors. Locked. No sound from the other side.

The elevator door closed behind him. Turning, he stabbed the button and waited for it to return.

Back on Wilshire, he continued to study the building. Lot of lights were on, including several on the third floor. A couple of weeks ago, the state had warned of impending power shortages, urged everyone to conserve. Either the Cossacks didn't care, or someone was working late.

190

He rounded the corner, returned to the Taurus, reversed direction, and parked with a clear view of the building's subterranean parking lot. Fighting back that old feeling: wasted hours, stakeout futility. But stakeouts were like Vegas slots: once in a great while something paid off, and what better basis for addiction?

Twenty-three minutes later, the lot's metal grate slid open and a battered Subaru emerged. Young black woman at the wheel, talking on a cell phone. Six minutes after that: a newish BMW. Young white guy with spiked hair – also gabbing on cell, oblivious, he narrowly missed colliding with a delivery truck. Both drivers traded insults and bird-flips. The streets were safe, tonight.

Milo waited another half-hour, was just about to split when the grate yawned once more and a soot-gray Lincoln Town Car nosed out. Vanity plates: CCCCCCC. Windows tinted well past the legal limit – even the driver's pane – but otherwise nice and conservative.

The Lincoln stopped at the red light at Wilshire, then turned west. Traffic was heavy enough for Milo to obtain cover two lengths behind, but sufficiently fluid to allow a nice, easy tail.

Perfect. For what it was worth.

He followed the gray Lincoln half a mile west to San Vicente Boulevard, then north to Melrose and west again on Robertson, where the Town Car pulled into the front lot of a restaurant on the southwest corner.

Brushed steel door. Matching steel nameplate above the door, engraved heavily:

Sangre de Leon

New place. The last time Milo had taken the time to look, an Indonesian–Irish fusion joint had occupied the corner. Before that had been some kind of Vietnamese bistro run by a celebrity chef from Bavaria and bankrolled by movie stars. Milo figured the patrons had never served in the military.

Before *that*, he recalled at least six other start-up trendolas in as many years, new owners refurbishing, grand opening, garnering the usual breathless puff pieces in *L.A. Magazine* and *Buzz*, only to close a few months later.

Bad-luck corner. Same for the site across the street – the

191

bamboo-faced one-story amorphoid that had once been a Pacific Rim seafood palace was now shuttered, a heavy chain drawn across its driveways.

Sangre de Leon. Lion's Blood. Appetizing. He wouldn't take bets on this one enduring longer than a bout of indigestion.

He found a dark spot across Robertson, parked diagonal to the restaurant, turned off his headlights. The rest of the decor was windowless gray stucco and sprigs of tall, bearded grass that looked like nothing other than dry weeds. An army of pink-jacketed valets – all good-looking and female – hovered at the mouth of the lot. Stingy lot; the seven Mercedes parked there filled it.

The Town Car's chauffeur – a big, thick bouncer type nearly as large as Georgie Nemerov's hunters – jumped out and sprang a rear door. A chesty, puffy-faced guy in his forties with sparse, curly hair got out first. His face looked as if it had been used as a waffle iron. Milo recognized Garvey Cossack right away. The guy had put on weight since his most recent newspaper photo, but not much else about him had changed. Next came a taller, soft-looking character with a shaved bullet head and a Frank Zappa mustache that drooped to his chin – little brother Bobo, minus his slicked-back hairdo. Middle-aged sap doing the youth-culture thing? Cranial skin as a proud badge of rebellion? Either way, the guy enjoyed mirror time.

Garvey Cossack wore a dark sport coat with padded shoulders over a black turtleneck, black slacks. Below the slacks, white running shoes – now there was a touch of elegance.

Bobo had on a too-small black leather bomber jacket, too-tight black jeans and black T-shirt, too-high black boots. Black-lensed shades, too. Call the paramedics, we've got an emergency overdose of cool.

A third man exited the Lincoln, and the big chauffeur let him close his own door.

Number Three was dressed the way businessmen used to dress in L.A. Dark suit, white shirt, undistinguished tie, normal shoes. Shorter than the Cossack brothers, he had narrow shoulders and a subservient stoop. Saggy, wrinkled face, though he didn't appear any older than the Cossacks. Minuscule oval eyeglasses and long, blond hair that shagged over his collar fought the Joe Corporate image. The top of his scalp was mostly bald spot.

Mini-Specs hung back as the Cossacks entered the restaurant, Garvey in a flat-footed waddle, Bobo swaggering and bopping his head in time to some private melody. The chauffeur returned to the car and began backing out, and Specs walked past the pink ladies' expectant smiles. The Town Car turned south on Robertson, drove a block, pulled to the curb, went dark.

Specs remained out in the lot for a few seconds, looking around – but at nothing in particular. Facing the Taurus, but Milo caught no sign the guy saw anything that bothered him. No, this one was just full of random nervous energy – hands flexing, neck rotating, mouth turned down, the tiny lenses of his glasses darting and catching street light, a pair of reflective eggs.

Guy made him think of a crooked accountant on audit day. Finally, Specs ran his finger under his collar, rotated his shoulders, and made his way to the pleasures of leonine hemoglobin.

No additional diners materialized during the thirty-seven minutes Milo sat there. When one of the untipped valets looked at her watch, stepped out to the sidewalk, and lit up a cigarette, he got out of the Taurus and loped across the street.

The girl was a gorgeous little red-haired thing with blue-blue eyes so vivid the color made its way through the night. Maybe twenty. She noticed Milo approaching, kept smoking. The cigarette was wrapped in black paper and had a gold tip. Shermans? Did they still make those?

She looked up when he was three feet away and smiled through the cloud of nicotine that swirled in the warm night air.

Smiling because Milo had his latest bribe visible. Two twenties folded between his index and tall fingers, backed by a freelance journalist cover story. Forty bucks was double what he'd paid the Pakistani POB clerk but the valet – her tag said Val – was a helluva lot cuter than the clerk. And as it turned out, a lot easier to deal with.

Ten minutes later he was back in the Taurus, cruising past the Town Car. Mr Chauffeur was snoozing with his mouth open. A shaved-head Latino guy. The redhead had supplied Mini-Specs's ID.

'Oh, that's Brad. He works with Mr Cossack and his brother.'

'Mr Cossack?'

'Mr Garvey Cossack. And his brother.' Blue-eyed glance back at the restaurant. 'He co-owns this place, along with . . .' A string of celebrity names followed. Milo pretended to be impressed.

'Must be a jumping place.'

'It was when it opened.'

'No more, huh?'

'You know,' she said, rolling her eyes.

'How's the food?'

The parking cutie smiled and smoked and shook her head. 'How would I know? It's like a hundred bucks a plate. Maybe when I get my first big part.'

Her laugh was derisive. She added: 'Maybe when pigs fly.' So young, so cynical.

'Hollywood,' said Milo.

'Yeah.' Val looked back again. All the other girls were loafing, and a few were smoking. Probably keeping their weight down, thought Milo. Any of them could've modeled.

Val lowered her voice to a whisper: 'Tell the truth, I hear the food sucks.'

'The name can't help. Lion's Blood.'

'Ick. Isn't that gross?'

'What kind of cuisine is it?'

'Ethiopian, I think. Or something African. Maybe also Latino, I dunno – Cuban, maybe? Sometimes they've got a band and from out here it sounds kind of Cuban.' Her hips pistoned, and she snapped her fingers. 'I hear it's on its way out.'

'Cuban music?'

'No, silly. This place.'

'Time for a new job?' said Milo.

'No prob, there's always bar mitzvahs.' Stubbing out her cigarette, she said, 'You don't happen to ever work for *Variety*, do you? Or the *Hollywood Reporter*?'

'Mostly I do wire service stuff.'

'Someone's interested in the restaurant?'

Milo shrugged. 'I drive around. You've got to dig if you wanna find oil.'

She looked at the Taurus and her next smile was ripe with sympathy. *Another L.A. loser.* 'Well, if you ever do *Variety*, remember this name: Chataqua Dale.'

Milo repeated it. 'Nice. But so is Val.'

A cloud of doubt washed over the blue eyes. 'You really think so? 'Cause I was wondering if Chataqua was maybe, you know, over the top.'

'No,' said Milo. 'It's great.'

'Thanks.' She touched his arm, let the cigarette drop to the pavement, ground out the butt, got a dreamy look in her eyes. Audition fever. 'Well, gotta go.'

'Thanks for your time,' said Milo, reaching into his pocket and slipping her another twenty.

'You are *soooo* nice,' she said.

'Not usually.'

'Oh, I bet you are – let me ask you, you meet people, right? Know any decent agents? 'Cause mine is an asshole.'

'Only agents of destruction,' he said.

Puzzlement lent the beautiful young face temporary complexity. Then her actor's instincts cut in: Still not comprehending, but recognizing a cue, she smiled and touched his arm again. 'Right. See you around.'

'Bye,' said Milo. 'By the way, what does Brad do?'

'Walks around with them,' she said.

'A walking-around guy.'

'You got it – they all need them.'

'Hollywood types?'

'Rich types with gross bodies.'

'Know Brad's last name?'

'Larner. Brad Larner. He's kind of a jerk.'

'How so?'

'He's just a jerk,' said Val. 'Not friendly, never smiles, never tips. A jerk.'

He drove the two blocks to Santa Monica Boulevard, made a right turn, and circled back to Melrose, this time approaching the corner from the east and parking just up from the shuttered Chinese place. The rest of the boulevard was taken up by art galleries, all closed, and the street was dark and quiet. He got out,

195

stepped over the Chinese place's heavy chain, and walked across a lot starting to sprout weeds through the cracks and dotted with mounds of dry dog shit. Finding himself a nice little vantage point behind one of the dead restaurant's gateposts, he waited, taking in the Chinese place's grimness up close – black paint flaking, bamboo shredding.

Another dream rent asunder; he liked that.

Nowhere to sit, so he continued to stand there, well concealed, watching nothing happen at Sangre de Leon for a long time. His knees and back began to hurt, and stretching and squatting seemed to make matters worse. Last Christmas, Rick had bought a treadmill for the spare bedroom, used it religiously every morning at five. Last month, he'd suggested that Milo give regular exercise a try. Milo hadn't argued, but neither had he complied. He was no good in the morning, usually pretended to be asleep when Rick left for the ER.

He checked his Timex. The Cossacks and Brad 'the jerk' Larner had been inside for over an hour, and no other patrons had materialized.

Larner was no doubt the Achievement House director's son. The harasser's son. Yet another link between the families. Daddy putting up Crazy Sister Caroline at Achievement House, buying jobs for himself *and* Junior.

Connections and money. So what else was new? Presidents were selected the same damn way. If any of this provided a hook to Janie Ingalls, he couldn't see it. But he knew – on a gut level – that it *did* matter. That Pierce Schwinn's forced retirement and his own transfer to West L.A. had resulted from more than Schwinn's dalliances with street whores.

Twenty-year-old fix, John G. Broussard doing the dirty work.

Schwinn had sat on whatever he'd known for two decades, pasted photos in an album, finally decided to break silence.

Why now?

Maybe because Broussard had reached the top and Schwinn wanted his revenge to be a gourmet dish.

Using Milo to do the dirty work . . .

Then he falls off a docile horse . . .

Headlights from the north end of Robertson slapped him out of

196

his rumination. Two sets of lights, a pair of vehicles approaching the Melrose intersection. The traffic signal turned amber. The first car passed through legally and the second one ran the red.

Both pulled up in front of Sangre de Leon.

Vehicle Number One was a discreet, black, Mercedes coupe – surprise, surprise! – whose license plate he copied down quickly. Out stepped the driver, another business-suit, moving so quickly the pink ladies had no time to get his door. He slipped a bill to the nearest valet, anyway, let Milo have a nice, clean look at him.

Older guy. Late sixties to midseventies, balding, with a sparse gray comb-over, wearing a boxy beige suit, a white shirt, and a dark tie. Medium height, medium build, clean-shaven, the skin falling away from the bone at jowls and neck. No expression on his face. Milo wondered if this was Larner, Senior. Or just a guy out for dinner.

If so, it wouldn't be a solo dinner, because the occupants of the second car nearly tripped over themselves to get to his side.

Vehicle Two was also black, but no feat of German engineering. Big, fat Crown Victoria sedan, anachronistically oversize. The only places Milo'd seen those things, recently, were government offices, but this one didn't have state-issue **e** plates.

But neither did lots of unmarkeds, and for a second he thought, *Department brass?* and experienced a rush of expectations met too easily: documenting cop honchos with the Cossacks, why the hell hadn't he remembered to bring a damn *camera?*

But the moment the first guy out of the Crown Victoria turned and showed his face, it was a whole different story.

Long, dark, lizard face under a black pompadour.

City Councilman Eduardo 'Ed the Germ' Bacilla, the official representative of a district that encompassed a chunk of downtown. He of the serious bad habits and poor work habits – Bacilla attended maybe one out of every five council meetings and a couple of years ago he'd been nabbed in Boyle Heights trying to buy powdered coke from an undercover narc. Quick and frantic negotiations with the DA's Office had led to the draconian sentence of public apology and public service: two months on graffiti-removal detail, Bacilla working alongside some of the very gang-bangers he'd favored with city-funded scam rehab programs. Lack of a felony conviction meant the councilman could keep his job, and a recall effort by a leftist homeboy reformer sputtered.

And now here was ol' Germ, kissing up to Tan Suit.

So was Crown Victoria Rider Two, and guess what: another civil stalwart.

This guy had looped his arm around Tan Suit's shoulder and was laughing about something. No expression on Suit's CEO face.

Mr Jocular was older, around Tan Suit's age, with white temples and a bushy, white mustache that concealed his upper lip. Tall and narrow-shouldered, with an onion-bulb body that a well-cut suit couldn't enhance, and the ice-eyed cunning of a cornered peccary.

City Councilman James 'Diamond Jim' Horne. He of the suspected kickbacks and briberies and ex-wives hush-moneyed to silence back in the good old days when domestic violence was still known as wife-beating.

Milo knew through the LAPD gravevine that Horne was a longtime, serious spouse-basher with a penchant for pulverizing without leaving marks. Like Germ Bacilla, Diamond Jim had always managed to squeak through without arrest or conviction. For over thirty years, he'd served a district that bordered Bacilla's, a north-central strip filled with ticky-tack houses and below-code apartments. Once solidly working-class white, Horne's constituency had turned 70 percent poor Hispanic, and the councilman had watched his vote pluralities tumble. From 90 percent to 70. A series of opponents with surnames ending in 'ez' had failed to topple Horne. The corrupt old bastard got the potholes fixed, and plenty else.

Germ and Diamond Jim, walking arm in arm with Tan Suit, heading for the steel door of Sangre de Leon.

Milo returned to the Taurus and, using the ID of a Pacific Division Vice detective he despised, pulled up the Mercedes coupe's plates.

He half expected another corporate shield, but the numbers came back matching a four-year-old Mercedes owned by a real-life person.

W.E. Obey

The three hundred block of Muirfield Road in Hancock Park.

Walter Obey. He of the billion-dollar fortune.

Nominally, Walt Obey was in the same business as the Cossacks – concrete and rebar and lumber and drywall. But Obey occupied a whole different galaxy from the Cossacks. Fifty years ago, Obey Construction began nailing up homes for returning GIs. The company was probably responsible for 10 percent of the tracts that snaked parallel to the freeways and sprawled across the smog-choked basin that the Chumash Indians had once called the Valley of Smoke.

Walt Obey and his wife, Barbara, were on the board of every museum, hospital, and civic organization that meant anything in the lip-gnawing, over-the-shoulder uncertainty known as L.A. Society.

Walt Obey was also a model of rectitude – Mr Upright in a business that claimed few saints.

The guy had to be at least eighty, but he looked a good deal younger. Good genes? Clean living?

Now here he was, supping with Germ and Diamond Jim.

The Cossacks and Brad Larner had been inside for one hour. No shock, it was their restaurant. Still the question hung: table for three, or six?

He obtained Sangre de Leon's number from Information and called the restaurant. Five rings later a bored, Central European-accented male voice said, 'Yes?'

'This is Mr Walter Obey's office. I've got a message for Mr Obey. He's dining with the Cossacks, I believe they're in a private room—'

'Yes, they are. I'll get the phone to him.' Eagerness to please had wiped out the boredom.

Milo hung up.

He drove home trying to piece it all together. The Cossacks and Walt Obey and two city councilmen noshing on designer grub. Brad Larner along as a gofer, or his dad's surrogate? Alex had pulled up something about the Cossacks trying to bring a football team to L.A., maybe reactivating the Coliseum. The scheme had died, as had nearly everything else the Cossacks had tried – movies, tearing down landmarks. On the face of it the brothers were losers. Yet they had enough clout to bring Walt Obey from Hancock Park to West Hollywood.

The Cossacks in their chauffeured Town Car with personalized plates screamed new money. But Obey, the real money man, drove himself in an anonymous, four-year-old sedan. The billionaire was so unobtrusive he could pass for your average, middling CPA.

What got vulgarians and bluenoses together? Something big. The Coliseum sat in Germ Bacilla's district, and next door was Diamond Jim Horne's domain. Was this one of those complicated deals that always managed to elude zoning laws and whatever else stood in its way? Taxpayers footing the bill for rich guys' indulgences? Something that might be jeopardized by the rehash of a twenty-year-old murder and the exposure of the Cossacks' role in covering up for their crazy sister and junkie-murderer Willie Burns?

Why *had* Georgie Nemerov gotten so antsy?

The only possible thread between Nemerov and the rest of it was the department.

And now the department was verifying his vacation time and maybe sending that Bartlett asshole to spook him.

Health facilitator. Meaning what? Be careful not to get *un*healthy?

Suddenly, he wanted very much to make someone else deathly ill.

When he pulled into his driveway, the white Porsche was parked up near the garage, little red alarm light blinking on the dash, extra-strength lock bar fixed to the steering column. Rick loved the car, was as careful with it as he was with everything else.

He found Rick at the kitchen table, still wearing his scrubs and eating warmed-up Chinese food from last night. A glass of red wine was at his elbow. He saw Milo and smiled and gave a weak wave and the two of them shared a brief hug, and Rick said, 'Working late?'

'The usual. How'd your day go?'

'The usual.'

'Heroics?'

'Hardly.' Rick pointed to the empty chair across the table. The final dark hairs in his dense cap of curls had faded to gray last summer, and his mustache was a silver toothbrush. Despite being a doctor and knowing better, he liked to tan out in the backyard and his skin had held on to summer color. He looked tired. Milo sat down opposite him and began picking at orange chicken.

'There's more in the refrigerator,' said Rick. 'The egg rolls, the rest of it.'

'No, I'll just take yours.'

Rick smiled. Weary.

'Bad stuff on shift?' said Milo.

'Not particularly. Couple of heart attacks, couple of false alarms, kid with a broken leg from falling off a Razor scooter, colon cancer patient with a serious gut bleed that kept us busy for a long time, woman with a darning needle in her eye, two auto accidents, one accidental shooting – we lost that one.'

'The usual trivia.'

'Exactly.' Rick pushed his food away. 'There was one thing. The shooting was the last case I pulled. I couldn't do anything for the poor guy, he came in flat, never beeped. Looks like he was cleaning his nine-millimeter, stared into the barrel, maybe making sure it was clear, and boom. The cops who came in with the body said they found gun oil and rags and one of those barrel-reaming tools on the table next to him. Bullet entered here.' Rick touched the center of his mustache, under his nose.

'An accident?' said Milo. 'Not suicide? Or anything else?'

'The cops who came in kept calling it an accident, maybe they knew something technical. It'll go to the coroner.'

'Sheriff's cops?' said Milo.

'No, you guys. It happened near Venice and Highland. But that's not what I want to tell you. The body had just gone to the morgue, and I came back to chart and the cops who brought the guy in were in the cubicle next door and I heard them talking. Going on about their pensions, sick leave, department benefits. Then one said something about a detective in West L.A. division who'd tested HIV-positive and put in for retirement. The other cop said, "Guess what goes 'round comes round." Then they both laughed. Not a joyful laugh. A mean laugh.'

Rick picked up a chopstick and seesawed it between two fingers. Looked into Milo's eyes. Touched Milo's hand.

Milo said, 'I haven't heard anything about that.'

'Didn't assume you had, or you'd have told me.'

Milo withdrew his hand, stood, and got himself a beer.

Rick stayed at the table, continued to play with the chopstick.

Tilting it deftly, precisely. A surgeon's grace.

Milo said, 'It's bullshit. I'da heard.'

'I just thought it was something you'd want to know.'

'Highland and Venice. What the hell would Wilshire Division know about West L.A.? What the hell would *blues* know about *Ds*?'

'Probably nothing . . . Big guy, is there something I should know? Some tight spot you've gotten yourself into?'

'Why? What does this have to do with me?' Milo didn't like the defensiveness in his own voice. Thinking: the goddamn department rumor mill. Then thinking: *Health Facilitator. You never know . . .*

Rick said, 'Okay,' and started to get up.

Milo said, 'Wait,' and came around and stood behind Rick and put his hands on Rick's shoulders. And told him the rest of it.

twenty-two

I got on the computer, typed in 'Paris Bartlett' as a keyphrase on several search engines, and came up with nothing.

Next, I tried 'Playa del Sol' and its English translation: *Sun Beach*, and connected to hundreds of resort links all over the world. Costa del Sol. Costa del Amor. Playa Negra. Playa Blanca. Playa Azul. Sun City. Sunrise Beach. Excursion packages, time shares, white sand, blue water, adults only, bring the kids. Also, a guy who'd devoted an obsessive site to the old song '*Cuando Caliente El Sol.*' The joys of the information age . . .

I stuck with it for hours, felt my eyes crossing and broke for a midnight sandwich, a beer, and a shower before returning to the screen. By 2 A.M., I was fighting sleep and nearly missed the article in a three-year-old issue of the *Resort Journal* elicited by yet another try at Playa del Sol. This time, I'd logged on to a pay service – a business-oriented data bank that I hadn't used since last fall, when I'd considered selling a lot of municipal bonds. I clicked my assent to pony up by credit card and continued.

What I got was a rear-of-the-magazine piece entitled 'Seeking the Good Life on Distant Shores: Americans Looking for Foreign Bargains Often Find Themselves on the Losing End.' The article recounted several real estate deals gone sour, among them a construction project down in Baja named Playa del Sol: high-end condos peddled to American retirees lured by American-style luxury living at Mexican prices. Two hundred units out of a planned four hundred fifty had been built and purchased. The first wave of retirees hadn't yet moved in when the Mexican government invoked a fine-print provision of an obscure regulation, confiscated the land, and sold it to a Saudi Arabian consortium who turned the condos into a hotel. The Playa del Sol Company, Ltd, incorporated in the Cayman Islands, dissolved itself and its American subsidiary, Playa Enterprises, declared Chapter 11. The retirees lost their money.

No comment from the president of Playa Enterprises, Michael Larner.

Recalling the obscure business journal references that had come up on my first search for Larner – magazines not in the Research Library's holdings – I looked for anything else I could find on the former Achievement House director and came across several other deals he'd put together during the past five years.

Larner's specialty was real estate syndication – getting moneyed people together to buy out incomplete building projects that had run into trouble. High-rise apartments in Atlanta, defunct country clubs in Colorado and New Mexico, a ski lodge in Vermont, a golf course in Arizona. Once the deal was inked, Larner took his cut and walked away.

All the subsequent articles had the rah-rah tone of paid ads. None mentioned the Mexican debacle, Playa Enterprises, or the Playa del Sol Company, Ltd. Larner's corporate face was now the ML Group.

No mention of the Cossack brothers, either. Or any of Larner's fellow venture capitalists, though showbiz and Wall Street affiliations were implied. The only other ML staffer named was Larner's son, Bradley, executive vice-president.

Using 'ML Group' as a keyphrase, I retraced all the search machines and obtained the exact same articles, plus one more: a two-year-old stroke job in a glossy rag titled *Southwest Leisure Builder*.

Centered amid the text was a color photo: Larners, father and son, posing on a bright day in Phoenix, wearing matching royal blue golf shirts, white canvas slacks, white smiles.

Michael Larner looked around sixty-five. Square-faced and florid, he wore wide steel-framed aviator's glasses turned to mirrors by the Arizona sun. His smile was self-satisfied and heralded by overly large capped teeth. He had a drinker's nose, a big, hard-looking belly, and meticulously styled white hair. A casting agent would've seen Venal Executive.

Bradley Larner was thinner and smaller and paler – barely a nuance of his father. Late thirties or early forties, he was also bespectacled, but his choice of eyewear ran to gold-framed, narrow, oval lenses so tiny they barely covered his irises. His hair was that lank, waxy blond destined to whiten, and it trailed past his shoulders. Less enthusiasm in his expression. Barely a smile at all, though to read the article, the Larners were riding the crest of the real estate wave.

Bradley Larner looked like a kid forced to sit for yet another obnoxious family snapshot.

An accompanying picture on the following page showed Michael Larner in an ice-cream suit, blue shirt, and pink tie posed next to a white-on-white Rolls-Royce Silver Spirit. To his father's right, Brad Larner perched atop a gold Harley-Davidson, wearing black leather.

The caption read: **Different generations, but the same flair for the Ultimate Ride.**

The Playa del Sol link meant 'Paris Bartlett' was likely an envoy to Milo from the Larners.

Warning him off the trail of Caroline Cossack.

Because the Larners and the Cossacks went way back.

The families had something else in common: big deals that often went bad. But all of them managed to stay on top, maintaining the good life.

The Ultimate Ride.

In the Cossacks' case, inherited wealth might've provided a nice safety blanket. Michael Larner, on the other hand, had bounced from job to job and industry to industry, leaving scandal or bankruptcy in his wake but always managing to position himself higher.

That smile, teeth as white and gleaming as his Rolls-Royce. A man willing to do whatever it took? Or friends in the right places? Or both.

Back when Larner had bent the rules and admitted Caroline Cossack to Achievement House, her brothers had been barely out of adolescence but already in the real estate business. Larner might have dealt initially with Garvey Cossack, Senior, but the relationship endured well after Senior's demise and found Larner working for men twenty-five years his junior. Then I thought of something: *Bradley* Larner was about the same age as the Cossack brothers. Was there some link there? Something that went beyond business?

When searching for school data on Caroline, Milo hadn't gotten very far with the local high schools. Because everyone was litigation-wary and watched episodic TV and believed cops without warrants were impotent.

Maybe also because Caroline's emotional problems meant she hadn't enjoyed much of a school history. But perhaps tracking her brothers would be easier.

The next morning, I was back at the library thumbing through *Who's Who*. Neither Bob Cossack nor Bradley Larner was listed, but Garvey Cossack had merited a biography: a single paragraph of puffery, mostly what I'd already learned from the Web.

Tucked among all the corporate braggadocio was Garvey's educational history. He'd completed two years of college at Cal State Northridge but hadn't graduated. Maybe that's why he'd bothered to list his high school. And the fact that he'd been student body treasurer during his senior year.

University High.

I checked with the reference desk and found that the library maintained three decades of local yearbooks in the reference section. Uni was as local as it got.

Finding the right volume wasn't hard. I estimated Garvey's age and nailed it on the second try.

His graduation picture revealed a full-faced, acne-plagued eighteen-year-old with long, wavy hair, wearing a light-colored turtleneck. Sandwiched between the top of the sweater's collar and the boy's meaty chin was a puka-shell necklace. His grin was mischievous.

Listed under his picture were memberships in the Business Club, the 'managerial staff ' of the football team, and something called the King's Men. But there was no mention of his being treasurer. According to the Student Council page, the treasurer was a girl named Sarah Buckley. Thumbing through the three preceding yearbooks taught me that Garvey Cossack had never served in any student-government capacity.

Petty fib for a middle-aged millionaire; that made it all the more interesting.

I located Robert 'Bobo' Cossack's headshot one class back. He'd come to photo day wearing a black shirt with a high collar and a choker-length chain. Equine face, hair darker and even longer than his brother's, a more severe blemish. Bobo wore a sullen expression and his eyes were half-shut. Sleepy or stoned – or trying to look the part. His attempts to grow a beard and mustache had resulted in a halo of dark fuzz around his chin and spidery wisps above his upper lip.

No affiliations below his picture other than the King's Men.

Also in the junior class was a very skinny Bradley Larner, wearing tinted aviator glasses, a button-down shirt, and peroxide surfer-do that obscured half his face. The part that was visible was as dispirited as Bobo Cossack's.

Another King's Man.

I searched the yearbook for mention of the club, found a listing in the roster of school service organizations but no details. Finally, in a breathless account of the homecoming game, I spotted a reference to '*the revelry, high jinks (and other good stuff) perpetrated by the King's Men.*'

An accompanying snapshot showed a group of six boys at the beach, wearing bathing trunks and striped beanies and clowning around with cross-eyed grins, goofy poses, behind-the-head rabbit ears. The beer cans in their hands had been blacked out clumsily. In one case, the Miller logo was still visible. The caption: **Surf's Up! but the King's Men crave other liquid entertainment! Partying at Zuma: G. Cossack, L. Chapman, R. Cossack, V. Coury, B. Larner, N. Hansen**.

The Cossack brothers had been high school party animals, and the Bel Air bash a couple of years later was just more of the same. And the link between them and the Larners had been forged on the sands of Zuma, not in the boardroom.

That made me wonder if the idea for secreting problematic sister Caroline might have originated with the boys, not their father. '*Hey, Dad, Brad's dad works at this place for weirdos, maybe he can help out.*'

I searched the yearbooks for mention or a picture of Caroline Cossack.

Nothing.

I drove around the pretty residential streets of Westwood, thinking about Pierce Schwinn and what he'd really wanted from Milo. Had the former detective finally decided to come clean with secrets held for two decades, as I'd suggested, or had he undertaken his own freelance investigation late in life and come up with new leads?

Either way, Schwinn hadn't been as serene as his second wife believed. Or as faithful: he'd found a confidante to mail the murder book.

As I'd told Milo, Ojai was a small town and it was doubtful Schwinn could've pulled off a regular assignation there without Marge finding out. But before he'd married Marge, he'd lived in Oxnard in a fleabag motel. Marge hadn't mentioned the name, but she had given us the site of Schwinn's minimum-wage job, and said Schwinn hadn't owned a car. Taking out the trash at Randall's Western Wear. Somewhere within walking distance.

The place was still in business, on Oxnard Boulevard.

I'd taken the scenic route because it was the quickest way and I had no stomach for the freeway: Sunset to PCH, then north on the coast highway past the L.A.–Ventura line and Deer Creek Road and the campgrounds of Sycamore Creek – fifteen miles of state land that kissed the ocean and separated the last private beach in Malibu from Oxnard. The water was sapphire blue under a chamber-of-commerce sky, and the bodies that graced the sand were brown and perfect.

At Las Posas Road, I avoided the eastern fork that swoops into glorious, green tables of farmland and up to the foothills of Camarillo and continued on Route 1.

Nature's beauty gave way, soon enough, to dinge and depression and seventy-five minutes after leaving the house I was enjoying the sights of central Oxnard.

Oxnard's a funny place. The town's beach sports a marina and luxury hotels and fishing excursions and tour boats to the Channel Islands. But the core is built around agriculture and the migrant workers whose dreadful lives put food on the nation's tables. The crime rate's high, and the air stinks of manure and pesticide. Once you get past the marina turnoff, Oxnard Boulevard is a low-rent artery lined with trailer parks, auto-parts yards, thrift shops, taco bars, taverns blaring Mexican music, and more Spanish than English on the signage.

Randall's Western Wear was a red barn in the center of the strip, stuck between Bernardo's Batteries and a windowless bar called El Guapo. Plenty of parking in back; only two pickups and an old Chrysler 300 in the lot.

Inside was the smell of leather and sawdust and sweat, ceiling-high racks of denim and flannel, Stetsons stacked like waffles, cowboy boots and belts on sale, one corner devoted to sacks of feed, a few saddles and bridles off in another. Travis Tritt's mellow baritone eased through scratchy speakers, trying to convince some woman of his good intentions.

Slow day in the ranch-duds biz. No customers, just two salesmen on duty, both white men in their thirties. One wore gray sweats, the other jeans and a black Harley-Davidson T-shirt. Both smoked behind the counter, showing no interest in my arrival.

I browsed, found a tooled cowhide belt that I liked, brought it to the counter and paid. Harley-D rang me up, offering no eye contact or conversation. As he handed back my credit card, I let my wallet open and showed him my LAPD consultant badge. It's a clip-on deal with the department's badge as a logo, not good for much and if you look closely it tells you that I'm no cop. But few people get past the insignia, and Harley was no exception.

'Police?' he said, as I closed the wallet. He wore a bad haircut like his own badge of honor, had a handlebar mustache that drooped to his chin, and a clogged-sinus voice. Stringy arms and stringy hair, a scatter of faded tattoos.

I said, 'Thought maybe you could help me with something.'
'With what?'
Sweats looked up. He was a few years younger than Harley, with a blond-gray crew cut, a square shelf of a chin finishing a florid face. Stocky build, quiet eyes. My guess was ex-military.

'A few questions about a guy who worked here a while back. Pierce Schwinn.'

'Him?' said Harley. 'He hasn't been here for what – coupla years?' He looked back at Sweats.

'Coupla,' Sweats agreed.

Harley looked at the belt. 'What, you bought that to get friendly or something?'

'I bought it because it's a nice belt,' I said. 'But I have no problem with being friendly. What do you remember about Schwinn?'

Harley frowned. 'When he worked here he was a bum. What's up with him now?'

'Have you seen him since he stopped working here?'

'Maybe once,' he said. 'Or maybe not. If he did come in, it was with his wife – that right?' Another consultation with Sweats.

'Probably.'

'Why?' said Harley. 'What he do?'

'Nothing. Just a routine investigation.' Even as I said it, I felt ridiculous, not to mention criminal. But if Milo could risk violations of the public order, so could I. 'So the last time Mr Schwinn worked here was a couple of years ago?'

'That's right.' Harley's smile was derisive. 'If you wanna call it work.'

'It wasn't?'

'Man,' he said, leaning on the counter, 'let me tell you: it was a gift. From our mom to him. She owns the place. He used to live down the block, at the Happy Night. Mom felt sorry for him, let him clean up for spare change.'

'The Happy Night Motel?' I said.

'Right down the block.'

'So it was a sympathy thing,' I said. 'From your mother.'

'She's got a soft heart,' said Harley. 'Ain't that so, Roger?'

Sweats nodded and smoked and turned up the volume on Travis Tritt. The singer's voice was plaintive and rich; I'd have been convinced.

'Schwinn have any friends?' I said.

'Nope.'

'What about Marge – the woman who married him.'

'She comes in for feed when she runs out on her bulk order,' said

Harley. 'Yeah, she married him, but that makes her his wife, not his friend.'

And when are you entering law school, F. Lee Picky?

I said, 'Marge met him here.'

'Guess so.' Harley's brows knitted. 'Haven't seen her either, for a while.'

Roger said, 'She's probably ordering off the Internet, like everyone. We gotta get with that.'

'Yeah,' said Harley, listlessly. 'So, c'mon, tell me, man, why're you asking about him? Someone off him or something?'

'No,' I said. 'He's dead, all right. Fell off a horse a few months ago.'

'That so. Well, she never mentioned it. Marge didn't.'

'When's the last time you saw her?'

Harley looked back at Roger. 'When's the last time I saw her?'

Roger shrugged. 'Maybe four, five months ago.'

'Mostly everyone orders bulk from suppliers,' said Harley. 'And the Internet. We do gotta get hooked up.'

'So Marge has been in since Schwinn died, but she never mentioned his death.'

'Probably – I couldn't swear to it, man. Listen, don't pin me down on any a this.'

Roger gave another sweat-suited shrug. 'Marge don't talk much, period.'

Travis Tritt bowed out and Pam Tillis weighed in about 'The Queen of Denial.'

Harley said, 'Is this about drugs, or something?'

'Why do you say that?'

Harley fidgeted. His brother said, 'What Vance means is that the Happy Night – everyone knows about it. People go in and out. You wanna do us a favor? Get it moved outta here. This block used to be a nice place.'

I kept my car in the Randall's lot and walked the block to the motel. The place was a twelve-unit gray stucco C built around a central courtyard and open to the street. The yard was tiled with crumbling bricks, didn't look as if it had been designed for parking, but four dirty compact cars and an equally grubby truck with a camper shell occupied the space. The office was off to the right – a cubicle that smelled of gym sweat manned by a young skin-headed Hispanic man wearing an aqua blue cowboy shirt with blood-red piping. Spangling on the yokes, too, but oily splotches in the armpits and ketchup-colored freckles across the front mitigated the garment's charm. Resting on the pleat was a heavy iron crucifix attached to a stainless-steel chain.

My entry rang a bell over the door and the clerk shot a look at me then glanced under the counter. Reflexively. Probably checking out the requisite pistol. Or just wanting to let me know he was armed. A sign on the wall behind him said CASH ONLY. Same message in Spanish, right below. He didn't move but his eyes jumped around and the left lid twitched. He couldn't be more than twenty-two or -three, could probably take the adrenaline surges and blood-pressure spikes for a few more years.

I showed him the badge, and he shook his head. Atop the counter was a *novella* – black-and-white photos of characters speaking in captions, storyboard laid out like a comic book. Upside down I caught a few words: '*sexualismo*', '*con pasión.*'

He said, 'Don' know nothin'.' Heavy accent.

'I haven't asked anything.'

'Don' know nothin'.'

'Good for you,' I said. 'Ignorance is bliss.'

His stare was dull.

'Pierce Schwinn,' I said. 'He used to live here.'

No answer.

I repeated the name.

'Don' know nothin'.'

'An old man, Anglo, white hair, white beard?'

Nothing.

'He used to work at Randall's.'

Uncomprehending look.

'Randall's Western Wear – down the block?'

'Don't know nothin'.'

'What's your name?'

'Don' kno—' Lights on in the brown eyes. 'Gustavo.'

'Gustavo what?'

'Gustavo Martinez Reyes.'

'You speak any English, Mr Martinez Reyes?'
Headshake.
'Anyone work here who does?'
'Don' know noth—'

So much for ace detective work. But I'd come this far, why not give Ojai another try – check out a place I knew Marge Schwinn had frequented. The shop where she'd bought the blue albums – *O'Neill & Chapin . . . over by the Celestial Café . . . from England . . . discontinued . . . I bought the last three.*

Maybe she hadn't. Or maybe Schwinn had also shopped for himself.

I continued to the next freeway on-ramp and was back on Highway 33 within minutes. The air was cold and clean, every color on full volume, and I could smell ripening fruit in the neighboring groves.

O'Neill & Chapin sat in one of those cozy commercial groupings that had sprouted along the road, this one a well-shaded segment just past the center of Ojai but several miles before the turnoff to Marge Schwinn's ranch. The shop was a minuscule, shingle-roofed, clapboard cottage dominated by live oaks. The boards were painted forest green, and the store was fronted by five feet of cobblestones running from the earthen curb to Dutch doors painted creamy mint. Gold leaf lettering across the front window proclaimed:

O'Neill & Chapin, Purveyors of Fine Paper and Pigments.
Est. 1986

Behind the windows were dark oak shutters. A sign leaning against the slats said:

On a buying trip in Europe. Back soon

I checked out the neighboring business. To the right was the candlery, also shuttered. Then Marta, Spiritual Counselor, and the Humanos Theosophic Institute. To the left was a one-story office building faced in river rock: chiropractor's office, a notary public-cum-insurance broker, a travel agent specializing in 'nature-friendly excursions.' Next to that, in a sunnier spot, sat an adobe cube with a wooden sign over the door.

Celestial Café

Gold stars danced around the edges of the signs. Lights flickered behind blue gingham curtains. It was nearly 3 P.M. and I'd fed neither my brain nor my gut. Times like this, I supposed, organic muffins and herbal tea wouldn't be half-bad.

But according to the blackboard mounted above the open kitchen, the café specialized in country French food – crêpes, quiche, soufflés, chocolate desserts. Real coffee, Lord almighty.

Some kind of New Age soundtrack – tinkly bells, flute, and harp – eased out of speakers set into the low, wood-beam ceiling. More blue gingham covered half a dozen tables. A woman with elaborately braided gray hair wearing a buckskin jacket over a crinkly, pink dress sat enjoying what looked to be ratatouille. No server was in sight, just a pasty-faced, heavyset, white-aproned woman wearing a blue bandana over her hair cutting vegetables in the kitchen. At her elbow was a six-burner Wolfe range, with one flame aglow under a cast-iron crêpe pan. Fresh batter had just been poured into the pan, and the cook stopped cutting long enough to grab a towel and take hold of the handle. Tilting deftly, she created a perfect disc that she slid onto a plate, then topped with creamed spinach. A dash of nutmeg, and the crêpe was rolled and placed on the counter. Then back to the vegetables.

The gray-haired woman got up and took the crêpe. 'Beautiful, Aimee.'

The cook nodded. She looked to be forty or so, had a squashed face and downturned eyes. The hairs that had peeked out from under the bandana were light brown and silver.

I smiled at her. Her face registered no expression, and she continued chopping. I read the blackboard. 'How about a mixed-cheese crêpe and coffee?'

She turned around, left the kitchen through a side door. I stood there, listening to bells and flute and harp.

Behind me, the gray-braided woman said, 'Don't worry, she'll be back.'

'I was wondering if it was something I said.'

She laughed. 'No, she's just shy. Heck of a cook, though.'

Aimee returned with a small wheel of white cheese. 'You can sit,' she said, in a very soft voice. 'I'll bring it to you.'

'Thanks much.' I tried another smile, and her mouth quivered upward for less than a second, and she began wiping the crêpe pan.

The gray-haired woman finished her meal just as Aimee brought me my plate, a mug of coffee, utensils wrapped in a heavy yellow linen napkin. She returned to her vegetables and the gray-braided woman said, 'Here you are, dear,' and paid her cash. No change exchanged. No credit card signs anywhere in the café.

I unfolded the napkin, looked at my plate. Two crêpes.

With her back to me, Aimee said, 'You only have to pay for one. I had lots of cheese.'

'Thank you,' I said. 'They look delicious.'

Chop chop chop.

I cut into the first crêpe and took a bite and flavor burst on my tongue. The coffee was the best I'd had in years, and I said so.

Chop chop chop.

I was working on the second crêpe when the front door opened, and a man walked in and headed for the counter.

Short, chubby, white-haired, he wore a purplish red polyester jumpsuit, zipped in front, with big floppy lapels. Crimson clogs and white-socks-clad stubby feet. His fingers were attenuated, too, the thumbs little more than arced nubs. His ruddy face was impish but peaceful – an elf in repose. A leather-thonged bolo tie was held in place by a big, shapeless purple rock. Flashing on his left hand was a huge gold pinkie ring set with a violet cabochon.

He looked to be in his midsixties, but I knew he was seventy-seven because I knew him. I also understood why he wore a single color: it was the only hue he could perceive in an otherwise black-and-white world. A rare form of color blindness was one of a host of physical anomalies he'd been born with. Some, like the shortened digits, were visible. Others, he'd assured me, were not.

Dr Wilbert Harrison, psychiatrist, anthropologist, philosopher, eternal student. A sweet and decent man, and even a murderous psychopath bent on revenge had recognized that, sparing Harrison

215

as he conducted a rampage against the doctors he believed had tormented him.

I hadn't been spared, and I'd met Bert Harrison years ago, trying to figure all of that out. Since then we talked occasionally – infrequently.

'Bert,' I said.

He turned, smiled. 'Alex!' Holding up a finger, he greeted Aimee. Without making eye contact, she poured him tea and selected an almond-crusted pastry from the glass case beneath the blackboard.

A regular.

He said, 'Thank you, darling,' sat down at my table, placed his cup and plate in front of him, and grasped my hand with both of his.

'Alex. So good to see you.'

'Good to see you too, Bert.'

'What have you been up to?'

'The usual. And you?'

Soft gray eyes twinkled. 'I've embarked on a new hobby. Ethnic instruments, the more esoteric the better. I've discovered eBay – how wonderful, the global economy in its finest form. I find bargains, wait like a child on Christmas Eve for the packages to arrive, then try to figure out how to play them. This week my project is a one-stringed curiosity from Cambodia. I haven't learned its proper name, yet. The seller billed it as a "Southeast Asian thingamajig." Sounds dreadful, so far – like a cat with indigestion, but I have no neighbors, per se.'

Harrison's home was a purple cottage, high on a hill above Ojai, bordered by olive groves and empty fields and nearly hidden by snarls of agave cactus. Bert's old Chevy station wagon sat in a dirt driveway, always freshly waxed. Each time I'd visited, the house's front door had been unlocked.

'Sounds like fun,' I said.

'It's great fun.' He bit into the pastry, let loose a flow of custard, licked his lips, wiped his chin. 'Delicious. What have *you* been doing for fun, Alex?'

Figuring out how to answer that must have done something to my face, because Harrison placed his hand atop mine and looked like a concerned parent.

'That bad, son?'

'Is it that obvious?'

'Oh, yes, Alex. Oh, yes indeed.'

I told him about Robin. He thought a while, and said, 'Sounds like small things have been amplified.'

'Not so small, Bert. She's really had it with my risk-taking behavior.'

'I was referring to *your* feelings. Your anxiety about Robin.'

'I know I'm being paranoid, but I keep flashing back to the last time she left.'

'She made a mistake,' he said. 'But she bore the brunt of it, and you might think about disconnecting yourself from her pain.'

'Her pain,' I said. 'Think it still bothers her after all these years?'

'If she allows herself to focus on it, my guess is she feels a good deal worse about it than you do.'

He'd met Robin twice, and yet I didn't feel him presumptuous. A few months after our house had burned down, we'd driven up to Santa Barbara for a change of scenery and had run into Bert at an antiquarian bookstore on State Street. He'd been browsing through eighteenth-century scientific treatises. In Latin. ('My current hobby, kids.') Dust had speckled the front of his jumpsuit.

'She loves you deeply,' he said. 'At least, she did when I saw her, and I have my doubts about that depth of feeling just vanishing.' He ate more pastry, picked almond slivers from his plate, and slipped them between his lips. 'The body language, the mind language, was all there. I remember thinking, "This is the girl for Alex." '

'I used to think so.'

'Cherish what you've got. My second wife was like that, accepted me with all my irregularities.'

'You think Robin accepts me, no matter what.'

'If she didn't, she'd have left long ago.'

'But putting her through more of my risk-taking would be cruel.'

He squeezed my hand. 'Life is like a bus stop, Alex. We map out our route but linger briefly between adventures. Only you can chart your itinerary – and hope God agrees with it. So what brings you to Ojai?'

'Enjoying the scenery.'

'Then come up to my house, let me show you my acquisitions.'

217

We finished our food and he insisted on paying. The old station wagon was parked out front, and I followed him into town and onto Signal Street, where we climbed past a drainage ditch paved with fieldstones and spanned by footbridges, up to the top of the road.

The front door to the purple house was open and shielded by a well-oxidized screen. Bert climbed the steps with agility and ushered me into the living room. The space was exactly as I remembered: small, dark, plank-floored, crammed with old furniture, shawls, throw pillows, an upright piano, the bay window lined with dusty bottles. But now there was no room to sit: a gigantic, hammered-bronze gong nudged the piano. Every couch and chair bore drums and bells and lyres and zithers and Pan pipes and harps and objects I couldn't identify. The floor space behind the piano bench was taken up by a six-foot dragon-shaped contraption topped with corrugated wood. Harrison ran a stick along the ridges and set off a percussive but melodic scale.

'Bali,' he said. 'I've learned "Old MacDonald" on it.' Sigh. 'One day, Mozart.'

He cleared instruments from a sagging sofa, and said, 'Be comfortable.'

As I sat, something metallic behind the couch caught my eye. A folded-up wheelchair.

Bert said, 'I'm storing it for a friend,' and settled his small frame on a hard-backed chair. The fingers of his right hand brushed against a pedal harp, but not hard enough to make a sound. 'Despite your stress you look well.'

'As do you.'

'Knock wood.' He rapped the rim of the harp, and this time a note rang out. 'G sharp . . . so you're just passing through? Next time, call and we can have lunch. Unless, of course, you need solitude.'

'No, I'd love to get together.'

'Of course, we all need solitude,' he said. 'The key is finding the right balance.'

'You live alone, Bert.'

'I have friends.'

'So do I.'

'Milo.'

'Milo and others.'

'Well, that's good – Alex, is there anything I can do for you?'

'No,' I said. 'Like what?'

'Anything, Alex.'

'If you could solve cold cases, that would be helpful.'

'Cold cases,' he said. 'A murder.'

I nodded.

'The body may be cold,' he said, 'but I wonder if the memory ever really cools. Care to tell me about it?'

I didn't. Yes, I did.

twenty-three

described the Ingalls murder without mentioning names or places or the murder book. But there was no sense withholding Milo's name. Bert Harrison had met Milo, had given a statement to Milo on the Bad Love case.

As I talked, he rarely allowed his gaze to wander from my face.

When I finished, he said, 'This girl – the one who poisoned the dog – sounds monstrous.'

'At the very least, severely disturbed.'

'First a dog, then a person . . . that's the typical pattern . . . though you have only the neighbor's accusation to go on.'

'The behavioral warning in the girl's chart is consistent with the neighbor's report. She didn't belong in that school, Bert. String-pulling by her family probably got her in – safe hiding during the investigation of the murder.'

He folded his hands in his lap. 'And no word on the other possible victim . . . I assume Milo's been looking for her.'

'No sign of her, yet,' I said. 'Most likely she's dead. The disturbed girl seems to have vanished, completely. No paper trail at all. That reeks of more string-pulling.'

'A supportive family,' he said.

'In terms of aiding and abetting.'

'Hmm . . . Alex, if the case was taken out of Milo's hands twenty years ago, how did he manage to be reassigned?'

'He was unofficially reassigned,' I said. 'By someone who knew we worked together and was sure I'd give him the message.'

'What message, Alex?'

I thought about how much to say. Told him about the murder book and its probable link to Pierce Schwinn.

220

'Pierce?' he said. 'So that's why you're here.'

'You knew him?'

'I did. I know his wife, Marge, as well. Sweet woman.'

'Milo and I were up at her ranch a few days ago,' I said. 'It's a good bet Schwinn assembled that book, but the only photos of his she claims to know about are nature shots.'

'Claims?' said Harrison. 'You doubt her?'

'She seemed truthful.'

'I'd believe her, Alex.'

'Why's that?'

'Because she's an honest woman.'

'And Schwinn?'

'I have nothing bad to say about him either.'

'How well did you know him, Bert?'

'We ran into each other from time to time. In town – shopping, at the Little Theater.'

'Are you aware of any confidante he might've had other than Marge? Someone he'd have trusted to send the book? Because it was mailed to me seven months after he died.'

'You're certain it emanated from Pierce?'

'The photos are LAPD crime-scene shots, probably purloined from old files. Schwinn was a shutterbug, used to bring his own camera to crime scenes in order to snap his own pictures. On top of that, Marge Schwinn said she purchased three identical blue leather albums for Pierce, over at O'Neill & Chapin. She showed us two but the third was missing and she had no idea where it was. That's what drew me back here. I wanted to speak to the shop's owners to see if they'd sold any others.'

'The owner,' he said, 'is a lovely woman named Roberta Bernstein, and she's in Europe. O'Neill & Chapin are her pet terriers.' He pressed a blunt little index finger to his lips. 'Sounds like the totality of evidence does point to Pierce . . .'

'But?'

'No buts, Alex. You've put together a solid argument.'

'Any idea who he might've passed it to?'

He crossed his legs, hooked a finger under the hem of a purple trouser leg. 'The only person I ever saw Pierce with was Marge. And as I said, I doubt she's involved.'

221

'Because she's honest.'

'And because Pierce was protective of her, Alex. I can't see him exposing her to something like that.'

'Sounds like you knew them both pretty well,' I said.

He smiled. 'I'm a psychiatrist. I'm allowed to theorize. No, we never really socialized, but this is a small town. You meet the same people over and over. I suppose I'm drawing upon Pierce's body language when they were together.'

'Protective.'

'Very much so. Marge seemed to take well to that. I found that interesting. She'd never lived with anyone before. Her family goes way back in this region, and she's taken care of that ranch nearly single-handedly for years. People of a certain age can get set in their ways, not take well to the demands of a relationship. But Marge seemed quite content with domestic life. They both did.'

'Did you know Pierce had been a detective?'

'Marge told me,' he said. 'Soon after Pierce moved in. I believe it was at the theater, as a matter of fact. Out in the lobby, during intermission. She introduced me, and we began chatting about a crime story in the newspaper – something down your way, bank robbers, a shoot-out, the criminals had escaped. Marge said something along the lines of "If Pierce were still on the force, he'd solve it." '

'How'd Pierce react to that?'

'If I recall correctly, *un*reactive. Didn't say much of anything. That's the way he usually was. Reserved.'

Milo had described Schwinn as verbally aggressive, prone to sermonizing. Lots had changed over twenty years.

I said, 'Marge told us Pierce had grown serene.'

'She'd know best . . . so Pierce was Milo's partner. How interesting. The world grows smaller yet.'

'The way he died,' I said. 'Falling off that horse. Any thoughts about that?'

He uncrossed his leg, tapped a rosy cheek, and allowed his hand to brush against an ornate concertina. 'You suspect something other than an accident? Why, Alex?'

'Because that's the way my mind works.'

'Ah,' he said.

I could hear Milo laughing.

'Small world,' he repeated. 'That's about all I can tell you . . . can I fix you some tea, Alex? Wait – you're a guitarist, aren't you? I've got something in back that might interest you. A turn-of-the-century Knutsen Hawaiian harp-guitar. Perhaps you can tell me how to tune the drone strings.'

His spare bedroom was filled with instruments and antique music stands, and I hung around for a while watching him fiddle and tinker, listened to him expound on music and rhythm and culture. He began to reminisce about his time in Chile. Ethnographic research in Indonesia, a summer of musicology in Salzburg, ministering to Israeli kibbutz children who'd been traumatized by terrorism.

No mention of his Santa Barbara days – the years he'd spent at a school for troubled kids, just a few miles away. The kind of place someone like Caroline Cossack might easily have ended up. That high-priced travesty had caused more problems than it had solved.

Bert had a selective memory for the positive. Perhaps that's why he'd seemed reluctant to imagine a young girl evincing brutality.

He stopped narrating and threw up his hands. 'I'm such a bore – you've probably begun wondering if I'm going senile.'

'I haven't at all, Bert.' Though I had thought: *He seems distracted.*

'The truth is, I have lost some short-term memory. But nothing beyond my age norms.'

'Your memory seems fine to me,' I said.

'That's kind of you to say . . .' He gestured around the room. 'All this – all these toys, Alex, they're a wonderful distraction. A boy needs a hobby.' Pudgy fingers took hold of my forearm. His grip was forceful. 'We both know that, don't we?'

I stuck around for tea, finally told him I needed to get back to L.A.

As he walked me to my car, he said, 'That girl. So monstrous, if it's true.'

'You seem skeptical.'

He nodded. 'I do find it hard to believe that a young female would be capable of such savagery.'

'I'm not saying she acted alone, Bert, or even initiated the murder. But she could've lured the victims, and either receded into the background or participated.'

'Any theories about the main perpetrator?'

'The girl had a boyfriend, six years older, with a criminal history, including murder.'

'Sexual murder?'

'No, an ambush killing.'

'I see,' he said. 'Any particular reason you didn't mention him, initially?'

'The cover-up's more likely related to the girl.'

'This fellow wasn't wealthy.'

'Young black street pusher.'

'I see – and what became of this murderous young felon?'

'He vanished, too.'

'A girl and a young man,' he said. 'That would change things. Psychosocially.'

'A killing team,' I said. 'One scenario is the two of them picked up the victims at the party and took them somewhere to be raped and murdered.'

'A Svengali-Trilby situation,' he said. 'Dominant male, submissive female . . . because that's what it usually takes to get an impressionable young female involved in extremely violent behavior. Nearly all sexual violence seems to emanate from the Y chromosome, doesn't it? What else do you know about this boyfriend?'

'Apart from being a junkie and a pusher, he was manipulative enough to get a street-smart bail bondsman to forgo a bond. And calculated enough to ambush the bondsman – that's the homicide he's wanted for. Still wanted. Another of Milo's open cases.'

'Sad convergence for Milo,' he said. 'A junkie in the strict sense – heroin?'

'Heroin was his first choice, but he was eclectic.'

'Hmm . . . then I suppose that would explain it.'

'Explain what?' I said.

'With sexual sadists, one usually thinks of alcohol or marijuana as the drugs of choice, correct? Something mild enough to take the edge off inhibition, but not sufficiently incapacitating to blunt the libido. Other drugs – amphetamines, cocaine – can foster violence, but that's usually more of a paranoid reaction. But heroin?' He shook his head. 'Opiates are the great pacifiers. Take away the necessity to steal in order to obtain heroin and no place would be safer than a city full of addicts. I've certainly never heard of a junkie acting out in such a sexually violent manner.'

'Not while high,' I said. 'But a heroin addict in need of a fix wouldn't be good company.'

'I suppose.' He scratched an ear. 'Even then, Alex, wouldn't the violence be impulsive – born of frustration? An addict would be interested in the needle, not luring and raping and cutting up young girls. Just garnering the concentration would be difficult, wouldn't you say? At least that's the way it was years ago when I worked with addicts.'

'When was that?'

'During my internship, I rotated through the Federal hospital in Lexington.'

'Where haven't you been, Bert?'

'Oh, lots of places . . . do forgive my rambling, Alex. What do I know about crime? You're the expert.'

As I got in the Seville, he said, 'What I told you before about Robin. I didn't mean to presume to instruct you how to live your life. I've presumed an awful lot today, haven't I?'

'I didn't take it that way, Bert.'

He sighed. 'I'm an old man, Alex. Most of the time I *feel* young – sometimes I wake up in the morning ready to dash to the lecture hall and take notes. Then I look in the mirror . . . the life cycle. One regresses. Loses one's sense of propriety. Forgive me.'

Tears welled in the gray eyes.

'There's nothing to forgive—'

'You're kind to say that.'

I placed a hand on his shoulder. Beneath the purple polyester he was soft and frail and small. 'Is everything okay, Bert?'

'Everything is as it should be.' He reached up and patted my hand. 'Lovely seeing you, son. Don't give up.'

'On the case?'

'On anything that matters.'

I drove down the hill, paused to look through the rearview

225

mirror. He remained standing in the driveway. Waved. A tired wave.

Definitely distracted, I thought as I drove away. And the sudden mood swings – the tears. A different Bert from the buoyant man I'd known.

The allusions to senility.

Nothing beyond my age norms.

As if he'd tested himself. Maybe he had.

An impressive man, afraid . . .

He called me *son* several times. I realized that for all his travels and adventures, the first-time mention of being married, he'd never spoken of having children.

Alone, in a house full of toys.

If I reached his age, how would I be living?

I got home just before dark, with a head full of road glare and lungs teeming with smog. No numeral blinked on my phone machine, but two messages had been left with my service: someone wanting to sell me earthquake insurance and a request to call Dr Allison Gwynn.

A young female voice answered at Allison's office.

'Hi, Dr Delaware, I'm Connie Martino, Dr Gwynn's psych assistant. She's in session right now but she told me to let you know that she'd like to speak with you. Her last patient's finished by eight and you can drop by the office if you'd like. Or let me know what works for you.'

'Eight works for me.'

'Great. I'll tell her.'

At seven-forty, I set out for Santa Monica. Allison Gwynn's building was on Montana Avenue, just east of the beach city's boutique row, a pale, one-story late-forties moderne affair with rounded corners and grilled slat windows and apricot-tinted accent lighting. A small patch of daylilies sprouted near the front door, bleached white by the night. Inside were four suites: a three-woman obstetric-gynecology group, a plastic surgeon, an endodontist, and, at the rear, A. GWYNN, PHD, AND ASSOCIATES.

Allison's waiting room was empty and smelled of face powder and perfume and the merest nuance of stress. The decor was soft chairs and thick wool carpeting and marine prints, everything tinted in variants of soft aqua and beige, as if someone were trying to bring the beach indoors. Halogen spots tuned to dim cast a golden white glow – the beach at twilight. Magazines were stacked neatly. A trio of red call buttons next to the door listed Allison's name above those of two assistants: C. MARTINO, MA, AND E. BRACHT, PHD. I rang in, and, a moment later, she opened the door.

Her black hair was tied back into a ponytail and she wore an ankle-length, navy crêpe dress above matte brown boots. The dress had a scoop neck that dipped just below her collarbone. The same meticulously applied makeup. Same diamond accents at wrist and neck and ears, but tension played around the big blue eyes. The first time I'd met her, she'd maintained steady eye contact. Now she was focused somewhere over my left shoulder.

'Sorry for bringing you all the way here,' she said, 'but I didn't want to talk over the phone.'

'I don't mind being here.'

Her eyebrows rose. 'Well, then, come in.'

Her inner office was more of the same maritime hues and compassionate lighting. The room was large enough for group therapy, but set up for individual work, with a desk in the corner, a sofa and a pair of facing easy chairs. She took one of the chairs, and I sat down opposite her. The navy dress covered most of her but clung to her body, and as she positioned herself I saw muscle and curve, the sweep of thigh, the tug of bosom.

Remembering her history with Michael Larner, I switched mental gears.

She said, 'This may turn out to be nothing, but given the seriousness of what you're doing, I thought it best that I tell you.'

She shifted in the chair, showed me another aspect of her figure. Not seductively; her mouth was set tight.

I said, 'I appreciate any help you can give me.'

The edge of her lower lip insinuated itself between her teeth, and she chewed. Her hands flexed. She shook her head.

Neither of us spoke. Two therapists measuring the silence.

She said, 'I recalled something right after we talked. I'd forgotten about it – or maybe it never really registered because at the time . . . I'm sure it's nothing, but a short while after Willie Burns left

Achievement House – maybe a week later – I was with *him*. Larner.
And he was angry about Willie. Worked up. I know because he
called me into his office and his anger was obvious. I never really
thought about it in terms of Willie because I had my own issues . . .'
She chewed her lip, again. 'Let me back up . . .'

Undoing her ponytail, she shook her hair loose in a sable billow,
tied it up again. Tucking her legs under her, she hugged herself and
studied the carpet.

'Larner had been bothering me for a while. It began soon after I
started volunteering. Nothing blatant – looks, smiles, little asides
about my clothes – how cute they were, what a nice healthy girl I
was. He'd pass me in the hall and pat me on the head or brush my
hip or chuck my chin. I knew what was going on, but what I didn't
realize was just how wrong it was.' She took hold of her hair,
smoothed the ends. 'I didn't want to leave Achievement House,
thought it would be a good summer experience. And even if I'd told
someone, what was he really doing to me?'

'Insidious,' I said.

'Insidious and devious and altogether creepy. I tried to avoid him.
For the most part, it worked. But that day – it was a Monday, I
remember that because I'd been to the beach over the weekend, had
gotten a tan. Willie Burns had been gone a good week, maybe
more. I remember asking about Willie because with him gone the
halls were quiet. When he worked, he'd usually be humming,
low-key, some kind of bluesy thing. He always looked stoned, but
he did have a good voice. And he was friendly, would generally look
up and smile, and say, "Hi." '

'Friendly to everyone?'

'To the kids. They seemed to like him, though I got the feeling
some of them were making fun of him – that drugged-out
demeanor. The only time he got furtive was when he was with
Caroline. Anyway, he was gone, and an older woman was doing his
job – an old Latina who didn't speak English. I asked people what
had happened to Willie, but no one seemed to know.'

She twisted in her chair, cupped one hand over a knee. 'That
Monday, I'd been delivering charts when Larner called me into his
office. Something about new filing procedures. That sounded
strange – why would the director want to talk to a student volunteer

about procedure? I didn't want to go, but I couldn't see any way out. If I refused, that would be insubordination. When I got there, Larner's secretary was out in front, and that made me feel better. But then she told me to go right in and closed the door after me. It was summer and I was wearing a sleeveless white sundress and my tan was pretty blatant and I just knew he'd say something about it and started to tell myself I was stupid for not covering up more. But Larner didn't even look at me. He was standing, sleeves rolled up, a cigar in one hand, his back turned, on the phone, listening. I stood near the door. He was rocking on his heels and clenching the phone tight – he was a big, pink disgusting thing, and his hands were tight around the receiver – mottled, like lunch meat. Then he half turned, but he still didn't acknowledge me. His face was different from all the other times I'd seen him. In the past he'd always smiled. Leered. Now he looked furious. Red-faced – he's naturally ruddy, but this time he was like a beet. I remember the contrast with his hair – he had this blond-white hair that looked as if he waxed it. I just stayed there, with my back against the door, and he barked something into the phone and slammed it down. All I caught was Willie Burns's name. Then something about "We'd better do something about it." Then he hung up.' She held out one hand. 'That's it. I never paid much attention to that, because it really wasn't the focus of my memories.'

'You had your own issues,' I said.

She lowered her head, then raised it very slowly. Her eyes were closed, and her face had lost color.

'After he slammed down the phone, he began to dial another number, then he saw me, gave me this surprised look – surprised and hateful. As if I wasn't supposed to be there. Then there it was – that smile of his. But the anger remained on his face, also, and the combination scared me – predatory. He came around from behind the desk, shook my hand, held on too long, told me to sit down, said something to the effect of "How's my favorite volunteer?" Then he walked behind me and just stood there, not talking or moving. I could smell his cigar, the smoke kept wafting toward me. To this day, I can't see a cigar without . . .'

She sprang up, strode to her own desk, and sat down, putting wood and space between us.

'He started talking – softly, in a singsong. How did I like working at Achievement House? Was I finding satisfaction? Had I thought about career choices? Maybe teaching would be good for me because I was clearly a people person. I didn't say much, he really didn't want answers. It was a monologue – droning, hypnotic. Then he stopped talking and I tensed up, and he said, "Don't be nervous, Allison. We're all friends, here." Nothing happened for what seemed to be forever. Then suddenly I felt his finger on my cheek, pressing, stroking, and he said something about my skin – how clean and fresh it was, how nice it was to see a young lady who cared about her hygiene.'

She caught hold of her hair with one hand and tugged hard. Then both hands slapped flat on the desk and she was staring at me – daring me to look away.

'He kept stroking,' she said. 'It was annoying – ticklish – and I twisted my head away. And then he chuckled and I looked up and I saw that it hadn't been his finger on my cheek. It was his thing – oh, listen to me, like a child – it was his *penis*, and he was rubbing it against my cheek, *pushing*. I was so freaked out that my mouth dropped open and that was the worst thing to do because he chuckled again and in it went and all of a sudden he was holding the back of my head with his other hand, the hand with the cigar, and the smoke wrapped around me, and he forced himself deeper into my mouth and I couldn't breathe, I was gagging. But my eyes were open, for some reason I kept them open, and I could see his white shirt and his tie – a striped tie, blue and black – and the bottom of his face, all that pink flab, quivering, his double chin and he was rocking on his heels again, but in a different way and the cigar smoke was burning my eyes and I started to cry.'

She turned icy and still. Didn't move for a long time. 'He didn't come. Thank God for that. I managed to wrench free first, made it to the door, ran out, never looked back. Drove home like a zombie, called in sick. Which wasn't much of a stretch because I felt sick as a dog. For the next few days, I took to bed. Threw up when my mother wasn't listening, lay there feeling degraded and scared and worst of all stupid – replaying it over and over, blaming myself. For the tan and the dress and not being on guard – I know it's never the

victim's fault, God knows how many times I've told that to *patients*.
But . . .'

'You were seventeen,' I said.

'I'm not sure I'd have handled it better – or felt differently – had
I been twenty-seven. Not at the level of consciousness twenty years
ago.' She slumped, loosened her hair again, fooled with it, flicked
something away from the corner of one eye.

'The worst part was how *alone* I felt. Abandoned, with no one in
my corner. I couldn't tell my parents, because I was too humiliated.
I told Larry Daschoff a sanitized version, because even though
Larry had been my mentor for the summer and he'd been kind and
helpful, he was a *man*. And I couldn't get rid of the feeling that I
was to blame. So I just kept calling in sick to Achievement House,
told my mother I had some kind of flu, stayed holed up in my room.
Obsessing about what had happened, dreaming about it – in the
dreams it was worse. In the dreams I *didn't* get away and Larner
came in my mouth and then he hit me and raped me and forced me
to smoke the cigar. Finally, I realized I was falling apart – was
wasting. I needed to do something. So I found out the name of the
school's chairman of the board – some downtown lawyer – Preston
something – and after agonizing about it for a whole week, I called
his office, got through after several attempts, and told him what had
happened. Only I didn't really tell him. I soft-pedaled it. Reduced it
to grabbing – the same story I told Larry.'

Larry had told me, *Mashing and groping.*

'How'd Preston react?' I said.

'He listened. Didn't say anything at all, at first. Didn't ask any
questions, which really upset me. I got the impression he thought I
was crazy. Finally, he said he'd get back to me. Two days later a
letter of dismissal arrived in the mail. I was being let go for poor
work habits and excessive absenteeism. I never showed the letter to
my parents, just told them I'd quit because the job wasn't challenging. They didn't care. My mother wanted me to swim at the club
and play tennis and meet guys. What she *wasn't* happy about was
that I just wanted to hang around the house and not be *social*. So
she arranged a family cruise to Alaska. Big luxury liner cruising past
the glaciers – baby otters nursing amid the ice floes. All that blue ice
wasn't as cold as my heart was that summer.'

231

She stood, returned to the easy chair, tried to look comfortable but couldn't pull it off.

'I've never told anyone what really happened. Not until now. But this was the wrong time and place, wasn't it? Using a stranger. I'm sorry.'

'Nothing to be sorry for, Allison.'

'All these years,' she said. 'And it still eats at me – not going after that piece of dirt. Who knows how many others he's done that to. What I could've prevented.'

'It would've been his word against yours, and he was in power,' I said. 'It wasn't your fault then, and it's not your fault, now.'

'Do you know how many women I've treated – how many patients I've helped deal with *exactly* this kind of thing? *Not* because I pursue those kinds of cases. *Not* because I'm using my patients to work through my own garbage. Because it's so damned *common*. I've helped my patients, but then when it comes to my own garbage, I repress. It's crazy, don't you think?'

'No,' I said. 'It's human. I've preached the virtues of talking it out, but when it comes to my own stuff, I usually go it alone.'

'Do you?'

I nodded.

'And you're going through something now, aren't you?'

I stared at her.

'Your eyes are sad,' she said.

'I'm going through a bit of something,' I said.

'Well, then,' she said, 'I guess we're kindred spirits. And I guess we'll leave it at that.'

She walked me to the waiting-room door. 'Like I told you the first time, you're just too good a listener, sir.'

'Occupational hazard.'

'Was it helpful? Telling you that Larner was angry about Willie Burns?'

'Yes,' I said. 'Thanks very much. I know it was an ordeal.'

She smiled. 'Not an ordeal, an experience. What you're going through – it has nothing to do with Caroline Cossack or Willie Burns, does it?'

I shook my head.

'Sorry,' she said. 'No more prying.' She reached for the doorknob and her shoulder brushed my arm. The contact sent something electrical down my arm. Suddenly I was rock-hard, fighting to keep my breathing even. To keep my hands off her.

She stared at me. No tension around the huge, blue eyes, just softness, sadness, maybe desire.

'It wasn't an ordeal,' she said. 'You said the right thing. Here's another confession: I was looking forward to seeing you again.'

'Me too,' I said.

I smiled and shrugged, and she did the same. Gracious mimickry.

'You too, *but*,' she said. 'That bit of something, right?'

I nodded.

'Well, maybe in another galaxy, Alex. You're very sweet. Good luck.'

'Good luck to you, too.'

She held the door open. Kept it open as I walked down the hall.

twenty-four

Milo woke up early the next morning, with the faces of the men at the Sangre de Leon meeting leering in his head. Thinking: *Too many ways to take it, not enough of me to go around.*

He stumbled to the shower, shaved, picked clothes randomly, got the coffee machine going, looked at the clock. Seven-thirteen. An emergency call had yanked Rick out of bed three hours ago. Milo had watched in the darkness as Rick slipped into the scrubs he kept neatly folded on a bedroom chair, picked up his Porsche keys from the nightstand, and padded out the door.

Rick stopped, returned to the bed, kissed Milo lightly on the forehead. Milo pretended to be sleeping, because he didn't feel like talking, not even 'Goodbye.'

The two of them had talked plenty all night, sitting up late at the kitchen table. Mostly Milo had blabbed and Rick had listened, maintaining a superficial calm, but Milo knew he was shaken by the Paris Bartlett encounter and the HIV rumor. All these years, and Milo's work had never intruded on their personal life.

Milo reassured him, and Rick nodded, complained of crushing fatigue and fell asleep the moment his head hit the pillow.

Milo cleaned up the Chinese takeout cartons and the dinner dishes and slipped into bed beside him, lying there for an hour or so, listening to Rick's even breathing, thinking.

The Cossacks, Walt Obey, Larner Junior, Germ Bacilla, Diamond Jim Horne.

Plus the player who *hadn't* shown up. He saw that face, clearly: a stoic ebony mask.

Smiley Bartlett, the personnel inquiry, and the HIV rumor said John G. Broussard's hand was in all of it.

He recalled Broussard – smelled Broussard's citrus cologne in the interview room, twenty years ago. The hand-stitched suit, all that confidence, taking charge. He and his pink pal – Poulsenn. Milo had no idea what had happened to *his* career, but look how far John G. had come.

A white man and a black man teamed up, and the black man had been the dominant partner.

A black man advancing that quickly, back in LAPD's bad old racist days. That had to mean Broussard had harpoons in all the right whales. Had probably used his IA dirt to build up leverage.

Mr Straight and Narrow. And he'd covered up Janie Ingalls and Lord knew what else. Milo had been part of it, allowed himself to be swept along, pretended he could forget about it.

Now he wondered what that had done to his soul.

He poured coffee but the muddy brew tasted like battery acid and he spit it out and gulped a glass of tap water. The light through the kitchen window was the yellow-gray of old phlegm.

He sat down, kept thinking about Broussard, a South Central guy who'd ended up in Hancock Park.

Neighbor to Walt Obey.

Every police chief before Broussard had lived in his own house, but John G. had convinced the mayor to give him an empty mansion on Irving Street, rent-free. The three-story edifice, donated to the city years ago by the heirs of a long-dead oil tycoon, was twelve thousand square feet of English Tudor with big lawns, a pool, and a tennis court. Milo knew because he'd done security years ago at a party for an ambassador – the envoy from some small Asian state that had since changed its name.

Set aside originally as a mayor's residence, the Irving house had sat dormant for years because the mayor's predecessor had his own place in Brentwood and the current mayor's even larger spread in Pacific Palisades was just fine, too.

John G. Broussard's crib, prior to his promotion, had been a too-small affair in Ladera Heights and John G. claimed he needed to be closer to headquarters.

Ladera Heights was a half-hour ride downtown, the mansion on Irving was fifteen minutes up Sixth Street. The mayor's drive from the Westside could stretch to over an hour, but no one saw the inconsistency in John G.'s logic, and the new chief got himself baronial lodgings.

Irving Street, less than a mile from Walt Obey's estate on Muirfield.

Obey was one of the mayor's big donors. Had supported Broussard for chief over three other candidates.

The mayor and Obey. Obey and Broussard. Obey and a bunch of lowlifes supping nouvelle-whatever cuisine in a private room at Sangre de Leon.

Private enterprise and municipal government and the long arm of the law arm in arm. And Schwinn had thrown him right into it.

He left his house, looking in all directions and over his shoulder, got into the rented Taurus, and drove north. IDing the asshole who claimed to be Paris Bartlett shouldn't be a problem, if his hunch about a department plant was true. Just head over to the police academy in Elysian Park and thumb through the face books. But that was too conspicuous; for all he knew it was his sneaky little trips to Parker Center and back to his West L.A. desk that had sicked the department on him in the first place. Besides, Bartlett was a minor player, just a messenger, and did it really matter who'd sent him?

Stay healthy . . .

Maybe he should return to Ojai and nose around a bit more up there. But what more could he learn? Schwinn was the Ojai link, and he was gone.

Falling off a goddamn horse . . .

He pulled over to the curb, yanked out his cell phone, got the number of the Ventura County morgue. Using an insurance-investigator lie, he spent the next half hour being bounced from desk to desk, trying to get the full facts on Schwinn's death.

Finally, a coroner's assistant who knew something got on the line. The death was written up just as Marge Schwinn had described: massive head injuries and fractured ribs consistent with a fall, copious blood on a nearby rock. Ruled accidental, no suspicious circumstances. No dope or booze in Schwinn's system. Or the horse's, the clerk added. An equine drug scan seemed thorough, and Milo told the CA so.

'Special request of the widow,' said the guy, a middle-aged-sounding guy named Olivas. 'She wanted the horse tested and was willing to pay for it.'

'She suspect something?'

'All it says here is that she requested a full drug scan on Akhbar – that's the horse. We had a vet in Santa Barbara do it, and she sent us the results. Mrs Schwinn got the bill.'

'So the horse was clean,' said Milo.

'As a whistle,' said Olivas. 'It busted itself up plenty, though – two broken legs and a torsion injury of the neck. When the widow got there, it was down on the ground moaning, pretty much out of it. She had it put down. What's up, the insurance company has problems with something?'

'No, just checking.'

'It was an accident, he was an old guy,' said Olivas. 'Riding a horse at his age, what was he thinking?'

'President Reagan rode when he was in his eighties.'

'Yeah, well, he had Secret Service guys to look after him. It's like old people driving cars – my dad's eighty-nine, blind as a bat at night, but he insists on getting behind the wheel and driving to L.A. to get authentic *menudo*. That kind of thing and idiots on cell phones, give me a break. You'd see what I see comes in here every day, you'd be scared.'

'I'm scared,' said Milo, hefting his phone.

'Pays to be scared.'

He craved caffeine and cholesterol, drove to Farmers Market at Fairfax and Third and had a green chili omelet and two stacks of toast at Du-Pars. Keeping his eye on a homeless guy in the next booth. The bum wore three jackets and hugged a battered, stringless guitar. The instrument made Milo think about Robin, but the psychosis in the homeless guy's eyes pulled him into the here and now.

They engaged in a staring contest until the homeless man finally threw down a couple of dollars and waddled off mumbling at unseen demons and Milo was able to enjoy his eggs.

Once again, he thought, *I've brought peace and light to the world.*

But then the waitress smiled with relief and gave him a

thumbs-up, and he realized he'd really accomplished something.

Still hungry, he ordered a stack of hotcakes, drained everything down with black coffee, walked around the market, dodging tourists, figuring the distraction might get his brain in gear. But it didn't, and after inspecting produce stands full of fruit he didn't recognize and buying a bag of jumbo cashews, he left the market, drove south on Fairfax, turned left on Sixth, at the old May Company building, now an adjunct of the art museum, and kept going east.

Chief John G. Broussard's official residence was beautifully tended, with grass as green as Ireland and more flower beds than Milo remembered from that diplomatic party. A flagpole had been erected smack in the middle of the lawn and the Stars and Stripes and the California Bear swooshed in the midday breeze.

No walls or fences or uniformed officer on patrol, but the driveway had been gated with wrought iron, and through the stout bars Milo saw a black-and-white cruiser, and behind that a late-model white Cadillac. The Caddy was probably Mrs Broussard's wheels. He recalled her as a trim, pretty woman with henna-tinted, cold-waved hair and the resigned look of a political spouse. What was her name . . . Bernadette . . . Bernadine? Did she and John G. have kids? Milo'd never heard of any, and he realized how little he knew about the chief's personal life. How little the chief doled out.

Seven blocks west and a half mile south was Walt Obey's address on Muirfield. The billionaire's nest sat at the end of the road, where Muirfield terminated on the southern border of the Wilshire Country Club. No house in sight, just ten-foot stone walls broken by an opaque, black steel gate studded with enormous bolts. Closed circuit TV camera on one post. The implication was a grand place on multiple acres, and Milo flashed to Baron Loetz's spread, neighbor to the Cossack party house. Did Obey spend time on his veranda, sipping gin and enjoying what God had given him?

Eighty years old and still taking meetings with hustlers like the Cossacks. Some big deal on the verge?

He found himself staring at Obey's gate. The TV camera remained immobile. The place was close enough for an athletic guy like John G. to jog over. Obey and Broussard on the veranda? Making plans. Running things. All of a sudden Milo felt very small and vulnerable. He rolled down the window, heard birds peeping, a plink of running water behind Obey's walls. Then the camera began to rotate. An automatic circuit, or maybe his presence had attracted attention. He backed up halfway down the block, whipped a U-turn, and got the hell out of there.

A few minutes later, he was parked on McCadden near Wilshire, cell phone hot against his ear. More DMV finagling gave him other addresses, and he had a look at all of them.

Michael Larner lived in a high-rise condo just east of Westwood, in the Wilshire Corridor. Pink stone and cheesy-looking brick, doorman out in front, an oversize fountain. Son Bradley's Santa Monica Canyon place turned out to be a smallish, blue frame house with stupendous ocean views and a FOR RENT sign out in front. No cars in the driveway, and the gardening looked a little lax, so Brad was living somewhere else.

Garvey Cossack Junior and brother Bob bunked together at a Carolwood address in Holmby Hills, not far, geographically, from Alex's place off Beverly Glen, but a whole different world financially.

Carolwood was a lovely, hilly block, leafy and sinuous, shaded by old-growth trees, one of the highest-priced stretches in L.A. Most of the houses were architectural masterpieces landscaped like botanical gardens, many of them cosseted by greenery and bearing that classy look that only came from durability.

The Cossack brothers' pad was an exceedingly vulgar, blue-tile-roofed and monstrously gabled heap of gray limestone perched atop a scarred dirt hill with no grass or trees in sight. Stone facing, only. The sides were lumpy stucco. Bad trowel job. Cheap-looking white metal fencing and an electric gate partitioned the front of the property from the street, but without benefit of vegetation the house sat in full view, baking in the sun, puffy flanks glaring white in spots.

A double-sized dumpster overflowing with trash advertised ongoing construction, but no workers were in sight, drapes covered the windows, and a mini car museum took up the rest of the massive driveway.

Plum-colored Rolls-Royce Corniche, black Humvee with blacked-out windows, red (what else?) Ferrari that came as close as

Milo had seen to a penis on wheels, a taxi-yellow Pantera, a pair of Dodge Vipers, one white with a blue center stripe, the other anthracite-gray striped orange, and a white Corvette convertible. All under a drooping, makeshift canvas awning that stretched across listing metal stilts. Off to the side, in the full sun, was a ten-year-old Honda that had to be the maid's wheels.

Big house and all those cars, but no landscaping. Just the kind of eyesore a couple of teenagers would put together if they tumbled into endless cash, and Milo was willing to bet the Cossacks had six figures' worth of stereo equipment inside, along with a state-of-the-art screening room, a pub, a game room or two. He was starting to think of them as a dual case of profound arrested development.

The house was exactly the kind of eyesore that would provoke neighbor complaints in a blue-chip district, meaning now he had something to look for.

He drove downtown to the Hall of Records, made it through the traffic by 2 P.M., and combed through the zoning-board complaint files. Sure enough, three gripes had been lodged against the Cossacks, all by Carolwood residents, irritated about noise and dirt and other indignities caused by 'protracted construction.' All dismissed for lack of cause.

He moved over to the property files, ran searches on the Cossacks, Walt Obey, both Larners. John G. Broussard.

Obey's holdings were protected by a cadre of holding companies, a firewall that would take weeks, if not months, to break through. Same for the Larners and the Cossacks, although a few pieces of real estate were held privately by each duo. In the case of the Larners it was half a dozen condos in a Marina del Rey building owned jointly by father and son. Sixteen strip malls in low-rent exurbs were registered to the Cossack brothers.

The boys living together, working together. How touching.

Nothing was registered to Sister Caroline.

Shifting gears for a moment, he pulled up Georgie Nemerov's records. The bail bondsman and his mother co-owned a single-family dwelling in Van Nuys that Milo recognized as the family home from twenty years ago, and a six-unit apartment in Granada Hills, also jointly registered to Ivana Nemerov. Whatever Georgie had or hadn't done, building a real estate empire didn't seem part of the equation.

John G. Broussard and his wife – Berna*delle* – had held on to the house in Ladera Heights as well as three contiguous lots on West 156th Street in Watts. Maybe the chief's or his wife's parents' place, an inheritance.

Once again: no empire. If John G. was trading for something, it wasn't land. Unless he was embedded somewhere in Walt Obey's corporate acreage.

He ran searches on Melinda Waters and mother Eileen and came up empty, was thinking about what else to do when the records clerk came over and told him the building was closing. He left and drove up and down Temple Street, past the place where Pierce Schwinn had spotted Tonya Stumpf strutting. The block was a Music Center parking lot now, filled with its daytime load of municipal workers' and litigants' vehicles, owing to the Court Building down the street. Lots of people, lots of movement, but Milo felt out of it – out of the rhythm.

He drove toward home, slowly, not caring about rush-hour toxins, street-work delays, notably stupid driving by what seemed to be fifty percent of his fellow commuters. All the urban niceties that usually drove up his blood pressure and made him wonder why the hell he'd chosen to live like this.

He was sitting at a red light at Highland when his phone rang. Alex's voice said, 'I got you. Good.'

'What's up?'

'Maybe nothing, but my source – the woman Michael Larner molested – called me again, and I met with her last night. Seems the day Larner made his move on her, he was angry about Willie Burns. Enraged, talking to someone about Burns. Willie had been gone from Achievement House for a few days so it sounds like Larner found out who Burns was, was steamed because Burns disappeared.'

'Enraged,' said Milo.

'That's how she describes it. She walked into his office just as he got off the phone, said Larner was flushed and agitated. Then he composed himself and turned his attention to her. Which could be more than a coincidence. Harassers and rapists often get stoked by

241

anger. Anyway, it's probably no big deal, but it does fit with our working hypothesis: the Cossack family contracted Larner to hide Caroline until Janie Ingalls's murder cooled down. Burns made contact with Caroline, then split, and the family panicked. But they never found him, he even managed to slip away after his dope arrest, because Boris Nemerov bailed him out immediately. Four months later he ambushed Nemerov.'

'Interesting,' said Milo. 'Good work.' He summarized what he'd seen at Sangre de Leon last night.

'Big money,' said Alex. 'Same old story. One more thing: when I was looking for Melinda Waters on the Internet, I got a few hits but dismissed them. Then I realized maybe I'd been too hasty about one in particular. An attorney in Santa Fe, New Mexico, specializing in bankruptcy and evictions. I'd been thinking about Melinda as a stoned-out truant, didn't see a pathway from that to a legal career, but your comment about her turning up with a family and picket fence got me thinking, so I pulled up her website again and checked her bio. She's thirty-eight years old, which would be exactly our Melinda's age. And she didn't graduate college until she was thirty-one, law school till thirty-four. Before that, she worked as a paralegal for three years but her résumé still leaves the years between eighteen and twenty-eight unaccounted for. Which would mesh with someone going through changes, pulling her life together. And get this: she was schooled in California. San Francisco State for undergrad, Hastings for law.'

'Hastings is a top school,' said Milo. 'Bowie Ingalls described Melinda as a loser.'

'Bowie Ingalls was not a sterling judge. And people change. If I didn't believe that, I'd choose another profession.'

'Bankruptcy and eviction . . . I guess anything's possible.'

'Maybe she's not our gal, but don't you think it's worth looking into?'

'Anything else interesting in her bio?'

'No. Married, two kids. Do they have picket fences in Santa Fe? Not that hard to find out. It's a ninety-minute flight to Albuquerque, another hour by car to Santa Fe, and Southwest Airlines has cheap flights.'

'Calling her on the phone would be too easy,' said Milo.

'If she's trying to put her past behind her, she may lie. There's a flight at seven-forty-five tomorrow morning. I booked two seats.'

'Manipulative. I'm proud of you.'

'It's cold there,' said Alex. 'Twenty to forty Fahrenheit, some snow on the ground. So bundle up.'

twenty-five

By seven-fifteen, Milo and I were at the back of a long queue at the Southwest Airlines gate. The terminal was Ellis Island minus the overcoats – weary posture, worried eyes, language-soup.

'Thought we had our seats,' he said, eyeing the front of the line.

'We have electronic tickets,' I said. 'Southwest's system is you wait for your seat assignment. They board in groups, give you little plastic number tags.'

'Great . . . I'll take half a dozen bagels, a rye sliced thin, and two onion rolls.'

The flight was booked full and cramped, but amiable, populated by seasoned, mostly easygoing passengers and flight attendants who fancied themselves stand-up comedians. We arrived early on a tarmac specked with snow and turned our watches ahead one hour. Sunport Airport was low-profile and blessedly quiet, done up in earth tones, turquoise, and mock adobe, and riddled with talismanic hints of a decimated Indian culture.

We picked up a Ford Escort at the Budget desk, and I drove north on Highway 25 toward Santa Fe, feeling the wind buffet the tiny car. Snow – clean white fluff – was banked up along the side of the road, but the asphalt was plowed clear and the sky was bluer and bigger than I'd ever imagined and when I opened the window to test the air, I got a faceful of pure, sweet chill.

'Nice,' I said.

Milo grunted.

City sprawl, fast-food franchises, and Indian casinos gave way soon enough to long, low vistas of desert, bounded by the purplish tips of the Sangre de Cristo Mountains and that vast sky that just seemed to grow bigger.

'Gorgeous,' I said.

'Hey, look at this,' said Milo. 'Seventy-five-mile-an-hour speed limit. Put some weight on that pedal.'

As we neared Santa Fe, the highway climbed and the altitude registers increased steadily to seven thousand feet. I was speeding across the highest of deserts, no cactus or sandy desolation. The mountains were green where the snow had melted and so were the lowlands, bearded by wind-hardy, drought-tolerant *piñon* trees, ancient and ragged and low to the ground – Darwinian victors – and the occasional vertical statement of bare-branch aspens. Millions of trees, tipped with white, not a cloud in the sky. I wondered if Melinda Waters, Attorney-at-Law, had woken up thinking this was going to be a great day. Would we be a petty annoyance or an intrusion she'd never forget?

I took the Saint Francis exit to Cerrilos Road and continued through the southern part of Santa Fe, which seemed not much different from any other small city, with shopping centers and auto dealers and gas stations and the type of businesses that hug highways. Melinda Waters's office was listed on a street called Paseo de Peralta, and my reading of the map I'd grabbed at the rental counter put that right off Cerrilos. But the address numerals didn't check out and I followed the signs north to City Center and the Plaza and suddenly we were in a different world. Narrow, winding streets, some of them cobbled, forced me to reduce my speed as I rolled past diamond-bright, one-story adobe and Spanish colonial buildings plastered in sienna and peach and dun and gold. Pools of melting ice glistened like opals. The luxuriant trees that lined the road had managed to shrug off all but reminiscent flecks of snow, and through their branches streamed the sky's blue smile.

Different businesses filled the north side: art galleries, sculpture and glass studios, gourmet cookware emporia, purveyors of fine foods, high-fashion clothing and hand-hewn furniture, custom picture framers. Cafés and restaurants never tainted by corporate logos abounded, promising everything from Southwestern to sushi.

SUVs were the steeds of choice, and sinuous, happy people in jeans and suede and boots that had never known the kiss of manure crowded the sidewalks.

We reached the central plaza, a square of tree-shaded green set up with a bandstand and surrounded by low-rise shops, drove past a covered breezeway where a couple of dozen down-parkaed Indians sat behind blankets of silver jewelry near the Palace of the Governors. Across the square was a massive blocky structure of fieldstone that seemed more European than American. More restaurants and galleries, a couple of luxury hotels, and suddenly Paseo de Peralta had disappeared.

'Very pretty,' said Milo, 'but you're going in circles.'

At Washington Avenue, in the shadow of a salmon-pink Scottish Rite temple, I spotted a white-haired couple in matched shearling jackets walking an English sheepdog that could've supplied the garment's linings, and asked directions. The man wore a plaid cap, and the woman's hair was long and braided and gray and set off by silver butterflies. She wore the kind of makeup meant to convey no makeup at all, had crinkly eyes and a ready smile. When I showed her the address she chuckled.

'You want the northern part of Paseo de Peralta – it horseshoes at the Plaza. Herb, where's this address, exactly?'

The man shared her mirth. At least I'd made someone happy. 'Right there, my friend – just up the block.'

Melinda Waters's law office occupied one of eight suites in a sand-colored adobe building that abutted an Italian taverna. The restaurant's chimney billowed storybook puffs of smoke and cooking smells that got my salivary glands going. Then I thought about what lay ahead, and my appetites shifted.

The units faced a large, open parking lot backed by a high berm and an opaque stand of trees, as if the property – the town itself – terminated at a forest. We parked and got out. The air was frigid and perfect.

Each office had its own entrance. A wooden post hung with shingles served as a directory. Four other lawyers, a psychotherapist, a practitioner of therapeutic massage, an antiquarian book dealer, a print gallery. How far was Ojai?

Melinda Waters's door was unlocked and her front room smelled of incense. Big rust-and-wine-colored chenille chairs with fringed pillows were arranged around a battered old, blackwood Chinese table. Atop the table were art books, magazines that worshipped style, a brass bowl full of hard candy, and straw baskets of potpourri. Would any of that ease the pain of bankruptcy and eviction?

Blocking the rear door, a round-faced Indian woman of thirty or so sat behind a weathered oak desk and pecked at a slate gray laptop. She wore a pink sweatshirt and big, dangling earrings – geometric and hard-edged and gold, more New York than New Mexico. As we approached her desk, she looked up without conveying much in the way of emotion and continued typing.

'How can I help you?'

'Is Ms Waters in?'

'Do you have an appointment?'

'No, ma'am,' said Milo, producing his card.

'L.A.,' said the receptionist. 'The police. You've come all that way to talk to Mel.'

'Yes, ma'am.'

Her eyes scanned the card. 'Homicide.' No surprise. No inflection at all. She reached for the phone.

Melinda Waters was five-five, curvy and chunky and busty in a tailored, moss-green pantsuit turned greener by the wall of maroon-bound law books behind her. Her eyes were a lighter green edged with gray and her hair was honey-blond, cut short and swept back from a well-formed face softened by full lips and the beginnings of a double chin. Big, round tortoiseshell eyeglasses were perfectly proportioned for the thin, straight nose upon which they rested. Her lips were glossed, her manicure was impressive, and the diamond ring on her finger looked to be two carats, minimum.

She barely looked at us, gave off an air of bored competence, but seemed to be working at that. The moment I saw her my heart jumped. Same face as in the Hollywood High yearbook. Milo knew it, too. His expression was pleasant, but cherry-sized lumps had formed where his jaw met his sideburns.

Melinda Waters stared at his card and waved us into two

cane-backed chairs that faced her desk.

Her private office was rust-colored and small – tiny, really, with barely enough room for the bookcase and the desk and a red lacquer stand off to one side, set with a single white orchid in a blue-and-white pot. The walls perpendicular to the books were hung with watercolor landscapes – green hills above the ocean, live oaks, fields of poppies. California dreaming. The rest of the space bore family photos. Melinda Waters with a slim, tall, dark-bearded man and two mischievous-looking boys, around six and eight. Skiing, scuba diving, horseback riding, fishing. The family that plays together . . .

'Homicide detectives. Well, this is certainly different.' Soft voice, edged with sarcasm. Under normal circumstances, she was probably the image of professionalism, but a quaver at the tail end said she wasn't pretending this was routine.

'Different from what, ma'am?' said Milo.

'From what I thought I'd be doing right before lunch. Frankly, I'm confused. I'm not working on any L.A. cases at all, let alone homicide. I specialize in tenants' rights and financial—'

'Janie Ingalls,' said Milo.

Melinda Waters's sigh stretched for a very long time.

She fiddled with papers and pens, closed her laptop, tamped her hair. Finally, she punched an intercom button on her phone, and said, 'Hold my calls please, Inez.'

Wheeling her chair back the few inches that remained between her and the law book backdrop, she said, 'That's a name from a long time ago. What happened to her?'

'You don't know?'

'Well,' she said, 'your card says homicide, so am I safe in assuming?'

'Very safe.'

Melinda Waters removed her glasses, made a fist, knuckled one eye. The glossy lips trembled. 'Oh, damn. I suppose I knew it all along. But . . . I didn't really – damn. Poor Janie . . . that is so . . . obscene.'

'Very,' said Milo.

She sat up straighter, as if drawing upon a reserve of strength.

Now her eyes were different – searching, analytical. 'And you're here, after all this time, because . . . ?'

'Because it remains an open case, Ms Waters.'

'Open or reopened?'

'It was never closed, officially.'

'You're not saying the L.A. police have been working on this for twenty years?'

'Does that matter, ma'am?'

'No . . . I suppose not. I'm rambling . . . this is really . . . this takes me by total surprise. Why are you here?'

'Because you were one of the last people to see Janie Ingalls alive, but no one ever took your statement. In fact, it was only recently we learned you hadn't been a victim, yourself.'

'A victim? You thought . . . oh, my.'

'You've been hard to locate, Ms Waters. So has your mother—'

'My mother died ten years ago,' she said. 'Lung cancer, back in Pennsylvania, where she was from. Before that, she had emphysema. She suffered a lot.'

'Sorry to hear that.'

'So was I,' said Waters. She picked a gold pen from several resting in a cloisonné cup, balanced it between the index fingers of both hands. The office was a jewel box, everything arranged with care. 'All this time you really thought I might be . . . how strange.' Weak smile. 'So I'm reborn, huh?'

The pen dropped and clattered to the desk. She snatched it up, placed it back in the cup.

'Ma'am, could you please tell us everything you remember about that night.'

'I did try to find out where Janie was. Called her father – you've met him?'

'He's dead too, ma'am.'

'How'd he die?'

'Car accident.'

'Driving drunk?'

'Yes.'

'No surprise there,' said Waters. 'What a lowlife, always plastered. He couldn't stand me, and the feeling was mutual. Probably because I knew he'd grope me if he had a chance, so I never gave

249

him one – always made sure to meet Janie outside her building.'

'He came on to you?' said Milo.

'I never gave him a chance, but his intentions were obvious – leering, undressing me mentally. Plus, I knew what he'd done to Janie.'

'He abused Janie sexually?'

'Only when he was drunk,' said Waters, in mocking singsong. 'She never told me until shortly before she was . . . before I last saw her. I think what made her talk about it was she'd had a bad experience a month or so before that. She was hitching, got picked up by some deviant who took her to a hotel downtown, tied her up, had his way with her. When she first told me about it, she didn't seem very upset. Kind of blasé, really, and at first I didn't believe her because Janie was always making things up. Then she pulled up her jeans and her top and showed me the rope marks where he'd tied up her ankles and her wrists. Her neck, too. When I saw that, I said, "Jesus, he could've strangled you." And she just clammed up and refused to say any more about it.'

'What did she tell you about the man who did this?'

'That he was young and nice-looking and drove a great car – that's why she said she went with him. But to tell the truth, she probably would've gone with anyone. A lot of the time Janie was out of it – stoned or drunk. She didn't have much in the way of inhibitions.'

She removed her glasses, played with the sidepieces, glanced at the photos of her family. 'Some lawyer I am, running my mouth. Before we go any further, I need your assurance that anything I tell you will be kept confidential. My husband's a semipublic figure.'

'What does he do?'

'Jim's an aide to the governor. Liaison to the Highway Department. I keep my maiden name for work, but anything unsavory could still be traced back to him.'

'I'll do my best, ma'am.'

Waters shook her head. 'That's not good enough.' She stood. 'I'm afraid this meeting is adjourned.'

Milo crossed his legs. 'Ms Waters, all we came here for are your recollections about Janie Ingalls. No assumption was made of any criminal involvement on your part—'

'You bet your boots no assumption was made.' Waters jabbed a finger. 'That didn't even cross my mind, for God's sake. But what happened to Janie twenty years ago isn't my problem. Safeguarding my privacy is. Please leave.'

'Ms Waters, you know as well as I do that I can't guarantee confidentiality. That's the DA's authority. I'm being honest, and I'd appreciate the same from you. If you've done nothing wrong, you have nothing to worry about. And refusing to cooperate won't shield your husband. If I wanted to complicate his life, all I'd have to do is talk to my boss and he'd make a call, and . . .'

He showed her his palms.

Waters slapped her hands on her hips. Her stare was cold and steady. 'Why are you doing this?'

'In order to find out who murdered Janie Ingalls. You're right about one thing. It was obscene. She was tortured, burned with cigarettes, mutilat—'

'No, no, no! None of that shock treatment, give me some *credit*.'

Milo's palms pressed together. 'This has become needlessly adversarial, Ms Waters. Just tell me what you know, and I'll do my utmost to keep you out of it. That's the best I can offer. The alternative means a bit more overtime for me and a lot more complication for you.'

'You have no jurisdiction in New Mexico,' said Melinda Waters. 'Technically, you're trespassing.'

'Technically, you're still a material witness, and last time I checked New Mexico had diplomatic relations with California.'

Waters looked at her family again, sat back down, put her glasses back on, mumbled, 'Shit.'

The three of us sat in silence for a full minute before she said, 'This isn't fair. I'm not proud of the kind of kid I was back then, and I'd like to forget it.'

I said, 'We've all been teenagers.'

'Well, I was a *rotten* teenager. A total screwup and a stoner, just like Janie. That's what drew us together. Bad behavior – Jesus, I don't think a day went by when we weren't getting loaded. And . . . other things that give me a migraine when I think about them. But I pulled myself out of it – in fact, the process *started* the day after Janie and I split up.'

'At the party?' said Milo.

Waters grabbed for another pen, changed her mind, played with a drawer-pull – lifting the brass and letting it drop, once, twice, three times.

She said, 'I've got kids of my own now. I set limits, am probably too strict because I know what's out there. In ten years, I haven't touched anything stronger than Chardonnay. I love my husband. He's going places. My practice is rewarding – I don't see why any of that should be derailed because of mistakes I made twenty years ago.'

'Neither do I,' said Milo. 'I'm not taking notes, and none of that goes in any file. I just want to know what happened to Janie Ingalls that Friday night. And anything else you can tell me about the man who raped her downtown.'

'I told you everything I know about him.'

'Young and nice-looking with a nice car.'

'The car could've been Janie's fantasy.'

'How young?'

'She didn't say.'

'Race?'

'I assume he was white, because Janie didn't say he wasn't. And she would've. She was a bit of a racist – got it from her father.'

'Any other physical description?'

'No.'

'A fancy car,' said Milo. 'What kind?'

'I think she said a Jaguar, but I can't be sure. With fur rugs – I do remember that because Janie talked about how her feet sank into the rug. But with Janie, who knows? I'm trying to tell you: she was always fantasizing.'

'About what?'

'Mostly about getting loaded and partying with rock stars.'

'That ever happen?'

She laughed. 'Not hardly. Janie was a sad little girl from the wrong part of Hollywood.'

'A young guy with a Jaguar,' said Milo. 'What else?'

'That's all I know,' said Waters. 'Really.'

'Which hotel did he take her to?'

'She just said it was downtown, in an area full of bums. She also

252

said the guy seemed to know the place – the desk clerk tossed him a key the moment he walked in. But she didn't think he was actually staying there because the room he took her to didn't look lived in. He wasn't keeping any clothes there, and the bed wasn't even covered. Just a mattress. And rope. He'd put the rope in a dresser drawer.'

'She didn't try to escape when she saw that?'

Waters shook her head. 'He gave her a joint on the ride over. A huge one, high-grade, maybe laced with hash, because she was really floating and that's what hash usually did to her. She told me the whole experience was like watching someone else. Even when he pushed her down on the bed and started tying her up.'

'Her arms and legs and her neck.'

'That's where the marks were.'

'What happened next?'

Anger flashed behind Waters's eyeglass lenses. 'What do you think? He did his thing with her. Used every orifice.'

'She said that?'

'In cruder terms.' The gray in her eyes had deepened, as if an internal light had been dampened. 'She said she knew what he was doing, but didn't even feel it.'

'And she was blasé about it.'

'At first she was. Later – a few days later – she got loaded on Southern Comfort and started talking about it again. Not crying. Angry. At herself. Do you know what *really* bugged her? Not so much what he did to her, she was out of it during the whole thing. What made her mad was that when he was finished, he didn't drive her all the way back home, just dropped her off in East Hollywood and she had to walk a couple of miles. *That* ticked her off. But even there, she blamed herself. Said something along the lines of, "It must be something about me, makes people treat me like that. Even *him*." I said, "Who's him?" and she got this really furious look on her face, and said, *"Him.* Bowie." *That* freaked me out – first the deviant, now incest. I asked her how long that had been going on, but she clammed up again. I kept nagging her to tell me, and finally she told me to shut up or she'd tell my mother what a slut I was.'

She laughed.

'Which was a viable threat. I was no poster child for wholesome living. And even though my mother was no Betty Crocker, she wasn't like Bowie, she would've cared. She would've come down on me, hard.'

'Bowie didn't care,' said Milo.

'Bowie was scum, total lowlife. I guess that explains why Janie would do anything to avoid going home.'

I thought of the bareness of Janie's room. Said, 'Did she have a crash pad, or somewhere else she stayed?'

'Nowhere permanent. She'd sleep at my house, crash once in a while in those abandoned apartments north of Hollywood Boulevard. Sometimes she'd be gone for days and wouldn't tell me where she'd been. Still, the day after the party, after Janie and I had split up, I called Bowie. I *despised* the ground that lowlife walked on, but even so, I wanted to know Janie was okay. That's what I was trying to tell you: I made an attempt. But no one answered.'

'When did you split up?'

'Soon after we got there. I *cared* about Janie. We were both so screwed up, that was our bond. I guess I had a bad feeling about the party – about her just disappearing in the middle of all that commotion. I never really forgot about her. Years later, when I was in college and learned how to use a computer, I tried to find her. Then after I got to law school and had access to legal databases, I tapped into all kinds of municipal records. California and the neighboring states. Property rolls, tax files, death notices. But she was nowhere—'

She picked up Milo's card. 'L.A. Homicide means she was murdered in L.A. So why wasn't an L.A. death notice ever filed?'

'Good question, ma'am.'

'Oh,' said Waters. She sat back. 'This is more than a reopened case, isn't it? Something got really screwed up.'

Milo shrugged.

'Great. Wonderful. This is going to suck me in and screw me up no matter what I do, isn't it?'

'I'll do my best to prevent that, ma'am.'

'You sound almost sincere.' She rubbed her forehead, took a bottle of Advil out of a desk drawer, extricated a tablet, and swallowed it dry. 'What else do you want from me?'

'The party,' said Milo. 'How'd you and Janie hear about it, for starters.'

'Just street talk, kids talking. There was always plenty of that, especially as the weekend approached. Everyone trying to figure out the best way to party hearty. So many of us hated our homes, would do anything to be away. Janie and I were a twosome, party-wise. Sometimes we'd end up at squat-raves – promoters sneaking into an abandoned building, or using an outdoors spot – some remote corner of Griffith Park, or Hansen Dam. We're talking bare minimum in terms of entertainment: some tone-deaf band playing for free, cheap munchies, lots of drugs. *Mostly* lots of drugs. Because the promoters were really dealers, and their main goal was bulk sales. Other times, though, it would turn out to be a real party, in someone's house. An open invitation, or even if it wasn't, there was usually no problem crashing.'

She smiled. 'Occasionally, we got bounced, but a girl could almost always crash and get away with it.'

'The party that night was one of those,' said Milo. 'Someone's house.'

'Someone's *big* house, a mansion, and the talk on the street was *mucho* drugs. Janie and I figured we'd check it out. To us a trip to Bel Air was like blasting off to a different planet. Janie was going on and on about partying with rich kids, maybe finding a rich boyfriend who'd give her all the dope she wanted. As I said, she loved to fantasize. The truth is we were both such losers, no wheels, no money. So we did what we always did: hitched. We didn't even have the address, guessed once we got to Bel Air we'd figure it out. I picked Janie up at her place Friday afternoon, and we hung out on Hollywood Boulevard most of the day – playing arcade games, shoplifting cosmetics, panhandling for spare change but we didn't get much. After dark, we walked back down to Sunset where the best hitching was, but the first corner we tried was near some hookers and they threatened to cut our asses, so we moved west – between La Brea and Fairfax, where all the guitar stores are. I remember that, because while we waited for a ride, we were looking at guitars in windows and saying how cool it would be if we started a girl band and got rich. No matter that neither of us had a lick of talent. Anyway, finally – we must've been waiting there over an hour – we got picked up.'

'What time?' said Milo.

'Must've been nine, ten.'

'Who picked you up?'

'A college student – nerdy type, said he went to Caltech, but he was heading to the U because he had a date with a girl there and that was really close to Bel Air. *He* had to tell us that, because we had no idea – I don't think either of us had ever been west of La Cienega, unless we were taking the bus straight to the beach, or, in my case, when I visited my father at the Navy base in Point Mugu. The nerd was a nice guy. Shy, probably picked us up on impulse and regretted it. Because we immediately started hassling him – turning the radio to our station, blasting it loud, teasing him – flirting. Asking him if he wanted to come to the party with us instead of some lame date with a college girl. Being real obnoxious. He got embarrassed, and that cracked us up. Also, we were hoping he might take us all the way to the party, because we still had no idea where it was. So we kept nagging him, but he said no, he liked his girlfriend. I remember Janie getting really rude about that, saying something to the effect of "She's probably colder than ice. I can give you something she can't." That was the *wrong* thing to say. He stopped the car at Stone Canyon and Sunset and ordered us out. I started to, but Janie held me back, started ragging on him to take us to the house, and that just made him angrier. Janie was like that, she could be extremely pushy, had a real talent for getting on people's nerves. The nerd started shouting and shoved Janie and we got out and she flipped him off as he drove away.'

'Stone Canyon and Sunset. Close to the party.'

'*We* didn't know that. We were ignorant. And drunk. Back on the boulevard, we'd also boosted a bottle of Southern Comfort, had guzzled our way through most of it. I hated the stuff, to me it tasted like peaches and cough syrup. But Janie loved it. It was her favorite high. She said it was what Janis Joplin had been into and she was into Janis Joplin because she had some idea that her mom had been like Janis Joplin, back in the hippie days. That she'd named Janie after Janis.'

'Another fantasy,' I said.

She nodded. 'She needed them. Her mom abandoned her – ran

away with a black guy when Janie was five or six, and Janie never saw her again. Maybe that's another reason Janie always made racist comments.'

Milo said, 'What'd the two of you do after you were dropped off?'

'Started walking up Stone Canyon and promptly got lost. There were no sidewalks, and the lighting was very bad. And no one was around to ask directions. All those incredible properties and not a soul in sight, none of the noises you hear in a real neighborhood. It was spooky. But we were having fun with it – an adventure. Once we saw a Bel Air Patrol car driving our way, so we hid behind some trees.'

She frowned. 'Complete idiocy. Thank God my boys aren't hearing this.'

'How'd you find the party?'

'We walked in circles for a while, finally ended up right where we started, back at Sunset. And that's when the second car picked us up. A Cadillac, turning onto Stone Canyon. The driver was a black guy, and I was sure Janie wouldn't want to get in – with her it was always "nigger" this, "nigger" that. But when the guy rolled down the window and shot us this big grin, and said, "You girls looking to party?" Janie was the first one in.'

'What do you remember about the driver?'

'Early twenties, tall, thin – for some reason when I think of him I always think of Jimi Hendrix. Not that he was Hendrix's spitting image, but there was a general resemblance. He had that rangy, mellow thing going on, loose and confident. Played his music really loud and moving his head in time.'

'A Cadillac,' said Milo.

'And a newer one but not a pimpmobile. Big conservative sedan, well taken care of, too. Shiny, fresh-smelling – sweet-smelling. Lilacs. Like it belonged to an old woman. I remember thinking that, wondering if he'd stolen it from an old woman. Because he sure didn't match the car, dressed the way he was in this ugly denim suit with rhinestones all over it, all these gold chains.'

'What color?'

'Something pale.'

Milo opened his briefcase, removed Willie Burns's mug shot, handed it across the desk.

Melinda Waters's eyes got big. 'That's him. *He's* the one who killed Janie?'

'He's someone we're looking for.'

'He's still out there?'

'Maybe.'

'Maybe? What does *that* mean?'

'It's been twenty years, and he was a heroin addict.'

'You're saying he'd have a poor life expectancy,' she said. 'But you're still looking for him . . . why *has* Janie's murder been reopened? What's the real reason?'

'I was the original detective on the case,' said Milo. 'I got transferred off. Now, I've been transferred back on.'

'Transferred back on by your department or you requested it yourself?' said Waters.

'Does it matter, ma'am?'

She smiled. 'It's personal, isn't it? You're trying to undo your own past.'

Milo smiled back, and Waters returned the mug shot. 'Wilbert Burns. So now I have a name.'

'He never introduced himself?'

'He called himself our new friend. I knew he was a junkie as well as a dealer. From how spacey he was – slurring his words. Driving *really* slow. His music was junkie music – slow jazz, this really draggy trumpet. Janie tried to change the station, but he put his hand on hers and she didn't try again.'

'How'd you know he was a dealer?' said Milo.

'He showed us his wares. Carried one of those men's purses and had it on the seat next to him. When we got in, he put it in his lap and after we were driving for a while, he zipped it open, and said, "How about a taste of something sweet, ladies?" Inside were envelopes of pills and little baggies full of white stuff – I couldn't tell you if it was coke or heroin. *That* stuff I stayed away from. For me it was just grass and alcohol, once in a while acid.'

'What about Janie?'

'Janie had no boundaries.'

'Did she sample Burns's wares?'

'Not in the car, but maybe later. Probably later. Because she and Burns got something going on right from the beginning. All three of us were in the front seat, Janie alongside Burns and me next to the door. The minute he started driving she started in – flipped her hair in his face, rested her hand on his leg, started moving it up.'

'How'd Burns react to that?'

'He loved it. Said, "Ooh, baby," stuff like that. Janie was giggling, both of them were laughing at nothing in particular.'

'Despite her racism,' I said.

'I couldn't believe it. I elbowed her a couple of times, as in, "What's going on?" But she ignored me. Burns drove to the party – he knew exactly where it was, but we had to park up the road because there were so many cars there.'

'Did he say anything about the party?' said Milo.

'He said he knew the people throwing it, that they were rich but cool, it was going to be the finest of the fine. Then, when we got there, he said something along the lines of, "Maybe the President'll show up." Because the house had huge pillars, like the White House. Janie thought that was hilarious. I was pretty put out by then, felt like Janie was shutting me out.'

'What happened next?'

'We went inside the house. It was vacant and rancid-smelling and pretty much trashed, with beer cans and bottles and Lord knows what else all over the place. Kids running around everywhere, no band, just loud tapes – a bunch of different stereos set up all over the place, really cacophonous, but no one seemed to care. Everyone was blasted, kids were walking around looking dazed, bumping into each other, girls were on their knees, going down on guys right in the middle of the dance floor, there'd be couples dancing and right next to them, other couples would be screwing, getting kicked, stepped on. Burns seemed to know a lot of people, got plenty of high fives as we walked through the crowd. Then this funny-looking, kind of dumpy girl showed up out of nowhere and latched on to him.'

'Funny-looking how?'

'Short, fat, zits. Odd – spaced-out. But he immediately got all kissy-kissy with her, and I could see Janie didn't like that.' Waters shook her head. 'She'd known the guy all of fifteen minutes, and she was jealous.'

'Janie do anything about that?'

'No, she just got this ticked-off look on her face. I could read it because I knew Janie. Burns didn't see it – or he didn't care. Threw one arm around the dumpy girl, the other around Janie, and led both of them off. That little purse of his bouncing on his shoulder.'

'And you?'

'I stayed behind. Someone handed me a beer and hands started groping me. Not delicately. It was dark, and whoever was doing it started to get rough, yanking at my clothes. I broke away, started walking around, looked for a quiet room to mellow out in, but there was none. Every inch of that place was party-time. Guys kept putting their hands all over me, once in a while someone would pull me hard onto the dance floor and rather than fight it, I'd just dance for a while, then make my escape. Then the lights went out and the house got even darker and I could barely see where I was stepping. The Southern Comfort in my system wasn't helping, either. I felt nauseous, dizzy, wanted to get out of there, looked some more for Janie, couldn't find her, and got angry at her for bailing on me. Finally, I told myself *forget* her and the next time someone pulled me onto a dance floor, I danced for a while. And when someone offered me a pill, I swallowed it. The next thing I remember is waking up on the floor of an upstairs bathroom, hearing shouts that the cops were going to roust the party and running out of there along with everyone else – it was like a stampede. Somehow I ended up in the back of someone's truck, bouncing along Sunset.'

'Whose truck?'

'A bunch of guys. Surfer types. They ended up at the beach, Santa Monica or Malibu, I couldn't tell you which. We partied some more, and I fell asleep on the sand. The next morning, I woke up and I was alone. Cold and wet and sick to my stomach. The sun was rising over the ocean and I suppose it was gorgeous but all I could think about was how lousy I felt. Then I thought about my father – stationed up at Mugu – and I started crying and got it into my head that I had to go see him. It took me four hitches to get up there and when I reached the base the sentry wouldn't let me through the gate. I started crying again. It had been a long time since I'd seen my dad. He'd remarried, and his new wife hated me. Or at least that's what my mother was always telling me. Whatever the truth was, he'd pretty much stopped calling. I bawled like a baby, and the sentry made a call and told me my dad wasn't there, he'd shipped out to Turkey three days before. I just broke down and I guess the sentry felt sorry for me because he gave me all the money in his pocket – thirty-three dollars and forty-nine cents.' She smiled. 'That I remember precisely.'

Reaching under her glasses, she fingered the inside corners of her eyes. 'Finally, someone was being nice to me. I never thanked him, never knew his name. Walked back to PCH, stuck out my thumb, caught a ride with some Mexicans heading over to Ventura to pick cabbage, just kept thumbing my way up the coast. My first stop was Santa Cruz, and I stayed there a while because it was beautiful and there was this retro-hippie thing going on, plenty of free food and parks to sleep in. Eventually, I moved on to San Francisco, Crescent City, Oregon, Seattle, back down to Sacramento. The next ten years are kind of a blur. Finally, I got it together – you don't want to know the boring details.'

'Like I said, we want to maintain your privacy.'

Melinda Waters laughed. 'Thanks for the thought.'

twenty-six

Milo asked her a few more questions – more gently, unproductively – then we left her sitting at her desk looking dazed. As I drove out of the lot, the smoke from the Italian restaurant's chimney caught my eye.

'Want lunch?' I said.

'I guess . . . yeah, why not.'

'No fast food, though. Let's aim high. We deserve it.'

'For what?'

'Making some progress.'

'You think so?'

The taverna across the street was divided into four small, white-washed rooms, each warmed by a beehive-shaped fireplace and topped by low ceilings striped with rough-hewn logs. We ordered beer, a mixed antipasto, spaghetti with capers and olives and garlic, and osso bucco from a lithe, young woman who seemed genuinely happy to serve us.

When she left, Milo said, 'Progress.'

'We can place Janie with Willie Burns and Caroline Cossack the night of the murder. You don't have doubts she was the dumpy girl, do you?'

He shook his head.

I said, 'Melinda's story also supplies a possible motive: jealousy. Caroline had a thing for Burns, thought Janie was moving in on her territory.'

'The eternal triangle leading to *that*?'

'The eternal triangle combined with dope and psychopathology and a low-inhibition party scene and Janie's racism. No shortage of

262

triggers. And something else fits: Janie's murder presented as a sadistic sex killing and we've been wondering why other victims haven't shown up. Because cold, sexual sadists don't quit. But if the murder resulted from a passion-of-the-moment flare-up, a sole victim would make sense.'

'Janie in the wrong place at the wrong time.'

'Melinda's description of Janie makes her the perfect victim: drugged-out, not too bright, prone to fantasy, a tendency to irritate people, a history of sexual abuse. Throw enough ingredients into the stew, toss in a few careless "niggers," and who knows.'

'What do you think about Janie's blasé reaction to the downtown rape?'

'Doesn't surprise me,' I said. 'People expect rape victims to react the way they do on TV. And sometimes that happens. But pseudo-calm is pretty common. Protective numbness. Given Janie's victimization by her father, it makes perfect sense.'

'For her it woulda been more of the same,' he said. 'Poor kid.'

He picked at his food, slid his plate away. 'There's a discrepancy between Janie's description of the rape as Melinda remembers it and what Schwinn told me. According to Melinda, the rapist dropped Janie off a couple of miles from her home. Schwinn's informant told *him* Janie'd been dumped in an alley and found unconscious by some wino.'

'That could've been Janie prettying up the picture,' I said. 'Grasping for a shred of dignity.'

'Pathetic,' he said.

'Any idea who Schwinn's informant was?'

'Nope. He never gave me a single bit of insider info. I kept waiting for him to clue me in, to help me learn the ropes, but we just went from call to call and when the time came for paperwork, he went home. And now here he is, pulling strings from the grave . . . If Janie made up the part about walking home, maybe the young guy in a Jag was bogus, too. Her not wanting to admit he was a drooling, scabby hunchback in a jalopy? The alleged wino.'

'Could be. But if she was being truthful, the Jag story's interesting. A young guy with hot wheels checking into a fleabag hotel wouldn't be safe. Unless he had connections. As in Daddy owns the place. And Janie told Melinda the clerk seemed to know the guy. It

263

might be interesting to know who held the deed on fleabag hotels twenty years ago.'

'You're thinking some real estate honcho. The Cossacks. Or Larner.' He told me about Playa del Sol, rubbed his face. 'I remember a few of the hotels down there. The scuzziest ones were on or near Main, between Third and Seventh. SRO flops, full of winos. The Exeter, the Columbus – there must've been a good half dozen, mostly propped up by Federal subsidies . . . so now I'm supposed to solve a twenty-year-old rape with no victim as well as a murder. Don't think so, Alex.'

'Just tossing out suggestions,' I said. 'Isn't that what you pay me for?'

He forced a smile. 'Sorry. I'm feeling hemmed in. Unable to do my usual investigative thing because it puts me in the crosshairs.'

'Paris Bartlett and the call from Personnel.'

'And the level of the players. That dinner with Obey, I don't imagine they were convening to crochet samplers. Bacilla and Horne live for graft, and if Walt Obey's involved in something, it has lots of zeros attached to it. Broussard wasn't at the restaurant, but his hand's been in this right from the beginning. He's Obey's neighbor, and Obey was one of his biggest supporters. All that makes me a *flea*. And guess what: a rumor's circulating around the department about an HIV-positive detective about to retire soon. "Stay healthy," huh?'

'Oh my,' I said. 'Subtle.'

'Cop's subtlety. We train with nightsticks, not scalpels. Looks like I couldn't have picked a worse time to stir the ashes, Alex. The hell of it is I've accomplished nothing . . . you finished? Let's get back to the smog. This city's too damn pretty.'

During the drive back to Albuquerque, he was glum and unreachable. The taverna's food had been excellent, but I'd finished more of my plate than he had, and that was a first.

He spent the flight to L.A. dozing. When we were back in the Seville, he said, 'Finding Melinda was progress in terms of motive, means, and opportunity. But what the hell's all that worth when I have no idea where my suspects are? If I had to bet, my money would be on Willie Burns in some unmarked grave. The money folks behind Caroline would have seen him as a threat, and even if they never got to him, there was his heroin habit. Crazy Caroline, who could also be dead, or anywhere from the Bahamas to Belize. Even if I found her, what could I prove? They'd bring in one of your colleagues, and she'd go right back to some plush-padded room.'

'Sounds bleak,' I said.

'Some therapist you are.'

'Reality therapy.'

'Reality is the curse of the sane.'

I took Sepulveda to Venice, got onto Motor Avenue going south, drove past Achievement House.

'Talk about subtle,' he said.

'It's a shortcut.'

'There are no shortcuts. Life is tedious and brutish . . . it can't hurt to look into those SROs. Something I can do without attracting attention. But don't expect anything. And don't get *yourself* in trouble thinking you can fight my battles.'

'Trouble, as in?'

'As in anything.'

Robin had left a message on my machine, sounding hurried and detached. The tour had moved on to Vancouver and she was staying at the Pacific Lodge Hotel. I called the number and connected to her room. A happy male voice answered.

'Sheridan,' I said.

'Yes?'

'It's Alex Delaware.'

'Oh. Hi. I'll go get Robin.'

'Where is she?'

'In the bathroom.'

'How's my dog?'

'Uh . . . great—'

'The reason I'm asking is because you seemed pretty in tune with him. Showing up prepared with a Milk-Bone. Very intuitive.'

'He – I like dogs.'

'Do you?' I said.

'Well, yeah.'

265

'Well, good for you.'

Silence. 'Let me tell Robin you're on the phone.'

'Gee, thanks,' I said, but he'd put down the receiver, and I was talking to dead air.

She came on the line a few moments later. 'Alex?'

'Hi,' I said.

'What's wrong?'

'With what?'

'Sheridan said you sounded upset.'

'Sheridan would know,' I said. 'Being a sensitive guy and all that.'

Silence. 'What's going on, Alex?'

'Nothing.'

'It's not nothing,' she said. 'Every time I call you're more . . .'

'Insensitive?' I said. 'As opposed to you-know-who?'

Longer silence. 'You can't be serious.'

'About what?'

'About *him*.' She laughed.

'Glad to amuse you.'

'Alex,' she said, 'if you only knew – I can't believe this. What's gotten into you?'

'Tough times bring out the best in me.'

'Why in the world would you even think that?' She laughed again, and that was probably what set me off.

'The guy shows up with a damned dog biscuit,' I said. 'Let me tell you, hon, men are pigs. Altruism like that always comes with strings—'

'You are being totally *ridiculous*—'

'Am I? Each time I call your room, he's right there—'

'Alex, this is *absurd*!'

'Okay, then. Sorry.' But there was nothing remorseful in my tone, and she knew it.

'What's gotten into you, Alex?'

I thought about that. Then a rush of anger clogged my throat, and out it came: 'I suppose I can be forgiven a bit of absurdity. The last time you left me didn't turn out so great.'

Silence.

'Oh . . . Alex.' Her voice broke on my name.

266

My jaw locked.

She said, 'I can't do this.'

Then she hung up.

I sat there, perversely satisfied, with a dead brain and a mouth full of bile. Then that sinking feeling set in: *Idiot, idiot!* I redialed her room. No answer. Tried the hotel operator again, was informed that Ms Castagna had gone out.

I pictured her running through the lobby, tear-streaked. What was the weather in Vancouver? Had she remembered her coat? Had Sheridan followed, ever ready with consolation?

'Sir?' said the operator. '*Would* you like her voice mail?'

'Uh . . . sure, why not.'

I was connected, listened to Robin's voice deliver a canned message. Waited for the beep.

Chose my words carefully, but ended up choking and letting the phone drop from my hand.

I moved to my office, drew the drapes, sat in gray-brown darkness, listened to the throbbing in my head.

A fine fix you've gotten yourself into, Alexander . . . the hell of it was Bert Harrison had warned me.

Bert was a wise man. Why hadn't I listened?

What to do . . . send flowers? No, that would insult Robin's intelligence, make matters worse.

Two tickets to Paris . . .

It took a long time before I was able to shove my feelings somewhere south of my ankles, turn suitably numb.

I stared at the wall, visualized myself as a speck of dirt, worked hard at disappearing.

I booted up the computer and downloaded Google, because that search engine could locate a hamburger joint on Pluto.

'Walter Obey' pulled up three hundred and some-odd hits, 90 percent of them pertaining to the billionaire, with a quarter of those repetitive. Most were newspaper and business journal articles, about evenly divided between coverage of Obey's philanthropic activities and his financial dealings.

Walter and Barbara Obey had contributed to the Philharmonic, the Music Center, Planned Parenthood, the Santa Monica Mountains Conservancy, the Humane Society, shelters for homeless youth, a slew of foundations raging battle against tragic diseases. The Sierra Club, too, which I found interesting for a developer.

I came up with no connection to organized sports nor to any link between any of the aborted plans to bring sports teams to L.A. In none of the articles was Obey's name mentioned alongside those of the Cossack brothers or the Larners. He and his wife socialized very little and lived an understated life – for billionaires. A single, albeit baronial, residence in Hancock Park, no live-in help, off-the-rack clothing, no expensive hobbies. Barbara drove a Volvo and volunteered at her church. If the press could be believed, both Obeys were as wholesome as milk.

One item, a year-old *Wall Street Journal* piece, did catch my eye: one of Obey's development companies, a privately held corporation named Advent Builders, had invested in a huge parcel of land south of the L.A. city limits – an unincorporated county area where the developer planned to build an entire community, complete with ethnically diverse, low-to-middle-income housing, public schools, well-landscaped commercial districts and industrial parks, 'comprehensive recreational facilities.'

Obey had taken ten years to accumulate fifteen thousand acres of contiguous lots and had spent millions to rid the earth of toxic waste left behind by a long-defunct county power depot. Unlike other empire-builders, he'd considered the environmental impact of his projects from the beginning, was out to crown his career with something culturally significant.

The new city was to be named Esperanza – Spanish for 'hope.'

I combined 'Esperanza' with each of the Cossack brothers' names and the Larners but came up with nothing. Tossing John G. Broussard into the mix proved no more fruitful. I tried 'Advent Properties' and 'Advent.' Still nothing on the Cossacks and the Larners, but a back-page construction journal article informed me that L.A.'s police chief had been hired as a security consultant to the Esperanza project. Broussard, hamstrung by city regulations, was working for free, but private shares in Advent had been gifted to the chief's wife and his only child, daughter, Joelle, a corporate attorney with a white-shoe downtown firm.

Broussard hadn't shown up at the private dinner but Milo's hunch was right on: the chief's hand was in everything.

The bitter aftertaste of my bad behavior with Robin kept rising like vomitus as I worked hard at concentrating on Obey and Broussard and the others and wondering what it could possibly mean.

'Comprehensive recreational facilities' could mean playgrounds for kids, or it was a buzzword for bringing pro football back to the L.A. environs.

Billionaire with a big dream – I could see that being the crowning glory of Obey's long career. And it made good sense to place the top cop on your masthead.

But if the PR about Obey's righteous mien and the size of his personal fortune was accurate, why would he waste time with the Cossacks, who alienated their neighbors and couldn't seem to get any projects off the ground? And in the case of the Larners, the association would be even more hazardous – they were outright hustlers tainted by the Playa del Sol debacle.

Unless Obey's balance sheets weren't as glowing as the press believed, and he needed financial backup for his dream. Even billionaires could lose sight of assets and debits, and Obey had spent a decade buying up land and financing and detoxifying his holdings without a single spadeful of Esperanza dirt dug.

Big dreams often meant cataclysmic problems.

I switched to several financial databases and probed for thorns in Obey's numerous gardens. At least seven separate corporations were listed under his leadership, including Advent. But only one outfit was publicly traded, a commercial leasing company named BWO Financing.

BWO. Probably stood for Barbara and Walt Obey. Homey. From everything I could tell, the company was doing great, with common stock trading at 95 percent of its high, preferred units paying consistent dividends, and solid ratings from Standard & Poor.

Still, Wall Street's top analysts had been known to be caught with their pin-striped trousers around their ankles, because, at root, they were dependent upon what companies told them. And because their interests lay in selling stock.

Was Obey's empire teetering and had he sought out the Cossacks and the Larners for support? Did the Cossacks and the Larners have enough to offer Obey?

Bacilla and Horne's involvement was puzzling. Obey's planned city was located outside city limits, so what use could a pair of councilmen be?

Unless plans had changed and the focus had shifted back to downtown.

Nothing really sat right. Then I thought of the cement that held it all together:

John G. Broussard's aid in covering up the Ingalls murder implied he'd had connections to the Cossacks and maybe the Larners. Walt Obey was one of the chief's major patrons. Maybe Broussard had put them all together, earned himself a big fat finder's fee in addition to the private stock assigned to his wife and daughter.

Had the chief concealed a substantial lump sum payment from public scrutiny? With Obey's multiple corporations as shield, concealing cash would've been easy enough.

Payoff. Payback. For all his power and status, John G. Broussard remained a civil servant whose salary and pension by themselves would relegate him to upper-middle-class status, at best. Playing with the big boys could mean so much more.

I imagined the deal: Walt Obey salvaging his dream, the Cossacks and the Larners offered a big-time social and economic leap upward, from strip malls and parking lots to the grandest of monuments.

For Chief Broussard and the councilmen, good old cash.

So much at stake.

And now Milo had the opportunity to blow it all to smithereens.

twenty-seven

'Interesting theory,' said Milo. 'I was wondering along the same lines, except that night Obey's body language was more grantor than grantee. Bacilla and Horne were kissing up to him big-time.'

I said, 'Bacilla and Horne would be supplicants any way you look at it because their political life depends on fat cats. And Obey's been alpha-dog with politicians for a long time. But you never had a chance to watch him interact with the Cossacks.'

'No,' he admitted.

We were at his kitchen table. I'd spent a miserable hour mulling how to mend things with Robin, had made another attempt to reach her at the hotel. Out. When I reached Milo he was on the way home from the Hall of Records with a briefcase full of photocopies. He'd combed through the property tax files and found fourteen fleabag hotels operating near Skid Row twenty years ago, but no ownership by the Cossacks or any of the other players.

'So much for that.' I scanned the tax roster he'd spread out between us. Then a name jumped out at me. A trio of Central Avenue hotels – the Excelsior, the Grande Royale, the Crossley – owned by Vance Coury and Associates.

'A kid by the name of Coury hung out with the Cossacks and Brad Larner back in high school,' I said. 'They all belonged to some club called the King's Men.'

'Coury,' he said. 'Never heard of him.'

He brought his laptop over from the laundry room office. A search yielded three hits on two men named Vance Coury. An eleven-year-old *Times* piece described a Vance Coury, sixty-one, of Westwood, as having been brought up by the city attorney on slumlord charges. Coury was described as 'the owner of several

271

buildings in the downtown and Westlake districts who had failed repeatedly to correct numerous building and safety violations.' One year prior to his indictment, Coury had been convicted of similar charges and sentenced, by a creative judge, to live in one of his own buildings for two weeks. He'd rehabbed a single unit in two days and set up housekeeping under protection by an armed guard. But Coury's empathy quotient hadn't risen a notch: he'd done nothing to improve his tenants' living conditions, and the judge lost patience. A follow-up article three weeks later reported that Coury had avoided a felony trial by collapsing in his attorney's office and dying of a stroke. An accompanying headshot showed a rail-thin, silver-haired, silver-bearded man with the defiant/frightened eyes of one scrambling to remember his latest tall tale.

Vance Coury, Jr, appeared in a two-year-old Sunday *Daily News* item, having contributed the custom paint job to the winning entry in a California hot rod contest. Coury, forty-two, owned an auto body shop in Van Nuys specializing in 'ground-up restoration of classic and specialty vehicles,' and his outfit had sprayed forty-five coats on a chopped and blown 1938 Dodge Roadster known as the Purple People Eater.

'Another father and son duo,' said Milo.

'Father owns the hotel, son makes use of the premises,' I said. 'And son was a pal of the Cossacks. Meaning he might very well have been at that party. Which turns the prism a whole new way. What if it went down this way: Janie separated from Melinda and tagged along with Burns and Caroline. Burns gave her some dope, introduced her to some of his rich-kid pals. All of a sudden, Janie finds herself face to face with Vance Coury, the Prince Charming who tied her up and raped her and dumped her in an alley like garbage. She freaks out, there's an altercation, and Coury, maybe with a little help from his friends, spirits Janie away before she can cause a scene. They subdue her and bring her somewhere secluded, and Coury thinks, hmm, why not take advantage of the situation? We know he's into bondage, and what would be more arousing than helplessness? He does his thing, and this time the others join in. It gets out of hand, goes really bad. Now they need to dump the body. Because of his father's properties, Coury's familiar with downtown, and he picks a spot he knows is quiet and relatively deserted late at night: the Beaudry on-ramp. He takes a buddy or two along, which would explain taking the risk of leaving Janie out in the open. With one person as lookout and to help with the body, the danger would've been minimized.'

Milo stared at the tax roster and placed his finger on Coury's name. 'Boys being boys. The Cossack brothers themselves, not just Caroline.'

'Them, Coury, Brad Larner, maybe the other members of the King's Men – I think their names were Chapman and Hansen.'

'A high school club.'

'A party club,' I said. 'Noted for liquid refreshment, high jinks and other good fun. Janie's murder took place a few years after graduation, but that doesn't mean the fun stopped.'

'So where do Caroline and Burns fit into a gang-bang killing?'

'Both had reason to dislike Janie. So they could've participated. The fact that Caroline was stashed at Achievement House indicates her involvement. So does Burns's disappearance. A gang-bang killing also meshes with the absence of a sequel. It took the right combination to turn things bad: dope, a defiant victim, and the ultimate adolescent drug – group conformity.'

'Adolescent?' he said. 'All the males were in their twenties.'

'Arrested development.'

'Funny you should say that. When I saw the Cossacks' current house, that's exactly what went through my mind.'

He described the eyesore mansion, the cars, the history of neighbor complaints.

'It also matches something else you said early on,' he added. 'Women tend to be affiliative. Caroline wouldn't have had the drive or the strength to slice Janie up by herself, but once Janie was incapacitated, a few cuts and burns would've been easy enough.'

'But Caroline's involvement – and Willie Burns's – created a new level of risk for the boys: two weak links who couldn't be counted on to keep their mouths shut. Caroline because of her mental instability and Burns because he was a junkie with a tendency to flap his gums. What if Burns found himself in a desperate situation – poor cash flow and a strong heroin jones? What if he tried to scratch up some money by blackmailing the others? To a street guy like Burns, a bunch of rich white boys with

273

a very nasty secret would've seemed perfect marks. That would explain Michael Larner's rage at Burns's disappearance. Burns had made himself a very viable threat to Larner's son, and now he was gone. Burns blackmailing would also explain his skipping on Boris Nemerov, even though he'd always been dependable before. Given all that, his paranoid rant about people being after him when he phoned Boris Nemerov makes perfect sense. Burns wasn't worried about going to jail. He'd been part of a brutal murder and had gotten on the wrong side of his coparticipants.'

Milo flipped his notepad open. 'Chapman and Hansen. Any first names?'

'All I read in the yearbook were initials, and I don't remember them.'

'High school,' he said. 'Oh, the glory days.'

'They *were* Garvey Cossack's glory days. He lied about being class treasurer.'

'Preparing for a career in finance . . . okay, let's go have a look at that yearbook.'

Within moments of our arrival, we'd filled out details on the other King's Men.

At eighteen, Vance Coury, Jr, had been a good-looking, dark-haired boy with heavy, black eyebrows, a curled-lip smile that bordered on sneer, and a piercing stare. A certain type of girl would've thought him hot.

'Teenage Lothario,' I said. Just as Janie described. 'Despite what Melinda said, she wasn't always fantasizing. Ten to one his dad owned a Jag twenty years ago.'

As with the Cossacks and Brad Larner, Coury's out-of-class interests had been limited: auto shop monitor and the King's Men.

L. Chapman turned out to be moon-faced Luke, a hulking, fair-haired boy with a vacant mien.

Nothing on his plate but the King's Men.

The last boy, Nicholas Dale Hansen, was a different story. A clean-cut, button-down youth with an ever-so-serious expression, 'Nick' Hansen had participated in the Junior Chamber of Commerce, Art Club, and the Boy Scouts. He'd also made honor roll for two semesters.

'The smart one in the group,' said Milo. 'Wonder if he was smart enough not to be there.'

'Or the brains behind the organization.'

We got hold of the *Who's Who* that had helped me locate the boys in the first place. No bios on anyone but Garvey Cossack, Jr.

'Coury's a Van Nuys fender-bender,' said Milo, 'so no big surprise there. And old Luke doesn't look like the brightest bulb in the chandelier. But personally, I'm disappointed in Nick Hansen. Maybe he didn't fulfill his promise.'

We left the library and sat out in front on a stone bench that ran along the reflecting pond flanking the entrance. I watched students come and go as Milo appropriated the identity of a Southwest Division Auto Theft detective and phoned DMV. It took some prodding to get the clerk to go back two decades, but when Milo hung up he'd filled two pages with scrawls: makes, models, owners, and addresses of record.

'Vance Coury, Sr, owned a Jaguar Mark 10 sedan, a Lincoln Continental, and a Camaro.'

'So Janie was right on,' I said. 'The Lincoln was probably the missus's wheels, and Vance, Jr, drove the Camaro. When he was out to impress girls, he took Daddy's car with the deep pile carpeting. Something that would set them at ease before he got them up in that room and pulled out the rope.'

'He's got himself a slew of wheels, now: eight registered vehicles, mostly classics, including a couple of vintage Ferraris.'

'You said the Cossacks had a Ferrari out in front of their house. Maybe the King's Men never went dormant, and Coury's bunking in.'

'Coury's home address is listed in Tarzana, but could be,' he said. 'And guess what: I was wrong about Nicholas Dale Hansen not living up to his capabilities. Drives a BMW 700 and lives in Beverly Hills on North Roxbury. Guess he just didn't want a bio.'

'Modest,' I said.

'Or he shuns the limelight,' he said. 'Because who knows what too much attention can do.'

'What about Luke Chapman?'

'Nothing on him. Never owned a car in California.'

'Meaning he hasn't lived in California for a while,' I said.

'Maybe the family moved out of state after high school. Or it's another disappearing act, voluntary or otherwise. If he was as dull as his picture implies, he would've been considered another weak link.'

'Snipping off loose ends,' he said.

'That makes me think of two other ends, both apparent accidents: Bowie Ingalls hitting that tree and Pierce Schwinn hitting that rock.'

'Oh, your imagination,' he said. 'So how'd the boys get the parents to stash Caroline?'

'She'd been the problem child for years. If she poisoned that dog, her parents probably had a sense the problem was serious. If the boys came to them feigning horror at something terrible Caroline had done, they might very well have believed it.'

'The *boys*,' he said. 'Bunch of sleazes and that Boy Scout. *He's* the one who interests me.'

'Merit badge for murder,' I said. 'What a concept.'

Walking back to the Seville, he said, 'Something that smells of evidence, I'm starting to feel like a real-life detective, gee whiz. The question is where to take it. Can't exactly march into the board-room at Cossack Development and accuse the brothers of being scumbag killers.'

'Can't confront John G. Broussard, either.'

'A working cop never mentions John G. Broussard in polite company. Did you see that piece in the paper about him this morning?'

'No.'

'The mayor approved him for a raise but the police commission has the authority and they say no way. Last few weeks, the *Times* has printed a few other less-than-complimentary comments about John G.'s management style.'

'Broussard's on the way out?' I said.

'Good chance. He must've finally annoyed the wrong people.' As we neared the parking structure, his cell phone squawked and he slapped it to his ear. 'Hello – hey, how's it – what? *When?* Where are you? Okay, just stay right there – no, just stay put, I'm with Alex over at the U, we'll be there in ten.'

He hung up and sped up to a jog. 'That was Rick. Someone stole the Porsche.'

'Where?' I said, matching his pace.

'Right out of the doctors' lot at Cedars. You know how he loves that car . . . he sounded shook up. C'mon, let's go.'

I broke speed laws and made it to the Cedars-Sinai complex in fifteen minutes. Rick was waiting at the corner of Beverly Boulevard and George Burns Avenue wearing a long white coat over blue scrubs. Except for surgeon's fingers that never ceased flexing, he was motionless.

As I pulled to the curb, Milo bounded out of the Seville, rushed to Rick's side, and listened as Rick talked. At a casual glance, they appeared to be two middle-aged men exhibiting no obvious physical affection but the bond between them was obvious to me and I wondered if anyone else could see it. Wondered about something else, too: Hot Dog Heaven, where Paris Bartlett had accosted Milo, was only a block away, and the fast-food stand's picnic tables afforded a full frontal view of the hospital. Sometimes Milo dropped in at Cedars to have lunch with Rick, or just to say hi. Had he been watched, and if so, for how long?

Then I thought about the two cops gabbing in the ER cubicle. Supposedly unaware of Rick's presence in the next booth. But maybe the chat about the HIV detective forced to retire *had* been for his benefit.

Throw in Bartlett's little display, the call from LAPD Personnel, and a stolen car, and it added up to psychological warfare.

As Milo and Rick talked, I sat in the driver's seat and looked around. All I saw was a flood of anonymous faces and cars, the usual L.A. ratio of one pedestrian to five hundred vehicles.

Rick stopped talking, slumped a bit. Milo patted his back and eyed the Seville. Rick got in back and Milo returned to the front passenger seat.

'Hey, Alex,' said Rick.

'Sorry about the car.'

He grimaced. 'An alarm and a steering lock, and it's gone.'

Milo glanced back at him. His eyes were cold, his neck cords were taut, and his mandible jutted like that of a fighting cur, straining to enter the pit.

I said, 'When did it happen?'

Rick said, 'I got to work at five A.M., didn't come out until two P.M., so sometime in between.'

'He thinks he might've been followed,' said Milo, 'driving to work.'

'It was probably nothing,' said Rick. 'But that early, you don't expect too many cars on the street and there was a set of headlights behind me when I pulled out to San Vincente and it stayed with me until I got to Third Street.'

'And you have no idea exactly when that started?' said Milo.

Rick sighed. 'I told you, no. I had an emergency splenectomy at six. My focus was on getting psyched up.' Rick's voice was steady. His fingers kept flexing. 'I really don't think it was anything, Milo. Probably some other early bird.'

'How many other cars do you usually see when you hit the early shift, Rick?'

'Usually none. But sometimes one or two – as I said, I don't pay attention. If the Porsche hadn't been ripped off, if you hadn't asked me about being tailed, I'd never have given it a thought.'

'*Give* it a thought,' said Milo. 'We've both got to think.'

'About what?'

'Watching our backs. Maybe even a temporary change of address.'

'Oh, come on,' said Rick.

'I'm serious.'

Silence. Rick said, 'Well, first things first. I need a rental car. Alex, would you be so kind as to drive me over to—'

'*I'll* take you,' said Milo. 'Drop us off a block from our house, Alex.' To Rick: 'You wait while I check out the premises. I'll pick you up in the Taurus and drive you to Budget. No, let's use another company, just to play it safe. I want to minimize any links between us.'

'You *can't* be serious,' said Rick.

'Drive, Alex.'

'Minimize *links*?' said Rick.

'Sorry,' said Milo. 'Right now putting a layer of separation between you and me is the nicest thing I can do for you.'

twenty-eight

Alex dropped Rick and Milo around the corner and drove off. Milo left Rick waiting under a Brazilian floss tree and walked to his house with his eyes on high beam. The rental Taurus sat alone in the driveway, and he gave it a cursory once-over. Nothing weird. Slipping behind the car, he made his way up the driveway, unholstered his gun, and unlatched the back door, feeling foolish. The alarm buzzed, a positive sign. He disarmed the system, covered each room as if stalking a suspect. Playing Robocop in his own domicile. Jesus.

Nothing had been disturbed that he could see and the junk in the spare bedroom closet was stacked just as he'd left it: on top of the movable floorboards that concealed the safe. Still, the prickly heat of paranoia coursed up and down his back. He hadn't relaxed a bit by the time he got in the Taurus and drove back to Rick.

Rick said, 'Everything okay, I assume.'

'Seems to be.'

'Milo, the Porsche probably had nothing to do with anything.'

'Maybe.'

'You don't think so?'

'I don't know what to think.'

'Well, given that,' said Rick, 'let's not get overly dramatic. After I get a rental, I'm going back to work, and afterward I'm coming home.'

Milo started up the Taurus but kept it in park. Rick cleared his throat, the way he did when he got impatient.

Milo said, 'What'd you do this morning, work-wise?'

'Why?'

'How many surgeries did you perform?'

'Three—'

'Was I there in the OR, telling you which scalpel to use?'

'Listen,' said Rick. Then he went silent.

Milo tapped the steering wheel.

Rick said, 'Fine, I accede to your superior knowledge of the rotten side of life. But expertise doesn't mean infallibility, Milo. If someone wanted to intimidate you, why steal *my* car?'

Because that's the way they think.

Milo didn't answer.

Rick said, 'It was a car theft, plain and simple. You always told me if a pro wanted the Porsche, he could get it no matter what I did.'

'There are pros, and there are pros,' said Milo.

'Meaning what?'

'Meaning I don't know what really happened to the Porsche, but I do know that I want you away from my mess. So stop giving me a hard time even though you think I'm being melodramatic. Worse comes to worst, I was an idiot and you were inconvenienced. What kind of rental car do you want?'

Rick frowned. 'Doesn't matter.' He tapped the Taurus's dashboard. 'One of these will be fine.'

'Anything but one of these,' said Milo. 'I don't want you in something that could be confused with mine. How about an SUV? This city, that's like joining the ant swarm.'

'As if I care,' said Rick, folding his arms across his chest. 'Sure, an SUV. Maybe I'll go hiking.'

'Not a bad idea. Take some time away from the city.'

Rick's head whipped around. 'You're serious. You really want me gone.'

'I want you safe.'

'Forget it, big guy, just dismiss the thought. I've got a solid week of shift plus built-in overtime. We've got bills to pay.'

'Get real,' said Milo. 'When's the last time we worried about making the bills?'

'Not since the Porsche was paid up. But now I'll probably need a new car and that'll mean new monthlies and we were talking about taking some time off and going to Europe this summer, so I need to stockpile revenue.'

Milo didn't answer.

Rick said, 'You *were* serious about Europe? I've been organizing my entire schedule with an eye toward taking a month off.'

'I was serious.'

'Maybe we should travel right now.'

Milo shook his head.

'Why not?' said Rick. 'If you're right, why stick around and be a target?'

'The weather,' said Milo. 'If I bother to lay out bucks for Europe, I want sunny weather.'

'Now you're a meteorologist.' Rick took hold of Milo's arm. 'What if your anxiety doesn't level off? Am I supposed to go into long-term exile?'

'It's not a matter of anxiety. It's my finely honed sense of threat.'

'That stupid rumor those cops were talking about? I've been thinking about that. For all you know, there is an HIV-positive detective in your division. Someone deep in the closet. Or those cretins were just flapping their gums the way cops do. I know, I see them all the time when they bring in suspects. Standing around drinking coffee and gabbing while we sew the poor devils up.'

'Another West L.A. gay detective,' said Milo. 'Sure, that's likely.'

'Who says he's gay? And, what, only you can be a celebrity?'

'Yeah, that's me, a star. Rick, it's more than the rumor—'

'That old case, I know. Maybe it was shunted aside all these years precisely because no one *gives* a hoot. What if you've just built it up in your head, Milo? With Alex's help.'

'What's that supposed to mean?'

'It means that you and Alex have this bizarre chemistry. The two of you put your heads together, and strange ideas start to pour out.'

'I've found Alex to be right more often than he's wrong. And what's the murder book, a schoolboy prank?'

'It's possible.'

Milo was silent.

'Fine,' said Rick. 'Let's not talk about this anymore. Get me a rental.'

Milo drove Melrose west to Doheny then north to Santa Monica Boulevard. Past the clubs he and Rick no longer patronized.

Rick said, 'Where exactly are you going?'

'Beverly Hills. The Hertz office at the Beverly Hilton.'

'As a well-known companion of mine always says, "Hoo-hah." Maybe I'll rent a Rolls.'

'Forget it, we've got bills to worry about.'

Rick stared at him and he stared back and they both broke into laughter. Milo knew it was temporary tension relief, more Band-Aid than cure. But that was fine.

Milo watched Rick drive away in the rental Volvo. The counter agent had been a good-looking blonde woman, and she'd taken one look at Rick, flirted outrageously, and upgraded him.

No meeting of the minds about where Rick would stay and for how long. Milo agreed to let it ride until tonight.

Alone, he drove downtown, to Skid Row. The fleabags that Vance Coury, Sr, had owned twenty years ago had all been situated on a two-block stretch of Main Street. The chance that any personnel from that era remained was nil, but what did he have to lose?

The moment he drove by each of the hotels, the iota of optimism vanished. The spots where the Excelsior and the Crossley had stood were now parking lots, and the Grande Royale was the Shining Light Mission.

He made his way back to the Hall of Records and pulled property tax records on all three parcels. The parking lots were leased to a Nevada corporation, but the land was owned by Concourse Elegance, Inc., which traced to Concourse Auto Restoration on Van Nuys Boulevard. Vance Coury's shop. Junior had inherited the buildings, torn two of them down and converted to low-hassle, income-churning asphalt.

The Shining Light Mission was interesting, though. The Shining Light Foundation was a nonprofit run by the Reverends Fred and Glenda Stephenson – a pair Milo knew because back in his uniform days he'd transported bums to their soup kitchen on San Pedro. He'd found the couple to be saints who put in twenty-hour days serving the poor. Coury probably donated the third lot as part of some sort of tax deal, in order to end up with the other two, free and clear.

Feeling like Don Quixote's dumber brother, he moved on to

282

death records. Sucked in his breath when he encountered unexpected success.

Luke Matthew Chapman had died in a drowning accident, twenty years ago, at the age of twenty-two.

Date of death: 14 December. Six months after Janie Ingalls's murder. Eight *days* prior to Caroline Cossack's final day at Achievement House and nine days prior to Boris Nemerov's execution.

He phoned the coroner's office, got hold of one of the few friendly voices at his disposal: a morgue assistant who'd come out of the closet after learning about Milo's travails. Milo was uncomfortable being viewed as inspirational, but the guy had come in handy from time to time.

Today, Darren asked no questions and went to pull the file. Milo wouldn't have been surprised to encounter another vanished folder, but a few minutes later he had the relevant data jotted down in his notepad:

Luke Chapman had parked his car on PCH and gone nightswimming at Zuma Beach. An illegal dip, because state sand was off-limits after dark and Chapman had had to scale a high link fence. Chapman's alcohol level was twice the legal limit, which made Milo wonder about his ability to climb the fence, but the coroner's theory was that 'this young, white, well-nourished male' had been caught in a riptide and lost coordination due to intoxication. Water in the lungs confirmed drowning. The corpse had washed up at the far end of Zuma, where public sand abutted Broad Beach. Multiple contusions and abrasions consistent with battery by surf and sand had been apparent. But no obvious signs of foul play.

No obvious signs unless you were prepared to interpret the bruises on Chapman's arms and legs and back as evidence of his having been forced down into the water. Knew Zuma had been one of the King's Men's party spots.

Milo recalled Chapman's vacant expression. The dumb kid in the group. Participating in Janie Ingalls's murder and sitting on the horror for months, but unable to get over it. Maybe he'd gotten loaded and blubbered the wrong thing to his buddies and made himself an extreme liability.

Bought himself the big blue kiss.

On the other hand, accidents happened . . .

Bowie Ingalls: man versus tree.

Pierce Schwinn: man versus rock.

Luke Chapman: man versus water.

What was left – fire? Suddenly Milo's head filled with images of Caroline Cossack and Wilbert Burns roasted alive. Bodies charred beyond recognition, the perfect obliteration of the past.

The King's Men. A nasty bunch of spoiled, rich party animals cleaning up after themselves and earning a nice, cushy twenty years.

More than cushy: Ferraris and chauffeurs, cribs in Holmby, dabbles in the film biz, private dinners with politicos and power brokers.

They'd gotten away with it.

These King's Men would've jumped at the chance to stomp Humpty Dumpty's skull.

The Cossack brothers, Specs Larner, Coury. And the smart one – Nicholas Dale Hansen. What was *he* about?

He looked the guy up in the property files. Nothing. What did that mean, he was leasing the house on North Roxbury?

He found himself a quiet corner in the basement of the building, hidden between stacks of old plot maps, made sure no one was around and took the risk of an NCIC call using the ID of a West Valley D-I named Korn – a punk he'd supervised two years ago, low on initiative, high on attitude.

Wasted risk: Nicholas Dale Hansen had no criminal history.

The only thing left to do was go home and play with his laptop. Or take a shortcut and ask Alex to do it – his friend, initially a computer Luddite, resistant to the whole notion of the Internet, had become quite the Web-surfing whiz.

He began the two-block walk to the city lot where he'd left the Taurus. Melting in with the afternoon pedestrian throng, dialing up his cell phone like every other lemming on the street. Probably giving himself ear cancer or something, but those were the breaks. Faking normal felt good.

Alex picked up on the first ring, and Milo thought he sounded disappointed. Waiting for a call from Robin? What was up with *that*?

Milo asked him about running a search on Nicholas Hansen, and Alex said, 'Funny you should ask.'

'Oh yeah, I forgot,' said Milo. 'I'm dealing with Nostradamus.'

'No, just a guy with spare time,' said Alex. 'Hansen wasn't hard to find, at all. Guess what he does for a living?'

'He looked kinda corporate in high school, so some hoo-hah financial thing with a bad smell to it?'

'He's an artist. A painter. Quite a good one, if the images posted by the New York gallery that handles him are accurate.'

'An artist and he leases in Beverly Hills and drives a big Beemer?'

'A successful artist,' said Alex. 'His prices range from ten to thirty thousand a canvas.'

'And what, he churns them out?'

'Doesn't look like it. I phoned the gallery pretending to be an interested collector, and he's sold out. They described his style as post-modern old masters. Hansen mixes his own pigments, makes his own frames and brushes, lays down layer after layer of paint and glaze. It's a time-consuming process and the owner said Hansen finishes four, five pictures a year. She implied she'd love to have more.'

'Four, five a year at his top fee means a hundred and fifty, max,' said Milo. 'A year's lease on a house in the flats could be more than that by itself.'

'Plus galleries usually take around thirty percent,' said Alex, 'so, no, it doesn't add up.' He paused. 'I hope you don't mind, but I drove by his house. It's a nice one – big old Spanish thing that hasn't been made over. The BMW's in the driveway. Freshly polished. Dark green, almost the exact same shade as my Seville.'

Milo laughed. 'Do I mind? Would it make a difference? No, it's fine unless you knocked on the door and accused the bastard of murder. Which, *I'd* love to do. Because, guess what, the plot curdles.'

He told Alex about Luke Chapman's drowning death.

'Another accident,' said Alex. 'Normally, I'd say "ah," but you've been crankier than usual.'

'Say it. I'll give you Novocaine before I start drilling.'

Alex let out an obligatory chuckle. 'I also got a brief look at Hansen. Or someone who's living at the same address. While I was driving by, a man came out the front door, went to the BMW, and removed a sheet of wood from the trunk. Nicholas Hansen paints on mahogany.'

'An artist,' said Milo, 'with independent income. Ambling out to his driveway in comfy clothes, doing whatever the hell he pleases. Life's sure fair, ain't it?'

There were things Milo wanted to do after dark, so he thanked Alex, told him to stay out of trouble, he'd call in the morning.

'Anything else I can do for you, big guy?'

Milo quashed the impulse to say, 'Stay out of trouble.' 'No, not right now.'

'Okay,' said Alex. He sounded disappointed. Milo wanted to ask about Robin, but he didn't.

Instead, he hung up, thinking about Janie Ingalls and how some lives were so short, so brutish, that it was a wonder God bothered.

He slogged through yet another rush-hour mess from downtown, wondering what to do with Rick and deciding that a nice hotel for a few days was the best solution. Rick would be profoundly unhappy, but he wouldn't scream. Rick never screamed, just tucked himself in psychologically and grew quiet and unreachable.

It wouldn't be fun, but in the end Rick would agree. All these years together, and they'd both learned to pick their battles.

He made it home by five o'clock.

Midway up his block, he stopped.

Something white was stationed in his driveway.

The Porsche.

He looked around, saw no strange cars on the block, gunned the Taurus, and swung it behind the pearly 928. From what he could tell the car was intact – no joyriding wounds or missing parts. More than intact – shiny and clean, as if it had been freshly washed. Rick kept it spotless, but Milo couldn't remember when he'd last scrubbed it down . . . last weekend. For most of the week, Rick had garaged the car, but the last two days he'd left it out to be ready when he hit the ER early. Two days' dirt would have shown itself easily on the white paint.

Someone had *detailed* the damn thing.

He surveyed the block, put his hand on his gun, got out cautiously, walked over to the Porsche and touched the car's convex flank.

Glossy. Washed and waxed.

A peek through the window added *freshly vacuumed* to the picture; he could see the tracks in the carpet.

Even the steering wheel lock had been put back. Then he saw something on the driver's seat.

A brown paper bag.

He gave the block another up-and-down, then kneeled down and examined the Porsche's underside. No ticking toys or tracers. Popping the trunk revealed an intact rear engine. He'd worked on the car himself, had rust-proofed the belly for all those cold-weather trips that had never materialized. He knew the Porsche's guts well. Nothing new.

He unlocked the driver's door, took a closer look at the bag. The paper mouth was open, and the content was visible.

A blue binder. Not shiny leather like Alex's little gift. Your basic blue cloth.

The same kind of binder the department used to employ before the switch to plastic.

He took hold of the top of the bag with his fingertips and carried it inside the house. Sat down in the living room, heart racing, hands icy, because he knew exactly what would be inside. Knew also that, despite the certainty, he'd be shocked.

His jaw hurt and his back ached as he opened the book to Janie Ingalls's case file.

Very thin file. Milo's own notes on top, followed by the official death shots, and yes, Schwinn had lifted the photo out of this set. Body drawings with every wound delineated, autopsy summary. Not originals, nice clean photocopies.

Then, nothing else. No tox screens or lab tests, no investigative reports by the Metro boys who'd supposedly taken over. So either that had been a lie, or pages had been left out.

He flipped to the postmortem summary. No mention of semen – of anything much. This had to be the sketchiest autopsy synopsis he'd ever read. 'This white, adolescent, well-nourished female's wounds were accomplished by sharp, single-bladed . . .' Thanks a heap.

No sign of the toxicology screen he'd requested. He didn't need

287

official confirmation; Melinda Waters had said Janie began the evening stoned.

No semen, no foreign blood types. Forget DNA.

But one detail in the autopsy summary did catch his eye: ligature marks around Janie's ankles, wrists, and throat.

Same pattern of restraints as in the hotel.

Vance Coury spotting Janie and going for an encore.

This time, adding his buddies to the mix.

He reread the file. Nothing revelatory, but someone wanted to make sure Milo saw it.

He settled his head with vodka and grapefruit juice, checked the mail, punched the phone machine.

One message from Rick, who'd made it easy for him by taking on an extra shift.

'I won't be through until tomorrow morning, probably crash in the doctors' room, maybe go for a drive afterward. Take care of yourself . . . I love you.'

'Me too,' Milo muttered to the empty house. Even alone, he had trouble saying it.

twenty-nine

I opened the door for Milo at 9 A.M., doing my best impression of awake and human. Last night, I'd woken up every couple of hours, thinking the kind of thoughts that erode your soul.

Three calls to Robin had gone unanswered. Her hotel refused to say if she'd checked out – guest security. Next stop, Denver. I pictured her on the bus, Spike sleeping in her lap, gazing out the window.

Thinking of me, or anything but?

Milo handed me the blue binder. I thumbed through it and led him into my office.

'Your typing wasn't any better back then,' I said. 'Any theories about who delivered it?'

'Someone with a talent for grand theft auto.'

'Same messenger who sent me the deluxe version?'

'Could be.'

'Doesn't sound like Schwinn's secret girlfriend,' I said. 'Or maybe I'm being sexist; I suppose women can steal cars, too.'

'This was no amateur. I print-powdered the wheel and the door handles. *Nada*. Nothing on the book other than my paws. They put the crooklock back on. Picked it, didn't slice it.'

'Same question,' I said. 'A criminal pro, the department, or a rogue cop?'

'A rogue cop would mean Schwinn had a buddy back then or made a new one. I never saw him hang with anyone. The other detectives seemed to shun him.'

'Any idea why?'

'At first, I figured it was his charming personality, but maybe everyone knew about his bad behavior, could see he was ready for a

289

fall. Everyone except me. I was a dumb-ass rookie caught up in my own paranoia. At the time I wondered if I'd been paired with him because I was seen as a pariah, too. Now, I'm sure of it.'

'Not that much of a pariah,' I said. 'They got rid of him and transferred you to West L.A.'

'Or I hadn't accrued enough time on the job to accumulate embarrassing information.'

'Or to develop street sources. Like the one who cued Schwinn right to Janie.'

He fingered the edge of the blue cloth binder. 'Another burnout cop . . . maybe. But why send this to me a week after the deluxe version?'

'More covering of the rear,' I said. 'Pacing himself. He couldn't be sure you'd be seduced. You started investigating and qualified for the next installment.'

'More installments coming?'

'Could be.'

He got up, circled the room, returned to the desk but remained on his feet. I'd kept the drapes drawn and a razor edge of light ran across his torso diagonally, a luminous wound.

I said, 'Here's yet another theory: the IA man who interrogated you along with Broussard – Poulsenn. Any idea what happened to him?'

'*Lester* Poulsenn,' he said. 'Been trying to recall his first name, and it just came to me. No, never heard of him again. Why?'

'Because the real target of renewing interest in the case could be Broussard. John G. built his career on an upright reputation, exposure of a cover-up would destroy him. Lester Poulsenn could have a good reason to resent Broussard. Think about it: a black man and a white man are partnered, but the black man is put in charge. Then the black man ascends to the top of the department ladder, and the white man's never heard from again. Was Poulsenn also drummed out due to bad behavior? Or maybe he wasn't good at keeping secrets. Either way, we could be talking about one disgruntled gentleman.'

'And Poulsenn would've known about *Schwinn's* resentment . . . yeah, it'd be interesting to know what happened to *his* career. I can't exactly waltz into Parker Center and stick my nose in the files . . .'

He frowned, called DMV and identified himself as someone named Lt Horacio Batista. A few minutes later, he had statistics on three Lester Poulsenns living in California, but all were too young to be the man who'd played second fiddle to John G. Broussard.

'He could've moved out of state,' I said, 'meaning he's probably not our man. Or he's yet another disappearing act.'

He got to his feet again and paced; the light razor bounced. Returning to the book, he touched a blue cover. 'Installments – hey, folks, join the murder book club.'

We divided up the workload this way:

1. I'd try to learn what I could about Lester Poulsenn, check newspaper microfilms for twenty- to twenty-five-year-old stories about misbehaving cops and chase down whatever details I could find about the disposition of their cases. A long shot, because the department kept corruption stories quiet, just as it had with Pierce Schwinn. Unless, as in the Rampart scandal or the Hollywood Division burglary case of ten years ago, the stink got too strong to mask.
2. Milo would go off to do his thing, not telling me what or where or when.

The search on my computer revealed no Lester Poulsenns who fit the bill. I made another futile call to Vancouver, comforted myself with self-pity, and drove to the U.

It took three hours to go through five years of microfilm, and I came up with several instances of felonious police officers. A pair of West Valley detectives had offered their services as contract killers. Both were serving life sentences in protective isolation at the state penitentiary at Pelican Bay. A Glendale traffic officer had been arrested for having sex with a thirteen-year-old baby-sitter. Ten years of jail, this prince was out by now, but an alliance with Schwinn and a child molester seemed unlikely. A female Pasadena gang officer had slept with several minor-age gang members, and two Van Nuys uniforms had been caught burglarizing pawnshops on their patrol route. Convictions and incarceration for all. In each instance a hookup with Schwinn seemed improbable. I copied down all the names, anyway, punched Lester Poulsenn's name into the periodicals index and felt my pupils dilate as a single reference popped into view.

Twenty-year-old reference.

> Poulsenn, L.L. Veteran LAPD detective
> found murdered in Watts.

The *Sacramento Bee*. I located the spool, jammed it into the machine, twirled like mad until I came to the story. Associated Press wire service piece. The L.A. papers hadn't picked it up.

The *Bee* had run it in a side column at the back of the main section titled 'Elsewhere in the State.' Sandwiched between the account of a dead black rhinoceros at the San Diego Zoo and a Berkeley bank robbery.

The date was 5 January. Fourteen days after Caroline Cossack had checked out of – or had been taken from – Achievement House.

I did an instant photocopy on the machine, then read the text.

(AP) Los Angeles police are investigating the shooting death of one of their own, in what appears to be a homicide and attempted cover-up by arson. The body of Lester Louis Poulsenn, formerly a detective with the department's Internal Affairs Unit and recently appointed to the Metro Major Crimes Unit, was found inside a burning house in Watts. Poulsenn, 39, a thirteen-year LAPD veteran, was discovered by firefighters dispatched to put out a blaze at the private residence on West 156th Street. A police spokesman said Poulsenn had been shot twice in the head in what appeared to be an execution-style killing.

'This is a rough neighborhood, with lots of gang activity,' said the source, who neither confirmed nor denied reports that Poulsenn had been in Watts on official business. The structure, a single-family dwelling that had been vacant for some time, was described as a total loss.

I kept spooling, in search of a follow-up.

Nothing. Which was crazy; nothing mobilizes a police department faster than a cop's murder. Yet local press coverage of Poulsenn's death had been suppressed, and no further official statements had been issued.

Recently transferred to Metro. Translation: Poulsenn had taken over the Ingalls case?

Twenty years ago, a pair of IA men had interrogated Milo. One had merited success, the other was dead seven months later.

A white man shot to death in a black neighborhood, just like Boris Nemerov. Dispatched execution-style, just like Boris Nemerov.

Arson cover-up. Milo had wondered out loud about fire. Beleaguered or not, he had perfect pitch.

I called him, got no answer at any of his numbers, thought about what to do.

Nice mild morning. Time to wash the car.

Two hours later, the Seville was as shiny as a '79 Seville could be, and I was hurtling over the Glen to the Valley. Mere cleanliness hadn't satisfied me. I'd waxed and hand-buffed the chesterfield-green paint, added detail spray, scrubbed the tires, the hubcaps, the beige vinyl top and matching upholstery, wiped down those crafty little simulated wood insets, vacuumed and shampooed the rugs. I bought the car fifteen years ago from the proverbial little old lady (a heavy-footed retired schoolteacher from Burbank, not Pasadena) and had pampered it since. Still, 105,000 miles had taken its toll, and one day I'd be forced to decide between an engine rebuild or something new.

No decision at all. No more changes of heart.

Concourse Auto Restorers was one of the many car-oriented businesses lining Van Nuys Boulevard between Riverside and Oxnard. Modest setup – not much more than a double tin-roofed garage behind an open lot filled with chrome and lacquer. A sign above the garage, done up in red Day-Glo Gothic lettering, advertised 'CUSTOM PAINT, PLATING, AND BODY-OFF RESTORATION' above a cartoonish rendering of an equally red, priapic Ferrari coupe. I parked on the street and made my way among muscle cars, hot rods, and one very white stretch Mercedes with its roof hacked off and a blue tarp spread across its interior. Years ago the state had passed laws restricting outdoor spray painting, but the air above Concourse Auto was chemically ripe.

Midway up the lot, two men in greasy T-shirts and baggy cutoffs were inspecting the doors of a seventies Stutz Blackhawk done up in the same copper finish as a gourmet frypan. Both were young and husky and Hispanic, with shaved heads and mustaches. Face masks hung around their necks. Their arms and the backs of their necks were brocaded with tattoos. The inkwork was dusky blue, square-edged and crude – prison handiwork. They barely raised their eyes as I passed, but both were paying attention. My nod evoked squints.

'Vance Coury?' I said.

'In there,' said the heavier of the two, curling a thumb toward the garage. His voice was high-pitched, and a teardrop tattoo dripped under one eye. That's supposed to mean you've murdered someone, but some people brag. This fellow had a hunched posture and flat eyes, and boasting didn't seem his style.

I moved on.

As I got closer to the garage, I saw that my first impression of a small lot had been wrong. A driveway ran to the left of the building, and it led to a rear half-acre of chain-linked dirt piled high with tires and fenders, bumpers and broken headlights and random garbage. Two spray booths were affixed to the rear outer wall of the garage, and a few intact cars were parked in the dirt, but most of the land was dumping ground.

I returned to the front of the structure. The garage door to the left was shut and bolted, a wall of corrugated iron. In the open right-hand bay sat a red, white, and blue Corvette Stingray. The 'Vette's windows were tinted amethyst, its nose had been lengthened a foot, a rear spoiler arced over the trunk, and twenty-inch, chrome-reversed wheels extended several inches wider than the body. Primer spots blemished the passenger side, and another shaved-head Latino crouched at one of them, hand-sanding. Yet another tattoo-boy sat at a workbench to the rear of the bay, arc-welding. The decor was raw walls, cement floor, bare bulbs, gasoline reek. Tacked to the wall beams were auto-parts calendars and foldouts of naked women with an emphasis upon luxuriant pubic hair and angles that bespoke an interest in amateur gynecology. A scattering of hard-core shots was dispersed among the collection; someone had a thing for skinny, crouching, supplicant blondes with dope-eyes performing oral sex.

The sander ignored me as I edged behind the 'Vette, avoided the sparks from the welding gun, and stepped into the sealed section of the garage. Half a black Porsche roadster occupied this bay – a racer sliced neatly in half so that the number 8 on the door had been bisected and turned into a 3. At the rear of the room, behind the truncated torso, a broad-shouldered man sat at a metal desk, phone nestled under his chin, fingers busy at a calculator.

Fortyish, he had long, thick silver hair slicked straight back and tucked behind his ears, incongruous too-black eyebrows, and an equally inky goatee. The bulb hanging above the desk greened an already olive complexion. Dark, brooding eyes were bottomed by pouches, his neck was creased and soft, and his face had long surrendered to flab. Remnants of the good-looking high school kid were hard to find, and I didn't want to stare. Because Vance Coury had his eyes on me, as he continued talking and calculating.

I walked over to the desk. Coury gave off a strong whiff of musky aftershave. His shirt was black silk crêpe with blousy sleeves rolled to the elbows and a high, stiff collar that nearly reached his earlobes. A gold chain flashed around his neck. A gold Rolex the size of a pizza banded a thick, hirsute wrist.

He studied me without acknowledging my presence. Stayed on the phone, listening, talking, listening some more, adjusting the instrument in the crook of his neck. Never ceasing the tapping of the calculator keys. The desk top was littered with papers. A half-empty bottle of Corona served as a paperweight.

I left him and strolled over to the demi-Porsche. The car retained no internal organs, was just half a shell. The edges had been smoothed and painted. Finished product; no one was intending to put this one back together again.

All the king's horses . . .

'Hey,' said a raspy voice behind me.

I turned. Coury said, 'What do you want?' Alert, yet disinterested. One hand rested on the calculator. The other was cupped and aimed at me, as if ready to collect something.

'I'm thinking of some custom work.'

'What kind of car?'

'Seville. Seventy-nine. Are you Mr Coury?'

He looked me over. 'Who referred you?'

'Read your name in an auto magazine,' I said. 'From what I could tell you seem to work on a lot of contest winners.'

'It happens,' he said. 'Seventy-nine Seville? A box. They built 'em on Chevy Two Nova chassis.'

'I know.'

'What do you want done to it?'

'I'm not sure.'

He smirked. 'Can't think of any contest you'd enter that in – unless it's one of those AIDS things.'

'AIDS things?'

'They're trying shows, now. To raise money for AIDS. Some little fruit came in, wanted me to cherry up his '45 BMW.'

'Take the job?' I said.

The cupped hand waved off the question. 'Seventy-nine Seville,' he said, as if offering a diagnosis. 'It's still gonna be a box unless we get radical. And then there's the engine. It sucks.'

'It's been good to me. No problems in fifteen years.'

'Any rust on the belly?'

'Nope. I take care of it.'

'Right,' he said.

I said, 'It's here, if you want to see it.'

He glanced down at the calculator. Punched numbers as I stood there. 'Where's here?'

'Out in front.'

He snickered. 'In front.' He stood to six-three. His upper body was massive, with meaty shoulders and a swelling gut, outsized for the narrow hips and long, stalky legs that supported it. Tight, black, plain-front slacks slimmed the legs further and accentuated the effect. On his feet were black crocodile boots with silver straps banding the shins. He came around the desk jangling. Walked right past me and out of the garage.

Out at the curb, he laughed.

'Tell you what, we wreck it, give you four hundred bucks, call it a day.'

I laughed back. 'Like I said, it's been good to me.'

'Then leave it the hell alone – what the hell would you want to do with this?'

'I was thinking about turning it into a convertible.'

'Figures,' he said. 'What, chain-saw the roof off?'

'Only car you can do that with is a Rolls Silver Cloud,' I said. 'Not enough tensile strength in any other chassis. I was figuring take the roof off, strengthen the frame, install an automatic soft-cover with a mohair liner, rechrome, and do a custom-color. You guys still doing lacquer?'

'Illegal,' he said. 'Listen, man, you want a convertible, go buy yourself one of those little Mazdas.'

'I want this car converted.'

He turned his back.

I said, 'Too complicated for you?'

He stopped. Caught his lower lip between his teeth and bit down. The pouches beneath his eyes rode up and obscured the bottom half of the irises. The two homeboys working on the Stutz looked our way.

Coury kept his lip between his teeth and rotated his jaw. 'Yeah, that's it,' he said. 'Too complicated.'

He left me standing there and walked back toward the lot. But he only made his way halfway through, paused by the Stutz. As I drove away he was watching.

thirty

Milo stared into his coffee cup, pretended the soil-colored liquid was a bog and he was sinking.

If this was a normal case, he'd have gotten himself backup. As much as he hated meetings and personalities and all the other crap that went with teamwork, multiple suspects demanded it.

An army of suspects on Janie. Six, with Luke Chapman dead. And then there was after-burn: Walt Obey and Germ Bacilla and Diamond Jim.

And the glue that held it all together: J.G. Broussard.

And now, yet another unknown: Alex's theory about a rogue cop.

Milo'd spent some time thinking about that, trying to come up with a possible name, but all he could conjure was an abstraction. Some ass-hole doing Pierce Schwinn's postmortem bidding, playing games and yanking his strings. Someone with the gall to rip off Rick's car and return it detailed, with a nice little gift.

Vance Coury was in the car biz and wasn't that a coincidence? But Coury sure wouldn't have delivered the real murder book.

So maybe the use of the car meant someone was pointing him *toward* Coury. Or was he really getting overly complicated now?

The anger that had percolated within him since the first murder book had surfaced kept rising in his gorge.

Coury. The bastard shaped up as a sadist and a rapist and a control freak. Maybe the dominant one in the group. If he and his rich buds were cornered, they'd be likely to ambush the enemy, cut his throat, and burn his body.

One army deserved another, and all *he* had was Alex.

He laughed silently. Or maybe he'd let out sound because the old lady in the second booth over looked up, startled, and stared at him

298

with that antsy expression that takes hold of people when they confront the weird.

Milo smiled at her, and she retracted her head behind her newspaper.

He was back at DuPars in Farmers Market, trying to sort things out. Vance Coury had stayed in his head because it had been Coury who'd raped Janie the first time and maybe initiated the scene that led to Janie's murder.

Normally, he'd have investigated the hell out of the guy. But . . . then something hit him. Maybe there *was* a safe way to learn more.

He threw money on the table and left the coffee shop. The old woman's stare followed his path to the door.

The Shining Light Mission was five stories of brick-faced stucco painted corn yellow and sided by rusting gray fire escapes. No friezework, no moldings, not the slightest nod to design. It reminded Milo of one of those drawings little kids do when asked to render a building. One big rectangle specked with little window squares. The place even tilted. As a hotel, the Grande Royale had been anything but.

Old men with collapsed jaws and runny eyes years past self-torment loitered in front and every one of them greeted Milo with the excessive amiability of the habitual miscreant.

Knowing exactly what he was – no way could he be taken for anything else. As he entered the mission, he wondered if the cop aura would stick after he left the department. Which might be sooner rather than later; going up against the chief wasn't a formula for career longevity.

Even an unpopular chief who might be leaving soon himself. Milo had been scouring the papers for Broussard stories, and this morning he'd found yet another one in the *Times*. Pontification on the chief's rejected raise by two members of the police commission. Defying the mayor who'd appointed them, which meant they were serious.

'*Chief Broussard represents a long-entrenched police culture that contributes to intracommunity tension.*'

Politico-blab for 'Update your résumé, J.G.'

Broussard had come into office in the aftermath of the Rampart scandal, and the commission had offered no hint at new corruption. The chief's problem was his personality. Arrogance as he bucked the commission at every turn. In that sense, the chief still thought like a cop: Civilian meddling was the enemy. But Broussard's imperious nature had alienated the wrong people, well past the point where even pals like the mayor and Walt Obey could help him.

Then again, maybe Broussard didn't care about losing his job, because he had something waiting in the wings.

Converting his unpaid position as security consultant to Obey's Esperanza project into a nice, fat corporate gig that would guarantee him long-term status and bucks, keep the wife in Cadillacs and whatever else floated her canoe.

If so, what was Obey getting out of the deal?

The Cossacks' participation as refinancers fit perfectly. They owed Broussard big-time for the Ingalls cover-up, would go with the flow. Could Alex be right about Obey getting himself into a financial bind, needing the brothers as white knights?

Any way you turned it, Milo knew he was a flea. What the hell, safety and security were for wimps.

He entered the mission lobby. The vaulted space had been converted to a TV room where a dozen or so bums sat slumped on folding chairs, staring at a movie on big-screen. The scene featured actors and actresses in long hair and beards and camel-colored robes wandering through a desert that looked like Palm Springs. Despite the camels. Some biblical epic that asked you to buy the Hebrews as blond and blue-eyed. Milo shifted his attention to the reception desk – maybe the very desk where Vance Coury had obtained the key to his rape den. The counter was topped by several plastic, screw-top cookie jars, and the bookcase behind it was jammed with red-bound Bibles with crosses on their spines. Off to the left were two brown-painted elevator doors. A metal-railed staircase ran straight back and hooked sharply to the right.

The place smelled of soup. Why did so many places dedicated to salvation smell of soup?

An old black guy, more cleaned up than the others, got up from his chair and limped over. 'I'm Edgar. May I help you, sir?'

Big bass voice but a little bandy-legged fellow wearing pressed khakis, a blue-gray plaid shirt buttoned to the neck, and sneakers. Bald except for tufts of kinky white cotton above his ears. White-white dentures made for smiling. The total effect was clownlike, benign.

Milo said, 'Is Reverend Fred or Reverend Glenda in?'

'Reverend Fred's at the City of Orange Mission, but Reverend Glenda's upstairs. Who shall I say is calling?'

The guy had a refined way of enunciating, and his eyes were clear and intelligent. Milo could see him doing butler time at some country club, kissing up to rich folk using perfect grammar. Different skin color, and maybe he'd have been the one getting served.

'Milo Sturgis.'

'And this is about, Mr Sturgis?'

'Personal.'

The old man regarded him with compassion. 'One moment, Mr Sturgis.' He made his way slowly up the stairs and returned a few minutes later. 'Reverend Glenda's waiting for you, Mr Sturgis. Next floor up, second door to the right.'

Sitting behind a small oak desk in a small, nearly empty office fitted with an ancient radiator and masked by yellowed venetian blinds, Glenda Stephenson looked exactly as she had ten years ago. Fifty pounds over-weight, way too much makeup, a teased-up meringue of brunette waves atop a broad, welcoming face. Same kind of clothes too: pink, dotted Swiss dress with a frothy collar. Every time Milo'd seen her she'd worn something frilly and inappropriate in that same soap-bar pink.

He didn't expect her to remember him but right away she said, 'Detective S! It's been so long! Why haven't you brought me anyone in so long?'

'Don't hang out much with the living these days, Rev,' said Milo. 'Been working Homicide for a long time.'

'Oh, dear,' said Glenda Stephenson. 'Well, how have you been with that?'

'It has its moments.'

'I'll just bet it does.'

'How's the soul-saving business, Reverend?'

301

Glenda grinned. 'There's never a lack of work.'

'I'll bet.'

'Sit down,' said Glenda Stephenson. 'Cup of coffee?'

Milo saw no urn or pot. Just an alms box on the desk, next to a neat stack of what looked to be government forms. Impulsively, he reached into his pocket, found a bill, dropped it in.

'Oh, that's not necessary,' said Glenda.

'I'm Catholic,' said Milo. 'Put me in a religious environment, and I have an urge to donate.'

Glenda giggled. Little girl's giggle. For some reason it wasn't as foolish coming out of that dinner-plate face as it should've been. 'Well, then come by often. There's never a lack of need, either. So . . . Edgar said this is personal?'

'In a way,' said Milo. 'Work and personal – what I mean is it needs to be kept confidential.'

Glenda sat forward, and her bosoms brushed the desk top. 'Of course. What's the matter, dear?'

'It's not about me,' said Milo. 'Not directly. But I am involved in a case that's . . . ticklish. A name came up, and I traced a connection to the mission. Vance Coury.'

Glenda sat back. Her chair creaked. 'The son or the father?'

'The son.'

'What has he done?'

'You don't sound surprised.'

In repose, Glenda's customary face was unlined – nothing filled wrinkles as well as fat. But now worry lines appeared at the periphery – etching the corners of her mouth, her eyes, her brow.

'Oh dear,' she said. 'Could this reflect in any way on the mission?'

'Not that I can see. I certainly wouldn't do anything to put you in a bad position, Reverend.'

'Oh, I know that, Milo. You were always the kindest. Taking time from your patrol to deliver sad souls. The way you held their arm, the way you . . . ministered to them.'

'I was trying to clean up the streets, and you were there. I'm afraid there's nothing pastoral in my makeup.'

'Oh, I think you're wrong,' said Glenda. 'I think you would've made a wonderful priest.'

Milo's face went hot. Blushing, for God's sake.

Glenda Stephenson said, 'Coury, the son . . . when Fred and I accepted the building, we had our reservations. Because you know we're grizzled old veterans of this neighborhood, knew darn well what his father had been like – everyone on Skid Row knew about his father.'

'Slumlord.'

'Slumlord and a mean man – never gave us a dime, and Milo, we asked. That's why we were shocked when a few months after he died we received a letter from the son's lawyer letting us know he was donating the hotel to the mission. I'm afraid our immediate response was to harbor uncharitable thoughts.'

'As in, what's the catch,' said Milo.

'Exactly. The father . . . no, I won't speak ill of the dead, but suffice it to say that charity didn't appear to be his strong point. And then there were the people he employed. They'd always made the lives of our men difficult. And the son had kept them on.'

'What people?'

'Angry young men from East L.A.,' said Glenda.

'Which gang?' said Milo.

She shook her head. 'You hear talk. Eighteenth Street, the Mexican Mafia, Nuestra Familia. I really don't know. But whoever they were, when they showed up on the street, they intimidated our men. Swaggering by, driving by. Sometimes they'd get out and demand money, become threatening.'

'Physically?'

'Once in a while someone got punched or pushed. Mostly it was psychological intimidation – looks, threats, verbal bullying. I suppose they felt entitled – territorial. Mr Coury – the father – had used them as rent collectors. When the son offered us the building, the first request we made on him was that he ask his crew to stay away from the men. Because we thought he was going to hold on to the other hotels, and we didn't want to be geographically close to that kind of environment. His lawyer said there'd be no problem, Coury was going to tear the buildings down and pave them for parking lots. It ended up being a very smooth transition. Our lawyer talked to his lawyer, papers were signed, and that was it. Fred and I kept waiting for some ulterior motive but the way our lawyer explained it, the son was in an inheritance tax bind and the Grande

Royale could be appraised in a manner that would serve his best interests.'

'Inflated appraisal?'

'No,' said Glenda. 'Fred and I wouldn't be party to that. In fact, we demanded to look at the most recent county assessments, and everything was in line. The Grande Royale was worth approximately twice what the other hotels were, so apparently it fit the son's tax needs. It wasn't the only thing he sold. Mr Coury, the father, had owned many properties. But the three hotels had been acquired as a package through some sort of government housing deal, so by donating the Royale, everything worked out.'

'Coury aiding the Lord's work,' said Milo.

'Funny, isn't it? The father acquired filthy lucre by oppressing the poor and now at least some of those profits have served to elevate the poor.'

'Happy ending, Reverend. Doesn't happen very often.'

'Oh, it does, Milo. You just have to know where to look.'

He talked to her a bit longer, stuffed more money in the alms box over her protests, and left.

Vance Coury had made good on his promise to keep the gang-bangers away from the Mission, and now that the two other hotels had been torn down for parking lots his need for rent collectors had disappeared.

But the gang thing intrigued Milo, and when he drove by the lots and took a look at the attendants, he saw shaved heads and skulking posture. Tattoos conspicuous enough to be visible from the curb.

thirty-one

What I'd seen of Vance Coury's demeanor synched with the profile of a domination rapist: surly, hypermacho, eager not to please. The supercharged ambience in which he operated fit, too: big engines, flashy paint, the photos of submissive fellatrices tacked to the walls of the garage. The mutilated Porsche.

A corrupt father completed the picture: Coury had been raised to take what he wanted. Throw in some like-minded buddies, and Janie Ingalls had been a rabbit in a dog pit.

Junior hadn't been interested in my patronage. Did he really regard the Seville as a hunk of junk? Or did those parking lots pay the bills and the auto-customizing business was recreational? Or a front . . . all those gang boys.

I headed for the city and thought about the bisected Porsche. Evisceration on display. The joy of destruction. Maybe I was interpreting too much, but the few minutes I'd spent with Coury had left me wary and creeped-out, and I kept checking the rearview mirror well past Mulholland.

Back at home, I imagined the party scene twenty years ago: Janie's encounter with Coury, amid the noise and the dope, the flash of recognition – pleasure for Coury, horror for Janie.

He moves in and takes over. The King's Men join in.

Including a King's Man who seemed different than the others?

The images Nicholas Hansen's gallery had posted on its website were still-lifes. Lush, luminously tinted assemblages of fruit and flowers, rendered meticulously. Hansen's work seemed galaxies away from the ruined sculpture assembled on the Beaudry on-ramp – from any brutality. But art was no immunization against evil.

305

Caravaggio had slain a man over a tennis game and Gauguin had slept with young Tahitian girls knowing he'd be infecting them with syphilis.

Still, Nick Hansen seemed to have taken a different path than the others, and deviance has always fascinated me.

It was nearly three, maybe past the New York gallery's closing time, but I phoned anyway, and got a young, female voice on the other end. The first time I'd contacted the gallery, I'd talked to an older woman and hadn't left my name, so here was a chance for some new dissembling.

I shifted into art-speak and presented myself as a collector of old masters drawings who'd run out of the sunlight-free space such treasures demanded and was considering switching to oils.

'Old masters oils?' said the young woman.

'A bit beyond my budget,' I said. 'But I *have* been impressed by some of the contemporary realism that's managed to assert itself among all the performance pieces. Nicholas Hansen, for example.'

'Oh, Nicholas's wonderful.'

'He's certainly not daunted by tradition,' I said. 'Could you tell me more about his background – is it rigidly academic?'

'Well,' she said, 'he did go to Yale. But we've always felt Nicholas transcends academic painting. There's something about his sensibilities. And the way he uses light.'

'Yes. Quite. I like his sense of composition.'

'That, too. He's simply first-rate. Unfortunately, we have no paintings by him in stock, at this time. If you could give me your name—'

'I always research an artist before I take the plunge. Would you happen to have some biographical information on Hansen that you could fax me?'

'Yes, of course,' she said. 'I'll get that right out to you. And about the academic aspect . . . Nicholas *is* well schooled, but please don't hold that against him. Despite his meticulousness and his way with paint as matter, there's a certain primal energy to his consciousness. You'd need to see the pictures in person to really appreciate that.'

'No doubt,' I said. 'There's nothing like in person.'

Five minutes later, my fax machine buzzed, disgorging Nicholas

Hansen's curriculum vitae. Education, awards, group and individual exhibitions, corporate collections, museum shows.

The man had accomplished plenty in two decades, and unlike his old pal Garvey Cossack he hadn't recounted any of it in a pumped-up biography. No mention of high school at all; Nicholas Hansen's account of his education began with college: Columbia University, where he'd received a BA in anthropology, summers filled with painting fellowships, a Masters of Fine Arts at Yale, and two years of postgraduate work at an atelier in Florence, Italy, learning classical painting technique. Among his museum shows were group spots at the Art Institute of Chicago and the Boston Museum of Fine Arts. Prominent names figured among those who collected his work.

An accomplished man. A polished man. Hard to fit that with Vance Coury's garage or the Cossacks' vulgar lifestyle. A gang-rape murder.

I went over the dates on Hansen's résumé. Saw something else that didn't fit.

Milo still wasn't answering any of his phones, so I tried to dispel my restlessness with a beer, then another. I carried the bottle down to the pond, thought about kicking back, decided to net leaves instead. For the next hour or so I pruned, raked, busied myself with mindless chores. I was just about to allow myself a moment of repose when the phone rang up in the house.

Robin? I ran up the stairs, grabbed the kitchen extension, heard Dr Bert Harrison's voice. 'Alex?'

'Bert. What's up?'

'It was nice to see you,' he said. 'After all this time. Just checking to see how you're doing.'

'Did I look that bad?'

'Oh, no, not bad, Alex. Perhaps a bit preoccupied. So . . .'

'Everything's rolling along.'

'Rolling along.'

'No, that's a lie, Bert. I screwed up with Robin.'

Silence.

I said, 'I should've followed your advice. Instead, I brought up the past.'

307

More dead air. 'I see . . .'

'She reacted just as you'd imagine. Maybe I wanted her to.'

'You're saying . . .'

'I really don't know what I'm saying, Bert. Listen, I appreciate your calling, but things are kind of . . . I don't feel like talking about it.'

'Forgive me,' he said.

Apologizing again.

'Nothing to forgive,' I said. 'You gave me good advice, I screwed up.'

'You made a mistake, son. Mistakes can be remedied.'

'Some.'

'Robin's a flexible woman.'

He'd met Robin twice. I said, 'Is that your natural optimism speaking?'

'No, it's an old man's intuition. Alex, I've made my share of mistakes, but after a few years one does get a sense for people. I'd hate to see you misled.'

'About Robin?'

'About anything,' he said. 'Another reason I'm calling is that I'm planning to travel. Perhaps for a while. Cambodia, Vietnam, some places I've been to, others I haven't.'

'Sounds great, Bert.'

'I didn't want you to try to reach me and not find me here.'

'I appreciate that.' Had I come across *that* needy?

'That sounds presumptuous, doesn't it?' he said. 'To think you'd call. But . . . just in case.'

'I appreciate your telling me, Bert.'

'Yes . . . well, then, good luck.'

'When are you leaving?' I said.

'Soon. As soon as final arrangements are complete.'

'Bon voyage,' I said. 'When you get back, give me a call. I'd love to hear about the trip.'

'Yes . . . may I offer one bit of advice, son?'

Please don't. 'Sure.'

'Try to season each day with a new perspective.'

'Okay,' I said.

'Bye, now, Alex.'

I placed the receiver back in its cradle. What had *that* been about? The more I thought about the conversation, the more it sounded like goodbye.

Bert going somewhere . . . he'd sounded sad. Those comments he'd made about senility. All the apologies.

Bert was a first-rate therapist, wise enough to know I hadn't wanted advice. But he offered a parting shot, anyway.

Try to season each day with a new perspective. Last words from an old friend facing deterioration? Taking a trip . . . a final journey?

There I was again, off on some worst-case tangent.

Keep it simple: the old man had always traveled, loved to travel. No reason to think his destination was anywhere but Southeast Asia . . .

The phone rang again. I switched it to speaker and Milo's voice, distant and flecked with static, filled the kitchen. 'Any new insights?'

'How about an actual fact?' I said. 'Nicholas Hansen couldn't have been involved in Janie's murder. Early in June he was finishing up his last year at Columbia. After he graduated, he went to Amsterdam and spent the summer at a life-drawing course at the Rijksmuseum.'

'That assumes he didn't come home for the weekend.'

'New York to L.A. for the weekend?'

'These were rich kids,' he said. 'Anything's possible, but I just don't see it. Hansen's different from the other King's Men. His life took a whole different turn, and unless you can uncover some present-day dealings with Coury and the Cossacks and Brad Larner, my bet is he distanced himself from the group and maintained that distance.'

'So he's no use to us.'

'On the contrary. *He* might be able to provide insights.'

'We just drop in and say we want to chat about his old pals the sex-killers?'

'Any other promising leads at the moment?' I said.

He didn't answer.

I said, 'So what'd you do today?'

'Nosed around about Coury, Junior. His daddy was the nasty piece of work the papers made him out to be. Used gang-bangers to collect the rent. And looks like Junior's continued the relationship. The dubious citizens working his parking lots have that homeboy thing going on.'

'Funny about that.' I told him about my visit to the garage.

'Chopping the Seville as a cover story?' he said. 'Did it ever occur to you Coury didn't want to do the job 'cause he wasn't buying your story? Jesus, Alex—'

'Why wouldn't he buy it?' I said.

'Because maybe someone in the enemy camp knows we've been snooping around the Ingalls case. You got the goddamned murder book in the first place because someone knew we worked together. Alex, that was goddamned stupid.'

'Coury wasn't suspicious, just apathetic,' I said, with more confidence than I felt. 'My take is that he doesn't need the money.'

'Was he doing other chop jobs?'

'Yes,' I admitted.

'Meaning he works, but he just didn't want to work with *you*. Alex, no more improvisation.'

'Fine,' I said. 'Gang connections would have given Coury ready personnel for odd jobs. Like taking care of Luke Chapman, and possibly Willie Burns and Caroline Cossack. Maybe Lester Poulsenn, too. I located him – safely, all computer work – and guess what, he died less than two weeks after Caroline left Achievement House. Shot in the head in a house in Watts, then the house was burned down. He'd just been transferred from IA to Metro, meaning maybe he was working on Janie's case, right?'

'Burned to death,' he said. His voice was tight. 'What was he doing in Watts?'

'The paper didn't say. Sacramento paper, by the way. A detective got murdered in L.A. but the L.A. papers didn't print a word about it.'

'The article say where in Watts?'

I read off the address.

No answer.

'You still there?'

'Yeah . . . okay, meet me in Beverly Hills in an hour. Time for art appreciation.'

thirty-two

Nicholas Hansen's green BMW sat in the cobbled driveway of the house on North Roxbury Drive. The street was lined with struggling elms. A few trees had given up, and their black branches cast ragged shadows on the sparkling sidewalks. The street was quiet but for a Beverly Hills symphony: teams of gardeners pampering the greenery of mansions up the block.

Milo was parked in a new rental car – a gray Oldsmobile sedan – six houses north of Hansen's vanilla hacienda. By the time I'd switched off the engine he was at my window.

'New wheels,' I said.

'Variety's the spice.' His face was pallid and sweaty.

'Something else happen to make you switch?'

'Contacting Hansen is a risk and maybe not a smart one. If he's still in touch with the others, everything hits the fan. If he's not, there may be no real payoff.'

'But you're going ahead, anyway.'

He yanked out a handkerchief and sopped moisture from his brow. 'The alternative is doing nothing. And who says I'm smart?'

When we reached Hansen's property, he scowled and peered through a window of the BMW. 'Clean. Meticulous.' As he stepped up to the door and stabbed the bell, he looked ready to tear something apart.

Nicholas Hansen answered wearing faded black sweats, white Nikes, and a distracted look. Brown and red paint stains on his fingers were the only clues to his occupation. He was tall and spare with an oddly fleshy face, looked closer to fifty than forty. Soft neck, basset eyes the color of river silt, grayish mouth stitched with wrinkles, a bald, blue-veined scalp ringed by a beige buzz. A

311

middle-aged crisis stoop rounded his shoulders. I'd have guessed a burnt-out lawyer taking a day off.

Milo flashed the badge, and Hansen's muddy eyes came alive. But his voice was low and mumbly. 'Police? About what?'

I was standing behind Milo, but not so far that I couldn't smell the alcohol breeze Hansen had let forth.

Milo said, 'High school.' His voice was rough, and he didn't use Hansen's name, hadn't even offered a cop's patronizing 'sir.'

'High school?' Hansen blinked, and the paint-stained fingers of one hand capped his bald head, as if he'd been afflicted by a sudden migraine.

'The King's Men,' said Milo. Hansen dropped the hand and rubbed his fingers together, dislodging a fleck of paint, inspecting his nails. 'I really don't understand – I'm working.'

Milo said, 'This is important.' He'd kept the badge in Hansen's face, and the artist took a step backward.

'The King's Men?' said Hansen. 'That was a very long time ago.'

Milo filled the space Hansen had vacated. 'Those who forget the past are condemned to repeat it, and all that.'

Hansen's hand floundered some more, ended up on the doorjamb. He shook his head. 'You've lost me, gentlemen.' His breath was ninety proof, and his nose was a relief map of busted capillaries.

'Be happy to clarify,' said Milo. He flicked his wrist, and sunlight bounced off the badge. 'I assume you don't want to talk out here in full view.'

Hansen shrank back some more. Milo was only an inch or so taller than Hansen, but he did something with his posture that increased the gap.

'I'm a painter, I'm in the middle of a painting,' Hansen insisted.

'I'm in the middle of a homicide investigation.'

Hansen's mouth slackened, revealing uneven, yellowed teeth. He shut his mouth quickly, looked at his watch, then over his shoulder.

'I'm a big art fan,' said Milo. 'Especially German Expressionism – all that anxiety.'

Hansen stared at him, stepped back farther. Milo remained in the dance, positioned himself inches from Hansen's worried eyes.

Hansen said, 'I hope this doesn't take long.'

★ ★ ★

The house was cool and dim, saturated with the geriatric reek of camphor. The chipped terracotta tiles of the entry hall floor continued up the steps of a narrow, brass-railed staircase. Thirteen-foot ceilings were crossed by carved oak beams. The wood was wormholed and aged nearly black. The walls were hand-troweled plaster two shades deeper than the external vanilla and dotted with empty niches. Smallish leaded windows, some with stained-glass insets picturing New Testament scenes, constricted the light. The colored panes projected rainbow dust beams. The furniture was heavy and dark and clumsy. No art on the walls. The place felt like some ill-attended church.

Nicholas Hansen motioned us to a sagging, fringed sofa uphol-stered in a scratchy tapestry fabric, sat down facing us in a bruised leather chair, and folded his hands in his lap.

'I really can't imagine what this could be about.'

'Let's start with the King's Men,' said Milo. 'You do remember them.'

Hansen gave his watch another glance. Cheap digital thing with a black plastic band.

'Busy day?' said Milo.

Hansen said, 'I may have to interrupt if my mother wakes up. She's dying of colon cancer, and the day nurse took the afternoon off.'

'Sorry,' said Milo, with as little sympathy as I'd ever heard him offer.

'She's eighty-seven,' said Hansen. 'Had me when she was forty-five. I always wondered how long I'd have her.' He plucked at a cuff of his sweatshirt. 'Yes, I remember the King's Men. Why would you connect me to them after all these years?'

'Your name came up in the course of our investigation.'

Hansen showed yellow teeth again. His eyes creased in concen-tration. 'My name came up in a murder investigation?'

'A very nasty murder.'

'Something recent?'

Milo crossed his legs. 'This will go more quickly if I ask the questions.'

Another man might've bristled. Hansen sat in place, like an

obedient child. 'Yes, of course. I'm just – the King's Men was just a stupid high school thing.' Slight slur in his voice. His eyes shot to the ceiling beams. A pliable man. The addition of booze made Milo's job easier.

Milo pulled out his notepad. When he clicked his pen open, Hansen was startled but he remained in place.

'Let's start with the basics: you were a member of the King's Men.'

'I'd really like to know how you . . . never mind, let's do this quickly,' said Hansen. 'Yes, I was a member. For my last two years at Uni. I arrived as a junior. My father was an executive with Standard Oil, we moved around a lot, had lived on the East Coast. During my junior year, Father was transferred to L.A., and we ended up renting a house in Westwood. I was pretty disoriented. It's a disorienting time, anyway, right? I guess I was irritated at my parents for uprooting me. I'd always been obedient – an only child, overly adult. I guess when I got to Uni I figured I'd rebel, and the King's Men seemed a good way to do it.'

'Why?'

'Because they were a bunch of goof-offs,' said Hansen. 'Rich kids who did nothing but drink and dope. They got the school to recognize them as a legitimate service club because one of their fathers owned real estate and he let the school use his empty lots for fund-raisers – car washes, bake sales, that kind of thing. But the Men weren't about service, just partying.'

'A dad with real estate,' said Milo. 'Vance Coury.'

'Yes, Vance's father.'

Hansen's voice rose at the word 'father,' and Milo waited for him to say more. When Hansen didn't, he said, 'When's the last time you saw Vance Coury?'

'High school graduation,' said Hansen. 'I haven't been in touch with any of them. That's why this whole thing is rather odd.'

Another glance upward. Hansen had never boned up on the body language of deception.

'You haven't seen any of them since graduation?' said Milo. 'Not once?'

'By the time we graduated, I was moving in another direction. They were all staying here, and I'd been accepted at Columbia. My

314

father wanted me to go to business school, but I finally accomplished a genuine rebellion and majored in anthropology. What I was really interested in was art, but that would've caused too much tumult. As is, Father was far from amused, but Mother was supportive.'

A third look at his watch, then a glance toward the stairs. Only child hoping for maternal reprieve.

Milo said, 'You didn't really answer the question. Have you seen any of the other King's Men since graduation?'

Hansen's muddy irises took yet another journey upward, and his mouth began to tremble. He tried to cover it with a smile. Crossed his legs, as if imitating Milo. The result was contortive, not casual.

'I never saw Vance or the Cossacks or Brad Larner. But there was another boy, Luke Chapman – though we're talking twenty years ago, for God's sake. Luke was . . . what is it you want to know, exactly?'

Milo's jaw tightened. His voice turned gentle and ominous. 'Luke was what?'

Hansen didn't answer.

Milo said, 'You do know he's dead.'

Hansen nodded. 'Very sad.'

'What were you going to say about him?'

'That he wasn't very bright.'

'When, after graduation, did you see him?'

'Look,' said Hansen. 'You need to understand the context. He – Luke – was no genius. Honestly, he was dull. Despite that, I'd always thought of him as the best of them. That's why – does this have to do with Luke's drowning?'

'When did you see Chapman?'

'Just once,' said Hansen.

'When?'

'My first year in grad school.'

'What month?'

'Winter break. December.'

'So just weeks before Chapman drowned.'

Hansen blanched and brought his eyes back to the carved beams. He sank in his chair and looked small. Incompetent liar. Painting had been a better choice than the corporate thing. Milo slapped his pad shut, shot to his feet, strode to Hansen and placed his hand on the back of Hansen's chair. Hansen looked ready to faint.

'Tell us about it,' said Milo.

'You're saying Luke was murdered? All those years ago . . . who do you suspect?'

'Tell us about the meeting with Chapman.'

'I – this is – ' Hansen shook his head. 'I could use a drink – may I get you something, as well?'

'No, but feel free to fortify yourself.'

Hansen braced himself on the arms of his chair and rose. Milo followed him across the tiled entry, across an adjoining dining room and through double doors. When the two of them returned, Hansen had both his hands wrapped around a squat, cut-crystal tumbler half-filled with whiskey. When he sat down, Milo resumed his stance behind the chair. Hansen twisted and looked up at him, drained most of the whiskey, rubbed the corners of his eyes.

'Start with where.'

'Right here – in the house.' Hansen emptied the glass. 'Luke and I hadn't been in contact. High school was long out of my conscious-ness. They were *stupid* kids. Stupid *rich* kids, and the thought that I'd found them cool was laughable. I was an East Coast nerd scared witless about making yet another lifestyle switch, thrown into a whole new world. Tanned bodies, loud smiles, social castes . . . it was a sudden overdose of *California*. Luke and I had World History together. He was flunking – he was this big blond lunk who could barely read or spell. I felt sorry for him so I helped him – gave him free tutoring. He was dull, but not a bad kid. Built like a fridge, but he never went out for sports because he preferred drinking and smoking dope. That was the essence of the Kingers. They made a big point of not engaging in anything *but* partying and at that specific time in my life that kind of abandon seemed attractive. So when Luke invited me to join the group, I jumped at it. It was somewhere to belong. I had nothing else.'

'Were you welcomed by the others?'

'Not with open arms, but they weren't bad,' said Hansen. 'Tested me out. I had to prove myself by drinking them under the table. That I could do, but I never really felt comfortable with them and maybe they sensed it because, toward the end, they got . . . distant. Also, there was the economic thing. They'd figured I was rich –

there'd been a rumor circulating that Father *owned* an oil company. When I told them the truth, they were clearly disappointed.'

Hansen passed the tumbler from hand to hand, stared at his knees. 'Listen to me, going on about myself.' He took a deep breath. 'That's the sum total: I hung out with them for the second half of my junior year and a bit into my senior year, then it tapered off. When I got into Columbia, that put them off. *They* were all planning to live off their parents' money in L.A. and keep partying.'

Milo said, 'So you were home on break and Luke Chapman just dropped in.'

'Yes, it was out of the blue,' said Hansen. 'I was spending my time holed up in my room drawing. Luke showed up unannounced, and Mother let him in.'

Hansen hefted the empty tumbler.

'What did he want?' said Milo.

Hansen stared at him.

'What was the topic, Nicholas?'

'He looked terrible,' said Hansen. 'Disheveled, unwashed – smelled like a barn. I didn't know what to make of it. Then he said, "Nick, man, you were the only one who ever helped me, and I need you to help me now." My first thought was he'd gotten some girl pregnant, needed guidance about where to get an abortion, something like that. I said, "What can I do for you." And that's when he broke down – just fell apart. Rocking and moaning and saying everything was fucked up.'

He held up the tumbler. 'I could use a refill?'

Milo turned to me. 'The bottle's on the counter. Nicholas and I will wait here.'

I entered the kitchen and poured two fingers from the bottle of Dalwhinnie single-malt on the counter. Taking in details as I made my way back: yellow walls, old white appliances, bare stainless-steel counters, empty dish drainers. I opened the refrigerator. Carton of milk, package of sweating bacon, something in a bowl that looked like calcified gruel. No food aromas, just that same mothball stink. The whiskey bottle had been three-quarters empty. Nicholas Hansen cared little for nutrition, was a solitary drinker.

Back in the living room, Milo was ignoring Hansen and flipping the pages of his notepad. Hansen sat paralytically still. I handed him the drink and he took it with both hands and gulped.

Milo said, 'Luke fell apart.'

'I asked him what was wrong but instead of telling me he pulled out a joint and started to light up. I grabbed it out of his hand, and said, "What do you think you're doing?" I guess I sounded irritated because he shrank back and said, "Oh, Nick, we really fucked up." And that's when he let it all out.'

Hansen finished the second Scotch.

Milo said, 'Go on.'

Hansen regarded the empty glass, seemed to be considering another shot, but placed the tumbler on a side table. 'He told me there'd been a party – a big one, some place in Bel Air, an empty house—'

'Whose house?'

'He didn't say and I didn't ask,' said Hansen. 'I didn't *want* to know.'

'Why not?' said Milo.

'Because I'd moved on, they were long gone from my consciousne—'

'What did Chapman tell you about the party?' said Milo.

Hansen was silent. Looked anywhere but at us.

We waited him out.

He said, 'Oh my.'

'Oh my, indeed,' said Milo.

Hansen snatched up the tumbler. 'I could use a—'

Milo said, 'No.'

'A girl got killed at the party. I really need another drink.'

'What was the girl's name?'

'*I don't know!*' Hansen's irises were wet – boggy mud.

'You don't know,' said Milo.

'All Luke said was there'd been a party and things had gotten wild and they'd been fooling around with a girl and things got even wilder and all of a sudden she was dead.'

'Fooling around.'

No answer.

'All of a sudden,' said Milo.

'That's how he put it,' said Hansen. Milo chuckled. Hansen recoiled, nearly dropped the tumbler.

'How was this *sudden* death brought about, Nick?'

Hansen bit his lip.

Milo barked, 'Come on.'

Hansen jumped in his chair and fumbled the glass again. 'Please – I don't know what happened – *Luke* didn't know what had happened. That was the point. He was confused – disoriented.'

'What did he tell you about the girl?'

'He said Vance tied her up, they were partying with her, then all of a sudden it was bloody. A bloody scene, like one of those movies we used to watch in high school – slasher movies. "Worse than that, Nick. It's much worse when it's real." I got sick to my stomach, said, "What the hell are you talking about?" Luke just babbled and blubbered and kept repeating that they'd fucked up.'

'Who?'

'All of them. The Kingers.'

'No name for the girl?'

'He said he'd never seen her before. She was someone Vance knew, and Vance noticed her and picked her up. Literally. Slung her over his shoulder and carried her down to the basement. She was stoned.'

'In the basement of the party house.'

'That's where they . . . fooled with her.'

'Fooled with her,' said Milo.

'I'm trying to be accurate. That's how Luke put it.'

'Did Chapman take part in the rape?'

Hansen mumbled.

'What's that?' demanded Milo.

'He wasn't sure, but he thought he did. He was stoned, too. Everyone was. He didn't remember, kept saying the whole thing was like a nightmare.'

'Especially for the girl,' said Milo.

'I didn't want to believe him,' said Hansen. 'I'd come home from Yale for ten days. The last thing I needed was this dropping in my lap. I figured it had been a dream – some sort of drug hallucination. Back when I'd known Luke he was always on something.'

'You said he wanted help from you. What kind of help?'

'He wanted to know what to do. I was a twenty-two-year-old *kid*, for Christ's sake, what position was I in to give him advice?'

Hansen's fingers tightened around the tumbler. 'He couldn't have picked a worse time to drop it on me. People were telling me I had talent, I was finally standing up to Father. The last thing I needed was to get sucked into some . . . horror. It was my *right* not to get sucked in. And I don't know why *you* feel you have a right to—'

'So you just dropped it,' said Milo. 'What'd you tell Chapman?'

'No,' said Hansen. 'That's wrong. I didn't drop it. Not completely. I told Luke to go home and keep all of it to himself, and when I figured things out, I'd get back to him.'

'He listened to you?'

Hansen nodded. 'It was what . . . he wanted to hear. He thanked me. After he left, I kept telling myself it had been the drugs talking. I *wanted* to drop it. But something happened to me that year – a painting class I'd taken. The teacher was an Austrian expatriate, a Holocaust survivor. He'd told me horror stories of all the good citizens who'd claimed to know nothing about what was going on. What liars they were. How Vienna had cheered when Hitler took power and everyone had turned a blind eye to atrocities. I remembered something he'd said: "The Austrians have convinced themselves that Hitler was German and Beethoven was Austrian." That stuck with me. I didn't want to be like that. So I went over to the library and checked out the newspapers for the time period Luke said the murder had taken place. But there was *nothing*. Not an article, not a single *word* about any girl being murdered in Bel Air. So I decided Luke *had* been freaking out.'

Hansen's shoulders dropped. He allowed himself a weak smile. Trying to relax. Milo played the silence and Hansen tightened up again. 'So you're saying there really . . . ?'

'Did you ever call Chapman back? Like you said you would?'

'I had nothing to tell him.'

'So what'd you do next?'

'I went back to Yale.'

'Chapman ever try to reach you at Yale?'

'No.'

'When were you in L.A. next?'

'Not for years. The next summer I was in France.'

'Avoiding L.A.?'

'No,' said Hansen. 'Looking for other things.'

'Such as?'

'Painting opportunities.'

'When did you move back to L.A.?'

'Three years ago, when Mother became ill.'

'Where were you living before that?'

'New York, Connecticut, Europe. I try to spend as much time as I can in Europe. Umbria, the light—'

'What about Austria?' said Milo.

Hansen's face lost color.

'So you're here to take care of your mother.'

'That's the *only* reason. When she passes, I'll sell the house and find myself somewhere peaceful.'

'Meanwhile,' said Milo, 'you and your old buddies are neighbors—'

'They're not my bud—'

'—ever make you nervous? Your being a semipublic figure and having a bunch of murderers knowing you're back in town?'

'I'm not semipublic,' said Hansen. 'I'm not any kind of public. I *paint*. Finish one canvas and start another. I never truly believed anything *happened*.'

'What did you think when you learned about Chapman drowning?'

'That it was an accident or suicide.'

'Why suicide?'

'Because he'd seemed so upset.'

'Suicide out of remorse?' said Milo.

Hansen didn't answer.

'You believed Chapman had been hallucinating, but you left town without trying to convince him there was nothing to worry about.'

'It wasn't my – what is it you *want* from me?'

'Details.'

'About what?'

'The murder.'

'I don't have any more details.'

'Why would Chapman feel remorse for something that never happened?'

'I don't know, I'm not a mind reader! This whole thing is insane. Not a word in the papers for twenty years, and all of a sudden someone cares?'

Milo consulted his pad. 'How'd you learn about Chapman's death?'

'Mother included it in her weekly letter.'

'How'd you feel about it?'

'What do you *think*? I felt *terrible*,' said Hansen. 'How *else* could I feel?'

'You felt terrible, then just forgot about it.'

Hansen rose out of his chair. Spittle whitened the corners of his lips.

'What was I *supposed* to do? Go to the police and repeat some far-fetched, stoned-out story? I was twenty-two, for Christ's sake.'

Milo flashed him a cold stare, and Hansen slumped back down. 'It's easy to judge.'

'Let's go over the details,' said Milo. 'The girl was raped in the basement. Where'd Chapman say they killed her?'

Hansen shot him a miserable look. 'He said there was a big property next door to the party house, an estate, no one living there. They brought her over there. He said she was unconscious. They took her into some wooded area and started talking about how they needed to make sure she didn't turn them in. That's when it got . . .'

'Bloody.'

Hansen covered his face and exhaled noisily.

'Who's "they"?' said Milo.

'All of them,' Hansen said through his fingers. 'The Kingers.'

'Who exactly was there? Names.'

'Vance and Luke, Garvey and Bob Cossack, Brad Larner. All of them.'

'The Kingers,' said Milo. 'Guys you don't see anymore. Guys you're not worried about being your neighbors.'

Hansen's hands dropped. 'Should I be worried?'

'It does seem odd,' said Milo. 'For three years you've been living in L.A. but you've never run into them.'

'It's a big city,' said Hansen. 'Big as you want it to be.'

'You don't run in the same social circles?'

'I don't have *any* social circle. I rarely leave the house. Everything's delivered – groceries, laundry. Painting and taking Mother to the doctor, that's my world.'

I thought: *Prison*.

Milo said, 'Have you followed the others' lives?'

'I know the Cossacks are builders of some kind – you see their names on construction signs. That's it.'

'No idea what Vance Coury's been up to?'

'No.'

'Brad Larner?'

'No.'

Milo wrote something down. 'So . . . your buddies took the nameless girl to the property next door and things just *kind* of got bloody.'

'They weren't my buddies.'

'Who did the actual killing?'

'Luke didn't say.'

'What about the rape? Who initiated that?'

'He – my impression was they all joined in.'

'But Chapman wasn't sure if he participated or not.'

'Maybe he was lying. Or in denial, I don't know,' said Hansen. 'Luke wasn't cruel but – I can see him getting carried along. But without the others, he never would've done anything like that. He told me he'd felt . . . immobilized – as if his feet were stuck. That's the way he phrased it. "My feet were stuck, Nick. Like in quicksand." '

'Can you see the others doing something like that on their own?'

'I don't know . . . I used to think of them as clowns . . . maybe. All I'm saying is Luke was a big softie. A big Baby Huey type of guy.'

'And the others?'

'The others weren't soft.'

'So,' said Milo, 'the murder started out as a way to silence the girl.'

Hansen nodded.

'But it progressed to something else, Nicholas. If you'd seen the body, you'd know that. It was something you wouldn't want to paint.'

'Oh, Lord,' said Hansen.

'Did Luke Chapman make any mention at all of who initiated the murder?'

Hansen shook his head.

'How about taking a guess?' said Milo. 'From what you remember about the Kingers' personalities.'

'Vance,' said Hansen, without hesitation. 'He was the leader. The most aggressive. Vance was the one who picked her up. If I had to guess, I'd say Vance was the first to cut her.'

Milo slapped his pad shut. His head shot forward. 'Who said anything about cutting, Nicholas?'

Hansen turned white. 'You said it – you said it was ugly.'

'Chapman told you they'd cut her, didn't he?'

'Maybe – he could've.'

Milo stood and stomped his way slowly toward Hansen on echoing tiles, came to a halt inches from Hansen's terrified face. Hansen's hands rose protectively.

'What else are you holding back, Nicholas?'

'Nothing! I'm doing my best—'

'Do better,' said Milo.

'I'm *trying*.' Hansen's voice took on a whine. 'It's twenty years ago. You're making me remember things I repressed because they disgusted me. I didn't *want* to hear details then, and I don't want to now.'

'Because you like pretty things,' said Milo. 'The wonderful world of art.'

Hansen clapped his hands against his temples and looked away from Milo. Milo got down on one knee and spoke into Hansen's right ear.

'Tell me about the cutting.'

'That's it. He just said they started cutting her.' Hansen's shoulders rose and fell, and he began weeping.

Milo gave him a moment of peace. Then he said, 'After they cut her, what?'

'They burned her. They burned her with cigarettes. Luke said he could hear her skin sizzle . . . oh God – I really thought he was . . .'

'Making it up.'

Hansen sniffed, wiped his nose with his sleeve, let his head fall. The back of his neck was glossy and creased, like canned tallow.

Milo said, 'They burned her, then what?'

'That's all. That really *is* all. Luke said it was like it became a game – he had to *think* of it as a game in order not to freak out completely. He said he'd watched and tried to pretend she was one of those inflatable dolls and they were playing with her. He said it seemed to go on forever until someone – I think it was Vance, I can't swear to it, but probably Vance – said she was dead and they needed to get her out of there. They bundled her up in something, put her in the trunk of Vance's Jaguar, and dumped her somewhere near downtown.'

'Pretty detailed for a hallucination,' said Milo.

Hansen didn't respond.

'Especially,' pressed Milo, 'for a dull guy like Chapman. You ever know him to be that imaginative?'

Hansen remained mute.

'Where'd they take her, Nicholas?'

'I don't *know* where – why the hell wasn't it in the *papers*?' Hansen balled a hand into a fist and raised it chest high. Making a stab at assertiveness. Milo remained crouched but somehow increased his dominance. Hansen shook his head and looked away and cried some more.

'What'd they do afterward?'

'Had coffee,' said Hansen. 'Some place in Hollywood. Coffee and pie. Luke said he tried eating but threw up in the bathroom.'

'What kind of pie?'

'I didn't ask. Why wasn't there anything in the *papers*?'

'What would your theory be about that, Nicholas?'

'What do you mean?' said Hansen.

'Given what you know about your buddies, what's your theory?'

'I don't see what you're getting at.'

Milo got up, stretched, rolled his neck, walked slowly to a leaded window, turned his back on Hansen. 'Think about the world you inhabit, Nicholas. You're a successful artist. You get thirty, forty thousand dollars for a painting. Who buys your stuff?'

'Thirty thousand isn't big-time in the art world,' said Hansen. 'Not compared to—'

'It's a lot of money for a painting,' said Milo. 'Who buys your stuff?'

'Collectors, but I don't see what that has to—'

'Yeah, yeah, people of taste and all that. But at forty grand a pop not just any collectors.'

'People of means,' said Hansen.

Milo turned suddenly, grinning. 'People with money, Nicholas.' He cleared his throat.

Hansen's muddy eyes rounded. 'You're saying someone was bribed to keep it quiet? Something that horrible could be – then for God's sake why didn't it *stay* quiet? Why is it coming to light now?'

'Give me a theory about that, too.'

'I don't have one.'

'Think.'

'It's in someone's best interests to go public?' said Hansen. He sat up. 'Bigger money's come into play? Is that what you're getting at?'

Milo returned to the sofa, sat back comfortably, flipped his pad open.

'Bigger money,' said Hansen. 'Meaning I'm a total *ass* for talking to you. You caught me off guard and used me—' He brightened suddenly. 'But you screwed *up*. You were obligated to offer me the presence of an attorney, so anything I've told you is inadmissible—'

'You watch too much TV, Nicholas. We're *obligated* to offer you a lawyer if we arrest you. Any reason we should arrest you, Nicholas?'

'No, no, of course not—'

Milo glanced at me. 'I suppose we could exercise the option. Obstruction of justice is a felony.' Back to Hansen: 'Charge like that, whether or not you got convicted, your life would change. But given that you've cooperated . . .'

Hansen's eyes sparked. He pawed at the scant hair above his ears. 'I need to be worried, don't I?'

'About what?'

'*Them.* Jesus, what have I done? I'm stuck here, can't *leave*, not with Mother—'

'With or without Mother, leaving would be a bad idea, Nicholas. If you've been straight – really told us everything – we'll do our best to keep you safe.'

'As if you give a damn.' Hansen got to his feet. 'Get out – leave me alone.'

Milo stayed seated. 'How about a look at your painting?'

'*What?*'

'I meant what I said,' said Milo. 'I do like art.'

'My studio's private space,' said Hansen. 'Get out!'

'Never show a fool an unfinished work?'

Hansen tottered. Laughed hollowly. 'You're no fool. You're a user. How do you live with yourself?'

Milo shrugged, and we headed for the door. He stopped a foot from the knob. 'By the way, the pictures on your gallery website are gorgeous. What is it the French call still-lifes – *nature morte*? Dead nature?'

'Now you're trying to diminish me.'

Milo reached for the door, and Hansen said, 'Fine, take a look. But I only have one painting in progress, and it needs work.'

We followed him up the brass-railed staircase to a long landing carpeted in defeated green shag. Three bedrooms on one end, a single, closed door off by itself on the north wing. A breakfast tray was set on the rug. A teapot and three plastic bowls: blood-colored jello, soft-boiled egg darkened to ochre, something brown and granular and crusted.

'Wait here,' said Hansen, 'I need to check on her.' He tiptoed to the door, cracked it open, looked inside, returned. 'Still sleeping. Okay, c'mon.'

His studio was the southernmost bedroom, a smallish space expanded by a ceiling raised to the rafters and a skylight that let in southern sun. The hardwood floors were painted white, as was his easel. White-lacquered flat file, white paint box and brush holders, glass jars filled with turpentine and thinner. Dots of color squeezed on a white porcelain palette fluttered in the milky atmosphere like exotic butterflies.

On the easel was an eleven-by-fourteen panel. Hansen had said his current painting needed work, but it looked finished to me. At the center of the composition was an exquisitely bellied, blue-and-white Ming vase, rendered so meticulously that I longed to touch the gloss. A jagged crack ran down the belly of the vase, and brimming over its lip were masses of flowers and vines, their brilliance accentuated – animated – by a burnt umber background that deepened to black at the edges.

Orchids and peonies and tulips and irises and blooms I couldn't identify. Hot colors, luminous striations, voluptuous petals, vaginal leaves, vermiform tendrils, all interspersed with ominous clots of sphagnum. The fissure implied incipient explosion. Flowers, what could be prettier? Hansen's blooms, gorgeous and boastful and flame-vivid as they were, said something else.

Gleam and hue fraying and wilting at the edges. From the shadows, the black, inexorable progress of rot.

Conditioned air blew through a ceiling vent, flat, artificial, filtered clean, but a stink reached my nostrils: the painting gave off the moist, squalid seduction of decay.

Milo wiped his brow, and said, 'You don't use a model.'

Hansen said, 'It's all in my head.'

Milo stepped closer to the easel. 'You alternate paint and glaze?'

Hansen stared at him. 'Don't tell me you paint.'

'Can't draw a straight line.' Milo got even nearer to the board and squinted. 'Kind of a Flemish thing going on – or maybe someone with an appreciation of Flemish, like Severin Roesen. But you're better than Roesen.'

'Hardly,' said Hansen, unmoved by the compliment. 'I'm a lot less than I was before you barged into my life. You *have* diminished me. I've diminished myself. Will you really protect me?'

'I'll do my best if you cooperate.' Milo straightened. 'Did Luke Chapman mention anyone else being present at the murder? Any of the other partygoers?'

Hansen's fleshy face quivered. 'Not here. Please.'

'Last question,' said Milo.

'No. He mentioned no one else.' Hansen sat down at the easel and rolled up his sleeves. 'You'll protect me,' he said in a dead voice. He selected a sable brush and smoothed its bristles. 'I'm going back to work. There are some real problems to work out.'

thirty-three

When we were back on Roxbury Drive, Milo said, 'Believe his story?'

'I do.'

'So do I,' he said, as we walked to our cars. 'I also believe I'm a hypocrite.'

'What do you mean?'

'Playing Grand Inquisitor with Hansen. Making him feel like shit because he repressed twenty-year-old memories. I did the same damn thing, with less of an excuse.'

'What's his excuse?' I said.

'He's weak. Cut him open you'll find a Silly Putty spine.'

'You sensed the weakness right away,' I said.

'You noticed that, huh? Yup, moved right in on ol' Nicky. Got a nose for weakness. Doesn't that make me pleasant company?'

When we reached the gray Olds, I said, 'I know you're going to tell me I'm laying more shrink stuff on you, but I don't believe your situation's comparable to Hansen's. He had access to firsthand information about the murder and kept it to himself for twenty years. In order to do that, he convinced himself Chapman had been hallucinating, but those details – cigarette burns, the way they moved Janie – say he knew better. Hansen engaged in two decades of self-delusion, and who knows what it did to his soul. You tried to do your job and were ordered off the case.'

'Following orders?' He gazed up the block absently.

'Fine,' I said. 'Torment yourself.'

'Hansen paints, I don't,' he said. 'We all need our hobbies . . .

listen, thanks for your time, but I need to sort things out, figure which way to go with this.'

'What about the main point we got from Hansen's story?' I said.

'Which is . . .'

'What you were getting at with that final question in the studio about anyone else being at the murder. Chapman spilled his guts to Hansen but made no mention of Caroline Cossack or Willie Burns. Meaning they probably weren't there. Despite that, the Cossacks stashed Caroline at Achievement House for six months and had her tagged with a behavioral warning. Burns returned to the streets, got busted for dope, took a big risk by getting himself a job at Achievement House. Maybe he skipped on Boris Nemerov because of what he'd seen at the party. If he went to jail on the drug beef, he'd be a sitting duck.'

'Burns as a witness.'

'Maybe he followed the King's Men because he figured there'd be more doping and he could peddle more merchandise. Caroline could've just been hanging with him. Or she wanted to hang out with her brothers – the odd little sister who'd always gotten shunted to the background. The initial motive for Janie's murder was to silence her. Luke Chapman may have died for the same reason. Caroline and Burns would've been extreme liabilities.'

'Victims, not murderers,' he said. 'And all the more likely to be dead.'

'Those two photos preceding Janie's death shot. A dead black guy and a mangled white female mental patient. Maybe whoever sent the book was trying to tell you about two other db's.'

'Except, as you pointed out, the dead black guy was in his forties, which would be Burns's age now, not twenty years ago.' He took hold of the door handle. 'I need to develop a few migraines over this. Ciao.'

'That's it?'

'What?' he said.

'You go your way, I go mine?' I said. 'Is there something you aren't telling me?'

His half-second hesitation belied his answer. 'I wish I *had* something not to tell, Alex – look, I appreciate your effort but we can go over theories till the Second Coming, and it won't move me any closer to solving Janie.'

'What will?'

'Like I said, I need to do some thinking.'

'Alone.'

'Sometimes,' he said, 'alone helps.'

I drove away wondering what he was keeping from me, peeved at being shut out. Thinking about what didn't await me at home turned irritation to dread, and before I knew it I was hunched over the wheel, driving too fast – going nowhere fast.

Nothing worse than a big house when you're alone. And I had no one to blame but myself.

I'd screwed things up, royally, despite Bert Harrison's wise counsel. Like most expert therapists, the old man wasn't one for offering unsolicited advice, but during my visit he'd made a point of warning me off the paranoia trail when it came to Robin.

'*Sounds like small things have been amplified . . . this is the girl for you.*' Had he sensed something – sniffed out nuances of my impending stupidity? Why the hell hadn't I listened to him?

A blast of honks jolted me. I'd been sitting at the green light at Walden and Sunset for who knew how long and the cute young woman in the VW Golf behind me thought that justified a snarl and a stiff finger.

I waved at her and sped off. She passed me, stopped talking on her cell phone long enough to flip me off again, nearly collided with the curb as her VW struggled with the winding road.

I wished her well and returned to thoughts of Bert Harrison. The other opinions the old man voiced that day – outwardly casual remarks tossed out at the tail end of my visit.

Coincidence or the old therapist's trick of harnessing the power of the parting word? I'd used it myself hundreds of times.

Bert's parting shot had been to bring up Caroline Cossack. Out of context – well after we'd stopped discussing the Ingalls case.

'*That girl. So monstrous, if it's true.*'

'*You seem skeptical.*'

'*I do find it hard to believe that a young female would be capable of such savagery.*'

Then Bert had gone on to express doubts about Willie Burns as a lust murderer.

'*A junkie in the strict sense – heroin? Opiates are the great pacifiers . . . I've certainly never heard of a junkie acting out in such a sexually violent manner.*'

Now it looked as if Bert had been right on.

Was all that the intuition of an exceptionally insightful man?

Or did Bert *know*?

Had Schwinn continued to work the Ingalls case for years after leaving the department? Had he told *Bert* about what he'd unearthed?

Bert had admitted knowing Schwinn but claimed the relationship was casual. Chance meetings in theater lobbies.

What if it was anything *but* casual?

Schwinn had fought his way out of drug addiction, and perhaps he'd done so on his own. But that kind of progress would've been helped along by treatment, and Bert Harrison had trained in addiction treatment at the Federal hospital in Lexington.

Schwinn as Bert's patient.

Psychotherapy. Where all kinds of secrets tumbled out.

If any of that was true, Bert had lied to me. And *that* could explain all those apologies he'd tendered. His contrition – so puzzling at the time that I'd wondered about Bert's deteriorating mental state.

Bert had *encouraged* my suspicions: '*One regresses. Loses one's sense of propriety. Forgive me.*'

'*There's nothing to forgive—*'

I remembered how he'd wiped away tears.

'*Is everything okay, Bert?*'

'*Everything is as it should be.*'

Seeking forgiveness because he knew he had to lie to me? Protecting Schwinn because of patient confidentiality?

But Schwinn had been buried seven months ago and any privilege had died along with his body. Perhaps Bert held himself to higher standards.

Or maybe he was protecting a *living* patient.

In drug treatment – the kind of intensive treatment Bert would've prescribed for a long-term addict like Schwinn – family members were included. And Marge was all the family Schwinn had had left.

Bert shielding Marge. It made sense. I strained to recall anything in our conversation that pointed to that and came up with something quickly: Bert had deflected any suggestion Marge could've mailed the murder book.

Protecting her, or had *Bert* been the messenger? A doctor honoring his patient's last wishes.

What if Janie's murder had eaten at Schwinn – corroded his late-in-life serenity – to the point where he felt impelled to stir up the ashes? Because even though the department had booted him out, and outwardly he'd made major life changes, Pierce Schwinn had held on to a detective's bulldog sensibilities.

Janie wasn't only a cold case, she'd been Schwinn's *last* case. One massive overdose of unfinished business. Perhaps Schwinn had connected the unsolved murder with his breakdown.

Bert would have wanted to help him with that.

The more I thought about it, the better it fit. Schwinn came to trust Bert, showed Bert the murder book, eventually bequeathed the album to his psychiatrist. Knowing Bert would do the right thing.

Bert's involvement would also explain why the blue-bound horror had been mailed to me. He'd met Milo a couple of times, but he knew me much better and was well aware of my relationship with Milo. For Bert, my handing over the book to Milo would have been a certainty.

Fingerprints wiped clean. I could see the old man doing that.

What I *couldn't* see was him driving down to L.A., stealing Rick's Porsche, and returning the car with the original Ingalls file on the front seat. The GTA combined with the HIV detective rumor and that weird encounter with the man who called himself Paris Bartlett had Big Blue written all over it.

Someone in the department. Or once associated with the department. Maybe even the cop buddy I'd hypothesized, stepping in once the wheels had begun to turn.

Theories. . . Bert had just called to let me know he was leaving town. A few days ago, he'd mentioned nothing about travel plans.

Escaping *because* of my visit? Bert and I weren't everyday acquaintances, there'd be no reason for him to notify me of his itinerary. Unless he was trying to distance himself from the fallout.

Or call me off.

By the time I made it to the bridle path that leads to my property, my head ached with conjecture. I pulled up in front of my house . . . our house. The damn thing looked cold, white . . . foreign. I sat in the Seville with the engine running. Turned the car around and drove back toward the Glen.

You *could* go home again, but what was the point?

My nerves were exposed wire sizzling with impulse. Maybe a long, pretty drive would help cool them down.

Alone.

Milo was right about that.

thirty-four

M ilo drove out of Beverly Hills, mulling over the interview with Nicholas Hansen.

The guy was pathetic, a momma's boy and a drunk, no big challenge browbeating him into spilling. But would Hansen change his story once he had time to stew, maybe call an attorney? Even if he did hold fast, his tale amounted to third-party hearsay.

Still Milo knew what he had to do: go home, transcribe his notes of the interview, making sure he got all the details down, then stash the transcription with all the other good stuff he kept to himself – the floor safe in his bedroom closet.

He took Palm Drive to Santa Monica, then the diagonal shortcut to Beverly, driving like a gangster's chauffeur – slower than usual, checking the scenery all around, scoping out the drivers sitting two, three, four car lengths behind the rented Olds. Taking a different route than usual – past La Cienega, then doubling back on Rosewood. As far as he could tell, everything clear.

One thing the Hansen interview *had* accomplished: Milo knew now that he couldn't let go of Janie.

All these years he'd coped with department bullshit and propped up his self-image with secret little pep talks, the psychobabble he'd never share with anyone. *You're different. Noble. Heroic, nonstereotypic gay warrior traversing a goddamn heterosexual universe.*

Rebel with a lost cause.

Maybe all that self-delusional swill was what had helped him conveniently forget Janie. But the moment Alex had shown him that death shot, his heartbeat and his sweat glands told him he'd lived nearly half his life as the worst kind of chump.

Conning himself.

335

Was that insight? If so, it sucked.

He laughed out loud because cursing lacked imagination. He and Hansen were two peas in the same cowardly, ass-covering pod. Alex, ever the shrink – ever the *friend* – had tried to spin it differently.

Thank you very much, Doctor, but that don't change the facts.

Yeah, old Nicholas was a moral mollusk, but meeting him had solidified things.

As he cruised through quiet West Hollywood streets, he formalized the next risky step: get closer to the murder by leaning on someone who'd actually been there. The choice of targets was: Brad Larner. Because twenty years after high school, Larner was low man among the King's Men, a loser who'd worked for Daddy, then regressed to lackeying for his buddies.

One of those walking-around guys. A jerk.

A follower. If Vance Coury and the Cossacks were sharks, Larner was a remora, ready to be plucked off the body corrupt.

Milo ached to get the bastard in a quiet little room. But Larner wasn't living at his own home, might very well be bunking with the Cossacks. The challenge was to snag him alone, away from the others.

A-hunting we will go.

Normally, even with his cop sensibilities, he might not have noticed the navy blue Saab heading his way down his own block. West Hollywood parking laws kept the streets fairly clear but permit parking was allowed and homeowners could grant guest passes, so it was by no means weird to see an unfamiliar vehicle stationed near the curb.

But today he'd mainlined adrenaline instead of vodka and was noticing everything. So when the blue Saab sped by him and he caught a half-second eyeful of the driver, he knew he'd have to confirm what his brain was telling him.

He lowered his speed, watched in his rearview as the Saab turned onto Rosewood and disappeared from view. Then he hooked a sharp U and went after it.

Thank God for the brand-new rental he'd picked up on the way home. The gray Dodge Polaris had sagging bumpers and poorly camouflaged dings all over its abused chassis. But with power to spare and windows tinted way past the legal limit, it was exactly what he needed. For this one, he'd forsaken Hertz and Avis and Budget and patronized a guy he knew who ran a yard full of clunkers on Sawtelle and Olympic, out past the 405 South. Budget wheels for the spiky-haircut-and-skinny-lapeled-black-suit types – *arriviste* thespians and screenwriters and would-be dot.com gajillionaires who thought it way cool to tool around L.A. in something outdated and ugly.

Milo stomped the gas, and the Polaris responded, laying down a nice little patch of vertebra-rattling speed. He followed the Saab's trajectory, making sure he didn't get too close when he spotted his quarry turning north on San Vicente. A medium-congestion traffic flow allowed him to settle five lengths behind the Saab and do a little creative swerving so he could keep his eye on the vehicle.

From what he could tell, just the one male at the wheel. Now it was time to confirm the rest of his first impression. The Saab continued past Melrose and Santa Monica, turned left on Sunset, and got stuck in a serious jam caused by orange CalTrans cones blocking off the right-hand lane.

Cones only, no work or workers in sight. The road agency was run by sadists and fools, but this time Milo blessed their mean little hearts as the congestion allowed him to jockey to the right, catch sight of the Saab's plates, copy them down. Traffic moved fifty feet. Milo cell phoned DMV, lied – Lord, he was getting good at it – *liked* it.

The plates came back to a one-year-old Saab owned by Craig Eiffel Bosc, address on Huston Street in North Hollywood, no wants or warrants.

The chrome sludge oozed another few yards, and Milo did some more rude maneuvering and managed to close the gap between the Dodge and the Saab to three cars. Three more stop-and-gos and a smooth but slow flow resumed and he was alongside the Saab, passing on the right, hoping the Dodge wouldn't register in his quarry's memory and if it did, that the blackened glass would cover him.

Another half a second was all he needed – mission accomplished.

The face was one he'd seen before. Mr Smiley. The asshole who'd accosted him at the hot dog stand, claiming to be Paris Bartlett.

Craig Eiffel Bosc.

Eiffel/Paris. Cute.

Bosc/Bartlett stymied him for a moment, then he got it: two varieties of pears.

How imaginative. Sell it to the networks.

Bosc/Bartlett was moving his head in time to music, oblivious, and Milo sped up, got two cars *ahead* of the Saab, used the next red light to peer through the intervening Toyota with its two little chicklets also bopping – to some bass-heavy hip-hop thing. He tried to get another look at Craig Eiffel Bosc but caught only the girls' hyperactivity and the Toyota's windshield glare. The right lane opened up and he eased back into it, allowed the Toyota and the Saab to pass.

Glancing to the left without moving his head as Smiley Pear zipped by. Then catching up and keeping pace with the Saab just long enough to take a mental snapshot.

Smiley was in shirtsleeves – deep blue shirt – with his sky-colored tie loosened, one paw on the wheel, the other wrapped around a big fat cigar. The Saab's windows were untinted but shut, and the interior was clouded with smoke. Not thick enough, though, to obscure the smile on Craig Eiffel Bosc's struggling-actor-handsome countenance.

Such a happy fellow, toking tobacco and cruising and grooving in his zippy little Swedish car on a sunny, California day.

On top of the world.

We'll see about that.

Craig Bosc took Coldwater Canyon into the Valley. Medium traffic made the tail easy. Not that Bosc would be looking out for him. The guy was no motor-pro – a real ninny for showing himself in plain view on Milo's block. The cigar and his grin said he couldn't even imagine the tables turning.

At Ventura, the Saab turned right and drove into Studio City, where it pulled into the parking lot of a twenty-four-hour yuppie gym on the south side of the boulevard. Craig Bosc got out with a blue bag and half jogged to the front. One good arm push and he was through the door and gone.

Milo looked around for a vantage point. A seafood restaurant across Ventura offered a perfect view of the gym and the Saab. The surf-and-turf special sounded enticing – he was hungry.

Ravenous.

He indulged himself with an upgrade from the special: extra big lobster, Alaskan crab legs, sixteen-ounce top sirloin, baked potato with sour cream and chives, a mountain of fried zucchini. All that washed down with Cokes instead of beer, because he needed his wits.

He ate slowly, figuring Bosc would be in there for at least an hour, doing the old body-beautiful thing. By the time he'd asked for the check and was working on his third coffee refill, the Saab was still in plain view. He threw down money, hazarded a trip to the men's room, left the restaurant, and sat in the Dodge for another half hour before Bosc emerged with wet hair. Back in his street clothes – the blue shirt and black slacks – minus the tie.

Bosc bounced over to the Saab, disarmed the alarm, but instead of getting in, stopped to check his reflection in the side window. Fluffing his hair. Undoing the shirt's second button. Milo watched the asshole show off that big smile for the glass audience – Bosc actually turned his head here and there. Appreciating his own damn face from multiple angles.

Then Bosc got in the Saab and did an L.A. thing: *drove* less than a block before pulling into another parking lot.

A bar. Little cedar-sided cube stuffed between a sushi bar and a bicycle shop. A painted sign above the cedar door labeled the place as **EXTRAS.** A banner to the right advertised the psychic benefits of happy hour.

Half a dozen cars in the lot. Not too many happy people?

But Craig Bosc was. Grinning as he parked next to a ten-year-old Datsun Z, got out, checked his teeth in the side mirror, rubbed them with his index finger, went inside.

EXTRAS. Milo'd never enjoyed the ambience, but he knew the bar by reputation. Watering hole for small-time actroids – pretty people who'd arrived in L.A. with a couple years of Stanislavski or

339

summer stock or college theater under their belts, fueled by Oscar fantasies but settling, a thousand cattle calls later, for the occasional walk-ons and crowd scenes and nonunion commercials that comprised 99.9 percent of movie work.

Craig Eiffel Bosc, Master Thespian.

Time for a bad review.

Bosc stayed in the bar for another hour and a half and emerged alone, walking a little more slowly and tripping once. When the guy resumed driving west on Ventura, he'd slowed to ten miles under the limit and was doing that dividing line nudge that made it clear he was under the influence.

A 502 stop would offer the opportunity for a face-to-face with Bosc, but pulling the turkey over for a deuce was the last thing Milo wanted. Being off duty, the most he could pull off would be a citizen's arrest. That meant holding on to Bosc while calling a patrol car, then having the blues take over and losing any hope of private time with Mr Smiles.

So he continued tailing the Saab and hoped Bosc wouldn't attract law enforcement attention or run someone over.

Another short ride – two blocks to a strip mall near Coldwater, where Bosc went shopping for groceries at a Ralphs, deposited two paper bags in the Saab's trunk, made a five-minute stop at a mailbox rentals place, and returned to the car with a stack of envelopes under his arm.

Mail drop, same setup as the West Hollywood POB where he'd registered as Playa del Sol. The tail resumed, with Milo two lengths behind as Bosc turned right on Coldwater, traveled north past Moorpark and Riverside, then east on Huston.

Quiet street, apartments and small houses. That made it a tough follow-along, even with the quarry oblivious and slightly intoxicated. Milo waited at the corner of Coldwater and Huston and kept his eye on the Saab. The blue car traveled one block, then another, before hooking left.

Hoping Bosc didn't live in some security building with a subterranean garage, Milo waited half a minute, wheeled his way up a block and a half, parked, got out and continued on foot toward the spot where he'd estimated the Saab had come to rest.

Luck was with him. The blue car was out in the open, sitting in the driveway of a one-story, white stucco bungalow.

The house had a cement lawn and no fence. A couple of scraggly palms brushing the front façade were the only concessions to green. The driveway was twenty feet of cracked slab, barely long enough for a single vehicle, and it ended at the house's left side. No backyard. The bungalow sat on a fractional lot – a sliver that had escaped tear-down and development – and behind the tiny house, on the rear-neighboring property, loomed a four-story apartment complex.

The glamour of Hollywood.

Milo returned to the Dodge and drove twenty feet past the bungalow. Plenty of parked cars here, but he managed to find a spot between a van and a pickup that afforded him a clean, diagonal view. Bosc's gym-bar-shopping excursion had taken up most of the afternoon, and the sun was beginning to drop. Milo sat there, his 9mm resting on his hip, the weapon substantial and cool and comforting, and he felt better than he had in a long time.

Maybe Bosc was in for the evening, because by 5 P.M. he hadn't shown himself, and lights had gone on in the white bungalow's front rooms. Lacy curtains obscured the details, but the fabric was sheer enough for Milo to make out flashes of movement.

Bosc shifting from room to room. Then, at nine, a window on the right side of the house went cathode-blue. TV.

Quiet night for Master Thespian.

Milo climbed out of the Polaris, stretched the stiffness from his joints, made his way across the street.

He rang the bell, and Bosc didn't even bother to shout out a 'Who's there?', just opened it wide.

The actor had changed into khaki shorts and a tight black T-shirt that hugged his actorly physique. One hand gripped a bottle of Coors Light. The other held a cigarette.

Casual, loose, eyes bloodshot and droopy. Until Milo's face registered and Bosc's well-formed mouth dropped open.

The actor didn't react to the roust like an actor would – like any kind of civilian would. His legs spread slightly and he planted his feet, the beer bottle jabbed at Milo's chin and the cigarette's glowing tip headed for Milo's eyes.

Split-second reaction. Tight little martial arts ballet.

Milo was mildly surprised, but he'd come ready for anything and retracted his head. The vicious kick he aimed at Bosc's groin landed true, as did the chop to the back of Bosc's neck, and the guy went down, putting an end to any debate.

By the time Bosc had stopped writhing on the floor and the green had gone out of his complexion, his hands were cuffed behind him and he was panting and struggling to choke out words and Milo was kicking the door shut. He lifted Bosc by the scruff and dumped him on the black leather couch that took up most of the living room. The rest of the decor was a white beanbag chair, a huge digital TV, expensive stereo toys, and a chrome-framed poster of a wound red Lamborghini Countach.

Bosc sprawled on the sofa, moaning. His eyes rolled back and he retched and Milo stepped back from the expected projectile puke. But Bosc just dry heaved a couple of times, got his eyes back on track, looked up at Milo.

And smiled.

And laughed.

'Something funny, Craig?' said Milo.

Bosc's lips moved a bit, and he struggled to talk through the grin. Sweat globules as big as jelly beans beaded up his forehead and rolled down his sculpted nose. He flicked one away with his tongue. Laughed again. Spit at Milo's feet. Coughed and said, 'Oh yeah. You're in *big* trouble.'

thirty-five

I sped up Highway 33, sucking in the grass-sweet air of Ojai. Thinking about Bert Harrison living here for decades, light-years from L.A. For all that, the old man had been unable to avoid the worst the city had to offer.

As I approached the bank of shops that included O'Neill & Chapin, I eased up on the gas pedal. The stationery shop was still shuttered and a CLOSED sign was propped in the window of the Celestial Café. Midway through town, I turned onto the road that led up to Bert's property, drove a hundred feet from his driveway, and parked behind a copse of eucalyptus.

Bert's old station wagon was parked out in front, which told me nothing. Perhaps he'd left for his overseas trip and had been driven to the airport. Or his departure was imminent, and I'd enter to find him packing.

Third choice: he'd lied about the journey, wanting to discourage me from returning.

I admired Bert, wasn't eager to examine the possibilities. Returning to the Seville, I swung back onto the highway. Ready to tap the source, directly.

The entry to Mecca Ranch was latched but unlocked. I freed the arm, drove through, closed the gate behind me, and motored up under the gaze of circling hawks – maybe the same birds I'd seen the first time.

The corral floated into view, glazed by afternoon sun. Marge Schwinn stood in the center of the ring, wearing a faded denim shirt, tight jeans and riding boots, her back to me. Talking to a big stallion the color of bittersweet chocolate. Nuzzling the animal, stroking its mane. The sound of my tires crunching the gravel made her turn. By the time I was out of the Seville, she'd left the enclosure and was heading toward me.

'Well, hello there, Dr Delaware.'

I returned the greeting, smiling and keeping my voice light. The first time I'd met her, Milo hadn't introduced me by name or profession. Suddenly I felt good about the trip.

She pulled a blue bandana from her jeans pocket, wiped both hands, offered the right one for a firm, hard shake. 'What brings you up here?'

'Follow-up.'

She pocketed the bandana and grinned. 'Someone think I'm crazy?'

'No, ma'am, just a few questions.' I was looking into the sun and turned my head. Marge's face was well shaded, but she squinted, and her eyes receded into a mesh of wrinkles. The denim shirt was tailored tight. Her breasts were small and high. That same combination of girlish body and old woman's face.

'What kind of questions, Doctor?'

'For starts, have you thought of anything new since Detective Sturgis and I visited?'

'About . . . ?'

'Anything your husband might've said about that unsolved murder we discussed.'

'Nope,' she said. 'Nothing about that.' Her eyes drifted to the corral. 'I'd love to chat, but I'm kind of in the middle of things.'

'Just a few more things. Including a sensitive topic, I'm afraid.'

She clamped both hands on hard, lean hips. 'What topic?'

'Your husband's drug addiction. Did he overcome his habit by himself?'

She dug a heel into the dirt and ground it hard. 'Like I told you, by the time I met him, Pierce was past all that.'

'Did he have any help getting there?'

A simple question, but she said, 'What do you mean?' She'd maintained the squint, but her eyes weren't shut tight enough to conceal the movement behind the lids. Quick shift down to the ground, then a sidelong journey to the right.

Another bad liar. Thank God for honest people.

'Did Pierce have any drug treatment?' I said. 'Was he ever under the care of a doctor?'

'He really didn't talk about those days.'

'Not at all?'

'He was past it. I didn't want to rake things up.'

'Didn't want to upset him,' I said.

She glanced over at the corral again.

I said, 'How did Pierce sleep?'

'Pardon?'

'Was Pierce a sound sleeper or did he have trouble settling down at night?'

'He was pretty much a—' She frowned. 'These are strange questions, Dr Delaware. Pierce is gone, what difference does it make how he slept?'

'Just general follow-up,' I said. 'What I'm interested in specifically is the week or so before the accident. Did he sleep well or was he restless?'

Her breath caught, and the hands on her hips whitened. 'What happened, *sir*, is what I told you: Pierce fell off Akhbar. Now he's gone and I'm the one has to live with that and I don't appreciate your raking all this up.'

'I'm sorry,' I said.

'You keep apologizing, but you don't stop asking.'

'Well,' I said, 'here's the thing. Maybe it was an accident, but you did ask for a drug scan on Akhbar. Paid the coroner quite a bit of money to do it.'

She took a step away from me, then another. Shook her head, plucked a piece of straw out of her hair. 'This is ridiculous.'

'Another thing,' I said. 'Detective Sturgis never introduced me by name, but you know who I am and what I do. I find that kind of curious.'

Her eyes widened and her chest heaved. 'He said you might do this.'

'Who did?'

No answer.

I said, 'Dr Harrison?'

She turned her back on me.

'Mrs Schwinn, don't you think we need to get to the bottom of things? Isn't that what Pierce would've wanted? Something was keeping him up at night, wasn't it? Unfinished business. Wasn't that the whole point of the murder book?'

'I don't know about any book.'

'Don't you?'

Her lips folded inward. She shook her head again, clenched her jaw, swiveled, and caught a faceful of sun. A tremor jogged through her upper body. Her legs were planted, and they absorbed the motion. She turned heel and half ran toward her house. But I followed her inside; she didn't try to stop me.

We sat in the exact same spots we'd occupied a few days ago: me on the living-room couch, she in the facing chair. The last time, Milo had done all the talking, as he usually does when I tag along, but now it was my game and, God help me, despite the anguish of the woman sitting across from me, I felt cruelly elated.

Marge Schwinn said, 'You guys are spooky. Mind readers.'

'We guys?'

'Head doctors.'

'Dr Harrison and I,' I said.

She didn't answer, and I went on: 'Dr Harrison warned you I might be back.'

'Dr Harrison does only good.'

I didn't argue.

She showed me her profile. 'Yes, he was the one who told me who you were – after I described you and that big detective, Sturgis. He said your being here might mean things would be different.'

'Different?'

'He said you were persistent. A good guesser.'

'You've known Dr Harrison for a while.'

'A while.' The living-room windows were open, and a whinny from out in the corral drifted in loud and clear. She muttered, 'Easy, baby.'

'Your relationship with Dr Harrison was professional,' I said.

'If you're asking was he my doctor, the answer is yes. He treated us both – Pierce and me. Separately, neither of us knew it at the time. With Pierce it was the drugs. With me it was . . . I was going through . . . a depression. A situational reaction, Dr Harrison called

346

it. After my mother passed. She was ninety-three, and I'd been taking care of her for so long that being alone was . . . all the responsibility started bearing down on me. I tried to go it alone, then it got to be too much. I knew what Dr Harrison was, had always liked his smile. So one day I got up the courage to talk to him.'

The admission – the confession of weakness – clenched her jaws. I said, 'Was Dr Harrison the one who introduced you to Pierce?'

'I met Pierce at the end of . . . by the time I was better, able to take care of things again. I was still talking to Dr Harrison from time to time but was off the antidepressants, just like he said I'd be.'

She leaned forward suddenly. 'Do you really know Dr H? Well enough to understand what kind of man he is? When we first started talking, he used to come over every day to see how I was doing. *Every day.* One time I came down with the flu and couldn't do my chores and he did them for me. Everything – vacuumed the house, washed and dried the dishes, fed the horses, cleaned up the stables. He did that for four days running, even made trips into town for supplies. If I'd paid him by the hour, I'd be dead broke.'

I knew Bert was a good man and a master therapist, but her account astonished me. I pictured him tiny, aged, purple-clad, sweeping and hosing horse stalls, and wondered what I'd have done in the same situation. Knew damn well I'd have fallen far short of that degree of caring.

What I was doing right now had nothing to *do* with caring. Not for the living.

How much was owed to the dead?

I said, 'So you met Pierce when things had smoothed out.' Sounding wooden, formulaic. *Shrinky.*

She nodded. 'Dr H told me I should get back into my old routine – said my old habits had been good ones. Before Mama got terminal, I used to drive into Oxnard and shop at Randall's for feed. Old Lady Randall used to work the counter and she and Mama were old friends and I used to like going in there and talking to her, hearing the way things used to be. Then Mrs Randall took sick and her boys started working the counter and I had nothing to say to them. That and my energies were flagging so I switched to a mail-order feed outfit that delivered. When Dr Harrison said it would be good for me to get out, I started going to Randall's again. That's where I met Pierce.'

She smiled. 'Maybe it was all part of his plan – Dr Harrison's. Knowing Pierce and me both. Figuring there'd be some kind of chemistry there. He always said no, but maybe he was being modest like he always is. Whatever the truth, there *was* a chemistry. *Must've* been,' 'cause the first time I saw Pierce he looked like nothing but an over-the-hill hippie and I'm an old Republican ranch girl, shook Ronald Reagan's hand, wouldn't normally be attracted to that type. But something about Pierce . . . he had a *nobility*. I know your detective friend probably told you stories about the way Pierce used to be, but he became a different man.'

I said, 'People change.'

'That's something I didn't learn till late in life. When Pierce finally got up the courage to ask me out for coffee, he was so shy about it, it was . . . almost cute.' She shrugged. 'Maybe we met at just the right time – the planets moving perfectly or something.' Tiny smile. 'Or maybe Dr Harrison's a tricky one.'

'When did you tell Dr Harrison you were seeing Pierce?'

'Pretty soon after. He said, "I know. Pierce told me. He feels the same way about you, Margie." That's when he told me he'd known Pierce for some time. Had been doing volunteer psychiatry at Oxnard Doctors' Hospital – counseling sick and injured people, burnt people – after the Montecito Fire they put in a burn unit and he was their psychiatrist. Pierce wasn't any of those things, he came into the emergency room having terrible seizures from his addiction. Dr Harrison detoxified him, then took him on as a patient. He told me all this because Pierce asked him to. Pierce had strong feelings about me but was deeply ashamed of his past, depended on Dr Harrison to clear the air. I still remember the way Dr H phrased it. "He's a good man, Margie, but he'll understand if this is too much baggage for you to carry." I said, "These hands have been hauling hay for forty years, I can carry plenty." After that, Pierce's shyness mostly left him, and we got close.' Her eyes misted. 'I never thought I'd find anyone, and now he's gone.'

She fumbled for the bandana and spit out laughter. 'Look at me, what a *sissy*. And look at *you*: I thought you guys were supposed to make people feel *better*.'

I sat there as she cried silently and wiped her eyes and cried some more. A sudden shadow streaked the facing wall, then vanished. I turned in time to see a hawk shoot up into the blue and disappear. Foot stomping and snorting sounded from the corral.

'Red-tails,' she said. 'They're good for the vermin, but the horses never get used to them.'

I said, 'Mrs Schwinn, what did Pierce tell you about the unsolved case?'

'That it was an unsolved case.'

'What else?'

'Nothing else. He didn't even tell me the girl's name. Just that she was a girl who got torn up and it was his case and he'd failed to solve it. I tried to get him to open up, but he wouldn't. Like I said, Pierce always wanted to shelter me from his old life.'

'But he talked to Dr Harrison about the case.'

'You'd have to ask Dr Harrison about that.'

'Dr Harrison never spoke to you about it?'

'He just said . . .' She trailed off and twisted so that all I could see was the outline of her jaw.

'Mrs Schwinn?'

'The only reason it came up in the first place was because of Pierce's sleep. He'd started having dreams. Nightmares.' She turned suddenly and faced me. 'How'd you *know* about that? What was it, a *real* good guess?'

'Pierce was a good man, and good men don't take well to corruption.'

'I don't know about any corruption.' Her voice lacked conviction.

'When did the nightmares start?' I said.

'A few months before he died. Two, three months.'

'Anything happen to bring them on?'

'Not that I saw. I thought we were happy. Dr Harrison told me he'd thought so, too, but turns out Pierce had never stopped being plagued – that's the word he used. *Plagued.*'

'By the case.'

'By failure. Dr Harrison said Pierce had been forced to walk away from the case when they railroaded him off the department. He said Pierce had fixed it in his mind that giving up had been some kind of mortal sin. He'd been punishing himself for years – the drugs, abusing his body, living like a bum. Dr H thought he'd helped Pierce get past it, but he'd been wrong, the nightmares came back. Pierce just couldn't let go.'

She gave me a long, hard stare. 'Pierce broke rules for years, always wondered if he'd have to pay one day. He loved being a detective but hated the police department. Didn't trust anyone. Including your friend, Sturgis. When he got railroaded, he was sure Sturgis had something to do with it.'

'When I was here with Detective Sturgis, you said Pierce had spoken kindly of him. Was that true?'

'Not strictly,' she said. 'Pierce never breathed a word to me about Sturgis or anyone else from his old life. These are all things he told Dr Harrison, and I was trying to keep Dr Harrison out of all this. But yes, Pierce had changed his opinion about Sturgis. Followed Sturgis's career and saw he was a good detective. Found out Sturgis was homosexual and figured he had to have a *lot* of courage to stay in the department.'

'What else did Dr Harrison tell you about the case?'

'Just that walking away had stuck in Pierce's brain like a cancer. That's what the nightmares were all about.'

'Chronic nightmares?' I said.

'Chronic enough. Sometimes they'd hit Pierce three, four times a week, other times he'd be okay for a stretch. Then boom, all over again. You couldn't predict, and that made it worse, because I never knew what to expect when my head hit the pillow. Things got to a point where I was scared to go to bed, started waking up at night myself.' Her smile was crooked. 'Kind of funny. I'd be lying there all wound up, unable to sleep, and Pierce'd be snoring away and I'd tell myself it was finally over. Then the next night . . .'

'Did Pierce say anything during the nightmares?'

'Not a word, he just moved – thrashed. That's how I'd know a fit was coming on: the bed would start moving – thumping, like an earthquake, Pierce's feet kicking the mattress. Lying on his back, kicking with his heels – like he was marching somewhere. Then his hands would shoot up.' She stretched her arms toward the ceiling. 'Like he was being arrested. Then his hands would slam down fast, start slapping the bed and waving around wild, and soon he'd be grunting and *punching* the mattress *and* kicking – his feet never stopped. Then he'd arch his back and freeze – like he was paralyzed, like he was building up steam to explode, and you could see his teeth gnashing and his eyes would pop real wide. But they weren't looking at anything, he was somewhere else – some hell only he could see. He'd hold that frozen pose for maybe ten seconds, then let go and start punching *himself* – in the chest, on the stomach, on the face. Sometimes, the next morning, he'd be bruised. I tried to stop him from hurting himself, but it was impossible, his arms were like iron rods, it was all I could do to jump out of the bed to avoid getting hit myself. So I'd just stand there and wait for him to finish. Just before he was finished, he'd let out a howl – this loud howl that would wake up the horses. *They'd* start mewling, and sometimes the *coyotes* would chime in. *That* was something to hear – coyotes screaming from miles away. Ever hear that? When a pack of them goes at it? It's not like a dog barking, it's a thousand creatures gone crazy. Ululation's the name for it. They're supposed to do it only when they're killing or mating, but Pierce's howling would get them going.'

She'd squeezed the bandana into a blue ball. Now she studied her fingers as they uncurled. 'Those coyotes were scared witless by the sound of Pierce's fear.'

She offered me a drink that I declined, got up and filled herself a glass of water from the kitchen tap. When she sat back down, I said, 'Did Pierce have any memory of the nightmares?'

'Nope. When the fit was over he'd just go back to sleep, and there'd be no mention of it. The first time that happened, I let it pass. The second time, I was shook up but still said nothing. The third time, I went to see Dr Harrison. He listened and didn't say much and that evening he came by, paid a visit to Pierce – alone, in Pierce's darkroom. After that, Pierce started seeing him for regular sessions again. About a week in, Dr H had me over to his house, and that's when he told me about Pierce struggling to live with failure.'

'So you and Pierce never talked about the case directly?'

'That's right.'

I said nothing.

She said, 'I know it's hard for you to understand, but that's

351

what we were like. Close as two people can be, but there were sides to each of us that we didn't get into. I realize it's not fashionable to hold on to privacy anymore. Everyone talks about everything to everyone else. But that's phony, isn't it? Everyone's got secret parts of their mind. Pierce and I were just honest about admitting it. And Dr Harrison said if that's the way we really wanted it, that was our choice.'

So Bert had tried to edge husband and wife toward more openness, and they'd resisted.

Marge Schwinn said, 'It was the same with Pierce's drug problem. He was too proud to expose himself to me, so he used Dr Harrison as a go-between. We were content with that. It kept things pleasant and positive between us.'

'Did you ever ask Dr Harrison about the unsolved murder?'

Strong headshake. 'I didn't want to know. I figured for it to plague Pierce it had to be really bad.'

'Did the nightmares ever clear up?'

'After Pierce started seeing Dr Harrison regularly again, they faded to maybe two, three times a month. Also, Pierce's photography hobby seemed to help, got him out of the house, got him some fresh air.'

'Was that Dr Harrison's idea?'

She smiled. 'Yes, he bought Pierce the camera, insisted on paying for it. He does that. Gives people things. There was a gal used to live in town, Marian Purveyance, ran the Celestial Café before Aimee Baker took charge of it. Marian came down with a muscle disease that wasted her away, and Dr Harrison was her main comfort. I used to visit Marian during her final days, and she told me Dr Harrison decided she needed a dog for companionship. But Marian was in no physical state to take care of a dog, so Dr Harrison found one for her – an old, half-lame retriever from the shelter that he kept at his house, fed, and bathed. He brought it over to Marian's for a few hours each day. That sweet old dog used to stretch out on Marian's bed, and Marian would lie there stroking it. Toward the end, Marian's fingers wouldn't work, and the dog must've known, because it rolled over right next to Marian and put its paw on Marian's hand so she'd have something to touch. Marian died with that old dog next to her, and a few weeks later the dog passed on.'

Her eyes were fierce. 'Do you get what I'm saying, young man? Dr Harrison *gives* people things. He gave Pierce that camera and gave me a bit of peace by letting me know the nightmares had nothing to do with me. Because I was wondering if they did. Maybe Pierce's being cooped up here with an old spinster after all those years on his own was having a bad effect on him. And – Lord forgive me – when I watched Pierce thrash around, I couldn't help wonder if he'd somehow backslid.'

'Into drug use.'

'I'm ashamed to admit it, but yes, that's exactly what I wondered. Because it was drug seizures that brought him into the hospital in the first place, and to my ignorant eye these looked like seizures. But Dr Harrison assured me they weren't. Said they were just bad nightmares. That it was Pierce's *old* life rearing its ugly old head. That I was nothing *but* good for Pierce and shouldn't ever think otherwise. That was a great relief.'

'So the nightmares thinned to two or three times a month.'

'That I could live with. When the thumping started, I'd just roll out of bed, go to the kitchen for a glass of water, walk outside to calm the horses, and when I'd return, Pierce'd be snoozing away. I'd hold his hand and warm it up – the nightmares always turned his hands icy. We'd lie there together and I'd listen to his breathing slow down and he'd let me hold him and warm him up and the night would pass.'

Another hawk's swoop striated the wall. She said, 'Those birds. They must *smell* something.'

'The nightmares thinned,' I said, 'but they returned the last few days before Pierce's death.'

'Yes,' she said, nearly choking on the word. 'And this time I started getting worried because Pierce didn't look so good in the morning. He was worn-out, kind of clumsy, slurring his words. That's why I blame myself for letting him take Akhbar. He was in no shape to ride, I shouldn't have allowed him to go off by himself. Maybe that time he did have some kind of seizure.'

'Why'd you test Akhbar for drugs?'

'That was just me being stupid. What I *really* wanted to do was have *Pierce* tested. Because despite what Dr Harrison had said when the nightmares came back, I let myself lose faith in Pierce, again. But after he died, I couldn't bring myself to come out and admit my suspicions. Not to Dr H or the coroner or anyone else, so instead I laid them on poor Akhbar. Figuring maybe once the subject of drugs came up, someone would catch on and test Pierce, too, and I'd know, once and for all.'

'They did test Pierce,' I said. 'It's standard procedure. The drug screen came back negative.'

'I know that, now. Dr Harrison told me. It was an accident, plain and simple. Though sometimes I still can't help thinking Pierce shouldn't have been riding alone. Because he *wasn't* looking good.'

'Any idea why that last week was rough for him?'

'No – and I don't want to know. I need to put all this behind me, and this isn't helping, so could we please stop?'

I thanked her and stood. 'How far from here did the accident occur?'

'Just a ways up the road.'

'I'd like to see the spot.'

'What for?'

'To get a feel for what happened.'

Her gaze was level. 'Do you know something you haven't told me?'

'No,' I said. 'Thanks for your time.'

'Don't thank me, it wasn't a favor.' She leaped up, walked past me to the door.

I said, 'The spot—'

'Get back on 33 heading east and take the second turnoff to the left. It's a dirt path that leads up a hill, then starts swooping down toward the arroyo. That's where it happened. Pierce and Akhbar tumbled from the rocks that look down into the arroyo and ended up at the bottom. It's a place Pierce and I rode together from time to time. When we did, I used to lead.'

'About Pierce's photography.'

'No,' she said. 'Please. No more questions. I showed you Pierce's darkroom and his pictures and everything else the first time you were here.'

'I was going to say he was talented, but one thing struck me. There were no people or animals in his shots.'

'Is that supposed to be some big psychological thing?'

'No, I just found it curious.'

'Did you? Well, I didn't. Didn't bother me one bit. Those pictures were beautiful.' She reached around me and shoved the door open. 'And when I asked Pierce about it, he had a very good answer. Said, "Margie, I'm trying to picture a perfect world." '

thirty-six

She stood by the Seville, waiting for me to leave.

I turned the ignition key, and said, 'Did Dr Harrison mention taking a vacation?'

'Him, a vacation? He never leaves. Why?'

'He told me he might be doing some traveling.'

'Well, he's certainly entitled to travel if he wants. Why don't you ask him? You're going there right now, aren't you? To check up on my story.'

'I'm going to talk to him about the unsolved case.'

'Whatever,' she said. 'Doesn't bother me being checked up on, because I'm not hiding anything. That's the thing about not letting yourself get involved in hopeless things. Less to worry about. The shame about my Pierce was he never really learned that.'

The turnoff she'd described led to an oak-shielded path barely wide enough for a golf cart. Branches scraped the Seville's flanks. I backed out, left the car on the side of the road, and hiked.

The spot where Pierce Schwinn had died was half a mile in, a dry gully scooped out of a granite ledge and backed by mountainside. A sere corridor that would fill during rainy seasons and transform to a green, rushing stream. Now, it was bleached the color of old bones and littered with silt, rocks and boulders, leathery leaves, snarls of wind-snapped branches. The largest rocks tended toward ragged and knife-edged and glinted in the sun. Up against them, a man's head wouldn't fare well.

I walked to the edge and stared down into the arroyo and listened to the silence, wondering what had caused a well-trained horse to lose its footing.

356

Contemplation and the warmth of the day lulled me into something just short of torpor. Then something behind me skittered and my heart jumped and the tip of my shoe curled over into open space and I had to jump back to avoid pitching over.

I regained my bearings in time to see a sand-colored lizard scurry into the brush. Stepping back from the ledge, I cleared my head before turning and walking away. By the time I reached the car, my breathing had nearly returned to normal.

I drove back to the center of Ojai, cruised to Signal Street, past the fieldstone-lined drainage ditch, and parked in the same eucalyptus grove, where I peered through blue shaggy leaves at Bert Harrison's house. Thinking about what I'd say to Bert if I found him. Thinking about Pierce Schwinn's nightmares, the demons that had come back to haunt him during the days before his death.

Bert knew why. Bert had known all along.

No movement from the old man's house. The station wagon was parked right where it had been. After a quarter-hour I decided it was time to make my way to the front door and deal with whatever I found, or didn't.

Just as I got out of the Seville, the door squeaked open and Bert stepped out onto his front porch in full purple regalia, cradling a large brown paper shopping bag in one arm. I grabbed the Seville's door before it clicked shut, hurried back behind the trees, and followed the old man's descent down the wooden staircase.

He loaded the bag on the station wagon's passenger seat, got behind the wheel, stalled a couple of times, finally fired the engine. Backing away from the house with excruciating slowness, he took a long time to complete a three-way turn. Battling with the wheel – manual steering. A small man, face intent, hands planted at 10 o'clock–2 o'clock, just the way they teach you in Driver's Ed. Sitting so low his head was barely visible above the door.

Crouching low, I waited until he drove past. The old Chevy's tired suspension wasn't up to the semipaved road, and it creaked and whined as it bounced by. Bert stared straight ahead, didn't notice me or the Seville. I waited till he'd passed from view, then jumped in my own chariot. Power steering gave me an edge, and I caught up in time to spot the wagon lurching east on 33.

I sat at the intersection as the Chevy diminished to a dust mote on the horizon. The empty road made following too risky. I was still wondering what to do when a pickup truck loaded with bags of fertilizer came to a rolling stop behind me. Two Hispanic men in cowboy hats – farmworkers. I motioned them around and they passed me and turned left. Interposing themselves between Bert and me.

I set out behind the truck, lagging a good ways behind.

A few miles later, at the 33–150 intersection, the truck kept going south and Bert managed a torturous, overcautious right onto 150. I stayed with him but increased my distance, barely able to keep the wagon in sight.

He drove another couple of miles, past private campgrounds and a trailer park and signs announcing the impending arrival of Lake Casitas. The public reservoir doubled as a recreational facility. For all I knew the paper bag was filled with breadcrumbs, and Bert was planning to feed the ducks.

But he veered off the road well before the lake, swinging north at a corner that housed a single-pump filling station and a one-room bait shop and grocery.

Another unmarked trail, this one dotted thinly with unpainted cabins, set well back from the road. A hand-painted sign at one of the first properties advertised homemade berry cobbler and firewood; after that, no messages. The underbrush grew thick here, nurtured by a shade canopy of ancient oaks and pittosporum and sycamores so twisted they seemed to writhe. Bert bounced along for another two miles, oblivious to my presence, before slowing, and turning left.

Keeping my eye on the spot where he'd disappeared, I pulled over and waited for two minutes, then followed.

He'd gone up a gravel drive that continued for two hundred feet, then angled to the left and vanished behind an unruly hedge of agave – the same spiky plants that fronted his own house. No building in sight. Once again, I parked and continued on foot, hoping the wagon's destination was measured in yards, not miles. Staying off the gravel for quiet's sake, and walking on the bordering greenery.

358

I spotted the Chevy another hundred feet up, stationed haphazardly in the dirt lot of a tin-roofed, green-boarded house. Larger than a cabin, maybe three rooms, with a sagging front porch and a stovepipe chimney. I edged closer, found myself a vantage point behind the continuing agave wall. The house was nestled by forest but sat on a dry-dirt clearing, probably a firebreak. Diminishing sunlight spattered the metal roof. A poorly shaped apricot tree grew near the front door, ungainly and ragged, but its branches were gravid with fruit.

I stayed there for nearly half an hour before Bert reemerged.

Pushing a man in a wheelchair. I recalled the chair in his living room.

Keeping it for a friend, he'd said.

Dr Harrison gives.

Despite the mildness of the afternoon, the man was wrapped in a blanket and wore a wide-brimmed straw hat. Bert pushed him slowly, and his head lolled. Bert stopped and said something to him. If the man heard, he gave no indication. Bert locked the chair, went over to the apricot tree, picked two apricots. He handed one to the man, who reached for it very slowly. Both of them ate. Bert held his hand to the man's mouth and the man spit the pit into his palm. Bert examined the seed, placed it in his pocket.

Bert finished his own apricot, pocketed that pit, too.

He stood there, looking up at the sky. The man in the wheelchair didn't budge.

Bert unlocked the chair, pushed it a few feet farther. Angled the chair and allowed me to catch a glimpse of the passenger's face.

Huge mirrored sunglasses below the straw hat dominated the upper half. The bottom was a cloud of gray beard. In between was skin the color of grilled eggplant.

I stepped out of the trees, made no attempt to muffle the crunch of my footsteps on gravel.

Bert turned abruptly. Locked eyes with me. Nodded.

Resigned.

I came closer. The man in the wheelchair said, 'Who's that?' in a low, raspy voice.

Bert said, 'The fellow I told you about.'

thirty-seven

Craig Bosc lay prone on his living-room carpet, smiling again. Plastic tie-cuffs from Milo's cop kit bound his ankles together, and another set linked to the metal cuffs around his wrists secured him to a stout sofa leg.

Not a hog-tie, Milo had pointed out, just a nice submissive position. Letting the guy know that any resistance would result in something more painful.

Bosc offered no comment. Hadn't uttered a word since telling Milo he was in big trouble.

Now his eyes were closed, and he kept the smile pasted on his face. Maybe acting, but not a drop of sweat on his movie star face. One of those psychopaths with a low arousal rate? Despite Milo's having the upper hand, Bosc looked too damn smug, and Milo felt moisture running down his own armpits.

He began searching the house. Bosc opened his eyes and laughed as Milo walked around the kitchen opening cabinets and drawers, checking Bosc's bachelor fridge – beer, wine, piña colada mix, three jars of salsa, an open can of chili-con-whatever. As Milo checked the freezer, Bosc chuckled again, but when Milo turned to look at him, the guy's eyes were shut tight and his body had gone loose and he might've been napping.

Nothing hidden behind the ice trays. Milo moved to the bedroom, found a closet full of designer duds, too many garments for the space, everything crammed together on cheap wire hangers, some stuff crumpled on the floor among two dozen pairs of shoes. On the top shelf were three tennis rackets, a hockey stick, an old deflated basketball, and a fuzzy, blackened leather thing that had once been a football. Joe Jock's sentimental memories.

A pair of thirty-pound Ivanko dumbbells sat in the corner, next to a sixty-inch TV, VCR-DVD combo. A mock-walnut video case held action thrillers and a few run-of-the-mill porno tapes in lurid boxes: busty blondes playing orifice-bingo.

Bosc's three-drawer dresser offered up rumpled underwear and socks and T-shirts and gym shorts. It wasn't till Milo hit the bottom drawer that things got interesting.

Buried beneath a collection of GAP sweatshirts were three guns: a 9mm identical to Milo's department issue, a sleek black Glock complete with German instructions, and a silver derringer in a black leather carrying case. All three loaded. Additional ammo was stored at the rear of the drawer.

Next to the guns was a small cache that added up to Bosc's personal history.

A North Hollywood High yearbook, fifteen years old, revealed that Craig Eiffel Bosc had played tight end for the varsity football squad, pitched relief for the baseball team, and served as a basketball point guard. Three letters. Bosc's grad shot showed him to be clean-cut and gorgeous, flashing that same cocky smile.

Next came a black leatheroid scrapbook with stick-on letters that spelled out **SIR CRAIG** on the cover. Inside were plastic-sheathed pages that made Milo flash to the murder book.

But nothing bloody here. The first page held a certificate from Valley College attesting that Bosc had earned a two-year associate degree in communications. From North Hollywood High to Valley. Both were within a bicycle ride to Bosc's house. Valley Boy hadn't moved around much.

Next came Bosc's honorable discharge from the Coast Guard; he'd been stationed at Avalon, on Catalina Island. Probably earned himself a nice golden tan while discharging his duty in scuba gear.

At the back of the album were five pages of Polaroids showing Bosc screwing a variety of women, all young and blonde and buxom, the emphasis upon close-up insertion and Bosc's grinning face as he kneaded breasts and pinched nipples and rear-ended his companions. The girls all wore sleepy expressions. None seemed to be playing for the camera.

Stoned cuties caught unawares. All appeared to be in their early to midtwenties, with big bleached hair and out-of-fashion do's that made Milo think *small-town cocktail waitress*. A few plain ones, one or two real lookers, for the most part an average-looking bunch. Not up to the level of the babes in the porno videos, but the same general type. Another indication Bosc had a limited range.

Milo searched for the hidden camera, figuring it would be focused on the bed, and found it quickly. Little pencil-lens gizmo concealed in the VCR box. Sophisticated bit of apparatus; it stood out among the general shoddiness of Bosc's apartment and made Milo wonder. Also stashed in the box were several tightly rolled joints and half a dozen tabs of Ecstasy.

Kiss the girls and make them stoned. Naughty, naughty.

He returned to the scrapbook, flipped to the next page. Wasn't really surprised at what he found, but still, the confirmation was unsettling and sweat gushed from every pore.

Certificate of Bosc's graduation from the L.A. Police Academy ten years ago. Then a group shot and an individual photo of Bosc in his probationer's uniform. Clean-cut, made-for-TV cop; that same obnoxious grin.

The subsequent paperwork recounted Bosc's LAPD progress. A couple years of North Hollywood patrol before promotion to Detective-I and transfer to Valley Auto Theft, where he'd spent three years as an investigator and left as a D-II.

Cars. Fast-track promotion for a hot-wire cowboy. Bastard probably had a collection of master keys to every known make and model hidden somewhere. With that kind of know-how and equipment, boosting Rick's Porsche and returning it vacuumed and wiped clean of prints would've been a sleepwalk for Detective Bosc.

After car-time, the guy had been moved downtown to Parker Center Records, then Administration.

Then a year with Internal Affairs.

Finally: a kick up to D-III and his current assignment.

Administrative Staff at Chief Broussard's office.

The bastard was an executive aide to John G.

Milo disconnected the pencil camera, brought it and the homemade pornos and the dope back to the living room. Bosc was still working on maintaining his mellow but Milo's footsteps opened his eyes and

362

when he saw what Milo was showing him, he flinched.

Then he recovered. Smiled. 'Gee, you must be a detective.'

Milo held an E-tab under Bosc's nose. 'Bad boy, Craig.'

'I'm supposed to be worried?'

'Pocketful of felonies, Georgie Porgie.'

'Another country heard from,' said Bosc.

'You think John G.'s gonna protect you? Something tells me the chief doesn't know about your film career.'

Bosc's eyes got hard and cold, offering a glimpse of the meanness that lurked beneath the pretty-boy façade.

He said, 'What I think is you're fucked.' Laughter. 'In the ass. Then again . . .'

Milo hefted the camera and the drugs.

Bosc said, 'You think you're seeing something, but you're not. None of that exists.' He shook his head and chuckled. 'You are *so* fucked.'

Milo laughed along with him. Stepped forward. Placed his foot on one of Bosc's shins and bore down.

Bosc cried out in agony. Tears filled his eyes as he struggled to twist away.

Milo lifted his shoe.

'You asshole-fuck,' Bosc panted. 'You stupid faggot fuck.'

'S'cuse me, Craig-o.'

'Go ahead,' said Bosc, catching his breath. 'You're only digging your own grave.'

Milo was silent.

Bosc's smile returned. 'You just don't get it, do you? This is L-fucking-A. It's not what you do, it's who you know.'

'Connections,' said Milo. 'Got yourself an agent yet?'

'If you had a brain, you'd be an ape,' said Bosc. 'You gain access to my premises with a clear B&E/kidnap combo, then add assault. We're talking major felony, prison time to the next millennium. You think any of that shit you're holding's going to stand up evidentiary-wise? I'll say you planted it.'

Milo fanned the photos. 'It's not my dick in these.'

'That's for sure,' said Bosc. 'Yours would be half the size and packed in fudge.'

Milo smiled.

363

'You're out of it, man,' said Bosc. 'Have been from the beginning, always will be. No matter how many 187s you close. No good deed goes unpunished, man. The longer you keep me here, the more screwed you are, and so is your shrink buddy.'

'What does he have to do with it?'

Bosc smiled and closed his eyes again, and for a moment Milo thought the guy would revert to silence. But a few seconds later, Bosc said, 'It's a game. You and the shrink are pawns.'

'Whose game?'

'Kings and bishops.'

'John G. and Walter Obey and the Cossack brothers?'

Bosc's eyes opened. Cold again. Colder. 'Stick your head up your ass and get yourself a clue. Now let me go, and maybe I'll help you out.' Snapping out the order.

Milo placed the contraband on a table. Paced the room, as if considering compliance.

Suddenly, he hurried back to Bosc's side, kneeled down next to Bosc, placed the tip of his finger on Bosc's shin. Precisely on the spot where his shoe had dug in.

Bosc began to sweat.

'Chess analogy,' said Milo. 'How erudite, Bobby Fischer. Now tell me why you ripped off my car and put on that show at the hot dog stand and rented a post-office box under Playa del Sol and were snooping around my house today.'

'All in a day's work,' said Bosc.

'At John G.'s request?'

Bosc didn't answer.

Milo pulled out his gun and pressed the barrel into the soft, tan flesh under Bosc's chin.

'Details,' he demanded.

Bosc's lips jammed shut.

Milo retracted the weapon. As Bosc laughed, Milo said, 'Your problem, Craig, is you think you're a knight, but you're a shit-eating pawn.' He rapped the butt of the gun against Bosc's shin, hard enough to evoke an audible crack.

He waited for Bosc to stop crying, then raised the gun again.

Bosc's panicked eyes followed the weapon's ascent, and he scrunched his eyes and sobbed out loud.

Milo said, 'Craig, Craig,' and began to lower the weapon.
Bosc yelled, 'Please, please, no!' Began jabbering.
Within minutes, Milo had what he wanted.
Good old Pavlovian conditioning. Would Alex be proud?

thirty-eight

Bert Harrison placed a hand on the shoulder of the man in the wheelchair. The man rolled his head and hummed. I saw my image doubled in his mirrored lenses. A pair of grim strangers.

I said, 'My name's Alex Delaware, Mr Burns.'

Willie Burns smiled and rolled his head again. Orienting to my voice the way a blind man does. The skin between his white beard and the huge lenses was cracked and scored, stretched tight over sharp bones. His hands were long and thin, purplish brown, the knuckles lumped arthritically, the nails long and yellowed and seamed. Across his legs was a soft, white blanket. Not much bulk beneath the fabric.

'Pleased to meet you,' he said. To Bert: 'Am I, Doc?'

'He won't hurt you, Bill. He will want to know things.'

'Things,' said Burns. 'Once upon a time.' He hummed some more. High-pitched voice, off-key but somehow sweet.

I said, 'Bert, I'm sorry I had to follow you—'

'As you said, you had to.'

'It was—'

'Alex,' he said, quieting me with a soft palm against my cheek. 'When I found out you were involved, I thought this might happen.'

'Found out? You sent me the murder book.'

Bert shook his head.

'You didn't?' I said. 'Then who?'

'I don't know, son. Pierce sent it to someone but never told me who. He never told me about the book, at all, until the week before he died. Then one day, he brought it to my house and showed it to me. I had no idea he'd gone that far.'

'Collecting mementoes.'

'Collecting nightmares,' said Bert. 'As he turned the pages, he cried.'

Willie Burns stared sightlessly at the treetops, humming.

'Where'd Schwinn get the photos, Bert?'

'Some were his own cases, others he stole from old police files. He'd been a thief for quite some time. His characterization, not mine. He shoplifted habitually, took jewelry and money and drugs from crime scenes, consorted with criminals and prostitutes.'

'He told you all this.'

'Over a very long period.'

'Confessing,' I said.

'I'm no priest, but he wanted salvation.'

'Did he get it?'

Bert shrugged. 'Last time I checked there were no Hail Marys in the psychiatric repertoire. I did my best.' He glanced at Willie Burns. 'How are you feeling today, Bill?'

'I'm feeling real good,' said Burns. 'Considering.' He shifted his face to the left. 'Nice breeze coming in from the hills, can you hear it? That plunking of the leaves, like a nice little mandolin. Like one of those boats in Venice.'

I listened. Saw no movement among the trees, heard nothing.

Bert said, 'Yes, it is pretty.'

Willie Burns said, 'You know, it's getting kinda thirsty out here. Maybe I could have something to drink, please?'

Bert said, 'Of course.'

I wheeled Burns back into the green board house. The front room was barely furnished – one couch along the window and two bright green folding chairs. Pole lamps guarded two corners. Framed magazine prints – garden scenes painted in Giverny colors – hung askew on plasterboard walls. Between the chairs, a wide pathway had been left for the chair, and the rubber wheels had left gray tracks that led to a door at the rear. No knob, just a kickplate.

Push door. Wheelchair-friendly.

The kitchen was an arbitrary space to the right: pine cabinets, sheet-metal counters, a two-burner stove upon which sat a copper-bottomed pot. Bert took a Diet Lemon Snapple from a bulbous, white refrigerator, wrestled with the lid, finally got it loose, and handed the bottle to Willie Burns. Burns gripped the bottle with both hands and drank down half, Adam's apple rising and falling with each gulp. Then he placed the glass against his face, rolled it back and forth along his skin, and let out a long breath.

'Thanks, Dr H.'

'My pleasure, Bill.' Bert looked at me. 'You might as well sit.'

I took one of the folding chairs. The house smelled of hickory chips and roasted garlic. A string of dried cloves hung above the stove, along with a necklace of dried chilies. I spotted other niceties: jars of dried beans, lentils, pasta. A hand-painted bread box. Gourmet touches in the vest-pocket galley.

I said, 'So you have no idea how the murder book got to me?'

Bert shook his head. 'I never knew you had anything to do with it until Marge told me you and Milo had been to visit and talked to her about an unsolved murder.' He began to lower himself onto the second folding chair, but straightened and stood. 'Let's get some air. You'll be okay for a few minutes, Bill?'

Burns said, 'More than okay.'

'We'll be right outside.'

'Enjoy the view.'

We walked into the shade of the surrounding trees.

Bert said, 'You need to know this: Bill doesn't have much longer. Nerve damage, brittle diabetes, serious circulation problems, hypertension. There's a limit to how much care I can give him, and he won't go to a hospital. The truth is no one can really help him. Too many systems down.'

He stopped and smoothed a purple lapel. 'He's a very old man at forty-three.'

'How long have you been taking care of him?' I said.

'A long time.'

'Nearly twenty years, I'd guess.'

He didn't answer. We walked some more, in slow, aimless circles. No sound issued from the forest. Not a trace of the music Willie Burns had heard.

'How'd you meet him?' I said.

'At a hospital in Oxnard.'

'Same place you met Schwinn.'

His eyes widened.

I said, 'I was just over at Marge's place.'

'Ah.' Once a shrink . . . 'Well, that's true,' he said. 'But Pierce's being there wasn't really a coincidence. He'd been tracking Bill for a while. Not very successfully. And not very consistently, because his amphetamine habit had rendered him pretty much incapacitated. Occasionally, he'd grow lucid, convince himself he was still a detective, make a stab at investigating, then he'd binge and drop out of sight. Somehow, over the years – through his criminal contacts – he managed to figure out that Bill had come up the coast. He knew Bill would need medical care and eventually, he pinpointed the hospital, though not until well after Bill had been discharged. But he began hanging around, checking himself in for spurious reasons. They had him tagged as an addicted hypochondriac.'

'He was trying to get access to Burns's records.'

Bert nodded. 'The hospital staff thought he was just another down-at-the-heels junkie out to steal drugs. As it turns out, he was really ill. An on-call neurologist who didn't know him ordered some testing and found a low-level seizure disorder – petit mal, mostly, some temporal symptoms, all due to drug toxicity. They prescribed anticonvulsants with mixed results, admitted him for short-term care several times, but I was never on duty during those periods. One day, he had a grand mal seizure out in the parking lot and they brought him into the ER and I *was* on call. One thing led to another.'

'Willie Burns needed medical care because he was burned in a house fire.'

Bert sighed. 'You're as skillful as ever, Alex.'

'A house on 156th Street in Watts. A neighborhood where a black man would be comfortable hiding out. Where a white face would stand out. A white police detective named Lester Poulsenn was assigned to guard Burns and Caroline Cossack and one night he was shot and the house was torched as cover. A high-ranking cop murdered but LAPD kept it quiet. Interesting, don't you think, Bert?'

He remained silent. I went on, 'It's a safe bet Poulsenn got ambushed by the people sent to get rid of Caroline and Willie. People who'd pulled off an ambush before and murdered a bail bondsman named Boris Nemerov. Burns's bondsman. Did he tell you about that?'

Nod. 'It came out in therapy. Bill felt guilty about causing Nemerov's death. He would have liked to come forward, to come clean about what he saw, but that would have put him in mortal danger.'

'What's his version of the ambush?'

'He phoned Nemerov for help because Nemerov had always been kind to him. He and Nemerov arranged a meeting, but Nemerov was followed and murdered and stuffed in the trunk of his car. Bill was hiding nearby, saw it all. Knew Nemerov's death would be blamed on him.'

'Why was Burns offered a police guard in the first place?'

'He had contacts in the police department. He'd worked as an informant.'

'But after Poulsenn's and Nemerov's murders the department let him dangle.'

'Contacts, Alex. Not friends.'

'The house was set on fire, but Burns and Caroline got away. How severe were their injuries?'

'She wasn't hurt, his were severe. He neglected the wounds, didn't seek care until months later. His feet had been scorched almost down to the tendons, multiple infections set in, at the time of admission the wounds were suppurating, gangrenous, flesh falling off the bone. Both feet were amputated immediately, but sepsis had spread up into the long bones and additional amputation was necessary. You could actually smell it, Alex. Like barbecue, the marrow had been *cooked*. We had some marvelous surgeons, and they managed to preserve half of one femur, a third of another, created skin flaps and grafted them. But Bill's lungs had also been burned, as had his trachea and his esophagus. He formed fibroid scars internally and removing the damaged tissue required additional multiple surgeries. We're talking years, Alex. He bore the agony in silence. I used to sit by the whirlpool as the skin sloughed off. Not a whimper. How he tolerated the pain I'll never know.'

'Was it the fire that blinded him?'

'No, that was the diabetes. He'd been ill for a while, had never been diagnosed. Made matters worse by indulging an addict's sweet tooth.'

'And the nerve damage? Heroin?'

'A bad batch of heroin. He scored it the day of the fire. Slipped away from Poulsenn and walked down the block to meet his supplier. That's how they traced him – something else he feels guilty for.'

'How'd he escape on burnt feet?'

'They stole a car. The girl drove. They managed to get out of the city, found themselves on Highway 1, hid out in a remote canyon in the hills above Malibu. At night, she sneaked into residential neighborhoods and scrounged in garbage cans. She tried to take care of him but his feet got worse and the pain caused him to shoot up that last hit of heroin. He lost consciousness, stayed that way for two days. Somehow she cared for him. At the end, she was trying to feed him grass and leaves. Gave him water from a nearby creek that added an intestinal parasite to his miseries. When I saw him in the burn ward, he weighed ninety-eight pounds. All that, and he'd withdrawn cold turkey. His survival's nothing short of a miracle.'

'So you became his doctor,' I said. 'And Schwinn's. And eventually, the two of them connected. Was that by design?'

'I listened to Bill's story, then Pierce's, finally put it all together. Of course, I never told either of them about the other – Pierce still thought of himself as a detective. Looking for Bill. Eventually – after much work – I got Bill's permission and confronted Pierce. It wasn't easy but . . . eventually they both came to understand that their lives were interwined.'

Matchmaking. Just as he'd done with Schwinn and Marge. The grand physician. *Giving.*

'You waited until it was clear Burns had nothing to fear from Schwinn,' I said. 'Meaning you learned the details of Janie Ingalls's murder. But all of you agreed not to pursue it. You became part of the cover-up. That's why you offered me all those apologies.'

'Alex,' he said. 'Some decisions are . . . these are shattered lives. I couldn't see any other way . . .'

'Schwinn changed things,' I said. 'Changed his mind about

keeping the secret. Any idea why he grew agitated about the murder during the weeks before his death? Why he sent out the murder book?'

'I've asked myself all that so many times, and the best I can come up with is the poor man felt he was going to die and had an urge to make peace.'

'Was he sick?'

'Nothing I could diagnose, but he came to me and complained about feeling weak. Shaky, out of focus. A month before his death, he began experiencing crushing headaches. The obvious possibility was a brain tumor, and I sent him up to the Sansum Clinic for an MRI. Negative, but the consulting neurologist did find some abnormal EEG patterns. But you know EEGs – so crude, hard to interpret. And his bloodwork was normal. I wondered about some late-term amphetamine sequelae. He'd been drug-free for years, but perhaps the self-abuse had taken its toll. Then, a week before the night terrors began, he blacked out.'

'Did Marge know about any of this?'

'Pierce insisted on keeping everything from her. Even hid his headache medication in a locked box in his darkroom. I tried to convince him to communicate with her more openly, but he was adamant. Their entire relationship was like that, Alex. Each of them talked to me, and I translated. In that sense, she was the perfect woman for him – stubborn, independent, fiercely private. He could be a profoundly *unmovable* man. Part of what made him a good detective, I suppose.'

'Do you think the night terrors were neurological, or unfinished business come back to haunt him?'

'Maybe both,' he said. 'Nothing unusual was found at his autopsy, but that means nothing. I've seen postmortem brain tissue that looks like Swiss cheese and turns out the patient was functioning perfectly. Then you come across perfectly healthy cerebral cortexes in people who fall apart neurologically. At the core, we humans defy logic. Isn't that why we both became doctors of the soul?'

'Is that what we are?'

'We are, son – Alex, I am sorry for concealing things from you. At the time I believed it was the right thing to do. But that girl . . . the killer's still out there.' Tears filled his eyes. 'One sets out to heal and ends up being complicit.'

I placed a hand on his narrow, soft shoulder.

He smiled. 'Therapeutic touch?'

'Friendship,' I said.

'The purchase of friendship,' he said. 'Cynics coined the term to demean what we do. Sometimes I wonder about the direction my own life has taken . . .'

We strolled toward the gravel pathway.

I said, 'What kind of relationship did Schwinn and Burns develop?'

'Once I knew Pierce could be trusted, I brought him out here. They began talking. Relating. Pierce ended up helping Bill. He'd come out from time to time, clean the house, wheel Bill around.'

'And now Pierce is gone, Burns remains as the last living witness to the Ingalls murder.'

Bert stared at the earth and kept walking.

I said, 'You call him Bill. What's his new surname?'

'Is that important?'

'It's going to come out eventually, Bert.'

'Is it?' he said, lacing his hands behind his back. He steered me toward the open space at the front of the house. 'Yes, I suppose it is. Alex, I know you need to talk to him, but as I told you, he has very little time left, and like most ex-addicts, his self-assessment is brutal.'

'I'll be mindful of that.'

'I know you will.'

'When we spoke earlier,' I said, 'you made a point of mentioning that heroin addicts were unlikely to be violent. You were trying to steer me away from Burns's trail. Caroline Cossack's, as well, by pointing out to me that females were unlikely to be involved in that kind of sexual homicide. All true, but how'd they end up witnessing the murder?'

'Bill came upon the scene once the poor girl was dead, saw what had been done to her.'

'Was Caroline with him?'

He hesitated. 'Yes. They were together at the party. She was allowed to be at the party *because* he was supervising her.'

'Supervising?'

'Keeping an eye on her. Her brothers paid him for that.'

'Drug pusher baby-sitting the strange little sister?' I said.

Bert nodded.

I said, 'So she tagged along with Burns, followed her brothers and their pals to the neighboring estate, came upon the kill spot. The killers saw them, had to be worried they'd unravel. Caroline, because her psychiatric history made her unreliable, Burns because he was a junkie. But instead of eliminating Caroline, they hospitalized her. Probably because even though the Cossacks had participated in murder, they couldn't quite bring themselves to murder their sister. They *would've* killed Burns, but he disappeared into the ghetto, and being rich white kids, they had no easy way to find him. Burns was scared, tried to make a big score, took too many risks and got arrested, made quick bail thanks to LAPD connections and Boris Nemerov's goodwill, and vanished again. But then, a few months later, he surfaced – got himself a job at Achievement House so he could see Caroline. The boys found out and decided the big step had to be taken. But before they could arrange the hit, Burns was gone again. He and Caroline managed to remain in contact. Eventually, he got her out of Achievement House, and the two of them hid out in Watts. How am I doing so far?'

'A-plus, Alex. As always.'

'But something doesn't make sense, Bert. Why would Burns put himself in terrible jeopardy by wangling a job at Achievement House? Why in the world would he risk his life?'

Bert smiled. 'Irrational, wasn't it? That's what I mean about human beings being hard to categorize.'

'Why'd he do it, Bert?'

'Very simple, Alex. He loved her. Still does.'

'Present tense?' I said. 'They're still together? Where is she?'

'They're very much together. And you've met her.'

He brought me back into the house. The front room was empty and the push door remained shut. Bert held it open, and I stepped into a corn yellow bedroom not much bigger than a closet.

Tiny bathroom off to one side. In the sleeping area were two single beds placed side by side, each made up with thin, white spreads. A stuffed bear sat atop a low dresser painted hospital green. The wheelchair was positioned at the foot of the nearer bed, and the man who called himself Bill remained seated, the nearly empty Snapple bottle in one hand, the other grasped by the pudgy, white fingers of a heavyset woman wearing an oversize, royal blue T-shirt and gray sweatpants.

Her downturned eyes were aimed at the bedspread, and my appearance didn't cause them to shift. She had a pasty, acne-scarred face – raw bread dough, pocked by airholes – and her flat nose nearly touched her upper lip. Faded brown hair striped with silver was tied back in a stub of a ponytail.

Aimee, the cook at the Celestial Café. She'd prepared my crêpes, doubled my portion without charging me extra, remained virtually mute.

Just as I'd finished my meal, Bert had come in. Nice coincidence; now I knew it had been anything but.

Marian Purveyance had owned the café until Aimee Baker took over.

He gives people things.

I said, 'Didn't know you were a restaurateur, Dr Harrison.'

Bert flushed nearly as purple as his jumpsuit. 'I used to fancy myself an investor, bought up a few local properties.'

'Including the land this house stands on,' I said. 'You even transplanted agaves.'

He kicked one foot with the other. 'That was years ago. You'd be amazed at the appreciation.'

'If you ever sold anything.'

'Well . . . the time has to be right.'

'Sure,' I said, and I found myself throwing my arms around the old man.

Aimee turned, and said, 'You're nice.'

Bill said, 'Which one you talking about, baby?'

'Both,' she said. 'Everyone's nice. The whole world is nice.'

thirty-nine

Detective III Craig Bosc whimpered. Vomit flecked his well-formed lips.

Milo said, 'I'll be right back. Don't think of leaving, lad.'

Bosc watched with panic as Milo collected the homemade videos and the dope and left. Milo brought the stash out to the rental Polaris, locked them in the trunk, and moved the car directly in front of Bosc's house. When he returned, the former auto cop hadn't budged.

He undid the leg restraint and hauled Bosc to his feet. Pressed his gun in the small of Bosc's back, making sure not to grow over-confident of his own dominance. Bosc was a fool, and he'd lost more than a bit of self-confidence, but he was also an athlete, young and strong and desperate. When he took hold of Bosc's arm he felt iron musculature.

'Now what?' said Bosc.

'Now, we take a ride.'

Bosc's body grew limp and Milo had to struggle to maintain his grip. Maybe a ploy . . . no, Bosc was really frightened. He'd passed wind and the stench filled the room and Milo eased him back on the couch, let him sit. Putting on the stone face, but he felt ashamed. What had he sunk to?

'Come on,' Bosc pleaded. 'I told you everything. Just let it be.'

'What do you take me for, Craig?'

'I take you for smart. You're supposed to be smart,' said Bosc.

'Exactly.'

'You can't be serious, this is crazy.' Genuine terror enflamed Bosc's eyes. Imagining the worst, because he, himself, was sorely lacking in the conscience department, and if the tables were turned . . .

The truth was Milo hadn't come up with a clear idea of what to do with the idiot. But that was no reason to allay Bosc's fears.

In a creepy, regretful voice, he said, 'There's really no choice, Craig.'

'Jesus,' said Bosc. 'We're both on the same team. Look: we're both . . . outsiders.'

'That so?'

'You know what I mean, man. You're on the outside because . . . you know. And I don't judge you for that, live and let live. Even when other guys put you down, I stood up for you. Said, look at the dude's solve rate, who the fuck cares what he does when he's – I kept telling them it's the job that counts. And you *do* your job, man. I *respect* that. There's been talk of promoting you, you've got a future, man, so don't blow it, no way you can get away with this. Why would you want to get *involved* in shit like this?'

'You've involved me,' said Milo.

'Come on, what did I really *do*? Followed a few orders and played some head games? Okay, it was wrong, sucked, granted, sorry, but no big deal, it was all just to – even that whole HIV rumor shit, man. And that wasn't my idea. I was against that. But all of it was just to – you know.'

'To get me focused.'

'Exact—'

'Well, I'm nice and focused now, Craig. Get up.' Milo backed up the command with a wave of the 9mm. Wondering what he'd do if Bosc complied because walking the guy outside to the rental car, even that short distance, would be risky in full daylight. Even in L.A., where a block was likely to be as devoid of people as one of Schwinn's nature photos.

'Please,' said Bosc. 'Don't do this, we're both—'

'Outsiders, yeah, yeah. How are *you* an outsider, Craig?'

'I'm artistic. Into different stuff than the typical morons in the department.'

'Cinematography?' said Milo.

'Drama – acting. I was in a rock video a few years back. The Zombie Nannies. Played a highway patrol chippie. Before that, I did a nonunion commercial for the transit authority. And art – paintings. I like art, man. Your typical department moron is into riding Harleys and pumping iron and drinking beer, I'm hitting the museums. I dig classical music – went to Austria couple of summers ago, to the Salzburg festival. Mozart, Beethoven, all that good stuff. You see what I'm trying to say? It's *because* I understand the art community that I get where *you're* coming from.'

'I'm an artist.'

'In a sense you are. Without the people in your community, art would go dead. It would be a fucked world, man – come on, don't *do* this. This is stupid, we're both worthwhile, we both have lots to live for.'

'Do we?'

'Sure,' said Bosc, voice smoothing at the nuance of calm in Milo's reply. 'Just think about it: there's lots of good stuff waiting for both of us.'

'Why,' said Milo, 'do I think you've taken a hostage negotiation course?'

Bosc smiled uneasily. 'You're dissing *me*, but I'm being *real* with *you*. Fine, I can dig that. I dissed you, played with your head, you're entitled. But focus on this: at this very moment I'm being realer than anyone you'll ever meet.'

Milo approached the sofa from one side, took hold of Bosc's T-shirt. 'Get up, or I'll shoot you in the kneecap.'

Bosc's smile dropped like a stone down a glacier hole. 'You take me out there, and I scream—'

'Then you'll die screaming.'

He yanked and Bosc stumbled to his feet and Milo marched him toward the door.

Bosc said, 'I give you credit, man, switching wheels the way you did. I thought I knew all the tricks, but you were too quick for me, I give you credit, give you full credit. Only there's something you *don't* know.'

'There's plenty I don't know, Craig,' said Milo. Figuring the guy was bargaining for time – another negotiation trick. If only he knew he was expending needless energy. Because eventually, he'd be let loose. What choice did Milo have? The question was where and when. And Bosc would reward the largesse with instant hatred and an overpowering bloodlust for revenge. Given Bosc's position in the department, he'd be very likely to do serious damage, and Milo knew he was screwed.

In big trouble, just as Bosc had gloated. But what choice had there been? Continue flopping around as others yanked the strings, Mr Meat Puppet?

He shoved Bosc toward the door. Bosc said, 'No, I mean something you should know right *now*. Specifically. For your own sake.'

'What's that?'

'You've gotta let me go, first.'

'Right.'

'I mean it, man. At this point, I've got nothing to lose, so you can do what the fuck you want to me and I'm not gonna tell you. Because why would I squander my last chip? Come on, make it easy for both of us and I'll tell you and save your friend's ass and we'll both forget any of this happened and be square.'

'My friend,' said Milo. Thinking: *Rick?* Jesus, it had been *Rick* Bosc tailed initially, *Rick's* car Bosc boosted. All these years he'd managed to keep Rick out of this world, and now . . .

He jammed the gun hard into the small of Bosc's back. Bosc gasped, but kept his voice cool. 'Your shrink friend Delaware. *You* switched cars, but he didn't. Still driving round in that green Caddy. I put a satellite tracer on it days ago, know exactly where the dude goes. It feeds into a computer, and I get the data, I know where the feed is. And let me tell you, man, he's been a traveling fool. Did he tell you he was gonna improvise?'

'Where'd he go?'

Long silence.

Milo poked even harder. Used his other hand to clamp the back of Bosc's neck.

'Uh-uh, no way,' Bosc gasped. 'You can fucking blow out my spine, do whatever bad stuff you want, but I'm not giving up my trump card. And something else. And this is the main issue: I'm not the only one knows where the dude is. Other people know, by now. Or they will, real soon. The bad guys. 'Cause the plan was to tell them, leave them one of those anonymous phone calls. We fucking set up your *buddy*, man. Not to hurt him, necessarily, just to use him, to get everyone together. Converging, you know? It was supposed to be perfectly timed, you were supposed to be in on it, too. That's what I was doing at your place today. I was gonna have another try at tagging your car, then you'd be called, too. To motivate you. But you weren't home, so I figured I'd try you later.'

'Bullshit,' said Milo. 'You were settled in for the night, work was the last thing on your mind.'

'Bullshit yourself, I'm a night owl, fucking Batman-Dracula, come alive when the sun goes down. The plan was perfect, only *you* screwed it by being too smart and switching cars, and now Delaware's out in the cold, man, and if you want to help him, there's only one thing you can do and you better do it quick.'

Milo twirled Bosc around, clamped Bosc's gullet at arm's length, aimed the gun at Bosc's groin.

'Go ahead,' said Bosc. 'Do your thing. I'm gonna hold on to my dignity.'

Staring back defiantly.

Sincere.

If the word could be applied to the bastard.

forty

Bert said, 'Yes, Aimee, the world is nice. Now how about you and I go over to the café, see if we can bake up something.'

Aimee smiled, kissed Bill on the forehead, and padded out of the room without a glance at me. Bert said, 'We'll be back in a short while. I'll bring you a sugarless brioche, Bill. Alex, what can I get you?'

'I'm fine.'

'I'll get you something. You may be hungry later.'

I sat on the bed, opposite the wheelchair. 'Good to meet you, Mr . . .'

'We're the Bakers, now,' said Bill. 'It was as good a name as any, and it made Aimee smile. Because one thing she could always do was cook and bake.'

'Bill Baker.'

He grinned and rolled his head. 'Sounds like a rich white man, huh? Bill Baker, attorney. Bill Baker, businessman.'

'It does have a ring to it,' I said.

'It does, indeed.' He grew serious. 'Before we start, I need you to know something. My Aimee, she's like a kid. Always been different, always been scorned. I used to scorn her, like everyone else. Back when I was pushing dope and her brothers used to buy product from me. I liked selling to them because it was a nice change of pace for a South Central junkie. I'd meet them up in the hills above Bel Air, and it was so gorgeous, nothing like my usual transaction locales. I used to call it the scenic route. Make some quick money and get a tour of the way the other side lives.'

The same hills where Bowie Ingalls had died in a single-car

encounter with a tree. The boys agreeing to meet *him* in a familiar spot.

I said, 'Did you have lots of clients on the Westside?'

'Enough. Anyway, that's how I met Aimee. Once in a while, the boys would bring her along. When their parents were in Europe or somewhere, which was a lot of the time, those parents were always gone. When they did bring her, they'd leave her in the car and make cruel comments. Embarrassed to be seen with her. To be related to her. I went along with the program. Back then, I had not an atom of compassion in my soul, was hollow, cold, manipulative, thinking only of me, me, me, and not very much of myself, at that. 'Cause if I'd really thought a lot about myself, I wouldn't have done the things I did.'

He raised his arms with effort. Compressed his face and pressed his palms together.

'I was a very bad person, sir. I can't say that I'm a good person now, and I don't give myself any credit for changing, because it was life that changed me.' A slow smile split his head. 'How much sin can a blind man with no feet get into? I'd like to think I wouldn't be bad, even with eyes and legs. But I can never be sure. I don't really feel sure of myself, here.' One hand lowered laboriously and touched his belly.

He laughed. 'Eye for an eye, leg for a leg. I ruined lots of lives, and now I'm paying for it. Almost ruined Aimee's life, too. Gave her dope – big dose of LSD, blotter acid. Her brothers' idea, but I didn't have to be talked into it. We forced her to swallow it, big joke, hahaha. She hollered and fussed and cried, and I stood around laughing with them.'

He drew a hand over sightless eyes.

'Poor little thing, hallucinated for four straight days. I think it might've changed her nervous system. Slowed her down even further, made her life even more difficult, and believe me, life had never been easy for that girl. Next time I saw her was her fourth day of freaking out. Garvey and Bobo wanted to score some mushrooms, and I was the candy man and I met them up in the hills the way we always did and there she was, sitting in the back of the car, but not still, like usual. She was rocking and moaning and crying her little eyes out. Garvey and Bobo just laughed, said she'd been tripping heavy since we blotted her, tried to plunge her hand in boiling water, had almost jumped out of a second-story window, they'd finally tied her down to the bed, she hadn't had a bath or eaten. Laughing about it, but they were worried because their parents were coming home and even though their parents didn't like her, they wouldn't have approved. So I brought her down with barbiturates.'

'Her parents didn't like her?' I said.

'Not one bit. She was different, looked it, acted it, and they were a nouveau riche family that made a big thing of looking good all the time. Country club and all that. Those boys were bad to the core, but they dressed well and combed their hair and used the right aftershave, and that made everyone happy. Aimee didn't know how to do any of that, couldn't be taught to fake it. She was less than a dog in that family, sir, and Garvey and Bobo took advantage of it. Did stuff and blamed it on her.'

'What kind of stuff?' I said.

'Anything that could get 'em in trouble – stealing money, peddling dope on the secondary market to other rich kids, setting fires for fun. They killed a dog, once. Bobo did. Neighbor's dog. Said it barked too much, annoyed him, so he tossed some poison meat at it, and after it died, he and Garvey had Caroline walk by the dog's gate a bunch of times when they were sure the neighbor was watching. So the neighbor would assume. Stuff like that. They bragged to me about it, thought it was funny. They talked about her like she was dirt. I don't know why I started feeling sorry for her 'cause really I was no better than them, but somehow I did. Something about her . . . I just felt sorry for her, can't explain it.'

'Obviously you weren't like them.'

'Kind of you to say so, but I know what I was.' He removed the mirrored sunglasses, revealed sunken black discs split by comma-shaped slits, scratched the bridge of his nose, replaced the glasses.

'You felt sorry for her and started baby-sitting her,' I said.

'No, I did it for the money,' he said. 'Told the boys I'd hang with her when the parents were out of town if they'd pay me. They laughed, and said, "You could turn her out, you should pay us, bro," figuring I wanted to do sexual things to her or maybe I was going to pimp her. And that was agreeable to them. I started coming by the house in my old Mercury Cougar and taking her places.'

'She just went along?'

'She was happy to be getting out. And she was like that – easygoing.'

'She wasn't in school?'

'Not since fifth grade. Severe learning problems, she was supposed to be tutored but never really was. She still can't really read much or do numbers. All she can do is cook and bake, but man, does she do that good, that's her God-given talent.'

'Where'd you take her?' I said.

'Everywhere. The zoo, the beach, parks, she'd keep me company when I did deals. Sometimes we'd just ride around and listen to music. I'd be high, but I never gave her anything again – not after I saw what that blotter did to her. Mostly, I'd talk – trying to teach her stuff. About street signs, the weather, animals. Life. She knew nothing, I never met anyone who knew less about the world. I was no intellectual, just a stupid junkie-pusher, but I had plenty to teach her, which tells you how pathetic her situation was.'

He craned his neck. 'Could I trouble you for another Diet Snapple, sir? Always thirsty. Sugar-diabetes.'

I brought him another open bottle, and he finished it within seconds and handed me the empty. 'Thank you much. The thing you should know is I never did anything sexual to her. Not once, never. Not that I get any credit for that. I was a junkie, and you being a doctor knows what that does to your sex urge. Then the diabetes took over, and the plumbing went south, so I haven't been much for sex in a long time. Still, I'd like to think it wouldn't have made a difference. Respecting her, you know? Not taking advantage of her.'

'Sounds like you respected her from the beginning.'

'I'd like to think so. You sound just like Dr H. Trying to tell me something good about myself . . . anyway, that's the story with my Aimee. I like that name for her, chose it for her. Her family gave her the old name and they treated her like dirt so she deserved a new beginning. Aimee means friend in French and I've always wanted to go to France, and that's what she's been to me, my only real friend. Outside of Dr H.'

He managed to place his hands on the wheels of the chair, rolled back an inch, and smiled. As if the merest movement was pleasure. 'I'm going to die soon, and it's nice knowing Dr Harrison will be here to take care of my Aimee.'

'He will.'

The smile dissipated. 'Course, he's old . . .'

'Have you and he made plans?'

'It hasn't come to that, yet,' said Bill. 'We better do it soon . . . I've chewed your ear off, and you don't want to know about my personal problems. You're here to find out what happened to the Ingalls girl.'

'Yes,' I said.

'Poor Janie,' he said. 'I can see her face as clear as day, right here.' Tapping a mirrored lens. 'Didn't know her, but I'd seen her around, thumbing on Sunset. She and this friend she was always with, this good-looking blonde. I figured the two of them were hooking, because the only girls still thumbing were hookers and runaways looking to be hookers. Turns out they were just careless girls. The night I found them, I was driving to the party, ready to do some heavy business, saw them standing around on Sunset all confused. Not on the Strip, Bel Air, 'cross the street from the U. They were just a walk from the party but had no idea. So I gave 'em a lift. I still think about that. What if I hadn't?'

'You brought them to the party, then what?'

He smiled. 'Move it right along? Yeah, I brought 'em, tried to get 'em high. Janie smoked some weed, dropped some pills, drank, the blonde one just drank. We hung around together a little, it was a lunatic scene, rich kids and crashers, everyone high and horny, doing their thing in that big, old, empty house. Then Aimee showed up. Attaching to me like she always did. She was there in the first place because I'd agreed to watch her. The parents were off in India, or some place. Had just bought a bigger house, and the boys decided to give themselves a little goodbye bash. Anyway, Janie and her friend – I think her name was Melissa, something like that – were getting into the scene.'

'Melinda Waters,' I said.

He cocked his head, like a guard dog on alert. 'So you know plenty.'

'I don't know how it happened.'

'How it happened is Janie got noticed. By one of the brothers' buddies, a mean kid. You know his name, too?'

'Vance Coury.'

'That's the one,' he said. 'Sweet piece of work, he wasn't any older than the others, but he had this seasoned bad guy's way about him. He noticed Janie, and that's the reason she died. Because he'd had her, before, wanted her again.'

'Had her how?' I said.

'He picked her up when she was thumbing. Took her to some hotel his old man owned downtown, tied her up, did her, whatever. He bragged about it.'

'To you?'

'To all of us. The brothers were with him, coupla other buddies, too. They'd come over to me to score, when Coury spotted Janie. She was off dancing, by herself, tank top half-off, pretty much in dreamland. Coury spots her and gives out this big grin, this big wolfy grin, and says, "Look at that, the slut." And the other boys check out Janie and nod, 'cause they know who she is, heard the story before, but Coury tells it again, anyway. How easy it was, like it was some safari and he'd bagged big game. Then he tells me not only did he do the slut but so did his old man. And the other guys crack up and tell me their daddies did her, too. Seems Janie's own dad was a lowlife scum who'd been selling her since she was twelve.'

Fighting revulsion, I said, 'The other guys' daddies. Do you remember which ones?'

'The brothers, for sure – Garvey and Bobo's old man, and this other creep, this nasty nerd named Brad something-or-other. He piped up and said his daddy'd had her, too. Laughing about it. Proud.'

'Brad Larner.'

'Never knew his last name. Skinny, pale nerd. Mean mouth.'

'Any other buddies in the group, that night?'

'One other, this big doofus, this surfer type . . . Luke. Luke the Nuke was my name for him cause he always looked bombed, would eat anything I sold him.'

'Luke Chapman,' I said. 'Had his father had sex with Janie?'

He thought. 'I don't recall his saying so . . . no, I don't think so, 'cause when the others were going on about it, he looked a little uneasy.'

Multigenerational rape. Michael Larner's assault on Allison Gwynn had been more than a passing fancy. Garvey Cossack, Sr, had harbored similar tastes and I was willing to bet Slumlord Coury played in that league, too.

Like father, like . . .

Bowie Ingalls had primed his only child by abusing her, then trafficking in her flesh. I thought about Milo's description of Janie's nearly empty room. A place she didn't, wouldn't think of as home.

Ingalls had been evil and calculating but stupid. Showing up at the meeting with his blackmail targets, drunk and overconfident.

I said, 'What happened when they finished bragging?'

'Coury made some crack about "Honor thy father." Went after Janie – just grabbed her and threw her over his shoulder. The others followed.'

'She resist?'

'Not much. Like I said, she was pretty much out of it. I took Aimee and got out of there. Not because I was a good man. But all that talk about ganging up on a girl, taking sloppy seconds from their daddies, made me feel . . . uncomfortable. Also, Aimee had to go to the bathroom, had been pulling at my arm for a while, complaining she needed to go. But finding a bathroom wasn't so easy in that place, every toilet was being used for getting high or having sex or throwing up or doing what a toilet's for. So, I took her out of the house, over to the backyard, all the way in back, to the bushes and trees, told her to go in there, I'd keep watch.'

He shrugged. The movement caused him pain, and he winced. 'I know it sounds crude, but we'd done that before, Aimee and me. I'd be driving her somewhere far from the city – we used to like to go up into the mountains, out in the San Gabriels or over in the West Valley near Thousand Oaks, or up on Mullholland Highway or Rambla Pacifica, top of Malibu. Anywhere we could find empty space and just enjoy the quiet. And no matter how many times I'd tell her to go to the bathroom *before* we set out, wouldn't you believe she'd have to go where there was no facilities?'

Big smile. 'Like a kid. So I was used to leading her into the bushes and keeping watch and that's what I did out in the backyard and when we were heading back to the house, we heard voices over the wall – her brother's voice, Garvey, whooping and laughing. Then the others. They were outside, too, going to the next-door property. I knew that because they'd taken me there, it was this huge place, acres, this estate, the owner was some rich European who was never there and most of the time the house was empty. They used to go there to party because no one would bother them. They had a way of getting in, this side gate, up toward the back with a bolt that was easy to wiggle loose and once you were back there you were so far from the house no one could spot you.'

'Party spot.'

'I partied with them, there,' he said. 'Like I said, I was the candy man. Anyway, Aimee wanted to tag along and go over there, like she always did – anything those boys did she thought was cool. No matter how they treated her, she'd want to be with them. I tried to talk her out of it, brought her back inside the party house and sat down and tried to groove on some music. 'Cause while Aimee was in the bushes, I'd shot up, was feeling mellow. But when I opened my eyes, she was gone, and I knew where she'd gone and I was responsible for her so I went after her. And found her. Looking. From behind some trees, into a clearing. She was shaking really bad, teeth chattering, and when I saw what she was looking at, I dug why.'

'How much time had passed since Coury had made a move for Janie?' I said.

'Hard to say. It felt like a long time, but I was going in and out – weaving, you know? Ever been on opiates?'

'When I was a kid I split myself open and they gave me Demerol to stitch me up.'

'Like it?'

'I liked it fine,' I said. 'Everything slowed down and pain turned into a warm glow.'

'So you know.' He rolled his head. 'It's like the best kiss. The sweetest kiss, straight from God's lips. All these years, even knowing what it did to my life, I *still* think about it . . . about the *idea* of doing it. And Lord help me, sometimes I pray that when I do die and if by some miracle I end up upstairs, there'll be this big syringe waiting for me.'

'What was Aimee looking at?'

'Janie.' His voice cracked on the name, and he rocked gently in his wheelchair. 'Oh, Lord, it was bad. Someone was holding a flashlight on her – Luke the Nuke – and the others were standing around, staring. They had her spread out on the ground, with her legs apart, and her head was nothing but blood and she was all cut up and burned and dead cigarettes and blood was all over the ground.'

'Did you see a weapon?'

'Coury and Bobo Cossack were holding knives. Big hunting knives, like you'd get in an army surplus store. Garvey had the pack of cigarettes – Kools. Trying to be hip.'

'What about Brad Larner?'

'He was just standing and staring. And the other one, this big dumb-looking dude, was behind him, freaked out, dead scared, you could see it all over his face. The others were more . . . frozen. Like they'd done something and now it was sinking in. Then Coury said, "We need to get the bitch outta here," and he told Brad to go to his car, get out these blankets he kept there. Then Aimee started retching out loud, and they all turned toward us, and Garvey said, "Oh, shit, you fucking moron!" and I grabbed Aimee and tried to get the hell out of there. But Garvey had got hold of her arm and wouldn't let go and I just wanted to be as far from there as I could so I left her with him and ran as fast as I could and got in my car and drove the hell out of there. I drove like a maniac, it's a miracle no cop pulled me over. Went over to the Marina, then east on Washington, sped all the way east to La Brea, then south into the ghetto.'

He smiled. 'Into the high-crime neighborhood. Watts. That's when I finally felt safe.'

'Then what?'

'Then nothing. I kept a low profile, ran out of money and smack, did what I knew how to do, and got busted.'

'You never thought about reporting the murder?'

'Sure,' he said. 'Rich kids from Bel Air and a black junkie felon tells the cops he just happened to see a white girl get carved up? Cops used to stop me for driving while black, run my license and reg, pull me out, have me do the spread for no reason. Even in my old Mercury Cougar, which was a piece of junk, appropriate for a black junkie felon.'

'That night,' I said, 'you had better wheels. Late-model white Cadillac.'

'You know that?' he said. 'You already know stuff?' Something new crept into his voice – an aftertone of menace. Hint of the man he'd once been. 'You having me go through the motions?'

'You're the first eyewitness we've found. I know about the Caddy because we located Melinda Waters, and she mentioned it. But she split from the party before the murder.'

His head rolled slowly, and he canted it away from me. 'The Caddy was a borrowed car. I maintained the Merc the way a junkie would and finally it broke down and I sold it for dope money. Next day I realized that without wheels I was nothing – good old junkie planning. I planned on boosting some wheels but hadn't gotten around to it, too stoned. So that night, I borrowed from a friend.'

'Nice car like that,' I said, 'must've been a good friend.'

'I had a few. And don't ask me who.'

'Was it the same friend who helped you escape?'

The mirrored shades tilted toward me. 'Some things I can't say.'

'It'll all going to come out,' I said.

'Maybe,' he said. 'If it happens by itself, it's not my responsibility. But some things I can't say.' He turned his head sharply toward the front of the house.

'Something's wrong,' he said. 'Aimee's coming, but that's not her usual walk.'

I heard nothing. Then: a faintest crunch – footsteps on gravel. Footsteps stopping and starting, as if someone was stumbling. But for the panic on his face, it would've floated right past me.

I left him and stepped into the front room, parted the drapes on a small, cloudy window, and looked out at the filmy, amber light of impending dusk.

Up the drive, maybe a hundred feet from the house, two men were walking Aimee and Bert toward us. Aimee and Bert's hands were up in the air as they marched forward reluctantly. Bert looked terrified. Aimee's pasty face was expressionless. She stopped suddenly and her escort prodded her with something and she winced and resumed walking.

Crunch.

One of the men was large and beefy, the other a head shorter and wiry. Both were Hispanic and wore cowboy hats. I'd seen them half an hour ago – in the pickup loaded with fertilizer that had interposed itself between Bert's car and mine, then dropped away at the 33–150 intersection.

Lucky break, I'd thought at the time, enabling me to use the truck for cover as I tailed Bert.

Bill called out, 'What's happening?'

I rushed back to him. 'Two cowboys have them at gunpoint.'

'Under the bed,' he said, waving his arms helplessly. 'Get it. Now.'

Barking the order. Sounding like anything but a junkie.

forty-one

The computer gizmo that read out the trace on Alex was right in Craig Bosc's Saab, hooked up to the dash, a cute little thing with a bright blue screen and a printer. It sputtered to life after Bosc punched a few keys.

Nineties guy, everything he needed, close at hand.

Milo hadn't found any printouts in Bosc's house, meaning Bosc had left those at his office. Or at someone else's.

As Bosc kept typing, the screen filled with readout – columns of numbers in a code that Bosc explained with no prodding. Bosc pushed another key, and the columns were replaced with what looked like blueprints. Vectors and loci, computerized map lines, everything loading at warp speed.

Bosc was sitting in the Saab's passenger seat. Hands free to work, but Milo had rebound his ankles, first, kept the gun at the back of Bosc's neck.

Promising to let him go when he'd done his bit for humanity.

Bosc thanked him as if he was Santa Claus with a bag full of goodies. The guy stank of fear, but you'd never know it from looking at him. Smiling, smiling, smiling. Gabbing technotalk as he worked.

Killing time and filling space; keep those psych tactics going.

His fingers rested. 'That's it, amigo. Look at the capital X, and you've got him.'

Milo studied the map. 'That's the best you can do?'

'That's pretty damn good,' said Bosc, offended. 'Within a hundred-yard radius.'

'Print it.'

★ ★ ★

392

His pocket filled with paper, Milo yanked Bosc out of the Saab and walked him to the rear of the car.

'Okay, Milo, we're just gonna forget this happened, right?'

'Right.'

'Could I have my legs back, please, Milo.'

The easy, repetitive use of his name filled Milo's head with enraged buzzing. He looked up and down the street, now graying. During the time Bosc had played with the computer, a single car had driven by. Young woman in a yellow Fiero, blonde and big-haired enough to be one of Bosc's unwitting home movie costars. But she sped by fast, went two blocks, disappeared, never returned.

Now the street was empty again. Thank God for L.A. alienation.

Milo popped the Saab's trunk, gave Bosc a swift, hard kick behind one knee and as Bosc collapsed predictably, shoved him inside, slammed the lid and walked away to the muffled drumbeat of Bosc thumping and screaming.

All that noise, someone would find him soon enough.

He hurried to the Polaris, checked the gas gauge, fired up, sped toward the 101 freeway, driving like a typical SoCal idiot: way too fast, steering with one hand, the other gripping his mobile phone as if it was a life preserver.

393

forty-two

A husky voice from outside the cabin bellowed, 'Everyone out, hands up.' A second later: 'No fucking around or we kill the retard and the old guy.'

I crouched closer to the window. 'We're coming out. I have to get him in the chair.'

'*Do* it.'

I returned to the bedroom, clamped my hands around the grips of Bill's wheelchair. I'd put a bright white stocking cap on his bald head and had covered him with two soft blankets, despite the heat.

Or maybe it wasn't that hot. I was sweat-drenched but he, the diabetic, remained freakishly dry.

A moment before, he'd prayed silently, lips quivering, hands hooked in the blankets.

He said, 'My, my, my' as I wheeled him forward. When we reached the door, the footrests of his chair nudged it open, and we stepped out into an amethyst twilight.

The pair of cowboys holding Aimee and Bert were twenty or so yards up the gravel drive, off center, closer to the western edge of the pathway, where the forest began. The sky was slate, and the foliage had deepened to olive drab. Flesh tones remained vivid; I saw the fear on Bert's face.

The bigger cowboy was positioned slightly in front of his partner. The pickup's driver. Midforties, five-eleven, with a potbelly that strained his ice-blue shirt, thick thighs that turned his blue jeans into sausage casing, a complexion the color of dirty copper, and a bristling, graying mustache. His hat was broad-brimmed, brown felt.

Bored demeanor, but even at this distance I could see the edgy movement around his eyes. He towered over Bert, held the old man by the scruff.

Just behind him, to the right, the smaller intruder maintained a grip on Aimee, clutching her sweatshirt from behind, stretching the fabric over the rolls and bulges of her torso. Younger, five-five, midtwenties, he wore a baggy black T-shirt and saggy black jeans too urban for his straw headpiece. The hat looked cheap, a hurried addition. He had a round face bottomed by a wispy goatee. Dull, distracted eyes. A mass of tattoos ran up his arms.

One of the car restorers at Vance Coury's garage.

The sun didn't move, but Bert Harrison's complexion grayed.

Aimee said, 'Billy, what's happening?' She made a move toward the chair but the small cowboy cuffed the back of her head. She flapped her arms clumsily. He said, 'Cool it, retard.'

'Bill—'

Bill said, 'Everything's cool, babe, we'll work it out.'

'Sure we will,' said the big cowboy, in the husky voice that had brought us out. A pack of cigarettes swelled one of the pockets of his shirt. Western shirt, with a contrasting white yoke, pearl buttons, still box-creased. He and his pal had dressed for the occasion. He said, 'Get the fuck over here, Willy.'

'Over where?' said Bill.

'Over here, Stevie Wonder.' Glancing at me: 'You – asshole – wheel him over here real slow – take your hands off the fucking chair, and I'll blow your fucking head off.'

'Then what?' said Bill.

'Then we take y'all somewhere.'

'Where?'

'Shut the fuck up.' To the smaller man: 'We'll load 'em in back with the shit. Under them tarps, like I showed you.'

Small said, 'Why don't we just do 'em here?' in a nasal voice.

The big man's chest swelled. Taking a deep breath. 'That's the plan, *mijo*.'

'What about the wheelchair?'

Big laughed. 'You can have the chair, okay? Give it to that kid of yours to play with.' To me: 'Wheel him.'

'Where's the truck?' I said.

'Shut up and wheel him.'

'*Is* there a truck?' I said. 'Or are we just taking a little walk?' Stalling, because that's what you did in situations like that. Because what was there to lose?

The big man yanked Bert's hair, and Bert's face creased with pain.

'I'll just do this old *payaso* right here, you keep talking. Blow out his eyes and make you fuck the sockets.'

I rolled the wheelchair forward. The tires caught in the gravel, kicked up rocks that pinged the spokes. I pretended to be stuck. My hands stayed wrapped around the grips.

Big maintained his hold on Bert and watched me closely. His companion's attention span wasn't as good, and I saw him glance off into the darkening trees.

'Bill?' said Aimee.

'*Bill?*' mimicked Big. 'That's what you call yourself now, Willie?'

'He's Bill Baker,' I said. 'Who do you think he is?'

Big's eyes slitted. 'Was I talking to *you*, asshole? Shut the fuck up and get the fuck over here.'

'Hey,' said Bill, cheerfully. 'What do you know? I thought I recognized that voice. Ignacio Vargas. Long time, Nacho. Hey, man.'

Recognition didn't trouble the big man. He smirked. 'Long time no see, nigger.'

'Real long time, Nacho. Doc, I used to sell this *vaquero* product. He was smart, never tasted, just distributed to his homeboys. Hey, Nacho, didn't you go off somewhere for a vacation – Lompoc? Or did you make it to Quentin?'

'Nigger,' said Vargas, 'before I went away I tried to party with you and the retard over at that house in Niggertown, but you got away. Now, here we are, after all those years. One a those . . . reunions. Who said you don't get a second chance?'

His mouth opened, displaying rows of broken, brown teeth.

Two decades of sanctuary, and I'd brought the enemy to the gates.

'You know what they say, amigo,' said Bill. 'If you don't succeed at first – but, hey, let the old guy go. He's just a doctor happens to treat me, got a bad heart, gonna kick soon, anyway, why bother?'

Bert had been staring at the gravel. Now his eyes climbed very gradually. Came to rest on me. Dispirited.

Bill said, 'Let her go, too. She can't hurt anybody.'

Bert shifted his weight and Nacho Vargas cuffed him again. 'No squirming around, Grampa. Yeah, I think I heard that one, before. If you don't succeed at first, make sure you kill the fucker dead the second time, then go out for a good meal. Come on, Whitebread, keep moving, then when I tell you to stop, let go the wheel and *slowly* put your hands up then get down on the ground and put your hands behind your head and eat dirt.'

I edged the chair another foot forward. Got stuck again. Freed the wheels.

Bill said, 'Nacho was intelligent-o, selling but never using. I could've learned from you, Nacho.'

'You couldn'ta learned nothing. You were stupid.'

I closed the space between us and Vargas to ten yards.

'I don't see any truck,' I said.

'There's a fucking *truck*,' said Small.

Vargas shot a disgusted look intended for his partner, but kept his eyes on me. He began tapping his boot impatiently. Shiny, needle-toed black boots that had never known stirrups; the jeans looked fresh, too. Big shopping spree.

A one-day costume, because you could never really wash out the blood.

Bill said, 'Nacho, my man, be smart: I got nothing to look forward to, put me out of my misery, but leave the old guy and Aimee and everyone else alone. Take me off in that truck of yours and do what you want with—'

'Like I need your fucking permission,' said Vargas.

Bill's head rolled. 'No you don't, no one's saying you do, it's just why not be smart, like I said, he's got a heart condition—'

'Maybe I should have him run around in circles till he drops dead. Save on bullets.' Vargas laughed, kept his gun hand behind Bert, lifted the other arm and jacked Bert up effortlessly. The old man's toes barely grazed the gravel. He'd gone deathly pale. A rag doll.

Vargas said, 'Hey, this is like playing puppet.' His gun hand shifted upward, too. Just an inch or so.

'Nacho, man—'

'Yeah, sure, we'll let everyone go. Maybe we'll let you go, too. Hey, that's a good idea – let's all go out and have a beer.' He snorted. 'She ain't the only retard.' The boot tapped faster. 'C'mon, c'mon, move it.'

I closed the gap to twenty feet, fifteen, exerted downward pressure that tipped the chair slightly, got stuck again.

'What the fu – you playing with me, Whitebread?'

'Sorry,' I said, in a tremulous voice. 'You told me to keep my hands – just a sec.'

Before Vargas could reply, Bert sagged in his grip, cried out in pain, clutched his chest. Vargas laughed, too clever to be taken in by an obvious ruse, but Bert kept thrashing, gave his head a hard shake, and the sudden movement tugged Vargas's arm down and Bert struggled to twist away. As Vargas tried to contain him, his gun hand rose and the weapon was visible. Sleek, black automatic. Aimed at the sky. Behind him, Small was cursing, his attention directed at the struggle. Aimee stared, too, not resisting.

The moment Bert had shown distress, I'd pushed the chair faster, got within five feet of Vargas. Stopped. Vargas continued to grope for Bert. I gave a low grunt.

Bill groped under the folds of the top blanket and pulled out the shotgun.

Old but clean Mossberg Mariner Eight-Shot Mini Combo with pistol grip and speed-feed. Extreme saw-off, barely any barrel left. I'd found it under the bed, where he'd said it would be, stored in a black canvas case coated with dust bunnies. Lying next to two rifles in similar housing and half a dozen boxes of ammo.

'Use the big shells,' he said. I'd loaded the weapon.

Then handed it over to a stiff-fingered blind man.

Vargas got a firm grip on Bert, but Bert saw the shotgun, turned, and bit down on Vargas's arm, and when Vargas bellowed and let go of him, he dropped to the ground and rolled away.

I muttered, 'Now,' and Bill yanked the trigger.

The explosion boxed my ears, and the recoil shoved the wheelchair into my groin as Bill's head snapped backward and connected with my midriff.

Nacho Vargas was blown away as if caught in a personalized tornado. The bottom half of his face turned to smoky, bloody dust, and a giant, ruby-pink orchid blossomed where his gullet and chest had once been. As he fell, white-flecked, red broth shot out through his back, spattering Aimee and the small cowboy, who looked stunned. I threw myself at him, swung one fist upward, connected under his nose, got hold of his groin with my other hand and twisted hard.

The whole thing had taken five seconds.

The small man went down, landed on his back, cried out in pain. His black T-shirt was grimed with what looked like steak tartare and bone bits and gobbets of something gray-pink and spongy I knew to be lung tissue. His gun – shiny and silver – remained entwined in his fingers, and I stomped his hand and kicked the weapon loose. The gun rolled away and I dived for it, slid into gore and skidded and went facedown into the gravel, feeling the buzz of impact, then searing pain along one half of my face, both elbows and knees.

I'd fallen atop the weapon, felt it biting into my chest. Now the damned thing would go off and blow a hole through me. What a dignified demise.

I rolled away, grabbed the gun, sprang to my feet, hurried back to the small man. He lay there, immobile, and I felt under his filth-encrusted jaw, got a slow steady pulse. The hand I'd stomped looked like a dead crab, and when I lifted his eyelids all I saw was white.

A few feet away, what had once been Nacho Vargas was an exhibit for the forensic pathology texts.

Aimee said, 'Careful.' Talking to Bill, not me. She was behind the chair now, had removed his watch cap, was stroking his head.

Bert was on his feet, tottering, holding Vargas's weapon with two hands. Staring at it with revulsion. His color made me unsure if the chest pains had been a total ruse.

I kept the silver gun trained on the unconscious man, heartbeat racing way beyond optimal, muscles pumped, head boiling.

Up close, he looked barely twenty.

Give it to that kid of yours to play with.

A young man with one kid, maybe a new father. Would he have helped Vargas dispatch all of us, then gone home and played with Junior?

He moaned, and my fingers tightened around the trigger.

Another moan, but he didn't move. I trained the gun on him, had to work at releasing the pressure in my fingers. Slowing my breathing, struggling to think clearly, sort things out.

The clearing around the house deepened to a sickening, syrupy gray. Bill sat there in the chair, the shotgun across his lap. Aimee and Bert stood by, silently. The small man didn't move. Silence settled around us. From somewhere off in the forest, a bird peeped.

A plan: I'd tie up the unconscious man, put him and the wheelchair in the trunk of the Seville, drive us all to some safe place – I'd figure out where along the way. No, first I'd call Milo from the house – I had to get them all in the house – the bloody gravel, the corpse with its yield of shredded body parts, would be dealt with later.

'Do you have any rope?' I asked Bill.

His mirrored glasses were off, and Aimee was dabbing at the gray hollows with a corner of the top blanket. Unmindful of the porridge that splotched her clothing and her face.

He said, 'No. Sorry.'

'Nothing to tie him with?'

'Sorry . . . the other one's alive?'

'Out cold but alive. I thought with that arsenal—'

'The arsenal was my . . . baggage . . . never really thought I'd use it . . .'

The shotgun had been clean, freshly oiled.

He must've read my mind, said, 'I taught my Aimee how to take care of it.'

Aimee recited: 'Ream the barrel, wipe it down, oil it up.'

'But no rope,' said Bill. 'Ain't that a hoot. Maybe we can shred some clothing.' Tired. One hand caressed the truncated shotgun.

Aimee mumbled.

'What's that, sugar?'

'There is rope. Kind of.'

'There is?' he said.

'Twine. I use it for my rolled roast.'

'Not strong enough, baby.'

'Oh,' she said. 'It holds in the roast.'

'Bert, come here and keep a close aim on him,' I said, pocketing the silver gun and pulling the small man to his feet. He was 130 pounds tops, but deadweight and the noradrenaline cool-down made dragging him to the house an ordeal.

I got him to the door, looked back. No one had followed. Nighttime turned the others to statuary.

'Inside,' I said. 'Let's take a look at that twine.'

forty-three

Bill was right about the cooking twine. Too flimsy. I used it anyway, sitting the small man in a chair in the front room and using both rolls to create a macramé mummy. He looked out of it, hopefully for a while. My heart started racing again.

I searched the small kitchen, found a crushed, nearly empty roll of duct tape beneath the sink, unspooled enough to run two tight bands around his body and the chair, at nipple and waist levels. What was left I used to bind his ankles together. He offered no resistance . . . how old was his kid?

I said, 'Where's the phone?'

Bert shuffled over to a corner, bent behind another chair, retrieved an old black dial phone, and handed it to me. He hadn't said a word since the shooting.

I lifted the receiver. No dial tone. 'Dead.'

Bert took the phone, jabbed the receiver button, dialed O. Shook his head.

'Do you generally have phone problems?'

'No, sir,' said Bill. 'Not that we use it much. Maybe—' He frowned. 'I know that smell.'

'What smell?' I said.

The concussion came from behind, from the rear of the house. The impact of something striking wood, followed by a loud sucking *swoosh!* Then the xylophone glissando of broken glass.

Bill turned toward the sound. Bert and I stared. Only Aimee seemed unconcerned.

Suddenly daylight – a false orange daylight – brightened the bedroom, followed by a rush of heat and the cellophane-snap of flames.

Fire licked the curtains, a zipper of it, running up to the ceiling and down to the floor.

I ran for the bedroom door, slammed it shut over the spreading inferno. Smoke seeped from under the panel. The odor hit: metallic, acrid, the chemical bitterness of a flash storm ripping open a polluted sky.

The smoke from beneath the door fattened from wisp to wormy coil to clouds, relentless and oily, white to gray to black. Within seconds, I could barely make out the forms of the other people.

The room grew furnace-hot.

The second firebomb hit. Again, from behind. Someone was stationed out back, in the forest, where the phone wires ran.

I grabbed hold of Bill's chair, waved frantically to Bert and Aimee's smoke-obscured silhouettes.

'Get out!' Knowing that what I was sending them to was unlikely to be safety. But the alternative was roasting alive.

No answer, and now I couldn't see them at all. I rolled Bill toward the front door. From behind came roaring protest. The door collapsed and flames shot forward as I shoved the wheelchair. Groping the air for Aimee and Bill. Screaming with clogged lungs: 'Someone's out there! Stay low—'

My words were choked off by convulsive coughing. I made it to the door, reached for the knob, and the hot metal broiled my hand.

Handicapped push door, idiot. I shouldered it hard, shoved Bill's chair, lurched outside, eyes burning, retching, coughing.

Running into the darkness and aiming the chair to the left as a bullet impacted against a front window.

Smoke billowed out of the house, a smothering curtain of it. Good cover, but poisonous. I ran as far from the gravel drive as possible, into the underbrush that formed at the house's eastern border. Racing with the chair, struggling to manipulate the contraption over rocks and vines, getting caught in the underbrush. Unable to free the chair.

Jammed. I lifted Bill out of the chair, slung him over my shoulder, and ran, adrenaline-stoked again, but his weight bore down and I could barely breathe and after ten steps I was on the verge of collapse.

My legs buckled. I visualized them as iron rods, forced them straight, lost my breath completely, stopped, shifted the load, panted and coughed. Feeling the dangle of Bill's ruined legs knocking against my thighs, the dry skin of one palm against the back of my neck as he held on tight.

He said something – I felt it rather than heard it – and I resumed carrying him into the forest. Pulled off ten more steps, counted each one, twenty, thirty, stopped again to force air into my lungs.

I looked back at the house. None of the Halloween glare of fire, just smoke, funnels of it, so dark it bled easily into the night sky.

Then the spot where the little green house had stood was suddenly engulfed by a crimson ball haloed in lime green.

The kerosene stink of a stale campground. Something igniting – the kitchen stove. The explosion threw me to the earth. Bill landed on top of me.

No sign of Aimee or Bert.

I stared back at the house, wondering if the fire would spread to the forest. Not good for the forest, but maybe good for us if it attracted attention.

Nothing but silence. No spread; the firebreak serving its purpose.

I rolled Bill off me and propped myself up on my elbows. His glasses had come loose. His mouth moved soundlessly.

I said, 'You okay?'

'I – yeah. Where's . . .'

'Let's keep moving.'

'Where is she?'

'She's fine, Bill, come on.'

'I need to—'

I got hold of his shoulder.

'Leave me here,' he said. 'Let me go, I've had enough.'

I began lifting him.

'Please,' he said.

My burned hand began to throb. Everything throbbed.

A raspy voice behind me said, 'Dead end, Mr Cadillac.'

404

forty-four

Vance Coury's silver hair caught moonlight. A black leather headband held it in place. The musk of his aftershave managed to seep through the scorched air.

He shone the flashlight in my face, shifted the beam to Bill, lowered it and held it at an angle that brightened the forest floor. As the white spots cleared from my eyes, I made out the rectangle in his right hand. Columnar snout. Machine pistol.

He said, 'Up.' Businesslike. Tying up loose ends.

He wore light-colored, grease-stained mechanics overalls – outfitted for messy work. Something flashed around his neck – probably the same gold chain I'd seen at the garage.

I got to my feet. My head still rang from the explosion.

'Walk.' He motioned to his right, back to the clearing.

'What about him?' I said.

'Oh, yeah, him.' He leveled the pistol downward, peppered Bill's frame with a burst that nearly cut the blind man in two.

The fragments of Bill's corpse bucked and flopped and were still.

Coury said, 'Any more questions?'

He marched me out of the forest. A pile of cinders, snarls of electrical conduit, random stacks of bricks, and twisted metal chairs were the remnants of the little green house. That and something contorted and charred, lashed and duct-taped to a chair.

'Playing with matches,' I said. 'Bet you liked that as a kid.'

'Walk.'

I stepped onto the gravel path. Keeping my head straight but moving my eyes back and forth. Nacho Vargas's corpse remained where it had fallen. No sign of Aimee or Bert.

405

A cloud of musk hit my nostrils, sickly sweet as a Sacher torte. Coury, walking close behind me.

'Where we going?' I said.

'Walk.'

'Walk where?'

'Shut up.'

'Where are we going?'

Silence.

Ten steps later, I tried again. 'Where we going?'

He said, 'You are *really* stupid.'

'Think so?' I said, reaching into my pocket and pulling out the short man's silver gun and wheeling fast.

Inertia caused him to pitch forward, and we nearly collided. He tried to step back, free the machine pistol, but couldn't get enough room to maneuver. Stumbled.

He hadn't bothered to pat me down. Overconfident rich kid who'd never grown up. All those years of getting away with bad stuff.

The little silver gun shot forward, as if of its own accord. Coury's goatee spread as his mouth opened in surprise.

I focused on his tonsils, shot three times, hit with every bullet.

I took his machine pistol and pocketed the silver gun, scurried off the gravel, found refuge behind a sycamore. Waited.

Nothing.

Stepping on greenery to muffle my footsteps, I inched forward, heading toward the road. Wondering who and what awaited me there.

I'd been overconfident, too, thinking Vargas and the small man had made up the entire army. Too important a job for a pair of thugs.

Coury had been a precise man who specialized in deconstructing high-priced machines and reconstituting them as works of art.

A good planner.

Send in the B team while the A team waits. Sacrifice the B team and attack from the rear.

Another ambush.

Coury had come himself to take care of Bill. Bill was a living witness, and eliminating him was the primary goal. The same went for Aimee. Had he taken care of her – and Bert – first? I hadn't heard gunfire as I carried Bill away, but the firebombs and the kerosene blast had filled my head with noise.

I walked five steps, stopped, repeated the pattern. The mouth of the gravel drive came into view.

Choice point, none of the options good.

I found nothing.

Just the Seville, all four tires slashed flat, hood open, distributor cap gone. Tire tracks – two sets, both deep and heavily treaded – said the pickup and another working vehicle had departed.

The nearest house was a quarter-mile up the road. I could barely make out yellow windows.

I was bloodstained and bloodied, one side of my face scraped raw, and my burnt hand hurt like hell. One look and the residents would probably bolt their doors and call the police.

Which was fine with me.

I almost made it before the rumble sounded.

Big engine, heading my way from Highway 150. Loud enough – close enough – for visibility, but no headlights.

I ran into the bushes, crouched behind a flurry of ferns, watched as the black Suburban sped past and slowed fifty feet before the entrance to Bill and Aimee's property.

It came to a halt. Rolled forward, twenty feet, stopped again.

A man got out. Big, very big.

Then another, slightly smaller but not by much. He gave some kind of hand signal, and the two of them pulled out weapons and hurried toward the entrance.

Anyone at the wheel? The Suburban's tinted windows augmented the night and made it impossible to tell. Now I knew that a run for the neighbors' house would be risky and wrong: Coury's shooting of Bill resonated in my head. Coury had pulled the trigger, but I'd been the angel of death, couldn't justify extending the combat to more innocents.

I crouched and waited. Tried to read my watch, but the crystal was shattered and the hands had been snapped off.

407

I counted off seconds. Had reached three thousand two hundred when the pair of big men returned.

'Shit,' said the shorter one. 'Goddammit.'

I stood, and said, 'Milo, don't shoot me.'

forty-five

Aimee and Bert sat in the third row of the Suburban. Aimee clutched Bert's sleeve. Bert's eyes lacked focus.

I got in next to Milo, in the second row.

At the wheel was Stevie the Samoan, the bounty hunter Georgie Nemerov called Yokuzuna. Next to him sat Red Yaakov, crew-cut head nearly brushing the roof.

'How'd you find us?' I said.

'The Seville car got tagged, and I got hold of the tagger.'

'Tagged?'

'Satellite locating device.'

'One of Coury's car gadgets?'

His hand on my shoulder was eloquent: *We'll talk later.*

Stevie drove to Highway 150 and pulled over just short of the 33 intersection, into a tree-shaded turnaround where three vehicles sat. Toward the rear, half-hidden by the night, was the pickup truck, front end facing the road, still loaded with fertilizer. A few feet away was a dark Lexus sedan. Another black SUV – a Chevy Tahoe – blocked both other vehicles.

Stevie dimmed his lights, and two men stepped from behind the Tahoe. A muscular, shaved-head Hispanic wearing a black muscle T-shirt, baggy black cargo pants and a big leather chest holster, and Georgie Nemerov in a sport coat, open-necked white shirt, rumpled slacks.

The muscular man's T-shirt read: BAIL ENFORCEMENT AGENT in big white letters. He and Nemerov approached the Suburban. Milo lowered his window, and Nemerov peered in, saw me, raised an eyebrow.

'Where's Coury?'

Milo said, 'With his ancestors.'

Nemerov tongued the inside of his cheek. 'You couldn't save him for me?'

'It was over by the time we got there, Georgie.'

Nemerov's eyebrow arched higher as he turned to me. 'I'm impressed, Doc. Want a job? The hours are long and the pay sucks.'

'Yeah,' said Yaakov, 'but de people you got to meet are deezgusting.'

Stevie laughed. Nemerov's smile widened reluctantly. 'I guess results are what counts.'

'Was there anyone else?' I said. 'Besides Coury?'

'Sure,' said Nemerov. 'Two other party animals.'

'Brad Larner,' said Milo. 'That Lexus is his. He and Coury arrived in it, Larner was driving. He was parked near the house, waiting for Coury, when we spotted him behind the truck. Dr Harrison and Caroline were tied up in the truck bed. Another guy was at the wheel.'

'Who?'

Nemerov said, 'Paragon of virtue named Emmet Cortez. I wrote a few tickets for him before he went away on manslaughter. Worked in the auto industry.'

'Painting hot rods,' I said.

'Chroming wheels.' Nemerov's grin was sudden, mirthless, icy. 'Now he's in that big garage in the sky.'

'Rendered inorganic,' said Stevie.

'Steel organic,' said Yaakov. 'Long as deyr someting left, he steel organic, right, Georgie.'

'You're being technical,' said Stevie.

'Let's change the subject,' said Nemerov.

forty-six

'Pancakes,' said Milo.

It was 10 A.M., the next morning, and we were at a coffee shop on Wilshire near Crescent Heights, a place where old people and gaunt young men pretending to write screenplays congregated. One half-mile west of the Cossack brothers' offices, but that hadn't been what drew us there.

We'd both been up all night, had returned to L.A. at 6 A.M., stopped at my house to shower and shave.

'Don't wanna wake Rick,' he'd explained.

'Isn't Rick up by now?'

'Why complicate things?'

He'd emerged from the guest bathroom, toweling his head and squinting. Wearing last night's clothes but looking frighteningly chipper. 'Breakfast,' he proclaimed. 'I know the place, they make these big, monster flappers with crunchy peanut butter and chocolate chips.'

'That's kid food,' I said.

'Maturity is highly overrated. I used to go there all the time. Believe me, Alex, this is what you need.'

'Used to go there?'

'Back when I wasn't watching my figure. Our endocrine systems are shot so we need sugar – my maternal grandfather ate pancakes every day, washed them down with three cups of coffee sweeter than cola, and he lived till ninety-eight. Woulda gone on a few more years, but he tumbled down a flight of stairs while ogling a woman.' He pushed an errant thatch of black hair out of his face. 'Unlikely to be my fate, but there are always variants.'

'You're uncommonly optimistic,' I said.

411

'Pancakes,' he said. 'C'mon, let's get going.'

I changed into fresh clothing, thinking about Aimee and Bert, all the unanswered questions.

Thinking about Robin. She'd called last night, from Denver, left a message at 11 P.M. I phoned back at 6:30, figuring to leave a message at her hotel, but the tour had moved on to Albuquerque.

Now, here we were, facing two stacks of peanut butter hotcakes the size of frypans. Breakfast that smelled eerily of Thai food. I corroded my gut with coffee, watched him douse his stack with maple syrup and begin sawing into it, then took hold of the syrup pitcher in my unburnt hand. The ER doctor at Oxnard Hospital had pronounced the burn 'first-degree plus. A little deeper and you would've made second.' As if I'd missed a goal. He'd administered salve and a bandage, swabbed my face with Neosporin, wrote me a scrip for antibiotics, and told me to avoid getting myself dirty.

Everyone at the hospital knew Bert Harrison. He and Aimee were given a private room near the emergency admissions desk, where they stayed for two hours. Milo and I had waited. Finally, Bert came out, and said, 'We're going to be here for a while. Go home.'

'You're sure?' I said.

'Very sure.' He pressed my hand between both of his, gave a hard squeeze, returned to the room.

Georgie Nemerov and his crew drove us to the spot at the entrance to Ojai where Milo had left his rental Dodge, then disappeared.

Milo had joined up with the bounty hunters, formulated a plan.

Lots of questions . . .

I tipped the pitcher, followed the syrup's drizzle, watched it pool and spread, picked up my fork. Milo's cell phone chirped. He clicked in, said, 'Yeah?' Listened for a while, hung up, stuffed his face with a wad of pancake. Melted chocolate frosted his lips.

I said, 'Who was that?'

'Georgie.'

'What's up?'

He cut loose another triangle of hotcake, chewed, swallowed, drank coffee. 'Seems there was an accident late last night. Eighty-third Street off Sepulveda, rental Buick hit a utility pole at high speed. Driver and occupant rendered inorganic.'

412

'Driver and occupant.'

'Two db's,' he said. 'You know what high-speed impact does to the human body.'

'Garvey and Bobo?' I said.

'That's the working hypothesis. Pending verification of dental records.'

'Eighty-third off Sepulveda. On the way to the airport?'

'Funny you should mention that, they did find tickets in the wreck. Pair of first-class passages to Zurich, hotel reservations at some place called the Bal du Lac. Sounds pretty, no?'

'Lovely,' I said. 'Maybe a ski vacation.'

'Could be – is there snow there, right now?'

'Don't know,' I said. 'It's probably raining in Paris.'

He motioned for a coffee refill, got a new pot, poured, and drank slowly.

'Just the two of them?' I said.

'Seems that way.'

'Odd, don't you think? They've got a full-time chauffeur and choose to drive themselves to the airport? Own a fleet of wheels and use a rental car.'

He shrugged.

'Also,' I went on, 'what would they be doing on a side street in Inglewood? That far south, you're heading for the airport, you stay on Sepulveda.'

He yawned, stretched, emptied his coffee cup. 'Want anything else?'

'Is it on the news, yet?'

'Nope.'

'But Georgie knows.'

No answer.

'Georgie has the inside track,' I said. 'Being a bail bondsman and all that.'

'That must be it,' he said. He brushed crumbs from his shirtfront.

I said, 'You've got syrup on your chin.'

'Thanks, Mom.' He threw money on the table and got up. 'How 'bout we take a little digestive stroll.'

'East on Wilshire,' I said. 'Up to Museum Row.'

413

'You are nailing those hypotheses, Professor. Time for Vegas.'

We walked to the pink granite building where the Cossack brothers had once played executive. Milo studied the façade for a long time, finally entered the lobby, stared down the guard, left, and returned to the front steps where I'd been waiting, pretending to feel civilized.

'Happy?' I said, as we headed back to the coffee shop.

'Ecstatic.'

We retraced our walk to the coffee shop, got into Milo's rental of the day – a black Mustang convertible – drove through the Miracle Mile and across La Brea and into the clean, open stretch of Wilshire that marked Hancock Park's northern border.

Milo steered with one finger. No sleep for two days but beyond alert. I had to fight to keep my eyes open. The Seville had been towed to a shop in Carpenteria. I'd phone in later today, get a report. Meanwhile, I'd drive Robin's truck. If I could stand the sweet smell of her permeating the cab.

He turned on Rossmore, drove south to Fifth Street, hooked back to Irving, and pulled over to the curb, six houses north of Sixth. On the other side was Chief Broussard's city-financed mansion. An immaculate white Cadillac sat in the driveway. A single plainclothesman stood guard, looking bored.

Milo stared at the house, same hostility as when he'd eye-zapped the guard in the Cossacks' lobby. Before I could ask what was up, he U-turned, headed south, then west to Muirfield, where he cruised slowly to the end of the block and stopped at a property concealed behind high stone walls.

'Walt Obey's place,' he said, before I could ask.

Stone walls. Just like the Loetz estate that neighbored the party house. The kill spot. Build walls, and you could get away with plenty.

Janie Ingalls abused by two generations of men. A closed-circuit camera atop one gatepost rotated.

Milo said, 'Say cheese.' Waved. Jammed the Mustang into DRIVE and sped away.

He dropped me back home, and I slept until 5 P.M., woke in time to

414

turn on the news. The Cossack brothers' deaths missed the network affiliate broadcasts but were featured an hour later on a local station's six o'clock spot.

The facts were just as Georgie Nemerov had reported: single-car accident, probably due to excessive speed. Thirty seconds of bio identified Garvey and Bobo as 'wealthy Westside developers' who'd built 'some controversial projects.' No identifying photos. No suspicion of foul play.

Another death occurred that night, but it never hit the L.A. news because it went down ninety miles north.

Santa Barbara News-Press item, forwarded to me by e-mail, with no accompanying message. The sender: sloppyslooth@sturgis.com. That was a new one.

The facts were straightforward: the body of a sixty-eight-year-old real estate executive named Michael Larner had been found two hours ago, slumped in the front seat of his BMW. The car had been driven into a wooded area just north of the Cabrillo exit off the 101, on the outskirts of Santa Barbara. A recently fired handgun sat in Larner's lap. He'd died of 'an apparent single wound to the head, consistent with self-infliction.'

Larner had come to Santa Barbara to identify the body of his son, Bradley, forty-two, the recent victim of a heart attack, who'd also – irony of ironies – succumbed in a car. Bradley's vehicle, a Lexus, had been discovered just a few miles away, on a quiet street on the north end of Montecito. The grieving father had left the morgue just after noon, and investigators had come up with no accounting of his whereabouts during the three hours leading up to his suicide.

A homeless man had discovered the body.

'I was going in there to take a nap,' reported the vagrant, identified as Langdon Bottinger, fifty-two. 'Knew something was wrong right away. Nice car like that, pushed up against a tree. I looked inside and knocked on the windows. But he was dead. I was in Vietnam, I know dead when I see it.'

forty-seven

After dropping Alex off, Milo turned on the Mustang's radio and dialed to KLOS. Classic rock. Van Halen doing 'Jump.'

Kicky little thing, the 'Stang. Something with a little zip.

'Used to be owned by Tom Cruise's gardener,' the multipierced girl at the alternative rental yard had told him. Night owl; she worked the midnight-to-eight shift.

'Great,' said Milo, pocketing the keys. 'Maybe it'll help on auditions.'

The girl nodded, knowingly. 'You go out for character roles?'

'Nah,' said Milo, heading for the car. 'Not enough character.'

He returned to John G. Broussard's digs on Irving, sat and watched for hours. The chief's wife emerged at 1:03 P.M., escorted to the driveway by a lady cop who held open the driver's door of the white Caddy. Mrs B drove toward Wilshire and was gone.

Leaving John G. alone in the house? Milo was fairly certain Broussard wasn't in the office; he'd phoned the chief's head-quarters, impersonated a honcho from Walt Obey's office, was told very politely that the chief wouldn't be in today.

No surprise, there. Yet another anti-Broussard piece had run in the morning *Times*. The Police Protective League griping about poor morale, dumping it all in Broussard's lap. Commentary by some law prof, psychoanalyzing Broussard. The clear implication was that the chief's temperament was a poor fit for modern-day policing. Whatever the hell that meant.

Add all that to the events of last night – and Craig Bosc's report to the chief – and Broussard had to know the walls were closing in.

John G. had always been the most cautious of men. So what was

416

he doing now? Upstairs in his bedroom closet, picking out a cool suit from a rack of dozens? It was almost as if he didn't care.

Maybe he didn't.

Milo kept watching the Tudor digs, stretched his legs, ready for the long haul. But five minutes later a dark green sedan – an unmarked Ford, blackwalls, pure LAPD – backed out of the driveway.

Solitary driver. A tall man, rigid at the wheel. The unmistakable outline of the chief's noble profile.

Broussard turned south, just like his wife had. Stopped at Wilshire and sat there for a long time, with his left-turn signal blinking – what a good example – waited for the traffic to thin before swinging smoothly onto the boulevard.

Heading east. So maybe he *was* going to work. Toughing it out, show the bastards.

One way to find out.

Broussard stuck precisely to the speed limit, gliding in the center lane, signaling his right turn on Western well within DMV parameters. He drove south, past Washington Boulevard, picked up the 10 East and engineered a textbook entry into the afternoon flow.

Freeway traffic was moderately heavy but steady, perfect tail situation, and Milo had no trouble keeping an eye on the Ford as it passed through the downtown interchange, stayed on the 10, and exited at Soto, in East L.A.

The coroner's office?

And Broussard did drive to the clean, cream morgue building on the west end of the County Hospital complex, but instead of turning in to park among the vans and the cop cars, he kept going, continued for another two miles. Made a perfect stop at a narrow street called San Elias, turned right, and did a 20 mph cruise through a residential neighborhood of tiny bungalows packaged by chain link.

Three blocks up San Elias, then the street dead-ended and the green Ford pulled over.

The terminus was marked by twenty-foot-high iron double gates, rich with flourishes and topped by Gothic arches. Above the peaks, the iron had been bent into lettering. Milo was a block away, couldn't make out what they spelled.

John G. Broussard parked the Ford, got out, locked it, tugged his suit jacket in place.

Not dressed for the office – the chief never showed up at Parker Center out of uniform. Lint-free, all those razor-presses, his chest festooned with ribbons. During ceremonial occasions, he wore his hat.

Thinking he was a fucking general or something, said the scoffers.

Today Broussard wore a navy suit tailored snugly to his trim physique, a TV blue shirt, and a gold tie so bright that it gleamed like jewelry from a block away. Perfect posture accentuated the chief's height as he walked to the big iron gates with a martial stride. As if presiding at some ceremony. Broussard paused, turned a handle, stepped through.

Milo waited five minutes before getting out. Looked over his shoulder several times as he covered the block on foot. Feeling antsy, despite himself. Something about Broussard . . .

When he was halfway to the gates, he made out the lettering.

Sacred Peace Memorial Park

The cemetery was bisected by a long straight pathway of decomposed granite, pink-beige against a bordering hedge of variegated boxwood. Hollywood junipers formed high green walls on three sides, too bright under a sickly gray sky. No orange trees in sight, but Milo could swear he smelled orange blossoms.

Twenty feet in, he came upon a statue of Jesus, benevolent and smiling, then a small limestone building marked OFFICE and fringed with beds of multicolored pansies. A wheelbarrow blocked half the path. An old Mexican man in khaki work clothes and a pith helmet stooped in front of the flowers. He turned briefly to look at Milo, touched the brim of the helmet, returned to weeding.

Milo circumvented the wheelbarrow, spotted the first row of gravestones, kept going.

Old-fashioned markers, upright, carved of stone, a few of them tilting, a handful decorated by sprigs of desiccated flowers. Milo's parents had been buried in a very different ambience, huge place, not far from Indianapolis, a suburban city of the dead bordered by industrial parks and shopping malls. Mock-colonial buildings with all the authenticity of Disneyland, endless rolling green turf fit for a championship golf course. The markers in his parents' cemetery were brass plaques embedded flat in the bluegrass, invisible until you got close. Even in death Bernard and Martha Sturgis had been loath to offend . . .

This place was flat and tiny and treeless except for the bordering junipers. Two naked acres, if that. Full up with gravestones, too – an old place. Nowhere to hide, and finding Broussard was easy enough.

The chief was standing off in a corner in the lower left quadrant of the cemetery. Second-to-last row, a snug, shady place. His back was to Milo as he faced a marker, big, dark hands laced behind his ramrod back.

Milo walked toward him, making no effort to squelch the sound of his footsteps. Broussard didn't turn.

When Milo got to the gravesite, the chief said, 'What took you so long?'

The stone that had occupied Broussard was charcoal granite edged with salmon pink and carved beautifully with a border of daisies.

Jane Marie Ingalls
MAY SHE FIND PEACE IN ETERNITY

Entry and exit dates spelled out a sixteen-year-three-month life span. A tiny smiling teddy bear had been chiseled above Janie's name.

A gray-blue juniper berry had lodged in the bevel that created the bear's left button eye. John G. Broussard stooped and plucked it out and placed it in a pocket of his jacket. The suit was double-breasted, blue with a maroon chalk stripe. Suppressed waist, high side vents, working buttonholes on the sleeves. *Look, Ma, I'm custom-made.* Milo remembered Broussard's terrific threads and poreless skin during the interrogation twenty years ago.

The thousandth time he'd thought about that day.

Up close, the chief hadn't changed much. The graying hair, a bit

419

of crease at the corner of his lips, but his complexion glowed with health, and his huge hands looked strong enough to crack walnuts.

Milo said, 'You come here a lot?'

'When I invest in something, I like to keep an eye on it.'

'Invest?'

'I bought the marker, Detective. Her father didn't care. She was going to end up in a potter's field.'

'Guilt offering,' said Milo.

Broussard remained still. Then he said, 'Detective Sturgis, I'm going to examine you for listening devices, so relax.'

'Sure,' said Milo, stifling the 'Yes, sir' on the tip of his tongue. No matter how hard he tried, Broussard made him feel small. He drew himself up as the chief turned, faced him, did an expert pat-down.

That figured. An ex-IA man would have experience with wires.

Finished, Broussard dropped his hands and maintained eye contact. 'So what is it you want to tell me?'

'I was hoping you'd have things to tell me.'

Broussard's lips didn't move, but a glint of amusement brightened his eyes. 'You'd like some sort of confessional statement?'

'If that's what's on your mind,' said Milo.

'What's on your mind, Detective?'

'I know about Willie Burns.'

'Do you?'

'The tax rolls say the place where he hid out on 156th – where your partner Poulsenn got nailed – was owned by your wife's mother. The night Willie took Janie Ingalls to the party he was driving a borrowed car. Brand-new white Cadillac, beautifully maintained. Your wife likes those, has owned six Caddies in the last twenty years, all white. Including the one she's driving at this very moment.'

Broussard stooped and brushed dust off Janie Ingalls's headstone.

'Burns was family,' said Milo.

'Was?' said Broussard.

'Very much *was*. It went down last night. Just like you choreographed.'

Broussard straightened. 'There are limits to protection. Even for family.'

'What was he, a cousin?'

'Nephew,' said the chief. 'Son of my wife's eldest brother. His siblings were all respectable. Everyone in the family went to college or learned a trade. Willie was the youngest. Something went wrong.'

'Sometimes it works out that way,' said Milo.

'Now you're sounding like that shrink friend of yours.'

'It rubs off.'

'Does it?' said Broussard.

'Yeah. Hanging around with the right people is good for the soul. Vice versa, too. Musta been a burden, you playing by the rules, taking all that racist crap, climbing the ranks, meanwhile Willie's going on his merry way shooting and selling smack. Lots of potential for bad PR. But you did your best to help him, anyway. That's why he never served much jail time. You hooked him up with Boris Nemerov, probably went his cash bonds. And at first he came through for Nemerov, kept you looking good.'

Broussard remained impassive.

Milo said, 'Musta been a strain, associating with a known felon.'

'I never broke the law.'

Milo's turn to keep quiet.

Broussard said, 'There's always flexibility in the law, Detective. Yes, I carried him. My wife adored him – remembered him as a cute little kid. To the family he was *still* the cute little kid. I was the only one seemed to realize he'd metamorphosed into a reprobate junkie. Maybe I should've seen it sooner. Or let him deal with the consequences earlier.'

The chief's posture relaxed a bit. Bastard was actually slumping.

Milo said, 'Then Willie got himself in a whole new level of trouble. Witnessed a very nasty 187 and got paranoid and told you they were going to pin it on him.'

'Not paranoia,' said Broussard. 'Reasonable apprehensiveness.' He gave a cold smile. 'Black junkie with a felony record versus rich white boys? No one intended to bring Willie to trial. The plan was to float rumors, plant evidence, have Willie OD somewhere, call in an anonymous tip, and close the case.'

'So Willie skipped on Boris, but you paid Boris off. Then you got Poulsenn assigned to the case, to cover it and control it, and meanwhile he could guard Willie and his girlfriend.'

421

'That was temporary. We were regrouping, assessing contingencies.'

'None of which included going after the real killers,' said Milo, surprised at the fury in his own voice. 'Maybe Schwinn and I wouldn't have solved it. On the other hand, maybe we *would've* pulled it off. We'll never know, will we? 'Cause you stepped in and sabotaged the whole goddamned thing. And don't tell me that was just because of Willie. Someone put the fix in for those rich kids. Someone you had to listen to.'

Broussard swiveled and faced him. 'You've got it all figured out.'

'I don't. That's why I'm here. Who was the fixer? Walt Obey? Janie was pimped by that piece of shit who called himself her father and used by two generations of rich scrotes, and who's richer than old Walt? Is that what doomed the investigation, John? Kindly, churchgoing Uncle Walt worried about having his nasty habits aired?'

Broussard's ebony face remained still. He stared past Milo. Let out a low, grumbling laugh.

'Happy to entertain, John,' said Milo. His hands were shaking, and he rolled them into fists.

'I'm going to educate you, Detective, about matters you don't understand. I've spent a lot of time in the company of rich folk, and it's true what they say. The rich *are* different. Life's little bumps get smoothed out for them, no one has the temerity to deny them anything. More often than not, their kids become monsters. Malignant entitlement. But there are exceptions, and Mr Obey's one of them. He's exactly what he claims to be: religious, straightforward, ethical, good father, faithful husband. Mr Obey grew rich through hard work and vision and luck – he'd be the first to emphasize the luck component, because he's also a humble man. So understand this: he had nothing to do with any cover-up. You mention the name Janie Ingalls, and he'll stare at you blankly.'

'Maybe I'll try that,' said Milo.

Broussard's jaw set. 'Stay away from that gentleman.'

'Is that an official order, Chief?'

'It's sound advice, Detective.'

'Then who?' said Milo. 'Who the hell fixed it?'

Broussard ran a finger under his collar. Full sun had brought the sweat out on his brow, and his skin glistened like a desert highway.

'It wasn't like that,' he said finally. 'No one ordered the Ingalls investigation stopped, per se. The directive – and it was a departmental directive, straight from the top, the *very* top – was to effect damage control on Pierce Schwinn's many years of felonious conduct. Because Schwinn was spinning out of control, heavily addicted to amphetamines, taking extreme risks. He was a ticking time bomb, and the department decided to defuse him. You just happened to get the wrong partner. It could've been worse for you. You were spared because you were a rookie and had never been observed participating in Schwinn's transgressions. Except for one instance, when you *were* observed picking up a known prostitute in your on-duty car and chauffering her and Schwinn around. But I chose to overlook that, Detective. I had you transferred to greener pastures rather than drummed out in disgrace.'

'Is this the dramatic moment where I'm supposed to thank you?' Milo cupped a hand to his ear. 'Where's the goddamn drumroll?'

Broussard's mouth curled downward in disgust. 'Suit yourself and be dense.'

'I didn't need your largesse, John. When I picked that hooker up I had no idea what was going to happen, figured her for an informant.'

Broussard smiled. 'I believe you, Detective. I had a pretty good notion that you wouldn't participate in any backseat calisthenics with a woman.'

Milo's face grew hot.

Broussard said, 'Don't get all indignant on me. I won't pretend to understand what you are, but it doesn't bother me. Life's too short for intolerance. I know what it's like to be on the outside, and I've given up on the whole idea of changing the way people feel. Let bigots feel any way they want to, as long as they don't misbehave.'

'You're a paragon of tolerance.'

'Not tolerance, constructive apathy. I don't care about your amusements – don't care about you, period, as long as you do your job.'

'When doing the job suits your interests,' said Milo.

Broussard didn't reply.

'You're an outsider, huh?' said Milo. 'For an outsider, you

scampered up the ladder pretty quickly.'

'Hard work and persistence,' said Broussard, sounding as if he'd recited it a million times before. 'And good luck. Plus a good deal of yassuh-mastah posterior-kissing.' He unbuttoned his collar and loosened his tie. Aiming for casual, just one of the guys. His bearing said otherwise. 'Back when I worked patrol, I used to tape pictures in my locker. Photographs of men I admired. Frederick Douglass, George Washington Carver, Ralph Bunche. One day I opened my locker and the pictures were ripped to shreds and the walls were decorated with *"Die, Nigger!"* and other genial messages. I pasted every one of those photos together, and if you go into my office today, you'll see them hanging behind my desk.'

'I'll have to take that on faith,' said Milo. 'Don't expect to be invited to your office anytime soon. Unlike that other worthy soul, Craig Bosc. I'm disappointed in you, John. Choosing a lowlife like that to run your errands.'

Broussard worked his lips. 'Craig has his talents. He went too far this time.'

'What was the idiot's assignment? Spook me into focusing on the Ingalls case, the old reverse psychology? Just in case sending Delaware the murder book wasn't enough to kick me in gear?'

'The *idiot's* directive,' said Broussard, 'was to aim you at the case and keep you focused. I thought you'd be interested, but for a while things seemed to be lagging. It *has* been twenty years.'

'So you steal my partner's car, float HIV-retirement rumors, have Bosc hit on me and make sure I get aimed at a POB that directs me to the Larners. Then you trail Dr Delaware and set Coury on his trail. He could've died last night, you manipulative sonofabitch.'

'He didn't,' said Broussard. 'And I don't deal in theoreticals. As I said, Craig grew overzealous. End of story.'

Milo cursed, caught his breath, bent, and caressed the top of Janie's grave. Broussard's shoulders tensed, as if the gesture was insulting.

'You buy a gravestone and think you're absolved, John. This poor little girl molders for two decades, and you've allowed yourself to grow righteous. Schwinn sent you the book, and you made me part of the chain letter via Dr Delaware. Why? It sure wasn't the search for justice.'

The chief's face returned to wooden. Milo visualized him wiping the murder book clean of prints, contemplating the 'contingencies,' finally deciding to forward the death shots to someone sure to pass them along. Using Alex to spook him, throw him off, wanting him to have to fight to regain his bearings, convince himself it was a noble quest.

And if Milo hadn't bitten, Broussard would've found another way. There'd never been any real choice.

'You've got a reputation,' said Broussard. 'As a contrarian. I thought it was wise to harness that.'

He shrugged, and the easy gesture turned Milo feverish. He locked his hands together, struggled not to hit Broussard, finally found his voice. 'Why'd you want the case solved now?'

'Times change.'

'What *changed* were your personal circumstances.' Milo jabbed a finger at the gravestone. 'You never gave a shit about Janie or the truth. Nailing Coury and the others became important because it was in your best interest, and boy, did you succeed. Bunch of dead guys in Ojai, couple more in S.B., the Cossacks bite it in Inglewood, and there's no reason to connect any of them. Now you're free to go about your merry way with Walt Obey's build-a-city game. That's what it's all about, isn't it, John? The old man's money. Fucking Esperanza.'

Broussard stiffened.

'Esperanza, what horseshit,' said Milo. 'It means "hope" and you're hoping it'll make you filthy-rich because you know you're a failure as chief, gonna have to leave the department soon under less-than-amiable circumstances, and Uncle Walt just happened to come up with an offer that'll make your pension seem like chump change. What's the deal, John? Chief of security for an entire city, maybe augmented by some bullshit corporate vice-presidency? Hell, Obey's probably tossing in preferred shares of the project that could shoot you into a whole new fiscal galaxy. Augmenting what he's already gifted to your wife and daughter. Man of color as co-owner of a *city* – ain't old Walt *liberal*. Everything was looking rosy until some nasty competition cropped up. Because Obey's grand scheme includes comprehensive recreational facilities aka finally bringing the NFL back to L.A. The old man pulls that off and Esperanza land values skyrocket and you're lunching at the country club and pretending the stiffs over there like you. But the Cossacks had other ideas. Wanted to rejuvenate the Coliseum, or some other downtown venue. Had Germ Bacilla and Diamond Jim Horne on their side, brought those two clowns to dinner at that stupid restaurant they own, did the whole private-room thing with Uncle Walt. Trying to convince Uncle Walt to cash in his chips and go along with them. Once upon Uncle Walt mighta blown off bullshit like that, but maybe this time he was willing to *listen*. The fact that he showed up at Sangre de Leon and didn't invite *you* says he was open-minded, and that had to spook you, John. Because even though the Cossacks had never pulled off anything close to that scope, this time they'd lined up decent financing and City Council support. And most important, Obey's losing steam. Because he's getting old and his wife's sick – really sick. Ain't that a hoot, John? You've come this far, and it could all come crumbling down.'

Broussard's eyes turned to cracks in asphalt. His lower jaw jutted forward, and Milo knew the chief was struggling not to hit *him*.

'You don't know what you're talking about, Detective.'

'John,' he said, 'I watched a portable dialysis van pull up early this morning on Muirfield. Mrs O's seriously not well. Old Barbara needs a machine to survive. Hubby's initiative is being sapped.'

Broussard's hand flew to the knot of his tie. He tugged it down farther, stared off into nowhere.

Milo said, 'Obey's owned the land for years, so even with his mortgages he can sell at a huge profit. He woulda tossed you a consolation prize, but basically you'd have been a controversial ex-chief forced out and looking around for a gig. Maybe some drugstore chain would hire you to oversee security.'

Broussard didn't answer.

'All those years of posterior-kissing,' said Milo. 'All that upright behavior.'

'What,' said Broussard, very softly, 'do you want?'

Milo ignored the question. 'You shrug off that twenty-year-old directive to shaft Schwinn as the reason the case got sidelined, but that's crap. Handing Janie's case to Lester Poulsenn was a dodge. An IA spook, like you, what the hell would Poulsenn know about a sex homicide?'

'Les worked homicide. Wilshire Division.'

'For how long?'

'Two years.'

Milo applauded silently. 'A whole twenty-four months chasing gang-bang shootings, and suddenly he's the one-man squad on a nasty 187 like Janie. His main gig was guarding Willie and Caroline in Watts because your family loved Willie.'

Broussard said, 'I walked on eggshells with that . . . with Willie. The family always pushed for him. I bought my wife a spanking new Sedan de Ville and she lent it to him. An IA man's car at the scene of a murder.'

A trace of whine had crept into the chief's voice. Suspect's defensiveness. The bastard's discomfort flooded Milo with joy. He said, 'What'd you tell the family when Willie disappeared?'

'That he'd burned up in the house. I wanted to put an end to it.' Broussard cocked his head to the right. Two rows over. 'Far as they're concerned, he's here. We had a quiet family ceremony.'

'Who's in the coffin?'

'I burned papers in my office, put the ashes in an urn and we buried it.'

'I believe you,' said Milo. 'I believe you'd do that.'

'As far as I knew, Willie really was dead. Lester died in that fire and the Russian got ambushed and I knew it all had to do with Willie, so why wouldn't Willie be dead? Then he calls me a week later, sounding half-dead, telling me he's burnt and sick, send him money. I hung up on him. I'd had enough. I figured he'd last, what – a few months? He had a serious addiction.'

'So you made him dead.'

'He did that to himself.'

'No, John, Vance Coury did that to him last night. Sliced him in half with a MAC 10. I buried him with my own hands – hey, if you want, I'll retrieve what's left of him, you can dig up that urn, and we'll make everything right.'

Broussard shook his head, very slowly. 'I thought you were smart, but you're stupid.'

Milo said, 'We're a good team, you and me, John. Between the two of us, we get everything tied up nice and neat. So who pushed Schwinn off that horse? Did you do it yourself or send a messenger, like old Craig? My guess is a messenger because a black face in Ojai would be conspicuous.'

'No one pushed him. He had an epileptic seizure and fell down a gully. Took the horse with him.'

'You were there?'

'Craig was there.'

'Ah,' said Milo. Thinking: Alex would laugh. If he'd reached the stage where he could laugh.

'Believe what you want,' said Broussard. 'That's what happened.'

'What I believe is Schwinn's sending you the book loosened your bowels. All these years you thought the guy was just a speed-freak burnout, and he turns out to have a long memory. And pictures.'

Broussard's smile was patronizing. 'Think logically: a few moments ago you constructed an elaborate theory about my desire to eliminate competition. If that's true, why would Schwinn's reactivating the Ingalls murder bother me? On the contrary, if the Cossacks could be implicated—'

'Except that Schwinn knew you'd put the original fix in. Once he was out of the way, you figured out a way to make everything work for you. You're nothing if not adaptable, John.'

Broussard sighed. 'Now you're being obstinate. As I told you, the directive was related to Schwinn's—'

'So what, John? If Walt Obey's half as righteous as you claim, he likes you because you've convinced him you're a choirboy. Schwinn comes forward, makes noises, sullies your rep, it's a threat to your executive wet dream. So he had to go, too. It's like bowling, isn't it? Human tenpins. Set 'em up, knock 'em down.'

'No,' said Broussard. 'I sent Craig to talk to Schwinn. To find out exactly what he knew. Why would I kill him? He could've been useful to me. Without him, I turned to you.'

'A seizure.'

Broussard nodded. 'Craig was driving to Schwinn's ranch, saw Schwinn ride his horse out the gates and followed along. There was a – there was contact, and Craig introduced himself and Schwinn got hostile. He'd wanted me to respond personally, not send a delegate. The man was presumptuous. Craig tried to reason with him. To get the facts of the case. Schwinn denied he'd had anything to do with the book, then he started to rave about DNA – finding semen samples, solving everything overnight.'

'Except there were no samples,' said Milo. 'Everything had been destroyed. Schwinn would've loved hearing that.'

'He was irrational, tried to charge Craig on horseback, but the horse wouldn't cooperate. Craig did his best to calm Schwinn down, but Schwinn started to dismount and suddenly his eyes rolled back in his head and he began salivating and convulsing. The horse must've panicked and lost its footing. It tumbled into the gully, Schwinn had one foot caught in the stirrup, got dragged, his head collided with a rock. Craig ran to help him, but it was too late.'

'So Craig left the scene.'

Broussard didn't answer.

'Terrific story,' said Milo. 'Forget building cities, John. Write a screenplay.'

'Maybe I will,' said Broussard. 'One day, when it's no longer raw.'

'When what isn't?'

'The pain. None of this has been easy for me.'

Broussard's left cheek ticked. He sighed. Injured nobility.

Milo hit him.

forty-eight

The blow connected square with the chief's nose and knocked him flat on his rear.

Broussard sat in the dust fronting Janie's grave, blood streaming from his nostrils, striping his Italian shirt, the beautiful golden tie, crimson deepening to rust as it met the pinstripe of his custom-made lapel.

He said, 'It's good I already have a broad nose.'

Smiling. Taking hold of the silk foulard in his breast pocket and wiping away the blood.

Making no attempt to get to his feet.

'You're immature, Detective. That's your problem, always has been. Reducing everything to black and white, the way a child does. Maybe it's tied in with your other problem. Generally arrested development.'

'Maturity's highly overrated,' said Milo. 'Mature people act like you.'

'I survive,' said Broussard. 'My grandfather never learned to read. My father went to college, then to music school, learned classical trombone but couldn't get a job so he worked his whole life as a porter at the Ambassador Hotel. Your problem can be concealed. You were born with unlimited opportunities, so spare me the pious lectures about morality. And don't even think about hitting me again. If you raise your hand to me, I'll shoot you and make up a plausible story to justify it.'

He patted his left hip, revealed the bulge under the pinstripe. Just a few subtle inches afforded by great tailoring.

'You could shoot me anyway,' said Milo. 'Sometime when I'm not expecting it.'

430

'I could, but I won't,' said Broussard. 'Unless you make it necessary.' He pressed silk to his nose. Blood continued to flow. 'If you act reasonably, I won't even send you the cleaning bill.'

'Meaning?'

'Meaning you've gotten it all out of your system and are prepared to return to work under new circumstances.'

'Such as?'

'We forget about this, you're promoted to lieutenant. Assigned to a division of your choosing.'

'Why would I want to push paper?' said Milo.

'No paper, you'll be a lieutenant detective,' said Broussard. 'Continue to work cases – challenging cases, but you pull a lieutenant's salary, enjoy a lieutenant's prestige.'

'That's not the way it works in the department.'

'I'm still the chief.' Broussard got to his feet, pretended to accidentally spread a flap of his double-breasted jacket, offered a full view of the 9mm nestled in a tooled-leather holster the color of fine brandy.

'You toss me a bone, and I go away,' said Milo.

'Why not?' said Broussard. 'Everything's been done that needs to be done. You solved the case, the bad guys are out of the picture, we all move on. What's the alternative, ruining both our lives? Because the worse you hurt me, the more pain you bring on yourself. I don't care how righteous you think you are, that's the way the world works. Think about Nixon and Clinton and all those other paragons of virtue. They got libraries, and all the people around them went down hard.'

Broussard stepped closer. Milo could smell his citrus aftershave and his sweat and the coppery tang of the blood that had finally begun to dry above his mouth.

'I've kept records,' said Milo. 'A paper trail hidden where even you'll never find it. Something happens to me—'

'Oh, please, look who's talking about screenplays,' said Broussard. 'You want to throw around threats? Think about Dr Silverman. Dr Delaware. Dr Harrison.' Broussard laughed. 'Sounds like a medical convention. You can be damaged beyond your wildest dreams. And to what end? What's the point?'

He flashed a smile. Winner's smile. A cold, damp wave of futility

431

washed over Milo. Sapped; the blow to Broussard's nose had taken more out of him than it had out of its recipient.

Winners and losers – the patterns were probably set in place back in nursery school.

He said, 'What about Bosc?'

'Craig has resigned from the department with substantial compensation, effective one week ago. He'll never go near you – that I can promise you.'

'He does, he's a dead man.'

'He realizes that. He's relocating to another city. Another state.' Broussard wiped away blood, checked his handkerchief, found a clean corner and made sure it showed when he tucked the silk square back in his breast pocket. Buttoning his shirt and knotting his tie, he advanced even closer to Milo.

Breathing slowly, evenly. The bastard had sweet breath, minty-fresh. No more sweat on his ebony face. His nose had started to swell, looked a little off kilter, but nothing you'd notice once he got cleaned up.

'So,' he said.

'Lieutenant,' said Milo.

'Fast-track promotion, Detective Sturgis, once you choose your division. You can take some vacation time or jump right into work. Think of it as mutually constructive adaptation.'

Milo stared into the flat, black eyes. Hating Broussard and admiring him. *O great guru of self-deception, teach me to live as you do . . .*

He said, 'Fuck your promotion. I'll drop everything, but I don't want anything from you.'

'How noble,' said Broussard. 'As if you had a choice.'

He turned and walked away.

Milo remained by the grave, let his eyes wander over Janie's stone. Goddamn teddy bear.

Knowing there was nothing he could do. If he wanted to stay in the department, he'd take the offer and why the hell not, because anyone who mattered was dead and he was tired, so tired, and what *was* the alternative?

Making a choice. Not sure of what it would do to him – to his soul.

Someone else might have convinced himself that was courage.

Someone else wouldn't feel this way.

forty-nine

Bert Harrison's call came at 9 A.M. I'd been sleeping and tried to push the fatigue out of my voice, but Bert knew he'd woken me up.

'Sorry, Alex. I'll call back—'

'No,' I said. 'How're you doing?'

'*I'm* fine,' he said. 'Aimee is . . . she'll eventually come to grips with the loss. We'd begun dealing with it, because Bill didn't have long, and I was trying to prepare her. Despite that, of course, the shock was traumatic. For her sake, I'm emphasizing the quickness of it. His feeling no pain.'

'I can back you up on that. It was instantaneous.'

'You saw it . . . you must be—'

'I'm fine, Bert.'

'Alex, I should've been honest with you all along. You deserved better from me.'

'You had your obligations,' I said. 'Patient-doctor confidentiality—'

'No, I—'

'It's all right, Bert.'

He laughed. 'Listen to us, Alex. Alphonse, Gaston, Alphonse Gaston . . . you're really okay, son?'

'I really am.'

'Because you bore the brunt of it as I stood by like a—'

'It's over,' I said, firmly.

'Yes,' he said. Several seconds passed. 'I need to tell you this, Alex: you're such a *good* young man. I find myself calling you "son" from time to time, because if I'd . . . oh, this is silly, I just called to see how you were getting on and to let you know we're coping. The human spirit and all that.'

'Indomitable,' I said.

'What's the alternative?'

Milo had come by last night, and we'd talked through sunrise. I'd been thinking a lot about alternatives. 'Thanks for calling, Bert. Let's get together. When things settle down.'

'Yes. Absolutely. We must.'

He sounded old and weak and I wanted to help him, and I said, 'Soon you'll be getting back to your instruments.'

'Pardon – oh, yes, definitely. As a matter of fact, I did get on-line early this morning. Came upon an old Portuguese *gitarra* on eBay that looks intriguing, if it can be restored. Tuned differently than a guitar, but you might be able to get some sound out of it. If I get it at the right price, I'll let you know and you can come up here and we'll make music.'

'Sounds like a plan,' I said. Happy to have any.

fifty

The next few days degraded to a blur of solitude and missed opportunity. I took a long time to muster the energy to call Robin, never found her in.

She didn't call back, not once, and I wondered if we'd descended to a new level.

I tried not to think about Janie Ingalls or any of the others, did a pretty decent job of cutting myself off, knew it was unlikely Allison Gwynn had read about Michael Larner's death in the *Santa Barbara News-Press* and that I should tell her. I couldn't dredge up the initiative for that, either.

I buried myself in housecleaning, yardwork, clumsy jogs, TV hypnosis, obligatory, tasteless meals, perusals of the morning paper – not a word of print about the bloody night in Ojai, the Larners, the Cossacks. Continued sniping at John G. Broussard by politicians and pundits was the only link to what had been my reality since receiving the murder book.

On an uncommonly mild Tuesday, I took an afternoon run and came back to find Robin sitting in the living room.

She had on a black T-shirt, black leather jeans, and the pair of lizard-skin boots I'd given her two birthdays ago. Her hair was long and loose, and she was made up and lipsticked and looked like a beautiful stranger.

When I went over to kiss her, I kept the bruised side of my face out of view. She offered me her lips but kept them closed. Her hand rested briefly on the back of my neck, then dropped off.

I sat down beside her. 'Tour over early?'

'I took a day off,' she said. 'Flew in from Omaha.'

'How's it going?'

435

She didn't answer. I took her hand. Her fingers were cool and limp as they brushed against my burnt palm.

'Before we get into anything,' she said, 'I'm going to tell you about Sheridan. He knew to bring a Milk-Bone because he'd met Spike before, has dogs of his own.'

'Robin, I'm—'

'Please, Alex. Just listen.'

I let go of her hand, sat back.

'Sheridan comes on strong,' she said, 'and his job puts him in close proximity to me, so I suppose I can understand your suspicions. But just for the record, he's a born-again Christian, married, has four kids under the age of six. He brings his entire family on tour with him, it's kind of a running joke with the rest of the crew. His wife's name is Bonnie, and she used to be a backup singer before she and Sheridan found religion. Both of them are what you'd expect from new converts: way too joyful, zealous, upright, quoting scripture. It's annoying, but everyone puts up with it because Sheridan's a nice person, and he's about the best tour coordinator in the business. When he does try to influence me it's in the form of not-so-subtle little asides about accepting Christ into my life, not sleazy little ploys to get in my pants. And yes, I know religious observance doesn't necessarily prevent bad behavior, but this guy means it. He's never come within a mile of anything remotely sexual. Most of the time when he's in my room, Bonnie's right there with him.'

'I'm sorry,' I said.

'I wasn't after an apology, Alex. I just wanted to tell you in person. So you wouldn't torture yourself.'

'Thank you.'

'What happened to your hand and your face?'

'Long story.'

'The same story,' she said.

'I suppose.'

'That's the other thing. The other reason I came by. Our situation. It's not simple, is it?'

'I missed you,' I said.

'I missed you, too. Still do. But . . .'

'There has to be a "but." '

'Don't be angry.'

'I'm not. I'm sad.'

'I am, too. If I didn't care about you, I'd have spared myself seeing you. Still, I'm not staying, Alex. A car is coming by to take me back to the airport and I'm rejoining the tour and remaining till the end. Which may stretch longer. We've been doing great, raising a bundle for the cause. There's been talk of a European extension.'

'Paris?' I said.

She began to cry.

I would've liked to join in, but there was no juice left in me.

We held hands for the rest of the hour, not moving from the couch except for the time when I got her a wad of tissues to wipe her eyes.

When the taxi arrived, she said, 'This isn't over. Let's see how it plays out.'

'Sure.'

I walked her to the door, stood on the terrace, and waved.

Three days later, I phoned Allison Gwynn's office and told her about Larner.

She said, 'Oh, my – it's going to take me some time to integrate this . . . I'm glad you told me. It was good of you to tell me.'

'I thought I should.'

'Are *you* okay?'

'I'm fine.'

'If *you* ever need someone to talk to . . .'

'I'll bear that in mind.'

'Do that,' she said. 'I mean it.'

THE IMPERIAL WAR MUSEUM BOOK OF

WAR BEHIND ENEMY LINES

THE IMPERIAL WAR MUSEUM BOOK OF

WAR BEHIND ENEMY LINES

Julian Thompson

SIDGWICK & JACKSON
Published in Association with
THE IMPERIAL WAR MUSEUM

First published 1998 by Sidgwick & Jackson

an imprint of Macmillan Publishers Ltd
25 Eccleston Place, London SW1W 9NF
and Basingstoke

Associated companies throughout the world

ISBN 0 283 06253 3

1 3 5 7 9 8 6 4 2

A CIP catalogue record for this book is available from
the British Library.

Typeset by SetSystems Ltd, Saffron Walden, Essex
Printed and bound in Great Britain by
Mackays of Chatham plc, Chatham, Kent

Contents

Contents

List of Illustrations

Section One

Captain P. J. D. McCraith who raised the Yeomanry Patrol in the Long-Range Desert Group in front of his Ford truck. (HU 71713)

Bagnold Sun Compass. (HU 71822)

Captain David Lloyd Owen with 'Tich' Cave on the back of a 30-cwt truck outside the Farouk Hotel in Siwa oasis, November 1941. (HU 25299)

A posed photograph of an LRDG Chevrolet truck. (E 12380)

LRDG Chevrolet truck shooting a dune. The truck behind is a Ford 30-cwt. (HU 25793)

Lieutenant-Colonel John Haselden dressed as an Arab coming out of the desert to meet an LRDG patrol. (HU 24997)

LRDG WACO aircraft. (HU 25081)

Y Patrol returning to Kufra after a successful incursion into enemy territory. (HU 25277)

David Stirling with men of G Patrol of the LRDG. (HU 69650)

An SAS jeep, heavily loaded with jerricans of fuel and water. (NA 676)

Lieutenant-Colonel Blair 'Paddy' Mayne. (AP 6069)

Section Two

Field Marshal Sir Archibald Wavell, then C-in-C India, talking to a Chindit officer. (IND 2088)

Major-General Orde Wingate taken just before his death. (HU 71286)

Maps

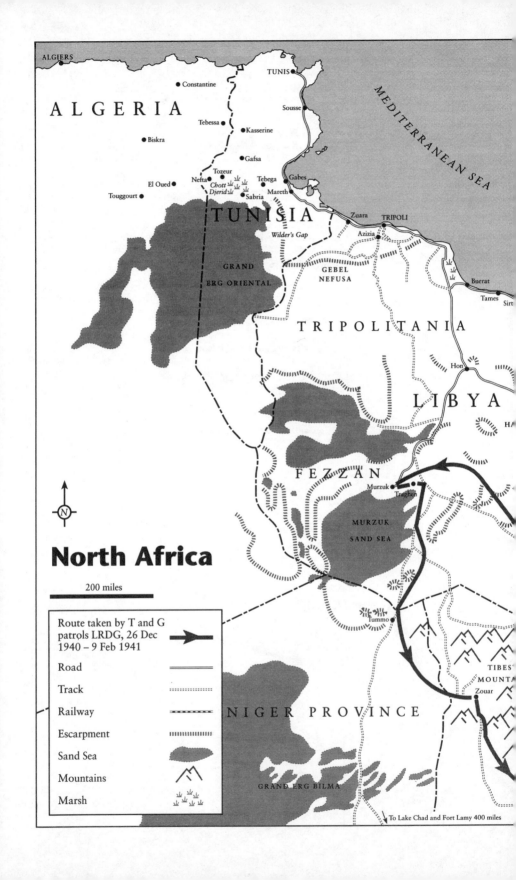

ALGIERS

Constantine

TUNIS

ALGERIA

Sousse

Tebessa

Kasserine

Biskra

Gafsa

Tozeur

Tebega

Gabes

El Oued

Nefta

Chott Djerid

Sabria

Mareth

TUNISIA

Touggourt

Zuara

TRIPOLI

Wilder's Gap

Azizia

GRAND ERG ORIENTAL

GEBEL NEFUSA

Buerat

Tames
Sirt

TRIPOLITANIA

LIBYA

Hon

HA

FEZZAN

Murzuk

Traghen

N

MURZUK SAND SEA

North Africa

200 miles

Tummo

TIBES'
MOUNTA

Zouar

NIGER PROVINCE

Route taken by T and G patrols LRDG, 26 Dec 1940 – 9 Feb 1941	➔
Road	———
Track	·········
Railway	—×—×—
Escarpment	ıııııııııııı
Sand Sea	▬
Mountains	⋀⋀
Marsh	⸙⸙⸙

GRAND ERG BILMA

To Lake Chad and Fort Lamy 400 miles

MEDITERRANEAN SEA

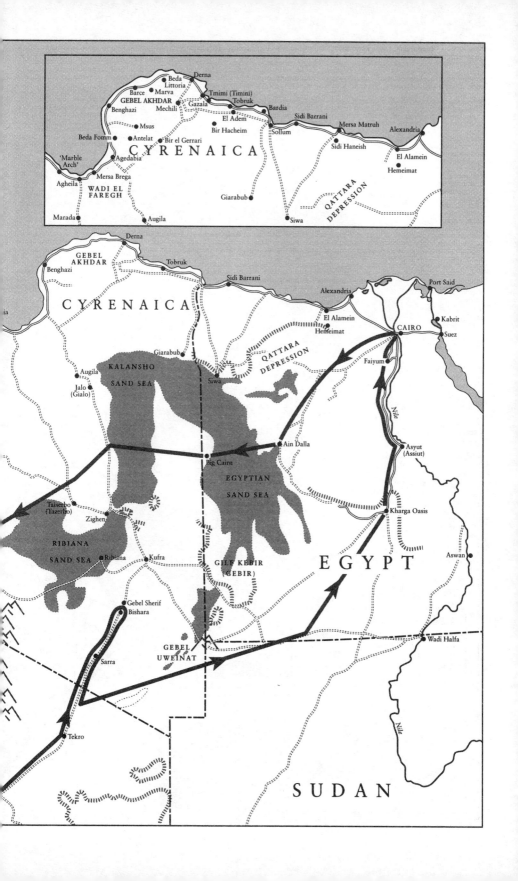

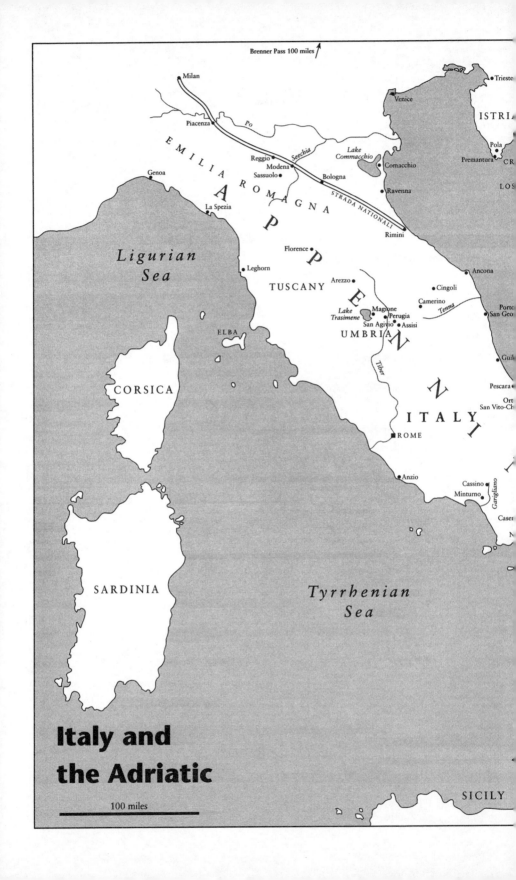

Brenner Pass 100 miles ↑

Milan

Trieste

Venice

ISTRIA

Piacenza

Po

E M I L I A   R O M A G N A

Pola

Premantura

CR

Reggio

Secchia

Lake *Commacchio*

Modena

Comacchio

Genoa

Sassuolo

Bologna

LOS

La Spezia

STRADA NATIONALI

Ravenna

A P P E N N I N E S

Rimini

Ligurian Sea

Florence

Leghorn

Ancona

Arezzo

Cingoli

TUSCANY

Camerino

Porto San Geo

Lake *Trasimene*

Magione

Tenna

Perugia

San Agivio

Assisi

Guil

UMBRIA

ELBA

Tiber

Pescara

CORSICA

I T A L Y

Ort San Vito-Ch

I

ROME

Anzio

Cassino

Gargliano

Minturno

Caser

N

Tyrrhenian Sea

SARDINIA

Italy and
the Adriatic

100 miles

SICILY

ZAGREB

YUGOSLAVIA

BELGRADE

Zara

D
A
L
M
A
T
I
A

Sarajevo

VIS

Dubrovnic

A
d
r
i
a
t
i
c
S
e
a

Drin

Termoli

Rodi

Shegnjin

Sannicandro

Foggia

Durazzo ■ TIRANA

Calitri

Pequin

Tragino Aquaduct

Bari

Elbasan

Shkumbin

erno

Sele

S

ALBANIA

Brindisi

Velona

Taranto

CORFU

Ionian
Sea

Gioia

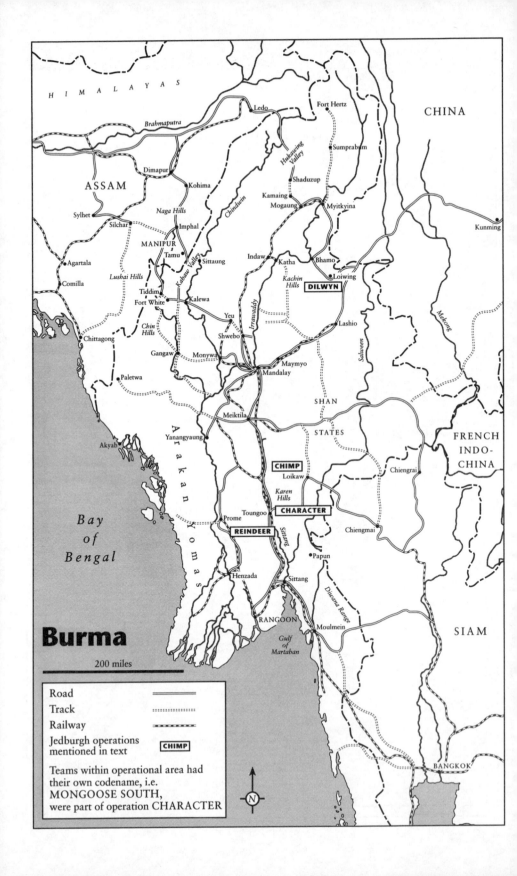

H I M A L A Y A S

Brahmaputra

Ledo

Fort Hertz

CHINA

Dimapur

Sumprabum

Hukawng
Valley

ASSAM

Shaduzup

Kamaing

Mogaung

Myitkyina

Kunming

Sylhet

Naga Hills

Silchar

Imphal

Chindwin

MANIPUR

Tamu

Sittaung

Indaw

Katha

Bhamo

Agartala

Kabaw Valley

Loiwing

Comilla

Lushai Hills

Kachin
Hills

DILWYN

Tiddim

Kalewa

Fort White

Yeu

Irrawaddy

Lashio

Chin
Hills

Shwebo

Saluveen

Chittagong

Gangaw

Monywa

Mekong

Paletwa

Maymyo

Mandalay

Akyab

Meiktila

SHAN

Yanangyaung

STATES

FRENCH
INDO-
CHINA

A
r
a
k
a
n

CHIMP

Loikaw

Chiengrai

Bay
of
Bengal

Y
o
m
a
s

Karen
Hills

CHARACTER

Prome

Toungoo

Chiengmai

REINDEER

Sittang

Papun

Henzada

Sittang

Dawna Range

Burma

RANGOON

Moulmein

SIAM

200 miles

Gulf
of
Martaban

Road	———————
Track	:::::::::::::::
Railway	·—·—·—·—·—
Jedburgh operations mentioned in text	CHIMP

Teams within operational area had
their own codename, i.e.
MONGOOSE SOUTH,
were part of operation CHARACTER

BANGKOK

N

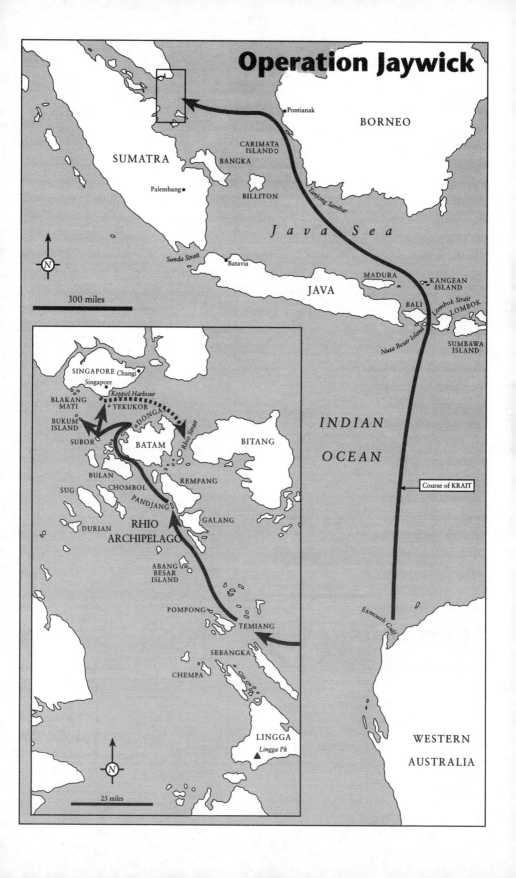

Operation Jaywick

BORNEO

Pontianak

SUMATRA

CARIMATA
ISLAND

BANGKA

Palembang

BILLITON

Tanjong Sambar

J a v a   S e a

Sunda Strait

Batavia

N

300 miles

JAVA

MADURA

KANGEAN
ISLAND

BALI

Lombok Strait

LOMBOK

Nusa Besar Island

SUMBAWA
ISLAND

SINGAPORE   Changi

Singapore

Keppel Harbour

BLAKANG
MATI

TEKUKOR

DONGAS

BUKUM
ISLAND

SUBOR

BATAM

Rhio Strait

BITANG

I N D I A N

BULAN

CHOMBOL

REMPANG

O C E A N

SUG

PANDJANG

GALANG

Course of KRAIT

DURIAN

RHIO
ARCHIPELAGO

ABANG
BESAR
ISLAND

POMPONG

TEMIANG

Exmouth Gulf

SEBANGKA

CHEMPA

LINGGA

Lingga Pk

WESTERN

AUSTRALIA

N

25 miles

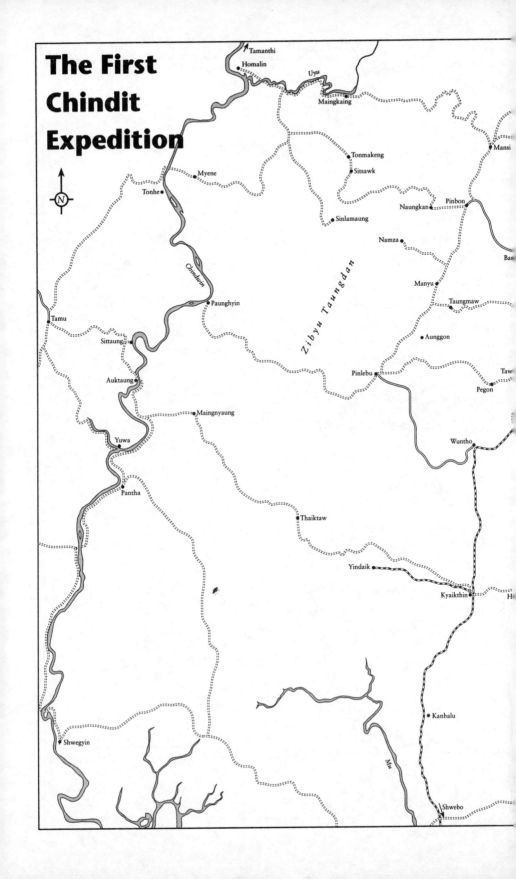

The First
Chindit
Expedition

N

Tamanthi
Homalin
Uyu
Maingkaing
Mansi
Myene
Tonmakeng
Sitsawk
Tonhe
Naungkan
Pinbon
Sinlamaung
Namza
Ba
Chindwin
Manyu
Paunghyin
Taungmaw
Tamu
Aunggon
Sittaung
Pinlebu
Taw
Auktaung
Pegon
Maingnyaung
Yuwa
Wuntho
Pantha
Thaiktaw
Yindaik
Kyaikthin
H
Kanbalu
Shwegyin
Mu
Shwebo

Zibyu Taungdan

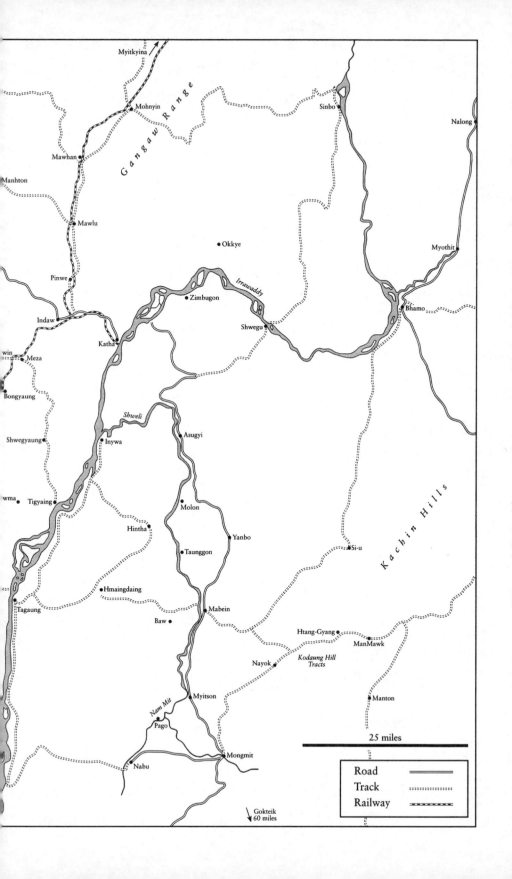

Myitkyina

Gangaw Range

Mohnyin

Sinbo

Nalong

Mawhan

Manhton

Mawlu

Okkye

Myothit

Pinwe

Irrawaddy

Zimbugon

Indaw

Shwegu

Bhamo

Katha

win Meza

Bongyaung

Shweli

Asugyi

Shwegyaung

Inywa

Kachin Hills

wma Tigyaing

Molon

Hintha

Yanbo

Taunggon

Si-u

Hmaingdaing

Tagaung

Mabein

Baw

Htang-Gyang

ManMawk

Nayok

Kodaung Hill Tracts

Manton

25 miles

Nam Mit

Myitson

Pago

Mongmit

Nabu

Road

Track

Railway

↓ Gokteik
60 miles

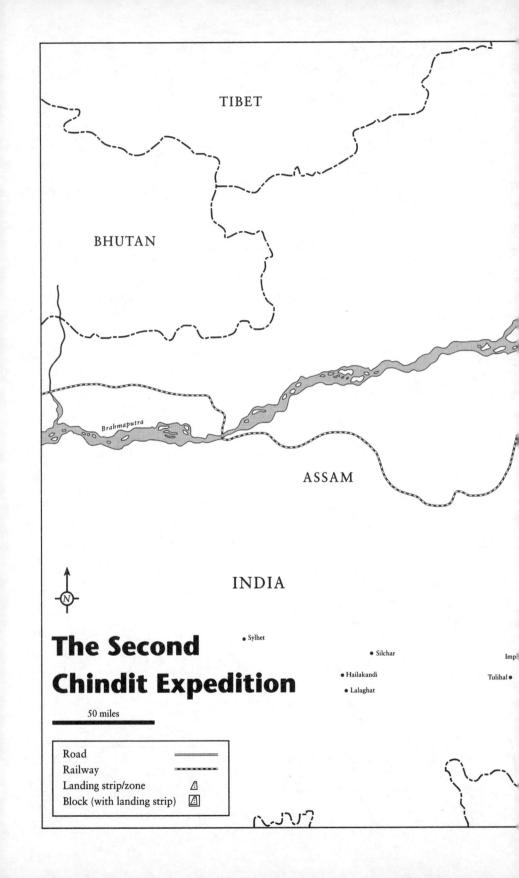

TIBET

BHUTAN

Brahmaputra

ASSAM

INDIA

The Second
Chindit Expedition

50 miles

Road	
Railway	
Landing strip/zone	
Block (with landing strip)	

Sylhet

Silchar

Imp

Hailakandi

Tulihal

Lalaghat

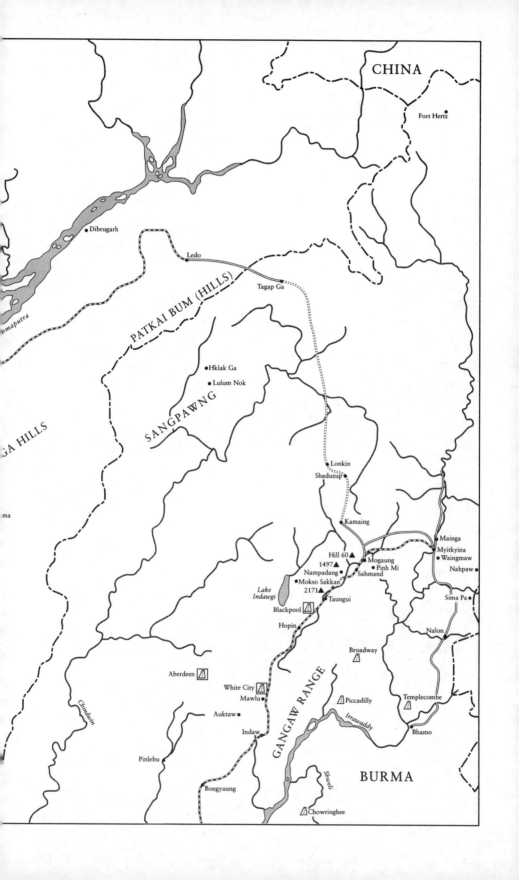

YUGOSLAVIA

B

ALBANIA

Florina

Thessaloniki
(Salonika)

THASOS

LEMNC

CORFU

PAXOS

LEFKAS

KEFALLONIA

SKIROS

A L

ZAKYNTHOS

Araxos

P E L O P O N N E S E

Corinth
Canal

Corinth

Megara

ATHENS

Piraeus

A

Katakolon
Pirgos

GIAROS

KEA

SIROS

KITHNOS

I O N I A N   S E A

SERIPHOS

C Y

SIPHNOS

P

GREECE

MILOS

N

KITHERA

**Greece and
the Aegean**

Maleme

Canea

He

100 miles

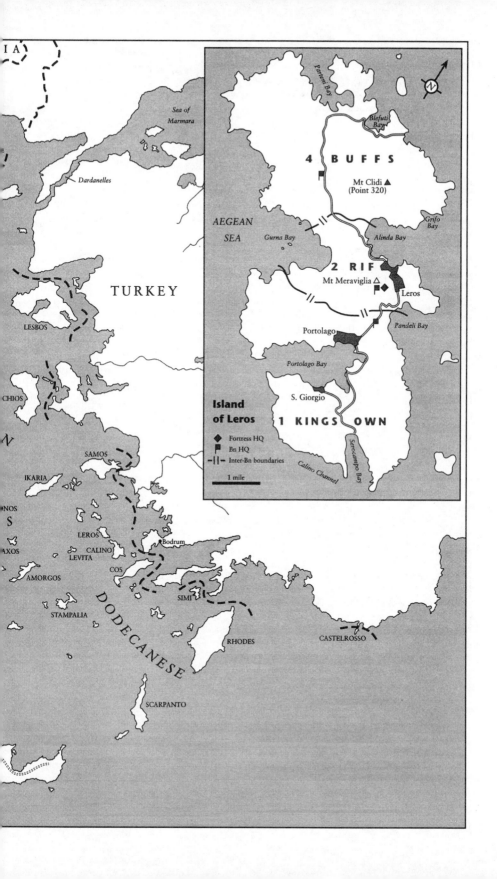

I A)

Sea of
Marmara

Dardanelles

AEGEAN
SEA

TURKEY

Parteni Bay

Blefuti
Bay

4   B U F F S

Mt Clidi ▲
(Point 320)

Grifo
Bay

Gurna Bay

Alinda Bay

2   R I F

Mt Meraviglia △
◆

Leros

Pandeli Bay

Portolago

Portolago Bay

S. Giorgio

1   K I N G S   O W N

LESBOS

**Island
of Leros**

◆   Fortress HQ
■   Bn HQ
–||– Inter-Bn boundaries

1 mile

Calino Channel

Serocampo Bay

CHIOS

N

SAMOS

IKARIA

S

NOS

LEROS

Bodrum

AXOS

CALINO

LEVITA

AMORGOS

COS

D O D E C A N E S E

SIMI

STAMPALIA

RHODES

CASTELROSSO

SCARPANTO

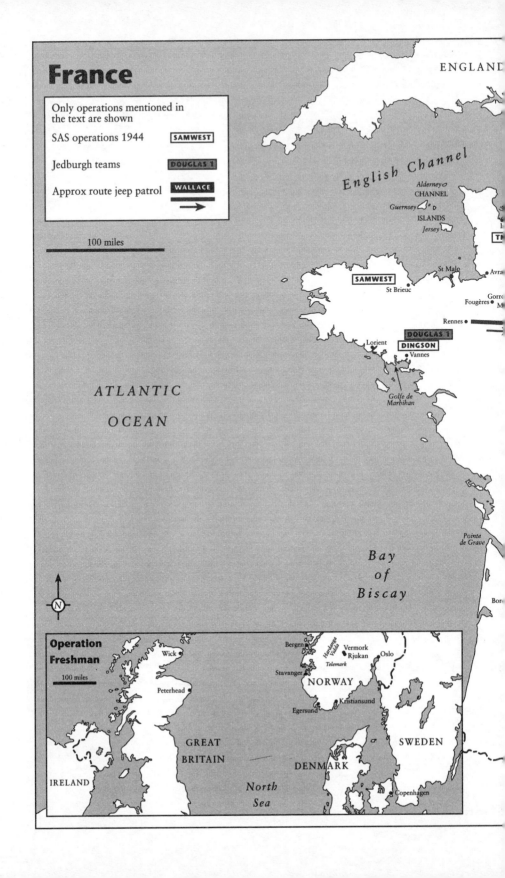

France

Only operations mentioned in the text are shown

SAS operations 1944   `SAMWEST`

Jedburgh teams   `DOUGLAS 1`

Approx route jeep patrol   `WALLACE`
→

100 miles

ENGLAND

English Channel

Alderney
CHANNEL
Guernsey
ISLANDS
Jersey

St Malo   Avra

`SAMWEST`
St Brieuc

Fougères   Gorro
M

Rennes

Lorient   `DOUGLAS 1`
`DINGSON`
Vannes

ATLANTIC

OCEAN

Golfe de Marbihan

Pointe de Grave

Bay of Biscay

Bor

N

Operation Freshman

100 miles

Wick

Peterhead

GREAT

BRITAIN

IRELAND

North Sea

Bergen
Hardanger Vidda
Vermork
Rjukan   Oslo
Telemark
Stavanger
NORWAY
Egersund   Kristiansund

SWEDEN

DENMARK

Copenhagen

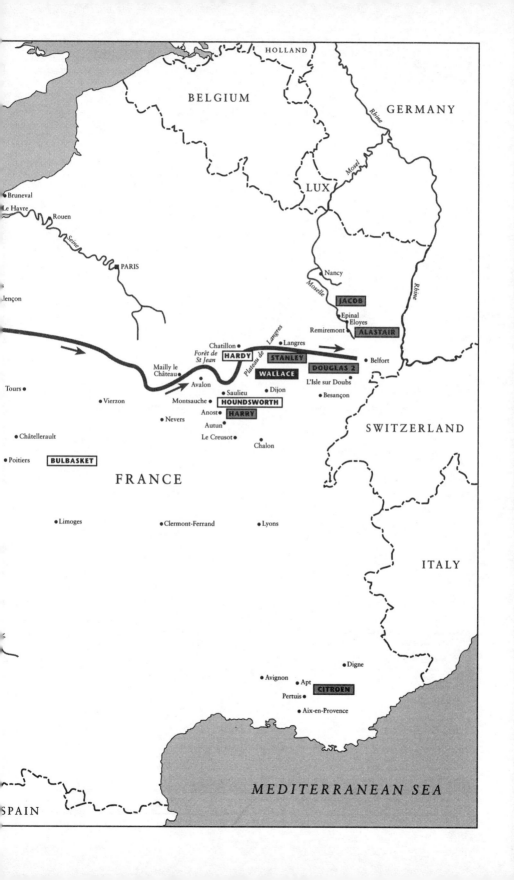

HOLLAND

BELGIUM

GERMANY

Rhine

LUX

Mosel

Bruneval
Le Havre
Rouen

Seine

PARIS

Nancy

Moselle

JACOB

lençon

Epinal
Eloyes
Remiremont

ALASTAIR

Chatillon
Langres

Langres

HARDY

Plateau de

STANLEY

Belfort

Mailly le
Château

*Forêt de
St Jean*

WALLACE

DOUGLAS 2

L'Isle sur Doubs

Tours

Avalon

Saulieu
Dijon

Besançon

Vierzon

Montsauche

HOUNDSWORTH

Nevers

Anost
Autun

HARRY

SWITZERLAND

Châtellerault

Le Creusot
Chalon

Poitiers

BULBASKET

FRANCE

Limoges

Clermont-Ferrand

Lyons

ITALY

Digne

Avignon
Apt

CITROEN

Pertuis

Aix-en-Provence

Rhine

SPAIN

MEDITERRANEAN SEA

Acknowledgements

It would not have been possible to write this book without the letters, diaries, accounts and taped interviews of the people I have quoted. My first acknowledgement must be to them. Their names are listed in the Index of Contributors, as are the names of copyright holders.

Next I must thank the senior members of the staff of the Imperial War Museum. Christopher Dowling, Keeper of the Department of Museum Services, was encouraging throughout the project. Roderick Suddaby, Keeper of the Department of Documents, gave me much wise advice and help. I am very grateful to him for allowing me to work in his department for so much of the time, and for pointing me in the direction of so many interesting collections; not least that of the late Major General Orde Wingate. Working in the Department of Documents was both stimulating and congenial thanks to the forbearance and kindness of the staff of the Department.

I would also like to thank Margaret Brooks (Keeper of the Sound Archive), Jane Carmichael (who was Keeper of the Photographic Archive at the time of my research), Gwynn Bayliss (Keeper of the Department of Printed Books), and all the staffs in the departments in whose archives I carried out my research. I am especially indebted to Mark Seaman of the Research and Information Office for the many days he spent going through my text in great detail. He also gave me hours of his time advising and putting me straight on a number of matters connected with behind-the-lines operations in the Second World War, as well as bringing to my attention some of the latest research material. His wide knowledge of procedures, training, methods of operating, and numerous other aspects of special forces techniques were invaluable to me. He assisted on the selection of photographs, including the one on the dust jacket. Without his help, I would have found my task immeasurably more difficult, and not least, would have committed a number of serious blunders which would have been pounced upon by the special forces fraternity.

I am equally appreciative of the help given to me by Major General David Lloyd Owen, whose extensive collection of Long Range Desert Group (LRDG) papers are the mainstay of the chapters on the LRDG. As well as spending a great deal of his time reading and correcting the chapters in which the LRDG appears, his guidance was absolutely essential. Having joined the LRDG in 1941, and commanded it from late 1943 to the end of the War in the Mediterranean, he is uniquely qualified to give advice on all aspects of LRDG operations. I must also thank him and the LRDG Association for granting permission to reproduce photographs HU 25299, HU 25793, HU 25081, HU 25277, HU 69650, HU 25273, HU 25268.

Colonel McCraith donated photograph HU 71713 to the Imperial War Museum and allowed me to use it in the book. Mrs N. Heath, widow of Lieutenant Commander Donald Davidson DSO RNVR, kindly donated the Jaywick photographs.

I am grateful to the following publishers/copyright owners for permission to quote extracts from the published works listed below:

David Higham Associates Limited, Shelford Bidwell, *The Chindit War: The Campaign in Burma 1944*, Hodder & Stoughton 1979.

Sage Publications Ltd, Shelford Bidwell in the *Journal of Contemporary History*, Volume 15.

Her Majesty's Stationery Office, F. A. E. Crew, *Medical History of The Second World War: Army Medical Services, Campaigns* Volume V.

Roy Farran, *Winged Dagger: Adventures on Special Service*, Fontana, 1956.

Robin Neillands, *The Dervish Wars: Gordon & Kitchener in the Sudan 1880–1898*, John Murray.

The Rt Hon. The Viscount Slim, Field Marshal the Viscount Slim, *Defeat Into Victory*, Corgi 1971.

John Verney, *Going to the Wars*, Collins, 1955, HarperCollins Publishers Limited.

A. P. Watt Ltd on behalf of Roland Huntford, *Scott and Amundsen: The Race to the South Pole*, Hodder & Stoughton 1979 (Pan 1983).

Phillip Ziegler, *Mountbatten*, William Collins Sons & Co, 1985, HarperCollins Publishers Limited.

William Armstrong of Sidgwick & Jackson has been most encouraging and supportive throughout. I am grateful to Chris Stewart, my editor, for his forbearance and advice; and also to the designer Wilf Dickie.

Jane Thompson's painstaking research and editorial advice was, as always, absolutely indispensable. The book would never have been finished without her support.

Prologue

The purpose of this book is to try to give the general reader some idea of what it was like for a soldier in the British Armed Forces in the Second World War to operate behind enemy lines. With one exception (Operation Jaywick) my definition of such a soldier is 'one who penetrated enemy's rear, but fought in uniform expecting to be treated by the enemy in accordance with the laws and usages of war'. This sets them apart from most SOE and OSS operations. I include Jaywick because it brings out certain features that I hope will interest the reader. It is also one of the few Special Forces operations in which a key participant kept a detailed day-to-day log.

I cannot cover all the behind the lines operations conducted by the British in the Second World War. Even attempting to do so would result in a 'dictionary' of such operations. For example I do not include the exploits of Wingate's Gideon Force in Abyssinia. This was an operation carried out under the auspices of SOE, and the bulk of the force was from the Sudan Defence Battalion and locally recruited Abyssinian troops.

Instead, I have picked out a selection from the extensive material in the Imperial War Museum which I hope will illustrate the principle of what I call 'return on investment', or otherwise, of these operations. Some collections are particularly rich, and hence much used in this book. The choice is mine, and no one else's.

After a lifetime of Commando soldiering, none of it in Special Forces, but having had Special Forces units under command on several operations, and been responsible for the SBS for two and a half years, I believe that I am in a position to offer an opinion on whether or not such forces give value for money based on my own experience. It is of course my opinion, and, therefore, open to being challenged.

Quotations The text contains many direct quotations from written documentary material and interview tapes. These are reproduced verbatim where possible, but obvious errors have been corrected and minor confusions clarified. It has not been thought necessary to indicate where quotations have been abridged.

Photographs   All the illustrations in this book have come from the Imperial War Museum, and have been listed with their reference after the caption.

1

Why Special Forces?

You wanted to get to the War. It was shameful not to have fired one's gun. It was a combination of duty and wanting excitement.

Oswin Craster

I wasn't prepared for the question 'Why do you want to join the Commandos?' He prompted me with the right answer; 'I suppose you want to have a crack at the Boche?'

George Jellicoe

Burma, July 1945: Rangoon had been in Allied hands since early May. The Japanese 28th Army, as dangerous as a cornered African bull buffalo, was trying to break out of the Pegu Yomas hills, cross the Sittang River, and head for a final stand in the far south of the Burma–Thailand peninsula. Three divisions of British, Indian and Gurkha soldiers deployed to destroy them. Aubrey Trofimov, who had operated behind enemy lines in France, was now behind the lines again in Team Mongoose South. He received a message that the Japanese were appearing on the west bank of the river, and some Karen levies were already fighting to stop them. He moved to join them on the Shwegyin River, a tributary of the Sittang, a good stop line to the west of the main river. He was allocated a section just under two miles long. They dug in.

The Japs would come out at dawn or sometimes just before dark, and they would come out in masses, some staying on the banks firing at us. They built rafts out of bamboo. It got to such point that the odds were a bit against us. We called in the RAF who were very effective so we found out later. One day we heard about Hiroshima, and thought 'that's it'. But the Japs hadn't heard about this. We went on fighting until well into September. By then we had established an airstrip. We received Japanese Officer POWs who we sent in to persuade the Japs that the war was over.

So ended one soldier's war behind enemy lines. By the time of the Japanese surrender, Aubrey Trofimov was just one of thousands serving, or who had served, in an array of special units in the British Forces. Their conception was brought about by two events five years before, and half a world away from Team Mongoose's last battles with the Japanese on the banks of the Shwegyin River. On 22 June 1940, France concluded an armistice with the Germans, and most of the British Expeditionary Force was back in the United Kingdom, having been evacuated from the Channel ports, notably Dunkirk, in May. Invasion appeared imminent. Also in June, Italy declared war on Britain and France. British garrisons and interests in the Middle East were threatened by Italian forces in North and East Africa. The most immediate menace was the large Italian army in Cyrenaica which greatly outnumbered the British force in Egypt. Alexandria was the base for the Mediterranean Fleet. In Cairo was the headquarters whose operational area stretched from the Balkans to Northern Rhodesia (present-day Zambia) and Algeria to Iran. Workshops, supply depots and reinforcement camps were situated all over the Nile Delta. To the east of the Nile lay the key waterway of the Suez Canal. Further east again, at the head of the Persian Gulf, were the Iranian oilfields, vital to Britain's war effort and very survival. Everywhere Britain, shorn of her ally France, was alone and at bay.

The first British special forces raised in the Second World War were the Commandos in Britain and the Long-Range Desert Group (LRDG) in Egypt, each with a very different purpose in mind. The story of the LRDG will be covered in the next and subsequent chapters. The Commandos were formed on the orders of Winston Churchill when France was still fighting. In a minute to the Chiefs of Staff on 5 June 1940 he wrote: 'I look to the Chiefs of Staff to propose me measures for a vigorous, enterprising, and ceaseless offensive against the whole German occupied coastline.' Starting on 9 June, the War Office sent out letters asking for volunteers to join a special force for mobile operations. There were some volunteers to hand already. When the Germans invaded Norway, ten independent companies were formed using volunteers from divisions and commands throughout the United Kingdom. The task of these companies was originally to mount ship-borne raids on the Norwegian coast to prevent the Germans setting up air and submarine bases. Half of them never got nearer to Norway than Gourock near Glasgow. Numbers 1 to 5 Companies, commanded by Lieutenant-

Colonel Colin Gubbins, after an extremely frustrating and fruitless month in Norway, were back in Scotland on 10 June 1940. Another source of commando volunteers was 5th Battalion Scots Guards, formed as a ski battalion to help the Finns against the Russians. The battalion was disbanded after the Norwegians and Swedes, both neutral at that time, refused to allow them to transit their territory.

For a time the commandos were grouped into Special Service (SS) Battalions, which was unfortunate in that the letters SS already stood for *Schutzstaffel*, Hitler's infamous black-shirted elite. Eventually the name for these units reverted to the original choice, commandos, after the Boer troops who had given the British army so much trouble in South Africa some forty years earlier. But the brigades into which the commandos were later formed retained the letters SS until the end of 1944.

The ink on the Franco-German Armistice was hardly dry, when on the night of 24/25 June the first raid on the French coast was carried out by a newly raised independent company specially formed for the operation, dubbed Number 11 Commando for the occasion. It was commanded by Major Tod, who had commanded Number 6 Independent Company. Tod would eventually command 2 Commando Brigade. Only one party saw any action of note. But coming so soon after the French capitulation, it signalled Britain's determination not to make peace with Germany, and was good for morale. The second raid, by men of Number 3 Commando and 11 Independent Company on Guernsey, was even less successful. Three men were left behind, and subsequently captured. Churchill commented, 'Let there be no more silly fiascos like that perpetrated at Guernsey.'

There now followed a lull in commando operations mounted from Britain, and apart from two raids on Norway, one in early 1941 and one in December of that year, the time until March 1942 was spent in training.

In truth, inspiring though the commando idea was, with its vision of striking at the enemy-held coast of Europe, there were subtler ways of achieving this using agents tasked by the Special Operations Executive (SOE), formed on Churchill's orders on 1 July 1940. Descending on the enemy, killing a few guards, blowing up the odd pillbox, and taking a handful of prisoners was not a cost-effective use of ships, craft and highly trained soldiers. The effect of these types of commando raid on enemy morale was negligible. One of the few exceptions was the St

Nazaire operation, the most successful and perhaps the greatest raid of all. Commando operations in the Middle East were even less effective than those in north-west Europe, for reasons which will be covered later. Starting with the Dieppe raid, commandos really came into their own from late 1942 onwards, fighting in most theatres of war, usually as part of the main battle. Increasingly they were given tasks on the flanks, or ahead of the main force, counting on their training and élan to overcome difficulties that might have daunted more conventional units. The Commando Association Battle Honours Flag in Westminster Abbey bears this out: thirty-four out of the thirty-eight engagements listed are major actions involving other forces in addition to commandos. Whatever the original intention, the majority of commandos did not operate behind the lines. Their actions, therefore, have no place here, except where they were operating in that capacity. But the early days of the commandos are interesting because some of the characters serving in them were to find their destiny in other units. One such was Lieutenant the Lord Jellicoe serving in the Coldstream Guards. A call went out for volunteers from London District and the Household Division to form Number 8 Commando. Jellicoe was interviewed by the commanding officer, Lieutenant-Colonel R. E. (Robert) Laycock of the Blues, in June 1940.

There was a troop from each Guards Regiment, and the 60th; lots of spriglets of the aristocracy, Randolph Churchill, and grander people from the old aristocracy. It was White's Club in the Army. That's where I first met David Stirling who was in the Scots Guards, Jock Lewes who was so influential in founding the SAS. David Stirling was known as the 'Giant Sloth' because on our voyage out to the Middle East in the *Glengyle* he spent the whole time in bed.

Our training was hard, but very few people fell out. We went to Lochailort to the Commando Course where 'Shimi' Lovat was the chief instructor. David Stirling's elder brother and David Niven were also on the course. It was very hard work and we learnt a lot. Some of the training included poaching deer on Lord Brocket's estate. He was known to be a bit of a Nazi sympathiser so we felt fully entitled to poach his deer. We did some long exercises in the hills. I then rejoined the commando at Inverary and at Largs. Then we went to the Isle of Arran. Here there were the three Glen Line ships converted for commando operations. Lord Keyes was in charge of combined operations. He kept pressing for the employment of the commandos.

Jellicoe went on to join the Special Air Service in the Western Desert and commanded the Special Boat Squadron in the Aegean.

James Sherwood was an RASC driver in London District. Lieutenant Roger Courtney came round seeking men for the commandos.

Courtney had been a white hunter in Kenya, in the Palestine Police, and had canoed almost the entire length of the White Nile from Lake Victoria to Egypt in a two-seater called the *Buttercup*. He was a very tough sort of man, very self-reliant, full of a love of adventure. Not a blustering, swaggering sort of pistol stuck in the belt type of bloke, but a straight-forward man with an adventurous spirit. We liked him and would have been prepared to go with him there and then.

Sherwood eventually found himself in Number 8 Commando with Randolph Churchill.

These were the days before the Commando Training Centre at Achnacarry. Each Commando set about training according to its own ideas. At that stage for the newcomer, the idea was to weed out those who could stand the pace from those who couldn't. Within 24 hours of arriving, we were formed up with all our gear, full pack, rifle, respirator, tin hat and all the rest of the paraphernalia and headed by Randolph Churchill who looked to us to be very fat and unfit, but who proved himself capable of taking anything we had to take. I remember the perspiration poured off him, he must have lost about a stone, on what turned out to be a speed march. I think the aim was to do something like seven miles in an hour. Which with all our gear was quite some going, especially for some of us from units like my own, the RASC, who had spent their time sitting behind the wheel of vehicles or on motor cycles. We belted out along the road going hell for leather for about an hour, after a brief stop, we turned round and did the same coming back. It was the return journey that weeded out those who couldn't take it. They just fell out. They were returned to unit the next day and we never saw them again.

Those who stayed the course carried on with the training. Everything at full pace, full pack, full equipment, losing weight rapidly and becoming fitter every day.

Jellicoe's remark about the Director of Combined Operations, Admiral of the Fleet Lord Keyes, pressing for tasks for the commandos, is indicative of one of the problems that many special forces organizations had to contend with throughout the Second World War. A special forces unit would form, usually because of enthusiastic backing from a very senior military commander, or even the prime minister. Adventurous spirits joined, often the best types, seeking action as soon as possible. After arduous training, lasting months, and often years without any prospect of action, or perhaps one minor, rather inconclusive foray, men in some of these special units would have the frustrating experience of hearing news of their original battalion or regiment in the thick of the fighting. This was not a universal experience in all special units, but common enough to be remarked upon, and there were a great number of these types of unit before the Second World War finished, particularly in the British Army. There are several reasons for this proliferation of what their detractors called 'private armies', a phenomenon not seen in the First World War.

By early 1942, the Second World War was being fought over a vast area, in many operational theatres. There were often open flanks, and a choice of approach: sea, land and air. Aircraft were capable of long ranges, carrying quite heavy loads. The technique of parachuting dispensed with the need for an airfield at the destination in order to launch troops into battle or deliver supplies. Gliders, loaded with troops, guns, supplies and even vehicles, could be towed by powered aircraft, and could land on terrain far too rough to accept the lightest aircraft.

The mechanization of armies resulted in long lines of communication. These were vulnerable to attack. The radios of the time were powerful, yet light enough to enable operations a long way behind enemy lines to be controlled, and information gathered and passed back to base. Trucks and jeeps capable of operating over harsh terrain were available.

The soldier in a Second World War special unit could often call upon a weight of fire power, and array of support, undreamed of by his forebears of just over twenty years before. Technology had produced small, light, hard-hitting weapons, such as the twin Vickers K gun, the shoulder-fired anti-tank weapon the PIAT, 2-inch and 3-inch mortars, and the .5-inch Browning machine-gun. Radio could be used to call for and control fighter-bombers to strike targets and provide fire support for small units far behind enemy lines. Transport aircraft or gliders could bring in supplies and reinforcements, and even evacuate casualties. In some cases a special forces soldier might even have vehicles flown in for his use.

Special forces had, and still have, three functions: offensive action; the gathering of intelligence; and operating with indigenous resistance groups, including transporting and escorting agents. The proliferation of 'private armies' in the Second World War led some people at the time, and ever since, to question their value. Among the most distinguished critics of special forces was Field Marshal Slim, one of the greatest field commanders on either side in the Second World War. As we shall see, he had good reason to view special forces with a jaundiced eye. His arguments against them, deployed in his book *Defeat into Victory*, are hard to fault. After condemning private armies as 'expensive, wasteful and unnecessary', he does concede that, 'There is, however, one kind of special unit which should be retained – that designed to be employed in small parties, usually behind the enemy, on tasks beyond the normal scope of warfare in the field.'[1]

The fairest way of judging the effectiveness of any special force would perhaps be its value in the form of 'return' set against the 'investment'. The 'return' is the strategic, operational or tactical effect on the battle, campaign, or even the war. The 'investment' is made up of a multitude of components, of which some are: the drain on limited manpower, including creaming off the best men from conventional units who will actually do most of the fighting; training time and effort; research and development of highly specialized equipment; and the diversion or expenditure of resources. These resources can include surface ships, submarines, aircraft, other army units, and the crews and soldiers manning them.

Almost invariably the first two special forces tasks, offensive action and intelligence gathering, produce the best 'return' when carried out as adjuncts of the campaign, or battle, being fought or about to be fought, by the main body of the army. There are a few examples of offensive action far removed from main force activity producing a good 'return', but these must be judged from a strategic point of view. The destruction of the heavy-water plant at Vemork in Norway, to impede the development of the German atom bomb, is one example; the blocking of the dry dock at St Nazaire, to deny the facility to heavy units of the German Navy, is another. Even the latter can be seen as an adjunct to a main force task: the winning of the Battle of the Atlantic. The raid by a parachute company to snatch the key components of a German *Würzburg* night fighter direction radar from Bruneval in northern France is an example of intelligence gathering, again in support of a main force task: the bomber offensive on Germany.

Arguably the same criteria can be applied to the third special forces function: actions with resistance movements. The effectiveness or otherwise of resistance movements is a contentious subject. But there is a perfectly respectable point of view which argues that few, if any, resistance movements conducted successful overt military operations (as opposed to clandestine activity), *unless operating in concert with a main, conventional force; even if that force was some distance away.* Undoubtedly the most effective resistance, or more properly, partisan forces, were those operating behind the German lines in the Soviet Union. Without the distraction of main force operations, a ruthless enemy like the Germans, and even more so the Japanese, could crush most attempts by resistance operatives to play soldiers, as happened in the Warsaw uprisings in August 1944, and on the Vercors Plateau in southern France in July 1944. In the former case the Soviet Army deliberately halted their offensive, and denied use of their airfields to the British and American allied air forces, in order that the Poles would be broken, and therefore unable to pose any resistance to a Russian takeover of Poland. In the latter example, there was no Allied force anywhere near the Vercors in July 1944.

To be effective the guerrilla or resistance force must be active. As Brigadier Michael Calvert, the outstanding Chindit commander, remarked:

> The main job of the soldier is to kill people. As a guerrilla you don't achieve anything by just being present. No regular force of any nation in the world is really frightened of guerrillas unless they can see the results in blown bridges, their friends being killed, or trucks being ambushed. There were cases in Burma, and elsewhere, for example in Europe, where missions just existed, were supplied by the RAF at great risk, and did nothing.

The idea of a guerrilla or resistance movement possibly supported by a 'private army' from a sponsor nation has often been seized upon, usually by politicians, in an effort to win cheaply, without the expense, in terms of blood and treasure, of the main battle. Unfortunately such expenditure is unavoidable if one wishes to defeat an equally strong and determined opponent. The point is that wars are won by main force navies, armies and air forces; especially armies. The activities of T. E.

Lawrence in the Arab Revolt in the First World War, so often hailed as the role model for the 'private armies' of the Second World War, were an adjunct to Allenby's operations against the Turks in Egypt and Palestine. Contrary to popular perception, Lawrence did not defeat the Turks in that theatre. His campaign was a sideshow, and it is arguable that Allenby would have won anyway, albeit with greater difficulty. Whereas, had the Turks not had to concentrate their energies against Allenby, it is likely that they would have smashed the Arab Revolt at their leisure.

By the end of 1940, the men who had volunteered for commandos with such enthusiasm in the wake of the defeat of France found themselves facing a future that did not seem to promise even a sideshow, let alone participation in the main event. Lack of resources, particularly landing craft, and the higher priorities of other theatres of war, meant that boredom and frustration set in among the commandos up in Scotland and elsewhere. But after Christmas, there was at last the prospect of action for some. George Jellicoe remembers the atmosphere in Number 8 Commando on the Island of Arran:

> The Grandees of the commandos did pretty well and they got their grand wives up and it was all very pleasant. But we were getting a bit fidgety. Then we got leave over Christmas which was embarkation leave before going out to the Middle East. But we had some very interesting people with us; there was Evelyn Waugh, and old Admiral Cowan who used to command the Mediterranean Fleet. He had come out as an observer, but was very actively engaged. It was an amusing crowd. Evelyn Waugh did not really fit in, he became much more of a misfit later on. He did extremely well in Crete and was extremely brave. He wasn't really suited for this type of thing. Neither was Randolph [Churchill], but it was a great help having him in the commando because it meant that views were received at a very high level.

Numbers 7, 8 and 11 Commandos, one troop of Number 3 Commando, and Courtney's Folbot Section went to the Middle East, as Force Z under Laycock. Mention will be made of them later in this story. The Folbot Section had been formed by Courtney as a private army within a private army. The early Folbots were canvas-skinned, wooden-framed canoes designed for civilian sporting use mainly on lakes and rivers. They had none of the navigation aids, spray covers, bow and stern buoyancy bags, or inflatable tubes on the gunwales to add stability, found on later versions. When Courtney had first proposed using these flimsy craft for operations, his ideas were dismissed as ludicrous by the staff of Combined Operations. He and another canoeist paddled out to HMS *Glengyle* one night in June 1940, and climbing her anchor chain, stole a gun cover. He delivered it to the Combined Operations staff ashore in the middle of a conference. With all of Britain bracing itself for invasion, he risked being shot by a trigger-happy sentry whose imagination had been stoked with stories of saboteurs and fifth column-ists. On another occasion he paddled up to *Glengyle*, and marked places on the hull where he would have placed limpet mines. This convinced the staff. James Sherwood had been recruited into Number 8 Commando by Courtney, but did not serve under him to begin with. After a while:

We were told that 8 troop was to be disbanded because our standard of training was not high enough. We were really angry. We couldn't see that we were responsible, it was our officers who were supposed to be training us. A lot of offensive language was used which under other circumstances would have been acted against. Our immediate concern was to avoid being Returned to Unit [RTU]. I happened to hear that a small Folbot section was being formed by Courtney. Without further ado half a dozen of us applied to see him at a hotel at Lamlash. He was looking for applicants for his section, it was not known as the SBS until some weeks later. We discovered this involved handling canoes. This was strange to the other chaps, but not to me. It had so happened when I was in Dublin in 1939 I had bought a two-seater Folbot canoe. I knew something about canoeing, and what is more on the Irish Sea, not on rivers, in various conditions, and I was confident in the water, though I was a lousy swimmer. But that didn't bother me, although it should have bothered other people. I was also keen on rock climbing, and mountaineering and mountain walking. Roger Courtney said, 'You're in.' I became part of the section. It consisted of Roger Courtney, at that time a Lieutenant in the Kings Royal Rifle Corps (KRRC), his second-in-command Robert Wilson, and about sixteen Other Ranks, by that time I was a Lance Corporal.

The training in the Firth of Clyde was pretty basic, and skills that would become commonplace later were unheard of. It mostly consisted of Folboting, compass work, map reading, night exercises and night landings north and south of Lamlash. These early types of canoe were highly unsuitable for winter work along the rocky coastline, in the sudden squalls and strong tides of the Clyde. Two men were lost off Corrie, north of Lamlash. They were never found, nor was the canoe. Originally it was planned that each Commando would have a Special Boat Section (SBS) of some thirty canoeists, but this never came to pass.

In October 1941 Commodore Lord Louis Mountbatten took over from Keyes as Director of Combined Operations. In March 1942 he was promoted to Vice Admiral and changed his title to Chief of Combined Operations (CCO). He was told by Churchill to revitalize the raiding programme, but that his main task was to plan the Allied invasion of France. His energy, enthusiasm and ability to drive a project through to its conclusion despite objections and difficulties resulted in a greatly increased number of raids during his time as Chief of Combined Operations. Not all of these were a success. Some of them were disasters, such as the raid on Dieppe in August 1942, and others potential catastrophes, such as the Alderney raid, planned for May 1942, but subsequently cancelled. This was because Mountbatten's character was seriously flawed, although he was personally brave, but as Andrew Roberts has written:

he was also a mendacious, intellectually limited hustler.[2]

He was immensely vain, and at Combined Operations Headquarters (COHQ), and everywhere else for that matter, surrounded himself with sycophants and friends. But despite their disparaging nickname 'Dickie Birds', many of the techniques, equipment and special units that were to be used on Allied amphibious operations in 1942 and thereafter were devised by COHQ. In August 1943, Mountbatten was elevated to Supreme Commander South-East Asia Command (SEAC), because at the time the reconquest of Burma and the East Indies was planned to be primarily by an amphibious operation.

By now in places outside Mountbatten's sphere of control, such as the North African desert, the Mediterranean and in Burma, an assortment of special units had operated behind the lines with a varying degree of success. The story of these, and subsequent operations in Italy, north-west Europe, the Aegean, Burma and the Far East will now be told.

2

The Long-Range Desert Group: June 1940 to November 1941

Extract from the latest despatch by General Wavell

I should like to take this opportunity to bring to notice a small body of men who have for a year past done inconspicuous but invaluable service, the Long Range Desert Group. It was formed under Major (now Colonel) Bagnold in July 1940, to reconnoitre the great Libyan desert on the western border of Egypt and the Sudan. Operating in small independent columns, the group has penetrated into nearly every part of desert Libya, an area comparable in size with that of India. Not only have patrols brought back much information, but they have attacked enemy forts, captured personnel, transport and grounded aircraft as far as 800 miles inside hostile territory. They have protected Egypt and the Sudan from any possibility of raids, and have caused the enemy, in a lively apprehension of their activities, to tie up considerable forces in the defence of distant outposts. Their journeys across vast regions of unexplored desert have entailed the crossing of physical obstacles and the endurance of summer temperatures, both of which have been achieved only by careful organisation, and a very high standard of enterprise, discipline, mechanical maintenance and desert navigation.

(Signed) Arthur Smith
Lt-Gen
25 Oct 41   CGS

The work done by the Long-Range Desert Group (LRDG) in their first year of existence, cited by Wavell in his report, established them as probably one of the most cost-effective special forces in the history of warfare. Their 'return on investment' was consistently better, and over a longer period, than any other British special forces unit in the Second World War. During the five years of its existence, the LRDG carried out more than two hundred operations behind enemy lines. Throughout those five years there were only two short periods of five months when no patrols were operating behind enemy lines.

The battles of the North African campaigns of 1940–43 were fought along the shores of the Mediterranean. Large forces could not penetrate far inland, mainly because their supplies were brought to them on the coastal roads and railways, and by sea. Winter rain falls occasionally on the coast. Here there are scattered strips of cultivated land, most evident in the coastal hills. Areas of scrub extend some thirty miles inland. No roads existed more than about a hundred miles inland, and these were few and far between.

The Libyan Desert covers western Egypt, north-west Sudan and practically the whole of Libya. It stretches a thousand miles southward from the Mediterranean, and more than a thousand miles west from the Nile Valley to the hills of Tunisia. Huge areas are covered by seas of giant dunes. In the south-east the surface is broken by the escarpment of the Gilf Kebir plateau, and the mountains of Uweinat, Kissu and Archenu. In the south-west, the Tibesti Mountains, rising to 10,000 feet, mark the border with Chad and Niger, then provinces of French Equatorial Africa and French West Africa respectively.

When Italy declared war on 10 June 1940, the British in Egypt faced a possible attack from Libya, and also from Eritrea and Abyssinia (now Ethiopia). Communication between Egypt and the Sudan lay through the Red Sea, which could be threatened or even closed by the Italian Navy, and along the Nile Valley, which could be attacked from the west. The Italians had based aircraft and motorized *Auto-Saharan* units capable of desert operations at Kufra Oasis, 650 miles from the Nile. It was feared that this force might attack Wadi Halfa, in the Nile Valley, in an attempt to cut the Egypt–Sudan line of communication. The Italians might also advance into Chad. Here lay some of the airfields used by the air route from British West Africa to the Middle East. Aircraft reinforcing the Middle East were unloaded from freighters at Takoradi in the Gold Coast (now Ghana) and flown across the sea to Nigeria, into Chad (Free French from August 1940), across the Sudan to Khartoum, and down the Nile Valley to Egypt.

In the First World War the frontiers of Egypt had been guarded by Light Car Patrols (LCP) in Ford cars. They had twice defeated Senussi tribesmen led by Germans and Turks. Now there was no such force at the disposal of General Sir Archibald Wavell, the General Officer Commanding-in-Chief Middle East; and any techniques they may have learned for driving in the desert had been forgotten by the soldiers in Egypt. Fortunately a man who had arrived in Cairo by mistake was about to put this right.

Major R. A. Bagnold Royal Signals had served as a sapper officer in France in the First World War, and between the wars in Egypt. Accompanied by a like-minded group of fellow officers, he had put his spare time in Egypt to good use. Bagnold remembered that they:

> drove model T Ford cars out into the desert at a time when people thought that cars were for use on roads, and there were no roads out into the Western Desert, only in the Delta. A group of Tank Corps, Engineer and Signals officers drove out into Libyan desert further than anyone before. We had to navigate by dead reckoning and the stars. It was like the ocean. Only the Egyptian part of the Libyan desert had been mapped.
>
> It [the desert] is waterless, therefore there are no people. It rains in one place on average once in about seventy years. There's a lot of water along the Mediterranean coast, but within fifty miles of the coast it doesn't rain. [In the desert] there are oases where artesian wells exist, from water that has fallen elsewhere.

Most of Bagnold's fellow officers and his superiors predicted that he would fail to cross the sand seas, would bog down, get lost, and would probably die of thirst. They were wrong, and these expeditions traversed much of the desert in Egypt to the Sudanese border, and into Italian territory in Cyrenaica. In the process they learned a great deal.

> The magnetic compass was unreliable, because you carried a lot of metal spare parts, like a spare back spring. When this was removed [to replace a broken part], the magnetic compass had to be reset. If you wanted to take a bearing, you had to stop, get out of the car and walk away. Which meant delay. It was quite hopeless for long-distance travel. As the sun shone all the time, and every day, it was obvious we could use the sun.

At first they employed the sun compass used by the LCPs of the First World War. This model was simply a modified sun-dial. It had a spike in the centre of a rotating dial on which was marked a pointer. The navigator took a bearing on a distant object, lined up the pointer on it, and drove keeping the shadow from the spike on the pointer on the dial. It had disadvantages. The sun's azimuth changes constantly, so about every twenty minutes they had to stop to adjust the bearing. The dial was not marked in degrees, so there was no accurate method of allowing for detours made necessary by impassable terrain. Bagnold modified the LCP sun compass, by adding a circular plate marked to show both bearing and sun's azimuth. A sun compass has the advantage over a magnetic compass that it gives true instead of magnetic bearings. The navigator rode in the front vehicle, with his map on a board overlaid with tracing paper. Thus he was able to record any deviations in course. Bagnold:

> We found that on a wiggly journey of a hundred miles, avoiding obstacles, going round sand dunes etc, we were very cross if the dead reckoning was wrong by a mile. The distance being measured by the speedometer of the car.

The navigation could be checked at night by taking sun or star shots with a theodolite, as a sailor uses a sextant at sea. They also learned a great deal about conservation of water:

> One lost water when the radiator began to boil, and blew water off through the overflow. So instead of having a free overflow pipe, we led the water into a can half full of water on the side of the car, so it would condense in the can. When that began to boil too it would spurt boiling water over the driver, who would have to stop. All we had to do was turn into wind, wait for perhaps a minute, there'd be a gurgling noise, and all the water would be sucked back into the radiator, which was full to the brim.

No one had tried crossing the big dunes of the Sand Sea in a vehicle, let alone a two-wheel drive 1920s Ford truck (lorry in the British parlance of the time). When they came across the first huge, whale-backed dune, Bagnold drove at it at forty miles an hour:

> A ... glaring wall of yellow shot up high ... in front of us. The lorry tipped violently backwards, and we rose as in a lift, smoothly and without vibration. We floated up.... All the accustomed car movements had ceased; only the speedometer told us we were still moving fast.... Instead of sticking deep in loose sand at the bottom as instinct and experience both

foretold, we were now . . . a hundred feet above the ground . . . nearing a smooth surface . . . nearly level.[1]

Over a number of years, Bagnold's trips had succeeded in crossing the Sand Sea for the first time. On one particular trip they covered over 6,000 miles. They learned the techniques of desert driving; how to tell the going by the colour of the sand; how to unstick bogged-in trucks; how to survive in this hostile environment.

Going round the junk shops in Cairo, we found heavy steel channels which were used in the First World War for roofing dugouts. They were about five feet long, one could carry one under each arm, just. You put them under the back wheels. During the Second World War every vehicle in the Army [in the desert] was equipped with sand channels. But the first time we used them successfully was in 1927.

Never in our peacetime travels had we imagined that war could ever reach the enormous empty solitudes of the inner desert, walled off by sheer distance, lack of water, and impassable seas of sand dunes. Little did we dream that any of the special equipment and techniques we had evolved for very long-distance travel, and for navigation, would ever be put to serious use. I may add without unfair criticism, that the army authorities shared in this lack of second sight. In peacetime our troops had never trained for a desert war, as officially we were never going to be at war with Italy.

When the Second World War started Bagnold, who had retired as a major, was recalled as a reservist and was on a troop ship bound for East Africa. Following a collision in the Mediterranean, it put into Port Said for extended repairs. He went to Cairo to visit friends:

A notice appeared in the *Egyptian Gazette*, announcing the return of Major Bagnold to Egypt, and expressing gratification at this evidence that the War Office was at last trying to fit square pegs into square holes. In reality I had landed in Egypt owing to the collision at sea, while on my way to Kenya, of which country I knew nothing useful at all.

Wavell got to hear of Bagnold's presence in Egypt and cancelled his posting to Kenya. At first he was sent to serve with the Armoured Division, the only fighting formation in the Middle East at that time. Later he held a signals appointment on Wavell's staff.

The coastal plateau, which the Army called the Western Desert, was firm and open; ideal country for mechanised troops, but totally unlike the broken, dune-infested country farther inland. Our army knew nothing of either the difficulties or the possibilities of operations in the vast dry hinterland. In the General Staff Offices in Cairo I could find only one small-scale map that extended beyond the western frontier of Egypt. It was dated 1915, and contained little more up-to-date information than Rohlfs [an early explorer] brought back in 1874.

The Italians declared war, France collapsed. It became important to discover whether the enemy intended using Kufra for offensive action against us. We had absolutely no contacts with the place, 700 miles away across the dunes and waterless desert, and no suitable aircraft that could do the double range. The only solution was to drive into inner Libya and find out. I took my courage in both hands and sent a note – I asked a friend to put it on the C.-in-C.'s desk. Within half an hour I was sent for and Wavell was alone.

He said, 'Tell me about this.'

He sat me in an armchair, and I told him what I thought was wrong. 'We ought to have some mobile ground scouting force, even a very small scouting force, to be able to penetrate the desert to the west of Egypt, so see what was going on. Because we had no information on what the Italians might be doing.'

He said, 'What if you find the Italians are not doing anything in the interior at all?'

I replied, without thinking, 'How about some piracy on the high desert?'

His rather stern face broke into a broad grin, 'Can you be ready in six weeks?'

'Yes, provided . . .'

'Yes I know, there'll be opposition and delay.'

He rang a bell, his Chief of Staff came in [Major General Arthur Smith].

'Arthur, Major Bagnold needs a talisman. Get this typed out and I'll sign it right away: "I wish that any request by Major Bagnold in person should be met instantly and without question."'

Within six weeks we had got together a volunteer force of New Zealanders. Their division had arrived in Egypt, and the ship carrying their arms and equipment had been sunk. So they were at a loose end. I chose them because I wanted responsible volunteers who knew how to look after things and maintain things, rather than the British Tommy who is apt to be wasteful.

Many New Zealanders were farmers, used to maintaining vehicles, and often owning a car; rare among the Tommies of the time. Bagnold organized his force into three patrols; R, T and W. Each consisted of two officers and about thirty men. Captain P. A. Clayton who had been one of Bagnold's desert companions pre-war commanded T Patrol. Captain E. C. Mitford commanded W Patrol, and Second Lieutenant D. G. Steele, R Patrol, originally the resupply patrol. Each patrol travelled in a 15-cwt light car, and ten 30-cwt trucks. Patrol weapons consisted of ten First World War Lewis guns, four Boys anti-tank rifles, one 37-mm Bofors light anti-aircraft gun, pistols and rifles. The Bofors was removed from its normal mount, and fitted so that it could fire astern or broadside from a specially modified 30-cwt truck. Later the patrol strength was halved to one officer and eighteen men in five or six trucks. The Lewis guns were replaced by Browning machine-guns and twin Vickers Ks, and the Boys and Bofors by .5-inch machine-guns and 20-mm Bredas.

The selection of trucks was made by Bagnold. Nothing the British motor industry produced at the time was suitable.

Harding-Newman [another of his pre-war desert expedition comrades] and I tested out a collection of the most likely American trucks, and I picked on an ordinary commercial Chevrolet 30-cwt model. By racing round to all the dealers in Egypt, Harding-Newman could raise only fourteen new truck chassis of our chosen type. The remaining nineteen had to be begged, second-hand, off the Egyptian Army. So had the sun compasses.

The navigators were trained by Lieutenant Kennedy Shaw, the Intelligence Officer, and Lance-Corporal Croucher, who had a Merchant Navy Mate's ticket. Communications were by Army Number 11 sets selected by Bagnold, a signals expert. The LRDG signallers using morse communicated over ranges of more than 1,000 miles, although the sets had originally been designed to work over a range of only thirty miles. All patrols took fitters and a range of spares. The fitters were capable of improvising parts for vehicles if necessary. Very rarely was a truck abandoned because it broke down.[2] Most trucks were lost to enemy action.

The first patrol was a small-scale reconnaissance led by Clayton in two light cars. Their task was to check the Jalo–Kufra track used by the Italians to supply Kufra and Uweinat from Benghazi. Having traversed the Egyptian Sand Sea, they crossed the frontier and entered territory new to them. After crossing a hundred miles of level gravel plain, and before striking the track, they encountered a second sand sea, not marked on Italian maps, the Kalansho Sand Sea. Captain Crichton-Stuart described it on a later patrol:

> This is but a continuation of the Egyptian Sand Sea, which from Siwa sweeps west into Libya, and south again. In shape it resembles an irregular horseshoe.

Clayton's men spent three days watching the track, the first of dozens of road-watch operations by the LRDG. They saw nothing. Later another patrol discovered that the Italians used an easier track further to the west. However, Clayton's reconnaissance had not been wasted. The route he had discovered, protected by the horseshoe of the Egyptian and Kalansho Sand Seas, was to be a favourite with the LRDG. He also brought encouraging news about the capacity of enemy aircraft to spot small groups of vehicles in the desert. He was overflown several times, apparently without being seen.

On 5 September 1940, the whole of the LRDG slipped out of Cairo. Bagnold:

> General Wavell came personally to wish us good hunting. He loved little enterprises of this kind.

The first leg was across the Egyptian Sand Sea to a cairn on the Egyptian–Libyan frontier, erected by Clayton in the 1930s, called Big Cairn. At Ain Dalla, east of the Sand Sea, the full loads were put on the trucks. Each carried two tons. Bagnold:

> From here we led up to the backs of the great dunes. To get a heavy truck up 200 to 300 feet of loose sand at a slope of 1 in 3, you have to charge it very fast. (I had selected the trucks with that in view; they could do fifty and more.) But it takes a lot of confidence to charge at full speed into what looks like a vertical wall of dazzling yellow. The drivers, overcautious, floundered axle-deep. That day we travelled only 10 miles, and I began to doubt if we should ever get across those endless sand ranges with those loads.
>
> But the New Zealanders were learning marvellously fast. Next day we did 30 more miles, and damaged only one truck. The following noon we topped the last dune, and looked out over the flat sand plains of Libya.

The route as far as the Big Cairn had been pioneered by Bagnold and Clayton in the 1930s. They had marked it on a published map, of which surely the Italians would have a copy. Bagnold expected the enemy to be waiting somewhere on the route, or at least be checking it from the air. But there was no sign of enemy activity. After being resupplied by R Patrol, the other two split, W to investigate to the north of Kufra, T to the south. R went back to their base at Siwa for another load of supplies.

W Patrol went through the Kalansho Sand Sea to the Jalo–Kufra track. They took the opportunity afforded by a sandstorm to visit two enemy air strips. Here they destroyed 2,500 gallons of fuel, took five prisoners, and captured the official mail which gave details of the Italian deployment in the inner desert. The heat at midday was stunning. All the pre-war Bagnold expeditions had been done in winter. Bagnold:

> We could not travel at midday at all, but lay under our trucks and gasped. Mitford's log read:
>
> > 'On this and the three preceding days there were a number of cases of heat stroke among the men. It was remarkable to notice in the shade of almost every stone a dead or dying bird.'
>
> Nor was it comforting to know that this kind of wind had killed three German explorers in this very area a few years before.

Clayton's T Patrol drove as far as the frontier post inside Chad Province at Tekro and found no sign of enemy activity en route. Bagnold:

> Our information changed things a great deal. The staff in Cairo decided that the role of the LRDG should now become a more offensive one. Graziani [the Italian General in charge of the enemy offensive into Egypt] was still at Sidi Barrani, short of transport, and we were to aggravate his worries. Wavell gave us a free hand to stir up trouble in any part of Libya we liked, with the object of drawing off as much enemy transport and troops as possible from the coastal front to defend their remote and useless inland garrisons.

Wavell was hatching his own plans, which would come to fruition with the O'Connor offensive in mid-December 1940, which eventually pushed the Italians out of Cyrenaica. Meanwhile Graziani remained supine at Sidi Barrani.

In October, R Patrol, led by now Captain Steele, laid mines on the track in the Gebel Uweinat area, which lies on the junction of the Libyan,

Egyptian and Sudanese borders. Here they found and destroyed an enemy bomb dump, and 160 drums of petrol. The next month, Captain Mitford's W Patrol attacked an Italian post near Uweinat. Lieutenant Sutherland and Trooper Willcox were awarded the MC and MM respectively, the first of many decorations to be awarded to the peerless soldiers of the New Zealand Expeditionary Force in the Second World War. Meanwhile, in the north, Captain Clayton's T Patrol attacked the fort at Auguila. Bagnold:

> The patrols worked by themselves, hundreds of miles from help. They seemed to the enemy to appear from nowhere, as if out of the fourth dimension, which, in a way the great empty desert was. The Sand Sea became our secret highway into Italian territory. I do not think they even found out how we got through. They had not bought Clayton's map after all. By simultaneous appearances at places 600 miles apart we managed to exaggerate our strength. Graziani had to provide armed escorts for all his supply columns in the interior of eastern Libya, and to patrol the long Kufra routes by air. Moreover the strength and armament of every garrison was greatly increased, which caused a still bigger demand for transport to keep them supplied.

The LRDG had achieved its aim in eastern Libya, with the exception of taking and holding Kufra. However, this would have to wait. The army in Egypt could not spare troops and transport to defend and supply a garrison in Kufra. Bagnold decided to attack Murzuk, the capital of the Fezzan, some 1,500 miles from Cairo and 500 miles south of Tripoli. The nearest friendly troops were the Free French in Chad. To preserve surprise it was necessary to avoid the one desert route found by the Italians, and the water holes. Bagnold selected a route north of the Ribiana Sand Sea and through the broken lava beds of the Haruj. Bagnold learned that:

> the Italians had tried and failed, but we did not take much account of that.

Because of the distance involved, Bagnold also decided to see if the Free French in Chad could send petrol by camel to a suitable RV north of the Tibesti Mountains. GHQ in Cairo had had no contact with the French in Chad since the fall of France six months before. Chad was one of the few Free French colonies, so it was important to find out if its garrison was prepared to help. Bagnold flew from Khartoum to Fort

Lamy on the shores of Lake Chad. Here he met Lieutenant-Colonel d'Ornano, the second-in-command in Chad, who with all his officers expressed keenness to take part in the war. In return for being allowed to join the raid with a few of his men, d'Ornano agreed to meet the LRDG patrols with a supply column.

At this stage the LRDG was reorganized. For a while the New Zealanders could not provide reinforcements for the LRDG, and some men were required back in their own units. Later more New Zealanders were released for the LRDG. In December 1940 officers and soldiers of 3rd Battalion Coldstream Guards and 2nd Battalion Scots Guards formed G Patrol under Captain M. D. D. Crichton-Stuart Scots Guards, taking over the vehicles and equipment of W Patrol. Crichton-Stuart wrote a vivid report, graded SECRET at the time, of G Patrol's first operation:

We spent three busy weeks learning the ways of the trucks, weapon training, doing a short training run in sand dunes near Fayum, and finally in detailed preparations for a great expedition which was shrouded in secrecy.

Christmas Day was spent in the old fashioned way. The next morning the Patrol Commander [Crichton-Stuart always refers to himself in the third person] announced that we were to start that afternoon and we would be away '40 days or more' – long enough to clear the thickest heads at any rate. At 2.45 p.m. on Boxing Day, the Patrol left the Citadel [in Cairo], together with a New Zealand Patrol [T] under Major P. A. Clayton who was for many years in the Egyptian Desert Survey. He, as senior patrol commander, commanded the whole expedition.

We carried as navigator Lieutenant W. Kennedy-Shaw, who had done as much desert travelling by camel and car as anyone alive, and who came from a Government archaeological job in Palestine.

In addition to the usual LRDG patrol weapons they took:

As a final, and most fortunate afterthought, a 2-inch mortar.

We also carried with us a famous old Senussi Chieftain, Sheikh Abd El Seif Al Nasr, one of the last to hold out against the Italians in Libya, together with his personal slave, a coal black gentleman, who was immediately and affectionately christened 'Midnight' by the Patrol. The old man welcomed this opportunity of a trip to his old tribal lands, so long as he got the chance to shoot an Italian or two.

At the first night stop the Patrol was briefed that the aim was a raid into the Fezzan in cooperation with the French, to coincide with the main advance of the Western Desert Force along the coast, under Lieutenant General Richard O'Connor, which had begun on 9 December 1940.

At Ain Dalla, they filled their water containers from the artesian well and:

> washed, and most of G Patrol shaved, as habits die hard. It was forbidden to use the carried water for washing and shaving.

The next morning the guardsmen encountered their first sand sea. Crichton-Stuart:

> The Egyptian Sand Sea, in area about the size of Ireland, stretches from Siwa Oasis almost to Sudan, along the Libyan frontier. Since the great disaster to Cambyses's army of 40,000 men, which attempted to invade Siwa from Luxor [in 522 BC], and disappeared to a man in the sand, it has been rather avoided by military bodies, and all but the fewest travellers. The Italians felt safe behind its impenetrability, but previous patrols had proved a way across, and we were now taking advantage of this secret to cross it. That night it froze, and was bitterly cold for the first few hours next morning, so that we were glad of the special sheepskin coats with which we had been issued.
>
> The parallel lines of dunes run almost north and south, rising to some 500 feet in the centre of the Sand Sea. Packed and shaped by the prevailing wind over thousands of years, this Sand Sea compares in shape and form with a great Atlantic swell, long rollers, crested here and there, with great troughs between. It is utterly lifeless, without a blade of grass or a stone to break the monotony of sand and sky.

By 31 December 1940, dunes began to lessen and the patrols camped a few miles short of the Libyan frontier.

> We had come about 500 miles from Cairo, nearly 150 miles across the Sand Sea. A few of us saw the New Year in round the camp fire, but most of us were in 'bed', for it was freezing again.

Away from the coast and enemy garrisons, it was usually quite safe to light camp fires and cook. David Lloyd Owen, who joined the LRDG later remembered:

Most of the battles in the desert went on within 50 miles of the coast. When we were a long way south, say 200 miles, at night we never bothered to put sentries out. Down south you hardly ever saw a track of a vehicle. And if you did we knew exactly who had made them; 1920 Bagnold's cars, or ourselves. We could read those tracks.

By 2 January 1941, T and G Patrols had crossed the gravel plain and the Kalansho Sand Sea. From their camp they could see the Kilo post on the main track from Kufra to Jalo.

It was the most dangerous spot on our route, as we or our tracks might be spotted by the daily air patrol the enemy was known to keep. For this reason we started off at first light next morning, in freezing weather again. We crossed the 'road' consisting of thousands of vehicle tracks spread over half a mile in wide formation, and ran on fast for many miles. With no windshields, at high speed, and in the bitter cold, conditions were almost arctic. The Patrol Commander, who with wise foresight had brought his Blue-Grey great-coat was best off. At last many miles west of the track we stopped for breakfast. This day, 3 January, we covered nearly 200 miles in all, over mostly good 'Serir' [gravel plain].

LRDG rations were wholesome. The daily ration scale is shown in Appendix A (page 423). It included menu suggestions, and breakfast might consist of porridge, or fried bacon with oatmeal fritter, the latter being porridge dropped into hot bacon fat.

On 5 January 1941, having covered 1,100 miles in nine days, Clayton left to contact the French. Kennedy-Shaw and Lieutenant Gibbs, Coldstream Guards, the second-in-command of G Patrol, went to reconnoitre a route to the north-east of the Tibesti Mountains.

The remainder under Crichton-Stuart spent some three days idly, but time was passed with a rifle meeting, a 2-inch mortar meeting, some PT, and some arms drill, the standard of the latter contrasting oddly with the beards and general turnout.

At midday on 7 January, Clayton returned laden with French and petrol. The leader of the French, Colonel d'Ornano, was a magnificent figure of a man, very tall, in native uniform, complete with burnous and monocle. The meeting was celebrated in Pernod. That evening there was a council of war, at which representatives of England, Scotland, New Zealand, France, and Libya attended.

There were two high spots. First the arrival of a long wireless message from Cairo giving fearsome and rather incredible details of the defences of Murzuk, from a document captured at Sidi Barrani. The other was when the old chieftain admitted that some years ago he had successfully besieged the place for two months. The result of the conference was a unanimous decision to make straight for Murzuk, missing a smaller Italian outpost called Uau el Kebir, which might give our presence away by wireless. For Murzuk was the capital of South-West Libya, and a worthier object for our surprise.

The town of Murzuk, set in a belt of palms, had an airfield protected by machine-gun posts, a stone fort and a sizeable garrison. Without artillery, the two patrols had little chance of capturing the fort, unless the garrison could be panicked into surrendering, but they could destroy any aircraft on the strip. The main danger lay in the fort summoning help from the Italian air base in Hon, 250 miles to the north. About five miles outside the town, Clayton and Kennedy-Shaw discovered, by questioning a local woman they met on the road, that the town was quiet, and their approach had not been noticed. Clayton judged that they would be unable to carry out close reconnaissance without disclosing their presence, and decided to attack at once. The plan was for T Patrol under Lieutenant Ballantyne to attack the airfield (aerodrome in 1940s terminology), while G Patrol with a troop of T Patrol under command was to keep the occupants of the fort busy. They had driven 1,440 miles to pay this call on the Italian garrison. Crichton-Stuart:

> As the column entered the belt of palms, a solitary cyclist met it. This gentleman, who proved to be the Postmaster, was added to the party with his bicycle. As the convoy approached the fort, above the main central tower of which the Italian flag flew proudly, the Guard turned out. We were rather sorry for them, but they probably never knew what hit them.

T Patrol detached from the column and headed for the airfield. G Patrol deployed in a semicircle east to west of the fort, about 250 to 500 yards off, and, with their trucks under cover, opened fire. After hitting some men, a car and a truck trying to enter the fort, no more confirmed hits were observed. However, Lieutenant Gibbs with both patrols' 2-inch mortars managed to lob some bombs on to the roof of the main tower, which started a fire and gutted the central block. Meanwhile intermittent fire was returned from the fort. Crichton- Stuart:

A huge column of black smoke from the direction of the aerodrome told us that the New Zealanders had been successful. On reaching the aerodrome they found the Italians running to man their posts. They forestalled one lot and knocked out another with their Bofors, after a little trouble. Unfortunately this machine-gun post killed Colonel d'Ornano, who was travelling with Clayton, when he ran on to it unexpectedly. When the remaining forty-odd Italians had been rounded up, the hangar was burnt, together with three fully loaded Reconnaissance Bombers, petrol, oil, bombs and other equipment. Finally four prisoners were selected from the rest, and Clayton fired a white flare as a signal for the withdrawal.

We never saw the signal, or sand had begun to blow, and the Italians had brought all their machine-guns to bear on us. Any movement brought down heavy fire. 'Midnight' made himself extremely unpopular with one post. He would fire his rifle (he had knocked off the sights because they obstructed his view), then stand up and shout abuse at his enemies. When the signal for withdrawal finally arrived at about 4 o'clock by hand, the Patrol Commander [Crichton-Stuart] had to run the gauntlet to get round the various posts. It seemed that we must suffer considerable casualties in extracting crews and trucks, and getting away in the soft sand. But God most opportunely sent the wind, as with the Armada, and the whole Patrol withdrew in a thick sandstorm to the aerodrome, where the Italian prisoners sat in a miserable huddle (we couldn't take them because of the problem of rations, and the French were very annoyed that we did not otherwise dispose of them). We called the roll. All the Patrol and trucks were present. One Guardsman was badly wounded in the leg, and several trucks were holed without serious damage. The New Zealanders had had a couple of their men slightly wounded, and Sergeant Hewson who commanded the New Zealand troop with our patrol was shot dead. We cut back on to the Hon road, on top of the escarpment where we had made our plan that morning. We buried Colonel d'Ornano and Sergeant Hewson together, while heavy firing continued from the fort, six miles away.

One of the French officers had been shot through the leg; he had however, cauterised the wound by applying the lighted end of his cigarette, and had not bothered to see the doctor.

Early next morning the patrols captured two Italian policemen on camels. They were from the small town of Traghen, thirty miles east of Murzuk. They were sent into town with a demand that the fort surrender:

Before a quarter of an hour had passed, a great clamour arose from the village, shouting and beating of drums. A few minutes later a procession approached carrying many flags and led by the local headman. Traghen surrendered according to ceremonial tradition.

After clearing the fort of documents and other military equipment, the patrols moved on, taking the documents for future examination and burning the equipment. A further two forts south of Murzuk were left alone after an initial probing attack, because they were too strongly held for the patrols equipped with unarmoured vehicles and nothing more formidable than a Bofors.

Clayton ended operations in the Fezzan in mid-January 1941, and drove south to Tummo on the French border. At this stage the Medical Officer's light truck broke down for lack of a spare. Ahead lay the prospect of a 1,000-mile tow to the Free French base at Faya, their next port of call. The badly wounded Guardsman Wilson was transferred to another truck. Part of the route lay over the rugged terrain of the foothills of the Tibesti Mountains. Crichton-Stuart:

> We learned the real meaning of '*terrain chaotique*' [marked on the French maps]. We came into the worst country we ever experienced. From broken rocky plateaux we dropped steeply into rock-bound valleys, only finding a way out with great difficulty by putting flat stones over the soft sandy patches between the stony going, and charging the trucks up the escarpments one by one. Somehow the tow kept up by masterly driving, even over giant sand dunes which choked the way between great black crags with vertical cliffs. We had to go round these, struggling through the soft dunes, and down steep sand slopes. The country was wild and magnificent, but not exactly ideal motoring: springs, tyres and drivers were hard tested.
>
> At last we wound our way, with great difficulty, down several broken black escarpments, in one of which Gibbs found caves full of rock paintings and carvings of animals. We came quite suddenly on a narrow plain through which a track ran east and west. We had struck the track to French West Africa – to Timbuctoo! But had covered only nine miles in the whole morning.

Eventually the patrols reached the Free French fort at Zouar situated in a broad green valley. It was day 22 of the patrol. Here Clayton found a message from Bagnold, who had flown from Cairo to Fort Lamy. It asked how many trucks were fit to join with the French who intended to attack Kufra Oasis. After the death of d'Ornano, Colonel Leclerc succeeded him in command of the Free French in Chad. His real name was the Vicomte de Haute Cloque, but he had adopted a *nom de guerre* to protect his family when he escaped from France. Eventually he was to lead his force in an epic march to join up with Montgomery's 8th Army in Tripoli in February 1943. He would enter Paris in August 1944 as a major general commanding a Free French armoured division. The start of his long march home was to be the seizure of Kufra. The LRDG was to come temporarily under his command. Crichton-Stuart:

> Kufra Oasis, or rather Oases, for there are a number of outlying smaller ones, is the largest and most important in Libya, dominating the whole of the south-east of the country. Bounded by sand seas to the north, west and east, and by 350 miles of barren desert, with only two single wells to Tekro, the nearest French outpost to the south, its natural defences were formidable enough. Add to this a very large stone fort with artillery, a garrison of some 1,200 to 1,400, and a squadron of bombers.

Bagnold flew up to Zouar from Fort Lamy. The next day he took Kennedy-Shaw, whose intelligence reports were needed in Cairo, and Guardsman Wilson with him. Wilson eventually arrived in hospital in Cairo, having flown, via Faya, Fort Lamy and Khartoum, some 7,000 miles.

The patrols arrived at Faya on 24 January to be inspected by Leclerc. Here they found a spare for the towed truck:

> Surely a record tow of over 900 miles over unexplored country, and a very fine feat of driving by Guardsman Roberts, Coldstream Guards.

recorded Crichton-Stuart.

> Meanwhile the Patrol Commanders conferred with Colonel Leclerc and his staff officer on the Kufra expedition. The two patrols were to act as an advance guard to the force, which comprised some 350–400 Senegalese armed with rifles and knives and led by French officers. They had few automatic weapons and one 75 mm portée [small portable gun]. Their transport consisted of a number of Bedfords [small British trucks], and all the lorries in Chad, commandeered, and they had insufficient petrol to get them back if the attack failed. They were to be supported by a Free French Squadron of Blenheims [obsolete British bombers], and two Lysanders [small British Army cooperation aircraft]. Over 350 miles against a well-

defended fort and garrison including guns. It was a desperate venture, but they were quite determined to strike the first blow for the Free French at any cost.

The two LRDG patrols left Faya on 27 January, reaching Tekro two days later. They went on to Sarra, where G Patrol remained in reserve for a day, while Clayton motored on to Bishara with T Patrol. G Patrol found the well at Sarra had been destroyed by the Italians, so clearly they had been alerted. The next day G Patrol drove about twenty-five miles north of Sarra. Crichton-Stuart:

We camped in the open plain, expecting to catch up Clayton by midday the following day. We were eating breakfast at sunrise, when the alarm was given: vehicles were heard, then seen approaching fast from the north. As we opened out for action, we recognised the New Zealand trucks, without Clayton, and with four trucks missing. They bore a tale of disaster.

They had reached Bishara the previous morning, to find the well blown in and fresh tracks around it. As they moved north-east towards the Gebel Sherif where they intended to lie up, they were spotted by an Italian reconnaissance plane. Clayton, however, was confident in his ability to lie up among rocks concealed from the air, after experience from previous patrols, and carried on. They dispersed and camouflaged in a rocky wadi between two gebels, posting sentries in the gebels. Later in the afternoon, the sentries reported vehicles approaching, and at the same time the reconnaissance plane began circling overhead. Just after Clayton had given the word to pack up, the plane dived on them, and heavy cannon and machine-gun fire was opened up on them from one end of the wadi, where the enemy seem to have got into position unseen. The cannon were using explosive [ammunition] and almost immediately three trucks were blown up, with their loads of petrol and ammunition. One was the truck on which Guardsmen Winchester and Easton were travelling [attached to T Patrol]. The latter was last seen manning his Lewis gun and firing steadily as the remaining trucks got out of the other end of the wadi. They were rallying there in preparation for a counter-attack, when three Savoia bombers and the reconnaissance plane attacked them with bombs and machine-guns. Clayton gave the order to disperse and go south down their old tracks.

When they eventually rallied, Clayton and his truck and crew, who were seen to stop after being machine-gunned from the air, were missing. Two men were slightly wounded, a corporal had been seen killed at his gun. The prisoners were all believed killed as they were on the trucks which had blown up. Easton, Winchester, a New Zealander Moore, and an RAOC fitter Tighe were missing.

Ballantyne, now in command of the patrol, and his men were all convinced that if the four had not been killed, as they thought most probable, they must all be prisoners. They believed the enemy to have two armoured cars, and a cannon mounted on a double tracked vehicle, together with trucked machine-gunners – the remaining Auto Saharan Company which we knew to be based at Kufra. Against these and the bombers the French were heading for disaster. Clayton's last instructions to Ballantyne had been for both patrols to return and warn the French, if he did not turn up.

Accordingly they continued south, taking Captain Mercer Nairne [the British Military Attaché in Chad who had flown up with Bagnold from Lamy, and remained with the LRDG] to interpret, while we finished our breakfast. [Like good members of the Brigade of Guards they were not to be panicked]. Then believing Easton and Winchester and the other two killed, or at least captured, and expecting the bombers at any time, we turned despondently south. Just south of Sarra at about 8.30 a.m. a cautious enemy reconnaissance plane spotted us, but as we continued to put more miles of good going between us and Kufra, we began to feel that the rumoured shortage of aero petrol in Kufra was true. It was nearly midday before we met the advance elements of the French. Finally quite late in the afternoon we found Colonel Leclerc some 40 miles north of Tekro.

Through Captain Mercer Nairne, Ballantyne told Colonel Leclerc his story. The latter listened attentively and asked if there was any chance of finding Clayton and the others. Ballantyne confirmed that the enemy were close on Clayton's tail when his truck was stopped, and reconfirmed his belief that there was no hope of finding the others. Then Colonel Leclerc asked what what was known of the Italian outposts at Gebel Uweinat. Finally he left to confer with his officers, asking Crichton-Stuart, Mercer Nairne and Ballantyne to rendezvous with him next morning to receive his decision. If the attack was postponed as it might have to be, the [LRDG] Patrols would not be able to remain because of shortage of rations and water. Another danger presented itself: with Clayton there might have been captured his maps, papers, codes, and plans of dumps, in which case the dump between Kufra and Uweinat that we were relying on, would more than likely be located and destroyed by the enemy before we could get there.

That evening we opened our first mail since Christmas. At the same time the Patrol Commander opened the 'Important Intelligence' from Cairo, to find much valuable information. Had Clayton waited for it, he would never have gone so gaily ahead, for we learnt that the Italians were on the alert and expecting attack, having intercepted some French wireless messages, and spotted a reconnaissance party earlier near Sarra.

Next morning, leaving the patrols where they were, the Patrol Commanders went forward to find Colonel Leclerc. There was a certain Gallic abandon about the French method of advance: no one knowing where their headquarters, or anyone else was, and everyone following a track of his own. They did not find Colonel Leclerc until late afternoon just south of Sarra. They gave him their intelligence, after which he released the patrols from his command. He would not abandon, but would only postpone, the advance on Kufra. According to the original contract, the attack would have taken place this night, and we were to have been released two or three days later. As it was the French could provide us with neither water, rations, nor petrol, so that we had to leave them to carry on alone. Crichton-Stuart agreed to take a French party to reconnoitre Uweinat on our way home, and to mark the way there, and also to leave one New Zealand truck with a second navigator, Lance-Corporal Kendall, with the French for ten days. Colonel Leclerc thanked them for what they had done in saving his own force from disaster, and promised to send a party up to the place of the ambush as soon as possible. Then they said farewell to him, and turned south again at sunset.

It was later learned that machine-gun fire punctured two tyres, the radiator and petrol tank on Clayton's truck. The crew changed the tyres, and refilled the radiator, but ran out of fuel. The aircraft continued to attack, and enemy ground troops followed up. Clayton was wounded in the arm, and he and two New Zealanders in his truck were forced to surrender. He was awarded the DSO for his leadership with the LRDG since its inception, and particularly the raid on Murzuk. He had only come from Tanganyika to help Bagnold get the LRDG started, and on return from this patrol was to have gone to the Transjordan Survey to finish his career and retire on a pension. Crichton-Stuart:

On the wireless from Cairo we heard that our codes were compromised. We also learned that Clayton had not had time to destroy his codes, maps, dump lists, and papers. An ingenious new code was improvised at the same time, based on the Regimental numbers of various Guardsmen.

The four men from T Patrol, who were missing believed killed, were a New Zealander (Trooper R. J. Moore), two guardsmen (Easton and

Winchester) and an RAOC fitter (Tighe). They hid among rocks until the enemy had gone. Moore persuaded them not to give themselves up, but to walk south along their old tracks, rather than north to Kufra, by far the shortest distance. They had a two-gallon can of water, and a tin of jam. Tighe who was feeling the effects of an old operation could not keep up and was left behind on the fifth day, with his share of water, to continue at his own pace. The other three reached Sarra on the sixth day. Tighe made Sarra a day later and was found three days later by a French reconnaissance party returning from Kufra. On the eighth day, Easton, who had struggled along bravely despite a wound in his neck, dropped behind. Moore and Winchester were spotted by two French aircraft, who could not land because of the rough ground but dropped food and a bottle of water to the two men. The food could not be found, and the cork had come out of the bottle, leaving a mouthful of water. Winchester became too weak to continue. Moore pushed on. Easton was found by the French reconnaissance party fifty-five miles south of Sarra, lying on the ground but still alive. Despite the efforts of a French doctor to save him, he died that evening. Winchester, delirious but still standing, was found ten miles farther on. Ten miles farther south they overtook Moore, who had been wounded in the foot but dressed it daily, still walking. He had covered 210 miles since the ambush at Gebel Sharif, and believed he could have reached Tekro, 80 miles away, in another three days. Eventually the three survivors were flown via Sarra and Fort Lamy to Khartoum, and on by boat to Cairo. Moore was awarded the DCM. Winchester returned to his patrol and eventually to 2nd Battalion Scots Guards.

Setting out on 4 February, the two LRDG patrols had 1,000 miles to go to reach their base in Cairo, via Uweinat and Kharga Oasis. On 8 February they found two LRDG trucks at Kharga waiting for them, loaded with fuel, cigarettes and chocolate. Crichton-Stuart:

We left Kharga about 3 o'clock in the afternoon; at the Patrol Commander's suggestion that it would be better to run up [*sic*, down actually] the Nile Valley by night, rather than struggle through the carts, buses and animals that blocked the road by day. Our road ran along with the many hundreds of parallel camel tracks of the Darb el Arbain, the great slave route of the old days from Darfur in the Sudan to the Nile Valley. Hundreds of camel skeletons marked the last stage of this terrible [slave] journey. Having a large meal after dark, we drove on with headlights to find the Egyptian Post on the outskirts of Assiut. Now we joined the Nile Valley, and drove steadily north alongside the moonlit river. Stopping for a mug of tea at 2 o'clock, we passed the southernmost line of pyramids to the south of Cairo as dawn broke. At 8.30 on 9 February, on the 45th day of the patrol we entered the Cairo Citadel. The order of the day was: Breakfast, Bath, Barber and Beer.

We had covered some 4,300 miles in all. It is for the record hunter to work out how many records we broke for an infantry patrol. We were more interested in six weeks' pay and five days' leave.

Record or no, this patrol established the reputation of the LRDG once and for all. They had proved they could go where others, particularly the enemy. could not. They could strike, or just watch, hundreds of miles behind enemy lines, appearing and disappearing as if by magic. Not only were they the first to take the field against the enemy, but above all their professionalism in everything they did was never surpassed, and seldom equalled by any other special force. Theirs was a yardstick by which one should gauge those that came after them. The LRDG needed adventurous spirits, but never tolerated 'cowboys'. They were utterly reliable. If they said that they would arrive at an exact spot in the desert 1,000 miles away at a certain time, they almost invariably did. They made their radios work over long distances. They got the messages through. This demanded high standards of driving, maintenance and navigation. This was the legacy of Bagnold and the early members of the LRDG: a capacity for taking pains; of thinking the problem through; an intellectual rather than what we would now call a 'gung-ho' approach.

While T and G Patrols had been on the Fezzan operation, Steele's R Patrol spent two months assisting the 6th Australian Divisional Cavalry Regiment [armoured cars] in preventing the besieged Italian garrison of Giarabub, 160 miles inland from Bardia, escaping or being resupplied overland. T Patrol took over for about three weeks, until Giarabub fell to an Australian assault during a sandstorm on 22 March 1941.

Meanwhile Kufra had fallen to Leclerc. His advanced guard reached the Oasis on 7 February. They seized the airstrip and the town. Leclerc defeated the Auto-Saharan Company, which withdrew leaving the garrison without mobile protection. The Italians retired into the fort. Leclerc had far too little food and fuel to maintain his force, but he hung on. With 101 Europeans and 300 native troops, and one 75-mm gun against 64 Italians and 352 Libyans, he besieged the fort, 500 miles from his own base with nothing in between. The garrison surrendered on 1 March, although they had sufficient supplies for weeks. Leclerc withdrew to Chad, leaving a small garrison at Kufra to live on the captured Italian supplies.

By now the Germans had come to the aid of their Italian allies. Rommel with the advance party of his Afrika Korps arrived in North Africa on 12 February 1941. By the end of April, the British were back on the Egyptian frontier and the whole of Cyrenaica except Tobruk was lost. The British had to keep the Germans out of Kufra, and two oases to the north, Tazerbo and Zighen. The LRDG under Bagnold was sent to occupy Kufra. It was not the LRDG's role to act as garrison troops, but there was no one else until troops from the Sudan Defence Force could be made available in July 1941. Bagnold:

> I was made military governor of the Oases, a resplendent title rather like Lord of the Isles. It was a tantalising situation. Kufra was ideally set to be a base (which it afterwards became) from which we could have reconnoitred and made raids on the long German supply road from Tripoli, and on Italian posts inland; but we were almost immobilised for lack of petrol.

Kufra was not one oasis but several, as Bagnold describes:

> Imagine northern Europe as an empty rainless desert of sand and rock with London as Tag [the site of the fort], a little area a few miles across, with shallow artesian well water, palm groves, villages and salt lakes, and with a population of 4,000 Cyrenaicans. The suburb of Tazerbo with another 1,000 inhabitants is north-west where Liverpool is. Zighen would be near Derby, and Rebiana near Bristol cut off by a sea of dunes. Cairo would be at Copenhagen, across a sand sea. Wadi Halfa [on the Nile] would be near Munich, with waterless desert in between.

The supply problem was eventually solved by running convoys from Wadi Halfa. American-built 10-ton trucks took two to three weeks to complete the 1,300-mile round trip. These 10-tonners were even better cross-country vehicles than the 30-cwt trucks used by the LRDG, especially over really bad rocky terrain. To the members of the LRDG, Kufra meant the main oasis around the fort at Tag, and over the years it was used as a base it provided a welcome break from the desert. Frank

Harrison remembered that one of the less attractive aspects of operating without washing for weeks and sometimes months was desert sores:

> ... big open sores, all over, particularly the legs. But when we got down to Kufra, which had a salt lake, and by the time you'd been there a week and gone in the lake every day, your sores all dried up.

By now the LRDG had been expanded by recruiting a Yeomanry Patrol (Y) and a Southern Rhodesian Patrol (S). The Group was reorganized into two squadrons: A Squadron consisted of G and Y Patrols, B Squadron of R, S and T Patrols. Initially B Squadron with LRDG headquarters went to Kufra and the outlying oases, while A Squadron under Mitford operated from Siwa under command of the Western Desert Force, renamed 8th Army in June 1941:

> Siwa was a sight I never forget; the palms, and Cleopatra's pool. The buildings in Siwa were white and dazzling in the sun,

remembers Alexander Stewart, a fitter with G Patrol.

In February Major G. L. Prendergast Royal Tank Regiment joined as second-in-command. He was another of Bagnold's fellow pre-war desert explorers. When Bagnold was posted to GHQ in Cairo in August, Prendergast became the commanding officer of the LRDG. He was a qualified pilot and solved the problem that plagues the commanding officer of any unit spread over vast distances, that of keeping in personal touch with his troops, and with his superior headquarters, in this case GHQ in Cairo. The RAF never had any light aircraft to spare, so Prendergast bought two little single-engined aircraft from an Egyptian pasha. These aircraft, built by the Western Aircraft Corporation of Ohio, WACOs for short, had a range of only 300 miles, but by using pre-dumped fuel, it was possible to reach the Nile from Kufra in one day instead of ten, and the trip to patrol outposts was shortened correspondingly. The RAF, always touchy about private air forces not under their control, especially one owned by the Army, initially refused to allow the LRDG aircraft to have roundels painted on them.

About this time the Chevrolets were beginning to need replacement because of wear and tear. The only available trucks were four-wheel-drive Fords, which could carry similar loads but were less manoeuvrable.

Like all the patrols, the Yeomanry had a character of their own.

Captain David Lloyd Owen The Queen's Royal Regiment (West Surrey) joined the Yeomanry Patrol in mid-1941.

I was in the Officer Cadet Training Unit [OCTU], as a training officer. I met a friend who told me about the LRDG. He was in the Coldstream Guards and joined Guards Patrol in December 40. I was excited about his description of the patrol to Fezzan working with the Free French. I wanted to get out of Cairo. I went for my first interview with Bagnold. I had very little knowledge of the desert. I was in Palestine when the war started. I was a company commander in the first campaign at Sidi Barrani, and Tobruk. But I knew very little about vehicles. I was Regimental signal officer; at the start of the war we had no wireless sets, we communicated in Palestine with flags, and heliographs and lights, and laid line. We went into battle laying line. It was useless.

Bagnold asked me questions to which I had no answer, I knew so little.

There was a vacancy in the Yeomanry Patrol. I was not Yeomanry, I was a regular officer in the Queen's Royal Regiment. I thought my chances of acceptance were nil. But Bagnold agreed to take me on. My problem was to convince my CO of the OCTU to release me.

I was accepted to command the Yeomanry Patrol, the original commander was wounded. I found myself commanding 25 men of jolly good Yeomanry Regiments and a few from the Commandos who were without a role in the ME.

But being formed of different kind of men, the commander [of the LRDG] had a lot of different kind of instruments available to him to do the job. For example the New Zealanders were terrific on vehicles. The Yeomanry were brought up with horses. A whole Yeomanry Division had been sent to Palestine. How futile.

The special characteristics of the Yeomanry Patrol were that they were cavalrymen and their role was gaining information, they were mostly countrymen, they were not scared of being alone in the dark, like some town men. They were used to being given general direction.

It was quite new to me. I had only been in the Army about two years. I had been shot at. But was pretty inexperienced. I had to rely very heavily on some of them because they had been operating for six months. There was a whole new technique to learn. For the first time you operate behind the enemy lines, even though you are in pretty flat country, you expect to see the enemy over every rise. You do not. You have to learn the art of learning moving without exhausting the men under your command in extremes of heat and sometimes in very cold weather. You have to nurture the water and petrol; you are completely on your own. You will get no help from anyone else. I learnt a great deal from Sgt Carningham, before the war he had been a chauffeur driving a Rolls-Royce. I last saw him in 1943, and we lost touch with him.

When I first joined they were refitting in Cairo having been brought back from Siwa. After this we went straight down to Kufra, the main base for the LRDG. The equipment was ten 30-cwt Chevrolets capable of carrying up to two tons of load, or even three tons, each having two or three men, mostly three on the vehicle. They were capable of travelling 1,800 miles and the patrol could exist up to six weeks on what the vehicle carried (water, food, ammunition and petrol). Water [was] unobtainable almost anywhere. You could get it in the main oases, of which there were very few. There were a few wells. But most of them had been poisoned by the Germans if up on the coast, or poisoned by ourselves. Or filthy or rancid. I can't remember drawing water except from oases.

One of the Yeomanry troopers recruited by Lloyd Owen was Roderick Matthews

Before the War in order to get free riding, I joined the North Somerset Yeomanry, we were sent out to Palestine which after a time became very tedious. A friend of mine joined the Yeomanry Patrol of the LRDG. About three months later my friend came back with Lloyd Owen looking for more recruits. I joined. Out of 400 volunteers, 12 were taken. I was interviewed by Captain Lloyd Owen. My role was to understudy navigating. I was a gunner. I later became a driver. Discipline in the LRDG was on the basis that everybody had to rely on each other. The biggest punishment was RTU. Some people couldn't live with being a long way off in the desert. But this happened to very few people. You joined someone's truck and the old hands told you what to do.

Fitters played a vital role in maintaining the efficiency of the LRDG; Private Alexander Stewart RAOC:

While in the transit camp Bagnold and Prendergast came round to recruit. While they were talking the bulk of the troops walked out, they weren't interested, but I had made friends with a Canadian called Jimmy Spencer, and he turned to me and said, 'Come on Scotty, let's give it a go.' So I joined the LRDG. I was attracted by the idea of lack of parades and drill. Bagnold and Prendergast were pleasant but firm. I joined the LRDG as a fitter. [This was before the days of the Royal Electrical and Mechanical Engineers.]

The next step was the journey to Kufra with the LRDG HQ. Our job was to maintain the trucks that came in from patrol. I loved the desert, and still do. The only thing I didn't like were the flies. Luckily they weren't everywhere. In the Kufra Oasis there were palm trees and a wonderful salt lake. The other patrols were working from Siwa.

The flies were not the only nuisance. A New Zealander, Gunner Grimsey, was stung three times by a scorpion which was quickly despatched. This scorpion became the model for the official LRDG badge, designed by Grimsey.

As soon as fuel supplies allowed, patrols explored towards the coast, gathering information on 'going', sites for airstrips, and water supplies, for the forthcoming British advance, planned for the autumn of 1941. T Patrol carried out a 1,200-mile round trip to the Gulf of Sirte, approaching close to the road being used by enemy convoys. S Patrol made a similar foray south of Agedabia. Neither patrol was discovered by the enemy.

In addition the LRDG transported British and Arab intelligence agents behind the lines from Siwa. A favourite place for agents to operate was the fertile plateau of the Gebel Akhdar (The Green Mountain) inland of the coastal bulge of Cyrenaica between Benghazi and Derna. Here the Italians had built a few settlements, and it was one of the more densely populated parts of Cyrenaica, 'dense' being relative in this context. Here agents could operate among the local population. The patrols ran a 'taxi service', delivering radio batteries, ammunition and explosives. They usually operated as half patrols, because it was uneconomical to go at full strength on what the LRDG regarded as the 'short' journeys from Siwa. 'Short' again being relative: the round trip was in the region of 800 miles.

Captain McCraith, Sherwood Rangers Yeomanry, had raised the Yeomanry Patrol which he handed over to Lloyd Owen in September 1941, on returning to his regiment. McCraith remembers that in June 1941:

I was ordered to take a British agent, Captain 'Taranto', up to the Gebel south-east of Slonta, some 200 miles within enemy-held territory, to a rendezvous with a pro-British Arab Sheikh who was one of Taranto's subagents. I took five trucks, and much against my better judgment, permitted Taranto to take with him his undesertworthy and spare-less light van which he wanted to use when he arrived up there to save himself a long walk in the great heat.

The outward journey of over 350 miles took two and a half days of hard driving and (except that on the first night 'Taranto' produced a bottle of Weasel Brand Gin, which appeared to be pure alcohol, and that in crossing an unavoidable and notoriously difficult area of rock and stone, we broke five or six main springs, using up all the spares we carried) we arrived in the Gebel without incident. We leaguered at a point in the hills beyond which we could go no further due to the fearful 'going'. I agreed to 'Taranto's' request for a volunteer fitter to accompany him on his mission, but would not agree to his suggestion that they both dressed up in German helmets and jackets which we had found among the debris of earlier battles on our way up. To have done so would have risked death as spies had they been captured.

'Taranto' set off stating that he would be returning in three days. Our leaguer, although fairly well hidden, was one from which it would not have been easy to have fought our way out had we been spotted either from the ground or from the air. But there was no other suitable hideout. My anxiety was increased when 'Taranto' did not return by the end of the third day. I began to suspect that he had been captured, and I imagined the subsequent suspicion and search that his capture would arouse. I decided to wait a further 24 hours. On the fourth day 'Taranto' and the fitter returned exhausted and on foot, the van having been irreparably damaged. It had taken 'Taranto' much time to find the Sheikh because he lost his way soon after leaving me. To prevent further delay he had been compelled to ask his way from an Italian soldier and thereafter drive a considerable distance along the main road, mingling with enemy convoys.

I was most anxious to leave for we had stayed long enough. Furthermore my medical orderly had a temperature of 105 degrees and another soldier a temperature not much lower. Both were delirious. Before leaving we were compelled to move across very difficult country to the abandoned van to camouflage it, and pinpoint its position for collection by the next patrol to visit the area.

An hour later on re-entering the rock and stone area, my truck broke a mainspring. With no further spares its abandonment appeared inevitable. But my Patrol Sergeant who was a skilled and ingenious fitter bound and wedged the spring with leather bootlaces, wire, metal and wood. He told

me to stop every quarter of an hour so that he could tighten up his Heath
Robinson contraption, and bet me a bottle of whisky he could get the truck
safely back to Siwa.

The constant halts to attend to the spring and the delirious patients were
most tedious. The return journey was uneventful, except that I was lucky
enough to get within 30 yards of a cheetah and her three cubs sitting
beneath a small bush in the middle of a large salt pan, before they sped
away. This was the second time within a few weeks that cheetah had been
seen by an LRDG patrol. It was confirmation that these rare, swift and
graceful creatures were not, as was hitherto believed, extinct in the Western
Desert. We arrived safely in Siwa and my Patrol Sergeant received his bottle
of whisky.

Stewart:

The LRDG was given the name 'Libyan Taxis Ltd', because we used to take
people, like Peniakoff (alias 'Popski') and others out into the Desert. Leave
them, and then pick them up on completion. 'Popski' used to be dressed as
an Arab and had an Arab guide. He had a radio transmitter. When we
dropped them, goats would mysteriously appear, and the two would set off
for caves in the Wadi Akarit. 'Popski' would walk up to the coast road near
Benghazi. One of his jobs was to get information to the POW in the camp
there so they could escape. He was successful sometimes. We transported
him a number of times, and we got to know him quite well.

'Popski' was a great man, a wonderful leader. He did great work in the
desert.

Vladimir Peniakoff ('Popski') was a Belgian émigré of Russian extraction. He was complex, colourful, and had a somewhat mysterious
background, particularly during the First World War, during which he
spent some time at Cambridge, where it was likely he was a pacifist. He
subsequently claimed that he served in the French Army in the latter
part of that war, although his sister insists that he was mobilized as a
chemist.[3] John Willett, for a time a GSO 2 Intelligence at Headquarters
8th Army, and a great friend of 'Popski', commented:

Popski was a little cavalier with the facts, and it is not always easy to
distentangle the truth.[4]

Between 1924 and the outbreak of the Second World War 'Popski'
worked for a sugar company in Egypt. In 1939 he was a tough, stocky,

forty-two-year-old. Having shed his pacifist ideas, he managed to wheedle his way into the Libyan Arab Force (LAF) as a company commander. This force consisted of Senussi Arabs, who had fled from Italian atrocities in Cyrenaica. In 1942, he was appointed to command an offshoot of the LAF, the Libyan Arab Force Commando. With twenty-two Senussis and a British sergeant, he operated in the Gebel Akhdar, where he was regarded with great affection by the Senussi tribesmen. For these operations he relied heavily on the LRDG for transport, whom he came to admire. Some found his 'Arab' approach to life, including 'creative' lying, disregard for time and mercurial moods extremely trying. He was, however, absolutely fearless, especially in battle, greatly respected by his men, and feared, rather than loved, by them. While most people would agree with Stewart's assessment of Popski's courage and effectiveness as an agent in the desert campaign until the end of 1942, he was less successful, acting independently as a sub-unit commander, later in the war.

The LRDG's Medical Officer based at Siwa during this period wrote in his journal about the problem of what to do with men who fell sick on patrol:

Most difficulties arose from the length of time the patrols were away – up to a month – and the distance they worked from the bases, from 800 to 1,000 miles. A patrol went out with a definite object and if that was not accomplished continuity of information to 8th Army would be broken, an agent might be missed, and lost, a patrol of SAS might be stranded with insufficient food and water. If a man had to return to base, it meant two out of five trucks taking him, as no trucks ever travelled singly, an inflexible rule. The big responsibility of making the decision lay with the patrol commander guided by the advice of the medical orderly. The latter if in difficulty signalled back to the MO who replied with further questions and advice. The orderly was given the final say, and on several occasions depleted patrols successfully carried out the job while the casualty returned.

The illness which gave the worst trouble was malaria developing while on patrol. [Siwa was a malarial area, and although he does not say so, this is possibly what the two in McCraith's patrol had.] During the fever bouts without shade or rest from rough going, vomiting, severe and intractable, developed adding to the dehydration from sweating, and making the taking of quinine impossible. To try and cool the patient, cloths soaked in drinking water and laid on him while he was fanned under the shelter of his truck eased some. At night with the coolness, it was often possible to get quinine down in sufficient quantities to improve matters.

Evacuation of sick and wounded was a further problem. After various trials it was found that if a truck were emptied and filled with sand until the springs were almost flat, and the patient laid in the sand deeply enough to fix his position, he travelled comfortably enough. One guardsman with a compound fracture of the tibia and fibula travelled over 1,000 miles like this [on the patrol to the Fezzan], and later returned to become a sergeant in his old patrol. On another occasion a lobar pneumonia travelled in this way for 450 miles over a period of three days.

Sitting cases were evacuated to a suitable point well away from the site of operations, where a small landing ground would be marked out for the Colonel [Prendergast] who flew out with or without the MO. His plane could carry two sitting cases and the pilot. On other occasions, e.g. a fractured spine in the middle of the sand sea, the patient was taken to the nearest flat space suitable for a larger plane [usually a Bombay], and evacuated to Cairo 800 miles away.

At times it was not possible to evacuate casualties whose wounds in normal circumstances would have merited immediate treatment. There were cases of men with severe compound fractures who had to spend days in plaster, or with abdominal wounds having to be treated as best they could, until they could be taken to an area for evacuation by air from a place hundreds of miles behind the lines. The LRDG Medical Officer also had interesting views on the efficacy of rum:

> The lime powder bought from Palestine with the rum issue, drunk as a long drink in the late afternoon after running [driving] in the heat all day, made an immediate change from extreme weariness and irritation to a tolerable attitude to another 2–3 hours' driving. This was so marked that when the rum ration was stopped, special permission was obtained to restart it. Lime alone does not have the same effect.

*

On 1 August Bagnold was promoted to full Colonel and sent to Cairo in a staff appointment. Prendergast took over, remaining in command until the end of the desert campaign. Experience showed that patrols of up to eleven trucks were too large, and more easily seen, particularly by aircraft. Each patrol was split in two, retaining their original letter, so, for example, T Patrol became T1 and T2.

Patrols did get spotted and chased from time to time; Alexander Stewart:

> On one occasion we were chased by German armoured cars, and the whole patrol was split up. While being chased we had a puncture. And everybody on the trucks must have thought we were going to be captured. But we were well ahead of the Germans, so we got out, frantically jacked up the truck and changed the wheel. We got away just as the Germans appeared over the dune.

There were also intentional clashes with the enemy, some of which did not go as planned. Captain Easonsmith of the Royal Tank Regiment had taken over R Patrol from Steele when the latter was promoted to Squadron commander. North-west of Mechili, in the southern foothills of the Gebel Akhdar, he discovered an Italian camp with four light tanks and about forty soft-skinned vehicles. He decided to lay an ambush and capture a prisoner for interrogation. Covered by two patrol vehicles, he staged a breakdown of his own truck on the track a mile or so from the enemy camp. The first convoy that appeared consisted of about sixteen trucks. The leading vehicle stopped, but before Easonsmith could grab the occupants, they ran off. Italians began jumping out of the other trucks. Easonsmith's gunner fired from the back of his truck, but his gun jammed after a few rounds. Easonsmith ran down the column hurling grenades under the trucks where the Italians were taking cover. He captured two men, but one was wounded and died. The survivor revealed that the Trieste Motorized Division was moving to Mechili. The patrol escaped without suffering any casualties having inflicted several. Easonsmith was to end up commanding the LRDG.

In November 1941, the whole of the LRDG came under command of the 8th Army for the British offensive, which aimed to drive Rommel out of Cyrenaica. Other special forces units were play a part in this, alongside the LRDG.

3

Sand and Sea: Desert and Mediterranean to the eve of Alamein – LRDG, SBS AND SAS

For over a year the LRDG had been the only effective force operating behind enemy lines in the Libyan Desert. Lloyd Owen describes operating in the desert:

We had some narrow brushes with the enemy. Troops on the ground or vehicles were usually easy to evade, because we were so well prepared. We could see them coming miles away. What we really feared was enemy aircraft. We hated them. With a patrol of five vehicles (cut from the original ten – too unwieldy), it was quite easy for two or three aircraft to take on the vehicles one by one and knock them out. You were then left with a long walk with very little water, if you were not wounded anyway. We tried to reduce the risk. What we did was to disperse as fast as we could, going flat out in any direction. We would all RV at the last place we had spent any time, e.g. last night stop, or lunch stop. This worked. With luck, you would get away with one vehicle destroyed, and the men killed or wounded, and you could go and pick them up. I was lucky, although I was attacked many times by aircraft.

There was a chance of getting help from Arabs in the Gebel Akhdar, in Cyrenaica colonised by the Italians, between Tobruk and Benghazi. They were keen to help us, and people like Peniakoff ('Popski'). All these people had been working with the locals. And the Senussi simply loathed the Italians who had treated them very badly.

Towards the west in Tunisia they were not helpful, and betrayed us. South you hardly ever saw anyone.

I felt the desert to be a marvellous place to be and operate in. I was left to get on with the task. No one told me what to do. We had to keep in touch by wireless with the HQ. One was working with excellent men. All volunteers for a job that was different. We worked in terrain in which we had complete mastery. We never thought we would get lost. We never even bothered to use maps they were so useless. We used a piece of paper and worked out our longitude and latitude within a mile or two, and fixed it using a theodolite at night. It was a free life, sometimes intense excitement, sometimes anxiety, sometimes boredom. There were many wonderful things. It was fascinating country. The great sand sea was a wonderful challenge. There were so many different kinds of terrain. Sometimes you were in rocky country and couldn't move more than ten miles in a day. Sometimes you could drive for 200 miles at 40 mph.

In November 1941 the LRDG were joined by another specially raised unit, the Special Air Service (SAS). The SAS had been formed from the remnants of one of the more ill-starred special forces formations of the Second World War: Layforce. Brigadier Robert Laycock's Force Z consisting of Numbers 7, 8 and 11 Commandos, a troop of Number 3 Commando, and Courtney's Folbot section had sailed from the Clyde on 31 January 1941 in the *Glengyle* and *Glenroy*. On arrival in Egypt in March 1941, Force Z was renamed Layforce and took under its wing two more Commandos, Numbers 50 and 52. These two, and Number 51, which had been disbanded, had been operating in Sudan, Eritrea, Abyssinia, and the eastern Mediterranean. Although they had given sterling service, they had also suffered a very frustrating time after a series of operations that had either turned sour or been cancelled at the last moment, including an abortive attempt to capture and hold the island of Castelorizzo in the Dodecanese as an MTB base for the Mediterranean Fleet. None of this had been their fault, and they had seized any opportunities for action offered. Their fortunes were not to improve after becoming part of Layforce.

The original task of Layforce was to take part in the capture of the island of Rhodes, as part of 6th Infantry Division. This operation was seen as the key to establishing control of the Aegean and, with luck, drawing Turkey into the war on the British side. The only member of Layforce to set foot on the island was Captain Courtney. His Folbot section had been training at Kabrit on the Great Bitter Lake. There, at the instigation of the staff at GHQ Middle East, he had teamed up with Lieutenant Commander Nigel Clogstoun-Willmott RN, who had been carrying out reconnaissance of the beaches on Rhodes through the periscope of a submarine. Clogstoun-Willmott, after experience in the Norwegian campaign the year before, knew that a beach had to be surveyed thoroughly before it could be approached by landing craft with any guarantee of success. Reefs, sandbars and runnels (a trench scoured out by tide or current) were hazards that could seriously hinder, if not ruin, an amphibious landing. A very shallow beach gradient would result in craft beaching hundreds, or even thousands of yards offshore, with a long wade to the waterline. The area above the waterline was also critical: soft sand, boggy clay, steep sea walls and sand dunes could all prevent vehicles getting off the beach. In daylight, sketches could be made through the submarine periscope to provide aids to pilotage such as the silhouette of the land behind the beach. Some enemy positions might be identified in the same way. Clogstoun-Willmott had persuaded GHQ Middle East that a proper beach survey had to be conducted by men taking soundings up to the waterline, and reconnoitring the beach and the exits to establish the suitability or otherwise of possible landing places. To GHQ in Cairo, whose baby the Rhodes landing was, Courtney's canoes provided the ideal way of carrying the survey party into the beach, and put the two in touch with each other. For two months on the Great Bitter Lake Courtney and Clogstoun-Willmott trained for their task.

Lance-Corporal James Sherwood was selected for the first Folbot operation on the grounds that he was not married.

We went to Alexandria to join the Submarine depot ship *Medway*. We canoed and practised in Alexandria harbour. We then embarked in the submarine *Triumph* and headed for Rhodes to carry out a reconnaissance by Folbot on the beaches where the landings were to be carried out. All this was very exciting because I had never been in a submarine before. I'd always seen them as rather romantic, rather than dangerous. I soon learnt that this wasn't so. My role was not to go ashore. That was Courtney's and Clogstoun-Willmott's as the officers. My job was to keep the two canoes [one spare] in good order, and to be up on the casing of the submarine for launching the canoe at night off the fore-planes of the submarine. Later a technique was developed which involved sitting in your canoe on the casing of the submarine, which slowly trimmed down and dived, until you floated off. It was much easier. With any kind of a sea running you had a hell of a job launching from the fore-plane, holding on to the canoe, while the submarine heaved and rolled in the seaway, and the chap who was going ashore tried to get into the canoe with all his gear.

Eventually they carried out four beach surveys. Clogstoun-Willmott did the first three, and Courtney the fourth. The technique was for one canoeist to swim in to the beach, while the other waited offshore. The swimmer occupied the front seat of the canoe for the paddle in and out from the beach. Entering the water had to be done carefully to avoid capsizing the canoe. Crawling forward over the bow became a favourite method of launching a swimmer from a canoe. These were the days before special suits for swimmers had been designed, and they wore long johns and a sailor's dark blue jersey liberally coated with periscope grease. A revolver, prismatic compass, a hooded torch in an issue condom, bags to carry sand and shingle specimens, a piece of slate and a chinagraph pencil completed the outfit.

The swimmer swam in using the breast-stroke – 'flippers' ('fins' to the professionals) had not been thought of yet. When his feet could touch bottom, the swimmer would test for depth and natural underwater obstacles: rocks and sandbars. He would swim and paddle the length of the beach to establish the gradient and nature of the bottom below the waterline, noting estimated depths on the slate. Techniques that became commonplace later in the War, such as taking lines of soundings with a small lead line, and recording them on a waterproof kneepad, had yet to come. If sentries were about, he might have to lie still in the water for minutes or even hours, until they went away, or abort the task if they remained. When all was clear, he would go up the beach collecting samples, and go as far inland as he needed to establish the location and suitability of beach exits. After several hours, cold and exhausted, he swam out to the canoe. He attracted his companion's attention by flashing his torch out to sea.

Once the swimmer was hauled in, the two would paddle out to rendezvous with the submarine; a welcome warm-up for the swimmer whose teeth would be chattering with cold from hours immersed in the cold early spring Mediterranean water. The rear paddler navigated by an aircraft compass fixed to the floor between his legs. When he judged that he had reached a position near the submarine, he flashed an infra-red torch, which could not be seen with the naked eye. Aboard the submarine a lookout scanned using a special optical device on which infra-red light showed up as a green spot. Once the rendezvous was made, the swimmers and canoe were hauled on to the submarine's casing and everything was taken down below through the forward torpedo loading hatch.

Unfortunately all these efforts on the part of Courtney and Clogstoun-Willmott were to no avail, although a number of useful lessons in beach survey techniques were learnt, and put into practice in the future. But the Rhodes landing was cancelled because the Germans had landed in Greece, and the ships and craft were needed to evacuate the British and Commonwealth troops from there, and subsequently from Crete. When the Germans invaded Crete on 20 May 1941, Numbers 7 and 50/52 Commandos were sent to Crete under Laycock's command, and arrived just in time to play a gallant but fruitless part in that débâcle. The majority went into the bag. Laycock was ordered to leave as he still had two of his Commandos elsewhere in the Middle East.

Number 11 Commando carried out one operation north of the Litani river in Lebanon to assist the Australians in their advance against the Vichy French in the Syrian campaign. Number 8 Commando carried out some ill-conceived raids on the North African coast. Lieutenant George Jellicoe:

> We transferred to Alexandria, they didn't know what to do with us. There were some abortive small raids in which I didn't take part. In May 1941 I was involved in a raid from Tobruk, by then besieged. We had an old Yangtse gunboat, the *Aphis*, carrying Number 8 Commando to attack a German airfield near Gazala about 80 miles behind the German lines besieging Tobruk. But this old lumbering gunboat was detected very early on by the enemy air force. We were extremely lucky not to be sunk. That was a failure. I can remember old Admiral Cowan shooting with a tommy-gun at these Italian bombers. He was seventy.

Admiral Cowan had retired from the Royal Navy in 1931 at the age of sixty. In 1940 he managed to persuade his friend Keyes to attach him to Number 8 Commando as their Naval Liaison officer. Eventually he joined the 18th Indian Cavalry, and was captured by the Italians at Bir Hacheim attempting to fight a tank armed with just a revolver. The Italians repatriated him on the grounds that he was too old to fight. He subsequently joined 2nd SS (Commando) Brigade in Italy, eventually being awarded a bar to his DSO. He had won his first DSO in Kitchener's campaign in the Sudan in 1898.

Jellicoe:

> Morale was rather low. We had had all these abortive things. We were disbanded. By that time I had got really bored with standing by for operations and not well-planned operations. Raiding a German airfield was not on in a slow gunboat. Carol Mather had a better idea. He fixed for us to go into the garrison in Tobruk. [From here] We could go in a small craft and raid the same airfield, just four of us. His idea was to walk back into the Tobruk garrison after destroying the aircraft. Luckily each time we set out, and we tried three times, the commander of the craft couldn't find the right place. If we had gone in we would have spent the rest of the war in a German or Italian 'jug' [jail].

Layforce was disbanded at the end of July 1941. George Jellicoe rejoined his battalion, 3rd Coldstream Guards, and fought with them in the desert for about a year. Many others from Layforce went back to their own regiments in disgust after nearly a year of boredom and frustration. Some graffiti on a troop deck in HMS *Glengyle* said it all:

> Never in the whole history of human endeavour, have so few been buggered about by so many.[1]

Some remained in the Special Boat Section, or joined the LRDG, or the SAS which was about to be formed. James Swanson of Number 11 Commando was as disillusioned as were many of his comrades:

> On the Litani River landing our Troop in reserve. We didn't see any action. I never saw any action with 11 Commando. The unit was disbanded. The LRDG was looking for volunteers. They were looking for drivers. I had an army licence. About six of us went to LRDG, and some to SAS. I had interview with Capt. Lloyd Owen, I didn't know that he had only just joined himself, so he could not tell us much about it.

Some members of Number 8 Commando waiting in Kabrit while the future of Layforce was being resolved, and with nothing better to do, decided to try parachuting. One of their number, Lieutenant Jock Lewes, Welsh Guards, had 'liberated' some parachutes en route to India, but off-loaded them at Alexandria by mistake. He persuaded the Royal Air Force to allow them to jump from a Vickers Valencia, an ancient biplane;

the same type being used for training by the fledgling parachute battalions in India. Although old, it was also slow, and therefore very suitable for basic parachute training. This did not help one of the would-be parachute soldiers, Lieutenant David Stirling, who hit the ground so hard that he was temporarily paralysed from the waist down and spent two months in hospital.

While there he pondered how best to improve the raiding that Number 8 Commando had been engaged in, hitherto with little success. He came to the conclusion that the numerous enemy bases, particularly airfields, strung out over hundreds of miles behind their lines were ideal targets. The way to get at them was by using the two open flanks, the desert to the south and the sea to the north. The latter had been used as an approach by the commandos, but their raids had been wasteful in resources. Large numbers of men had been transported in sizeable vessels, accompanied by valuable escorts, to attack perhaps one target. The very size of the expedition made detection by the enemy easier.

Escorts were now in short supply after the losses suffered by the Royal Navy in the Greece and Crete evacuations. A number of smaller parties, each no more than four or five men, inserted by parachute, submarine, fishing boat or vehicle would have a greater chance of achieving surprise, and furthermore could attack a number of targets simultaneously. He thought in terms of 200 troops attacking thirty different targets in one night. He was striving for a better 'return on investment' although he did not express it like that. It was important that the force came directly under the C.-in-C. He produced a paper setting down his ideas.

When he was fit enough to walk, he bluffed his way into GHQ and, armed with his paper, bearded Major-General Ritchie, the Deputy Chief of Staff to General Auchinleck, Wavell's successor as C.-in-C. Middle East. His nerve paid off. He was summoned by Auchinleck, promoted to Captain, and told to raise a force of sixty-five men and drop behind enemy lines from Bombay aircraft, which would be allocated to him, to attack airfields. The operation was to be mounted two days before the offensive by 8th Army, Operation Crusader, four months hence. The force was to be known as L Detachment Special Air Service Brigade; a totally imaginary formation that existed only in the fertile brain of Brigadier Dudley Clarke responsible for deception in the Middle East. He was trying to persuade the enemy that a fully equipped airborne brigade was stationed in the theatre. Real parachutists, albeit the only ones in the Middle East, were the icing on the bogus cake Clarke was baking.

Stirling managed to extract Lewes from Tobruk where Number 8 Commando was now operating. He recruited most of his men from Layforce, and some from the battalion of his own regiment, the Scots Guards. Most of the founder members of L Detachment had operational experience, and had done a good deal of night training. The training instituted by Stirling was very tough indeed, and included long marches with heavy loads.

Lieutenant Jock Lewes was responsible for parachute training. He was not a parachute training instructor, and had only ever done one jump. The only British parachute schools then in existence were at Ringway, near Manchester, and Delhi in India. Both were far too busy to spare instructors. There was, through no fault of the SAS, a certain amount of 'reinventing of the wheel' about their parachute training in Egypt. Two men were killed when the snap-links connecting the strops on their parachutes to the static wire in the Bombay aircraft twisted sideways and were forced open. So when the men jumped, they were, unknown to themselves until it was too late, disconnected from the aircraft and their parachutes failed to deploy. When the SAS appealed to Ringway for advice, they received some training notes which indicated that the Parachute School had had a fatal accident caused by exactly the same problem almost a year before. The remedy was a safety pin.

Lewes was not the type to be deterred by this or any other difficulty. He was an Australian, an Oxford rowing blue, and as President of the University Boat Club had led his university eight to their first win over Cambridge after several years of Cambridge victories. George Jellicoe, who was to join the SAS nearly a year later, said of him:

David always said that without Jock Lewes the thing would never have got off the ground. He was a marvellous trainer, and had the ability to choose the right people. He invented the Lewes bomb, which we used to destroy aircraft. The three of them had extraordinary qualities. David grasped the heaven-sent opportunity presented by the open desert flank, and recognised that the clumsy commando tactics attacking by sea was not the right way to go about it; his persuasiveness, his ability to get to the top; his extraordinary powers of leadership. I felt very much under his spell. He was one of the most remarkable people I have ever met in my life. Then there was Paddy Mayne, brave as ten lions, a tactical genius.

Captain R. B. (Paddy) Mayne was an Irish Rugby International, and a fine boxer. He was the type that flourishes in war, and spends most of the time in trouble when not kept busy on operations. He could not attend the first meeting of the newly formed SAS because he was under close arrest for knocking out the commanding officer of his previous unit. He eventually became one of the two most highly decorated officers of the British Army in the Second World War, with four DSOs, the other being Lieutenant-Colonel Alastair Pearson of the Parachute Regiment.

Another of the first officers to join from Number 8 Commando was a Cambridge rowing blue, Tom Langton of the Irish Guards. The light and dark blue background of the SAS parachute wings, based on the Cambridge and Oxford rowing colours, was chosen by him and Jock Lewes.

The first raid by the SAS was planned for the moonless night of 17/18 November 1941. Five parties were to be dropped to attack five forward fighter and bomber strips at Timini and Gazala. The dropping zones (DZs) were to be about twelve miles south of the objective. From the DZ the teams were to move to a lying-up place and to spend the day observing their objectives. That night they were to attack simultaneously. Each team carried about sixty combined incendiary and explosive bombs, with delay time pencils. After the attack the teams were to rendezvous with a patrol of the LRDG south of the Trig el Abd.

Meanwhile the whole of the LRDG, who were also to be kept very busy in support of 8th Army's offensive, moved from Kufra to Siwa to reduce the time taken to reach their operational areas. The LRDG were to watch enemy movements in the desert south of the Gebel Akhdar and the approaches to Jalo Oasis from the north. In addition R1 Patrol, under Captain Easonsmith, was to pick up Stirling's men after their raid, while Captain Hunter's T2 Patrol was to drop Captain Haselden and two Arabs in the foothills of the Gebel, and pick them up three weeks later. Haselden was a cotton broker and had been born and brought up in Egypt. He spoke fluent Arabic, and took part in a number of operations behind enemy lines.

Haselden headed for the coast to signal to the submarines *Torbay* and *Talisman* carrying a party of commandos, consisting of the remnants of Number 11 Commando, commanded by Lieutenant-Colonel G. C. T. Keyes, Royal Scots Greys, the son of Admiral of the Fleet Lord Keyes. The commandos would land in rubber dinghies from the submarines, kill Rommel in his house in the village of Beda Littoria, and sabotage a number of key communications facilities. Haselden would lead Keyes's men to Rommel's house. This behind enemy lines operation, like that of Stirling's, was timed for the night of 17/18 November, and aimed to cause maximum disruption to the enemy before Operation Crusader. Laycock, travelling in the *Talisman*, landed in a co-ordinating role. Why it was necessary to have such a senior officer on this raid is not clear. Almost every venture by Layforce, or any part of it, seemed to have been doomed to failure. This last gasp by them was no exception.

Haselden was on the beach when Keyes's group from *Torbay* landed with some difficulty through the heavy surf running that night. Of Laycock's group, only seven got ashore. Because of the need to co-ordinate the operation with the start of Crusader, Laycock decided not to wait for the remainder of the *Talisman* group to land. After lying up that day, Keyes was to move off to attack Rommel's house, and Lieutenant Cook was to sabotage the telephone lines south of Cirene. Laycock stayed at the rendezvous in case the remainder arrived that night.

At nightfall on 15 November, the parties set off in pouring rain which continued for the next forty-eight hours. The eighteen-mile approach march, over that and the following night, was long, cold and wet. Before long everybody was soaking, and walking through ankle-deep mud, or slipping on greasy rocks. They lay up during the daytime in a cave, and in a small wood. On the night of 17/18 November at around 23.30, Keyes party of approximately thirty men approached the house. Keyes and Sergeant Terry were leading, about fifty yards ahead. As the main body led by Captain Campbell, a fluent German speaker, passed a small hut a dog began to bark. An Italian came out. Campbell shouted at him in German that they were Germans on patrol. The Italian went back into his hut.

Keyes's plan was for him, Campbell and Terry to enter the house, while the remainder stayed outside to watch the various exits. Unable to get in through the windows or any back or side doors, Campbell knocked on the front door, and in German, demanded entry. A sentry opened it. Keyes advanced on him, but the German grasped the muzzle of his tommy-gun, and backed against a wall, jamming himself between the inner and outer doors of the main entrance. Keyes could not draw his fighting knife, and neither Campbell nor Terry could get behind the

German to stab him in the throat in the approved manner, because Keyes was in the way. Campbell shot the sentry with his .38 revolver, as this would make less noise than Keyes's tommy-gun. A man came clattering down the stairs, but fled followed by a burst from Terry's tommy-gun. After checking one of the many rooms off the main hall, and finding it empty, Keyes opened a door under which the light was shining. Inside were about ten Germans in steel helmets. Keyes fired a few rounds, and Campbell told him he would throw a grenade. Keyes held the door shut. Campbell pulled the pin. Keyes opened the door. As Campbell lobbed the grenade, the Germans fired, hitting Keyes who fell instantly. Campbell shut the door, the grenade exploded, followed by silence. Terry and Campbell carried Keyes outside where he died. Campbell went back inside, and round to the back, where he was shot in the leg by one of his own men thinking he was a German. He ordered his men to withdraw leaving him behind.

Terry and some of the party reached the rendezvous and met Laycock. Cook did not appear, and later it was learned that he had been taken prisoner. *Torbay* arrived on the evening of 18 November, but heavy surf prevented the party getting off the beach. The submarine, however, managed to send a boat in with food and water, and a message that it would return the following night at another beach close by. During the following day, parties of Italians and Germans probed the area. After an exchange of fire in which an officer was wounded, Laycock ordered the party to disperse in small groups. They were to go to the alternative beach where *Talisman* would come in that night, or to the place where the LRDG was due to meet Haselden, or hide in the Gebel to await the arrival of 8th Army. Laycock and Terry spent the next forty-one days walking back to the 8th Army's lines and reached them on Christmas Day 1941. They existed on food provided by friendly Senussi tribesmen. Water was not a problem because it rained almost every day. Every other member of the commando party was taken prisoner or killed by Arabs.

Haselden got away. Part of Hunter's T2 Patrol had clashed with a very strong Italian party. After the ensuing firefight, Hunter and three New Zealanders were missing. One of his trucks returned to warn the remainder of the patrol who reported by radio to LRDG Headquarters, and was ordered to withdraw to Siwa. Croucher, now commissioned as a second lieutenant, was sent with three trucks to the RV to pick up

Haselden's party. He found him waiting for him with Hunter who had evaded capture. The New Zealanders had been taken prisoner.

The house raided by Keyes had never been used by Rommel. Campbell had his leg amputated in a prisoner-of-war camp. Laycock was sent back to Britain to take command of the Special Service Brigade. Keyes was awarded a posthumous Victoria Cross. Bad planning and poor intelligence had resulted in the total failure of the operation, and the loss of thirty or so highly trained men. This raid showed that even eighteen months after the raising of the commandos, they still had a great deal to learn. Although there was much to admire about their enthusiasm and courage, there was also a great deal that was amateurish about the way they went about their business, as this disaster showed. Once again, the need for good intelligence for special forces operations was highlighted.

The other diversionary raid, by Stirling, on the same night as the Rommel raid, was also chaotic but had a happier ending. In spite of bad weather reports which led to Stirling being advised to cancel or postpone the operation, he decided to go, having first taken soundings from his officers. The high winds raised sandstorms, so the pilots of the five Bombay aircraft missed the DZs. After taking evasive action because of the intensity of the enemy flak, the aircraft dropped their sticks of parachutists. Winds gusting over 45 m.p.h. blew the parachutists miles out into the desert. Eventually twenty-two men including Stirling out of the sixty who had set out turned up at David Lloyd Owen's Y 2 patrol position.

My role was to watch a track and report movement, both vehicle and aircraft until given further orders. In the event, I spent 10 days sitting there and saw nothing. Then Paddy Mayne was seen walking across the desert with about nine men, and a couple of days later David Stirling and some more men came walking through me. One very interesting thing arose from my meeting David Stirling that morning, David told me all about the operation and that it had been a total failure. He was a remarkable man. He never gave in to failure and was determined to make the next operation a success. I turned over in my mind; 'Why the hell do this ridiculous parachuting, why didn't they let us take them to where they wanted to go? We could take them like a taxi to do the job. We could push off while they did their task, and then pick them up at an agreed rendezvous.' We discussed this while having a mug of tea laced with rum in the dawn. He was a little doubtful. I then took him to the next RV to meet up with Jake

Easonsmith who was detailed to take him to Siwa and thence to Cairo. A week or so later David told me he had been so immensely impressed by Jake and his patrol, he decided that he would work with us, and they did until the end of 1942, when they got their own transport. These were months of great success.

'On 24 November the role of the LRDG was suddenly changed,' records a report entitled 'Some Account of the part played by the LRDG in the operations of 8 Army in Cyrenaica November–December 1941'. The report continues:

Owing presumably to the somewhat critical situation in the north, 8 Army issued us orders to 'act with the utmost vigour offensively against any enemy targets or communications within your reach', adding that the most effective areas were the Mechili Gadd el Ahmar to El Adem and the coastal road in the Agedabia region.

These reports, Secret at the time they were written, continue up to 29 March 1943, later just being called 'LRDG's Part in the 8th Army's Offensive' (sometimes 'Operations'), or just 'LRDG Operations'. The situation certainly was critical. Operation Crusader, on which such high hopes had been pinned, was going badly. Auchinleck had relieved Lieutenant-General Sir Alan Cunningham of command of the 8th Army, and taken personal command of the battle. Eventually he placed Ritchie in command of 8th Army. The LRDG Account continues:

To give effect to 8 Army's orders the following steps were taken. Y1 [Captain Simms] and Y2 [Captain Lloyd Owen] were told to join and attack roads in the Mechili–Derna–Gazala area. G1 [Captain Hay, Cold-stream Guards, who had taken over from Crichton-Stuart who had returned to his regiment] and G2 [Lieutenant Timpson] also to join and attack the Agedabia Road, and S2 [Second Lieutenant Olivey] and R2 [Second Lieutenant Browne, an old LRDG hand, newly commissioned] together to work on the Benghazi–Barce–Marua road.

The other patrols were to continue with their original tasks.

Guardsmen Cyril 'Lofty' Richardson, Coldstream Guards, was a member of G1 Patrol. He wrote in his diary:

We had fresh orders wirelessed through to us to go to a certain map reference near the coast between Agedabia and Benghazi and meet the other half of our patrol. We moved off in the middle of the afternoon, choosing this time because owing to the heat haze it would be very difficult for hostile aircraft to spot us.

After skirting a salt marsh they were attacked by an Italian bomber but escaped any damage:

About four o'clock we had stopped to check our course again, when from our right we saw diving straight for us another plane. The recognition signal for our own planes was at the time that they should fly with their wheels down. We were happy that this one had its wheels down all right. But we soon learnt it was a JU 87 out for a bit of fun. We split up as soon as he opened up on us, going in all directions. Being the leading truck, he gave us all his attention for about 10 minutes, the longest 10 minutes I have ever spent in my life. We twisted and turned all over the desert dodging his bursts of lead. I got a few shots at him before my gun mounting broke and my Vickers went flying over the side of the truck. He then left us alone and concentrated on the rest, dive bombing at his leisure. He kept us busy for at least half an hour. When he had gone it took us nearly two hours to find each other. We carried on until about nine o'clock that night, and it was dark when we reached our meeting place.

After two days spent waiting for the other half of the patrol, they were ordered by radio from Siwa to attack the road on their own:

We arrived just as the sun was setting and hid behind a little mound about fifty yards from the main road, but found much to our disappointment the trucks were at least two miles apart. It was useless for us to fire at just one truck, so our officer had a brain-wave. He decided that we should get on to the main road and drive down it towards Agedabia until we found something worth hitting. Just as the last vehicle pulled on to the road, along came a closed-up convoy of about eight trucks. We could do nothing with these as we were already moving down the road towards them. I felt pretty helpless without my gun, which we failed to find after the encounter with the JU 87. I just held my breath and hoped for the best. The centre truck of that convoy was an AA gun manned by six Germans. They had a good look at us, but did not stop, needless to say neither did we.

After five or six miles passing odd lorries we saw our prey; a house on the side of the road, with lorries parked all around it. I think it was an ordnance yard or petrol filling station. By now it was just about dark, and as each lorry of ours pulled off the road, they fired with everything they had into the house and parked lorries. What effect it had on those lorry drivers we did not stop to see. But seeing as it took place some six hundred miles behind their lines [by road], it must have upset them rather.

We put eight miles between us and the road when we stopped and signalled through to HQ [at Siwa] telling them we were awaiting fresh orders. We had our rum issue, and listened to the news over the wireless while our cook prepared our tea and bully-beef stew.

The new orders soon came through: 'Do the same again tomorrow night.' As soon as we had finished our dinner, we returned to our hiding place in the wadi. The next day we had quite a few planes flying around but they failed to spot us. Just after four o'clock we left the wadi, bound this time for a spot further south. The sun had just set when we pulled up behind a little hillock no more than twenty-five yards from the road. We could hear the drivers singing we were that close. We decided this time on ground action. We mounted the guns along the top of the ridge, and waited for a suitable target. The vehicles were at even greater intervals than the previous night. So we picked on a big oil tanker and trailer and let him have it good. We waited hoping for another customer, but all traffic stopped. They must have heard or seen the firing, because nothing else came our way. So once more we did a flit into the night. Ten miles from the road we stopped, lit fires, cooked our dinner, and sent a message through to HQ. As soon as our meal was over we moved off again travelling all night; stopping only for a rum ration, and to take a bearing on some star. About nine o'clock the next morning we reached the Trigh el Abd and lay up all day.

At three o'clock that afternoon we had a message telling us that our position was 'unhealthy', and to make our way back to Siwa. No sooner had we arrived [three days later], we were told we would be out again within a few days.

The LRDG Report:

On 29th [November] S2 and R2 carried out an attack carefully planned by Olivey, on the Barce–Marua road. In all nine lorries with trailers were destroyed, a number of enemy killed, and the telephone wires cut. Just after the attack on the first vehicle had begun (in the dark), Olivey noticed it was marked with a red cross. He was trying to stop his men from firing when a posse of men with rifles and a sub-machine-gun tumbled out of the back of the truck and opened up on our Patrol.

Not content with this success, Olivey's Rhodesians and Browne's New

Zealanders attacked four trucks further up the road, putting all of them out of action. They chose a 30-foot-high cutting to mount an ambush on two more trucks and trailers, and a fuel tanker. They destroyed all the vehicles and killed all the occupants, except one badly wounded man. Having cut all the telephone wires they turned south without suffering any casualties. Olivey was awarded the Military Cross, and a New Zealander and a Rhodesian the Military Medal. Olivey was to play a leading role in the LRDG right up to the last day of the War against Germany. The LRDG Report continues:

> The two Ys had joined up on November 25th and had for three days been scouring the area allotted to them without finding any suitable targets. They decided to attack the Mechili–Derna road. The Patrols moved off separately at dawn on 29th, and Y2 captured a truck containing three Italians coming from a post at El Azziat. One spoke good English, and with the information obtained from him, it was decided to attack the post. One Yeoman who had been left as a 'horse holder' with his truck, feeling he was missing the fun, shouted to his Italian prisoner, 'Here, look after this truck', and dashed off to join the party.

On 30 November Y2 made a successful attack on the main road between Tmimi and Gazala, returning to Siwa on 3 December. Y1 attacked a vehicle park near Sid Saleh, damaging about fifteen vehicles, before returning to Siwa on 6 December.

In mid-December Rommel disengaged and began withdrawing to Agedabia. In order to try to cut him off, as the Italians had been the year before by O'Connor, 8th Army sent columns across the desert south of the Gebel Akhdar. These included 22nd Guards Brigade and three patrols allocated as navigators and flank guards to this brigade: T1 (Major Ballantyne), R1 (Captain Easonsmith) and R2 (Second Lieutenant Browne and later Second Lieutenant Croucher). Ballantyne had to wait for two weeks at Bir Hacheim while the Guards disengaged from the battle west of Tobruk. During this time, he was bombed and strafed by German aircraft. Second Lieutenant Freyberg Grenadier Guards (son of Major-General Bernard Freyberg commanding the New Zealand Division and attached to the LRDG) was wounded slightly in one of these attacks. Easonsmith took the opportunity en route to the RV at Bir Hacheim to attack an enemy anti-tank unit and inflict casualties without taking any himself.

Meanwhile Hay (G1) and Lloyd Owen (Y2) were harassing enemy transport on the Agedabia–Benghazi road with considerable success. By now the enemy were thoroughly alerted, and obliged to escort their convoys; a drain on their resources. Lloyd Owen returned to Siwa without suffering any losses.

'Lofty' Richardson in G1 takes up the tale of his patrol:

We moved out from Siwa on 10th December arriving at our old hide-out [near Beda Fomm] on the morning of 14th without mishap. On the same afternoon vehicles were sighted heading straight for us. We got orders to prepare our trucks for a quick get off, and to stand by our guns. But we need not have bothered for it was only a half of Y Patrol sent by the HQ to operate with us.

They reached the road when it was dark, and parked about forty yards away:

The Lewis gunners and a sergeant and the officer [Hay] with a tommy-gun each, walked down to the roadside to wait for a suitable target. We waited for at least half an hour for a decent sized catch to come along. It was a big covered truck with a trailer loaded, we later found out, with shells. The fireworks were soon over, and the officer threw some sort of candle [incendiary] with what he thought was a three-minute fuse into the back of the lorry. The fuse turned out to be three seconds, and the whole area was lit up like daylight. These candles burn furiously for about half an hour normally, but we were hardly a mile from the road when we heard a terrific explosion. The lorry or what was left of it was burning furiously, and for the next half-hour we heard a series of explosions. We stopped and had our dinner a few miles from the road as usual, then set off again. This time we went further north where the escarpment [the west of the Gebel Akhdar] was much higher and afforded new and better cover.

We laid up in a wadi all day, and unlike the last time, not only were there planes about, but vehicles patrolling the flat between us and the road. About four o'clock as we were leaving our hiding place, the scout car of Y Patrol came up. They had been hiding about half a mile from us and we did not know it. They thought the vehicles moving about our front were us until they saw us emerge from the wadi.

Both patrols waited for the enemy vehicles which, according to 'Lofty' Richardson, by their tracks must have been six- or eight-wheeled armoured cars to buzz off. In the meantime they [Y Patrol] told us their doings the previous night. They finished up on the road about 10 miles from our position. While waiting for a suitable target, we had opened up. This caused all the traffic to stop and congest. They managed to burn one oil tanker and destroy three other lorries.

We moved off at about five o'clock not feeling so cheerful as last night. The thought of running into armoured cars in our soft Ford V8s did not appeal to me or any of the others. We reached the road without difficulty just as it got dark. The traffic tonight was a lot thicker, vehicles were only three or four hundred yards apart. But patrolling at regular intervals were armoured cars. Things were definitely getting too warm for us in this area. But we decided to have one last crack at them before finding fresh hunting grounds. This time we chose a big diesel towing a staff car. The Lewis gunners lay beside the road waiting for it to approach, this time we had to be very careful because of the armoured cars. But everything went off OK. We did a hasty withdrawal, stopping about ten or twelve miles away as usual for dinner. Once more we were travelling all night.

They had been told that by 17 December a force of Indian and South African armoured cars, one of the columns mentioned earlier, sent south of the Gebel in the attempt to cut off Rommel's retreat, would reach the place for which G1 Patrol was now heading. 'Lofty' Richardson:

So when at about eight o'clock the following morning we almost ran into some South African trucks everyone was quite sure that we had met our own force. There were no shots fired at us as we approached. The first three trucks [of G1 patrol] were roughly two or three hundred yards from these supposed Indians. The other two were about three hundred yards behind us. Everyone was feeling sleepy and hungry and we were not as careful as we should have been. The officer drove forward and disappeared over a rise in the ground. Everyone was walking round their trucks trying to keep warm. All at once the fun started; although I did not think it fun at the time. Machine-guns opened up from about four places, and I made a dive for the rear of the truck with two other members of the crew. The last two trucks with their crews were fortunate they did a quick about turn and got away over a rise in the ground. That was the last we saw of them.

It was useless trying to climb into the truck, the lead was flying about all over the place. The three of us made ourselves as small as possible and spent a very uncomfortable time while the supposed Indians peppered our truck. A section of them came to collect us, or to bury us. None of us at that moment had been hit. Seeing we were definitely at their mercy, we stood up to give ourselves up. But one fellow must have been nervous for seeing us move to stand up, let fly firing from the hip. He put a burst through the ankle of the chap [Guardsman Chapman, Coldstream Guards] on my right. But all credit to the German front-line soldiers; within two minutes they had applied first-aid dressings. Chapman's ankle was in a bad way, the bullets had gone in the heel and blood and pieces of bone had come out of his lace holes.

The two surviving G1 Patrol trucks and six men got back to Siwa. 'Lofty' Richardson and the men in the leading three trucks were taken back to Agedabia:

We could, I think, have escaped easily on this journey, for we had only three guards in the back of the truck with us, and only one or two men in each of our trucks which were being brought with us. But we could not have done it with poor old Chapman. He must have suffered terribly on that rough track, but never once did a moan escape his lips.

Chapman was put in hospital and left behind by the Axis forces when they retreated from Agedabia. He was evacuated to Egypt by advancing British troops. The rest of the G1 Patrol prisoners were handed over to the Italians who treated them far worse than the German front-line troops. Richardson judged that they had one more chance to escape when they were being taken to Benghazi in a 30-cwt truck with two escorts in front and seven in the back. 'Lofty' Richardson:

Plans were made as soon as we moved off, as to what member of the escort each man should handle, who was to drive the truck, in what direction we should go, etc. We decided to act on a signal from our officer. About thirty miles from Agedabia, we began passing the derelict trucks we had smashed up on our raids. This was an ideal spot for our break, we knew every inch of this country. Other trucks on the road were few at this time of day, and the chances of them following us fewer still. But when we reached the outskirts of Benghazi we were still awaiting the signal. Whether he got the wind up, or afraid of the responsibility of any of us getting hurt or shot in our attempt, I do not know.[2]

By now Jalo had been taken by a mixed force known as E Force under Brigadier Reid. LRDG patrols S1 (Captain Holliman), S2 and T2 were sent to Jalo to operate temporarily under Reid's command. He had orders to advance to the Agedabia area in concert with 8th Army's push to Benghazi. It would help him if the enemy aircraft on Agedabia airfield were eliminated. This gave Stirling his chance to try again, and with the LRDG this time he planned two raids on Sirte and Agheila airfields, and a further one on Agedabia a week later. These would be followed by two more raids on Sirte and Agheila when the attack on Benghazi was in full swing.

On the outward journey with S1, Stirling's party was attacked by an Italian aircraft, but suffered no casualties. He therefore decided to send Mayne to the satellite airfield at Tamet, and attack the one at Sirte himself. The Italians got wind of Stirling's attack when his night reconnaissance of the target was spotted. They immediately evacuated the Sirte airfield. Mayne had better luck. The LRDG Report:

> An attack was made by the parachutists [SAS] on the LG [landing ground] at Wadi Tamet on the night of 14th. This was most successful; 24 aircraft were destroyed or badly damaged; a petrol and a bomb store were both destroyed and the buildings on the LG shot up.

Mayne had actually damaged one aircraft with his bare hands. He had seen one with lights on in the cockpit, and looking in saw it was unoccupied. Taking a fancy to the instrument panel as a souvenir, he climbed in and wrenched it out. The half-patrol responsible for collecting Stirling had not been idle. The LRDG Report:

> While the attack was in progress half our patrol had driven eastwards along the main road to pick up Capt Stirling (OC SAS troops), who had been dropped the previous night. Stirling was successfully collected, and on the return journey the road was mined behind the patrol, and one vehicle carrying ammunition was seen to blow up shortly afterwards.

T2 Patrol under Lieutenant Morris (in Hunter's absence) took the SAS party under Captain Lewes to the Agheila airfield raid. Morris also had a task to attack Mersa Brega, about fifty miles east of Agheila on the coast road. The LRDG Report:

> On December 13 the parachutists were dropped [the LRDG refer to them in this way although they were being delivered courtesy of the LRDG and not the RAF] with a Lancia truck of their own and two LRDG cars with

their crews at a point 12 miles south-east of El Agheila. Morris himself then spent the next two days reconnoitring the coastal road and approaches to Mersa Brega. As a result of this he decided that the only way to attack Mersa Brega was along the coast road. On the evening of the 16th, having by then been rejoined by the parachutists, who had found the LG at El Agheila unoccupied, Morris made up a 'convoy' of vehicles and drove it eastwards along the main road. This 'convoy' was headed by the Lancia, followed immediately by Morris's own truck with its lights shining on the Lancia; the rest of the patrol following. In this order they drove for nine miles along the main road passing 47 enemy vehicles en route. Arriving at Mersa Brega, they found about 30 vehicles drawn up by the roadside and some 60 troops standing around them. These were attacked for some 20 minutes, most of the firing being at about 30 yards range. At the end of this time Morris drew off with no casualties to his own party. Owing to the roadside salt marshes the patrol had to follow the main road for another 10 miles before they could get off it to the south. During this run Corporal Garvin in the last truck laid mines on the road to stop pursuit. From the explosions heard it is estimated that at least seven vehicles were blown up.

The SAS party under Captain Fraser was taken in by Olivey. Before he did so, he and a 25-pounder gun section under Lieutenant Eitzen attacked a small Italian fort at Gtafia. After a few rounds from the 25-pounder, the garrison fled. Two machine-guns and four prisoners were taken. Three days later Olivey took a party of SAS to a point nine miles from Agedabia whence they made a night attack on the airstrip there, and destroyed 37 aircraft, being picked up on the 22nd at a prearranged rendezvous. The LRDG Report:

> Unfortunately on their return journey to Jalo, the party was suddenly attacked by two RAF aircraft while halted in the Wadi el Faregh. Corporal Ashby and Private Riggs were killed.

On this first series of raids the SAS had accounted for sixty-one aircraft. Stirling's faith in his concept of raids by small parties had been triumphantly vindicated. But without the professionalism and desert skills of the LRDG his ideas would have been stillborn.

Stirling and Mayne's second visit to Sirte and Tamet was a repeat of the first. Stirling was unable to reach the airfield because the road was jammed with German armour and vehicles. He was lucky not to have been killed or captured. An Italian sentry tried to shoot him when he failed to give the correct reply to a challenge, but there was a click instead of a bang; possibly a faulty round. Mayne's luck held and he destroyed twenty-seven aircraft at Tamet.

Fraser and Lewes were taken by Morris (T2 Patrol) to raid the strips at Nofilia and 'Marble Arch'. Mussolini had built a triumphal arch at Ras Lanuf as a monument to his African conquests. This pompous edifice commemorating the generally less than heroic performance of Italian troops, and its similarity to the arch at the top of Park Lane in London, tickled the British soldiers' sense of humour; 'Marble Arch' it became and was known throughout the 8th Army. The LRDG Report:

> He [Morris] dropped the first party near the 'Marble Arch' and having taken the second party to Nofilia, picked them up two days later.

Lewes had bad luck at Nofilia, he had placed a bomb with a half-hour delay fuse on one aircraft, and was about to place a bomb on the next when the first exploded prematurely. Under heavy fire, Lewes's party withdrew. The LRDG Report:

> On December 31, the Patrol was on its way back to collect the first 'Marble Arch' party when they were attacked by a Messerschmitt. Shortly after two Stukas joined the chase and the attack was kept up by relays of aircraft for most of the morning. Although there was not enough cover to hide the men still less the trucks, the patrol had only one casualty, Lt Lewes (of the parachutists) being killed, and all but one of the vehicles being burnt out. During the attacks the trucks had become widely separated, and although Morris and some of his patrol were able to get back to Jalo on the one surviving vehicle, nine LRDG men and one parachutist found themselves at evening the best part of 200 miles from their base.

The death of Lewes was a considerable loss to the SAS. He was a man of action but also intellect, and a special forces unit needs both.

After walking more than 200 miles in eight days the nine LRDG men reached Augila, an oasis, near Jalo; the SAS man fell out near the Agheila–Marada road with almost raw feet. Extracts from some of their debriefing reports give an idea of their ordeal. Trooper Martin:

> When the planes departed we found that it would be impossible to salvage anything from the trucks due to exploding ammunition. However, Pte Bassett had had the foresight to take with him approximately 3 gallons of

water when he originally left his truck. So with this, plus 9 biscuits and one chocolate ration, we set out to walk to Augila. During that afternoon we walked approximately seven miles.

The aircraft were still in the vicinity during that afternoon. Gunner Stutterd:

We saw two more Stukas approaching. Down again behind some bushes not big enough to cover a scorpion, and spent a very unpleasant time here, while the planes circled and played around.

Martin:

At dusk we started walking in earnest and by 7.30 on the morning of Jan 1st 1942 we estimated we had covered 30 miles. At midnight we toasted the New Year in with a sup of water each. We could see the RAF paying their respects to the Luftwaffe at what we thought was the 'Marble Arch' drome. We continued walking until 7 a.m. on the morning of 2nd Jan. We estimated we had covered another 30 miles.

By now they were about fifteen miles east of the road to Marada. Gunner Walsh:

Cpl White [SAS] decided to leave us, heading back to the Marada Road, in hopes of capturing a truck. Actually I think his feet were too far gone, and he decided to give himself up and not hinder the party. Rather a noble act I think.

Martin:

Most of our footwear had worn out, and we had to make moccasins out of a greatcoat. We had eaten some snails, and had sucked some Gibbs Dentifrice, this helped to keep our mouths fresh. The cold was nearly unbearable, and when we did rest, we climbed on top of each other. Naturally the outside men growled a bit. By 06.30 hrs 3rd Jan we estimated we had covered another 30 miles, and it was here we saw a light [of a fire] north of us. By this time we had reduced our ration to three eighths of a pint per man per day. After discussion we decided to walk to the fire. After approximately three hours walking we decided to rest, but Cpl Garven, Trooper Brown, Gunner Stutterd and myself carried on.

Stutterd:

We marched for an hour or so and came to some very moist ground in the swamp. Our thirst by this time was getting very bad and we dug a small hole looking for water. Trooper Brown carried on towards the fire, saying he would fire a shot if he found anything. After a while we struck water and found to our disgust it was far too salt to drink. At his stage I heard a shot and we headed for it. After an hour's walking, we found Brown with four Arabs, and it was not long before we were gargling the small drop of water they had with them, and eating a few dates. One of the Arabs informed us that there was a spring 3 kilometres away. He volunteered to show us the way. The 3 kms turned out to be about 6 miles. On arrival there, the Senussi, who were camped there, could not do enough for us. We had been there about an hour when the rest of the party arrived also.

Trooper Ramsay:

We arrived [at the Senussi Camp] at about 1500 hours, and enjoyed large drinks of water.

Signalman Fair:

It tasted better to me than a glass of cold beer in Groppi's Cairo.

Ramsay:

Just as we arrived we observed two trucks some distance away, and not knowing if they were friendly or not we hid. That night one of the natives told us they were English trucks. He had spoken to some of the personnel and they had given him some tea.

After a fairly comfortable night round a large fire, we decided to wait until the following afternoon in case the trucks returned, and if they did not to start marching again that night. Corporal Garven and Trooper Brown went out to a hill where they hoped to see the trucks if they returned and signal to them. The trucks did appear several miles away, but all efforts to attract them failed.

They continued walking from 1.30 p.m. on 4 January to 6.30 a.m. the next day carrying with them four gallons of water. After a brief stop to boil some water and stir in some of the chocolate ration, they pushed on. By now they were very weak, and they carried the water can in relays of six minutes each. Martin:

At 5 p.m. 5 Jan it started to rain, so it was unanimously agreed to drop our tin of water and make an all-out effort for Augila [which they estimated was about 25 miles away]. By 4 a.m. 6 Jan we were still 'in the blue'. Fatigue was now starting to take its toll, and we were finding it increasingly difficult to make a start after each rest. Trooper Brown and myself decided to carry on a bit further, thinking we just could not be far from Augila. After three hours' walking, there was still no sign of the oasis, so we decided to return to the rest of the party. No sooner had we turned than the wind increased, and inside an hour we were enveloped in a severe sandstorm.

As it would be impossible to retrace their tracks in the storm, and having been heading south-east into the wind when they left the others, they turned into the wind and continued on a south-easterly course. The only compass was with the navigator Private Bassett with the other group. Martin continues:

During the afternoon we sighted the sun for a moment and were amazed to find we were walking north-west. Obviously the wind had changed, and we had not noticed it. After dusk, after again turning south-east, we struck some tracks and tried to follow them. We lost them when it became dark, and rested until the moon came up. We started walking towards and slightly to the right of it, until fatigue got the better of us, and we stopped to rest. We woke just before dawn, and were amazed to find the sun showed signs of getting up behind us. We must have turned about during the night. Retracing our steps yet again, we were beginning to despair a bit, when we were overjoyed to see, far away, on our left what we thought was an armoured car. Hurrying to the best of our ability we arrived after two hours' walking. The two auxiliary water tanks were full, so we sat in the car and drank sparingly for about an hour and a half. We also raked around and found some cigarette butts which we put in Brown's pipe and smoked.

At 9.30 a.m. 7 Jan we left the car and followed in its tracks in what we knew was the direction of Augila. We had passed this car on our way out from Gialo [Jalo]. At approximately midday we sighted Augila Oasis, and walked towards it. Whether it was fatigue, relief or anything else, I do not know, but the White Fort took a bit of reaching. When we did arrive, the natives were very good to us, and promised to look for the rest of the party.

Stutterd was in the party still resting when Troopers Brown and Martin had decided to go on:

We were at the time following a track which exactly coincided with our compass bearing. The next morning spirits were getting fairly low, thirst was troubling us badly and our feet were getting almost unbearably sore. Our marching spells were cut to a fraction, and everyone was very tired.

Just after midday, Stutterd sighted palm trees, but hesitated before saying anything. Their eyes were sore and they 'were seeing things'. However, it was the oasis.

> We made the place which proved to be Augila at dusk. We found an empty Arab garden and a hut which we appropriated for the night. We lit a fire, boiled some turnips and onions, had a glorious drink out of the well. After spending the most comfortable night since 30th December, we cooked some more turnips and onions, had some date tea and set off for the fort. On the way we met two Arab policemen who took charge of us and led us to their barracks. Too much praise cannot be given to these Arabs for the way they treated us.

On arrival they found the others. A message was sent to Jalo by one of the Arab policemen and Major Steele came to pick them up. Trooper Martin ended his report with four observations:

1. Hunger did not unduly worry any of us.
2. The best type of footwear appeared to be slippers as worn by the natives, not chapplies [sandals].
3. It would be OK if each man had a compass and map of the locality in which he is working. I have omitted to mention that we were lucky to have both in our party [i.e. one of each for the whole party].
4. Lastly, that grumbling and grousing were not features of our trip. Everyone was helpful to one another.

Private Bassett the navigator was awarded the DCM and Gunner Sanders the MM.

*

Captain Fraser's SAS party, having found the 'Marble Arch' strip empty, waited for six days at their RV for Morris's patrol to collect them. With their water running out, they decided to walk the 200 miles to Jalo. They arrived after eight days.

Both the LRDG and the SAS continued operating together during the period when Rommel mounted his counter-offensive and pushed the 8th Army back, through Benghazi to the Gazala line some thirty miles west of Tobruk. The LRDG, having moved the whole group forward to Jalo by early January, had to withdraw by the end of the month to re-establish bases at Siwa and Kufra.

These moves did not disrupt LRDG operations, but in early February 1942 most patrols were pulled back to Cairo for refitting and re-equipping. The Ford trucks were replaced by new, specially modified Chevrolets. Before going to Cairo G2 (Timpson) and Y2 (Lloyd Owen) each made one more sortie from Siwa. Timpson's spent four days watching and reporting on the enemy traffic east of Barce. When he returned to Siwa he had picked up a number of troops who had been hiding in the Gebel Akhdar, having been overtaken by Rommel's rapid advance. He arrived back in Siwa with forty-seven passengers on his four trucks, including the Arab Mudir of Slonta, his two wives, one child, some chickens and a goat.

Lloyd Owen was tasked to find out if the enemy was building up his supply dumps east and north-east of Agedabia in preparation for an advance on Tobruk. He brought back some useful information despite the difficulties of operating in such open country, and on one occasion was chased by enemy vehicles for about twenty miles, before eventually returning to Siwa.

Frank Harrison was Lloyd Owen's driver:

Siwa had the most beautiful water. Imagine, you've been out on patrol for three, four, five weeks. You're dirty and dusty. You've never had a wash. We never used to shave of course. About the only thing we did was clean our teeth, usually with the dregs of some [tea]. We'd come back from patrol, and these magnificent pools. There was figure of eight pool, there was bubbly pool, like I would imagine a Jacuzzi today. It was crystal clear water, eight, ten feet deep. You could toss a coin in and see it go all the way to the bottom. Well, just to pull your lorry alongside the pool, and fall out into the pool was wonderful. We must have stunk to high heaven.

Starting in early March the LRDG maintained a watch on the road thirty-five miles west of Agheila and five miles east of 'Marble Arch'. This continued up to 21 July 1942. Lloyd Owen:

This was a watch on the only tarmac road that ran from Tripoli to Alexandria. The lifeline of both armies. We set up a watch on that road and reported in detail every vehicle for months on end. On roadwatch one might be on duty for a fortnight [or longer]. For half the time you were sitting hidden in a wadi, thinking about when you could next have a drink of water, or brew up. You couldn't brew up in daylight because of the flies.

Flies were a problem near any area used by the armies, or by the local population. They covered food and drink. Deep in the desert there were no flies.

The road watch position near 'Marble Arch' had been first noted on a reconnaissance from Kufra nine months before. LRDG Report:

> At this point a wadi leads down towards the road from the high ground to the south of it. In the wadi and in the smaller side-wadis there is good cover and vehicles can be effectively camouflaged. At its north-east end the wadi leads out on to a flat plain, across which, about two and a half miles from the wadi mouth the road runs. The usual procedure is that the patrol vehicles are hidden in the wadi and every morning about 3.30 a.m. two men go down to the road where they remain for 24 hours.

The patrol vehicles on road watch were often hidden several miles from the road. The LRDG thought nothing of walking a dozen miles at the beginning and end of each twenty-four-hour stint. They would be laden with greatcoats, water and personal weapons. The LRDG Report:

> The plain is flat and without cover other than sparse scrub about two feet high in which the watchers have to hide themselves as well as they can. Except in a sandstorm it is impossible to move about during daylight, and once they have selected their hideout the watchers must remain in it, lying at full length until dusk. By day they are some 300–400 yards from the road; after dark it is easy to approach to within 20 or 30 yards, but details of traffic are difficult to distinguish. The risk of watchers being seen is considerable. Arabs with goats and camels occasionally pass down the wadi and on the road itself repair gangs are a danger. On a number of occasions convoys have pulled off the road onto the plains for meals or to camp for the night.

Private Alexander Stewart:

> On another road watch our patrol was miles behind the enemy lines getting information about the Axis movement back and forth on the coast road. We did a twenty-four-hour watch on the road, as close as we could. A German convoy came along, pulled off the road, and stopped. Once again our hearts stopped. About a hundred yards from us they walked towards us. Some just dropped their trousers, others had a leak. Then they returned to their trucks.

Corporal Roderick Matthews:

During the German retreat from Alamein they camped all round us, we were in a bush. They did not find us.

Frank Harrison:

The 8th Army had a continuous feed-back of all movements on the road. The worst part of the road watch was hanging about. The heat was absolutely dreadful. You couldn't walk around because this left tracks. This wore a path which showed up from the air. You just lay under your camouflage and sweated it out.

If tanks or large numbers of enemy troops were seen going towards the front, the patrol would send a radio message to LRDG Headquarters at Siwa. By the time the enemy column had reached Agedabia, its whereabouts would be known to GHQ in Cairo. When a patrol had been relieved and was well clear, it radioed a full report of what it had seen. This information was invaluable in building up the intelligence plot in GHQ. In order to keep the road watch going without a break, three patrols were allocated to this task.

While the LRDG and the SAS were attacking or watching the enemy behind the lines from the desert, the SBS attacked from the sea. Some of their operations were successful, some were not. There seems to have been a lack of co-ordination of their activities, particularly after December 1941 when Roger Courtney was sent back to Britain to take charge of Number 2 SBS operations there.

James Sherwood:

For about a year after the Rhodes recce we continued to live in the *Medway*. Jobs were few and far between. We went out in submarines with a canoe embarked, sometimes on spec, on a full wartime patrol, which lasted anything up to three weeks. Maybe one or two of the Section with a Folbot, without an officer.

They just said, 'You two are going out on that op, you're going out in that submarine, leaving so-and-so and you're going to do this or that, whatever it was, or you're going on spec and taking the canoe, and if the commander of the submarine sees something ashore that he thinks could justify some action by you blokes, then you're under his command.' This worked very satisfactorily.

The only snag was that any operations we did were just a one-off lasting one night, and we then had to endure everything the submarine might suffer on a normal offensive wartime patrol, attacking enemy shipping, being depth-charged and so on which wasn't always amusing, in fact very frightening. Anyhow we were stuck with this and made the best of it. For the rest of the patrol we'd volunteer as look-outs on the bridge, a good opportunity to get some fresh air at night when the submarine was on the surface charging her batteries. We'd take a turn on the fore or after plane controls, sometimes helping with decoding in the wireless office, or anything else we were asked to do.

On one occasion we were lying off Benghazi in *Triumph*, the skipper sent for us and said, 'There's a ship in the harbour which you two blokes can go and sink if you'd like.' By that time we had limpet mines. So we said, 'Right, we'll have a go.' With some apprehension I must admit. We had a look through the periscope by day, and there was the ship. By dusk the scene had changed. The skipper decided that rather than send us ashore it was far easier to fire a torpedo to sink this bally thing. So we didn't go ashore, which is probably just as well. I don't think we'd have come back.

The submarines were operating out of Alexandria covering the eastern Mediterranean as far as the overlap with 10th Submarine Flotilla operating out of Malta. They carried out reconnaissance of areas of the coast on which information was required, along the North African, Greek and Yugoslav coasts. They put intelligence agents ashore – Greeks, Yugoslavs, even on one occasion a Pole.

What he was doing going ashore in Greece I never discovered. The people we put ashore were [involved in sabotage operations], but we never were told much in case of capture. They took wireless sets and explosives. Whether these chaps came back I never discovered. They went ashore in civilian clothes. On one occasion, on the plains of Marathon on the coast of Greece, the chap got into the canoe wearing an ordinary burberry type raincoat, a soft grey felt hat, collar, tie, shoes and everything else just as though he were going for a walk or shopping expedition into town. I was in uniform. We were about a mile offshore. We did a reconnaissance during the day through the periscope. We were allowed very brief looks just to get the lie of the land, and to see if there were any enemy posts to be avoided. You can't keep a periscope up [for long] a mile off the enemy coast without risk to the submarine. Two of us each with our civilian in front, us paddling at the back, landed on the beach, quiet dark night, no moon, fairly calm sea. Out they stepped, as if they were getting out of a pleasure rowboat to a seaside resort, got on to the beach, unloaded their gear, hid it under bushes, and vanished. We returned to the submarine. That was a typical operation landing agents.

The role operating from submarines came to an end after about a year. The SBS then used MTBs. Their operations were confined to some mostly abortive attempts to land along the coast of Egypt and Libya. During the summer of 1942, when the Germans had reached Alamein, the Navy had withdrawn through the Suez Canal, and the Army was burning its files in Cairo. Sherwood remembers:

There was an air of defeatism around. There was talk of evacuation to Palestine. We were miles from the action. When everybody seemed to be talking of pulling out, the SBS went in the reverse direction.

The SBS officers having billeted themselves in Alexandria hatched a number of offensive operations against the Germans, using MTBs. Sherwood went on one of these:

Who had selected the landing place I know not. It turned out to be a large German camp. The MTB crept in. We had one Folbot and an enormous blow-up RAF life raft, which held six men. In this contraption we gyrated our way gently towards the shore from the MTB which unfortunately had been heard from the shore. Within minutes of landing, Very lights were fired lighting up the whole area. A gun opened up on the MTB. We still went ahead and landed on the beach. We couldn't see anybody moving about. The Very lights went out, the gun stopped firing, perhaps thinking that what had been there had sheered off. We expected Germans to be running all over the place. Nothing happened. Our object was to place thermite [incendiary] bombs on the petrol tanks of any lorries we came across. We split up into pairs. There was no plan. We had two officers with us. It was just, 'You go that way, you go there, you go there, and rendezvous on the beach at 02.00.'

There was no sign of life despite the gun firing and the Very lights. It was a moonless night. I and my colleague went up through some sandhills to the edge of a bluff overlooking the beach. We were about to scramble over the top when we saw a giant figure approaching silhouetted against the starlight. It was a German sentry with his rifle slung. He looked over the bluff, while we crouched like a pair of rabbits in the sand with our pistols ready to drop this bloke should he spot us. He came on and stood about four feet away. He never saw us. He turned and walked away.

By now a great deal of time had passed, so we made our way back to where we had left the canoe and the raft. All but two of the blokes were there. They hadn't achieved anything either. We found the blow-up raft had a puncture. Fortunately it had a pump. I found that it made a ghastly metallic squeaking noise. So having got away with it so far, we were certain someone would hear and investigate. But they didn't. We got the wretched thing inflated, and launched ourselves off. We left the canoe upside down covered with sand in case the other two got away, and be able to paddle along the coast back to the British lines which would have been possible, with care, at night. We learned later they didn't come back.

Afloat on the dark sea, periodically working the squeaky pump to keep the raft from deflating, we looked in vain for the MTB. We didn't have any binoculars, and were relying on spotting its silhouette against the starlit sky. But there was no sign of her. The raft was almost unmanageable. It had short wooden paddles, and we progressed in a series of whirls out to sea. We decided that if the worst came to the worst, we'd paddle on by night, land by day and lie up, and eventually get back to our own side. It was getting close to the rendezvous time with the MTB, when she started up. Immediately we pin-pointed her. She hadn't spotted us. Why the Germans didn't open up again I don't know. We got on board and the skipper said he'd hang around till about first light in the hope the other two would turn up. He couldn't afford to stay after that, and even then would have to run back to Alexandria in daylight. They didn't come back. Later we learned they had planted some plastic bombs on lorries which had gone off, but they'd got themselves captured as well. We got back to Alexandria. It [the raid] didn't really achieve anything, except we felt at least we were trying to do some operations. No great result came from it, one or two lorries blown up.

The SBS returned to Kabrit on completion of these largely wasteful and badly planned operations to find that the SAS had designs on them.

We didn't want to join the SAS. However in the end their greater strength prevailed, and we were absorbed into the SAS, while still known as the SBS.

According to Sherwood, Stirling had greater 'pull' than Courtney. Perhaps the SAS had been more successful.

We were told, 'Right, you'll all be doing a parachute jump.' I and another chap were determined not to be bludgeoned into parachute jumping or belonging to the SAS, or anything. So we asked for an interview with the CO at the time, Michael Kealey. Roger Courtney had returned to England to start Number 2 SBS. We said we would not do a parachute jump, and would return to our units if necessary. He didn't call our bluff, luckily. We stayed, the only two who didn't make a jump. We felt we'd made a stand for the poor old SBS. Later we were to do a jump at Courtney's behest back in England.

This description of the absorption of Courtney's old SBS by the SAS has taken the story forward to the period after the 8th Army had been forced back on the Alamein position in early July. Before their 'shotgun wedding', the SBS had accompanied an SAS raid on shipping in Benghazi harbour in March 1942, but this was aborted because of bad weather. The SAS and SBS were to have another attempt at Benghazi in September 1942; a raid which was to include James Sherwood, and is described in the next chapter.

Meanwhile the LRDG's excellent work had been acknowledged by a letter from the Chief of the General Staff to the Commander-in-Chief Middle East addressed to Prendergast:

MOST SECRET AND PERSONAL

GHQ MEF
7th April 1942

Lt-Col Prendergast
Headquarters
LRDG

The Commander-in-Chief directs me to say how impressed he is with the work of the LRDG in carrying out of [sic] their deep reconnaissances along the TRIPOLI–BENGHAZI road and elsewhere.

The information which they are producing is of the utmost value to us at the present time.

The Commander-in-Chief would like you to convey his appreciation to the Officers and Other Ranks concerned.

Lieutenant-General
Chief of the General Staff

Copy to 8th Army
(To be destroyed after reading)

In the LRDG Report for the period 19 April to 26 May 1942 appears the comment:

Of recent weeks, LRDG has found itself more and more in the position of 'universal aunts' to anyone who has business in the desert behind enemy lines. An increasing stream of commandos (European and Arab), L Detachment [SAS], bogus Germans, lost travellers, escape scheme promoters, stranded aviators etc., has continued to arrive at SIWA needing petrol, rations, maintenance, information, training, accommodation, and supplies of all kinds.

The fall of Tobruk on 21 June 1942, and subsequent withdrawal of 8th Army to the Alamein position, resulted in the LRDG having to withdraw from Siwa to Kufra and Fayum. The move from Siwa had many disadvantages. It deprived the LRDG of their forward base for patrolling into Libya. Now the only approaches were from the east through the Alamein line, or across the bad going of the salt flats of the Qattara Depression, or from Kufra in the south.

*

Captain George Jellicoe had joined the SAS in time to take part in their operations in mid 1942:

About three weeks before the German offensive which led to the disorderly retreat to Alamein, I was evacuated to the CCS at Tobruk and from there to the General Hospital Alexandria. We had a really beautiful nurse only 24 years old, she nearly became the Duchess of Wellington, but she married really well. Then David Stirling asked me to join him. I went to Beirut on sick leave and got malaria. Then I got sent to an Australian Hospital with male nurses, no beautiful nurses. I don't think I've ever got out of a hospital quicker. I then joined L Detachment of the SAS.

Stirling required me as his 2ic, to try to get the organisation and administration better. Also I spoke French, and Stirling had just got a French detachment of Free French under a marvellous commander Georges Bergé. Very soon I found myself on operations. Much more fun than administration.

My first op with Stirling was June 1942 on German airfields on Crete and North Africa. There were about five attacks on airfields in North Africa in which the French were involved as well as the rest of the SAS. These were to coincide with the passage of two convoys to Malta, which was extremely hard pressed. One convoy from the east and one from the west. David asked me to go with Georges Bergé and three of his men, and a Greek officer, to attack one of the airfields on Crete at Heraklion.

We took passage in a Greek submarine, the *Triton*, a bit long in the tooth. I wouldn't recommend a voyage in an old French-built Greek submarine. The submarine surfaced at night, we had two rubber boats and paddled in. There was no one on the beach. After landing two of us swam out with the rubber boats, filled them with shingle and deflated them so they sank and there was no trace of them. Then we had aimed to get into position from where we could observe the airfield that night. But we were further away than we planned because of the wind which had resulted in our being launched from the submarine further out than expected. The going was very rough and we had far more equipment than we could carry. So we disembarrassed ourselves of some of it. We lay up that day, but not where we could see the airfield. We tried to get in that night, but not having observed it before, we ran into a German patrol, who fired on us. So surprise was lost. So we moved to a position from which we could observe the airfield properly. We did this the next day, and moved to a place where we thought we could get through. The wire round this airfield was pretty deep, about 20 feet. As we were cutting our way through, we were challenged by a German patrol. I didn't know what to do. If we had fired all surprise would have been lost. But the French Sergeant was inspired. He lay on his back and started to snore. The patrol moved on. We later learned from a captured document that they had taken us for drunken Cretan peasants. Then two Blenheims [bombers] came over to bomb the airfield. It had been arranged that they would bomb it if we hadn't got onto it the first night. That also helped us, and in the resulting confusion, we cut ourselves through and placed our charges. We destroyed a Feisler Storch and about 23 JU 88s. We marched out in what we thought was good German formation. We had the pleasure of hearing the explosions going up as we moved off.

It was less pleasant in the morning when we were lying up not having navigated very well. We were quickly discovered by Cretans, who told us that about 80 hostages had been shot as a reprisal, including the Greek governor of Crete. We later learned that when Paddy Leigh Fermor captured the German General Kreipe in Crete he was at pains to leave messages that this had been carried out by the British. We had a long walk back across the island. It took us three nights. That went fine. We kept ourselves to ourselves. We crossed the Masara Plain east of Tymbaki. As usual a Cretan found us. Georges Bergé was suspicious of him. But our Greek guide said he was OK. Shortly after that Georges asked me to go off with Petrakis our guide to meet the agent where we would re-embark.

So I went off with Petrakis and made the contact. Petrakis's feet had given out, so I returned alone by night to the valley where I thought I had left my French friends and could not find them. After a great deal of searching and by daylight I found the right place. I was immediately suspicious, because some of their belongings were neatly laid out. I thought this is not how my French friends behave, there is something wrong. At that moment three boys ran up shouting, and I gathered something had gone wrong. What had happened was that by sheer misfortune we had met one of the few quislings in Crete. He had sent one of his boys running into Timbaki to tell the Germans that there were British troops there.

As Bergé was getting ready to move, he found himself surrounded by two companies of Germans. They tried to shoot their way out. One Frenchman was killed, one wounded and Bergé decided to surrender. Georges finished up in Colditz with David Stirling. Georges Bergé was a great loss. I was evacuated three nights later, and joined up with two other parties, SBS. They had not been so lucky. One airfield, Timbaki, had no aircraft on it, one by Maleme was so heavily defended that they couldn't get on to it. We were taken off from the south coast by boat commanded by a marvellous man called John Campbell RNVR. As we went out in a rubber boat, another boat came in and we were hailed, and a voice said, 'I am Paddy Leigh Fermor, who are you?' I shouted back, 'I am George Jellicoe. Good luck to you.' That's the first time I have ever met him. We got back to Mersa Matruh one day before the Germans took Mersa Matruh [28 June 1942].

By now the SAS had been equipped with jeeps, still a novelty in the Middle East. Stirling fitted them with Vickers K guns. These had been fitted in Gloster Gladiator biplane fighters, now obsolete so their guns were spare. They were twin .303-inch guns with a very high rate of fire, 1,200 rounds per minute each. Each jeep had a pair in the front and a pair at the back. The jeep was easier to learn to drive across country than the LRDG trucks, and easier to maintain; so it suited the SAS. In order to compensate for the jeep's lack of range, because unlike the LRDG trucks it could not carry large amounts of petrol, fuel had to be pre-dumped out in the desert for SAS use, or carried in three-ton vehicles of which the SAS had acquired twenty.

George Jellicoe was on some of the earlier raids when the Vickers K guns were used:

I was very badly bitten by ticks on Crete and went into hospital, where there was a beautiful nurse. After that I was asked by David to carry out a series of raids behind the German lines. We were helped by the LRDG. I took the convoy to 8th Army HQ and then just north of the Qattara Depression to just north of Siwa. From there we carried out a series of raids on German airfields; Paddy Mayne and David with their usual success. I wasn't much good. I then went with some Free French and laid ambushes on the coast road, but nothing came along. Then as part of one of the operations I went with three jeeps and two people who later became MPs, Stephen Hastings and Carol Mather, to attack the most easterly of the German airfields nearest to the Alamein lines, the furthest from our base. Robin Gurdon of the LRDG was with us to attack the next one. Because we had to leave in daylight to cover the distance, we were bounced by fighters. Robin was killed. Two of our jeeps were destroyed by the first attack. I managed to hide my jeep in a wadi. We had to bring the whole party back in one jeep. The radiator was holed, so we stuffed it with plastic explosive and peed into the radiator to top it up. We eventually got back.

Then David carried out one of the more spectacular raids on Sidi Haneish. He took a force of about 17 jeeps. We approached under cover of dark, and formed up into two columns, Paddy Mayne was leading one, and I the other. We broke our way on to the airfield shooting our way round it. They shot back, and one chap was killed. We drove off after doing a lot of damage, about 30–35 aircraft. We lay up during the daytime, split into small groups. Unfortunately one of the French jeeps was spotted, shot up by aircraft and a very fine officer was killed. He was a great loss.

While Jellicoe's group was lying up well hidden:

A German Feisler Storch landed right by us, not more than 600 yards from us. Two people got out and had a pee. We realised that in our jeeps we could get to the plane before they could, and we captured them. One was a German doctor, and as it turned out I had had lunch with his parents in Bremen when I was driving from Bremen with the son of the Crown Prince in 1936.

My days in the desert were drawing to an end because I had trouble with my ligament locking. And it went again on this raid. Our doctor diagnosed one problem, the German doctor another. They were both right, because I had two problems. The German doctor eventually escaped with his companion. I was pleased. We went to look for them, but we didn't find the two Germans.

I was evacuated in one of three Bombays which had flown out to take some of us back. I missed the great Benghazi raid and the Tobruk raid which went wrong.

The 8th Army had held off Rommel at the first battle of Alamein, between 1 and 25 July, now both Armies broke off the battle while they prepared for the next phase. There was little respite for the LRDG and the SAS.

4

The Desert: From the eve of Alamein to Tunisia – LRDG, SAS and SBS

The success of the LRDG and SAS against the German and Italian lines of communication and airfields raises the intriguing question: why did the enemy not follow suit with similar operations? Early in the campaign Bagnold was concerned that the Italian *Auto-Saharan* companies might try raiding the Sudan and the bases in the Nile Valley. He and Prendergast had met one of these companies during their 1932 expedition, and had been most impressed. However, the Italians, despite actually having the only specially equipped long-range desert units in the Libyan Desert when they went to war, were amazingly unimaginative and timid when it came to using them. This is surprising because in other special forces activities, such as underwater attacks on ships, they were remarkably courageous and successful.

The Germans only tried it once. By a quirk of fate the man they chose to lead the expedition had accompanied Clayton and Kennedy Shaw on some of their pre-war desert forays: the Hungarian-born Count Ladislas de Almasy. In 1941 he was a captain in the Luftwaffe, and was given permission by Rommel to insert two German agents into Cairo. His party consisted of six, including himself, and the two agents, whom he calls 'Pit' and 'Pan'. He set off in mid-May 1942, and chose to go from Jalo via Kufra, but avoiding it because it was occupied by the British, and follow the route which he had explored across the Gilf Kebir plateau to Kharga Oasis and the Nile. Unknown to him, this was exactly the same way taken by T and G Patrols on their return from the Fezzan; and by other LRDG patrols subsequently. Almasy kept a diary. The first entry on 15 May 1942 gives his transport plan:

15 May 1942.

I shall drive with only 2 station wagons ('Inspector' and 'President') and 2 commercials ('Maria' and 'Purzel'). The latter two must be sacrificed. 'Purzel' will travel 800 km, 'Maria' a further 500. The last 200 km to the objective I must do with only one vehicle. There and back 400 km, can that be managed?

16 May 1942

The big surprise: due E of GIOF (main village of Kufra) 104 fresh truck tracks! I had no idea that enemy columns were running east from Kufra. They must come directly from the Gilf Kebir then?

17 May 1942

Here too are hundreds of older tracks in the direction of Gilf Kufra. The puzzle is solved: the trucks have come from the Wadi Halfa. The assumption hitherto held, that Kufra is supplied from the south from French territory, is not correct.

That the Axis did not know that the British had been driving to and from Kufra and the Nile for a year after the LRDG had moved into the Oasis was astonishing. If they did know, plainly they had not told Almasy; not very helpful if they hoped him to reach Egypt undetected. He also had problems with morale and training, both of which were not up to LRDG standards:

I have to see that Wohrmann [his signaller] keeps his log book up to date. He has no initiative, and I have to keep on asking and ordering everything. The men still cannot understand anyway that, despite experiences in the sea of sand, a long-range expedition through this realm of death is nothing else than a flight, flight from the desert itself.

Since Wohrmann is not capable of reckoning bearings and distances for me, I am continually forced to stop and check the distances on the useless Italian map.

He also had something to say on that score:

No mapping was done here outside the Depression and the Gebel Kufra. What were they [the Italians] doing from 1931 to 1939 then?

On 18 May he came across some British vehicles left behind with full tanks:

The vehicles are not abandoned but parked. On the front one are chalked the words, 'Refuelled for return'.

Gradually I understand what is happening: the enemy column goes from Wadi Halfa the first third of the distance, and leaves a number of vehicles there, which have supplied petrol for the whole column up to that point. Then the journey continues to here, the second third of the distance, and here these six trucks stay behind with empty petrol drums. When the column returns from Kufra, these trucks are collected, therefore their tanks are full.

Almasy drained the tanks of all but one of the British trucks and topped up his tanks. The next day he had problems finding his way. He found the innumerable British tracks confusing when trying to find his tracks of his previous visit before the war.

19 May 1942
Depressed spirits in our camp.
20 May 1942
I am rather worried as to how we shall get over the difficult part of my former entry into the Gilf but my old tracks – which, moreover, the British patrol also followed – lead us surely.

and later on the same day:

Altogether, except for Munz, the men cannot drive, only Koerper shows good driving ability.

He made better progress on 21 May and was approaching the Dachla Oasis having made 230 km that day:

Wireless communication has broken down again. Wohrmann reports that the transformer is not working. The men mess about with it for an hour, then came in, with the thing still out of action, to our one-pot supper. Three radio-operators and a mechanic are not in a position to find out what is wrong! In this undertaking I always have to do absolutely everything myself.

On 22 May in the vicinity of Kharga Oasis, he was beginning to worry about his fuel supply:

I have scarcely enough petrol to get back. Everything was discussed and planned in detail, I was only to radio and they would drop fuel, water and food for me in any grid square I liked. Now the instrument which is tuned in to our point of departure has fallen out, and the called station the other end does not answer!

He decided to conserve fuel by driving through Kharga Oasis on the road instead of over the dunes. The next evening Almasy, who spoke Arabic, bluffed his way past the nightwatchman posted in the small main square in the town.

Having dropped off the two agents just short of Assiut on the Nile, from where they were to make their own way into Cairo, he turned to retrace his route back to Jalo. Almasy's party returned through the square at Kharga without incident. In the Gilf Kebir he plotted the site for an airstrip, 'for an operation against the starting point of the enemy supply line'. That day he nearly ran into a column of 28 Sudan Defence Force (SDF) trucks camped in a wadi. All that day was spent trying to keep clear of the SDF column who were travelling in the same direction. Having allowed them to get ahead of him, Almasy discovered that the SDF column had bivouaced just in front of the one entrance to the only wadi leading out of the mountains:

> I stopped only a moment and waved up Munz with the car, and Koerper with his [station wagon] alongside, 'Close all windows and follow quite quietly, and just behind me. No shooting, at most salute.'
>
> They both grin, 'Yes, Sir.'
>
> I gave the Leica to Wohrmann, 'Take a photo in passing. I'll lean back so that you can make the exposure past me.'
>
> They were the same beautiful Chevrolet trucks. The men are preparing bivouacs for the night. The sun was deep down so they could hardly recognize the markings on our vehicles. I saluted with hand raised, and the Sudanese rise to return the salute. They are tall thin Negroes from the White Nile. This quaint meeting was over in a few seconds. Exactly 12 km [further on], the left back tyre was punctured; good job it did not happen near the enemy column.

They had some tense hours on 27 May wondering if they were going to find a depot they had made on the outward trip. But Almasy's navigation was good, on this stretch, after a distance of 300 kilometres, his dead reckoning was out by a mere 600 metres. However, the next day they took the wrong route, and spent most of it getting back on course. Almasy was not helped by having no one else in his party who could navigate, and also having to make sure he did not run into British patrols. At noon on 29 May they arrived back at Jalo, fourteen days after setting out. Almasy's trip had been an epic achievement, especially as he had to carry the whole venture on his shoulders, for lack of any desert expertise among his seemingly incompetent comrades. The British suspected that Almasy would attempt to penetrate to the Nile.

Lloyd Owen:

We knew where they were likely to go, because we knew where he had been before the War. I remember that operation, and being told to lay off Almasy.

Almasy's two agents were contacted by two future Presidents of Egypt, Lieutenants Anwar Sadat and Gamal Nasser of the Egyptian Army. Presumably both assumed that the Germans would be a more benign occupying power than the British. The agents, whose whereabouts were known to the British, were allowed to continue transmitting on their radio, until the information being picked up by intercept was of no further value, then they were arrested.

There are a number of explanations for Rommel's reluctance to send long-range penetration patrols behind the British lines. Only when 8th Army was operating west of Tobruk were their lines of communication as extended as his. The main British depots and airfields in the Delta were in populated areas where enemy patrols stood no chance of operating without being seen and caught. With the exception of Almasy, he had no one in his army with the expertise to operate deep in the desert. Finally, he was almost always short of fuel, and probably felt he could not spare any for long-range patrols.

With Rommel only sixty miles from Alexandria, his supply line was at its longest in the whole desert war. He received most of his supplies through Benghazi and Tobruk. If these ports could be damaged, he would be forced to rely on Tripoli, 1,200 miles to the west, as his main port. The British made plans to attack Benghazi and Tobruk. In addition Jalo was to be taken to provide a base for future operations by the SAS. All these schemes were to involve the LRDG as guides for the raiding force. At the same time the LRDG was to raid the airfield at Barce. Stirling and many LRDG officers were concerned that the raids on Tobruk and Benghazi were on too large a scale, the plans were too complicated, and that security was so poor that the intended targets were common knowledge in the bars in Cairo.

The aim of the raid on Tobruk was to destroy oil storage tanks, ammunition dumps, repair facilities and harbour defences and installations. The force was led by Lieutenant-Colonel Haselden, who had conceived the idea. Lloyd Owen's patrol would guide the force to the outskirts of Tobruk. Haselden was to drive into Tobruk in three trucks, carrying ninety commandos and SAS disguised as British prisoners of war, with their weapons hidden. Their escorts would be in German uniform, including some Palestinian Jews of German extraction to do any talking that was necessary. Under cover of an air raid, Haselden's party was to capture coastal and flak guns to the south of the harbour, and hold a bridgehead there. Offshore would be waiting two destroyers, *Sikh* and *Zulu*, eighteen MTBs, three MLs, eight Hunt class destroyers, and the anti-aircraft cruiser *Coventry*. On a signal from Haselden, about 350 men of the 11th Battalion Royal Marines and men from other units including sappers would land from *Sikh* and *Zulu* by craft, and from some of the MTBs. Together with Haselden's men, they would destroy the various targets in Tobruk. On completion, the whole force, other than the LRDG, would withdraw by MTBs and destroyers. Lloyd Owen was to wait outside Tobruk and seal off the entrance road. On a radio signal from Haselden he was to attack a radio direction station, remove a vital part of the equipment, and cut communications, before withdrawing himself.

On 6 September Haselden's party, led by Lloyd Owen, left Kufra, arriving on the outskirts of Tobruk on the evening of 13 September. Lieutenant Tom Langton, Irish Guards, lately in Number 8 Commando, and now in the SAS, was one of those in the trucks carrying the bogus prisoners headed for the town. He and other ex-Number 8 Commando men were familiar with Tobruk having been besieged there earlier in the campaign. Langton's job on arrival in Tobruk was to signal by Aldis lamp to the MTBs coming to the east promontory of Tobruk harbour. Tom Langton wrote in an unpublished memoir:

We solemnly shook hands with David Lloyd Owen and waved farewell to his merry band. I walked back to the third truck and slowly donned a long German overcoat and put the German forage cap on my head. I climbed up on to the seat beside the driver, and stuck my head out through the opening in the cab roof. I felt no fear at this stage, just excitement and a deep sense of the inevitability of the whole thing which had been growing on me ever since we left Cairo, and throughout the desert journey via Kufra. The men who were arranging themselves on the floor of the open truck, hiding their weapons under their legs, and trying hard to look like prisoners, appeared to have much the same feeling. There was none of the banter and ribaldry of the dress rehearsal of the night before, and only Lofty had his perpetual grin on his face, and was singing quietly to himself:

'If you go down to Tobruk tonight,

You're sure of a big surprise.'

As the trucks drove towards Tobruk, there was a moment of farce. Frank Harrison, David Lloyd Owen's driver:

We'd seen the commandos drive away in three-ton trucks. We saw a motor bike chase after them. Lloyd Owen said, 'We must get the motor bike.' We tore after it, and it vanished into a little wadi. When we got there we found it full of 'Eyeties' in a fifteen-hundredweight out looking for firewood. It was stuck in the sand. They'd seen the three-tonners pass, and sent the motor cycle to get them to give them a tow. In fact the motor bike couldn't catch the three-tonners so we needn't have bothered.

So we were stuck with these Italian prisoners. We drove to the outskirts of Tobruk. There we had to wait for further instructions.

Haselden's party took a wrong turning in Tobruk, and were late arriving at the point where they were to leave the trucks. Langton, having debussed, threw his German overcoat and cap into an empty sangar. It took longer than planned to clear some of the enemy positions, imposing further delays. One of Langton's men became the first casualty when on being challenged by his own side, he forgot the password and was shot through the thigh. Langton, already late, then missed his way, so did not have time to collect his Aldis lamp from an officer who was signalling from the other promontory. Why he did not have it with him is a mystery. He signalled with his torch instead.

Haselden's men had captured some of the coastal guns, but lost them to determined counter-attacks from a garrison that was much stronger and more alert than expected. The attack from landward may have taken them by surprise, but the approach from sea did not. As *Sikh* and *Zulu* and the MTBs approached, the searchlights which had been pointing at the sky at the departing RAF bombers swung down and picked out the ships offshore.

The first wave of 11th Battalion RM had already been launched. They were being taken ashore in wooden lighters, of which only one in three had an engine. Each powered lighter towed two engineless craft. In the rough seas, engines failed, and craft broke up, drowning the occupants. The Commanding Officer's craft started to founder and his one radio failed to work. He could not therefore warn the two destroyers that everything was going badly wrong. They closed the beach to cut down the journey for the lighters returning to collect the second wave. When the searchlights dipped down, *Sikh* and *Zulu* were caught in the beams, as were the first wave of 11th Battalion RM, or those still afloat, still 800 yards from the beach. Only seventy marines under Major Jack Hedley made the shore, two miles west of the correct beach. They put up a stout fight, in the course of which Hedley, a Bisley champion pistol shot, accounted for five of the enemy with five rounds of his revolver. By 8.30 a.m. there were only twenty-one marines alive. Hedley led them to some caves intending to lie up for the rest of the day and make for their own lines after dark. They were discovered and captured just before nightfall. Hedley was told by the garrison commander that the Germans had been expecting them.

Haselden had been killed during the night. *Sikh* was so badly damaged she was scuttled. *Zulu* and *Coventry* were sunk by bombing on the return to Alexandria, as were six out of the twenty-one MTBs and MLs. Only ninety marines returned to Egypt.

Outside the town Lloyd Owen waited for the signal from Haselden that never came. All night his patrol listened to the sound of fierce fighting in Tobruk. When dawn came, Lloyd Owen gave the order to withdraw. Frank Harrison, David Lloyd Owen's driver:

> We drove through a huge German Army camp. The cooks were just getting up. Odd fellows walking about, going to the lavatories and having a wash. We just drove through them waving. They waved back. Why not? Five trucks driving through your camp, in the early morning, waving to you, why not wave back? Can't possibly be enemy, all that way behind German lines. Impossible.

Apart from Lloyd Owen's patrol, few of those who went into Tobruk by land or sea got out: Lieutenant Lanark, Scots Guards, with two others, Langton with six, and one other. Langton wrote to his parents from hospital on 21 November 1942:

> At dawn, I and some others found our retreat cut off, and there was nothing for it but to make for the hills and wadis to the east. We split up into small parties, and that night started off to get through the perimeter wire. The

next morning found us hiding in a cave in a wadi, quite exhausted, after forcing our way through the well-defended perimeter of Tobruk – wire, tank traps, minefields, more wire, alert sentries, and deep rocky wadis, which made the going incredibly hard.

The party consisted of Langton, Sergeant Evans of the Welsh Guards, who had been in Langton's troop in Layforce, Corporal Wilson and four others: a private, whom Langton describes as a 'Geordie Black Sheep'; two Fusiliers, identical twins, called Leslie; and an Austrian Jew whom they called 'Kennedy'. He told them his real name was Hillman. He had operated in German uniform before, been captured, and escaped. It is likely that Hillman was not his name either, merely one given to him by the British Army as a cover. He had emigrated to Palestine before the war. Langton:

Between us and the fighting line were over 300 miles, most of which was waterless desert, all occupied by the enemy. Between the seven of us we had a small tin of cheese, one bar of chocolate, four biscuits, and not quite four pints of water. On top of all this 'Kennedy''s left boot was in pieces, and he had torn his foot on barbed wire. There were only two saving graces. One was that we had been told that if we should find ourselves left behind, we'd be picked up if we reached a certain point north of Bardia by a particular date. The other: the knowledge that there were Arabs living between Tobruk and Bardia who were friendly to the British. Where they were, and how many of them, we did not know.

That night we made for the road, and walked brazenly along it, rather in the hope of finding a deserted truck we could pinch. None came our way, and after a brush with some sentries near a camp, we hid up for the day in a cave. Next night the road again, but this time more in the hope of finding water or food. Eventually we found a tin which had water in it – or at any rate half water, half petrol. It was delicious. The third night we decided to make for the sea, and try our luck there.

Near the sea they found a waterhole, but so salty, it burnt their lips. Later they broke into a deserted Arab hut, and found some haricot beans, some flour and a tin of foul-tasting water with a dead rat in the bottom. The next day they hid in a cave by the sea. By now they had been evading for five days. The following night they decided to head for the road again, and try to hold up the first single truck they encountered. As they set off, they heard a dog bark, and walked towards the sound.

We staggered over a ridge, and there below us was a row of shapeless tents nestling in one of the dips which are the beginnings of the giant wadis. Our first excitement was tempered with discretion. We did not know for certain whether these people were friendly, nor did we know if the villages were watched. One fact was a great boon: 'Kennedy' spoke perfect Arabic. Furthermore he spoke it with a Palestinian accent. The Libyan Arabs would know that he wasn't a disguised Italian.

The Italians would sometimes approach an Arab village dressed in British uniforms and ask for help. The next day, the villagers would be taken away, never to be seen again.

The first time we adopted an approach drill which we kept to on future occasions. 'Kennedy' went in first to make peace with the village, followed at a distance of twenty yards or so by either myself or the sergeant with pistol ready. On this occasion we were in luck and found a ready welcome.

They were given biscuits and marmalade, and as much water as they could drink:

I don't think I shall ever forget that meal. We set upon it like animals, quite unashamedly, and could feel the strength returning to our bodies.

Later we were to learn through 'Kennedy' how to conduct ourselves as visitors.

Before dawn they set off, loaded with biscuits, their water bottles full, and 'Kennedy' sporting a pair of new German boots. They pushed on, lying up by day and moving by night, finding an Arab village each night, where they were given food. Langton had a considerable sum of Italian money, but most villagers refused to take it, preferring a note addressed to the British Forces saying that they had been of assistance. It was now long past the limit for the pick-up north of Bardia.

I began to get mentally distressed which proved far more trying than any physical distress I had suffered up to that date. What were we to do? We knew there were no more Arabs after Bardia. We hadn't got the food or water to get round Bardia and Sollum [250 miles from the lines]. Anyhow there wasn't much chance of a party of seven to get through the enemy lines. If we stayed in the wadis north of Bardia, it would be difficult to get the Arabs to keep us for any length of time, and although I believed the British were going to attack at Alamein, it might not be until the end of

November or later. Perhaps they did not intend to come further than Matruh. Maybe – gloomy thought – Rommel had succeeded in breaking the Alamein line – maybe anything!

At last we came to the coast north of Bardia, and an Arab told us that there was an English soldier and an Indian hiding not far away. I sent them a note, and that evening the Arab led them to us. That was how we met Chatta Singh Rowat, and 'Fortune' smiled on us again.

Chatta Singh Rawat, an Indian soldier, had been taken when Tobruk had been captured by Rommel on 21 June 1942, and had escaped soon afterwards, but was caught on the perimeter. After escaping again, he had been picked up attempting to find water in Sollum. His captors threatened him with death if he tried to escape again. He walked out that night, and had been at large for ten weeks when Langton's party met him. With him was Private Watler of Haselden's party, who had escaped from Tobruk after the raid.

Chatta and Watler led them to a large wadi, the Wadi Kattara, where the two had been living for a week, and which was to be:

our home for four weeks. Its sides were about 600 feet high, steep and rocky. Its bottom was sandy and scrub-covered, and about 250 feet wide. At the top [end], about a mile or more inland, it ended in an abrupt cliff, out of which a stream of clear water trickled. Fig trees and a small Arab plantation formed a small arbour surrounded on three sides by cliffs. At the sea end was a small sandy beach, and here, about halfway up the side of the wadi, was the little cave which for four weeks I shared with the Indian. The rest of the party lived in a larger cave about 200 feet further inland, except for Sgt Evans who lived alone in a cave near ours.

'Geordie Black Sheep' disappeared soon after their arrival.

For the last week before we reached Wadi Kattara, we had begun to get somewhat irritable. The mental worry over what to do next gnawed at me. I strictly forbade bickering, and made everyone apologise for 'snapping' at each other. I had to do quite a bit of apologising myself. The real cause of it was 'Geordie Black Sheep', just why it is hard to say, except he hadn't got the guts for the job, and spent his whole time whining and 'If onlying – if only we had this, if only we could do that', which we were all inclined to do, and which was extremely annoying for all those who weren't doing it at the moment. He got worse and worse, and eventually started to refuse to obey my orders, for which he was severely rebuked by me and abused by the others. We were not really sorry therefore when he disappeared one morning. After making sure he had not fallen over the cliff, I bothered no more, especially as 'Kennedy' told me he had asked him exhaustively about life in POW camps.

Life in the wadi was not exactly exhilarating.

They ate rice, macaroni, or chapattis made from flour and water. The amount of food varied depending on what the Arabs could spare from their own meagre stocks. They would watch for shoals of fish when the sea was calm, and stun them using German grenades provided by the Arabs. Using a barrel of petrol washed up on the beach and dry brush wood they made a signal fire in a triangle, to try and attract friendly aircraft passing overhead on frequent night raids to Tobruk, and other Axis positions to the west.

For several nights we got no reply. One night they came back flying very low. We poured on the petrol and lit up. I sat on the water's edge flashing optimistically with my torch. Sure enough a plane circled over us. He dropped a flare out to sea, and another. Watler shouted, 'If he drops another, he's sure to have seen us.' There was a whistle, a swish and a roar, and I was running up the wadi with bits of rock and sand whizzing all around me; three bombs and a delayed-action one that went off at midnight.

I realised that one of our possible ways of rescue was hopeless. That left two: to go and risk getting through, or to stay and await the coming of the 'push'.

They decided to stay for a while longer:

But all was not perfect in this troglodyte existence and a series of troubles led up to our final decision to depart.

Sergeant Evans contracted bad dysentery. He tried to persuade Langton to make a break for it, just the two of them, and try to steal a truck to drive through the lines at night, or to the Gebel where he thought they might find agents. But Langton felt responsible for the others and would not leave them. Evans's dysentery got worse, he was in great pain, and could not move a few yards without doubling up in agony. Eventually Langton persuaded him to give himself up.

We escorted him to the track and last saw him bravely struggling along towards the road, with a blanket over his shoulders. I have not heard of him yet, but sincerely hope he was picked up and treated well, for he was immensely brave, and never complained although he must have gone through agony. A tall and strong fellow as a rule, he looked like a haggard old man when he left us.

Evans was picked up and spent the rest of the War as a POW. Chatta Singh became difficult and moody. Clearly he was an independent type, and began to resent the others, although they parted good friends:

When we eventually left him, we had an affectionate parting and Chatta wept copiously.

The incident which confirmed Langton in his decision to leave was a visit by Italians to the Arab camp and the arrest of three of the men; for selling eggs on the road without a licence it later transpired. But this was enough for him. The two Leslies succumbed to dysentery just before the party set off on 23 October, leaving Corporal Wilson, Watler and 'Kennedy' to accompany Langton. After more desperate struggles to survive, they were picked up on 13 November, at Hemeimat, well behind the original British lines at Alamein. By this time the 8th Army had reached Tobruk. But Langton had swung south to the Qattara depression and had been bypassed.

Five days later, Lanark, the sole survivor of his party of three, was picked up by a British armoured car.

Almost every aspect of the Tobruk raid had been chaotic, and perhaps the seaborne landing was the worst of all. From lack of thorough reconnaissance, to the use of lighters to land troops, it epitomized the half-baked manner in which almost all amphibious operations were conducted in the Middle East at the time. There was a shortage of landing craft in the theatre of operations, but the staffs at GHQ who planned and sanctioned these raids should have known better, and not tried to make bricks without straw. In this, and other ways connected with these types of operation, they deserved the nickname 'The Short-Range Desert Group' given to them by the LRDG, or the 'Short-Range Shepheards Group', alluding to Shepheards Hotel in Cairo where they allegedly spent most of their time.

The Benghazi raid led by Stirling was only marginally better planned. James Sherwood of the SBS which had been hijacked into the SAS took part. (Allowance must be made for Sherwood's dislike of the SAS, but there are aspects of his account which have an undeniable ring of truth):

In August of 1942 we were told that an operation was being mounted by the SAS in September in which the SBS would take part. This would involve a long drive south up the Nile valley to Assiut; from there we would strike west across the desert south of the Sand Sea for the oasis of Kufra, for an attack on Benghazi to divert the Germans and Italians from Alamein. The same night there was to be a similar assault on Tobruk.

We set off. We had canoes on our trucks. The SAS went ahead. They hadn't given us any maps. The only instruction we had was to leave the Nile valley at Assiut, strike the desert track for the oasis at Kharga, take a westerly bearing, and follow that for some hundreds of miles, until we struck the Wadi Halfa–Kufra track. Here we would turn right, and we were told we would recognise it by the enormous number of vehicle tracks in the sand. The track could be miles wide depending on how many vehicles used it. If a vehicle stuck, the others would go round it to find firmer sand to drive on. We just followed this jumble of tracks for several days, until we struck another great conglomeration of tracks, we never did see how wide it was across, coming in from our left, which we rightly assumed, although with no great confidence at the time, must be the Wadi Halfa–Kufra track. In due course we got to Kufra.

I suppose we couldn't have got lost anyway. If we had, someone from the SAS would have said, 'Isn't the SBS supposed to be with us? Perhaps we'd better send someone back to try to find them.'

At Kufra we had two or three days to gather our forces and get ourselves together. Here we discovered our role. While the SAS kept Benghazi occupied, we were to assemble our canoes on the side of the harbour, paddle out and sink the ships there with limpet mines. Nobody was enthusiastic about this apart from the fact that we didn't want to be with the SAS anyway. A great deal of grumbling and moaning went on, quite amusing in retrospect, very irritating at the time. On 13th September 1942, we motored in trucks down the escarpment in the pitch dark towards Benghazi. We and the SAS were perched on our canoes in their bags in a 3-ton lorry, with a whole lot of explosives under the canoes. We were half asleep, dozing on top of these canoes and explosives with the blokes grumbling at one another, 'Get your bloody boots out of the way', sort of thing. When the truck stopped, one chap hopped over the side and had a crap at the side of the road, while the truck waited and the others went past. I can't remember any apprehension, just the coldness of the night, and everybody thoroughly out of sorts with one another.

An RAF raid had been arranged to keep Benghazi quiet until the SAS/ SBS force had got into the town.

The whole thing went wrong. We saw the raid from afar, and watched the fun and games, and fireworks and bombs, when we were still trundling down the escarpment hopelessly late. For better or worse David Stirling decided the operation would be carried on. We had a guide with us, some Arab who was supposed to know the way. He didn't know where he was, neither did anyone else. We went down the escarpment with headlights full on, Stirling hoped to bluff his way, that nobody [no enemy] would be stupid enough to come down with their headlights on.

We came on a proper road. Ahead you could see a striped pole. David Stirling got out, and walked up to this pole just to see what was going on, all the headlights beamed away behind him. He was a very brave bloke. He quickly found out. Instead of Italians being there, the Germans were waiting for us. They knew all about it. They opened up with everything they'd got. The extraordinary thing was that they scored very few hits. Just as well because sitting on our explosives we would have disappeared in a big bang.

We were told to get out of it, every man for himself, in jeep and lorry as best we could. There was a great deal of confusion, backing and filling of trucks trying to turn round. Shot and stuff flying all over the place without anybody, except one jeep, hit in the petrol tank, which went up in flames, adding to the already illuminated scene. We headed out of it, having achieved nothing at all; a complete fiasco, the whole operation.

At break of day we were all haring hell for leather across this big gravelly plain, trying to get to the Gebel area where there were ravines for conceal-ment before the planes got up to look for us. We weren't in time. They got the fighters up, strafing and bombing. I can remember lorries with great clouds of dust driving faster than they'd ever driven in their lives before, all trying to reach cover before the worst happened. None of us were hit. Some of us would bale out of the trucks when we thought a plane was diving on us and ran like hell. But the plane wasn't diving on us, it was after another truck which it didn't catch. The driver of our truck would slow up so we could catch him, and we all jumped aboard, and off again. Eventually we gained the shelter of the Gebel, the planes having turned back presumably to rearm and come after us again.

The first sight that greeted us when we got to a particularly deep ravine,

Captain P. J. D. McCraith who raised the Yeomanry Patrol in the Long Range Desert Group in front of his Ford truck. Captain 'Taranto' asleep on top. (HU 71713)

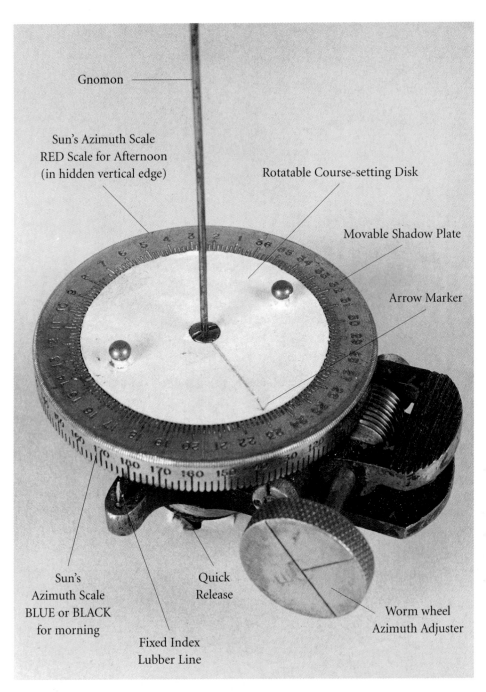

Gnomon

Sun's Azimuth Scale
RED Scale for Afternoon
(in hidden vertical edge)

Rotatable Course-setting Disk

Movable Shadow Plate

Arrow Marker

Sun's
Azimuth Scale
BLUE or BLACK
for morning

Quick
Release

Fixed Index
Lubber Line

Worm wheel
Azimuth Adjuster

Bagnold Sun Compass. The shadow that the Gnomon casts on the Shadow Plate is the
actual true bearing in which the vehicle is heading. The Azimuth Circle can be rotated
and set against the Lubber Line to match the sun's azimuth for the particular time of day
which is found by referring to tables issued for the purpose. The compass is mounted
so that the Lubber Line, as in a ship's or yacht's compass, is fixed pointing forward on an
exact fore and aft line. Wherever the vehicle points, so will the Lubber line. (HU 71822)

Captain David Lloyd Owen with 'Tich' Cave on the back of a 30-cwt truck outside the Farouk Hotel in Siwa oasis, November 1941. (HU 25299)

A posed photograph of an LRDG Chevrolet truck. The gunner beside the driver is manning an Italian Breda, with the Lewis gunner behind the driver. The condenser can is the cylindrical container with the tube in the top. The sand channels are hooked on the side of the truck below the Lewis gunner. (E 12380)

LRDG Chevrolet truck shooting a dune. The truck behind is a Ford 30-cwt. (HU 25793)

Lieutenant-Colonel John Haselden dressed as an Arab coming out of the desert to meet an LRDG patrol. (HU 24997)

LRDG WACO aircraft. (HU 25081)

Y Patrol returning to Kufra after a successful incursion into enemy territory.
Back row, left to right: Trooper 'Tankie' Babb (RTR), Corporal Jack Harris
(Somerset Yeomanry), Gunner James Patch (RA), Sergeant Derek 'Hutch' Hutchins
(Somerset Yeomanry), Lance-Corporal Arthur 'Tich' Cave MM (Somerset Yeomanry),
Lance-Corporal Brian Springford (Somerset Yeomanry), Trooper Kenneth Tinckler
(Cheshire Yeomanry), Craftsman Alf Tighe MM (REME), Trooper 'Jesus' Armstrong (?).
Front row, left to right: Private 'Darkie' Devine (Seaforths?), Private John 'Daisy' McKay
(Seaforths), Trooper F. Gordon 'Harry' Harrison (Yorks Hussars), Private William
'Jock' Fraser (Seaforths), Trooper L. D. 'Mickey' Coombs (Somerset Yeomanry),
Trooper Robert Davies (? Yeomanry), Trooper 'Bomski' Cashin (Cheshire
Yeomanry). (HU 25277)

David Stirling with men of G Patrol of the LRDG. The man standing in the vehicle is probably Guardsman G. T. 'Ginger' Blaney LRDG. The remainder, *left to right*, are: Guardsman Archie Gibson LRDG, Reg Seekings SAS, Guardsman Jack Crossley LRDG, Johnny Cooper SAS, David Stirling SAS, Craftsman R. N. Scott LRDG, Rose LRDG, Guardsman Archie Murray LRDG. Date and place unknown. (HU 69650)

An SAS jeep, heavily loaded with jerricans of fuel and water. The man nearest the camera is manning the .50-inch Browning heavy machine-gun. The driver has a single Vickers K gun mounted in front of him, and a twin Vickers K behind him. (NA 676)

Lieutenant-Colonel Blair 'Paddy' Mayne. (AP 6069)

was a group of SAS blokes with a fire going, cooking breakfast as though on a picnic. We didn't stop there. It was a daft place to be. We'd two officers with us, and we went up the ravine as far as we could. For the whole of the day we lay up under camouflage netting. Nothing spotted us. The rest of the force had a fearful dusting about a mile or two west of us which went on all day, machine-gunning and bombing. How many were lost then I don't know; very few at the encounter at the border post, but a lot altogether.

We lay up all day. We'd received a message from Stirling, 'The operation all off. Head for Kufra as best you can.'

Off they set. Having halted when they found the track, the truck refused to start. The driver was badly burned when the engine caught fire while trying to get it going by priming the carburettor with petrol. His mate volunteered to stay with him, and was taken prisoner by the Italians. The driver died. The officer with the party decided they would walk out to Kufra, some 500 miles away. Luckily they found a well of filthy water full of worms, but drinkable. At the well they must have been spotted by Arabs, although they didn't see them, some of their kit was stolen. The Arabs made contact with Stirling, who sent a message with one of them to wait at the well. Eventually Stirling appeared in a jeep. After more delays, an abandoned truck located by Stirling was got going, the patrol loaded up, and reached Kufra. Here they were bombed by the Luftwaffe. But eventually the whole party reached Cairo via the Wadi Halfa.

Captain Malcolm Pleydell was the doctor with the force on the Benghazi raid. A letter written on 6 October, after the raid, gives some idea of what being a medical officer with the SAS could be like, and what casualties had to put up with:

It's funny having to do all the anaesthetics and operating oneself, although I occasionally have an orderly to assist. I started off with a fractured femur, which I had to carry on with us on the back of a lorry. I had to keep him well under with morphia. Then I had two men wounded driving over a thermos bomb, one with extensive and second-degree burns over chest, abdomen, arms and legs; he died quietly during the night. The other with an amputation, I gave two pints of plasma and he lived. Not bad amputating with an officer to help me, and the dust blowing. We had to hurry to catch up with the others, it was hell to watch three legs and a stump being flung up in the air and falling back each time the lorry hit a bump; so we had to tie their legs down with a rope. The dust was thrown up and fell all over them, so they quickly became yellow, and we had to stop now and then to bathe their faces to let them breathe.

Later on I had a case of multiple wounds, not too bad; one shot through the lung, for which there was little to do; one with a compound fracture of the humerus, radius and ulna, with the arm shattered in two places. I left the arm on. As a last case I had a retention of urine due to the perineal urethra being shot away. I had to do a supra pubic cystotomy eventually, being unable to find the proximal end of the urethra. It was a devil. Again I was alone and two spencer wells, two scalpels, and one forceps. With nobody retracting and no retractors it's damned difficult to see what you are doing. I did muscle splitting and blunt dissection got down to the bladder with no bleeding.

We had no room for stretcher cases as we had lost a good deal of our transport, so I had to leave them with an Italian orderly who had given himself up. I brought back two major wounded and all the minor cases. One was the chap with a shattered arm and the other with multiple wounds. They both made the long trek home OK.

The attack on Jalo had not been planned to coincide with those on Tobruk and Benghazi. The enemy had time to prepare. The Sudan Defence Force was led to Jalo by two LRDG patrols, but having lost surprise failed to take the objective.

The fourth raid, that on Barce airfield, purely an LRDG affair, was a success. The operation was commanded by Major Jake Easonsmith, with T1 Patrol (Captain Wilder) and G1 Patrol (Captain Timpson). By now the LRDG also had some jeeps, and the total party was carried in twelve trucks and five jeeps. With them was Major Peniakoff ('Popski') and two of his Senussis. The outward journey of 1,155 miles, starting at Faiyum on 2 September, took them across the Egyptian and Kalansho Sand Seas, before swinging north to the Gebel Akhdar. Early in the crossing of the Egyptian Sand Sea, a G1 jeep overturned, fracturing Timpson's skull and a guardsman's spine. Fortunately, Captain Lawson, the LRDG medical officer, was with this patrol, and he probably saved the guardsman's life. The two men were evacuated by air from Big Cairn.

This delayed the party, but they were fifteen miles from Barce on 13 September, the day planned for the raid. Easonsmith took 'Popski' and his two Arabs forward to reconnoitre the airfield, before returning to brief the patrols. After dark, Easonsmith and the patrols set off. A native sentry who challenged them at a police guardpost was taken prisoner. An Italian officer who came out was shot, and the remainder of the guard took off into the night. 'Popski' met the patrols at the rendezvous, but without his two Arabs who may still have been on their reconnaissance. On the main road to Barce, the patrols met two light tanks. Fortunately the tanks held their fire until the leading vehicle was level, at which the LRDG opened fire, and the whole party got past in the confusion.

Close to Barce, the patrols separated; T1 to attack the airfield, and G1 the barracks. Easonsmith drove off with two jeeps to beat up the town. T1, having set fire to a fuel dump, and a tanker and trailer, drove round the airfield in single file firing incendiary ammunition at all the aircraft. A corporal in the last truck placed bombs on any aircraft not burning. Despite enemy fire the patrol spent an hour on the airfield without taking any casualties. They destroyed thirty-five aircraft.

The Italians tried to block the exit road from the airfield. Some extremely hairy driving ensued. Wilder rammed an Italian light tank, pushing it out of the way. After trying to immobilize the tank by throwing grenades under it, Wilder and his crew transferred from their wrecked truck to a jeep following behind. One of his crew was badly wounded, and another was seized by the Italians in the mayhem. The jeep in which Wilder was now travelling failed to take a corner, hit the kerb and overturned, pinning everybody, including Wilder, underneath either unconscious or injured. The crew of the next truck along managed to pull them clear and revive them before they reached the rendezvous.

The crew of another truck following Wilder had jumped on to the tank he had rammed, and put it out of action by climbing on to it and dropping grenades down the turret. They immobilized another tank before eventually finding their way to the rendezvous. One other truck, cut off by armoured vehicles, was set on fire as it desperately raced up another road, and crashed into a concrete shelter. The driver was thrown by the force of the impact into the shelter and taken prisoner by the Italian occupants. The other three members of the crew, one of whom was badly wounded, were also taken prisoner.

G1 Patrol had attacked the barracks to distract as many as possible of the Italians from T1's attack on the airfield, while Easonsmith created chaos in the town, lobbing grenades at troops in the streets, and destroying twelve vehicles in a transport park.

After meeting at the rendezvous, the whole party set off southwards. T1 had lost six men and three vehicles, and G1 four men and one truck. Just before dawn the party was ambushed at 'Popski''s drop-off point from the night before by about 150 Tripolitanian troops. Fortunately they mostly missed, but damaged a truck, and wounded three men, including 'Popski'. While the fitters were trying to repair this truck, which had been towed clear, and two others which had been damaged before the raid and left behind, the Tripolitanian soldiers attacked again. Easonsmith charged them with his jeep and drove them off. This allowed the fuel and stores to be taken off, and the trucks planted with time bombs. With the onset of daylight, the enemy air force put in an appearance and set about the patrols. The LRDG were crossing an area of rough scrub country where it was very difficult to take evasive action, or drive fast. From mid-morning until nightfall, the enemy air attacks continued. By last light, only one truck and two jeeps remained working. Captain Lawson, the Medical Officer, took a jeep and a truck with six wounded men, a navigator and a driver, and eventually reached a landing strip near the Kalansho Sand Sea, where they found Lloyd Owen who had been sent to meet them. Roderick Matthews, Y1 Patrol:

> Our next job was to go to LG 125 [landing ground] and pick up the survivors of a raid under Doc Lawson. We found them with one truck and got the RAF to pick them up.

The wounded were evacuated by air to Cairo by RAF Bombay transport aircraft.

Trooper Jopling, a New Zealander, and nine guardsmen began walking to Bir el Gerrari, in the middle of the Gebel, where G1 Patrol had left a vehicle on the way to Barce. While Easonsmith loaded the remaining jeep with water and rations, and with fourteen men also walked towards Bir el Gerrari. After covering eighty miles, they unexpectedly met S2 Patrol. They reported that Jopling's party had not reached Bir el Gerrari, so Easonsmith and S2 searched for three days. He found only eight guardsmen – Jopling and one guardsman were missing. The two, desperately short of water, had nearly made the rendezvous, but thinking they were too late, turned north, eventually stopping at an Arab camp, and were turned over to the Italians. Jopling, whose leg had turned gangrenous, and his companion had covered some 150 miles, mostly at night navigating by the stars.

Eventually Easonsmith also met S2 who had with them two guardsmen of the four missing when G1 withdrew from Barce. They had walked out of town.

All the LRDG patrols that had taken part in the Tobruk, Benghazi, Jalo and Barce operations ended up in Kufra.

Lloyd Owen:

> On our return there was a great mass of LRDG [there]. We had only just been there a day or two, when the Germans sent six Heinkels to bomb us because the GHQ communiqué had done exactly what we had asked them not to do, they announced that these raids had taken place and had been mounted from Kufra. We had implored them not to mention this. The LRDG and SAS fired with everything we had. Six came over, four failed to get back. I was standing watching when I was bowled over by a .5-inch round. I was flown back to Cairo and spent two months in hospital.

There were several other casualties. Alexander Stewart, a fitter with G1 Patrol, and just back from the Barce raid:

> Dish Harkness was letting them have it with a .5 browning and he fell back shot through the chest.

For their efforts in the Barce raid, Easonsmith and Wilder were awarded the DSO, Lawson the MC, and three New Zealanders the MM.

After the Benghazi raid, Stirling was summoned to meet the Prime Minister who was visiting the Middle East, and General Sir Harold Alexander who had just replaced Auchinleck as Commander-in-Chief. It was after this meeting that the SAS was officially recognized as part of the British Army as 1st Special Air Service Regiment with Stirling commanding as a lieutenant-colonel.

A bright young lieutenant-colonel, John Hackett of the 8th Hussars, who had recently been wounded, had been brought in to co-ordinate the activities of all the 'funnies', as they were sometimes called. Described by Montgomery's Chief of Staff, Major General Freddie de Guingand, as 'that dashing cavalry and later paratroop commander', 'Shan' Hackett remembered:

> The last thing I wanted to do was this. I was having the time of my life in the desert. I wrote to Freddie de Guingand and protested. You don't take a

horse busy training for a flat race just before the meeting and start training him for jumps. But I was sent to GHQ as GSO 1 Raiding Forces.

We had to reorganise this lot, and they were a lot of prima donnas. They were splendid. In addition to the LRDG, a wonderful unequalled deep recce lot, and David Stirling's SAS, the 'blowers-up', we had the Greek Sacred Squadron [Regiment], my goodness that was a party. Then we acquired a team of Turkish-speaking assassins. We kept them on ice to murder German generals if they got down through the Caucasus. I tried to make special operations comprehensible to senior commanders and palatable to them. This took a lot of doing. It was then I hatched 'Popski'. He was a Belgian national although Russian by birth. I found him in Cairo not doing very much, he had been wounded in the Tobruk show [*sic*; author's note: Barce actually], and had just come out of hospital with a grudge against the General Staff and the world in general. He was longing to get on with the war. So I set him up in what we called for the benefit of the War Establishments Committee by the somewhat pompous title of Number 1 Long-Range Demolition Squadron. That was to get them to take it seriously. We got it through in lightning time. We had discussion about what actually to call this outfit, we couldn't use this long name. So I said, 'Unless you can think of a suitable name, I am going to call you Popski's Private Army.'

'Done,' said 'Popski'.

The birth of the SAS as an 'official' regiment was accompanied by an order to double its strength. Montgomery refused to allow Stirling to recruit from 8th Army which was preparing for the forthcoming offensive at Alamein. He was forced to find his men from reinforcement depots, who would need much training before they were fit for operations. He put all his experienced men in a squadron under Mayne, and charged him with continuing with operations. Stirling also took over the Greek Sacred Regiment, formed by Greek Army officers who had escaped from Greece after the German invasion.

One of Hackett's concerns was keeping these units from conflicting with each other. The LRDG operational report comments on the problem of maintaining road watch where there were increasingly active enemy patrols:

undoubtedly as a result of the 'beating up' of the road by the SAS, though the incompatibility of road watching and beating up had been repeatedly stressed by us at GHQ.

Another outcome of the increase in size of the SAS Regiment was a need to define the roles of the LRDG and SAS. It was decided that the LRDG should carry out long-range reconnaissance tasks, and the SAS the shorter-range attacks on enemy communications and airfields, for which their training and equipment made them especially suitable. It was left open to the LRDG to make similar attacks on long-range targets. At the time of the Battle of Alamein, LRDG offensive operations were limited to the area west of Longitude 20 degrees East, which ran more or less down the eastern side of the Gulf of Sirte. For this reason the LRDG operations until December 1942 were restricted to reconnaissance, 'taxi service' and road watch.

The road watch began again a week after the start of the Battle of Alamein. LRDG report:

> By 10th November, the effects of the Battle of Alamein were beginning to show, enemy transport was streaming westwards at a rate which reached 3,500 a day. These figures and the absence of an eastward movement of fighting troops confirmed the belief that Rommel intended to evacuate Cyrenaica.

Enemy patrols forced the road watch to be lifted for about four days, by which time it was decided to double bank the patrols to maintain continuity at all costs, so valuable was the information that the LRDG was providing for 8th Army and GHQ Middle East. Timpson (G1) and Tinker (T2) left Kufra to join Sweeting (G2) and Talbot (R2). The LRDG report:

> Both had trouble on the way north. By this time the enemy were fully aware of the use we and the SAS were making of the Marada–Zella gap, and had laid mines and were maintaining patrols in it. Tinker lost a truck on a mine and one man had a leg broken. The following day Timpson lost four trucks and twelve men in an engagement with an enemy patrol. Tinker returned to Kufra with the wounded, but Timpson continued with his reduced force and established a watch on November 30th, maintaining it until December 14th. This was one of the outstanding achievements of the LRDG. Everything was against Timpson, he had lost half his patrol, he was short of rations, the weather was vile, the area was full of enemy troops, and his other officer was ill with a poisoned hand.

On 4 December, 8th Army sent a signal to Prendergast:

Army Commander congratulates you on fine achievements of your patrols and wishes them to know how very important their successes are at this time. Keep it up.

At the beginning of December, LRDG were asked by 8th Army to provide a patrol to guide a force in outflanking Rommel's position at Agheila. Browne (R1) contacted XXX Corps and guided 4th Light Armoured Brigade and the New Zealand Division in a hook round Rommel's southern flank, but he had pulled out. Browne led the New Zealand Division on a second hook near Marble Arch, but again Rommel had slipped away.

In spite of Rommel's withdrawal, the LRDG operating behind the lines had frequent contacts with enemy. Browne was switched to reconnaissance of routes for the 8th Army. He was badly shaken and his passenger killed when his jeep ran over mine. His second-in-command, McLauchlan, took over the patrol. A few days later he ran into an enemy armoured car patrol, and he lost one truck and had four men taken prisoner, although he skilfully avoided capture. Browne, who had been a founder member of the LRDG, was awarded the MC.

Some months previously, the LRDG had been reinforced by the four patrols of the Indian Long-Range Squadron, ILRS for short. On 10 December Popski's Private Army (PPA) also came under command of the LRDG. The LRDG Report commented: 'So far it [PPA] has not been engaged on active operations.' For the next month the LRDG spent most of its energies on reconnaissance of the routes that 8th Army would use for their advance to Tripoli and Tunisia.

From the start of Montgomery's advance from Alamein, the SAS had been tasked with harassing the enemy during their withdrawal. By mid-November, Mayne's A Squadron had been joined by Major Street's B Squadron fresh from training at Kabrit. Because of the swift advance of 8th Army, only a few raids were carried out by A squadron. But B Squadron had several clashes with the enemy, who gave as good as they got, inflicting large numbers of casualties; of their ten officers, one was killed and six captured.

By the time the 8th Army entered Tripoli on 23 January 1943, the LRDG had moved its base from Kufra, which was now too far away, to Hon, 300 miles south-east of Tripoli. Later the LRDG set up an advanced base at Azizia. Dumps were established near the Tunisian frontier in preparation for the next phase. Easonsmith had flown to visit the Allied Headquarters in Algiers, established since the Anglo-American landings in Morocco and Algeria the previous November, Operation Torch. He arranged for supplies for the LRDG to be made available at Tozeur. By now, as a result of Operation Torch, most of the French in North Africa were back in the war on the Allied side.

Montgomery told the LRDG that he wanted them to make a careful and detailed reconnaissance of southern Tunisia to provide 'going' maps in case 8th Army needed to bypass the strongly held Mareth Line and make a left hook on Gabes. Ten patrols were engaged on this task during January and February, and built up a very accurate and detailed picture of the terrain.

These reconnaissance forays were 'not done without incident', recorded the LRDG Report. Tinker and 'Popski' left most of T2 and the PPA in a base while they reconnoitred the Tebega Gap, through which the Mareth Line was to be outflanked later. When they returned they found that all Tinker's vehicles had been destroyed by enemy aircraft. His men had moved to another base camp occupied by a mixed bag of PPA, French parachutists and SAS, totalling, with the LRDG, thirty-seven men and five jeeps. But there was insufficient petrol to take all five jeeps more than a hundred miles. Tinker took three jeeps, two wounded men and enough petrol for 150 miles and set out for Sabria Oasis which he hoped was held by the French. The remaining men followed on foot with their rations and water loaded on the other two jeeps. The Germans still held Sabria, so Tinker had to go on to Tozeur. To save fuel, he crossed the salt marshes of the Chott (lake) Djerid, the first vehicle ever to do so. Sixteen miles short of Tozeur, he stopped at the small village of Nefta, and from here telephoned the French at Tozeur who brought him petrol. Having filled two of his jeeps, he sent them back to the walking party. He went on to Gafsa, beyond Tozeur, to get transport from the Americans, and use their radio to report to 8th Army. The Americans at Gafsa sent him a further hundred miles on to Tebessa. Here his story was greeted with disbelief, but eventually the Americans lent him two jeeps and allowed him to contact 8th Army. That done, Tinker went back and collected the walkers. The two jeeps he had sent back had missed them, but turned up at Tozeur the next day. When Tinker returned the jeeps to Tebessa, he found a message from 8th Army telling him to return to Tripoli by air. Leaving his men in Tunisia with

1st Army, he was flown back to Tripoli in time to help in the planning for the left hook round the Mareth Line. Tinker was awarded a well-deserved MC.

Meanwhile the SAS planned four operations behind the lines. Two were to harass the enemy lines of communication, and two were reconnaissance. Stirling accompanied a patrol tasked to operate in northern Tunisia, and cut the Sousse railway line. He also aimed to link up with his eldest brother, Bill, who had formed 2nd SAS Regiment operating with 1st Army. Going through the Gabes Gap they were spotted from the air. German troops captured them in their lying-up position that night. Stirling slipped away but was betrayed by an Arab shepherd. This time there was no escape and he ended up in Colditz. Others of his party subsequently managed to escape and evade recapture. The loss of Stirling was a severe blow to the SAS, not least because he hardly ever wrote anything down, and no one in his Regiment had much idea of his future plans beyond the series of operations under way at the moment, or even in some cases where patrols were at that time, or their tasks. He was also a great loss to the British Army. Apart from all the other works of destruction achieved by the SAS they accounted for nearly 400 aircraft in just over a year. Mayne's personal score was over twice that of any Allied fighter ace of the Second World War.

*

Under Lieutenant Bruce, Scots Guards, G Patrol, the last of the LRDG's long reconnaissance patrols, had set out on 3 February 1943 in four Chevrolets and two jeeps. Because of losses, the two Guards patrols had been amalgamated. Bruce wrote an account.

> Our orders were to reconnoitre an area of country to the south-east, south, and west of the Chott el Djerid, about which nothing was then known by 8th Army. General Montgomery had looked well ahead, so plenty of time was allowed for our task, unlike the previous reconnaissance of G1 Patrol when we found ourselves with an area a third the size of Scotland to cover in six days.

On 9 February they reached the edge of the Grand Erg Oriental (the Eastern Sand Sea of the Sahara), most of it then regarded as impassable,

> but we slipped through one of the few places where the outer edge of dunes

was passable. So our star shoot which gave us our exact position to within half a mile told us.

The next three days would have been hell for anyone in a hurry. We made 50 miles through appalling going, and despite magnificent driving we broke many springs and three steering assemblies, which [Alexander] Stewart changed most skilfully, though finishing his spares in doing so.

A few days later they were to encounter the Tunisian Arabs, very different from the Senussi.

February 13th lived up to its superstitious date, and gave us the surprise of two sudden and violent attacks by Arab bands. We were moving off after breakfast, when bullets started whistling about, coming from apparently nowhere, but really from the thick bushes near where we'd spent the night. Three of our six trucks stuck in soft sand – at one moment all but one jeep were *ensablés*, an excellently expressive word we learned later from the French; and we felt in a very awkward position – and would have been – if the enemy had followed up their attack with the same skill with which they started it.

Firing went on for over two hours, before we drove them off, during which time all I saw of the enemy were two flashes of white, as Arabs darted from one bush to another. There must have been many of them, but they had not automatic weapons. Some of their old French ammunition, which we found afterwards, could be heard droning past apparently not much faster than bumble bees. We took to our feet in the end and made a final advance across some open ground, which none of us will forget. One comment I heard afterwards, 'I wouldn't have missed that for a quid.'

That night, having posted guards, close firing broke out again.

This time our mysterious opponents – for we never found out, and probably never will know, who they were – got to within about ten yards of our trucks, which we'd parked purposely in a small open space. Jennings was wounded in the chest and Blaney in the leg before we brought our great fire power to bear on them, and drove them off. Pte Murphy was magnificent and beyond all praise in his care for the wounded, but we had to get them to the nearest doctor as soon as possible. It was hard to tell how serious Jennings's wound was, he was amazingly cheerful and brave.

We weighted down one of the 30-cwt trucks with sandbags and made it into a makeshift ambulance and proceeded for Tozeur, where we had been ordered to go for supplies and petrol, [planning on] being able to complete most of our reconnaissance by sorties in our jeeps, and to wireless back the news as we went.

That very day the Germans had launched their counter-attack at Kasserine, some thirty-five miles north of Tozeur. When Bruce's patrol entered Nefta Oasis, fifteen miles from Tozeur:

The last Allied forces had evacuated the Oasis the day before, and the local French civilians were what they called, '*en attendant les Boches*', whose movements they were following by telephone. We were hissed as we drove down the street, so we may have been taken for the first Germans.

Having topped up, and sent their wounded to Tozeur for treatment, they set out that night for the Oasis of El Oued 120 miles to the west, in Algeria, taking their wounded with them.

We stopped to wish '*bonne chance*' to the postmaster at Nefta. Guardsman Crossley (Coldstream Guards) suddenly remembered his stamp collection; and insisted on buying some samples from an amazed official, who was expecting the Boche. The enemy arrived there the next morning.

In Algeria they started meeting units of the French Colonial Army, including:

a battery of the French Foreign Legion who were proceeding eastwards rather vaguely, though full of *ésprit*, to meet the enemy. My driver, McNabola, a great character, soon found himself talking to a *Légionnaire* whose home was two streets away from his in Dublin – a goodish coincidence on the edge of the Sahara.

At Touggourt, beyond El Oued, they found a large French garrison which made them most welcome, and took good care of their wounded. Bruce decided that he would return by a different route to avoid the bad going of the outward journey. He opted for a long swing round to the south and east of the Grand Erg Oriental. But first they had to get spares, fuel and rations. Taking Alexander Stewart, the fitter, and five others they headed north for Constantine, 300 miles as the crow flies, much further by track and road. On the way they met some Americans at Biskra. This was the first meeting between an 8th Army unit and the Americans, and actually before they met 'officially' with much trumpeting in the press, because, as Bruce remarks, it was:

Two months before the much published meeting on the Gafsa–Gabes road.

They spent six days in Constantine, waiting for the spares to be flown from Tripoli. They enjoyed being the object of much curiosity, in their beards, Arab headdress, and sand-coloured jeeps, bristling with machine-guns. Their return trip south of the Grand Erg went without incident, although:

The 260 miles to Ghadames were the most difficult of our return journey. We passed the great silent dune masses of the Erg Oriental, impassable at most places even to camels. We had to cut through places where the dunes had buried the very bad track; and it was only thanks to the excellent drill which the patrol had learned in their crossings of the Egyptian Sand Sea that we took two and a half days where the French reckoned to take eight or nine.

At Ghadames, a beautiful oasis, south of Tripoli, in peacetime an Italian tourist resort and showplace:

The visitors' book in the hotel began with the name of the Crown Prince of Italy, and ended with those of all of G Patrol.

They motored into Hon on 12 March, having covered 3,515 miles in five weeks and two days, making a total for some of the patrol of over 9,990 miles of desert travel in the four and a half months since leaving the Egyptian Delta at the start of Montgomery's offensive.

The last operation carried out by the LRDG in the desert was navigating Freyberg's New Zealand Corps outflanking the Mareth Line. The task was given to the New Zealanders of Tinker's T2 Patrol in two jeeps. The New Zealand Corps passed through Wilder's Gap, found two months earlier by another New Zealander, Captain Wilder, who was then commanding T1 Patrol. Outflanked, but after very hard fighting, Rommel withdrew, abandoning the Mareth Line. Montgomery wrote to Prendergast:

Without your careful and reliable reports the launching of the 'left hook' by the NZ Div would have been a leap in the dark; with the information they produced, the operation could be planned with some certainty and as you know went off without a hitch.

The Axis forces were now pinned into a corner of Tunisia, and there was no more scope for long-range patrols. The LRDG were sent back to Egypt to rest and reorganize.

Lieutenant Bruce:

We knew that great changes were in store, and all guessed that our days in the desert were ending. It had been our home for so long, sometimes friend, sometimes enemy, always constant companion, that I do not think one of us left it without some regret, and some gratitude for great experience.

As we left the open desert for the road, for the last time, Crossley, our navigator, spoke for us all: 'It's like saying goodbye to an old schoolmaster, who was very severe and frightening, but whom one knew one was very fond of.'

For two and a half years, as the armies advanced and retreated along the coast, the LRDG had been the kings of the vast inner desert. They and the SBS were now bound for a very different war in the Aegean. The SAS were to operate in Italy and, ultimately, in north-west Europe.

5

Canoe Operations, 1942

In 1941, some fourteen raids and reconnaissance operations had been conducted in the Mediterranean and ten on the coasts of Norway and France. Canoes had played a part in some, but by no means the majority of these. However, canoe operations had become established as one method of operating behind the lines, or at such long range from base that some of their exploits qualify as 'behind the lines'. These operations continued to include reconnaissance, sabotage and special missions. A number of different units carried out these roles, and there was, as yet, no strict demarcation which decided who did what. Techniques and equipment had also improved since the early Folbot days.

Lieutenant James Foot joined Number 2 SBS in Ardrossan in Scotland in March 1942. It had emerged from 101 Troop, the commando boat troop, which was formed in Britain after Roger Courtney had taken his SBS to the Middle East in early 1941. After initial training, which lasted about eight weeks, they were sent to work up with submarines in a training flotilla to practise launching canoes by floating off from the casing, having first brought the canoes up from below through the torpedo loading hatch. James Foot:

> Finding the submarine on return was always a problem. Having paddled out on a compass bearing, we could do one of three things: use a coloured signal lamp shone to seaward, or drop grenades at a minute interval while they listened for these on their hydrophones, or a can on a tube with a handle on the top. When this was wound it made a clanking sound which the submarine could pick up on the hydrophones.

The noise made by this rudimentary device, called a 'bong stick' or 'bongle', could be picked up by the hydrophones up to twelve miles away if conditions were favourable. It is still in service with the SBS today.

James Foot:

The Navy were very loath to leave you, and stayed on the surface far longer than prudence demanded. As a last resort if you hadn't been picked up by first light, in theory, you paddled straight out to sea, and the submarine would stick its periscope up near you which would tell you they knew where you were, and would surface and pick you up after dark.

At end of training, the whole unit moved to HMS *Dolphin*. Here a COPP [Combined Operations Pilotage Party] was assembled ready to go to the Mediterranean to carry out the marking of beaches for the Torch landings. We sailed in a convoy from the Clyde. We arrived in Gibraltar, and lived in HMS *Maidstone*, a submarine depot ship.

The SBS element sent to Gibraltar was commanded by Captain Godfrey Courtney, brother of Roger, and consisted of eight or nine officers and about twelve other ranks.

Here three of us, Captain Courtney, Lieutenant Livingstone and I were told to take four canoes and get them on board HMS *Seraph*, an S class submarine. We were not told what we were to do. In the evening, five Americans passed the mess we were using as our HQ, and shortly after we were called to the Wardroom and introduced to the party. They were Major General Mark Clark, Brigadier General Lemnitzer, Colonel Hamlin, Colonel Holmes, and Captain Wright of the US Navy. They told us we were to take them ashore in French North Africa, 60 miles west of Algiers.

Here Major General Mark Clark, the second-in-command to General Eisenhower for the Allied landings in Morocco and Algeria, Operation Torch, was to have discussions with the French Major General Charles Mast on the likely reactions by the Vichy French to the forthcoming invasion.

We sailed shortly afterwards, at dusk, and proceeded on the surface into the Mediterranean. That evening we instructed the Americans in the use of canoes, inside the submarine, up on the casing, and paddled around close to the boat. Having satisfied ourselves that they knew how the paddles worked, we got back on board and went on our way. We sailed on the night of 19 October 1942, and arrived off the beach at about 0400 on 21st October. During the following day while submerged, we carried out a periscope recce of the beach, including making a silhouette drawing to help with navigation.

The next evening we surfaced and waited for a light to appear as a guiding light from a house on the shore. At about midnight it appeared, the submarine proceeded towards the shore, and the canoes were launched. In the first was Lieutenant Livingstone with Colonel Holmes, I followed with Brigadier General Lemnitzer, followed by Captain Wright and Colonel Hamlin, and finally General Clark was going with Captain Courtney. Unfortunately Captain Courtney's canoe was damaged on launching. He had to call back Captain Wright and Colonel Hamlin, and he and Clark changed places with them. Livingstone led the party in. We kept in sight of each other and had no problems. On reaching the beach the recognition signal was exchanged with the shore party. We carried the canoes up the beach, through the woods and into a house where our canoes were locked up in a safe place. We went in, were given a drink, and were introduced to the members of the French party; not by name, I had no idea who they were. Then we were shown up to a room and had some sleep.

At dawn we were woken up with nice French breakfast and coffee. We were told not to show ourselves at the window, and not to come down unless called for. All the servants had been sent away. During the morning I was called down to check over the canoes for damage and repair what I could, particularly Courtney's. We carried small repair kits in the canoes. The rest of the day we slept, while the Americans and French were in conference. We were to leave as soon as possible after dark. We had just got the boats out into the courtyard, when a message arrived to say the police were on the way. We hurriedly put the boats back into the locked store. We were shown into a cellar. It was dark and we all sat round with our backs to the wall. The three of us providing protection for the Americans sat facing the trap door, with our Thompson sub-machine-guns. If we were discovered, the Americans would try to bribe the police with gold, we carried about $2,000. Only as a last resort were we to shoot our way out.

We could hear the arguments going on upstairs. It seemed a long time. Courtney got a fit of coughing. General Mark Clark passed something to him and said, 'Here "Jumbo" suck this.' This seemed to do the trick. There was rather an ominous comment from the General, who was obviously playing with his carbine, 'How does this damn thing work?' Courtney said, 'For God's sake just leave it to us.' When we got out, Courtney asked what he had been given for his cough, and the General said, 'It's a bit of chewing gum that I've been chewing all day.' Courtney replied, 'I wondered why it didn't taste of anything.'

It was decided to get away as quickly as possible, as the police had said that they weren't satisfied and would be back. We carried the boats to the shore, and to our dismay we found that there was a lot of surf. This is not normally the case on this bit of coast. You get an onshore wind in the afternoon, but when the sun goes down, it tends to change round and blow off the land out to sea. Any sea kicked up by an onshore wind dies away. But on this particular evening it didn't happen. We decided we would have to get away anyway. We called up the submarine on the walkie-talkie, and explained the position, asking them to come in as close as they could. They came in so close, I could see *Seraph* with the naked eye from the shore.

Initially our getaway was not successful. I don't think a trained SBS crew would have had much difficulty. We would have swum the canoes out, and got in when we were beyond the surf line. You keep the canoe bows on to the waves. Once through, you climb on over the stern. The surf was too high to paddle a canoe through from the beach. First Courtney and Clark tried to launch in the normal manner. The surf overturned them. We had to go in and salvage the paddles, without the latter we wouldn't get away. I remember being told, 'Forget about the General, get the paddles.' We signalled the submarine and told them we would wait for a few minutes to see if the sea would subside. I was told to count the waves. You get a lull after a certain number of waves. Having established what we thought was a pattern, we decided to have another go. By now the French had come down to the beach, and we asked them to wade out with each canoe, to chest height, and hold it while the crew climbed in. We decided to put General Clark with Captain Wright in the first canoe, as they had the most knowledge of the forthcoming operation, and get them away first. We got them away safely by wading out, pushing the canoe as far we could. I and Colonel Holmes got away after the second attempt, as did Courtney and Lemnitzer. Livingstone and Hamlin got away at the first attempt. The sea was dropping all the time. The submarine was very close in, not more than 400 yards off. We all got aboard quite easily. Except that most of the gold, and some papers were sunk just off the beach [when the first canoe capsized]. A signal was sent to the American Embassy in Algiers to send someone to make sure nothing was washed up on the beach.

The United States had maintained diplomatic relations with the Vichy Government, and Mr Murphy the American Consul had established secret contacts with known anti-Vichy elements in Algeria. He had arranged the meeting between Clark and Mast.

As the party embarked in the submarine:

We noticed two lots of car headlights approach the house. It was the police. We learned that the French had said they had been holding a little party, with girls involved, to explain why they were cagey the first time the police visited.

On the first morning after leaving North Africa, a Catalina came out from Gibraltar, landed alongside *Seraph*, which had surfaced, and picked up the American party. Clark was flown to Gibraltar and to London. The French had given the Americans details of the defences and the likely attitude of the French and colonial troops.

We arrived back in Gibraltar on 25 October. We all got along with Clark and Lemnitzer very well. They treated us like equals. They took their orders from us. It was our job to get them ashore. At the time we were given very little information about the importance of the meeting between the Americans and the French. We understood that the Americans wanted to contact the French to find out the likely reactions. But we were not told anything about where the landings were going to take place, or when. As we knew that the other SBS and COPP parties were away doing reconnaissance trips the operation couldn't be very far off. We knew nothing that could possibly have been of use to the Germans if we had been picked up. We were given to understand that the French attitude might be hostile to the British after the action against the French Fleet at Oran [see *The Imperial War Museum Book of the War at Sea*]. But we saw nothing of that among the people we met at the house. They knew three of us were British.

On 27 October the same party were again told to take canoes to *Seraph*. That evening they sailed, once again with captain Wright USN accompanied by Colonel Gaylord United States Army, a fluent French speaker. The other American officers had returned to London to continue planning Torch. The mission was to collect the French General Giraud from southern France. He had been captured in 1940, but had escaped to Vichy France from Germany in April 1942. The Americans wanted him to take command of all the French troops in North Africa as soon as possible after the Torch landings, to ensure their loyalty to the Allied cause. General Giraud agreed to be picked up from the French coast just before the landings, but insisted that he would not be picked up by a British submarine, it must be an American one. It was decided that Captain Wright USN would pretend to be in command of *Seraph*, although Lieutenant Jewell RN was actually the Captain. After rehearsing Gaylord in canoe drills off the Spanish coast, Foot remembers that:

We continued to run up to the French coast, and on 4 November we had still received no instructions on when and where to meet the General. We didn't know if we were to go in and collect him, or he would come out in a boat. We received a message that evening giving us an RV. During the day we closed the coast and made a periscope recce. Although the original signal said he was coming out by motor boat, we still had to be prepared for the possibility of collecting him from the beach.

We surfaced in the evening, and began to close the shore. We hadn't gone far before we were forced to dive because we were heading for a mass of French fishing boats. After they had passed, we surfaced again and went on towards the shore. Again we hadn't gone very far when we spotted a darkened ship passing astern of us at high speed, it was an E-boat. We stopped. They didn't see us and made off. On we went again. At about midnight we saw a light, which flashed 'one hour'. We waited, and after a while we spotted a white boat heading out to sea, but it wasn't heading directly for us.

After some discussion, a dim light was shone towards the boat and it closed with the submarine. The sea state was such that when the boat came alongside, it was washed up over the saddle-tank of the submarine, and the General nearly fell into the water. Foot:

> He was met on the casing by Captain Wright. The submarine was flying the Stars and Stripes. He was taken below very quickly before he could realise that the majority of those aboard were British.

They had been told that the General did not speak English. Once clear of the coast, a signal was to be sent to Gibraltar to say that the operation was successful. But the transmitter was not working and the message could not be sent. The date of the invasion was close at hand, and they had to get General Giraud taken off by Catalina, so he could play his allotted part in the operation. Jewell took a risk and sailed on the surface by daylight, in the hope that they would be spotted by a friendly aircraft. Eventually they were seen by a Catalina reconnaissance aircraft from Gibraltar and a message was sent by light to land alongside, and take off the General and his party.

> I was detailed to take General Giraud across to the Catalina by canoe. We launched the canoe and I got into the front seat. General Giraud was a very tall man, and couldn't get his legs in. He sat on the back, and the stability

was practically nil. I could take only three strokes with the paddle, and then had to steady the canoe by laying the paddle across the canoe. The situation was made worse by the Catalina, its engines still running, moving away from me faster than I could paddle. I had been told I would be court martialled if I tipped the General in. The submarine saw what was happening and they signalled the Catalina to stop engines. Eventually I got alongside, and made some comment to the airman on board to the effect that they were welcome to the General who was a silly old b— who had nearly capsized me. As he climbed aboard the Catalina, he turned and said, 'Well thank you very much Lieutenant, I am sorry I caused you so many problems.' I was horrified, he spoke perfect English, and must have heard everything we had said aboard *Seraph*. I paddled like hell away in the other direction.

The beach reconnaissances for Torch were done by COPPs and some SBS canoeists in an organization known as Party Inhuman, commanded by Clogstoun-Willmott. Teams of COPPs and SBS were taken in five submarines to positions off five different beaches a week before the landings. From here they only did periscope recces and drew panorama sketches to enable to them to find the correct beaches on the night. They were not allowed to land, or carry out a proper beach survey (as described in Chapter 3) for fear of compromise, and this decision was to cause chaos on some of the beaches.

On the night of the operation, 8 November 1942, the SBS and COPPs provided navigational guidance for the landing craft bound for beaches being used by the British in the vicinity of Oran and Algiers. Navigation on the purely American beaches in the vicinity of Casablanca was an American responsibility. This was the first of many times that COPPs and SBS provided navigational guidance in amphibious operations in many theatres for the rest of the Second World War.

Sergeant Stan Weatherall was in one of two SBS teams taken in by the submarine *Ursula*. Weatherall was dropped off the Bay of Arzeu, and the other party about fifty miles to the west. Weatherall had with him a COPP navigator, who sat behind him:

The navigator took us in on a compass bearing, and anchored about 200 yards off the beach with a small kedge. The submarine went out 8–10 miles to act as beacon for the convoys. The first landing craft had one of the Party Inhuman officers aboard to guide them. Then we used the infra-red Aldis lamp to guide them in. We began sending 'Z' by morse from about midnight. [They were marking Z Beach.] The craft should have arrived at 1 o'clock, they were about 10 minutes late. Not too bad. We stayed there sending 'Z', so they didn't run into us. At daylight we landed.

Because this was the first major Allied amphibious operation of the War, it is understandable that there were plenty of mistakes, and chaos reigned on some of the beaches. Fortunately the French response was badly co-ordinated. The orders from Vichy were confused, so although individual unit commanders resisted the invasion, many others did not. As feared, the French Navy, still smarting after the sinking and damage of their fleet by the British in 1940, fought fiercely for a while. One of the causes of the problems on the beaches was the lack of proper beach survey and reconnaissance, mentioned earlier. For example, on X Beach the sand was so soft, vehicles could not drive inland, until special tracking had been landed. On Y Beach, the existence of a sand bar fifteen to twenty yards offshore was discovered only when the first vehicle drove off the leading craft when it grounded, straight into water so deep it was completely submerged. Clogstoun-Willmott was able to use these and other examples to press for proper beach surveys in future, and also for more time for training. Lack of training had been a factor in the decision not to allow any reconnaissance ashore.

At the end of November 1942 most of the SBS were sent home, but Stan Weatherall and Livingstone, now a captain, were sent on a typical SBS sabotage raid in the submarine HMS *Ursula* on twenty-one-day patrol to Genoa. The submarine was on a normal patrol, but embarked one canoe and crew. At sea, the SBS team were told that the Blue Express railway line, which runs up the west coast of Italy and into France, was to be cut. The submarine took them to within 1,200 yards of a beach by a little village west of Savona, between Genoa and San Remo. Stan Weatherall:

We got into the canoe with our gear and explosives. Having landed on the beach, we carried the canoe up to a small sea wall at the edge of the cove. As we crouched behind the wall, a courting couple come down the road, a few yards from where were hiding. Opposite to us was a big house with gates and a big garden with lots of bushes; ideal to hide our canoe. But these two stood kissing and cuddling for about half an hour, before they poddled off [*sic*]. Captain Livingstone nipped across the road and cut the wire holding the gates shut. We hid the canoe in the bushes in this big garden.

The best place to derail a train is in a tunnel. But they could not get down on to the track from where they were because the cutting was too steep. So they approached the line through some houses further along. As they neared a wooden hut alongside the track they heard voices; they paused, and an Italian soldier came out on to the balcony, made water right by where they were standing, and went back inside. From here they could see the tunnel about a hundred yards along the track.

> There was a sentry at the top and one at the bottom. They periodically called to one another. We couldn't do the job in the tunnel. We walked in the other direction to a curve in the line on an embankment. The engine weight on a curve is mainly on the outside rail. So we placed a charge sufficient to blow a six-foot gap on the outer rail. We also put charges on the pylon carrying the electric power, on a ring main. This was to be detonated by a pressure switch on the railway line. We made our way back to our canoe. We had to cut our way through some wire netting to get back to the road. We met an Italian soldier on the road. He must have been drunk because he took no notice of us. It saved his life. A bit further down the road there was a group of people talking. Livingstone was a Corpus Christi Don and whistled some Italian tune as we walked past. We made our way to the canoe and back to the submarine before the moon came up without any trouble.
>
> At about midnight I was called up on to the bridge to see a train coming down the track with a small light on the front. Suddenly there was a hell of a flash. I expect the train toppled down the twenty-foot embankment into the back gardens of the houses by the track.
>
> The captain of the submarine never expected to see us back. He gave me a piece of jam tart.

In Britain yet another canoe unit had been formed, this time almost by subterfuge, by Major H. G. 'Blondie' Hasler, Royal Marines. Hasler, a keen small-boat sailor in peacetime, had sent a paper on small-boat attack to COHQ. They had turned it down. Then the news of the Italian attacks on warships in the Mediterranean had revived interest in COHQ in small-boat attacks on shipping. Hasler was appointed to one of Mountbatten's brainchildren, the Combined Operations Development Centre (CODC) at Southsea. From there he was sent to form his own unit, because CODC had decided to develop an existing Italian explosive motor boat for British use. An Italian MTM (standing for *Motoscafi da*

Turismo Modificati, modified touring motor boat) had sunk the British cruiser *York* off Crete in March 1941. The Germans and the Japanese also used them with varying success, the latter as suicide craft. Even if not intended as suicide craft, the effect was often the same, and casualties were heavy. In both the Italian and German versions, the single crew baled out before the boat hit the target and detonated the explosive with which the hull was packed.

Captain Jock Stewart, bored with life in a Royal Marine Heavy Anti-Aircraft Battery, applied to join Hasler, whom he had met before, without knowing what he was joining other than it was something 'special'. He was sent to Major Hasler's Party, as it was known at first, as the second-in-command. The British version of the MTM was as bizarre and suicidal as all the other explosive motor boats. Jock Stewart:

> It was a very small fast motor boat, the driver aimed his boat at the target. Just before hitting, he pulled a lever. The raft at the back which was part of his seat, fell off, and dragged him out of the boat. The boat went on to the target. The driver had to drag himself on to the raft so that he would be out of the water before the explosion. Hasler used this as a chance to develop a canoe, because he felt that the driver of the boat would have a greater chance of escape if there was someone nearby in a canoe who could pick him up. He thought quite rightly that the explosive motor boat would take a very long time to develop. So to keep his unit employed he wanted canoes, and at the back of his mind he always had this idea of attacking enemy ships in harbour by stealth in a canoe.

The British explosive motor boat was never used in action, but Hasler's canoes were, which had been his intention in the first place. In August 1942, Lieutenants Pritchard-Gordon and MacKinnon were at the RM Small Arms Course at Gosport, after being commissioned. One day they and all the others on the course were told that a Major X would be visiting and that all young men without close domestic ties should be present to hear what he had to say. Major X was Major Hasler. Bill Pritchard-Gordon:

> I was not selected as one of his two lieutenants, and MacKinnon and I were congratulating ourselves on not being selected at the bar in the mess, when we were summoned to the Commanding Officer's office. We were told to get packed, because the CO of the school had overruled Hasler and told him that we were the people he wanted. Hasler laid great score on

knowledge of small boats, and a knowledge of light mechanical engineering. He emphasised the ability to work as an individual in a small team. I had some experience of canoes as a small boy, and was an adequate swimmer.

Having joined at Southsea, the unit only consisted of Hasler, Captain Stewart, MacKinnon and myself. We started to do testing of the very limited equipment for what was an as yet unformed unit. It wasn't for about three months that we went to select volunteers from the RM Divisions. I was happy to find that Cpl King who as a PT instructor had given me hell as a recruit at Plymouth was to be in my section. He became a friend. MacKinnon became my closest ever friend.

Hasler's party was called the RM Beach Patrol Detachment to begin with and then became the Royal Marine Boom Patrol Detachment as a cover name. The unit was based at Southsea. From here the boom that protected the Solent stretched from the mainland to Seaview on the Isle of Wight. Pritchard-Gordon:

> We trained in the area of that boom with canoeists every night and it would be perfectly natural for people to assume that we guarded the boom. Never did I come across anyone who doubted that we defended the boom, and could dive to repair it.

They trained in underwater attack and, as at that time there was no special underwater swimming equipment, they used Davis Escape Apparatus, a compressed-air system designed to allow men to escape from a submarine stuck on the bottom, and come straight to the surface. The Davis Apparatus, with all its projections, was very dangerous when working under obstructions and in a confined space. For underwater attack they had to use oxygen in a closed circuit, not compressed air because this leaves bubbles on the surface. The problem with using oxygen in a closed-circuit system is that the diver exhales carbon dioxide, which produces a build-up of this gas in the system. Eventually the diver can experience hallucination leading to irrational behaviour, or even death through carbon dioxide poisoning. The RMBPD lost an officer in this way. The carbon dioxide can be 'scrubbed' by being passed through soda lime. However, if this becomes wet, through leakage of sea water, it turns into a lethal 'cocktail' of quicklime. Attack diving was, and is, despite vastly improved techniques, a very different proposition from recreational scuba diving as enjoyed by thousands of people today.

To begin with the training was done in Folbots, which earlier canoeists had found inadequate. Hasler's design, based on years of experience in small boats, and with ship attack as his main objective, differed from the SBS canoes, as the COPP canoes were different again. In particular Hasler wanted a canoe that could be launched in rough water, with the crew sitting in it, with cockpit covers closed round them. Pritchard-Gordon:

> The Folbots were totally unsuitable for the job. It was essential that a fully loaded canoe could be pulled along over a beach, not just a sandy one, to get it under cover. The only thing the Folbots did for the RMBPD was to teach us to canoe in all conditions, and navigate. They were hopeless for lifting into a mother craft or into a submarine. They provided the basic seamanship for the new type of boats which eventually we got. These had timbered decks and keels, they were collapsible for stowing in the submarine, and you could stow them full of all the gear you needed on operations. The two men could sit in the fully loaded canoe and be hoisted outboard and lowered into the sea from a submarine using the submarine's gun. This is exactly what happened on the submarine which took MacKinnon's section and Major Hasler on Operation Frankton [the raid on Bordeaux].

Their first night-navigation training was carried out in the Solent. There were of course no lights on buoys or ashore because of the blackout. In autumn 1942 an operation was conceived in COHQ: the first operation by Hasler's unit – and about four months before they were ready, according to Pritchard-Gordon.

> Morale was very high. Each canoe crew were very close to each other. We were a very small unit, only 24 strong. We lived in billets and knew each other very well. When Mountbatten wanted the job done, MacKinnon's section was the only section available, mine was away. My section was intended for the explosive motor boats, and intended to be parachuted with the driver sitting in it. To this end my section went away some time after this to take a parachuting course at Ringway.

The targets were German ships known, by reading the signals from the Japanese Embassy in Berlin to Tokyo, to be taking special equipment to Japan from the Bordeaux–Bassens docks, some seventy-one miles up the Gironde River. An attack by commandos was ruled out as far too expensive in effort and investment. The area was well defended, and some estimates put the number of troops required at 20,000. After the

Dieppe fiasco that August, the planners were chary about large-scale raids against a target of this type, especially as it was so far inland. A bombing attack from the air would have caused too many civilian casualties. COHQ gave the task to Hasler. His canoeists were to be launched from a submarine at the mouth of the Gironde, paddle up the river, which would take several days, place limpet mines on the ships, and escape overland using the already established escape system set up by MI9 working with the French Resistance for shot-down aircrew.

An approach up the Gironde River was dependent on a particular combination of tide and moon, which occurred at the end of November 1942. Although Hasler was given two months' warning for the task, the RMBPD had been in existence for only two and a half months. There was much to be done: training in the new canoes; practising with the limpet mines; training with submarines; and escape and evasion. The technique of lifting the canoes over the side from a submarine involved a four-foot girder placed in the muzzle of the gun, with a tackle on the end. The canoe, weighing some 480 lb, with two crew and kit, was lifted up from the casing, and the gun trained outboard, allowing the canoe to be lowered into the water. Hasler had always had doubts about approaching ships in a canoe, even at night, preferring an underwater attack by swimmers carrying limpet mines from canoes some way off; hence his inclusion of diving training from the very beginning. But suitable equipment, although on the drawing board, was not yet available.

Attaching a limpet mine from a canoe requires plenty of practice. When the canoe comes alongside the ship, one canoeist holds his craft in place against the tide or current, by clamping on to the metal hull of the target with a strong magnet. The trick is to avoid a loud 'clunk', as the magnet attaches itself. Meanwhile the other canoeist lowers a pre-fused limpet down the side of the hull using a steel hook. The aim is to fix it at about six feet, the length of the hook. The deeper down the better, to obtain the maximum water tamping effect on the explosion. Again, avoiding a 'thunk' as the limpet fixes on is advisable, and not always achievable. After fixing a limpet, or several, depending on the size of the ship, the canoe is paddled, or allowed to drift to the next target.

Number One Section under MacKinnon trained in the River Thames and in Scotland, with Jock Stewart as the training officer. Hasler joined

MacKinnon in the Clyde when they started training with submarines. From time to time Lieutenant Commander le Strange, the planning officer at COHQ, brought up information about Bordeaux. All this time only three people in the unit knew the target: Hasler, le Strange, and Stewart.

> We planned off aerial photographs. But several days would elapse after the final briefing before their arrival at Bordeaux. So the ships might have moved berth. We also tried to find lying-up places on shore for the canoes as they went up river. We thought it best for the canoes to go in two sections; one section one side of the Gironde and one on the other. What we didn't realise there was a tidal race at the mouth of the Gironde. We should have done.

Hasler with MacKinnon's section boarded HMS/M *Tuna* on 30 November 1942. The Section was not briefed on the operation until they got aboard. Jock Stewart:

> We had had a party the night before to allow the chaps who had worked very hard to relax. I was feeling very hung-over the next morning, and when Sergeant Wallace, MacKinnon's number two, reported to me, he said:
>> 'You've got chalk on your face, sir.'
>> That was the last time I saw Wallace. He was captured and shot.

Five canoes were launched from *Tuna* on Monday 7 December 1942, south of the mouth of the Gironde River in the Bay of Biscay: *Catfish* (Major Hasler and Marine Sparks), and *Cuttlefish* (Lieutenant Mac-Kinnon and Marine Conway) heading for the west bank at Bordeaux; *Crayfish* (Corporal Laver and Marine Mills) and *Coalfish* (Sergeant Wallace and Marine Ewart) heading for the east bank at Bordeaux; *Conger* (Corporal Sheard and Marine Moffat) heading for the north and south keys at Bassens. The sixth canoe, *Cachalot*, crewed by Marines Ellery and Fisher, also heading for Bassens, was damaged in the torpedo hatch, and could not be launched.

After three hours' paddling with the flood tide under their tails, they saw the white water of a tide race ahead; short, steep waves breaking on shallows as the flood tide pushed in. Hasler rafted everyone together for some advice on how to cope with this unforeseen hazard. *Coalfish* failed to make it on the first attempt and was never seen again. *Conger* capsized at the second attempt. Corporal Sheard and Marine Moffat were each towed by *Catfish* and *Crayfish* to within a mile of the shore on Pointe de Grave, where the lighthouse marks the entrance to the river. The light had suddenly been switched on, and was so bright they all thought they must have been seen. The two men set off to swim ashore, but they never made it.

After seven hours' paddling, with daylight approaching, *Cuttlefish* became separated from the other two survivors, who had found a lying-up position for the day. MacKinnon and Conway pressed on for three nights, until their canoe was sunk by an underwater obstacle. They set off to make their way home via Spain.

The crews of *Catfish* and *Crayfish* spent the day in a hide, under camouflage nets. During the day, they were visited by Frenchmen. They started paddling late that night, because it took three and a half hours to drag the loaded canoes across three-quarters of a mile of mud. Again they lay up for the day. To take advantage of the remaining three hours of flood tide at the end of that day, they took a risk and set off at dusk. They were spotted by a French farmer, but it is unlikely that he betrayed them. At dawn the next day, they were still too far away to find a base from which they could attack the ships. Another nine-mile paddle the next night brought them to a suitable advance base position. These lying-up positions were either behind banks, over which the canoes had to be carried, or among reeds, which dried out as the tide ebbed. In the advanced base, they armed the limpets, and kept an eye on two ships moored 800 yards across the river.

With limpets set for 9 hours and 15 minutes, they set out, *Catfish* for the west bank quays, and *Crayfish* for the east bank. Drifting with the flood, after the moon had set, Hasler and Sparks in *Catfish* placed three limpets on a large cargo ship, and two on a mine destroyer, two on a smaller merchantman, and one on an oil tanker. At one stage, as they drifted, a sentry swung the beam of his torch on to them, holding it steady for what seemed like an eternity until the tide floated them out of his sight behind another ship. Perhaps thinking the canoe was a floating log, he snapped off his light and turned away.

Corporal Laver and Marine Mills in *Crayfish* found the east quays empty, and floated down on the now ebbing tide to place four limpets on each of the two ships opposite their advanced base. Both crews paddled downstream as fast as they could go, beached well before first light, and set off in their pairs on separate escape routes. Since leaving *Tuna*, they had paddled ninety-one miles.

Four ships were damaged, and in dock for several months, although according to German reports they were empty at the time. The damage to the mine destroyer was negligible, perhaps because her sides were especially designed to withstand underwater explosions. The other limpets probably failed to explode, or perhaps they fell off, before detonation.

Jock Stewart:

> I knew a little of what was going on because an RM officer on the staff told me the number of ships they got. Then later he told me that 'Blondie' was on the escape route. It wasn't until after the operation that the other half of the RMBPD was told that it was our people who had carried out the operation at Bordeaux which had been reported in the newspapers. Although they suspected.

Hasler and Sparks returned to England in April 1943, through the Resistance escape line 'Marie-Claire'. Only after the War was the fate of the other four crews discovered. Sergeant Wallace and Marine Ewart in *Coalfish* had actually paddled through the tide race that first night, but had been swept inshore after several hours' paddling, and capsized in surf. They were captured by men from a flak battery. Their canoe was found, but during five days of interrogation they did not reveal their objective. Early on 12 December, a few hours before the limpets exploded, they were shot in Bordeaux, despite being in uniform when captured.

Of *Conger*'s crew, Marine Moffat's body was washed ashore, but Corporal Sheard's body was never found. *Cuttlefish*'s crew, Lieutenant MacKinnon and Marine Conway, had put some thirty miles between themselves and Bordeaux, and were being hidden in a hospital, when they were arrested by the French police and handed over to the Germans. Corporal Laver and Marine Mills, the other successful canoe crew, in *Crayfish*, were on the run for two days before being picked up by the French police and handed to the Germans. All four – MacKinnon, Conway, Laver and Mills – were in civilian clothes when captured. They were shot in Paris in March 1943. The burial certificates of all six shot by the Germans were annotated, 'found drowned in Bordeaux harbour'. Although the four in civilian clothes ran the risk of being executed, the two in uniform were executed under the terms of Hitler's Commando Order of 18 October 1942. It was kept secret by the Germans at the time. Part of it read:

> From now on all men operating against German troops in so-called Commando raids in Europe or in Africa are to be annihilated to the last man. This is to be carried out whether they be soldiers in uniform, or saboteurs, with or without arms; and whether fighting or seeking to escape; and it is equally immaterial whether they come into action from ships and aircraft, or whether they land by parachute. Even if these individuals on discovery make obvious their intention of giving themselves up as prisoners, no pardon is on any account to be given.

The order specifically excluded enemy soldiers taken prisoner in open battle, in large-scale attacks, major assault landings or airborne operations. Neither did it apply to aircrew who baled out.

General Jodl, Chief of the Operations Staff of the German High Command, and one of Hitler's closest military advisers, took some pains to keep this order secret. His directive on 19 October 1942 included the passages below, which are a clear indication of a wish to cover up a monstrous edict:

> This order is intended for Commanders only and is under no circumstances to fall into enemy hands.
>
> The Headquarters mentioned in the distribution list are responsible that all parts of the order, or extracts taken from it, which are issued are again withdrawn and, together with this copy, destroyed.

While waiting for Hasler's return, Stewart had continued with trials and training:

> On Blondie Hasler's last day before the operation, we discussed the future of the unit. He said, 'I don't think we will be able to put on another op like this again. We will not be able to go alongside a ship in a canoe. Will you develop some form of swimming attack so we can reach the target under water. I have put in to CODC the design for an underwater glider. You are to try to do something about the swimming side of this.'

Stewart began to work on a light waterproof suit for attack divers. The suit was designed by Mr Goram, the chief rubber technologist of Dunlop, and made of stretchable rubber; the man entered through the neck. It was tested in the Eastney swimming baths. At this time attack divers swam using the breast stroke. Lieutenant Bruce Wright, Royal Canadian Navy, an Olympic swimmer, had been sent to join them, and was to have brought some fins designed by him. Unfortunately they were sent by sea, while he had flown across in a bomber, and the ship was sunk.

> Wright explained to Goram what the fins looked like. The RMBPD had already experimented with a tiny Italian fin about six inches long, which was not very good, and a larger pair made of canvas, which broke the first time they were used. Bruce Wright sketched the type of fin he was bringing. Goram went away and designed a set of fins that could be attached to the suit, and developed a breathing set that went on the swimmer's shoulders, and not on the chest as in the case of the Davis kit. Goram designed the swim suit, fins and breathing set. That was the beginning of the frogman.

Pritchard-Gordon had also been busy. The RMBPD had been asked by COHQ to look at a lake south of the Gironde used as a base by a flying boat which passed information about convoys back to U-boat headquarters. The plan involved dropping canoes on the side of the lake and paddling out to destroy the aircraft. Stewart said the plan was not possible because the lake was surrounded by forest. Instead he suggested that swimmers be parachuted on to the lake. Goram of Dunlop produced a small inflatable raft. This could drop with the man like a kitbag with a normal parachute soldier. It was designed in two parts; one to keep explosives dry; the other to inflate when you hit the water. A swimmer could lie on the raft, and propel himself out to the aircraft using fins.

Pritchard-Gordon was sent to practise dropping into Loch Leven and swimming with what he calls 'an inflatable suitcase' to place limpet mines on the flying boats. Fortunately this fantastic scheme was cancelled when the aircraft moved to another area. Pritchard-Gordon, with a section of sixteen men, was sent to the Middle East under command of Flag Officer Levant and Eastern Mediterranean to engage enemy shipping in the Mediterranean and Aegean, to clear the way for raids on the Aegean Islands.

From about this time, the tasks undertaken by the variety of canoe units that now existed began to be more specialized, depending on the type of unit. The RMBPD were best fitted for ship-attack and harbour sabotage. The Special Boat Section concentrated on sabotage and reconnaissance above the high-water mark. The COPPs covered beach survey and reconnaissance. Although the demarcation was not rigid, this is how they would operate for the rest of the war.

In early 1943, the biggest British operation behind the lines in the war so far was about to start: in Burma.

6

Operation Longcloth:
The First Chindit* Expedition

We were marching down to Imphal, and he said, 'You know, God gives man strange instruments to do his will.' Because these were not very high, but two very low-grade battalions which Wingate was going to take into the middle of Burma to fight the all-conquering Japanese.

Michael Calvert

At the end of May 1942, the emaciated, malaria-ridden rearguard of a defeated British Army Corps (Burcorps) marched into Imphal in Assam at the finish of a nine-hundred-mile retreat; expelled from Burma by the Japanese. Thus ended the first round in what was to become not only the longest campaign fought by the British Army in the Second World War, but also the longest land campaign involving Britain or the United States in the entire war against Japan. Although by the end some 100,000 British troops fought in Burma and Assam, by far the greatest number of soldiers under British command came from the many races in the Indian Army: Gurkhas, Sikhs, Pathans, Jats, Rajputs and Madrassis to name but some, albeit mostly led by British officers. In addition, some 90,000 West and East Africans fought in Burma, as did Karens, Kachins, Chins and Chinese. Eventual victory was gained by one of the most multiracial collections of soldiers in history: what was to become 14th Army, commanded by Lieutenant General, later General, Sir William 'Bill' Slim.

---

* Chindit: a mispronunciation of Chinthe, the mythical beast which stands guard outside the temples and monasteries of Burma, and which Wingate chose as his Brigade formation sign.

That May, morale in this defeated army was low. The Japanese had swept all before them, seemingly irresistible. To the end of the campaign, even when their reputation for invincibility had been punctured, they were respected as formidable foes.

Major Neville Hogan, a Karen who served from the first to the last day of the war in Burma, remarked that the Japanese were:

> Animals – but great soldiers, great fighting soldiers. Their battle drill was fantastic. You couldn't help but admire them. If they were ambushed, they were at you in 20 to 30 seconds, then pounding you with their mortars, and in frontal attacks they would just come on and on. We killed them but admired them.

Lieutenant-Colonel Desmond Whyte, a doctor with the Chindits:

> We underestimated the Japanese to begin with. They worshipped the Emperor as a God. They wished to die in his service. They had utter disregard of danger, and devious tactics; one could not help but admire them. In the early days they really were an invincible force until we had learnt jungle craft and battle craft and realised that we were superior. They were utterly ruthless and without compassion. I found a friend pinioned to a teak tree with a bayonet through both the left and right wrist. And the lower limbs missing, eaten by hungry jackals. The aim was to make us so terrified that we wouldn't wish to continue fighting. It had the opposite effect.

The Japanese did not follow up into Assam. Their reconnaissance persuaded them that the terrain on the Assam–Burma border was so rugged that large formed bodies of troops would be unable to penetrate it and be supplied with the necessities of war. The Japanese were content to remain in Burma, east of the Chindwin River, with just patrols on the western side. The British aim was to retake Burma but, to begin with, they simply had neither the strength nor means to do so. Having experienced the horrors of tramping along the rudimentary track from Kalewa to Imphal, they shared the Japanese view of the difficulties imposed by the terrain. So for some time the British anticipated that their reconquest of Burma would mainly consist of an amphibious operation culminating in the recapture of Rangoon; not, as eventually happened, an overland thrust mounted from Assam. The Americans encouraged the aim of reconquest, not because they were in the least interested in the British regaining part of their Empire – far from it – but because the Japanese occupation of all but a tiny corner of Burma blocked the route from Rangoon to China: by rail and road to Lashio and thence along the Burma Road. The Americans were thus prevented from supplying their ally Chiang Kai-shek, and his Nationalist Chinese Army, except by air from Assam.

To understand how the war in Burma was fought we must look at the terrain and climate. North Burma, the part we are particularly concerned with, is formed by the Irrawaddy basin and its tributary the Chindwin. To the west lie the Chin and Naga hills; in the north, in the region of Myitkyina, the terrain is mountainous. More mountains lie to the east, forming the watershed between the Irrawaddy and Salween rivers. There are scarcely any roads. The mountain ranges, densely covered with thick jungle, run from north to south, with swift rivers flowing in deep ravines. Sometimes the valleys open out into thickly wooded plains, dotted with low hills. In the flatter areas Burmese peasants cultivate rice in paddy fields. In the Irrawaddy valley there are large stretches of open paddy, millet and groundnut fields, and clumps of Toddy palm trees.

Because the lie of the land in the whole country runs north–south, the communications run in the same direction. Waterways were, and are, the chief means of transport. The railway ran up the centre of Burma from Rangoon to Mandalay, where it branched off to Lashio, Myitkyina and Ye-u. A motor road ran from Mandalay to Lashio, and north to join the Burma Road. From Mandalay, an all-weather road led to Myitkyina, and unmetalled roads to Sumprabum and Mogaung. Apart from these two, there were only tracks in North Burma. There were no rail connections between Burma and India, and only one underdeveloped road. The section from Imphal to Kalewa, some 185 miles, was a mixture of cart track and bridleway.

In the 'cold weather' in Burma and Assam brought by the north-east monsoon, from the middle of October to the end of March, the weather is dry and pleasant. In April and May temperatures rise so that at noon the heat strikes like an open oven, with high humidity. The south-west monsoon arrives in mid-May, petering out during September and October. Heavy rain swells the rivers, flooding valleys and flat areas; thick cloud, thunderstorms and turbulence make flying hazardous; malaria and dysentery flourish. In one year, 1943–44, British and other Allied troops recorded 250,000 cases of malaria and dysentery.

On to this stage stepped one of the most controversial commanders in the history of the British Army: Orde Wingate. As a result of 'string pulling' by his influential friends, he had been sent out to Burma in early 1942, the War Office in London having first asked General Wavell, the Commander-in-Chief India, if he wanted him. Wavell, whose operational responsibilities also included Burma, knew Wingate. He had served in Abyssinia when Wavell was Commander-in-Chief Middle East. Here, and in Palestine before the War, Wingate had been a successful commander of guerrilla-type operations. He had nearly been court-martialled twice, and had attempted to commit suicide once. Wavell had, however, recognized his talents, and encouraged and supported him. Always enthusiastic about unorthodox ideas, Wavell promoted Wingate to colonel, and sent him to the Bush Warfare School at Maymyo, north-east of Mandalay, to see if he could organize long-range penetration operations against the advancing Japanese. Here he met an equally remarkable character, Major Mike Calvert, Royal Engineers.

In late 1940, Calvert had been sent to Australia to train Australian Independent Companies in anticipation of the Japanese entering the war. In October 1941 he was sent to Burma to Mission 204 to try to maintain Chiang Kai-shek's guerrilla activity in China, to keep the Japanese so occupied there that they would not attack the British possessions in the Far East. Mission 204 trained the Chinese in demolition techniques:

> The school at Maymyo had been given the cover name of Bush Warfare School, so that people would think we were training people to fight in the jungle. Of course in the areas in which these cadres would fight there was no jungle at all, so we did not train them for jungle fighting. However, being commandant of the Bush Warfare School, I was supposed to be the expert on jungle warfare from then on. There is no jungle in China except on the borders of Indo-China and in the Island of Hainan.

Many of the officers trained at Maymyo who did go into China spent a frustrating war doing very little because the Chinese were fearful of Japanese reprisals. For example, after an Australian officer blew up a bridge, the Japanese immediately hanged a hundred villagers – men, women and children – from the telephone posts along the railway. After

trying again at the insistence of his headquarters, the Japanese responded
by hanging a thousand of the local villagers.

After the Japanese invaded Burma, Calvert attacked them at Henzada,
on the Irrawaddy north of Rangoon, and blew up some trains. On his
return to Maymyo he met Wingate for the first time.

> There was a man sitting at my desk. He got up and said, 'I'm Wingate.'
>
> I said, 'I'm Calvert, and that's my desk.'
>
> He said, 'I'm sorry.'
>
> I'd never heard of Wingate. He took me for walks, I found that when he
> talked about guerrilla warfare he was miles ahead of anybody I had met in
> his theories and his knowledge.

With the advance of the Japanese, the days of the Bush Warfare
School were numbered. Meanwhile Wingate had tried, unsuccessfully, to
organize the infiltration of small columns behind the enemy lines. He
also did a great deal of thinking, and produced two papers on long-
range penetration warfare in Burma, before being forced to retire to
India. Here he proposed to Wavell that a brigade operating behind the
Japanese lines in the jungle terrain would cause damage to the enemy
out of all proportion to their numbers. They could be supplied by air,
thus dispensing with a long and vulnerable line of communications. The
Japanese communications on the other hand would be ideal targets for
this 'long-range penetration' force. Wavell approved, and authorized the
raising of 77 Indian Infantry Brigade. One of its earliest members was
Calvert, by then just out of Burma.

He had been ordered to form a 'commando battalion' by General Sir
Harold Alexander, who had been sent out to command all British troops
in Burma. Calvert's Commando was formed from his bush warfare
instructors and any available troops in the area of Maymyo, including
men in detention. Having fought in the area of Mandalay, they formed
part of the rearguard on the withdrawal to the Chindwin and beyond.
On his arrival in India:

> Wingate sent for me and George Dunlop who had also been on the retreat
> from Burma. We were both suffering from malnutrition and disease. He
> said he was forming this brigade and would like us to help, and could I
> please bring as many people from the Bush Warfare School as possible. The
> training of the Brigade was initially carried out by the members of the staff
> of the School.

Space does not permit a detailed analysis of Wingate's character. But the Chindits, as his Long-Range Penetration Brigade, and later Division, came to be called, were so much his creation and to a degree an extension of his personality, that we must pause in the narrative to comment upon this extraordinary and enigmatic man. Wingate has been likened to T. E. Lawrence. In some ways he was more like General Gordon who was killed in Khartoum in January 1885, after being besieged by the Mahdi. Both thought nothing of flouting or questioning orders with which they disagreed; or of insubordination, which they would not tolerate for a moment from their juniors. Both were deeply religious, to the point of fanaticism, believing they were chosen by God, and therefore any attempt to frustrate them in their purpose was tantamount to blasphemy. Sir Evelyn, later Lord, Baring, the British Representative in Cairo, once said of Gordon, 'It is not easy to deal with a man who, in moments of difficulty, takes his instructions from Isaiah.'[1] He might have been speaking of Wingate. Both Wingate and Gordon were fortunate in having tolerant superiors, who recognized the remarkable men they were. For Wingate did have many attributes that would have qualified him to rank as a great commander and man. Unfortunately he was also flawed.

It is difficult to get a dispassionate judgement on him from anyone with whom he came in contact. He was usually either hated or worshipped. To this day those in the latter category usually react furiously to any criticism of 'their leader'. A former Chindit brigadier, who, in his own memoirs, quite mildly questioned some of Wingate's decisions, received a letter from an ex-Chindit comparing him with St Peter denying Christ thrice before the crucifixion.

Egotistical, obsessive, subject to dark depression and loss of self-control, Wingate behaved as if all the world was against him, particularly those in authority, whom he often treated with barely concealed contempt. But despite his beard, unkempt appearance, and rudeness, Wingate had influence where it mattered to a degree which is at odds with his image as a rebellious and maverick Messiah. His cousin General Sir Reginald (Rex) Wingate pressed Wingate's case with General Sir Hastings Ismay, who as head of the Military Wing of the War Cabinet Secretariat had direct access to Churchill. Rex, as he signed himself, also wrote on Wingate's behalf to his 'old friend Archie Wavell' and to another friend, Brigadier Sim, a member of the King's household. The

Secretary of State for India, L. S. Amery, took a great interest in Wingate, as did Harold Laski, Chairman of the Labour Party Executive with access to the Leader of the Labour Party and Deputy Prime Minister, Clement Attlee. When Wingate caught typhoid before his second expedition, Churchill sent him personal telegrams of encouragement. Few majors (Wingate's substantive rank) in the British Army's history can ever have had such clout with the influential and powerful.

The staffs he bullied unmercifully. In doing so, he alienated many who were trying to help him. When Wingate tried to browbeat a member of Mountbatten's staff at the start of his second expedition, Mountbatten riposted:

> Your astounding telegram to Joubert has made me realise how you have achieved such amazing success in getting yourself disliked by people who are only too ready to be on your side.

His behaviour was all too often not that of a great captain. Yet he was a loving husband, who wrote affectionate letters to his wife in terms that are free of the stilted style so prevalent at the time, addressing her as 'Beloved', or 'Sweetheart'. She returned his adoration of her in full measure. He was aware of his uncertain temper, and once wrote:

> remember dear twin, I love you as no one else I know or have ever known; there is a peculiar bond between us that has stood the test of rage and violence on my part.

And in another letter referring to the officer commanding the Gurkha Defence Platoon in his headquarters, missing after the first expedition:

> Rose behaved with the greatest courage and unselfishness. He was devoted to his Gurkhas and owes his present absence to that devotion – otherwise he would have come in my boat as I asked him to do. I often lost my temper with him & even struck him – but he understood.

Many of the younger, perhaps more impressionable, officers and soldiers responded to his magnetism, although by no means all; and it must be borne in mind that even majors were young by present-day standards, often in their early to mid-twenties, while many lieutenant-colonels and some brigadiers were in their late twenties and early thirties. Private Charles Aves, about twelve years younger than most of the men in his battalion, the 13th King's (Liverpool) Regiment, remembered meeting him for the first time:

> We heard about this man Wingate of Abyssinia. We thought he must be a freak who had done very well as a guerrilla in Ethiopia. He came to see us in Secunderabad and addressed us. He created a great effect on most of us. I felt I was in the presence of somebody really extraordinary. The type of person I had never come across before. He exuded an aura of power. And yet he didn't speak in that manner, he spoke quietly and convincingly, and we gradually came to the conclusion that he was talking about that we were going to be trained to infiltrate the Japanese lines in Burma and in fact we were going to be the first troops to fight back since the débâcle of the loss of Burma. He realigned our perceptions of what was possible for ordinary people like ourselves. He lifted us. We were left realising that our cushy life in India was coming to an end.
>
> He told us we were to be in for a very hard time training. We were going to show the Japanese we could do better. We were in awe of him. He convinced us that we could do it. He was a great man.

Major Frank Turner was a mule transport officer:

> Wingate was not the nicest chap in the world. We were not all gifted as he was gifted. He was small, and not good looking. He was an eccentric. But there was something about him that made him different. But he never asked you to do something that he could not do, or was afraid to do. He did not look the part. He looked scruffy. He grew a beard and it wasn't quite right for him. He had a short temper. He had an inability to understand. I have the greatest admiration for him. I am proud to have been sought out to serve with him. I was not a volunteer.

Wingate, as a pre-war gunner officer, knew a great deal about horses, and cared for animals. Hogan remembers him visiting his battalion of the Burma Rifles, and was due to come to the

> Officers' Mess for dinner. But he inspected the animal transport lines first. He then drove off, saying that the lines were in bad condition, and he wasn't going to eat with the officers if they couldn't look after their animals.

Some officers, particularly in Gurkha battalions, loathed him. Lieutenant Denis Gudgeon of the 3/2nd Gurkha Rifles was one:

> He was a very aesthetic man, not very tall, with a slight stoop. He carried a flit gun [an anti-insect repellant-spraying device] with him everywhere. He

also carried an alarm clock with him all the time. We thought he was mad. We did not like him, not many of the Gurkha officers liked him. He was aloof. He never said very much. He issued reams of instructions. We were terrified of him.

Wingate in his turn disliked the Indian Army, of which the Gurkhas were a part. Although he tolerated Gurkhas in his formations, because they had no caste fads about food, he refused to have any other Indian units. After his first expedition, Wingate was summoned by Churchill to the Allied conference at Quebec. Here he referred to the Indian Army as a 'system of outdoor relief'. As John Masters, a 4th Gurkha, eventually a Chindit Brigade Commander, and well-known author, remarked in his book, *The Road Past Mandalay*, 'If we had [known], we would certainly have asked to draw our dole in less draughty places than Keren, Cassino and Prome'; three of the many battles in the Second World War in which the Indian Army fought with distinction.[2]

Dominic Neill was also an officer in 3/2nd Gurkhas. After Wingate's first expedition, he fought in the Arakan with 3/2nd Gurkhas, and after the Second World War in Malaya and Borneo with 2/2nd Gurkhas, and instructed at the Jungle Warfare School in Malaya. By the end of all this, he had seen the average British and Gurkha soldier change from the mediocre jungle fighter of 1942 to surpass the Japanese by 1944, and become among the best in the world by the mid-1960s; and had himself played a part in the process. His views on Wingate, whom he could not abide, were tempered by years of operating, and training others to fight, in the jungle. In the process he acquired vastly more experience than Wingate and most other ex-Chindits in this particular art. Although a 3/2nd Gurkha, he had been sent to one of the King's (Liverpool) Regiment columns with muleteers from the 10th Gurkhas. He remembered his first meeting with Wingate:

> He was very interested in the mules, but he ignored my Gurkha muleteers completely. This appalled me. As the Brigade commander he should have at least attempted to speak to newly arrived young Gurkhas and make them feel at home.

Wingate's views on the Indian Army were without doubt influenced by obstructionism among many of the staff at GHQ in Delhi, and bad officers in some field units. Calvert, whom Wingate put in command of one of the Gurkha columns, replacing one of their own British officers, remembered:

> We were told by the Gurkhas that they would have to halt for two and a half hours to cook their meal. So Wingate gave a demonstration. He gathered the battalion round him. He couldn't speak Gurkhali, though he tried to learn. He did it all by mime. He took some dry sticks out of his pack, lit them, put some more on until he had a good fire. He then set his alarm clock, poured water from his bottle into the canteen, and measured out some rice from his sock. We always carried rice in a sock. He hummed some Arabic or Jewish songs while he waited for 20 minutes. After 20 minutes the water would be boiled away. He stirred the rice, took a spoonful, blew on it to cool it and ate it. A great smile went across his face, and all the Gurkhas smiled with him. He converted them in one go how to make rice in 20 minutes.

Squadron Leader T. P. O'Brien, a Royal Air Force liaison officer on the second Wingate expedition, was not impressed by him:

> Most officers spoke of him in terms reserved for a deity, but the brief contacts I had with him would never have tempted me to pray to him for aid; in the first place he would probably not even hear the prayer, being so engrossed in his own thoughts, and if he did happen to listen, any solution he offered would probably have been more dangerous than the original problem. I don't think of his original mind, compelling oratory, fanatical dedication, the aura of his personality and other such characteristics which his admirers point to, but to his lack of common humanity.

Lieutenant George Borrow, on the other hand, wrote home to his parents:

> Our Brigadier – O. C. Wingate – is a genius and a name to be remembered. He is an all or nothing man, who doesn't know the meaning of 'fear', 'can't', 'impossible', etc. and one who will brook no delay when he gives an order. What he wants he gets. I think he is the personification of the man we all ought to be.

Perhaps Calvert, who knew him better than most, sums up Wingate best:

> If a man is doing a hell of a lot, he will make enemies. In a particular cemetery I saw a large gravestone, 'So-and-so, loved by all'. Underneath someone had carved: 'Did fuck all'.

Not even his worst enemy could accuse Wingate of the latter.

*

The material given to Wingate with which to forge his Long-Range Penetration Force was hardly promising, the only qualification many of them possessed was either excessive age or youth; and a very low standard of training. Major R. B. G. Bromhead was Wingate's Brigade Major (Chief of Staff), and later a column commander in 77 Brigade. In a paper after the first expedition he wrote:

The troops available were:

One British Battalion [13th King's (Liverpool) Regiment]. This battalion was raised for coastal defence in the United Kingdom and sent to India for internal security purposes only. Average age was 33 and not in their wildest dreams could they have considered themselves a picked force.

One Gurkha Battalion [3/2nd Gurkha Rifles]. This battalion was formed and made up to strength through lack of trained men with 11-month recruits of whom the average age was [under] eighteen. Once again, not in their wildest dreams could they have considered themselves picked men.

One Burmese Battalion [2nd Battalion Burma Rifles]. This battalion was composed of men of the Burmese Army who had been through the first campaign and won their way back to India and, as such, they were seasoned troops.

The Sabotage Group [142nd Commando Company]. The Group was raised from commandos originally intended for the 104 Military Mission in China; volunteers from every regular regiment in India, and made up to strength by drafts from home [UK]. These men could, on the whole, be said to be picked men and proved to be the best troops in the force.

The Mule Leader element. It was decided that the mule leaders required for the force over and above those first line mules [i.e. mules belonging to battalions already] would be found from an extra company of recruits raised from a Gurkha Battalion. Almost without exception these too were too young and ill-trained for the job.

George Borrow, The Royal Sussex Regiment, attached to the 13th King's, would not have disagreed with Bromhead; he wrote to his parents:

This King's Battalion is a Battalion mainly of married men drawn from the dock workers of Liverpool. They are great workers and stickers once on the job, but often a bit self-pitying that such old men should be called upon to do such active work.

Wingate commented on the 13th King's (Liverpool) during training in the report written after his first expedition:

Within three weeks of entering the jungle in the monsoon, 30 per cent of the King's were either in or trying to enter hospital. Four weeks later their Sick Parade reached the peak figure of 70 per cent. With the co-operation of the doctors certain measures were taken and the Sick Parade numbers rapidly fell until, towards the end of training, they were less than 3 per cent.

Wingate singled out the Burma Rifles for praise:

I have never had under my command in the Field as good a body of men as the 2nd Burma Rifles. The Burman hillman is an ideal soldier for aggressive reconnaissance. He is not ideal in defence. He is not ideal if ordered to attack a strongly held position. But in carrying out rapid, bold and intelligent patrols in the face of the enemy, in obtaining local information, in making propaganda, in handling boats, in living off the country, and in loyal service to his officers he is without equal.... There appeared to be little difference between Karens, Kachins and Chins in general excellence.

The Burma Rifles were recruited from only those three tribes. Most, but by no means all, Burmans either supported the Japanese, fondly imagining that in the event of their eventual victory, they would grant independence to Burma, or were too afraid to side openly with the British. However, many Burmese villagers sold food to Wingate's men, particularly when the Chindits withdrew at the end of the first expedition. When they saw that the British were winning, the pro-Japanese Burmese changed sides. The Karens, Kachins and Chins were strongly pro-British, loathed the Burmese, and do so to this day.

The Indian Army was the largest volunteer army the world has ever seen. But by 1942, its units actually in India were neither well trained nor was their morale high. Not only had there been an enormous expansion, but since 1940 the Indian Army had been 'milked' of experienced officers and NCOs to provide drafts for Indian formations fighting in the Middle East. One of the reasons for the poor showing of Indian troops in the Malayan campaign that had just ended was the lack of good officers and NCOs. Any battle experience these soldiers might have acquired as a result of the fighting in Malaya was lost because all of them became prisoners of the Japanese. From 1943 onwards the standards of both training and morale rose, but Dominic Neill, having experienced the low period in the Indian Army's history, is scathing, both about his own basic officer training and that in the Regimental Depot:

> We were not well trained. I had spent one year in a junior soldiers battalion. We did very little training. I was then commissioned into the Indian Army. At Bangalore [the Officer Training Centre], the training was not up to standard, we did foot and bicycle drill, and trained in elementary tactics for the North-West Frontier. We trained with wooden machine-guns and wooden 2-inch mortars, we really learnt very little indeed. We had no weapon training. Map reading training was very poor. When I joined the Regimental centre [of the 2nd Gurkhas] I was in charge of recruit training, I knew nothing, my recruits knew nothing. My company commander had been a tea planter, and his military knowledge was very limited. We had no officer training and no language training. When I joined Wingate's Brigade I hoped I would get more training; I did not. I was 21 years old and untrained in charge of 50 equally inept young Gurkhas.
>
> The training that the Brigade had received had finished by the time we joined. I found out by questioning what it had consisted of. I was told, river crossing and tactical drills. On contact with the enemy a bugle was blown, the troops would disperse, under sub-unit commanders, and return to their former halting place. I could not believe my ears. I and my Gurkha muleteers received no tactical training whatsoever until I came face to face with the Japanese.
>
> We were badly trained, badly led, and the plans were over-optimistic.

The report Wingate wrote after the First Chindit Expedition contains frequent references to the low standards of training of most of the officers and soldiers in his brigade during their operations in Burma. The reader is entitled to ask whose fault was that? The answer is, of course, ultimately and solely, the commander's, Wingate's. Any brigade commander who is given a free hand and six months to turn men who have completed basic training into competent soldiers has only himself to blame if they are not up to his self-imposed standards.

Wingate organized his Brigade into two groups and seven columns.

The Southern (Number 1) Group (Lieutenant-Colonel L. A. Alexander) consisted of Numbers 1 (Major G. Dunlop) and 2 Column (Major A. Emmett), and 142 Commando Company (Major J. B. Jeffries). The Northern (Number 2 Group) (Lieutenant-Colonel S. A. Cooke) consisted of Column Numbers 3 (Major J. M. Calvert), 4 (Major Conran and later Major R. B. G. Bromhead), 5 (Major B. E. Fergusson), 7 (Major K. D. Gilkes) and 8 (Major W. P. Scott), the 2nd Burma Rifles (Lieutenant-Colonel L. G. Wheeler), and an Independent Mission, consisting of a platoon of Burma Rifles, under Captain Herring. Number 6 Column was broken up to replace casualties during training.

Each column consisted of about four hundred men, built around an infantry company. To this were added: a small headquarters; a reconnaissance platoon of the Burma Rifles; two mortars and two Vickers machine-guns; a mule transport platoon; an air liaison detachment of one RAF officer and radio operators to communicate with the air base whence resupply would come; a sabotage squad; a doctor and a couple of orderlies; and a radio detachment to communicate with other columns or Brigade Headquarters. The lieutenant-colonel commanding each group accompanied one of his columns.

Wingate's tactical concept was that columns should march independently, be self-supporting for a week, and be supplied by air. By adopting this organization he aimed for mobility and security. The mobility was to be achieved by not having wheeled transport, and without being tied to an overland line of communication they could, in theory, go where they wished. The security was based on the difficulty the enemy would have finding mobile columns in the jungles and teak forests of northern Burma, and on the ability of the column to disperse into smaller groups. Wingate planned to concentrate as many columns as were necessary to carry out a specific task. The orders for concentration and the rendezvous would be given by radio.

In battle the column often proved to be unwieldy, inflexible and uneconomic. An organization of four hundred men produced just over a hundred bayonets and some sabotage squads to engage the enemy, supported by two 3-inch mortars and two Vickers machine-guns. When the dispersion drill, about which Neill was so contemptuous, was tried without warning in the confusion of an unexpected contact with the enemy, the result was often chaos. It usually worked if proper orders could be given first, and disseminated to all soldiers.

The training was physically hard, and particularly so for men who had spent the war so far in static guard duties. Charles Aves of 13th King's (Liverpool):

> We went to Saugor near Jhansi. The jungle surrounding it was similar to that of the area of Burma in which we were to operate. We did long marches, all through the night. We had bad and inadequate food. The monsoon started. We were never dry, night or day. There were mud holes four or five feet deep. It was an appalling month. We had our first casualties. A number of men in camp returning to their tents were drowned in what had been a small stream which had become a swollen torrent. I and plenty of soldiers went down with malaria, and lots of people went down with dysentery.
>
> Those of us who had taken to the training and stuck it we called 'PKs' or 'pukka King's', those that opted out we called 'jossers'.

Aves also gives us a sympathetic portrait of Wingate:

> Many of the officers hated Wingate. I overheard an officer say to another officer referring to Wingate, 'This man is mad . . .'
>
> One day Wingate decided to hold a church service in the jungle. I was introduced by my Column Commander, Major Gilkes, to Wingate to discuss the hymns we would sing, which I would accompany on my accordion. I stood next to him as he conducted the first part of the service. I found him kind and considerate. Whenever we met on a one-to-one basis, which was not very often, he would ask how I was getting on.
>
> On one occasion he said, 'How are you finding the rations?'
>
> I replied, 'There is not enough. We are hungry all the time.'
>
> He just nodded his head. He said, 'You will be pleased to know that we are going on general service rations. There will be more food and more variety.'
>
> He went on his way. I felt proud to have spoken to Brigadier Wingate.

Although the food supplied during training may have improved after Wingate's conversation with Aves, the rations throughout 77 Brigade's time on operations in Burma were inadequate. Designed as emergency rations for parachute troops for two or three days only, each man had a daily allowance of: 12 ounces of Shakapura biscuits, rather like large dog biscuits; 2 ounces of cheese; 1 ounce of milk powder; 9 ounces of compressed almonds and raisins; 1 ounce of acid drops or chocolate;

¾ ounce of tea; 4 ounces of sugar; ½ ounce of salt; two packets of ten cigarettes; a box of matches; and for the Gurkhas and Burmese troops, rice if available. There was no meat in the ration.

Bromhead commented:

> The ration was designed to give 3,000 calories, the remaining 1,000 calories considered necessary would be obtained from game, or local purchase in villages.

Not only was a daily intake of 4,000 calories insufficient for men marching long distances under heavy load, but it was very rarely achievable anyway. Killing game in the quantities needed to provide even one meagre meal for 400 men would have taken days of effort, during which time the column would have made no progress, and the sound of shots would have risked compromise. The proposition also assumed a level of bushcraft and hunting skills which few in 77 Brigade, or anywhere else in the British or Indian Army, came within miles of meeting. A column on the move could not spare the time to stop very often to buy food from villages, assuming the village had enough spare to sell. The lack of food was to have dire consequences.

Calvert and the other column commanders trained their men in the basing-up or bivouacing drills that would become a daily feature of life on Chindit operations:

> The column commander would be near the front, and he would find a suitable place. You couldn't hesitate for long with 400 men behind you. He'd choose a place to bivouac. Some of the essentials were water and bamboo to feed the mules. Provided it was possible to combine it with water, we would try to find a place with fairly high ground so our signal sets would carry the 200 miles back to India. We would set up a defensive position off the path, while the rearguard marched on as a deception, before brushing away the footprints, and setting up an ambush [to catch any Japanese following up].
>
> Within five minutes of getting in every unit would be lighting fires. We had been trained in this detail by Wingate who pointed out that often as we got in the rains used to come at about four or five o'clock. He told us to collect dry sticks from the previous night's fire and put them in our pack. The wireless would be set up. The direction of the aerials was very important – a lot of units in the British and Indian armies didn't understand that. The column commander would sit down and his batman would bring him a

mug of hot sweet tea. And the signals would start coming in. The first signal out would give the position of the column back to the base in India.

The muleteers, one to each two mules, would go and cut bamboo for their mules. The men would go to fill their water bottles. The upper bit of the stream was for water bottles, the next piece down for mules, then for washing, and the lowest for defecating. We always tried to use running water for latrines, so it would be washed away and not give our position away.

We rarely stayed in a bivouac for more than one night; occasionally for two to three days. After the column commander had given orders, the column would settle down to eat and sleep. While the fires were still alight, we'd make a second quantity of tea, and put this in our water bottles, before burying the water bottle in leaves or earth just beside where one slept. In the mornings, before light, you drank warm tea and ate some Shakapura biscuit. The routines were carried out with few words being spoken, 400 men and 120 animals going into their places with no fuss. The same in the morning, I [as a column commander] would like to start the column just before dawn and get if possible two hours' marching away from our previous bivouac before we settled down to breakfast.

Underlying all the training was Wingate's firm belief that his Long-Range Penetration Force would outdo the Japanese. Calvert:

I don't want to be too hard on the British and Indian armies at the time, but they were to a large extent demoralised, they thought the Jap was invincible. There were well-meaning posters up all over India showing a cruel Japanese bayoneting children. Instead of making people want to fight the Japanese, it made them frightened. We had to build up the morale of the British to remember they were tough. I think this was why Wingate said that beards would be allowed. I personally would not allow mournful beards. I insisted we should have aggressive beards, like conquistadores.

Some people, like Neill and his Gurkha muleteers, were having to learn completely new skills:

I had never seen a mule in my life before. But we started to love our mules. I did take part in a final exercise. I joined 8 Column, commanded by Major Scott of the King's (known as 'Scotty', although not to his face). He was an excellent chap, and gave my men a very warm welcome. I was given a British sergeant and 20 British Other Ranks to lead the first line mules of 8 Column. The first line carried the support weapons, heavy wireless set, ammo, and spare LMGs. The second line carried bedding, spare rations. All were to be under my command. The sergeant was ex 17/21 Lancers and knew a great deal about horses, less about mules, but his knowledge was invaluable. The exercise was a hundred-mile march. What the scheme was about I have no idea. From start to finish of my time in 8 Column [with one exception] I was never called to one of 'Scotty''s O Groups. My orders came to me piecemeal via the Sergeant Major.

Wavell originally intended to use 77 Brigade ahead of an attack across the River Chindwin by IV Corps from Assam, itself part of an Allied advance by the Chinese from Yunnan across the Salween, and the American General Stilwell's Chinese–American forces south from Ledo. He wanted 77 Brigade to enter Burma in mid February 1943, cut the railway between Shwebo and Myitkyina, harass the enemy in the Shwebo area and, if possible, cross the Irrawaddy to cut the enemy communications with the Salween front. When it became apparent that mainly for administrative reasons no attack would be possible for some months, Wingate pressed to be allowed to continue with his part. He gave six reasons: first, his theories needed to be tested; second, any delay might be bad for morale in his Brigade; third, he could test whether the Burmese would co-operate in the liberation of their country; fourth, his operations would prevent a Japanese offensive on Fort Hertz, the last British outpost in Burma; fifth, Japanese infiltration across the Chindwin would be stopped; and sixth, he could interrupt any Japanese plan for an offensive against Assam.

Wavell agreed that Wingate should go ahead as planned, leaving Imphal on 8 February 1943. He also gave orders for another LRP brigade, 111 Indian Infantry Brigade to be raised. When 77 Brigade came out of Burma, 111 Brigade would be available to go in in the same role.

During January 1943, Wingate's Brigade had moved forward to Imphal. Charles Aves:

In January 1943, we travelled across India to Comilla and on to Dimapur. This took 12 days. From there we marched to Kohima, taking 8 days. It was beautiful country. Winding roads up to Kohima at 5,000 feet. We did it at night. The lorries used it by day carrying supplies to Kohima and Imphal. We slept by day. We then went on to Imphal. While there an advanced group of Burma riflemen and a few British soldiers were formed as a recce group to go in advance of the main force. A friend of mine was in this

group. He learned a few Karen phrases. He taught me some phrases which
came in useful later on.

Dominic Neill:

At Kohima, I called my senior Gurkha in for orders. He was drunk. The
following morning he was charged with being drunk on active service. He
was sent to Brigade HQ in disgrace. This meant I had no Gurkha officer.
My next in line was a havildar [sergeant], who was overweight and
overpromoted, called Limbu. I felt sorry for my men, with a very inexperienced young British officer from a different regiment. 'Scotty' required the
British sergeant and me to ride our chargers up and down the column on
the march to supervise the inexperienced young muleteers. We got to
Imphal about mid-January '43. Here we camped for about 10 days. We had
a visit from Wavell. When Wavell finished he gave us a pep talk, and ended
by saying, 'God bless you.' If he had had a crystal ball, he might have said
'God help you', because that is what we needed when we got deep inside
Burma.

Denis Gudgeon:

At Dimapur we met Major Calvert our column commander. I was
immensely impressed by Calvert. He was a dynamic character. We went
every day to the Imphal golf club, where Wingate had spread maps of
Burma on the floor and familiarised ourselves. We had to take our boots
off and walk around in our socks.

Wingate's report:

The Brigade arrived at Imphal during one of the rainy periods which do in
actual fact occur throughout the year at that place. In order that the troops
might not be softened by the cinema in Imphal, they were bivouacked some
seven miles north of the township.

Wingate had decided that the Northern Group including his own
headquarters, and consisting of 2,200 men and 850 mules, would cross
the Chindwin at Tonhe, traverse the steep Zibyu Taugdan range, cut the
Shwebo–Myitkyina railway between Bongyaung and Nankan, and cross
the Irrawaddy at Tigyaing. The Southern Group, consisting of 1,000 men
and 250 mules, would cross the Chindwin thirty-five miles further south
at Auktaung, march to cut the railway at Kyaikthin, cross the Irrawaddy
near Tagaung, and make for Mongmit. The Southern Group was to cross

the Chindwin a day before the Northern Group in the hope that the Japanese who were known to be in the locality would think this was part of an outflanking attack on Kalewa. Other diversionary operations were also mounted as part of a double bluff aimed at convincing the Japanese that the northern crossing at Tonhe was itself a diversion for the crossing in the south.

Before reaching the Chindwin, Dominic Neill remembers that:

Wingate sent a signal saying that once across the Chindwin, any man who was wounded and couldn't march would be left in a friendly village to his fate. I thought, on the eve of battle to give an order like that would cause men's morale to dip. I know that the British soldiers were not best pleased to hear what their fate might be, for my part I never passed the message on to my Gurkhas. In those days none of them spoke English. In the Indian Army we had always made such a thing of looking after wounded and saving them whenever possible, this edict from Wingate went down badly [with the officers]. Having received that boost to our morale, we started crossing the river. The mules were taken across ten or so tethered to the stern of boats. That night I remember feeling very excited. That night and the following day, and many days following, were quiet. We all wore bush hats, khaki clothes, boots, packs, 1937 pattern web equipment.

In his report, Wingate says that:

All this [the need to leave wounded behind] was thoroughly explained to every officer and man by myself in person, before leaving India. In fact it was made part of training.

Although some of Wingate's statements need to be taken with a pinch of salt, this assertion is borne out by others, who add that all were offered the chance of opting out. Because he arrived after most of the training had been completed, Neill possibly missed this briefing.

Both groups crossed the Chindwin without interference, and took preplanned supply drops. Denis Gudgeon with Number 3 Column:

We were lucky, it was in broad daylight but there was no Japanese air activity. We marched 20 miles and had our first supply drop. I arranged the distribution of the supplies; rice, biscuits, ammunition, fodder for mules, and petrol for the charging engines for the batteries for the wireless sets.

Dominic Neill:

Our first supply drop was the first I had ever seen. The sacks of mule fodder and rice were free dropped, without parachutes. Each weighed about 120 lb. After the drop we moved due east to what we called the escarpment [the Zibyu Taungdan]. The track was narrow, and it was hellish for the mules. They got bad wither galls [suppurating sores between the shoulder-blades caused by loads chafing], which became gangrenous. The stench of their galls was dreadful, it was like walking alongside a rotting corpse.

Galls were not the only problem with mules. Frank Turner was a mule transport officer with Wingate's second expedition, but his comments are valid for both:

A mule is product of donkey stallion and pony mare. The hinny is a product of a pony stallion and a donkey mare. We had them too. To the soldiers a mule was a mule. The mule could kick, at both ends. The main sickness problem with mules was diarrhoea, caused by eating green bamboo. This was sweet, and they loved it. That [the liquid droppings] stayed on the mule's hindquarters and hardened in the sun, so he was attacked by mosquitoes and flies. He became lame after a while; the front end working beautifully, back end not. If lame, I would despatch that mule, having transferred his load if it was an important one, such as a radio set. Our chaps would have mule steaks that night if we could have fire. I shot the mule, no one else in the whole brigade was allowed to do it. I did it with my revolver. I did not eat meat, I had been a vegetarian for years.

Charles Aves:

We crossed the River Chindwin with our mules and bullocks, and walked and walked, carrying very heavy packs. The men who survived the training were not special men, some were about 32 years old. It was like an adventure, I was not afraid at that stage. I liked the jungle. We could deal with the jungle.

Despite Aves's confident assertion, Wingate was not impressed by the standards of jungle skills, which were pretty low despite some six months' training:

March discipline was bad. Columns made a trail through the jungle of cigarette cartons, and other packings that would have been too liberal for a paper chase.... Whenever opportunity occurred in the course of the approach march to the railway, I personally lectured all officers on these and other points.

The Southern Group crossed two nights later. The Chindits had their first contact with the enemy near Maingnyaung, some mule loads were lost, and the whole group made a detour and reached the railway at Kyaikthin later than planned. On approaching the railway, the Southern Group split to attack different parts of the line. Number 1 Column destroyed a bridge north of Kyaikthin. Group Headquarters and Number 2 Column chose to march alongside a spur railway line in daylight because it was the easiest approach to the main line. Not content with that, they bivouacked within 200 yards of the line. The Japanese seldom allowed carelessness of this sort to go unpunished, and this was no exception. They brought up a company and ambushed the column as it was leaving the bivouac area. Colonel Alexander ordered the ambush cleared with the bayonet, but this was not attempted. The bulk of the force might have been saved, but the Column commander added to the mayhem by changing the rendezvous in the middle of the battle. Number 2 Column, having dispersed, never reassembled. Most of the men eventually recrossed the Chindwin safely. Some managed to join Alexander, with Group Headquarters and Number 1 Column at the group RV near Hinthaw, and together they crossed the Irrawaddy opposite Tagaung unopposed.

Meanwhile the Northern Group had acquired an elephant with its mahout from a Japanese occupied village at Sinlamaung. At Tonmakeng, while waiting for a supply drop, Wingate had sent Columns 3, 7 and 8 to attack Sinlamaung. The enemy had just left, but the columns were able to breakfast on Japanese rations.

On 1 March the whole Northern Group had reached a position five miles to the west of Pinbon. From here, Wingate sent Calvert (3 Column) and Fergusson (5 Column) to attack the railway, while Bromhead (4 Column) was to ambush the road out of Pinbon, and then march to join Wingate at Indaw. Meanwhile Gilkes (7 Column) and Scott (8 Column) were to demonstrate towards Pinlebu to draw the Japanese attention away from the railway.

On 4 March, Bromhead's column was about to move to Indaw, when Wingate changed his mind, and ordered him to join 7 and 8 Columns in the Pinlebu area. On his way south, Bromhead clashed with an enemy patrol:

> although we beat them off, our only radio got a bullet [*sic*]. Since the Japs used soft-nosed bullets, it was the end of that radio. The Column was split

by the encounter, but all reached the RV that evening, and we sat down to consider our situation. No communications, little food and no way of getting more, except courtesy of the locals, and the British officers of the (Gurkha) column reported very poor morale. What to do?

We could not influence the war, so I decided to turn back.

Sad to say it was the Gurkhas in the column who had panicked. Wingate in his report had:

No adverse comment to pass on his [Bromhead's] conduct which showed judgement and courage throughout.

On 6 March, Fergusson demolished the railway bridge at Bongyaung, which he calls Bonchaung in his report to Wingate. In a fight with fifteen Japanese in a lorry, in which all but one enemy were killed, Lieutenant Kerr and four men were badly wounded. Fergusson:

I left them in a village from which the villagers had run away, surrounded by food and water.... At 21.00 hours the bridge was blown. The end of a 100 ft span rested in the river, and the central 40 ft span fell completely.

In another place where the line ran through a gorge, thousands of tons of rock were brought down across the rails by demolitions set by Fergusson's column. Of the five left by Fergusson, all were taken prisoner by the Japanese. Kerr was the only one to survive.

Calvert after bumping the Japanese and driving them off with casualties to them reported:

We had destroyed three bridges and cut the line in 70 places and left numerous booby traps with 3-inch mortar bombs as bursting charges, and lost no man or equipment. We were very pleased with ourselves and it had been a good birthday party for me.

Both columns then crossed the railway to their own RVs, and marched to cross the Irrawaddy at Tigyaung, some twenty-five miles away. It was now a month since 77 Brigade had crossed the Chindwin, and although Wingate was encouraged by what had been achieved so far, he did not believe it was enough to constitute convincing proof of the effectiveness of LRP operations. While pondering his next move, he received radio reports that the Southern Group was crossing the Irrawaddy at Tagaung, and Calvert and Fergusson were approaching the river at Tigyaung.

Calvert and Fergusson told him that if they crossed at once, they would be unopposed, and sought permission to do so.

Wingate gave his permission, and decided to follow with the rest of the brigade. This was a very bold but risky decision to take. Once across, his withdrawal route would be over two major rivers which the Japanese would be bound to watch. Furthermore, following a clash at a supply drop south of Tamshaw, the Japanese were aware for the first time that the brigade was being resupplied by air. The Japanese commander of 15th Army could now withdraw any patrols searching for Wingate's line of communication, and concentrate on hunting the columns.

Fergusson crossed the Irrawaddy without incident. Calvert's crossing was discovered and his column was attacked. Most of his mules and supplies had to be left behind. 'This is where we lost our elephant, it stampeded with his mahout, and cut down [through] our mules,' recorded Denis Gudgeon.

The Irrawaddy is a formidable obstacle. Wingate's report on the place where he crossed:

> The Irrawaddy varies from 500 yards to 1600 yards in width. There is always a great flow of water, sometimes resulting in rapid current for a short distance, at other places a steady current from bank to bank.... On average we found that given country boats with skilled native paddlers, the process of loading, crossing, unloading and returning occupied one hour.... Fighter patrols by the RAF squadron at Imphal flew down the river on the 18th keeping away possible enemy launches. At Inywa on the east bank were a number of [pro-Japanese] Burma Defence Army, but these gentry preferred to remain behind closed doors.

Wingate had managed to get 2,000 men and 1,000 mules across this river, no mean feat; but as he admitted in his report, 'the ease and quickness of the crossing gave us little idea of the real difficulty'.

Anticipating that he would eventually operate across the Irrawaddy, Wingate had earlier allowed Captain Herring to take a platoon of Kachins of the Burma Rifles into the Kachin Hills, to see if the tribesmen were ripe for a rising against the Japanese. Depending on his answer, Wingate would decide whether or not to take his brigade into Kachin territory. Wingate had told Herring to RV with the Southern Group on the Shweli River on 25 March and report. Herring reached the hills north-east of Bhamo on 15 March without encountering any Japanese.

He decided that a rising on a far greater scale than expected could be organized providing weapons and ammunition could be dropped. Herring's radio set lacked the power to get through to Wingate, and could not pass on this information. He went to the RV, but despite waiting until 29 March, saw no one from 77 Brigade. On 18 April he made contact with 2nd Burma Rifles miles north of the RV, and reported his findings. By then Wingate's Brigade had dispersed.

As Wingate had marched east, he had found that the country between the Irrawaddy and the Shweli consisted of an area of hot, waterless jungle, with many tracks on which the enemy armoured vehicles could operate. His columns were meeting more and more Japanese, constantly having to keep on the move, and exhausting men and animals who were desperately short of water. On 24 March he was ordered to withdraw by IV Corps commander, who explained that any operations further east would be difficult to supply by air.

Dominic Neill recalled this period:

'Scotty' told me we would be shortly returning to India. He said it would be a good idea to kill one of the mules for rations. I chose the sickliest animal, and shot it between the eyes with my pistol. She dropped stone dead at my feet. Unfortunately the meat was tough, and sour. We never tried to eat our mules again. We were only about 70 miles from the China border. Thoughts of our return to India were very much in our mind. I really wondered why we had come into Burma. We in 8 Column had done absolutely nothing. A minor contact in Baw, and that was it. We had marched a very long way for nothing.

At about this time, Dominic Neill was involved in a minor skirmish which served to reinforce his views on Wingate's methods:

We marched in single file. No one seemed to worry in Wingate's brigade if troops bunched. Any infantryman knows that if you bunch you present a target and will suffer heavily if hit.

The vegetation was a mixture of primary and secondary jungle, and some lantau and some sal. It was not very thick. One could see ahead and to a flank. There was rifle fire ahead, and rounds were hitting the trees ahead of me. I saw the British Other Ranks ahead running back shouting 'Japs'. Suddenly I saw a Jap at about 20 yards. A British Other Rank got in the way, the Jap fired, but missed. There was confusion in extreme up front. The leading platoon came rushing back with a look of terror in their eyes. The sight of fleeing soldiers is very infectious. My men, in sympathy, turned about, and started running. I shouted at them in Nepali, 'Don't run'. Bless their souls, they stopped, and broke into a walk. I now found myself as rearguard. The Japs did not follow up.

Later, Neill:

asked the lead platoon commander what had happened. He told me they had bumped two Japanese, only two, the Japs had fired, and the leading platoon had followed out Wingate's dispersal drill to the letter. The only thing missing was the bugle call. Wingate had really opened a Pandora's box when he instituted that dispersal drill. It was an absolute shambles. A lot of young men in 8 Column hung their heads in shame that night.

I did not hear the sound of our rifles fired. I thought that if a field commander teaches bad tricks in training it is guaranteed that troops will behave badly on contact with the enemy for the first time. It was a lesson that was hoisted in by me, and no doubt by many others.

On 26 March Wingate gave his orders to withdraw. Before crossing the Irrawaddy he had ordered Calvert and Fergusson to join forces and destroy the Gokteik Gorge viaduct on the Lashio road. Fergusson was recalled from this task, but Calvert, on receiving the withdraw order, first tried to cross the Shweli and move to Bhamo. Finding the Shweli crossing held by the enemy, he organized a supply drop, thoroughly briefed his column in his usual laconic fashion, having divided them into nine groups; Calvert's report for 29 March 1943:

I called all officers together and went over their routes with them. I then made the following points:-
1. March methodically and don't overtire yourselves or men, as lack of sleep and tiredness makes cowards of us all.
2. If you are up against a problem, if possible sit down, and make a cup of tea, and it usually gets solved.
3. Don't whatever you do in trying to avoid the Japs, and through the fear of the Japs, get more casualties through drowning or lack of water or food than ever you would have done if you had fought them for these.
4. If you can't find boats in one place try again in another. If all fails make rafts of bamboo as big as you like and at night push off.
5. Don't allow this hunted feeling or the feeling of a child running ever faster down a dark lane get you. If you get overanxious, stop and rest; the Japs aren't all that keen in [sic] chasing people in the hot weather.

6. Make maps for all your men giving the direction and distances: e.g. River – mts – river – mts – Chindwin.

7. When you come in, don't look like a defeated army. It is very important to show the highest morale, drill and discipline as we pass the front line troops. Overdo the drill and saluting procedure.

8. Don't come back with stories of how this or that ran away. We have all been subjected to a very great strain in which many units in other circumstances have surrendered. That is of course out of the question. Let us keep our dirty washing to ourselves on our return.

9. We will be of great use on our return in the way of passing on information. So 'surface' at times at villages to obtain this.

10. 3 Column RV is at Sittaung. I expect all Group Commanders to arrive there complete at any time from the 12th onwards.

On the following day they dispersed. His report for 30 March:

As soon as all was fixed up all officers, VCOs and GCOs drank a health to the King and Bde in rum at midday, shook hands, and wished each other luck. Then some with heavy hearts departed in the various directions, but not very far due to the rum. My Gp remained to the last to clear up.

He took the most dangerous route himself, and attacked the railway as he passed. Thanks to Calvert's careful briefing and preparation, most of his column recrossed the Chindwin in good heart weeks before the others who had done far less fighting; some of his men were not so lucky.

Denis Gudgeon:

Calvert had ordered us to build 'Sapper Sampans', a framework of bamboo and covered with ground sheets. I was in the rearguard. Our ground sheets were rotten and of my party of 12, the only one [apart from him] who could swim was a Burma Rifleman. I aborted the crossing, and we marched up and down the Irrawaddy for several days, eventually getting to a village. We hid in thick undergrowth nearby and the Burma Rifleman negotiated for a boat and boatman. And after a lot of hard bargaining, I paid some silver rupees for him to ferry us across, we all got across safely. I had no maps, but had a prismatic compass. I became progressively weaker, and in the end had to order my men to leave me. I was on my own, and knew I was fairly near the River Chindwin. I waylaid a Burmese man selling fish. He promised a boat and that he would get me to the British lines. In fact he took me to the village, and handed me over to the local Burmese Militia.

They took me to the Japanese, and this fisherman got a reward of 50 rupees. I was rude to the first Japanese I met by not stopping reading when he came into the room. He interrogated me holding his sword to my throat for about four hours. I said that I belonged to a normal unit. Luckily they believed me. They took me to Rangoon, where I was interrogated again, then to Rangoon Central Jail where I spent the next two years.

Wingate ordered all the columns except Calvert's to RV east of the Irrawaddy and cross at Inywa. Fergusson's column became involved in a firefight with Japanese in a village which they had entered at night. Fergusson ordered dispersal and, except for Fergusson and about fifty of his men, most of the column managed to make the Brigade RV. The columns carried some RAF dinghies on mules, which were inflated on the river bank, but these were insufficient to carry the whole brigade across. A tour of Inywa village produced twenty country boats, and sufficient paddles for half of them.

Wingate's report:

> The villagers reported a force of 200 Japanese living in the village one mile upstream on the opposite bank. All therefore depended on crossing in sufficient force to deliver an attack on this force before it became aware of what was happening. A certain number of native rowers had been rounded up and were helping. Wherever BORs [British other ranks] or officers were attempting to cross unaided, they were floundering about, some making no progress, others being carried so far downstream as to make it impossible for their boats to return for several hours.

This is not the only place in his report that Wingate comments in a self-justifying and condescending tone on the poor watermanship of his troops. One wonders why, knowing he would be crossing large rivers in Burma, he did not train his men properly during the six months in India. Indeed in his report in a rare display of humility, he admits that he neglected swimming and boating training; perhaps he was not as prescient as some of his supporters believed.

Part of Number 7 Column was sent across to secure the far bank. Charles Aves was one of them:

> I was in the third boat. As we approached the other side the Japs opened up with mortars, machine-guns and rifles. I was lucky, my boat wasn't hit. The boat behind me was, and everybody was drowned. When I got ashore,

we crawled up the bank. There I found one of the officers eating cheese out of a tin, and unconcerned. The firing was from about 400 yards away, and we couldn't see any enemy. This officer told me to go out and fire grenades at the enemy. I had never used a grenade launcher before, and hadn't got one on me. He found one and some more grenades, I only had two. I crawled out on my own. Not another soldier was within sight. I couldn't see the enemy. I did not know what to do so I returned to find the party forming up to move off. Sixty-five of us had landed in this area: three officers, Captain Oakes, a lieutenant and a second-lieutenant, four sergeants, two or three corporals and fifty privates. We went to the designated RV inland. It was in deep jungle area. We waited for about 24 hours and no one else turned up.

Wingate's report:

At this point the native oarsmen all scurried for safety. Nothing could induce them to function either then or for days to come. We were left with a small number of country boats with perhaps a dozen oarsmen who knew enough to avoid capsizing them and who could do the round journey in perhaps an hour and a half . . . assuming no further interference from the enemy.

Wingate could make no such assumption, and as his brigade at the RV numbered some thousand men, it would have taken about two and a half days to get every man and a minimum of equipment across, even without Japanese interference. 'I therefore decided to abandon the crossing,' he reported and, after considering other options:

To break down into Dispersal Groups and fan out, crossing the Irrawaddy on as extended a line as possible, more or less simultaneously.

I therefore held a short sad meeting with Column Commanders and Colonel Cooke. I told them that I intended to withdraw at once to a secure bivouac in the forest and that they were to follow suit. . . . I then bid them goodbye and marched my Headquarters away from the bank.

This calm account written up after the event may well describe what occurred subsequently, but is not how Neill remembers the scene by the river:

I saw a group led by Wingate in a huge solar topi and his enormous beard, his eyes staring. As he passed me, he shouted, 'Disperse, disperse, get back to India.' Those were his exact words. I thought the man had gone stark staring mad. Here we were a force of 700 strong [actually nearer 1,000], with a platoon already across the river, and he wasn't prepared to cross. I realise that we would have taken casualties crossing, but far fewer than we eventually did in small groups and getting piecemeal to India. Our Column marched east away from India, talk about the Grand Old Duke of York.

In his report Wingate says he had considered continuing to cross as an option, or crossing elsewhere as a formed body; and he may have done. But it must be remembered that most reports are written in such a way as to cast the author, or commander, in the best possible light. Wingate's was no exception. He wrote as eloquently as he spoke, saying after this expedition, 'Everything is propaganda.' He maintained that dispersal was the best course, and added that columns which eventually crossed as a body were later forced to break down into dispersal groups in order to evade the Japanese. Reports are of course also written with the benefit of hindsight, and events that fit the ideas of the writer can be highlighted, and those that do not, disregarded or played down.

Dominic Neill:

> At this point I was ordered to release the mules and chargers because they would hinder us on our march out. I wondered what would happen to our animals. My charger started nuzzling my face. I was glad it was dark and no one [could] see; the tears were running down my face.
>
> The next day off we marched leaving our mules and chargers, except one wireless mule. My beloved horse followed for hours until he moved into a field of sugar cane. I looked at my Syce [groom], and he was weeping too.

Neill's best friend in the Column was Lieutenant Sprague, of 142 Commando Company. He had previous battle experience in Number 1 Commando, and was a very competent soldier:

> I asked 'Tag' Sprague if he would accompany me and my Gurkhas with his commando BORs should we split up. He agreed. So we had the final air drop of 10 days' rations. I was called to my first O Group. A big day. Confirmation; we were to split up into small groups. Wingate had played his last ace card. He had taken us so far and wasn't going to take us back. For that I have never forgiven him.
>
> The single radio was to go with 'Scotty''s group. He asked us to tell him our chosen group, so he could issue us with maps. 'Tag' and I told him we

would go north to the Irrawaddy, and between the big villages of Bhamo and Katha. We would cross there, and once across, we would head West for the Chindwin. 'Tag' took our maps and compass. I remembered my map reading lessons at Bangalore, riding round the bazaar on a bicycle. Now in the middle of a wilderness I was required to take my small group of ill-trained Gurkhas over hundreds of miles of inhospitable terrain, through the hunting parties of Japs. We knew that the Japs would make every effort to stop us escaping. I had grave doubts about my ability to get my chaps back. But 'Tag' was my rod and staff.

Charles Aves on the other bank of the Irrawaddy was very hungry:

It was obvious we would have to get some more food. We hadn't had an air drop for days. Some men were dispirited. I encouraged one of my friends by asking him what about his mother who was waiting for him to come home. We took his pack and rifle. Eventually he did get back.

We had to go to a village to get food. The officers had money and maps. They were able to buy cooked rice wrapped in a banana leaf. We made our way due west to the Chindwin.

Poor soldiering led to Aves's party being split up:

In a bivouac, two of us were brewing up, I and Corporal Hickman. We were pretty tired. We heard scampering feet and the two sentries ran past us, I went to run, as everybody seemed to be running. Corporal Hickman said, 'Don't go.' We paused and saw the Japanese approaching. Corporal Hickman said, 'Let's go.' Off we went leaving our packs behind. As we ran we picked up a pack each from a spot some distance away, we didn't know whose they were. We clambered up behind some rocks, with a few others of our party, and fired where the Japanese were. They did not reply. There were 11 of us, one officer, one sergeant, Corporal Hickman, and eight privates. The rest had run. We withdrew up a dried river bed. Between us we had two water bottles. We looked into the pack I had taken, it had all the maps for the way to the Chindwin. It belonged to Captain Oakes, he had left it behind. The pack that Corporal Hickman had belonged to the other officer. In that were 300 rupees in silver. There were the maps and money left behind by people who should not have left them behind. Lucky for us! But two water bottles was not enough, so the officer said we would have to go back. We went back, as we got nearer we could hear the Japs shouting. They make a lot of noise. They must have been looting the men's packs left behind. The officer changed his mind, and decided we would make due west as quickly as possible. This 11 were pretty fit. After two hours we rested overnight. We had to cross the railway line. The officer said we would hole up and watch to see if there were any Japs. There was a canal about 12 feet wide alongside the railway.

We waited one night and the next day, before crossing the following night. The officer could see some smoke about 300 yards down the railway line which he took to be a Jap camp. We eased our way into the canal and as silently as possible crossed the track. We had just got into the bushes when about 20 yards away there was a shout. It was a Jap sentry. We froze. There was no moon. I saw coming towards me what I thought was the fluorescent tip of a weapon. It was my sergeant with a compass. We got through safely. We marched on day after day. We were very lucky and went to the villages, this is where the Burmese phrases I had been taught came in handy. We had the money and the maps. So we could find the villages, and money to pay for food. We were treated very well, except in one village. I always went to the village first with the officer. At this one village, we felt uneasy. We always looked around to see if anybody disappeared. But here we knew there was something wrong. We got out. It turned out that a party ahead of us had been attacked in this village by the Japanese.

The rest of the journey towards the Chindwin went without incident. As we neared the river we met a patrol of the Seaforth Highlanders, looking for us. This patrol had been attacked by Japs the day before and was looking for them to revenge themselves on them. Our officer offered to help. But to our intense relief they refused saying that they were here to help us to safety not to get us killed. They showed us the way to the boats which they had used to cross. We paddled north to an area with a camp where we were fed. We walked on and then got transport to Imphal. We were buoyant, and felt wonderful. We were put into hospital, where I and some others went down with malaria. I was delirious for 48 hours. I came to in a wonderful bed of sheets, and was nursed by the Matron, Agnes McGeary. To my great pleasure, Brigadier Wingate came round. He said, 'I'm glad to see you're here.' I told him the story about the packs. He said, 'We won't wash our dirty linen in public, will we?'

I have never told this story before

At Imphal we got all our back mail. The officer who brought us out had a letter from his wife Joy, who he had spoken to us about on our way out; she was on the stage at the London Palladium telling him that she had fallen in love with someone else. Later he blew himself up with a grenade in a dugout.

Dominic Neill's party had a harder time:

'Tag' and I with my fifty-two Gurkhas and nine or so of his chaps split from 8 Column, I packed 10 days' rations into my pack. When I put it on, its weight absolutely staggered me. I was given 400 rupees in silver pieces from 'Scotty''s treasure chest. I put these in my pouch. They weighed a 'ton'.

Each escape group had half a dozen soldiers from the Burma Rifles Recce Platoon, ours were led by a Lance-Naik [Lance-Corporal] Tun Tin, a Karen. He spoke excellent English. We took three days to reach the Irrawaddy. We reached the village of Zimbugon on the Irrawaddy. We sent Tun Tin and some Burma Riflemen in plain clothes, which they all carried. Eventually he reported that the villagers were friendly. The headman promised to give us early warning of Jap approach, but it would take about a day to produce enough boats to carry us across.

We waited, and on the night 11/12 April 1943, four or five boats arrived. One boatman did a recce of the far bank first. It took about half an hour to cross. We arrived at about 21.00 hours. We paid and thanked the boatmen, and moved off to some high ground covered in jungle. I felt elated at crossing this huge barrier and being on our way home. As the crow flies we had about 200 miles to go to reach the Chindwin, and the monsoon was due to break in late May, early June, and the minor rivers would become tremendous barriers. So we had to get a move on.

After stopping for food at what they thought was a friendly village they set off again and Neill saw a villager on a bicycle peddling off ahead of them on the track they were using. He thought nothing of it.

We had not gone far from the village when an ambush exploded to our left. I roared to my men, 'Take cover right.' I was utterly shocked. I had never been taught counter-ambush drills. I did not know what to do. A Jap machine-gunner was firing from opposite me across the track. The bullets were cutting branches above my head. I now know with experience gained later in the war, and in Malaya during the emergency, I could have rolled up that ambush in a few seconds. But on that hot morning, such remedial action was beyond me. I remember hearing the Jap changing his magazine. I resolved to move the next time he did so. When he did, I shouted, 'Up, follow me.' Some of my men were running parallel with me, and some behind. No sign of Tag or Tun Tin.

Then I saw Tag just ahead. I felt relieved, so early in the retreat it would have been very bad for my morale. I suggested to Tag that we laid an ambush for the follow-up Japs, and allow stragglers to catch up. He refused. If we had hung around, the Japs would have had time to surround us. We had two British Offrs, 11 GORs [Gurkha Other Ranks], six of Tag's BORs, and one of Tun Tin's riflemen, all the others were missing. I felt I had failed my men completely. It was a heavy weight of guilt to carry.

I later found that most of the rest of my men had bumped into 8 Column's support platoon, and got back to India with them. The chaps separated from us had no maps and no compasses. Many years later, I heard that one of my NCOs was captured and died in captivity, another survived captivity.

I took over a tommy-gun from Corporal White, he was delighted, because my rifle was lighter. I vowed that night that by hook or by crook I would learn proper contact drills, and teach my soldiers, so never again would we be put in such a position. Later in the War and in two subsequent campaigns my Gurkha soldiers and I were able to kill a very great number of enemy as a direct result of lessons learned.

But when I was put to the test again on that gruelling retreat I was to fail once more. Some of the ridges went up to 4,000 feet. The BORs wanted to go to places where supplies had been pre-dropped for us to pick up. Sergeant Sennett said the BORs could not exist on rations from villages, and must have British rations.

Tag and I thought this would be suicide. The Japs would have seen where the drops had taken place, and be waiting for us. Tag explained this, but eventually acquiesced with Sergeant Sennett's request to take a party of BORs off to find these DZs, and march into China. He gave them maps. Sennett had a compass already. They were never seen or heard of again.

I was personally glad when Tag's men went. Their morale had gone. The BORs had lost confidence in our ability to make the Chindwin. Apart from our dwindling physical strength, we were now only 14 in number. After Tag's men left we had about 16 miles as the crow flies to reach the Myitkyina–Rangoon railway. It was very hard going. To protect our maps from being soaked with sweat, I kept them in our mess tins. We only looked at our maps at halts. We were often out in our reckoning. We were very tired, we had not had a single day's rest since leaving Imphal over two months before. We all had lice. Crossing a dusty road, we brushed out our tracks with a branch. We crossed the railway line, and headed for the Mesa river. In the forest we heard the sound of domestic cocks crowing. We hid near the village, and sent in our one Burma Rifleman, Mong San. He returned with a little rice, and a chicken. We moved on as fast as we could.

We reached the Mesa river which was quite shallow, and crossed it. From there the escarpment was 20 miles in a straight line. God knows how many miles it was in marching.

The [Burma Rifle] men's knowledge of what we could eat in the jungle turned out to be Tag's and my salvation. One particular fern we boiled with our rice. We only used game trails at this stage. When moving along, when the late afternoon approached, we moved away into thick cover, and lay down to sleep. My blanket was always wet from sweat. It was cold at night. One night it rained. I badgered the Almighty from dawn to dusk to give us the strength to escape.

One day we met some buffaloes in a Forest Reserve. Tag aimed and with one shot killed one buffalo, the others ran off. We knew we must eat the buffalo as soon as possible and vanish from the scene. A large fire was built, and the animal butchered. We hung and smoked some of the meat, while we roasted the remainder on wooden skewers. The Gurkhas knew exactly what to do. Apart from hide, blood and bones, and strips of smoked meat, the buffalo had disappeared. Our stomachs were distended. It was good to feel so full. We hung the strips of smoked meat on our packs. We occasionally chewed them on the march, or while preparing our evening meal. Some kept our strips too long, they stank. But we ate them.

We had to avoid the Jap garrisons in the villages, and it was now mid May. Our progress became slower and slower. We could manage only 45 minutes walking followed by a 15-minute halt, in every hour. We thought to use our outward route across the Zibyu Taungdan (escarpment) would be too dangerous, because the Japs would ambush it. We heard later that other parties were ambushed on it. We found a river which joined the Uyu river which flowed into the Chindwin. The river was either knee deep in water or ankle deep in soft sand. Tag was struck by fever, but his strong will and spirit kept him going. Only a Jap bullet would stop us now. We marched for 30 minutes and halted for 30 minutes. After this stage we reckoned we were in the Chin area and risked entering a village. The headman gave us some food in return for rupees.

It was a race against time and the monsoon. When we reached the Chindwin could we cross it, our men were all non-swimmers? Would the Japs cut us off at the final hurdle? We decided to move towards the river on a track we had used on the outward journey. Suddenly ahead we saw an elephant with a mahout, and a howdah with a man in it dressed in white, he picked up a rifle and started to shoot at us. The elephant was towing a small truck with about 15 Japs in it. We couldn't take the risk of fighting it out with the Japs. I roared out, 'Follow me', and we ran off. I dared not look back. I was constantly waiting to be hit. But I wasn't. We ran remarkably quickly despite our weak condition. We appeared to be keeping together. Eventually, the Japs had ceased firing. No one was following. In a dip in the ground we reorganised. Only my orderly was missing. There was nothing we could do for him. We walked on.

One Naik got malaria, we thought he was going to die. We shared out his equipment. We would not leave him. Fortunately he could walk, we could not have carried him in our state.

As they neared the Chindwin:

At about 13.00 hours we met a villager, who said that all boats had been collected by the Japs and taken to Homalin about 20 miles away. Our spirits, which had risen, sank. Morale was rock bottom. We went forward to the Chindwin and saw the river of our dreams. At this point the river was about 250 yards wide and very fast flowing. Tag and I could have probably swum across with weapons and equipment. But our men could not swim. We would not leave them.

We decided to build rafts. But I thought, 'Try to think of something else.' As I stood looking over the river, I heard a call in Nepali, 'Who is that?'

'The 3/2nd Gurkhas,' I shouted back. 'Have you got a boat?'

'One.'

'Send it across as quickly as you can.'

I assumed it was a V Force Levy who recruited Gurkhas. The villager was still standing there. He cried out the boat was coming. It was small, and would take four men. We sent four across. After a while, it came back. We sent four more. Eventually it came back, there were now five of us. Tag and I waited having sent three over. We were now on our own. We hid wondering if at the eleventh hour the Japs would catch us. At last it came back and we got in. We came upon a V Force Post, commanded by a young Captain. I asked him what date it was. He told me 6 June. We had long lost any idea of what day it was. [V Force manned an outpost line along the Chindwin.]

That night we had a meal of Meat & Veg Stew, a real treat, some Shakapura biscuits and a pound tin of jam. It was the most marvellous meal I have ever had. We were lucky not to have tummy problems.

I was proud that all our group had come back with all our weapons. The V Force commander told us that some Chindit parties had thrown away their weapons to lighten their loads.

We had an easy march with a mule to carry our packs to a 3/10th

Gurkha Rifles base. Then the next day on by truck. Before we left the Adjutant told us that the V Force base had sent a signal saying that they had sent a patrol across the river, and discovered that a Jap platoon-strength patrol had been tracking us for about a week, possibly since our contact with the elephant. This patrol must have been close on our heels, as they arrived at the crossing point only half an hour after we had crossed the river. In war men's fate hangs by a thin thread. Had we waited to construct rafts, we would have been caught. Had I not been standing by the river and been seen by the Gurkha levy, we would not have survived. They might have come upon us when Tag and I were alone. The Almighty or Lady Luck looked favourably upon us. On arrival at our next stop at a Forward Supply Depot we were given a meal. As we ate, it started to rain, the drops coming down like stair rods. This was no shower, it was the monsoon proper, against which we had been racing. We had beaten it by two days.

I got my maps out, and reckoned that from the railhead at Dimapur where we started marching to the Shweli River and back to the 3/10th Gurkhas' post was give or take a march of 1,000 miles. I found in the Forward Supply Depot a four-pound tin of plum jam, we ate it without any biscuits in about five minutes.

We went to Imphal in trucks, and on to a hospital at IV Corps. On the way we passed Corps HQ, and from out of an office tent three staff officers appeared, one of them said, 'He must be from Longcloth'.

They didn't welcome us.

We were checked over and had our beards cut off. Wingate visited. I stood at attention, he said, 'Oh I see you're out.'

I nearly replied, 'And no thanks to you sir.'

Fortunately I held my peace, and didn't get myself into trouble.

That was the last time I saw him. He could at least have asked how we got out and what had happened to us. But no. We were expecting to be debriefed by intelligence from IV Corps. Not a bit of it. No one gave a damn. We said that we did not expect to see any press reports of the expedition. We were wrong, there were banner headlines, about Wingate's expedition had done this and that. We had achieved nothing. We had been kicked out by the Japs.

Neill is being harsh, but not overly so. General Auchinleck, who took over from Wavell in August 1942, when the latter became Viceroy of India, was no fan of Wingate's, but in his covering note to Wingate's Report he wrote:

Results Achieved by 77 Indian Infantry Brigade in the Spring of 1943

Our ability to re-enter Burma, and the inability of the Japanese to stop us was demonstrated to the Burmese.

The railway Mandalay–Myitkyina was put out of action for a period of four weeks and the Japanese were forced to use the longer and more limited L of C via Bhamo.

Between six and eight Japanese battalions were drawn off from any other operations which the Japanese may have contemplated; and the activities of 77 Indian Infantry Brigade may have prevented them continuing their advance beyond Sumprabum [i.e. to Fort Hertz].

Much valuable information, both as regards the topography of the country and conditions of life in occupied Burma, was gained.

The operations had a good morale effect on our own troops generally and on the public, both in India and abroad.

The second and third paragraphs of Auchinleck's assessment above were actually irrelevant, although he did not know it then, because the Japanese had no plans to advance on Fort Hertz or, at that time, on Imphal. However, they now took note that, contrary to their earlier assessment, the grain of the country astride the Chindwin could be crossed by large bodies of troops. They set about making plans to do so in 1944. Unfortunately for the Japanese, they had neither air superiority nor sufficient air transport, so, for this and other reasons, their offensive ended in disaster. Ironically, this miscalculation by the Japanese was perhaps one of the two most important outcomes of Operation Longcloth.

The other was the importance of air supply, and that it could be made to work. Provided the Allies maintained air superiority, air supply was the key to restoring tactical and strategic freedom to the Allies in Burma for the rest of the War. Furthermore, provided Allied commanders and troops remained resolute, the favourite Japanese tactic of hooking behind units, which they had practised with such demoralizing effect when they threw the British out of Burma, would no longer be decisive. The 'cut off' unit could be supplied by air, and cut the Japanese off in their turn. Wingate was not the only man in India, or elsewhere, to understand the potential of air supply; he was, however, the first to demonstrate its effectiveness on operations.

The effect of Longcloth on morale is more difficult to gauge. Although the more fervent of Wingate's supporters claim that he alone showed that the Japanese could be beaten at their own game, it would be wrong to imagine that others were not training their men to do just that, as extracts from a letter from Brigadier Curtis dated 7 April 1943 (when Wingate was still in Burma) to one of the commanding officers in his own brigade make clear:

> Some words of advice from one who has seen a good deal of the Nips [Japanese]. They are a tough proposition. If you sit still they will give you hell, and then hook round your flanks, probably the weak one. You must be aggressive from the outset, and you must *always* have at least one coy out in front seeking out the Jap. Fortunately he gives many opportunities of ambushing him. You must seize them and hit him. There *must* be no firing from your main position before you are actually being attacked, and for goodness sake make your men hold their fire to the last possible moment. The Jap hates the bayonet. An immediate counter-attack with the bayonet will always succeed.

Others had also noted the paradox: the Japanese, who made so much of the Samurai spirit, with their obsession with swords, and the habit of practising bayonet drill on their prisoners, greatly feared being on the wrong end of a bayonet themselves. It was one of the few tactics that would sometimes make them run.

Wingate's dispersal group started out on the return to the Chindwin forty-three strong and marched into India with thirty-four. Out of some 3,000 who marched into Burma in February, 2,182 had returned four months later. Of the some 1,000 missing, about 450 were battle casualties. About 120 Kachins and Shans remained in their home areas with Wingate's permission. Of the remaining 430, most fell into enemy hands. Led by Major Gilkes, 150 men of Number 7 Column marched into China, minus those who had crossed the Irrawaddy before Wingate gave the disperse order. With Gilkes were some of Fergusson's Number 5 Column. They were all flown back to India by the United States Army Air Force. The Burma Rifles marched to Fort Hertz, in the very northern tip of Burma, collecting Captain Herring's platoon on the way. The Burma Rifles lost their commanding officer in a skirmish in a village, as recounted in their report:

> The enemy garrison was soon cleared from the village and confused fighting in the jungle followed. Lieut Duncan Menzies and one BOR [British Other

Rank] were found in the village bound with strong rope. Their faces and heads had been shaved and Jap helmets put on their heads. Before withdrawing from the village the enemy shot them. The BOR was dead and Lieut Menzies dying of a severe stomach wound. He showed great bravery and in spite of great pain was able to give information of Jap movements and of a party of 5 Column. Lt-Col Wheeler gave him morphia to put him out of his suffering. Burif HQ Group were on the point of withdrawing further to the hills, when a stray Jap bullet hit Lt-Col L. G. Wheeler in the head and penetrated his brain.

Number 8 Column and part of Number 5 reached the Chindwin at Tamanthi and Tonhe. The Southern Group, having tried to reach Fort Hertz, eventually returned across the Chindwin. Few of the men who marched in were fit for operations again.

Wingate's major error was in taking his whole brigade across the Irrawaddy into the Shweli–Irrawaddy triangle. The crossing by the Southern Group had been seen by the Japanese, and Calvert's crossing had been attacked. For Wingate to follow with the remaining columns nine days later was foolhardy, and showed his limitations as a brigade commander when faced with a tactical problem. He could, and should, have found out what the country between the Irrawaddy and Shweli rivers was like by asking people who knew the area, of which there were several in India. Had Wingate received Herring's report about the Kachins he might have taken his whole force into the Kachin Hills to foment trouble for the Japanese. Unable to be fully supplied by air, he would eventually have had to withdraw into China, leaving the tribes-people to the mercy of the Japanese. But they remained unmolested and free to help the LRP and similar groups in 1944 and up to the end of the War.

In his covering letter to Wingate's report, Auchinleck stated:

I wish to emphasize that this report is the report of the Commander 77 Indian Infantry Brigade to the Commander 4 Corps. It contains opinions with which I am not necessarily in full agreement.

Certain remarks which are unsuitable in a report of this nature have been deleted. While passages of questionable propriety remain, I have decided to sanction a limited distribution in order the Commanders should have without delay the benefit of the great quantity of valuable information it contains.

The report, 'Secret' at the time, does contain a wealth of information, besides revealing just how eccentric and obsessive Wingate was. Few other senior commanders, when commenting on the rations, and the biscuits in particular, would include:

> The roughage in it [the Shakapura biscuit] is a great element in prompting healthy action of the bowel. Personally I have never passed better looking stools.

Or when inveighing against issuing cigarettes, declaim:

> Doctors' recommendations on this subject are biased as they are all inveterate smokers.

Whether his praise for the Shakapura biscuit is an oblique defence of the totally inadequate ration, or merely another tilt at his superiors, we shall never know.

In his covering letter, Auchinleck also included an assessment of the functions of LRP Groups:

> Long-Range Penetration Groups must be considered in their proper perspective. They are detachments from the main forces and their operations must be governed by the same principles as for all other detachments. They are of value if they contain superior forces away from the main effort, or if their operations, offensive or destructive, have an effect on the enemy's conduct of the main battle. As detachments, therefore, Long-Range Penetration Groups should be few in number and as small in size as is consistent with the achievement of this object; and their commanders must direct and subordinate their actions to the achievement of success by the main effort.

In a nutshell, Auchinleck was talking about the principle of 'return on investment'. He was not opposed to 'special forces' in principle. He was a big enough man to distribute a report which contained passages with which he did not agree. He had after all given Stirling permission to raise the SAS in the Middle East. He had seen what small detachments like the LRDG and SAS could do in the desert, and supported their activities wholeheartedly. He was sounding a warning note that LRP groups should not be allowed to grow too large, or become a 'private army' with their own strategic agenda. No doubt his eye had been drawn to the conclusion in Wingate's report, which included a proposal to:

> Take, at once, measures to raise not less than six Long-Range Groups out of the proper materials. (The strength of each Group should be in the neighbourhood of 3,000 all ranks.)

One of the Wingate myths that endures to this day is that the Longcloth report was suppressed. This is drivel, as Auchinleck's covering letter quoted above demonstrates.

On 18 August 1943, the very day that Auchinleck signed this letter in New Delhi, Orde Wingate was in Quebec. Here Roosevelt and Churchill, together with with the Anglo-American Combined Chiefs of Staff would listen to him expounding his theory of how the war in Burma should be conducted. Auchinleck was about to have his instructions on Long-Range Penetration Groups overturned, by someone even more powerful than the Commander-in-Chief India.

7

Operation Thursday: The Second Chindit Expedition

I want this time to have a respectable codename, and not one
produced by some facetious clerk at GHQ India as was done on
the last occasion. . . . For this [operation] I suggest Thursday.

Orde Wingate in a note to Mountbatten
dated 13 November 1943

No patrol is to report the jungle impenetrable, until it has
penetrated it.

Orde Wingate

Wingate's report on Operation Longcloth was shown to Churchill by the
Secretary of State for India, Leo Amery. Churchill ordered Wingate
home, and having interviewed him, was so impressed that he decided to
take him to the Allied conference in Quebec. Here Wingate convinced
Churchill, the President of the United States, Franklin Roosevelt, and
the British and American Chiefs of Staff that his tactics of long-range
penetration could play a crucial role in winning the war in Burma. If
one was seeking proof of Wingate's intellect and eloquence, there is no
better example than his ability to persuade soldiers of the calibre of
General George C. Marshall, the US Army Chief of Staff, and Field
Marshal Sir Alan Brooke, the Chief of the Imperial General Staff, to give
him their support. In this respect he was very like the man with whom
he is so often compared: T. E. Lawrence. Wingate was promised the
resources he asked for, and more, was promoted to major general, and
returned to India.

At Quebec it was also decided to set up South-East Asia Command
(SEAC) under a supreme commander (Supremo), Admiral Lord Louis

Mountbatten. Its theatre of operations comprised Burma, Malaya and Sumatra, and, for clandestine operations only, Thailand and French Indo-China (now Vietnam, Cambodia and Laos).

As alluded to in the previous chapter, the American enthusiasm for a campaign in Burma was based solely on their aim of supporting Chiang Kai-shek. At that stage in the war, they saw the Nationalist Chinese as key players in the strategy to defeat Japan. To this end they poured in weapons and equipment. Chiang Kai-shek, having discerned that the Japanese were going to lose the war, decided his first priority was to keep his armies out of the fighting as much as possible, to preserve them for the next war, against the Chinese Communists. It was to take some time before the staffs in Washington realized just what Chiang Kai-shek intended. Meanwhile Lieutenant General Joseph W. Stilwell, United States Army, who commanded United States and Chinese Forces in the China–Burma–India theatre, made plans for the seizure of Myitkyina, the strategic key to northern Burma. With Myitkyina taken, Assam could be linked to China by a road from Ledo to the old Burma Road. Stilwell, who spoke fluent Chinese, after four tours of duty in China, was highly regarded by General Marshall. He was crusty, personally brave, and hated the British with a burning intensity he rarely bothered to conceal. Nicknamed 'Vinegar Joe', he liked to portray himself as a soldier's soldier, but his treatment of troops under his command, British or American, manifested little understanding of what makes soldiers 'tick'. He seems to have had more rapport with the Chinese, who he realized, if properly trained, equipped and led, would make competent soldiers.

To provide troops for Wingate, the crack, battle-hardened 70th Infantry Division, with its many regular battalions, was broken up. After fighting in North Africa, this Division had been sent to India to train for the war in Burma. The staff at GHQ Delhi were infuriated that this division was to be given to the man they called 'Robin Hood', or 'Tarzan', to carry out what they believed were his crack-pot schemes. To Wingate the decision was one in the eye for the detested staff. The divisional commander, Major General G. W. Symes, senior to Wingate, and who had been specially selected to take over the division in Tobruk, was understandably upset, as entries from his diary reveal:

Tuesday 31st August [1943]
Went to see Jack Winterton who told me that the Div was probably being

converted into Long-Range Penetration Groups – on the line of Wingate's force (77 Bde) in Burma. It looks very like it and if it is true is a very sad blow for the Div will cease to exist as such. Still we shall see.

Wednesday 1st September

My forebodings confirmed. Apparently it is an order from Washington – Wingate has been there & sold his idea.

Sunday 19th September

Had one and half hours' talk with Wingate. Quite amicable – no reason why it should be otherwise – but it didn't sound too good & I think his administrative organisation is unworkable. Still I must think it over.

Many officers in Symes's position would have refused to serve under Wingate, who was both his junior and lacked his battle experience, particularly when it became clear that the division would not fight as a formation. Symes, however, showed commendable loyalty by remaining, thus Wingate owed him a great deal, not least for getting the administration of the force on to an even keel. Neither Wingate nor his Brigadier General Staff (BGS – chief of staff in all but name), Brigadier D. Tulloch, was sufficiently experienced at staff work, especially running the administration of a large formation. Tulloch wrote later:

> Wingate had a liking for General Symes, a liking and respect, but he did not give him his full confidence at that or any other time.

Symes was offered the job of deputy commander, always an unenviable role. Despite misgivings he buckled down to the task.

Monday 20th September

To GHQ went in to see the C-in-C (Auk) at 9.45. On thinking matters over I had come to the conclusion that anything unworkable would soon show itself & that to make any opposition now would appear to be obstructionist. Wingate although possessing boundless self-confidence is lacking in administrative & organisation knowledge, and knowing it, has an inferiority complex on the matter. Auk asked my views & I told him. He agreed & said that he particularly wanted me to 'play' if I felt that I could so as to add some balance & experience. But if at any time I felt that I couldn't I was to come to him.

Friday 24th September

Div HQ is to be broken up & the intention is that the Div Commander [i.e. Symes himself] shall not command his troops except in action & shall not be responsible for their training. I shall be in an intolerable position & shall have to part with Wingate. I hope it doesn't arise as I like the show

& believe in it, but I feel that the projected organisation is an impossible one for any Div Commander. Also told the Auk this later in the morning.

For a commander not to be responsible for the training of the troops he is to take into battle, unless of course he has taken command only at the last moment, is plain barmy. But of course to begin with it was not Wingate's intention that Symes should command them in action, and if he gave Symes the impression that he would, while he, Wingate, was still about, as implied by the diary extract above, he was not truthful. However, once established in Burma, Wingate hoped to force his superiors to acknowledge that his force was actually a corps of two divisions, for in early March 1944 he wrote to Symes:

In future we shall have six brigades in the forward area i.e. two divisions. I consider we ought to form a new divisional staff to control 14, 23, and the WA Brigades for administration and training to start with, and later to take over command in the field.

This division will be the second division of Special Force in the field and should be allotted a number. I suggest that you take command of it with your Headquarters. . . .

The two divisions up here will then constitute an Army Corps of LRP. We need not put in for an establishment [official authorization] for this, as we already have it in the shape of a Commander & staff with a few deficiencies, but it should be recognised as an Army Corps and be given the number and status. This point should be raised in about a fortnight's time with 11th Army Group. If we have been successful in the coming crucial fortnight, there will be no grounds whatsoever for refusing it. I shall ~~use maximum pressure~~ [Wingate's correction] expect to obtain it, as it is a matter of simple justice and common sense. If we have not succeeded, I do not suppose they will listen to any suggestions of the kind.

If I want you to take this matter up with SEAC [South-East Asia Command], I will send a signal referring to this letter and asking you to do so.

But this devious plotting was months off, and as yet unrevealed by Wingate, when Symes, who must have had the patience of a saint, wrote:

12th October (Tuesday)
Wingate has got typhoid, which means about three weeks in hospital and six weeks' rest. A nuisance at this time as I am not completely in the picture.

21st October (Thursday)

Wingate is on Dangerously Ill list & won't be fit until Jan at earliest, which is really at most awkward time. Lentaigne (111 Bde) is being made my deputy – as a Maj Gen.

Wingate's 'Special Force', also named 3rd Indian Infantry Division as a deception measure in an attempt to conceal its long-range penetration role, consisted of six brigades and other supporting units. Thus this maverick major-general, who eighteen months previously had been a major, and who had never commanded so much as a battalion in battle, had been given charge of what was in reality a small corps, equivalent to two infantry divisions; and was soon plotting his own elevation to Lieutenant-General as implied in his letter to Symes. Special Force consisted of:

3rd West African Brigade	(Column 10)
(*Brigadier A. H. Gillmore* succeeded by *Brigadier Abdy Ricketts*)	
6th Battalion Nigeria Regiment	(Columns 39 & 66)
7th Battalion Nigeria Regiment	(Columns 29 & 35)
12th Battalion Nigeria Regiment	(Columns 12 & 43)
14th British Infantry Brigade (ex 70 Division)	(Column 59)
(*Brigadier Thomas Brodie*)	
54th Field Company Royal Engineers	(Support)
1st Battalion Bedfordshire & Hertfordshire Regiment	(Columns 16 & 61)
7th Battalion Royal Leicestershire Regiment	(Columns 47 & 74)
2nd Battalion The Black Watch	(Columns 42 & 73)
2nd Battalion York & Lancaster Regiment	(Columns 65 & 84)
16th British Infantry Brigade (ex 70 Division)	(Column 99)
(*Brigadier Bernard Fergusson*)	
51/69 Field Regiments Royal Artillery (as infantry)	(Columns 51 & 69)
2nd Field Company Royal Engineers	(Support)
2nd Battalion The Queen's Royal Regiment	(Columns 21 & 22)
2nd Battalion Royal Leicestershire Regiment	(Columns 17 & 71)
45th Reconnaissance Regiment (as infantry)	(Columns 45 & 54)
23rd British Infantry Brigade (ex 70 Division)	(Column 32)
(*Brigadier Lance Perowne*)	
60th Field Regiment Royal Artillery (as infantry)	(Columns 60 & 68)
12th Field Company Royal Engineers	(Support)

2nd Battalion Duke of Wellington's Regiment	(Columns 33 & 76)
4th Battalion The Border Regiment	(Columns 34 & 55)
1st Battalion Essex Regiment	(Columns 44 & 56)

77th Indian Infantry Brigade (Column 25)
   (*Brigadier Michael Calvert*)
Mixed Field Company Royal Engineers/Royal Indian Engineers

1st Battalion King's Regiment (Liverpool)	(Columns 81 & 82)
1st Battalion Lancashire Fusiliers	(Columns 20 & 50)
1st Battalion South Staffordshire Regiment	(Columns 38 & 80)
3rd Battalion 6th Gurkha Rifles	(Columns 36 & 63)
3rd Battalion 9th Gurkha Rifles (to 111 Bde later)	(Columns 57 & 93)
142 Company Hong Kong Volunteers	(Support)

111th Indian Infantry Brigade (Column 48)
   (*Brigadier 'Joe' Lentaigne* succeeded by *Major 'Jack' Masters* and *Brigadier 'Jumbo' Morris*)
Mixed Field Company Royal Engineers/Royal Indian Engineers

2nd Battalion King's Own Royal Regiment	(Columns 41 & 46)
1st Battalion Cameronians	(Columns 26 & 90)
3rd Battalion 4th Gurkha Rifles	(Columns 30 & 40)
4th Battalion 9th Gurkha Rifles (MORRISFORCE)	(Columns 49 & 94)

Other units included:
BLADET (Commando Engineers) (Major Blain)
DAHFORCE (Kachin Levies) (Lieutenant Colonel Herring)
2nd Battalion Burma Rifles
Four troops 160th Field Regiment Royal Artillery (in gunner role)
Four troops 69th Light Anti-Aircraft Regiment Royal Artillery (in gunner role)
Logistic Units

Where possible the numbering of columns followed the old battalion numbering system; for example the Black Watch were the 42nd and 73rd of Foot. If this was not possible, the numbers were combinations of regimental numbers or just arbitrary. Each brigade headquarters made up one column. Despite the lessons of the first expedition, the unwieldy column organization was retained for the second, although some battalion commanders made their own changes to it, as best they could.

For a while Wingate also had command of a 3,000-strong American infantry regiment (in reality about a brigade). Officially saddled with the typically bizarre American title 5307th Provisional Unit, it was more romantically known as 'Merrill's Marauders', after its commander Brigadier-General Frank D. Merrill, a Stilwell appointee.

Wingate's British and Gurkha battalions, many of whom had previous battle experience, and were in a different league from the low-quality troops of his first brigade, set about training for their new role. Lieutenant-Colonel Graves-Morris, commanding 2nd York & Lancasters, described his battalion's water training on an 800-yard-wide river:

> Every effort was made to teach all ranks to swim and to practise the improvisation of boats. Major Robertson RE ran a course for all officers in the art of boat making from ground sheets and bamboo, how to work outboard motors, the use of toggle ropes, methods of crossing rivers, and how to handle infantry assault boats. These lessons were then handed on [sic] to the men, and on 10th January both columns carried out a silent river crossing without mishap.

There was a drill for everything, as Hogan of the 2nd Burma Rifles recalls:

> For example, to go to the loo, go in pairs, backs to the column, only a small distance out.

Experience had shown that those whose modesty demanded that they go out of sight to relieve themselves sometimes got left behind and lost when the column moved off after a short halt.

The force was also introduced to a new ration, the American K Ration. Captain Paddy Dobney was the Administrative Officer of 84 Column:

> It was designed specially as a one-man pack ration. Each meal of the day, breakfast, dinner and supper, came in a separate pack about the size of the average book. So if a man had five days' rations, he had 15 packs to carry. Each pack was clearly marked and the inner wrapping was waxed. Not only was it waterproof, but the wrapping burnt easily, thus ensuring at least a warm drink under the wettest conditions.
>
> Each meal pack was different. Breakfast offered a fruit bar, a 4 oz tin of bacon and egg hash, a small packet of biscuits, and a packet of coffee powder. However, the British soldier does not like coffee, and this had to be supplemented by tea, powdered milk and sugar; all issued in miniature canvas bags. The dinner pack contained a 4 oz tin of processed cheese,

more biscuits, a small packet of Dextrose tablets, so revolting even the mules refused them, and a packet of lemonade powder. Supper gave us a 4 oz tin of meat loaf, biscuits, a chocolate bar, and a packet of soup powder. There were also packets of cigarettes. In one pack there was a small packet of toilet paper.

The whole ration was cleverly designed, no doubt after much thought by dietitians and scientists, and much of it was synthetic. Everything could be eaten hot or cold. It was easy to distribute and made each man self-supporting. When we first had it dropped to us during training, we were thrilled with it. It was however designed for consumption for a maximum of seven days. In Burma we liked it for the first 20 days, tolerated it for the next 20, and for the remaining 100 days loathed the sight of every packet. With very few exceptions, it formed our only meals for five, long, hungry months.

In fact the K ration, intended to sustain assault troops for a few days until better sustenance could be brought forward, contained very few more calories than the ration issued on the first expedition, and without the benefit of roughage provided by Wingate's delight, the Shakapura biscuit. Fergusson, on being asked to command a brigade for the second expedition, had told Wingate that he would not take troops into Burma again on the starvation fare of the first. Wingate promised something far better. When Fergusson saw the K ration, he realized that Wingate had lied to him.

In early January 1944, Fergusson tendered his resignation, over the matter of rations, and because Wingate had not fulfilled the second promise he made to him: that the insertion of the Long-Range Penetration Force would be followed up with more troops, so that there would not be a withdrawal as there had been last time.[1] Fergusson learned this when his Brigade was moving by train into Assam from where they would march into Burma. He flew to see Wingate to challenge him with failing to meet his conditions. He also handed him a note, which does not mention rations, but contains the paragaphs:

3. I am convinced that without a 'follow-up', the expedition would be disastrous, and I long to hear that it is postponed until a 'follow-up' is possible. The effect on Burmans of a second withdrawal would seriously affect their co-operation when the withdrawal of Burma is finally undertaken.

4. I command a Brigade where morale is very high. I believe it would be a breach of faith on my part to lead it into the expedition as at present contemplated, and I am prepared to resign my command of it if necessary. I wish, however, to share the fortunes of my men, and would like to accompany it if it is put under the command of another.

Wingate handed him a note saying:

I note that unless the forces made to exploit the LRP operations planned for Spring 1944 are materially increased you do not feel it right to remain in command of your Brigade while it pursues its allotted role in these operations.

I am unable to give you any assurance of any particular degree of support for a particular operation. All I am justified in asserting is that it will be my endeavour only to order justifiable operations.

In view of your letter, I wish you to carry out the following orders:

(a) Do not discuss the matter with anyone.
(b) Be prepared to hand over command to Colonel Rome or other officer selected by me.
(c) When relieved, leave your Brigade and report to HQ Special Force for duty without any delay.
(d) In the meantime continue to carry out my orders.

Fergusson was eventually persuaded to withdraw his resignation by Mountbatten, and was glad he did.[2] Subsequently, according to Fergusson, Wingate told him that when 16th Brigade had captured Indaw, Slim was going to fly in two divisions. As Fergusson wrote later: 'At times the truth was simply not in him.'[3] Because, if Wingate did tell Fergusson this, he did so knowing that he had been told by Slim that he would not get more than a brigade to reinforce Special Force. Wingate had been badgering Slim to release 26th Division, and to immobilize 50th Parachute Brigade to release its resources to him. Among Wingate's papers is a copy of a signal from Slim to 11th Army Group, dated 21 January 1944, which reads:

Have seen Wingate. I have already considered use up to one bde [brigade] to take advantage of favourable situation created by Special Force. 26 Div were trg [training] for this. Am prepared to risk *one bn* [battalion] to ensure Special Force remain in certain areas and *to follow up by one bde if real opportunity for exploiting from 4 Corps*. I will decide on purely military repeat purely military grounds when and if any bns go in. I shall decide. I cannot accept situation in any other terms. Wingate realises this. . . . Do not agree immobilization of 50 Parachute Bde. [Author's italics.]

This decision stood, despite Wingate appealing direct to Mountbatten, which he was to do on a number of occasions.

Most Chindits in his new force had an unwavering faith in Wingate, and quickly fell under the spell of his personality. Lieutenant Sealy, a platoon commander in the Lancashire Fusiliers, wrote:

I saw, met, listened to Wingate on probably not more than two dozen occasions. Yet he made a deeper and more lasting impression on me than almost anyone else I have met. There was no charisma – but most certainly there was something really compelling about him. An uncanny feeling that what he said was right and that what he intended to do would inevitably be done. He seemed a man apart – in isolation – self-contained. I do not recall that he was imposing in appearance or even spoke particularly well when addressing troops, but on the other hand he seemed able to impart his own intense convictions to his listeners. I know that there was a general feeling that with him in command anything he said we could do – we could do. We believed in him. On a few occasions when on liaison duty, I found myself alone with him in the back of a staff car, he almost invariably sang hymns to himself. He never spoke to me in a conversational sense, but this did not strike me as being at all out of the way at the time. He was so outside my experience of people that I was, I suppose, prepared not to be surprised at anything about him.

Lieutenant Durant, Royal Artillery, attached to Number 80 Column (South Staffordshires) and commanding their machine-gun (Vickers) platoon, wrote about Wingate to his parents after the second expedition:

He was a man in whose presence anyone from Lt General to Pte felt uncomfortable. He spared no one in his criticisms and never used soft words to his victims.

I never heard Wingate use the expressions: 'it seems to me', 'it is probably that', 'in my opinion', or any others so beloved of lecturers. With him it was always, 'the Japs' reaction will be', 'the result of this will be', 'such and such cannot happen', always with complete confidence in his predictions and reasoning. There was something awe-inspiring in his certainty and his dogmatism, yet something which inspired the fullest confidence, so that one went away saying, 'With him in command we cannot fail.'

Wingate's stock with his Chindits soared even higher when he acquired something which was, and still is, anathema to the RAF: a private air force. General 'Hap' Arnold, the Chief of Staff of the United States Army Air Force (USAAF), there was no such thing as the United States Air Force then, was so horrified at Wingate's account of leaving wounded behind, that he not only agreed to the latter's request for light aircraft for casualty evacuation, he did much more. The result was Colonel Cochran's Number 1 Air Commando USAAF. It consisted of a hundred CG-4A WACO gliders; a hundred short take-off and landing (STOL) L-5s and L-1s; thirty P-51A Mustangs fighter-bombers; twenty B-25 Mitchell medium bombers; twenty C-47 (DC-3) Dakotas and twelve UC-64 Norseman transport aircraft; and six Sikorsky helicopters, the first ever to take part in operations. The Air Commando had a mandate from Arnold for only ninety days' operations, and lacked the maintenance back-up for anything more. It also needed help from the RAF Dakotas to meet the supply requirements of the whole Chindit force, and to tow gliders when large numbers were required for a big lift.

The arrival of Number 1 Air Commando was a tremendous boost to morale. Every Chindit knew that badly wounded or sick on the previous expedition at best were left to the mercy of villagers who might, or might not, turn them over to the Japanese; at worst they were left to die. Now, there was a good chance of being flown out. According to Squadron Leader O'Brien, the RAF Liaison Officer with 111th Brigade, Wingate also told them that:

> The planes are our artillery. They will bomb and destroy the targets you produce.

As a gunner, he should have known better than to make such a promise. There is no doubt that the close air support provided by Cochran was first class, as was the control by RAF pilots with the columns, talking the aircraft in to attack the target over the radio. Together they did wonders, and as a result the Chindits developed considerable faith in air support. They realized that taking sufficient artillery in by glider to support the whole force was out of the question, especially when columns were on the move. However, the Chindits were to learn that, dedicated and skilled though the airmen were, they sometimes missed. Artillery fire can be adjusted on to the target by the observer, talking over the radio to the gun position, and it matters not if the first rounds miss. Once a complete air strike sortie has delivered its ordnance, missed and pulled away, even observed strikes cannot be adjusted. Also artillery fire, if available, is on tap whatever the weather, by day or night.

In the months before the Chindits were eventually committed to battle, numerous plans for their employment were made, only to be discarded as the strategic picture unfolded. Gradually the more grandiose flights of fancy were whittled down, until at one stage in the planning process the Chindits were to assist with Stilwell's advance on Myitkyina, and also with IV Corps's attack from Assam across the Chindwin, and XV Corps's in the Arakan. However, when it became apparent from the breaking of enemy codes and captured documents that the Japanese were also planning attacks in the latter two areas, as a result of their change of heart alluded to in the last chapter, Slim shrewdly decided to receive them on the ground of his own choosing, around Imphal in Assam and north of Buthidaung in the Arakan, and cancelled both corps attacks. This left Stilwell's effort as the only offensive action planned for the first half of 1944. Stilwell, concerned that his Chinese troops would not be aggressive enough, wanted American troops to give some bite to his offensive. Having been refused any American units by Marshall, he demanded Merrill's Marauders back from the British. Wingate's response to an American officer bearing the news was, 'You can tell General Stilwell he can stick his Americans up his arse.'[4]

However, he soon calmed down and acceded, knowing full well that in supporting Stilwell lay his best hope of achieving his own aspirations. These included the seizure of the airfield at Indaw, which he hoped he could use as a lever to persuade Slim to fly in a whole infantry division for further operations in north Burma; under his command, naturally. This concept had at one time figured in the myriad plans at GHQ Delhi under the codename Tarzan, the staff's dig at Wingate, alluding to his nickname. Resuscitating the Tarzan plan by hook or by crook was to remain one of Wingate's obsessions until the day he died. Originally, only three Chindit brigades were to deploy, the other three being used to relieve them. They would be relieved in the field in their turn by the first three and so on. But Wingate was determined to get his whole force committed as soon as possible. In this way, Slim, if short of troops, would not be able to take any of them away from him.

Wingate constantly 'bellyached' to Mountbatten about the tasks assigned to Special Force, going behind Slim's, his Army Commander's, back, as well as Giffard's, the Army Group Commander. Because he had been told at the Quebec conference that Special Force would be used in support of both IVth and XVth Corps's attacks, both 'claws of the pincer' as he put it, he imagined that these plans would remain set in concrete despite a changing operational situation. What he did not know, of course, because he was not privy to it, was the intelligence that the Japanese were about to attack. Signals intelligence of this sensitivity (Magic and Ultra) was known down the chain of command as far as Slim, and no lower. Wingate, imbued with his sense of divine mission, considered that he, and he alone, had the solution to victory in Burma. When he realized that 'both claws' were not about to attack, he pestered Mountbatten with a series of long, rambling letters which included threats to resign and suggestions that the LRP operation should be cancelled. After a meeting on 8 February, Mountbatten replied with remarkable restraint, as shown by extracts from a letter written to Wingate on the following day:

I must also ask you for your assurance that you are fully prepared to carry on with the LRPG [sic] operations on the basis of your present directive, which was prepared without any suggestion of continental operations on the scale you now propose.

I am sure you had no intention of 'putting me on the spot' last night, but the fact remains that *you suggested that your LRPG operations should not go on* unless the present idea of World Strategy were changed by the Chiefs of Staff!! [sic] [Author's italics]

This crossed with a letter from Wingate, dated 10 February 1944, which includes the paragraph:

Finally, I would like to know that it is appreciated that if this operation Thursday succeeds, an attempt will immediately be made to raise a minimum of *ten new LRP Brigades from both airborne divisions and normal divisions of good quality.* There is no justification whatever for making Culverin[5] an excuse for refusing this. [Author's italics]

There were no airborne divisions in South-East Asia, only one brigade. The only British Airborne *Divisions* (1st and 6th) were in Britain preparing for the invasion of north-west Europe (author's italics). Implying, in a letter to the Supreme Commander, that he, Wingate, knew how to employ them better than anyone else merely demonstrates how unbalanced Wingate could be. It is a measure of the degree to which his attendance at Quebec had gone to his head, and his overweening arrogance, that Wingate attempted to influence operational and strategic planning in the whole South-East Asia Theatre. Unfortunately he was not privy to all the factors involved. Nor does he seem to understand that strategic and other plans are not sacrosanct, and may be changed as fresh information and events unfold.

Mountbatten, who, according to his biographer, often shrank from confrontation, did not sack Wingate.[6] 'Mountbatten's penchant for the heroic, the eccentric and the larger-than-life ensured that he never wholly lost his admiration for this remarkable man.'[7] In the end Wingate was given three tasks: to help Stilwell's advance on Myitkyina by drawing off and disorganizing the Japanese opposing him and by preventing reinforcements reaching them; to create a favourable situation for the Chinese Army in Yunnan to advance across the Salween; and to inflict maximum confusion, damage and loss on the Japanese in north Burma. According to Tulloch, Wingate cherished a private aim to reconquer Burma and hold it down to a line roughly corresponding with the 24 degree parallel, including Indaw.

To fulfil these tasks Wingate decided on three targets: Indaw; the railway from Mandalay to Myitkyina; and the road from Bhamo to Myitkyina. He also decided that with one exception, he would fly his brigades into Burma by glider and Dakota into four landing zones (LZs). Three of these were named after famous streets: Piccadilly in London, Chowringhee in Calcutta and Broadway in New York; and the fourth after a Somerset village, Templecombe. Early glider loads would include sappers and light bulldozers to convert the LZs into strips capable of accepting Dakotas. These landing strips would be selected in areas clear of jungle, some distance from the brigade objectives, so that these would not be compromised by the landings which the Japanese would inevitably discover. In breaking the cardinal rule of airborne operations, land on or right by your objective, Wingate was relying on the brigades approaching their targets under cover of the jungle. He also rejected the use of parachute troops to seize, clear and hold the landing strips in advance of the glider landings. In a special appendix to his report on

Operation Longcloth he waxed enthusiastically about parachute troops, stating at the end:

To sum up, Long-Range Penetration is the indispensable preliminary to the use of parachute or airborne forces and will provide the most economical and effectual use of them.

By using gliders he was to follow his precept in part, but clearly changed his mind about parachute troops because in a letter to Mountbatten dated 27 December 1943, he said:

Parachutists are becoming obsolete in war, and I trust this will soon be recognised.

In his note covering subjects he intended raising at a meeting with Mountbatten on 11 January 1944, he somewhat impertinently wrote:

Orders to be Given by the Supreme Commander

(a) The absurd wastage of transport aircraft on the Parachute Brigade is to cease. . . . These aircraft are NOT to be reallocated on any pretext whatsoever without direct reference to the Supreme Commander.

He returned to the charge in an appreciation dated 10 February 1944:

The Parachute Brigade [in India] is obsolete in as much as there is no function for parachutists in War.

This claim was made not long before three of the biggest parachute operations in history: Normandy, Arnhem and the Rhine Crossing. On what he based these amazing assertions, other than prejudice and ignorance, is not clear.

His plan was as follows:

Fergusson's 16th Brigade, march from the Ledo road, starting in February, and secure the two airfields at Indaw. On the way he was to destroy the Japanese garrison at Lonkin, on the right flank of Stilwell's route south.

Calvert's 77th Brigade, land by glider at Broadway and Piccadilly, and having marched to the railway, set up a block.

Lentaigne's 111st Brigade, land by glider at Piccadilly, and head for the area south of Indaw, and by road blocks and demolitions, to protect the southern approaches of 16th Brigade's operations there. Bladet was to operate in the same area and demolish certain railway bridges.

Morris's 4/9th Gurkha Rifles (Morrisforce) land by glider at Chow-ringhee, march to mountains east of the Bhamo–Myitkyina Road and carry out raids on the road.

Herring's Dahforce, land by glider at Templecombe, raise guerrilla bands from the Kachins, and support Morrisforce.

Wingate had directed that each brigade was to select what he called a 'stronghold', near its operating area, and in a place inaccessible to wheeled transport. The stronghold should cover, but not necessarily include within its perimeter, an airstrip and a supply DZ. He hoped that the Japanese would attack the strongholds. They would be unable to bring up heavy artillery or tanks, and would have supply problems. Whereas the Chindits could be supplied by air, be supported by fighter-bomber ground attack, and by artillery flown in by glider or Dakota. Each garrison was to have a 'floater' company outside the stronghold to act as its eyes and ears and attack the enemy as he approached. Brigades were to be prepared to despatch additional 'floater' companies or even columns to attack the enemy's rear and flanks as he approached the stronghold. In a Training Memorandum dated 20 February 1944, Wingate wrote:

> The stronghold is a machan overlooking a kid tied up to entice the Japanese tiger.

Floater columns were not a Wingate invention. When Wingate had first mooted the idea of strongholds, Slim had sent him to talk to Lieutenant-General Scoones, commanding IV Corps, who had devised a method of defence using mobile detachments concealed outside defended localities, to do just what Chindit 'floater' units were to do.

Although, as recounted earlier, Wingate asked for 'normal' troops to be flown in to garrison the strongholds, in order to release the Chindits for operations outside, Slim told him he could have the 3/9th Gurkha Rifles, some artillery, and nothing more. Wingate still hoped that if all went well, he would get his reinforcements anyway.

Before each brigade set out, the next of kin of every man received a letter from the War Office like the one to the wife of Captain the Reverend Miller, the senior chaplain with 111th Brigade:

> Dear Madam
>
> It is probable that you will not receive any letters from your husband

No: 154997   *Rank:* Revd.   *Name:* Miller W. H.

for some time to come. This does not mean that he is unwell. For the
present, however, the type of operations in which he is taking part make it
impossible for him to write to you, but he will do so as soon as he can.
Please, however, go on writing to him as your letters will greatly cheer him,
and please ask his relations and friends to write to him too. If you use his
normal address, your letters will be delivered. Until he can write to you
himself, a letter similar to this will be sent once a month.

Fergusson's Brigade drove in trucks along the Ledo Road, still under
construction as far as Tagap Ga, in American trucks driven by Chinese.
Captain Rodney Tatchell, a sapper with 21 Column:

> It required two Chinese to drive these vehicles, one to steer and the other
> to change gear. It was only possible to move on the Ledo Road by night,
> and it was not possible to move at all unless a vehicle had four-wheel drive
> and chains on all wheels. On one side of the road there was usually a
> precipice often littered with wrecked vehicles that had gone over the side
> and been abandoned. The night we went up the road, it was pouring with
> rain and the mud was more than axle deep.

Sapper J. Snell, also with 21 Column, remembers Wingate meeting
the Brigade at the debussing point and addressing them:

> You are about to start on the toughest march that has ever been attempted.
> For the first month you will travel through the rain belt, where it rains
> almost every day of the year. You will cross the Naga Hills, some of which
> are over 8,000 feet high. After you have crossed the Chindwin, the hills will
> get smaller, the rainfall will be less but the jungle will go on and on. You
> won't all come back; but if this going seems tough just remember that after
> it is all over you will have forgotten the hardships and will remember only
> the achievements. It is not natural for Europeans to march in this climate
> and then sleep on the ground in damp blankets, so take care of your bodies
> first, and then your weapons. Nature will be your biggest enemy. Don't
> strain yourself, if you can't go any further pass the word to your officer and
> he will halt. Good luck and God be with you.

Perhaps the worst stretch of the march was from Tagap to Hkalak.
Columns averaged nine days to cover the thirty-five miles. Each man
was carrying around 70 lb, and this increased as their equipment became
saturated with rainwater. In his official report Fergusson wrote:

The rain was torrential and almost continuous; the gradients were often one in two; no single stretch of level going a hundred yards long existed between Tagap and Hkalak, and few thereafter.... The cold was intense, particularly at bivouacs over 5,000 feet. A dry bivouac was practically unknown. Leeches, which were innumerable, were the least trying of the conditions.

Rodney Tatchell on the ninth day:

Now we faced the worst stretch of all – the long, steep, heartbreaking climb up to Hkalak Ga. A crest which appeared to promise that the summit was about to be reached invariably turned out to be a false crest. The high rain forest cast a dim twilight; it was rare to be able to see more than 30 yards in any direction. Only once, I remember, did we come to a spot where suddenly we emerged to behold a glorious distant panorama of jungle-covered mountains. We all gasped as we came upon this unexpected vision.

The Chindits marched in silence; Signalman George Hill, with 21 Column:

We were not allowed to speak even in whispers. Even the mules had been 'debrayed' to keep them quiet. It was not possible to silence the battery-charging engine, but at least this was always in the centre of the night bivouac circle, when the terrain allowed for such to be formed.

Unless we were in a particularly sensitive area we were allowed to light fires for limited periods in order to provide ourselves with a hot drink and meal. Fires didn't really constitute any great danger, since the density of the jungle effectively screened them, as it did us, from being seen from other than a very short distance away. Smoke in daylight might be spotted from the air. Fortunately smoke does not indicate nationality, and could just as easily have been produced by the Burmese. All traces of fire had to be obliterated before we moved on.

Rodney Tatchell remembers that one supply drop:

to our joy, included our first mail. Almost the first envelope I opened was an Income Tax demand; the Inland Revenue has indeed a long arm.

Columns marched in single file, and 400 men with some 70 animals made a 'snake' up to a mile long. However slow the pace at the front, the men in the rear had to march flat out. Gaps occurred, as animals were led round or over fallen trees. When the gaps became large, they had to be reported by passing the word forward from man to man. The messages sometimes became garbled in passing, as Rodney Tatchell recorded:

> The original message, 'There is a gap in the column', reached the Adjutant as 'There is a Jap in the column'. On hearing this delivered deadpan by a rifleman, the Adjutant spun round, 'No, where?'

As well as the rain forest in which they often encountered fallen trees of ten-foot girth and more, Tatchell remembers other types of jungle on the march to and beyond the Chindwin, where there was no rain forest:

> There was bamboo. If it was green bamboo, progress was not too difficult. Dead (yellow) bamboo on the other hand was the very devil since usually it had collapsed and formed an almost impenetrable waist-high obstacle. This called for a great deal of slashing with dahs [a Burmese machete-type knife] or a long detour. Finally there was teak forest. This was fairly easy, if noisy, going because our passage during the then dry season, through the huge dead teak leaves covering the ground, set up a fearful roar. To add to the din there were in the teak forests myriads of cicadas which, on one's approach, raised a noise like a million alarm clocks. Apart from this, going through teak forest was rather like a stroll through Richmond Park.
>
> Our prime object [on this part of the march] was to avoid habitation. That meant keeping often along the high ridges where there was little or no water. Even on our march from Hkalak to Lulum Nok [about halfway to the Chindwin from the Ledo Road] we had difficulty in finding water and often had to dig for it in dry stream beds. The only good thing about dead bamboo was by cutting between the nodes, one usually could find a cupful of brackish water plus a few spiders. I even greedily lapped up dew which had collected in the large fallen teak leaves.
>
> Lack of food was almost permanent. We were supposed to receive a supply drop every five days, but often the tactical situation prevented a drop. Even when we did have one, we were lucky if, out of the five days' rations dropped, we picked up three, owing to the parachutes getting caught up in very high trees, or drifting away into inaccessible gorges.

George Hill's column reached the Chindwin on 1 March. They crossed in boats, which with their outboard engines and sapper crews had been flown in and landed on a convenient sandbank by gliders. It being the dry season, the river was low.

The most memorable thing about this crossing was not the crossing itself, but was the sight of Brigadier Fergusson walking along the 'beach' wearing nothing but a towel around his middle, but still with his inevitable monocle, accompanied by General Wingate with his horrible pith helmet. The latter had flown in by light plane the day before to watch the crossing, and flew out again on the day of 21 Column's crossing.

Wingate sent a signal to the leading battalion of 16th Brigade, the veteran, battle-hardened 2nd Royal Leicesters, saying 'Well done Leicesters. Hannibal eclipsed.' The Leicesters, whose badge was a tiger and were known as the 'Tigers', were in the words of Shelford Bidwell: 'a typical example of an old fashioned regiment of British infantry; élite, self-regarding, self-confident. They were not particularly honoured by being Chindits: if asked, they might have answered that the Chindits were honoured by the inclusion of the Leicesters.'[8] Most of them had not fallen under Wingate's spell, and their Commanding Officer, Lieutenant-Colonel Wilkinson, dismissed the signal by saying that all such references were over his head.

From the Chindwin to Indaw the distance was about 150 miles in a straight line, but more like 400 on the route taken by 16th Brigade. Fergusson could not possibly arrive in his operational area by 15 March, the deadline set by Wingate. In accordance with his orders, Fergusson detached two Columns, Numbers 51 and 69, to attack the Japanese garrison at Lonkin. They arrived to find it abandoned, except for a small rearguard, who were turned out after a brief skirmish. This diversion, from what modern soldiers call the main point of effort, resulted in the two columns arriving in the operational area ten days after the others. Other than a small patrol clash, Columns 51 and 69 were to see no further action.

While Fergussson's brigade was slogging towards Indaw, the fly-in of the leading Chindit brigade, Calverts 77th, started after dark on 5 March. Before this the Japanese Air Force had taken a severe pasting at the hands of Cochran's P-51s. They had deployed forward out of their bases in Siam to support the Japanese offensive in Assam, and Cochran's pilots destroyed twenty-six aircraft on the ground. A few days later, Cochran again caught the Japanese Air Force napping, and his P-51s and B-25s, with RAF assistance, destroyed over thirty aircraft, damaging several more. As a result, when the Dakotas and the even more vulnerable gliders started operating by day, the Japanese Air Force had been hard hit. There was no subsequent let-up in the intensity of the Allied air effort aimed at keeping enemy aircraft away from the area of Thursday operations.

The usual tense moments before men about to be launched into battle were heightened on the afternoon of 5 March at Hailakandi airfield. It had been decided that the LZs would not be overflown at all after a reconnaissance on 12 February. Whether or not this was a ban imposed personally by Wingate is not clear. He also refused to use parachute troops, even in the pathfinder role, despite it being standard practice for Allied airborne operations to be preceded by pathfinders to mark the DZs and landing zones. So he was committing Cochran's leading glider pilots to landing, at night, into a landing zone which had not been reconnoitred, cleared or marked with lights; and without benefit of recent air photographic coverage. According to Tulloch, in an unpublished typescript:

> On the morning of 5 March, Cochran had a premonition that the Japs had somehow got wind of our intended operation, and without consulting Wingate for he hoped his fears were groundless [or possibly because he knew he would be forbidden to do so] despatched an aircraft to take photographs of Piccadilly and Broadway.

It was as well he did. Piccadilly was blocked, as it later transpired, by foresters drying out logs after cutting. The Japanese suspected nothing, although in fairness Wingate could not possibly have known that at the time. His reaction shocked Slim, and others who had come to see Calvert off. He threw a tantrum saying that the whole operation had been betrayed, and refused to go ahead. Calvert said he was willing to take his complete brigade into Broadway, and this was agreed, but not before Slim had led Wingate aside in an effort to calm him down. Air Marshal Sir John Baldwin the Commander of the 3rd Tactical Air Force was also present. In 1952, Slim wrote in a letter to a fellow officer from the 6th Gurkhas, Slim's own regiment:

> Wingate urged very strongly that the whole fly-in should be cancelled. I then asked Calvert if *he* was prepared to go. He was. So I overruled Wingate with Baldwin's agreement and sent them off.

Wingate turned on Slim and said, 'The responsibility is yours.' Slim wrote in his book *Defeat into Victory*:

I knew it was. . . . I would have given a great deal if Wingate, or anybody else, could have relieved me of the duty of decision. But that is a burden the commander himself must bear.[9]

Wingate's version of events, in his covering letter to the Report on Air Borne Movements of two brigades of Special Force on Operation Thursday dated 19 March 1944, is very different, and bears all the hallmarks of the 'creative' writing at which he was so adept. He starts by saying:

In view of the fact that a large number of people had necessarily been informed of the operation it was only too possible that the design had been penetrated by the Japanese. This photograph appears to afford definite evidence that such was the case. I therefore consulted with the Army Commander [Slim] who agreed my arguments and left me to decide for myself so far as I myself was concerned.

He goes on to say:

Of the four airfields which it was proposed to use, only one could have been known to the Japanese by any means other than direct revelation of the details of the plan. That one was Piccadilly, for the simple reason that photographs of this airfield had appeared in *Life* [magazine] in June 1943, and apart from this the Japanese were well aware at the time that the place had been used in the manner described in the periodical.

Therefore the blocking of Piccadilly by the enemy did not necessarily imply any knowledge of the plan and the fact that none of the other three had been blocked (as far as we were aware) entitled one to hope that this interference of the enemy was merely a routine measure taken in consequence of a general scare of airborne landings.

The Army Commander and the Air Marshal were both in full agreement with me that the plan should proceed, cutting out Piccadilly.

Within a week of issuing this report Wingate was dead, and was not available to be challenged on the contents. Most people who knew both Wingate and Slim believe Slim's account.

On 13 March, after the fly-in of the leading brigades, Wingate wrote a MOST SECRET AND PERSONAL, pontifical letter to Mountbatten, about the work of Cochran's aircrew. He used phraseology which managed to praise Number 1 Air Commando and at the same time be self-serving and, in one paragraph, could be read to mean that Wingate had sanctioned the air photography of the LZs. It also reveals his obsessive belief that he was the victim of a conspiracy, as extracts show:

> I am reporting to you on the value of No. 1 Air Commando and the work it has done, because you will not receive a correct and comprehensive report on this subject from anyone else, and it is of the utmost importance that you should receive one.
>
> It is also of the utmost importance that you and no one else should pass on the true report of their activities and functions to the PM [Prime Minister], General Arnold and other persons who are interested, and who should receive true and not incorrect information.[10]

Later in the same letter he writes:

> It was Cochran's photographs which revealed the occupation of Piccadilly by the enemy in time to prevent a major holocaust.

By this time, seven days after the fly-in, it was known that the enemy had not had any part to play in the blocking of Piccadilly, as has been alluded to earlier.

*

Calvert's leading four Dakotas, each towing two gliders, took off at 6.12 p.m. In the eight gliders were Colonel Alison USAAF, a ground control party with radios, and covering troops of 1st Battalion the King's Regiment, under Lieutenant-Colonel Scott ('Scotty'), a column commander on the first expedition. They landed at Broadway after a flight of two and a half hours. Fifteen minutes later Brigadier Calvert and advance headquarters 77th Brigade arrived. The advance party laid out a flare path just before the arrival of the main body. The fly-in of the main body was chaotic. Deep ruts in the LZ concealed by thick grass caused many gliders to crash. Others landing before the wreckage could be cleared added to the mayhem. The concept of one tug aircraft towing two gliders had been introduced after insufficient trials. Many pilots had never towed two gliders in daylight, let alone at night. Many of the gliders were overloaded or badly loaded, as troops had taken more equipment on board than listed in the manifests. To clear the mountains on each side of the Chindwin the aircraft had to climb to 10,000 feet. Engines straining at full power overheated, developed faults, and some pilots realizing they would never clear the high ground cast off their tows. The results were as follows:

First Wave (52 gliders)

4 broke loose near Lalaghat.

2 returned to Imphal when the tug cut them off owing to petrol trouble.

2 returned to base as the tug developed electrical trouble.

8 landed in enemy territory east of the Chindwin. Personnel of two returned to the Chindwin and arrived safely. Personnel of another two marched on to join their unit at Broadway, and those of another two were taken prisoner. The remaining two were never traced.

2 were prematurely released near Broadway by the tug aircraft and crashed half a mile from the landing zone in the jungle, all but two being killed.

34 landed safely on the dropping zone [*sic*]. Total casualties: 2 killed; 34 wounded.

Second Wave (9 gliders)

8 recalled

1 landed across the strip – containing a bulldozer and a crew of 2 who had a miraculous escape.

At dawn on 6 March some 400 all ranks were in Broadway.[11]

The miraculous escape is also described in Otway's *Airborne Forces*:

When the first flight of gliders was complete it was decided to accept no more gliders that night and the codeword agreed for the cancellation of the operation was sent to Lalaghat. This message was not received until 02.27 hours, by which time nine gliders of the second wave, now flying at single tow, were already on their way. Eight were recalled and landed at base. The ninth, containing a bulldozer, was released over Broadway. This one, landing at speed, overshot the strip, discharging its load into the jungle as it stuck between two trees. The co-pilots [*sic*] were lifted bodily as the nose raised to emit the bulldozer, they were unhurt. The bulldozer was destroyed.

By the standards of the Sicily landings and the great Allied airborne operations yet to come, casualties were light. The dispersed crash-landings in enemy territory served to confuse the Japanese as to the true objective, as had happened previously in Sicily, and would to do so again on other airborne operations.

The codeword for the cancellation of the operation was Soya Link, an ersatz sausage made of soya, which featured all too often at breakfast during the Second World War and for some years afterwards, and was universally loathed by British soldiers. The meaning of the codeword was 'trouble at Broadway, cancel the operation'. Radio communications to Lalaghat were bad that night. Calvert had no option but to send that signal, knowing that one word had a chance of cutting through the roar of the static, whereas a long explanation would be garbled. Understandably it caused consternation at Lalaghat, not least to Wingate. Slim wrote in a letter to Gibbs:

> When 'Soya Links' [sic] came over the blower, Wingate said to me, 'You are responsible for this' – as indeed I was.

For the soldiers sitting helpless in the gliders wallowing in the turbulence, the fly-in was usually an alarming, sick-making experience, and bad enough, but the landing was often worse. The landing at Broadway that first night has been described by Private 'Vin' Worrall of the King's (Liverpool):

> I felt a terrific crash and an awful draught. With utter amazement I goggled out of the tail of the glider. It had been ripped clean off taking Pop Quinn and L/Cpl Kelly with it. Another horrible jolt shook the glider, and with a tearing and splintering of metal and canvas we went careering through the trees.

The next morning Calvert sent the codeword, Pork Sausage, indicating that all was well. By evening a 1,400-yard strip was ready. At 6 p.m. the Dakotas took off from Lalaghat and Hailakandi. At 8 p.m. the first Dakota piloted by Brigadier General Donald Old USAAF touched down on Broadway. Lieutenant Durant, wrote home:

> In my plane I had 8 men, 4 mules, and a complete Vickers with ammunition, rather an unpleasant mule/man ratio. The inside of the plane was fitted with bamboo poles and the idea was to get the mules in pairs well

forward and box them in pens, lashing the bamboo so close that they could not move however much they got thrown about. It took a very long time to make clear to the mules what was required. Eventually by cajoling them with handfuls of corn, and by turning out the lights inside the plane so they couldn't see what they were getting in to, we managed to get three of them secured, but the fourth was as obstinate as only a mule can be. Eventually we managed to put a bit of sacking over his head and led him very fast in circles until he didn't know whether he was coming or going. When he was really dazed, we pushed him up the ramp into the plane and lashed him in before he realised what was happening.

We had our last meal in Assam from a field kitchen set up by the strip, strolled back to the planes and lay on the grass beside them waiting for the hour to get aboard. At last the long, weary months of training and preparation were over.

At the end of the line the first Dakota started to roar as the engines came to life. We swung our packs and equipment into our plane, number 7, and the RAF pilots gave us a last word of advice – strap yourselves in, if a mule breaks loose, shoot it, hang on when I tell you we're landing – and the doors closed on us. The engines started, and all four mules made frantic but vain efforts to force themselves through the sides of the aircraft. Sweat stood out on my brow, and I clutched my revolver in anticipation, but the mule team succeeded in calming them. From the windows I could see the orange lights of the flarepath, and the green and red lights of the ship [aircraft] taking off before us. We taxied up into position, and with throttles open started the take-off. As the plane rushed forward, the most truculent of the mules leant to the side, his hooves got off the floor matting and on to the aluminium. He slipped and was on the floor thrashing about before we could do anything. This naturally upset the other three and they began lashing out until the place was bedlam. I had visions of having to ask the pilot to turn back. By superhuman efforts we got the mule on his feet, soothed the others with soft words and corn, tightened the lashings, and peace was restored. By this time we were airborne.

We had to climb to 10,000 feet to clear the Chin Hills, and it became uncomfortably cold. I was extremely glad when the pilot told us over the inter-comm to prepare for landing. Through the window we saw an amazing sight. On the ground were the long lights of the flare path, flanked by lights of planes that had already landed, while every now and then a bright signal lamp flashed out instructions, or a jeep's headlights lit up the crowds of hurrying men. We bumped as we landed, and the wheels bit into the ground. The doors were flung open, we tossed loads out, cut the mules loose, and pushed them unceremoniously out into the night. I looked round and could hardly believe my eyes. Here we were, behind Jap lines, within 30 minutes' flying time of Jap aerodromes, and there were more lights than show in Calcutta. Every five minutes a huge transport would land, or an empty one take off; over a loudspeaker instructions and orders boomed out; tow jeeps dashed about replacing burnt-out flares; torches flashed and men shouted; the only jarring notes were the skeletons of the gliders which had crashed the night before.

The same night the fly-in of 111th Brigade began. Initially this Brigade was intended for Piccadilly, but Wingate had decided that to relieve congestion in Broadway; he would send 111th Brigade to Chowringhee, despite the landing zone being on the wrong side of the Irrawaddy relative to this brigade's objective. By the morning of 8 March brigade headquarters, 4/9th Gurkha Rifles (Morrisforce), and 3/4th Gurkha Rifles had arrived in Chowringhee. On 9 March, after a visit to Chowringhee, Wingate changed his mind and ordered the rest of 111th Brigade (1st Cameronians and 2nd King's Own) to fly into Broadway. With them also flew in Dahforce, because information about their intended landing zone, Templecombe, was considered too scanty. Wingate made a wise decision, since the Japanese Air Force had flown over Chowringhee on the 8th, and one of their airfields was only fifteen miles away. But the result was that Dahforce and about a third of 111th Brigade had to cross the Irrawaddy before reaching their operational areas. That and the additional distance the Cameronians and the King's Own had to march resulted in 111th Brigade arriving too late to interfere with the Japanese moving north to attack Fergusson. Thanks to recalcitrant mules baulking at swimming the mile-wide Irrawaddy, Lentaigne's crossing went so slowly that at the end of two days he only had his headquarters and Number 30 Column on the west bank. Eventually, with reports of Japanese approaching in strength, he sent Number 40 Column, most of the mules and support weapons to join Morris who was marching east. Major D. S. McCutcheon, 3/4th Gurkha Rifles, the second-in-command of 40 Column, remembers the scene:

The Bn split on 12th March and did not come together until they reformed in Dehra Dun in the latter half of August. This splitting was a dismal moment and appeared to be a sorry end to an operation that had started on a note of high endeavour. Both columns left for their new roles with feelings of loneliness and it was with a sensation of gloom that they watched each other's fires across the Irrawaddy that night.

Lentaigne, the Brigade Commander, and 'Jack' Masters, his Brigade Major, must have felt equally depressed; they were both 4th Gurkhas.

Of all the Chindits landed in the first lifts, only Morrisforce had arrived complete at its correct LZ. However, despite the set-backs the operation so far had been a triumph for Wingate. The fly-in had been completed without enemy opposition. Over seven nights 650 Dakota and glider sorties had landed about 9,000 men 1,350 animals, 250 tons of stores, and a light anti-aircraft and 25-pounder battery in the heart of Japanese-held north Burma. It was the biggest behind-the-lines oper-ation in the War to date; and there was more to come. Wingate issued an order of the day, part of which read:

> Our first task is fulfilled. We have inflicted a complete surprise upon the enemy. All our Columns are inside the enemy's guts. The time has come to reap the fruit of the advantage we have gained. The enemy will react with violence. We will oppose him with the resolve to reconquer our territory of Northern Burma. Let us thank God for the great success He had vouchsafed us and press forward with our sword in our enemy's ribs to expel him from our territory.

Many of his men were inspired when this message was read out to them. The 2nd Royal Leicester's War Diary merely recorded: 'Long corrupt message from Force [Wingate], impossible to decipher, but something in it about guts and God'.

Calvert meanwhile was marching to the valley along which ran the railway supplying the Japanese division facing Stilwell in the north. Calvert was without doubt the finest of all Wingate's brigade command-ers, and one of the few people with any influence over him. Lieutenant Durant told his parents:

> He is about 5 ft 9 ins tall, immensely broad and looks what he is – an Olympic swimmer and first-rate boxer. He has a disconcerting habit of staring at you when you speak to him, and yet not appearing to hear a word. His lectures were always painfully slow and hesitant and during training he gave the impression of taking a long time to make up his mind; in action things were very different. His manner and attitude are always the

same if he is talking to a CO, subaltern or private soldier. No one could hope to serve under a finer man.

Calvert had left 3/9th Gurkha Rifles to garrison Broadway, with both columns of the 1st King's (Liverpool) as 'floaters' outside. He took the 1st South Staffs and 3/6th Gurkha Rifles to set up a block on the railway near Mawlu. The two columns (Numbers 20 and 50) of the 1st Lancashire Fusiliers were given independent tasks to be carried out on their way to the railway. On completion of these, they would become the 'floaters' for the railway block. Lieutenant Hugh Patterson, Royal Engineers, commanded the Commando Platoon with 50 Column:

On 12th and 13th March we crossed the Gangaw Range, climbing to nearly 4,000 feet – quite a job with 70 lb of equipment on one's back. We were now only ten miles from the railway, but it took us two more days to reach it, as the going was so bad. After cutting through very thick jungle, the head of our column reached the main road running parallel with the railway. At this point they were ambushed by a small party of the Burma Traitor Army (BTA) [Burmese Nationalists opposing the British] and a few Japs. By the time those had been disposed of it was about 18.30 on 15th March.

I set off with my demolition party for the railway bridge over the Ledan Chaung. I took about twenty of my commandos, and was given a platoon, and a machine-gun detachment as protection. Six mules carried the explosives. I wanted to reach the bridge before dark, so took a risk and walked straight down the main road.

My orders were to blow the bridge as soon as possible if the Japs knew we were there. Otherwise I was to wait, and try to bag a train on the bridge as well. The bridge was ready for blowing by about 21.00, and I had to blow it as we had had a scrap two hours before. I very much wanted to wait for a train, so tried to get in touch with the column commander on the wireless, but without success. Sergeant Kemp and I lit a fuse each to make sure, and I remember him saying as we walked down the line, 'This is something I've wanted to do all my life, Sir.' Next moment we were both blown flat by the blast of the explosion. Bits of metal and brick hummed through the air and thudded down all round, but luckily no one was hit. The bridge was a satisfactory mess – all spans and pillars destroyed, and a big crater in the north abutment. We finished off by laying a lot of booby traps and time bombs to discourage repair parties.

Mike Calvert heard it [the bang] away to the south and sent us a signal, 'Both saw and heard your bang – keep it up.'

Patterson withdrew and ambushed the road all night, but had no contact with the enemy. On the night of the 16th Patterson's commandos were let loose on Mawhun railway station, burning ten coaches and wagons, and blowing the overhead water tanks and pump house.

That same day, Calvert had arrived at the small village of Henu, which he had chosen as the site for his block. Durant wrote to his parents describing the typically confused infantry fighting that followed their arrival:

By the greatest stroke of luck the Japs had not anticipated our move and at first light on the 16th we moved into the area we were to occupy for the next 7 weeks. This consisted of a group of about 7 small hills to the north and east of which was thick wood, and to the west the road and railway and then open paddy, and to the south paddy, and in the distance Mawlu.

I was on a hill at the bottom of which ran the road and railway, not more than 200 yards away, but 100 yards to the south was a hill covered with bush and unoccupied by us. That afternoon Major Jefferies the [column] rifle company commander sent for me and said the CO had given orders to move 2 platoons and the Medium Machine-Guns [his platoon] on to this hill, as it was a key point. So at about 17.00 hours we moved and began digging. As no tools had been dropped we had to rely on entrenching tools and machetes, so progress was slow.

[Overleaf] is a rough diagram showing A the hill we were first on, and B the hill we moved to that evening. Across the road, only about 100 yards away was a third hill C on the highest point of which was a small Pagoda, and on the Southern end were 4 large wooden buildings raised on stilts off the ground. This hill completely dominated us, but there was no time that night to occupy it and so it was left unreconnoitred.

That night we got no sleep for we were too busy digging in, and at dawn we stood to in the foxholes we had dug. I had hardly put my equipment on before a terrific yammering began on the hill opposite, and I remarked to my sergeant that the 'locals' were making a lot of noise. To see what it was all about, I strolled down to the forward section positions when to my amazement I saw six Japs equally unconcerned, walking down the hill opposite towards the road. They weren't more than 80 yards from me, so snatching a bren gun from one of my men, who was unsighted by the thick bushes, I fired a magazine off from the hip. I think that in my excitement I missed the lot, but it certainly gave them the surprise of their lives. At that moment firing broke out behind me and Noel Day [a platoon commander]

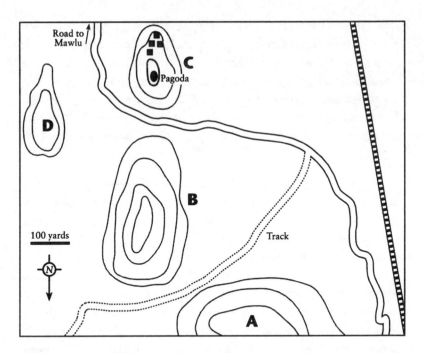

Map of Henu area from sketch by Lieutenant Durant in letter to his parents

came running forward to say that some Japs had infiltrated on to the hill A (which was lightly held after we had moved out the night before), and had killed two of his men and wounded one.

I moved a Vickers back and sprayed the area, flushing out six Japs who made off down the hill towards the railway, two never making it but the rest getting away. After this there was an hour's quiet, but then one of my platoon reported several Japs moving towards us across the open paddy from the direction of Mawlu. I moved both Vickers up into positions from which they could do the most damage and for the next two hours we were engaging groups of Japs as they doubled from cover to cover. We killed quite a number of them, including an officer who stood up and waving his sword urged his men on, but there was a company of them, and plenty of covered approaches so that they eventually reached the dead ground behind the hill(s) in front of us.

At about 11.00 hours heavy rifle and LMG fire opened up on us from hill C – Pagoda Hill – and at the same time we came under grenade and mortar fire from hill D where a Jap platoon had taken up position. For the next four hours we had a very unpleasant time indeed. We couldn't see the

Jap and there were very few parts of the hill that weren't under fire. Casualties were mounting. I had to move the Vickers every half hour or so as the Jap was doing his best to knock them out. He put a burst across one gun which hit the man firing it in the thigh, another in the foot, and ripped a box of ammunition into shreds. However, we silenced one of their LMGs and from occasional screams knew we were inflicting casualties. By now a third of us were casualties, including the rifle company commander 2nd-in-C who was hit in both feet, and one of the platoon commanders who was hit through the buttocks. We were extremely glad to get a message over the wireless that the Brigadier was on his way with two companies of Gurkhas, and would counter-attack any feature held by the Japs.

The next hour was absolute hell. The Japs stepped up their mortaring and grenading and it became quite obvious that at any moment they might rush the road and attack from Pagoda Hill. Consequently the arrival of the Brigadier at 16.00 hours resembled the moment in an American film when the police with sirens screaming wildly speed up in time to help the hero, whilst the audience applauds wildly. The first we knew of his arrival was when the firing on our left stopped and we saw the Gurkhas attacking hill D, and the Brigadier himself came striding up our hill, rifle and bayonet in hand, took a quick look round and said to Major Jefferies, 'How many men can you spare to attack Pagoda Hill?'

'About 20.'

'Right, we'll go straight up'

George Cairns the mortar officer and I hearing this picked up some grenades, got out our revolvers, and prepared to go too. We had been shot at all day, everyone felt like getting into the Japs and exacting a bit of retribution, besides I was very keen to see just how many casualties my guns had inflicted on the enemy. Seeing me ready to go, my platoon sergeant (Jenkins) picked up a Sten and I knew it was no good ordering him not to come. The Japs on Pagoda Hill were now a bit concerned over the arrival of the Gurkhas and we were not fired on as we doubled down the forward slopes of our hill on to the road. As we got to the bottom, the Brigadier said to me, 'Take a party round to the left and clear the houses,' and to Jefferies, 'Take the right side and the Pagoda.'

I went up the hill like a two-year-old, and halfway up met a path which led round the left of the hill, about 12 feet below the Pagoda, obviously finishing by the houses. Shouting over my shoulder for the sergeant to follow up with the party, I doubled along the path, rounded the corner and came into view of the houses.

To this day I'm not quite certain what I expected to see – the place deserted, or the Japs on the run I suppose, but what I actually saw was a Jap section climbing out of their trenches under the nearest house and coming straight at me; the leading two with bayonets fixed and rather unfriendly expressions being about 20 yards on my right. I fired my revolver twice and nothing happened – I was later to find the hammer had worked loose.

It is strange how at a moment like that the mind can think of a hundred things during the space of a split second. Even as I ran forward, my brain was working faster than it has ever done before or since. I realised my sergeant was a good 30 yards behind, out of sight round the corner, and the men with him probably a bit behind that; time was too short for them to be of any help. I had a four-second [time delay] grenade in my hand, but it was obviously useless against the two leading Japs because in considerably less than four seconds they were going to be embarrassingly close. I also knew that if I stopped or turned round I was asking to be shot.

This didn't leave me much choice, so I took the pin out of the grenade, and still running forward, threw it over the heads of the first two among the Japs scrambling out from under the house, did a swerve to the left, and took a flying leap over the side of the hill. As I swerved, I felt as if I had been violently kicked on the knee, and although I never heard the shot, I realised I had been hit. I was only 12 feet down the hill with no cover at all, and for a ghastly moment I imagined myself crippled and unable to move, having to lie there while the Japs following up got to work on me with their bayonets. I remember saying to myself as I anxiously looked up the hill, 'What the hell did I volunteer to come here for? This is the last time I shall do anything like this unasked.' But no one appeared, and I moved back along the hill about 30 yards and climbed on to the path just below the Pagoda.

My sergeant told me later what happened after I'd jumped. He had come round the corner with two or three men and they had shot the leading two Japs. The grenade I had thrown had caused some casualties and the remaining Japs were moving back round the west side of the hill. Seeing no sign of me, the Sergeant thought I had been captured and was being bustled away by the Japs. He went berserk, grenading like a lunatic until the side of the hill was clear; and moving back round the side of the hill, was relieved to see me there.

The first thing I saw on reaching the path was a horrible hand-to-hand struggle further up the hill. George Cairns and a Jap were struggling and choking on the ground. As I picked up a Jap rifle and climbed up towards them, I saw George break free and picking up a rifle and bayonet stab the Jap again and again like a mad man. It was only when I got near that I saw he himself had already been bayoneted twice through the side and that his left arm was hanging on by a few strips of muscle. How he had found the strength to fight was a miracle, but the effort had been too much and he died the next morning. There were now a lot of our dead and Jap dead lying about, and our wounded were crying for help. But the Japs still held the top of the hill and things were looking critical. We might have been pushed back if the Brigadier had not shouted, 'Come on now, one more effort, you've got them on the run.'

The last few grenades were produced and thrown, and with bayonet, kukri, machete and revolver we stumbled up the last few yards, and before we knew what was happening the Japs were running. It was almost dusk, and as the men began to dig in ready to face the expected counter-attack, I sat down while someone put a field dressing on my leg. The hill was a horrid sight littered with Jap dead, and already the ones who had been killed earlier in the day were black with flies. Stretcher-bearers were removing our wounded and our mercifully very few dead. Noel Day had been killed, shot through the back of the head by a Jap feigning dead. On trying to repeat the ruse he was spotted by Noel's platoon sergeant who promptly kicked his head in. We found out then what we were never afterwards to forget – it doesn't pay to leave wounded Japs breathing.

I made my way back to the RAP and had my leg dressed, was given a shot of morphia and told to rest, but on getting back to my hill and rolling up in a blanket, I found it impossible to sleep. Every time I closed my eyes I saw morphia-raised images of such appalling incidents that I hurriedly awoke myself.

That morning the Brigadier summoned more of the Brigade into the block.

Lieutenant George Cairns was awarded the Victoria Cross.

Further Japanese counter-attacks were beaten off at a total cost of fifty-nine casualties to the South Staffords. The garrison of the block, shortly to be christened the White City because it soon became festooned with supply parachutes, dug in and roofed their trenches with sleepers torn from the railway line. A Dakota strip was constructed. Sandbags and barbed wire were dropped, engineer plant flown in, and soon a very strong position, complete with four 25-pounder guns, six light anti-aircraft guns and four anti-tank guns was constructed.

All the while 16th Brigade had still been plodding south. Fergusson set up a stronghold near Taungle on 13 March, but on the 18th Wingate told him to move to Calvert's assistance at Henu. When 77th Brigade successfully repulsed the Japanese, Wingate changed Fergusson's orders again, and told him to continue with his original task, the seizure of Indaw, but not before two of his columns had marched some way in response to his earlier order to go to Henu, and had to be recalled. On this the first, and as it proved, only, time that Wingate sought to fight a formation battle, he did not make a good fist of it. He also moved Fergusson's stronghold, Aberdeen, by about two miles, telling him that he would fly in 14th Brigade when the strip was ready. Fergusson asked to be allowed to rest his Brigade before advancing on Indaw; the long march and malaria were starting to take their toll. Wingate rightly refused, worried that the Japanese would reinforce Indaw. His fears were justified, because by 21 March they had a strong brigade there. If Wingate wanted Indaw so badly, in the hope of resuscitating the Tarzan plan, the question must be asked why give the task to a brigade that had to march over 400 miles to get there? Why did he not seize Indaw by *coup de main*, following the airborne principle of landing on, or right by, the objective; and do so before landings elsewhere had alerted the Japanese to what he might be up to? At Indaw, as elsewhere, he failed to use his airborne assets, gliders and Dakotas, properly because he was so obsessed with the long-range penetration techniques he had pioneered. He seemed unable to grasp that the tasks he was giving his Chindits were less and less the guerrilla-type operations of his first expedition, and more like 'conventional' airborne operations, albeit a long way behind enemy lines.

Fergusson, given to understand by Wingate that 14th Brigade would be available to support him, and furthermore that a whole division was to be flown into the Indaw area (the Tarzan plan), set off for Indaw. Once again Wingate had lied to him.

The attack on Indaw failed. There were two airfields there, Indaw West and Indaw East. Fergusson had an over-complicated plan involving an approach on four separate routes, which is fair enough, but he did not attack concentrated. Furthermore the two columns sent to attack Lonkin were still ten days away. For lack of time he failed to send reconnaissance ahead of his columns. The vagaries of communications technology at the time, in that terrain, meant that messages from column to column, if more than a few thousand yards apart, often had to be relayed through the base station in Assam. Command and control by the brigade commander of dispersed columns, which could communicate only when they stopped to erect aerials, was slow and laborious. A further complication, which a proper reconnaissance would have revealed, was a complete lack of water on the approaches to Indaw from the north. The force approaching Indaw needed about 3,000 gallons of water a day for men and mules. In an attempt to draw water from Indaw lake, Number 45 Column bumped the Japanese at the village of Thetkegyin, north of the lake. After a stiff fight, the Column was forced to withdraw. For some reason the Column's Reconnaissance Troop had been given the job of guarding the mules during the battle; surely the wrong place for them to be. After listening to the sounds of battle ahead, and despatching some Japanese who had infiltrated the mule harbour area, they moved up to join the Column. They passed through an area where some mules carrying flame-throwers had been hit by mortar fire. In the ensuing inferno, sapper explosives and other ammunition had exploded, and set the forest on fire. Trooper Aylen was one of the Reconnaissance Troop:

> The ground was blackened and still smouldering. Two dying mules lay in the middle of the track. As we reached the mules we were greeted by a burst of machine-gun fire. We dived for cover by the side of the track. One of our number had been killed outright. As we lay in cover trying to locate the enemy, grenades, mortar bombs, and ammunition which lay scattered about with the abandoned equipment kept exploding. Presently we received the order to move on again, the enemy machine-gunner had evidently cleared off. The next sight which greeted us was a row of dead Japs who were lying on the smouldering ground. I counted 26 bodies. Two of our own casualties lay beside a fallen log.

Having made contact with the column, the reconnaissance troop was ordered to form the rearguard for the withdrawal, after an engagement which had lasted all day.

> Our position from lack of water was becoming desperate. A man's normal requirements in the tropical heat was ten to twelve pints daily. We had had only one water bottle, about 2½ pints all day. We had also used a lot of ammunition. So next morning [after leaguering for the night], we were

given orders that if a Jap patrol appeared, we were not to fire, but to let it pass.

About an hour or so after sunrise, one of our section signified silence, and there creeping up the opposite side of the track was a Jap machine-gun patrol of about 30 men. A mule brayed, and the Japs turned and came back in our direction.

Aylen's section lay hidden in a small hollow, out of sight, but with no cover from fire. Another section lay on a ridge to their right. The Japanese began firing bursts into the hollow:

> We soon realised that they were listening for sound then firing in that direction, and that our only hope lay in keeping dead quiet. Had we returned the fire with our rifles, this would have merely revealed the position of the section, and the next few bursts would have disposed of us. Instead of returning fire, we stealthily fixed our bayonets, loosened the pins of our grenades, and awaited the expected bayonet attack. The Jap machine-gunner began calling out in English, 'Come up here Johnnie. Come on; I've got something for you.' This we answered with silence. As the sun rose higher in the sky, we felt the pangs of thirst more acutely.

This deadly game of cat and mouse went on until about midday, with three men of the reconnaissance troop killed, and Aylen's section sergeant hit five times in the foot and ankle. Then, perhaps because the Japanese had run out of ammunition, they withdrew. Aylen's section rejoined the column which had found some water by digging in a dried-out river bed.

> This was distributed among the men in spoonfuls. On the way back I passed some men of another troop. It was heartbreaking to see their gaunt and bearded faces, with eyes protruding from shrunken flesh. While our troop had been mostly static the previous day, these men had been running about in action.
>
> Early in the afternoon the Japs returned with reinforcements. But this time our Vickers was brought into action. Immediately an enemy machine-gun opened up, it was silenced by our Vickers, whose masterly note gave us a feeling of security. This engagement lasted about an hour, after which the enemy retired to lick his wounds. An officer went out to inspect the damage inflicted largely by our Vickers, and counted 26 Jap bodies. Three of our men had been killed on the Vickers. The fourth man to take over, Trooper

Flynn, was awarded the MM for his part in this action. Once more we had a respite, this time of longer duration.

More water was found, by digging deeper in the river bed. As the column moved to take up a better position, a running fight developed, but they reached their destination covered by fire from some troops within the column who had arrived ahead of them. A Japanese attack was repulsed by fire from the column's 3-inch mortars. The next morning the column pulled out to withdraw to Aberdeen, without further interference from the enemy. That night they found some water in a stream. After another thirsty and foodless day, they reached the banks of the river which they had left five days earlier. Aylen:

> Throughout the night I kept waking and taking gulps out of my water bottle. Out of curiosity I counted the number of mugfulls I consumed that evening. It came to 15 pints.

The 2nd Royal Leicesters nearly took Indaw East. Wilkinson, whose elbow had been shattered by a bullet in an earlier engagement at Auktaw, but refused evacuation, fought a model battle. As a skilled and experienced infantryman, he had modified the clumsy column system, so that mules and other impedimenta could be quickly leaguered up or marched separately, and the two rifle companies, plus all his mortars and Vickers machine-guns, concentrated. Thus the Leicesters could fight as a battalion, albeit a small one, with no third company. Wilkinson reached the edge of the airfield, and dug in by a water-filled chaung to wait the Japanese attack. For two days and three nights his steady veterans cut down the massed hordes of screaming Japanese as they obligingly mounted frontal attack after frontal attack. The close support of Cochran's aircraft was skilfully applied to increase the firepower of the Leicesters. Had 45 Column managed to join Wilkinson as planned, he might have succeeded in capturing the airfield. The Leicesters were ordered to withdraw by Fergusson, as part of the general pull back of 16th Brigade to Aberdeen, which, falsely as it turned out, was reported as being under attack by 1,000 Japanese.

By now Calvert had captured Mawlu to increase his elbow room at the White City, and both 14th Brigade and 3rd West African Brigade were starting to arrive at Aberdeen. Wingate's sixth brigade, 23rd Brigade, had been removed from his command to operate in a short-range penetration role on the rear of the Japanese attacking Imphal.

Meanwhile Morrisforce had started operating in the Kachin Hills and on 24 March had blown their first bridge near Sikaw, and damaged another in the same vicinity. Some days before, on their way to this task, Peter Cane's Number 94 Column had met:

> some traffic in the form of an elephant surmounted by two thoroughly scared employees of the Nippon Burma Trading Corporation. They were Burmese ex Bombay Burma Trading Corporation employees and obviously expected to have their heads cut off (how near they were to this I don't suppose they will ever know). We were turning over in our minds General Wingate's strict orders to treat the local inhabitants with leniency and mercy as opposed to the attractive idea of having an elephant to carry our packs, when another elephant complete with a load of humanity arrived, followed by yet a third bearing a sick but very beautiful Burmese girl. We could not slaughter them all, or indeed manage a baggage train of three elephants unless certain of their complete co-operation. Jumbo number 3 decided this for us by squealing loudly and charging wildly off into the jungle.

Cane decided to take the Burmese with them for a day's march, and give them misleading information about the column's destination before releasing them. They were released the next day. Later 94 Column picked up some Shans in one of the Kachin villages, sent to spy for the Japanese it transpired later. One of these was identified:

> as the Thugyi of Kwehaungdon on the Shweli, famous for his spy activities against the British during the 1942 retreat. Since then he had spent his time rounding up ex-Burifs [Burma Riflemen] and particularly survivors from Gen Wingate's expedition. We warned these Shans that an attempt to escape would result in their instant death. An attempt to get away by bolting downhill was made, but the Thugyi's servant was the only one to get away. The remainder were cut down or shot. I had heard that the Gurkhas were very quick in using the kukri. They were quick, but the kukris must have been blunt I fear, or they were very inexpert at finishing their victims off.

Dahforce had originally been destined for Templecombe in five gliders. Here Major Shan Lone, a Kachin member of Force 136, had been parachuted in to prepare for their reception. Herring had overflown Templecombe on 12 March to try to make visual contact with the ground party, but Shan Lone, thinking the two American light aircraft were enemy, had not responded to Herring's waving. Hence Dahforce was landed at Broadway in three Dakotas, but because of the lack of space, without the several thousand pounds of arms, ammunition and explosives, and five radio sets, that should have flown in with them.

On arrival at the Irrawaddy, the majority of the rations, and all the boats dropped to them, fell into the jungle and were not recovered. Herring's report:

> We crossed the Irrawaddy the following morning using a Kachin boat and several Shan boats which arrived on the scene. In spite of kind treatment and an adequate reward the Shans informed the enemy of our presence and of the composition of our party. Apparently both Lazumtang [one of Herring's Kachins] and myself had been recognised as having passed this way last year and prices were put on our heads by the Japanese.

The party lost their one radio when the mule carrying it stampeded into the jungle as they were crossing the Bhamo–Myitkyina road. Having gone ahead to meet Shan Lone on the night of 22/23 March, and able once more to signal to Force Headquarters using the SOE sets, Herring reported that:

> Main body Dahforce arrived Nahpaw evening 25th in somewhat exhausted condition and just in time for a battle the next night.

By now Wingate was dead. He had visited Broadway on 24 March, and called in at Imphal on his way to Lalaghat. The B-25 in which he was flying never arrived. A search party was sent out to investigate reports of a crashed aircraft, and found the wreckage of a B-25. By it was Wingate's Wolseley pattern solar helmet. There were no survivors. Tulloch wrote in his diary:

> God what enemies we have & now I shall have to fight them alone.
>
> It is sad to think that on this occasion I pressed him no less than four times not to take this particular trip and he nearly weakened and called it off, he himself had a strong premonition of disaster and before taking off went back to his office on purpose to speak to his stenographer and pat him on the back, telling him he had worked wonderfully well for him and apologising for having cursed him at times.

Rodney Tatchell:

I think we all felt that the carpet had been pulled from under our feet; the bottom had fallen out of the campaign. Nevertheless I must record the first reaction among the troops of my column, exhausted and demoralised as they were, was one of relief. Wingate was certainly a slave driver; he himself had limitless powers of endurance and expected similar qualities in those who served under him. Perhaps his successor, it was felt, might prove to be more human; or at least less superhuman.

Hugh Patterson learned of Wingate's death when he was flown into the White City to be briefed by Calvert on future demolition tasks outside the block:

Just before I left, George Massey, the Brigade Intelligence Officer, told me that Wingate was dead. It was a dreadful blow, and we felt that no one could replace him, and we would get orders from people who didn't know his plans and didn't understand his methods. Our fears were justified, and the Chindits really died with Wingate. Mountbatten sent us the following signal:

'General Wingate has been killed in the hour of his triumph. The Allies have lost one of the most forceful and dynamic personalities this war has produced. You have lost the finest and most inspiring leader a force could have wished for, and I have lost a personal friend and faithful supporter.

He has lit a torch. Together we must grasp it and carry it forward. Out of your gallant and hazardous expedition will grow the final reconquest of Burma and the ultimate defeat of Japan.

He was so proud of you. I know you will live up to his expectations.'

We set off with heavy hearts.

What almost every Chindit wanted to know was who was to be Wingate's successor. Slim later wrote:

It is an interesting sidelight on a strange personality that, after his death, three different officers each informed me that Wingate had told him that he was to be his successor should one be required. I have no doubt at all that they were speaking the truth.[12]

8

Operation Thursday:
The Second Chindit Expedition;
supporting 'Vinegar Joe'

When Wingate was reported missing, his deputy, Major General Symes, naturally immediately came forward from rear headquarters to main headquarters at Sylhet. The next day, before Wingate's death had been confirmed, Symes recorded in his diary:

25th March (Saturday)
Up 7.30 [a.m.]. Alison [second-in-command to Cochran] has aircraft out searching, as there is no news of Wingate or his machine. At about 10 [a.m.] news that a burnt-out aircraft has been spotted near Pabram which is half way between Silchar and Imphal in the hills slightly north of a direct course from Imphal to Sylhet. Search parties have gone out by every available means but there seems to be slender hope. Tulloch then rang up Army HQ [14th Army] to talk to Slim & returned to me saying that (1) as he was completely in the picture Gen Slim had said that he was to take command (2) that it was no reflection on me (3) that he (Tulloch) had suggested that as Lentaigne was more in Gen Wingate's mind than anyone else, he should be withdrawn from the field at the earliest possible time & take command of the operations (4) that Gen Slim had agreed.

An astounding message & an astonishing way of conveying it. I have known and sensed that Tulloch has been in opposition to me all the time & has made no effort to keep me in the picture. Reason I don't know other than he knew I disagreed with some – or most – of the administrative methods. Anyhow there was no object, profit or decorum in arguing so I summoned the Anson and flew to Comilla after lunch to see Slim. I saw him at 4 & asked him where I stood. He professed that he didn't know that I was in these parts before. He then told me that until he told Tulloch to take comd he didn't know I was there. *Then* Tulloch told him & he didn't alter it because he didn't know what my status was. He then told me that the suggestion re Lentaigne came from Tulloch (but hedged afterwards) & he had agreed because he hadn't thought about me at all.

I pointed out that by his action he had superseded me & that had created a difficult situation. He said that he hadn't meant that at all & had made the decision hurriedly & had not had time to think it out – in other words he [missing section here]

26th March (Sunday)

Up 7.30. Tulloch arrived during the morning but I held little converse with him. There was no object in so doing. After lunch Slim rang me up & asked me to see Giffard [General Sir George Giffard, C.-in-C. 11th Army Group, Slim's immediate superior and presumably visiting Slim at the time] so I went over to Army HQ. There I saw Giffard who was very pleasant (he isn't a Slim) & who said that Slim wanted to put in Lentaigne & that he, Giffard, had decided to back Slim as under the circumstances he didn't think I was sufficiently in the operational picture & Slim thought Lentaigne was. Well that was that. I told him that I didn't agree, that I was as much in the operational picture as anyone else, knew all the training & could do the job. The root trouble as it came out was that I had been appt Deputy Comd & had not been told that I should *not* succeed Wingate if anything happened. He had apparently discussed the eventuality with other people but had never told me. *Otherwise* I should never have remained. . . . Giffard told me that there was no job for me out here but that he would cable the CIGS (& show me the draft) explaining why I had become spare & asking that I be given a Div.

Tulloch claims in his diary that Wingate had told him that he, Tulloch, was to take over in the event of Wingate's death. But Tulloch, possibly recognizing that he was far from suitable, never having commanded anything more than a gunner troop, nominated Lentaigne. Symes went home but never got a divisional command. This honest, loyal and able soldier, who had been appointed to command 70th Division after proving himself in battle as a brigade commander, had fallen victim to Tulloch's machinations. Tulloch knew perfectly well that Symes had a low opinion of him and the quality of his staff work, and suspected that if Symes took command he would have been sacked. His duplicity did him no good, because Lentaigne, who was appointed to succeed Wingate, had little time for Tulloch either. Having been appointed Deputy Commander Special Force, and replaced as chief of staff by Colonel Henry Alexander, Tulloch was increasingly sidelined by Lentaigne. At one point Tulloch sent a long signal to Lentaigne which included the demand:

Either trust me or sack me.

And ended:

Insist on a vote of confidence or else appoint my successor forthwith. Continual messages don't argue, obey orders etc. are NOT repeat NOT justified. We are going flat out to produce best answer out of a BUGGERS MUDDLE.

Despite this, Tulloch loyally supported his new boss, as Lentaigne acknowledged when he, Tulloch, resigned after the second expedition. In a long letter to Alexander on 26 July 1944, Tulloch wrote:

I am going quietly (I have told the Gen [*sic*] to get rid of me as soon as it suits him, as I have obviously lost his confidence).

And in a letter to Slim:

Let it suffice to say that I feel that to remain would prove an embarrassment to Lentaigne who, I now find, was not an admirer of Wingate.

Tulloch subsequently held a series of second-rate staff jobs in India and Britain, followed by one major general's appointment as Commander Singapore Base District. He retired in 1957, and died in 1974. In 1965 he wrote to Otto Heilbrunn, with whom he had started to co-operate on a book about Wingate:

After Wingate's death I was made the scapegoat (being his only close friend) and was insulted, demoted, ignored and generally treated as so many of Wingate's enemies longed to treat him. I grew to hate these faceless people more than the Japanese and went through a period of frustration and fury which have left on me an indelible mark. Indeed, so far as Wingate is concerned my mind is, more than probably, not normal.

Morris was appointed as the next commander of 111th Brigade, but as he was far away with his own force on the Burma–China border, he did not actually take command until the Chindits had been withdrawn. That part of 111th Brigade west of the Irrawaddy (2nd King's Own, 1st Cameronians, and 30 Column of 3/4th Gurkha Rifles) would be commanded until the end of the Chindit campaign by Major 'Jack' Masters, Lentaigne's Brigade Major.

Before Wingate's death, General Kawabe, the Japanese commander of Burma Area Army, had ordered the commander of 24th Brigade, Major General Hyashi, to clear the railway line. He was given sufficient troops to bring his command up to the equivalent of a division. Hyashi had been responsible for repulsing Fergusson's attack on Indaw. On the night of 5/6 April he set out to eliminate the White City block, starting with a heavy bombardment. The fighting in and around the White City lasted for eleven days and nights.

William Merchant was a private in the Commando Company in 20 Column of 1st Battalion Lancashire Fusiliers in 77th Brigade, and spent a total of seven weeks in the block.

> The Japs shelled the block and then attacked at night. The wire was very thick, sometimes 100 yards thick, and usually at least 30 feet thick. We crawled in between and booby trapped it and mined it. There were hundreds of Jap bodies hanging on the wire. The Japs would shout at us, trying to draw our fire. They attacked using bangalore torpedoes. The guns and mortars fired at them. My job was to fire grenades from an EY rifle at the Japanese from a small slit trench at night. I used to spend all day priming grenades. One night I fired over 100 grenades. The Japs were very brave but stupid – they'd attack the same place every night. They came across the paddy banging and shouting. I was wounded in the back with shrapnel. My mate had been wounded earlier, so I was the odd one out. The Sergeant used to say, 'Wait until someone is killed, and you can muck in with his mate.' The trouble was most seemed to be killed or wounded in pairs because they shared the same slit trench.

The Japanese force investing the White City included a 150 mm mortar (nearly 6-inch calibre) which fired a 200 lb bomb. Merchant was in one of the patrols sent to find and destroy it:

> Patrolling to find the place from which the 6-inch mortar was firing, we went out through a zig-zag in the wire, which was closed up behind us. We found some weapon pits dug for the Japanese to wait in while forming up to attack. We booby trapped them. We found tins of fish, Japanese cigarettes, and photos of their wives and children. We took the fish and cigarettes, but didn't take the photos because if the Japs had taken us they would have killed us. We were told that if it looked as if we were to be taken

prisoner, we should put a grenade to our chests and kill ourselves. Because the Japanese would torture us.

In attacks the Japanese would throw themselves on the wire so others could run over them. On one occasion they got in and overran [positions] on OP hill, in the morning we went up and turfed them out, killed the lot of them from where they had occupied our bunkers. In the dark the jackals would come up and eat the bodies on the wire. The crows would come by day.

The following night, we were relieved by 3rd West African Bde who had landed at Aberdeen and marched in.

Sergeant Shaw was the newly appointed Vickers machine-gun platoon sergeant in Number 12 Column in 12th Battalion Nigeria Regiment, 3rd West African Brigade. In contrast to Indian Army battalions which had few British officers, and where all NCOs and many of the junior officers were Indian or Gurkha, West African battalions had no African officers, and were led by a large contingent of British officers and NCOs seconded (loaned) from the British Army. Shaw's parent regiment was the Royal Sussex into which he had fraudulently enlisted after being discharged from the Welsh Guards for persistent bad behaviour in the 1930s. His first sight of the White City was when he was sitting on his pack:

watching a line of men and mules going to and from a stream. British, Africans, Asiatics, with every white man bearded. Upon the bank stood a succinct notice:

DEAD JAPS IN THE WATER
ALL WATER MUST BE CHLORINATED

A European asked my name, and wearily I told him. 'Stand up when you speak to an officer.'

I stared, for like every other human in sight he was bare from the waist up. He should have tattooed pips, and I nearly said so. As I rose, another white man appeared and shook hands. It was my new CO, Colonel Hughes, and a gentleman.

In the 14th Army, whose soldiers called themselves 'The Forgotten Army', the 90,000 West and East Africans who fought in Burma are truly forgotten today. The West African battalions had been originally raised for ceremonial and policing duties in their home countries. When well led, with understanding and by example, they performed splendidly. Naturally acclimatized to heat and humidity, and with an in-built immunity to many tropical diseases, the Africans played a valuable part in the Burma campaign.

Shaw remembered the scene inside the block:

> Pitted with craters, and with all shrubs flattened, the few skeleton trees still upright were subnude [*sic*]. Everywhere lay the filth and litter of war – opened tins, empty boxes, cartridge cases by the thousand. Hastily dug latrines were mere holes. You'd find several nationalities squatting together and trying to converse, you waited and squatted over the first vacancy.
>
> Although completely surrounded by the frustrated enemy, there was no 'Mafeking' atmosphere, for supplies arrived nightly. Bofors guns, artillery, jeeps and mules were brought in. Sick and wounded were evacuated by light plane. In fact, far from besieging, the encircling Japanese were in frequent uproar when perambulating Chindits pounced from nowhere, took a smack, and withdrew at speed.
>
> Enmeshed in Dannert wire were bodies, grotesque and distorted. Within touching distance were naked Japanese – suicides who had crawled up to sever the wire. Behind them were others, but fully accoutred, their skulls grinning inside their steel helmets. I remained staring, for there was something puzzling about the remains. Captain Bence explained, 'Hellish stink, and we had to use flame-throwers. Couldn't recover them – the wire's full of boobys [traps].' Among the ghastly skeletons hopped a small brown bird with a sparrow-like cheep.

The move of part of 3rd West African and 16th Brigades to the White City, on Lentaigne's orders, allowed Calvert to operate in a mobile role outside the block, harassing the Japanese attackers in the rear and cutting their communications. Trooper Aylen in the Reconnaissance Troop of 45 Reconnaissance Regiment, originally in Fergusson's Brigade and now under Calvert:

> We now set about harassing the besiegers in a new way. Their supplies and reinforcements came from the south either by road or rail, and we were now to put a temporary block on both. A spot was chosen south of White City where the road ran within a mile or so of the railway line. The Gurkhas were to put a block on one and the [West] Africans on the other, while our column was to bivouac in between as a reserve.

Calvert changed the plan, and leaving the Africans and Gurkhas on the two blocks, Aylen's column was ordered to attack the Japanese outside the block to take the pressure off the defenders inside the White City. When the column bumped the Japanese positions:

Within a moment there was a steady rattle of machine-guns and the sound of bursting grenades in front.

Aylen's troop was given the task of protecting column HQ.

Presently column HQ was subjected to an intense mortar bombardment. The position had been given away by the sound of the mules. Many of the mules were killed or wounded. The Vickers gun had meanwhile been placed near our section position, manned by Trooper Flynn who had previously earned his MM in our first engagement about a fortnight previously. He took his gun into an open space where he was completely unprotected from enemy fire and poured fire into enemy as he spotted them moving round our flanks. Mortar bombs were bursting all round us. We could hear the Jap mortar officer shouting the order to fire, followed by the sound of the cartridge. About ten seconds later a bomb would burst in our vicinity. The number two on the Vickers was hit by a bomb that shattered a tree stump behind which he was lying. Presently the battle in our vicinity began in earnest. Enemy had penetrated to the right of where we lay, and a hail of fire poured into our positions. I felt a sharp pain in my knuckles and a slight tug at my chest. I looked up dreading to see our Vickers gunner slumped over his gun, but he was still in the same position pouring intermittent streams of fire into the enemy, regardless of the storm raging round him. The fire died down and presently our column commander and the Brigadier [Calvert] came round. They were coolly walking round the positions. I looked down to find my shirt soaked in blood from a gash in the chest.

Calvert ordered the column back in support of the road and rail blocks. They found that the West Africans had been busy during their absence. They had mined the road and ambushed seven Jap trucks loaded with troops and supplies wiping out nearly the whole convoy. Aylen:

They [the West Africans] gleefully pointed out the remains of the lorries and dead Japs, and we began to feel a real affection for our black comrades in arms.

Hugh Patterson, commanding 50 Column's commando platoon, spent two weeks ambushing parties of Japanese in the infantry role:

I had only one proper 'sapper' job to do – the blocking of the road and tracks south of the White City to prevent movement of motor transport to and from the block. During this operation I had a rather amusing experience, which was typical of our daily routine. I was with Pat Scofield (later killed at Mogaung) and Dick Sealy whose platoon was to cover our party while we laid mines and felled trees on the tracks. We were about to start one such job when we heard lorries on a road further to the east across the railway; strictly speaking out of our area. But we thought we would go overland and try to catch them.

We arrived at the road through very thick jungle. Pat Scofield and I eased our way out to find ourselves in the midst of a crown of Nips resting by the roadside who were as surprised as we were. We crawled back about ten yards, and all lay down. We could see the Japs without them seeing us. We hoped they would follow us in, but they just chattered excitedly and appeared to do nothing in particular. I couldn't see how many there were, but it was enough to give us a good battle, and our job was to blow up roads, so we signalled the Bren-gunner to stand by while Pat Scofield and I gave them some grenades. The Nips ran like hell when we stood up to throw, but we bagged four with the Bren and bombs.

Meanwhile Calvert had been attacking the Japanese at Mawlu about a mile south of the White City. On 17 April the Japanese made their last attack on the White City. Hyashi was killed leading the attack on a white horse. The Japanese penetrated the defences but were killed by machine-gun fire and in hand-to-hand fighting by the South Staffordshires and Hughes's West Africans.

Durant commanding the machine-gun platoon in the South Staffs 80 Column later wrote to his parents:

The Jap made his last big attack on the block when at dawn he put in a battalion attack against OP hill which was held only by a platoon [of South Staffs] under a rather precious 35-year-old peacetime decorator. From our hill we got a grandstand view of the attack and mowed down a number of Japs attacking from the north. By sheer weight of numbers they broke through the wire on to OP hill, and only a magnificent show by the platoon prevented the hill being overrun. Eventually David Scholey (the Platoon Commander) and 16 men, all that were left of his platoon, held off the attack until a counter-attack force of W. Africans arrived and cleared the hill. When the Jap withdrew one was left trapped in a trench on the hill and was being grenaded by about 20 men. Instead of surrendering he suddenly leapt out and with a rifle and bayonet charged the many people standing around. A West African dropped his rifle, picked up a wooden box containing twelve grenades and batted him over the head – end of 'suicide Joe'. David Scholey got the very deserved immediate award of the MC, but was tragically killed at Mogaung.

The successful defence of White City throughout had been greatly assisted by artillery flown into the Dakota strip alongside the railway, and by the bold and imaginative use of fighter-bombers sometimes close in to friendly troops, to break up attacks and hit Japanese troops forming up their gun positions and troop concentrations. A Japanese force of divisional strength had been defeated by seven battalions: four British, two West African and one Gurkha. While the Japanese withdrew to lick their wounds and reorganize, plans were being hatched by Slim which were to have a profound effect on the Chindits.

During the siege of the White City, 111th Brigade had destroyed enemy dumps near Pinbon. The fly-in of 14th Brigade had been completed and they had demolished the rail bridge at Bonchaung and other bridges on the line to Indaw, while the 2nd Leicesters had held a block on the Pinwe–Mawlu road south of the White City. By the end of April, 14th Brigade had destroyed twenty-one dumps of supplies and ammunition, including 15,000 gallons of fuel, and cut the railway in sixteen places. Indaw West was finally taken by 16th Brigade on 27 April. But the airfield, which was neither drained nor surfaced, was useless. Fergusson was ordered to abandon it after having destroyed as many installations in the area as possible.

On the Bhamo road, Morrisforce had demolished the bridge over the Taiping River, and damaged the Bhamo–Myitkyina road. He had been attacked by a Japanese battalion near Nalong on 1 May, which forced him to withdraw into the hills. Dahforce resumed operations in the Nahpaw area, successfully ambushing enemy columns on two occasions.

Lieutenant-Colonel Graves-Morris, commanding 2nd York & Lancasters in 14th Brigade, had, like the Commanding Officer of the 2nd Leicesters, organized his two columns so that they could amalgamate and fight as a battalion, or as separate 'Battle Groups', with what he calls the 'soft skin' element (the men and animals not needed in action) centralized. At Bonchaung (Bongyaung) he hoped to blow the bridge and the line while a Japanese troop train was actually crossing. From his report:

> Major Downward with 65 Column laid an ambush in the gorge south of Bonchaung station, and prepared an iron girder bridge of 40-foot span for demolition in front of the engine. The whole trap was set and 65 Column in position when Major Downward and Major Bruce walking up the line after inspecting the ambush noticed a short distance ahead two scouts of a Japanese patrol walking towards them, eyes down. Major Downward and Major Bruce took cover and each accounted for his man. The chances of surprise were now gone, and soon the remainder of the Jap patrol were seen cautiously working their way up the railway line. An over-ambitious sentry opened fire on them too early with his Bren gun, and so 65 Column's location became known and they were subjected to a night of sniping. The girder bridge was blown during the evening to ensure that some damage was done to the railway.

While the two columns of the York & Lancasters were completing their demolition tasks, Graves-Morris records:

> The soft skins of both columns were together some two miles east of the railway. During the afternoon a Japanese platoon had followed them to their jungle hideout, but fortunately owing to their characteristic habit of screaming and shouting before attacking gave warning of their approach.

Captain Paddy Dobney, the administrative officer with 84 Column, was in command of the 'soft skins':

> At the first sight of our frenzied opponents, all hell was let loose as our weapons caught them in the short open space to our front. Quite by chance the Japanese officer leading the attack, brandishing his sword, as was their custom, burst through the jungle screen exactly opposite me.

The first attack was beaten off. During the battle, according to Graves-Morris:

> Lieutenant Shuttleworth moved with a Bren gun from 13 Platoon [one of the two guarding the area]. Unfortunately the gun jammed during the next Japanese attack and Lieutenant Shuttleworth was killed outright. He was the youngest officer with the column.

The Japanese remained circling round the perimeter for another hour and a half, sniping from trees, until the return of the Battle Groups from the demolition of the bridge.

Major Shiell [who had been sent ahead with the wounded] and his small escort encountered a small party of Japs in approaching the bivouac area and engaged them. The timely action of Lieutenant Johnston and 65 Recce Platoon who quickly killed three Japs eased the situation and enabled the party to reach the questionable security of the night bivouac. The light failed soon after the arrival of the Battle Groups, so there was little opportunity of elaborate defensive arrangements. We lay in uneasy lines of bodies on the slope of the hillside, with our wounded in the centre. We had little water and the needs of the wounded were acute. The animals had not drunk for 24 hours, and the men had fought a battle, and had no refill for the same period. There could be no cooking, and the evening meal was cold and glum. The elation of our success was tempered by our casualties.

As Graves-Morris records, with the onset of day:

The next problem was the evacuation of the wounded, and the map showed there were suitable paddy fields on the banks of the [River] Meza which could be converted into a landing strip for light planes. This entailed a gruelling climb up a steep gradient with a merciless sun beating down through the leafless plane trees and a choking dust. The casualties on improvised stretchers had to be manhandled by men already so weighed down by equipment that additional stretchers had to be made to carry their packs by even more men. It took nearly a full platoon to carry one casualty, as the stretcher-bearers needed frequent relief. Many of the men had now not drawn water for over 24 hours, and only undrinkable blackish water appeared from the holes dug in a chaung at the midday halt. However, it was known that the columns were marching to water, and they struggled on in the parching dusty heat, finally to be rewarded with a bivouac by a river. The animals went mad at the sight of water, their thirst seemed unsatiable, and they had to be dragged away for fear this sudden immoderate drinking would have ill-effects.

By 23 April Graves-Morris's columns were moving towards Indaw, in common with the other columns of 14th Brigade. He had been told that:

The columns were not to become committed to a major action, nor to risk the incurrence of undue casualties. The Japanese dumps and installations were to be destroyed if possible, but not if the operation jeopardised the safety of the future operations of the columns.

There are those who believe that by not concentrating 14th Brigade and smashing the Japanese who were reorganizing for another attempt on the White City, an opportunity was lost to alter the balance of forces in the Railway Valley. Calvert had since late 1943 been advocating training and employing LRP brigades to fight concentrated, using their fighting power to destroy the enemy, rather than indulging in hit and run tactics. He wrote a paper to this effect on 18 November 1943, and sent it to Headquarters Special Force. Calvert trained his Brigade 'how to reform from columns into a brigade and fight as normal battalions'. There is no evidence that his ideas were adopted to this extent by any other brigade, although it seems that Wingate was also thinking along these lines at the time of his death; too late, the guerrilla legacy was still strong in the Chindits. After all, they had spent months practising it in training, and without some direction from the top it was too much to ask that they abandon these tactics overnight.

Morrisforce initially achieved some notable successes on the Bhamo Road, used by the Japanese to supply their forces opposing Stilwell. Major Peter Cane commanding 94 Column in Morrisforce described the operations around Nalong on the Bhamo Road in his report:

> Nalong was the centre of a road construction company, and also a staging camp for motor transport convoys, including forage collection on a large scale. 49 Column was to attack from the north, while we were to attack from the south. This was the start of operations which might have and indeed should have resulted in the strangling of Myitkyina's only remaining lifeline; unfortunately the operations ended in a bitterly disappointing failure.

Nalong is situated where the Bhamo Road crosses the Mole Chaung. From the 2,900-foot-high Hpumpyen–Loimawk Ridge it was possible to see the whole Nalong basin, with four villages including Nalong itself. Peter Cane:

> These were all Jap staging camps, and during our stay we saw them house over 1,500 Japs and 300 trucks. They were mostly dispersed under the many trees and in and around the villages. Bombing or strafing would have

Field Marshal Sir Archibald Wavell (*centre*), then C.-in-C. India, talking to a Chindit officer before the First Chindit Expedition, with to his left Major Bernard Fergusson, commander Number 5 Column. Fergusson's cap badge has been obscured by the censor. (IND 2088)

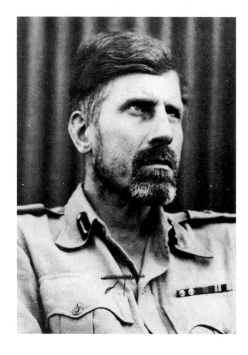

Major-General Orde Wingate taken just before his death. (HU 71286)

Wingate in sun
helmet with Colonel
Frank Merrill of
Merrill's Marauders,
and Lieutenant
Colonel Scott.
(MH 7864)

Wingate briefing
aircrew of Number 1
Air Commando
USAAF. Wingate's
Adc Captain George
Borrow holds up the
map on the left.
On Wingate's left
with arms folded
and cap askew, is
Colonel Cochran.
(MH 7877)

A mule being
loaded into a
Dakota C-47.
(EA 20831)

A sick man being loaded into an L-5 light aircraft in Burma. (SF 7947)

Two British soldiers and a Gurkha being evacuated from Burma. (HU 67284)

Chindits of 54 Column, 16th Infantry Brigade, carrying a wounded man on a stretcher. (KY 481781)

L-5 on an airstrip
in Burma.
(SE 7936)

Chindits on the
march in Burma.
(SF 7929)

Chindits brewing up.
(IND 2289)

Brigadier Mike Calvert (nearest camera) giving orders to Lieutenant-Colonel Shaw in Mogaung. Major Lumley with carbine under his arm. (MH 7287)

Major-General 'Joe' Lentaigne. (IND 3426)

Smoke rising after Stukas attack Leros. (HU 71385)

Members of 2 SAS who arrived in Termoli after the port had been captured by 1 SRS, and numbers 3 and 40 (RM) Commando. In front, *left to right*: Major 'Sandy' Scratchley, and Captain Roy Farran with a German Schmeisser sub-machine-gun. The censor has blacked out their badges. (E 26182)

Ashley Greenwood dressed as a Turkish peasant after his escape from Leros. (HU 25273)

Corporal Horner after promotion to Sergeant. (SR 325)

SB Squadron loading a caique before a raid in the Aegean. (E 29103)

Two SB Squadron soldiers preparing to land on the Simi raid. (E 29040)

Left to right: Major the Earl Jellicoe, Captain Chevilier, and a Greek officer on board the SB Squadron Headquarters boat *Tewfik*. (HU 71413)

An MTB and caiques in a wooded cove in the Aegean. (HU 71403)

MV *La Palma*, one of the two vessels of the LRDG's private navy in Bari. (HU 25268)

destroyed any vehicles there, and there did not seem to be enough slit trenches to hold more than half the personnel.

It seemed an ideal place for two columns to operate, the plan being to let a large convoy into Nalong, block the road north and south, and call for direct air support. This wonderful opportunity occurred twice, and is the object of considerable recrimination in that we were not permitted to take advantage of it.

On 22 April, the first attack on Nalong took place, with air support. Cane:

Practically the entire garrison of Nalong had fled into the jungle and there was minimum opposition.

At this stage 49 Column was sent off to liaise with Dahforce, while 94 Column having burnt the remaining villages was to retire to the Hpumpyen feature to await the return of 49, and a repeat performance. Peter Cane:

Next day we watched the Nips swarming round the bridge, which had been completely burned, and trying to rebuild it with more than one elephant to help. Watching these Nips was more than we could bear, and while recces on the road to the south were seeking demolition points, we planned to use Blackburn's support weapons with a rifle covering force to tease the 'sons of Nippon'.

A highly successful engagement by the column's two Vickers machine-guns and two 3-inch mortars ensued. The enemy were chased around Nalong by fire, and their counter-attack was stopped in the same way. However, when the Japanese brought up 75 mm guns, and with the column's guns and mortars out of ammunition, Cane withdrew to Hpumpyen.

He then had a frustrating time when his requests for air action against road convoys were refused. Having decided on demolition instead, in an attempt to block the road, 94 Column was denied sufficient explosive to make a good job of it, and the enemy were still seen crossing the Mole Chaung, probably fording it, for the bridge had not been repaired. Peter Cane:

We blew what we had prepared and called for air strafing. This demand was acknowledged and we were bitterly disappointed when nothing came.

But things were to get worse; on the night of the 21st we called again in no uncertain language for air action and the support of another column. As these messages were going off, more headlights were seen approaching Nalong and we counted 183 new motor transport arriving. This made 300 trucks in the Nalong basin, and we continued to tell the world, who appeared to be fighting against us, what wonderful opportunities were being missed.

Cane's frustrations were to continue. Headquarters Special Force (the Chindit HQ in Assam), for some reason consistently refused the air support that might have made all the difference to Morrisforce's operations. As fast as Cane blew sections of road, the Japanese, who had brought up a bulldozer, filled in the gaps. In one place:

> considering that 35 to 40 yards of road had been dropped down the hillside, they had made a wonderful job of it; they had blasted and bulldozed a completely new stretch of road out of the hill, and covered the surface with sleepers bound with wire. We threw ourselves into destroying this as soon as we could. The sleepers became a bonfire; we dug more explosive into the newly bulldozed road. We were severely handicapped by lack of earth augurs and camouflet, for which we had continually asked, but no supplies other than [by] an occasional single-engined aircraft were forthcoming.

Eventually the Japanese brought up reinforcements and, heavily outnumbered, Cane was forced to withdraw. But he did have the satisfaction of hearing the Japanese attempting to outflank him, running into the pangyi fields that his column had planted for just that eventuality.

Herring's Dahforce, which was busily engaged in harassing the Japanese and distracting them from concentrating on Morrisforce, was also having its problems with Special Force Headquarters not providing the support requested. The situation was not helped because Herring and Morris did not see eye to eye on a number of important matters. Herring wrote about him later:

> He really upset Dahforce when he once referred to them as labourers within the context of preparing a landing strip. Tact was not his strong point.

Up to now Stilwell had shown little interest in Morrisforce and Dahforce, both carrying out operations aimed at assisting his advance on Myitkyina, however indirectly in the latter case. Now Slim, on

Mountbatten's orders, directed that the whole Chindit effort, less 23rd Brigade, was to concentrate on assisting Stilwell to capture the objectives given him by the combined United States and British Chiefs of Staff: Mogaung, Myitkyina and open the road to China. As a result Lentaigne directed that Aberdeen, the White City and Broadway would be abandoned. Masters's 111th Brigade had already been ordered to establish a block, Blackpool, on the road and railway between Hopin and Pinbaw. Because this was close to Stilwell's area of operations, it would remain and be reinforced by 3/9th Gurkha Rifles and 1st King's (Liverpool) Regiment from 77th Brigade; the latter to be the floater battalion for 111th Brigade. In addition 77th Brigade and 3rd West African Brigade would march north to protect Blackpool from the east and west respectively. The 14th Brigade was to take over White City, close it down, and move north to assist in the protection of Blackpool. Fergusson's 16th Brigade was to be flown out. The Aberdeen garrison, 6th Nigerian Regiment, was to march to join 111th Brigade.

During his march north, Calvert reorganized his Brigade, as he later recorded in his report, by far the best and most perceptive of any produced by the Chindit brigades:

Reorganisation of the Colns [sic] into Battalions

I had found from our experience at and around the Block [White City] the men tended to fight better as a bn [battalion] than as a coln [column]. This was natural as it was ingrained in all that a 200-year-old bn could never utterly fail, whereas officers and men had not so much faith in a hybrid coln denoted by a number.... We therefore reorganised ... into a more normal battalion organisation of 3 coys of 3 platoons of 3 sections plus a support coy. This gave bn commanders great power of manoeuvre, and gave the men, especially the reinforcements, greater knowledge and confidence in what they were doing.... I feel, now, that the time has come when the coln, which was organised for a special raiding purpose, should cease to exist as an entity.

Slim had taken 23rd Brigade away from Special Force command, to operate against the rear of Japanese 15th Army on the Chindwin front attacking Imphal and Kohima. This brigade never joined their fellow Chindits in north Burma. Instead it was used very effectively against the lines of communication of Japanese 31st Division investing Kohima. The effect on Japanese morale, when their supply columns of mules found themselves being ambushed in what they thought was 'friendly' country, was considerable. One military historian has commented: 'This, rather than the static defence of "Strongholds", was much nearer the sort of activity which Wingate had envisaged when he created the Special Force.'[1]

Wingate had always maintained that, because of the strain of operating behind the lines, LRP brigades should be evacuated after ninety days. Fergusson's Brigade had been in since 5 February, and were out not long after the ninety-day deadline. Other brigades were to stay a great deal longer than that. But already many of the Chindits in brigades who had flown into Burma well after 16th Brigade were very tired, as William Merchant recalls:

By now [early May] I was ill with malaria, they gave me twenty mepacrine tablets. I was delirious. They thought I might have cerebral malaria. The Brigade was going to take Mogaung, but I wasn't fit to march. They took me to a slit trench by the strip to fly me out to Aberdeen, and on from there to India. Every time the pilot tried to take off, the Japs shelled the strip. So they carried me, a sergeant who had lost both legs, and a West Indian without an arm, back to the slit trench. Eventually, they left us in the plane, and when there was a lull, the American pilot who returned to the trench dashed out, and took off. When we landed at Aberdeen, it was bombed by nine Japanese bombers. They left me, because I couldn't run for cover. Then I was put in a tent. The next day I was flown out to Sylhet. I was there for about a week, and given liquid quinine. I weighed just under 8 stone.

Hugh Patterson:

Our fate was still undecided, but we knew we were to march north-east. Most of us were very tired, worn down with malaria, and feeling the strain – especially the officers. When we started retracing our steps to Broadway, there is no doubt we were all hoping we would be flown out of there. The brigade halted about 12 miles west of Broadway on May 6th and waited to learn their fate from General Lentaigne, who had flown in to give Mike Calvert his orders.

On 5th May I felt the malaria coming on again and developed a sharp pain in the knee, which got so bad that I could hardly walk. The brigade Senior Medical Officer had a look and ordered me out.

On 8th May I left the column with a few other sick and sorry and hobbled to Broadway. It was only twelve miles, but it is not a march I care to remember. I did not like leaving my platoon, but as it turned out, I should have been a serious drag on them if I had stayed, since the knee developed septic arthritis, immobilising me completely.

Trooper Aylen was among those flown out of Broadway because his chest wound prevented him from carrying a pack:

> When our plane landed at Sylhet we knew that all our troubles were over. We had the luxury of spring beds and white sheets, and best of all, the realisation that we could now relax in safety without having to be on the alert for every sight and sound around us.

Captain Rodney Tatchell of 21 Column in 16th Brigade:

> At last we had our orders to emplane. What bliss it was to lie on a cold metal floor and to know that every few minutes we were covering what would have been several days' march – but in the reverse direction, back to India. At Comilla in East Bengal [now Bangladesh], I was given the distressing news that the plane carrying the rest of my platoon had not reached Imphal and nothing was known of its fate.

Everybody in the Chindits suffered from malaria at some time. Reports and accounts mention it time after time. The majority with benign malaria soldiered on, and had usually recovered within about seven days. It was commonplace for men with high temperatures to take part in attacks, patrols and other duties. Evacuation was reserved for acute cases, or those with cerebral malaria, if they had not died first. Sometimes men with a severe dose of malaria had to be left while a column completed its task, as happened to ten men from a 77th Brigade column operating outside the White City. They were left hidden, awaiting a relief party from the stronghold. The next evening a Japanese patrol found them.

> The soldiers had five minutes bayonet practice before their supper. Only one man escaped and when he staggered into the Namaan observation post, his reason had nearly gone. Somehow he had hidden from sight under a comrade's dead body and had managed to lie still for a night and the best part of a day, while Japanese soldiers had laughed round their fires, and sentries had strolled among the dead.[2]

Almost the last that Sergeant Shaw saw of the White City as he marched out was:

a note pinned to a sandbag by some humorist. It was an advertisement from an old newspaper:

WHITE CITY STADIUM, GREYHOUND RACING TONIGHT

From Mawlu, Graves-Morris watched the final evacuation of the White City with 84 Column which was responsible for protecting the southern approaches to the block:

> There was considerable [Allied] air activity during the day, and it was of great interest to watch the direct air support trying to tempt the Japanese AA gun in the neighbourhood to open up so that it could be spotted and destroyed [so that it would not threaten the fly-out that night].
>
> It will remain a mystery why the Japanese took no steps to interfere with the air evacuation of the White City. A theory is that they interpreted the activity as reinforcements being flown in, and satisfied themselves by continuing their plans for a large-scale attack a few days later.
>
> It was an eerie night. The sight of Dakotas landing and taking off in the moonlight was fascinating, and there was always the expectancy that at any moment a different sound would interrupt, but eventually in the peace of a summer's night, troops, 25-pounder guns, and a quantity of other weapons and stores were ferried back to India. A heavily mined and booby-trapped fortress was left for the inquisitive Jap to investigate. On the morning of 10 May the codeword 'Strawberry' was received indicating that the evacuation had been successfully completed.

Graves-Morris along with the rest of 14th Brigade marched north to assist in the establishment of the Blackpool block. Now began the most testing time for the Chindits, operating under Stilwell's direct command. His unconcealed loathing of the 'effete Limeys', whose fighting qualities he denigrated, filtered down to his incompetent staff. They were examples of the worst type of staff officer, totally unsympathetic to the problems of the troops, bullying pushers of paper, who appeared to be unable to read a map. Major J. F. F. Barnes, a British liaison officer with Stilwell in a secret report on 26 July 1944, commented that the staff work in his headquarters:

> compared with the staff work of an equivalent British formation, was not good. There was a lamentable lack of co-ordination between the various branches of the staff who seemed to work very much in water-tight compartments. . . .

Their method of issuing orders was, to me, queer. On one occasion it was decided that a Chinese battalion should put in an attack. This order was transmitted to the American officer with the Chinese by telephone by the equivalent of a GSO 1 (Operations) in the following manner. 'Listen Wilkie, the heat's on, has that percolated?'

Stilwell and his staff shared the view of the majority of their countrymen at that time: any problem could be solved by throwing men and *matériel* at it, regardless of the cost. Only two decades later, in Vietnam, would they learn that this was not always the right answer.

When the Japanese discovered that the White City had been abandoned, the newly arrived 53rd Division was placed under command of Lieutenant General Honda's 33rd Army, and sent north up the railway to pursue the Chindit columns towards Blackpool, and destroy the block.

Wingate preached that 'strongholds' should be sited in inaccessible terrain, well away from Japanese lines of communication, so the enemy would find it difficult to move strong forces to eliminate them, whereas the defenders would be supplied by air. Whether the Japanese would actually bother to attack a 'stronghold', unless it posed a threat, was another matter, one which was never put to the test. The White City was a 'block' not a 'stronghold', because it sat right on the road and railway and impeded the Japanese line of communication. They had to attack it, even though it did not completely sever their communications because they could still use the River Irrawaddy. Blackpool was also a block, but nothing like as strongly constructed as the White City with its belts of barbed wire up to thirty yards deep, mines and booby traps, and bunkers roofed with railway sleepers. Although it covered part of the railway by artillery fire, it could not dominate the road; but the Japanese could use the railway and road to bring up their force from the south.

To begin with the attacks on Blackpool were sporadic, because the Japanese II/146th Battalion was the only enemy in the vicinity. But, because the 'floater' columns had not arrived yet, the Japanese were able to reconnoitre the approaches and establish artillery OPs at their leisure. 'Jack' Masters, commanding 111th Brigade, wrote to his ex boss, Lentaigne, regularly. In the chatty style of his letters one can detect the close and trusting relationship that often exists between a brigade commander and his brigade major. In his letter of 13 May 1944, he wrote:

The Japs have been behaving oddly. They march up the road and round the edge of it [the block].

After the Japanese had started ranging the block using artillery:

I made the tactical error of warning the DC pilots though, and they all made shocking landings. Two crashed – one burst into flames immediately. Shortly after the other over-ran [shot] the strip. A Jap raiding party of 4 men slipped through and burnt the second crashed DC with grenades. . . . There was some musketry fire as these buggers, trying to get away, ran into 81 [Column], but very little alarm. Work only stopped for 5 minutes in all. The DC pilots on the ground fairly leaped to it, and as the burning DC had burnt out the strip illumination, there was no light. So one [further] DC crashed off into the darkness and burst his wing, and is now sitting here. . . .

Thank you very much for your letter of 12 May which was salvaged from the flames – also the cigarettes which mean more to me in this static role than much fine gold.

As units of Major General Takeda's Japanese 53rd Division arrived and were pitched into the fight, 'the battle gathered momentum', in the words of 'Jack' Masters, 'like a flywheel, a noisy flywheel worked by a rackety motor'.[3] Lieutenant-Colonel Desmond Whyte RAMC was the SMO of 111th Brigade:

We had to block the railway, and hold at all costs, as ordered by Stilwell. We dug in to defend the high ground. We had an air drop of barbed wire. We began to prepare an airstrip 1,500 feet long outside the wire for Dakotas. The enemy attacked on the second night in the north. There was bloody fighting. At dawn the wire was littered with Japanese dead. That day it was hot, and the corpses burst as they putrefied; the stench and the myriads of flies. They attacked in the same place the next night and took hundreds of casualties. They broke through in a few places. We sustained casualties, but very light. They came back a third time the next night, same again. We hadn't slept. My dressing station was beginning to fill up. Then three days' silence. The Americans with a light bulldozer flown in on first plane flattened strip. Dakotas came in every night. We had strong searchlights. There were some nasty accidents, but most planes got in with reinforcements, ammunition. We got four 25-pounders in.

The enemy were still letting us alone. We managed to get in two AA guns, the enemy flew 15 planes over and dropped bombs with heavy casualties. Then silence. Then we heard the Japanese 100 and 105 mm guns ranging on us. The Americans flew over to try to find them without success. The Japanese began to plaster us. We hadn't sufficient strength to attack the guns. The shelling buried men alive. I and my doctors, now six, because the whole brigade was there, operated in the mud. The monsoon had started. Mules stampeded in the thunderstorms. There was very little to eat. The stench of the bodies on the wire did not improve things. The enemy turned his AA guns on the Dakotas. They flew off never to appear again. We were trapped. We knew the end could not be far off. The enemy had learned his lesson, he came in from the south. A creeping barrage came across us. We knew what it meant, he would come in behind it.

On 20 May the garrison was reinforced by 3/9th Gurkha Rifles, commanded by Lieutenant-Colonel Alec Harper, an officer of the Deccan Horse. He had volunteered for the Chindits and had been Cane's second in command on the Bhamo Road with Morrisforce. When the commanding officer of 3/9th Gurkha Rifles fell sick at Broadway and was evacuated, Harper replaced him. As the Broadway garrison 3/9th Gurkhas had been spared most of the long marches endured by other Chindit battalions, they were fit, fresh and at full strength. Harper considered that many Chindits were already debilitated by the training when they entered Burma. As late additions to the Special Force, 3/9th Gurkha Rifles had been spared much of this training, so had Harper. In an interesting aside on the disadvantages of overtraining, Harper wrote:

I missed all the training, joining just before the move to Assam. I think I was fitter than many who had undergone the training!

His method of moving to join 111th Brigade showed a certain cavalry panache:

We marched across the open paddy fields in open formation, me on a white pony as I had a violent fever. We saw no Japs and met a British patrol half way over. The Japs must have withdrawn to re-group after their first attack.

The monsoon had now arrived, and slowed up the approach of 14th Brigade; Graves-Morris describing one section of the march:

The columns had to climb from 600 feet to 3,400 feet in a distance of 12 miles and the track became very muddy and slippery. There were incessant small chaungs to cross, and the two sides became oozing quagmires through which the muleteers gallantly struggled, coaxing their animals and wrestling with the loads. On 16 May the going became so bad that some mules and their loads went rolling down the slopes, and to prevent serious loss, steps revetted with stakes and logs had to be cut to provide footing.

For the remainder of the Chindit campaign, the elements became at times a worse enemy than the Japanese; Graves-Morris:

For the next fourteen weeks, men and animals were to struggle on through the monsoon in the face of increased sickness and weakness from lack of food. The tearful cry of the Mule Officer, 'Oh my God, they must get us out now', as he saw his wretched charges slipping and falling on the muddy slopes was to become a hollow mockery in the days to come as conditions steadily worsened. He was to see his precious mules weaken and die of exhaustion, flounder to their bellies in mud and swamp to be dispatched mercifully by an officer's rifle as they pitifully and gamely tried to struggle up. We were all to see once robust men waste away to skin and bone, and to fall exhausted from sickness and weariness, to die before they could be evacuated. We were all to see the devastating effect of continuous rain, jungle gloom, mud, and toiling back-breaking marches was to have on men's minds, as many cheerful normal men, became depraved [sic], collapsed, and asked to be left to die, or even hastened their end by their own hands.

The fighting at Blackpool, often at close quarters, with tommy-gun, bomb, Bren, rifle and bayonet continued for seventeen days. The Japanese overran key positions, 111th Brigade's counter-attacks were thrown back, or failed to hold the positions retaken with so much effort. Lieutenant Rhodes-James, the cypher officer at 111th Brigade Headquarters, described one counter-attack:

Sergeant Donald of the Cameronians took a platoon and charged the slope. It was a magnificent effort. Donald was wounded but he carried on, and the Japs were swept off the top. He reported back to our commander trembling all over. 'I'm not a wee bit afraid, Sir. I'm just shivering with excitement.' That effort earned him a DCM. But it was impossible to hold the position in the face of the Jap mortar fire, and the gallant platoon was forced to withdraw.

The chaplain in Brigade Headquarters, the Reverend Miller, remembered the utter exhaustion of the troops:

The poor chaps were so utterly worn out and exhausted that they could hardly walk, let alone run. It was a pitiful sight. The whole block was a sea of mud, and steps revetted into the hillside had long since collapsed. The only way to get from place to place was to grip an overhanging branch or piece of bamboo in the hopes it would hold firm.

Heavy Japanese flak and the monsoon combined to prevent the block from being resupplied by air. Help from the other columns was still some way off. Time after time the Japanese overran vital ground, and ejecting them became progressively more difficult with the dwindling garrison. Masters had allocated cricket terminology to much of key terrain in and around his block, and used it in a letter written afterwards to Lentaigne on 28 May 1944, including a diagram:

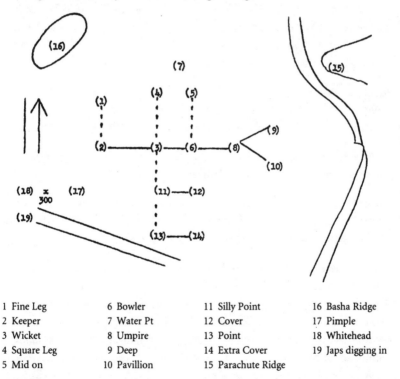

1 Fine Leg	6 Bowler	11 Silly Point	16 Basha Ridge
2 Keeper	7 Water Pt	12 Cover	17 Pimple
3 Wicket	8 Umpire	13 Point	18 Whitehead
4 Square Leg	9 Deep	14 Extra Cover	19 Japs digging in
5 Mid on	10 Pavillion	15 Parachute Ridge	

I organised a counter-attack with 2 pls [platoons] with mortar and MMG support. No more than 2 pls could be manoeuvred in the restricted and steep ground.

These pls, led PERSONALLY by Lt-Col Scott and Lt-Col Thompson were held up by enemy LMGs in SILLY POINT and by mortar and arty [artillery].

Enemy arty which was extremely well handled continued to cause severe casualties.

The position at about 07.30 hours was that the enemy was in possession of SILLY POINT (11), while my counter-attack was held up some 40 yards north of it. Further enemy parties were working down towards (12), had overrun (13), and were working down on (14). (1) and (2) remained under heavy and accurate fire. The whole ridge from KEEPER–UMPIRE was being heavily shelled. All remaining elements were holding this line including Bde HQ, engineers, etc.

At 08.00 hours I decided that as I could no longer receive rations or ammunition and as my ammunition was getting low and rations were already out, my only hope was another counter-attack to clear my southern perimeter. I decided against this course, considering the operation had no hope of success, and at 08.00 hours ordered withdrawal of all sick, Bde HQ and reserve elements of all columns. I ordered the remains of 90 Column and field artillery who had been holding their positions in the face of heavy infantry and artillery attacks to withdraw.

Masters' plan was to withdraw to Mokso Sakkan, east of Lake Indawgyi, using the classic tactic of leapfrogging the battalions back through a series of lay-back positions. Desmond Whyte:

I was with my wounded. The blind were tied to someone who could see. Those we couldn't get out we left behind.

Masters gave orders that those too badly wounded to move were to be shot; those who were still conscious being given a shot of morphia first. The withdrawal did not go to plan; Alec Harper:

On Jack Masters' instructions I went down to the 'back gate', told one company commander where to put his lay-back, and told the mule drivers to saddle up all they could and follow along. They did not have time to bring many. We were under shellfire. I also showed the same company commander the route out, perfectly simple, straight up the chaung, quite a good track. I then went back to bring out the others. Unfortunately when the leading company came out, some idiot on the brigade staff misdirected them with a totally unnecessary detour along the sides of the hills south-west of the chaung. A Jap section fired on the retreating column with an LMG causing more confusion and a few casualties. It was here that one of my company commanders had to shoot one of his men who had his jaw blown off.

Masters was the last to leave his block, with Harper and his Battalion HQ:

While the rest of the Brigade went off on this unplanned detour, Jack and I followed up the right road [*sic*], only to find no one there. I then made a little rearguard with my Battalion HQ where the track crossed the chaung. We were not followed up. I did catch a Gurkha who was supporting (nearly carrying) a British sergeant, and getting left behind in the process, leave his charge on the ground when he thought no one was looking. He went back for the sergeant, who looked much relieved, and the Gurkha very shame-faced. A bit further on, a mile perhaps, the Brigade rejoined the right track after its wanderings. Were Jack and I relieved to see them!

From then on the leapfrogging tactics worked. The Japanese did not follow up 111th Brigade; perhaps General Takeda was just glad to see them go. They did however deal with any wounded they found alive in their usual way; Hogan:

I was in the rearguard. We could hear the wounded being bayoneted by the Japs, asking to be killed; we could hear the screams.

Desmond Whyte remembers that the withdrawal to Mokso Sakkan took three days of:

nightmare dragging through the mud. The nearest troops were by Indawgyi Lake. The RAF brought in a Sunderland flying boat [two] in several sorties to take out the wounded and sick.

Before 111th Brigade arrived they were delighted to be met by 7th Nigerian Regiment. Miller:

When a mule slipped over the Khud-side, it was a giant of a West African who picked it up and set it down on the path again. When there were steps to be hewn out of the steep and slippery mountainside, the West African was there. When the sick and wounded were so exhausted that they could only sink down by the track, it was the West African who bore them to safety on his wide strong shoulders. When men were dying from hunger, a West African would be the first to share his own rations. As far as I know no one has sung their praise in this campaign. But their unwearied, unselfish and Christ-like service will not be forgotten by the men who came to rely on them.

The action at Blackpool had cost 111th Brigade 70 killed, 50 wounded and 100 missing. 'Jack' Masters concluded his letter of 28 May to Lentaigne:

> I much regret I was unable to carry out your orders to hold Blackpool until further orders. My failure was due in the [first] instance to the desertion of SILLY POINT by its garrison, but I feel that its fall could not have been long delayed in view of:
>
> (1) No floaters.
> (2) No food.
> (3) No ammunition.
> (4) No DAS [Direct Air Support – air attacks on enemy].
> (5) Considerable casualties and no replacements.

In the north, to Stilwell's delight, Merrill's Marauders had seized Myitkyina South Airfield. Stilwell, believing that the town was held by only 350 Japanese, immediately made plans to fly his Chinese troops in and capture the town. In fact, Myitkyina was held by 3,500 Japanese, and subsequently reinforced with another 500. Stilwell refused the offer of the fresh, full-strength 36th Indian Infantry Division, waiting to his north to support him. He wanted the honour of capturing Myitkyina to go solely to his Chinese–American force. He was, however, very happy to use the Chindits to further this aim; presumably on the basis that their part in the enterprise could more easily be concealed from the cloud of American war correspondents that inhabited his headquarters. So he ordered the Chindits to concentrate their efforts on capturing Mogaung, and assisting with the capture of Myitkyina, while retaining their block on the railway valley. He was livid when he learned that Blackpool had been abandoned without his permission, thus releasing Japanese troops to reinforce Myitkyina and Mogaung, and allowing them to open up their lines of communication. He rounded on Lentaigne and threw in his face Wingate's assessment that strongholds could be maintained despite the monsoon. Lentaigne had to remind him of the difference between a block and a stronghold.

The outcome was that Lentaigne was ordered to instruct Morris to attack the Japanese garrisons in the villages of Waingmaw and Maingna on the east bank of the Irrawaddy opposite Myitkyina, while Calvert was to attack Mogaung. Meanwhile 14th Brigade, having covered the reorganization of 111th Brigade at Mokso Sakkan, was to protect the southern half of Indawgyi Lake with 3rd West African Brigade. Having completed reorganization, 111th Brigade was to protect the northern half of the lake. The scene was set for the final and unhappiest act in the Chindit drama.

Some indication of the difficulties Lentaigne had to endure at this time are reflected in a letter he wrote to Slim on 19 June 1944:

> General Stilwell has little or no American troops, while his Chinese do not act on his orders unless it suits their purpose to do so. Stilwell consequently relies on us to pull his chestnuts out of the fire. While perfectly willing and anxious to do everything that is humanly possible, there is a limit to the capabilities of our men, and this has now been reached.... The only remedy I can suggest is our early relief by 36 Division, or for somebody with military knowledge on a much higher level [perhaps a hint that this should not be Mountbatten, a sailor], to come here at once, examine the situation on its merits, and give General Stilwell orders as to the future conduct of the campaign....
>
> I know you no longer command Stilwell, and that I may be accused of going behind his back....

A letter from 'Jack' Masters to Lentaigne gives an idea of how depleted his brigade was:

> As regards strength, 81, 41, 26 [Columns] are each the fighting strength of a coy. Scotty, who is no sluggard, says his men are in appalling condition.... Scotty says his coln is in a worse state than the men he brought out last year.

By now Merrill's Marauders were if anything in a worse physical state than the Chindits. Stilwell filled their depleted ranks with United States Army road construction engineers, who ran from the Japanese on several occasions. Stilwell sacked Merrill, and placed his own chief of staff, Brigadier General Haydon C. Boatner in command of the rag-bag Chinese–American Task Force of about divisional size.

One of the many drawbacks of operating under Stilwell was that his intelligence branch was perhaps the most useless section of his appalling staff. Major Barnes commented that they were:

> inclined to take their information at face value and did not appear to sift it sufficiently...

They consistently underestimated the Japanese strengths as Morris-force were to learn only too well. Morrisforce War Diary:

> *30 May 44*
> 49 and 40 Columns moved straight in to take over (reported unoccupied)
> Waingmaw. But found the Jap garrison in force.
> All columns very tired but pressed by commanding general Myitkyina Task
> Force [Boatner] to take maximum offensive action against Waingmaw.
> Planned another immediate attack.

Peter Cane in 94 Column's report:

> We had to lead the three-column attack on Waingmaw and were to start
> off that night.

Morrisforce War Diary:

> *2 June*
> 94 held up; running on to well defended area and 40 Column driven back
> to starting line of attack by 09.00 hours. No drop of ammunition. Two
> counter-attacks on 94 driven off, one with fair casualties. When it was
> obvious no further advance could be made all withdrew to Hoton very
> short of ammunition. These unrecced attacks were continually forced on
> Morrisforce at insistence, usually at no notice at all, by Brigadier General
> Boatner US Army. They achieved nothing tactical ever.

These two attacks were merely the beginning of Morrisforce's troubles.
Peter Cane:

> For the next month we were trying to take on about 450 Japs in excellent
> dug-in positions and short of nothing. We had no heavy support weapons
> and the ammunition supply for our light weapons was at times a hard
> enough question.
>
> Eight times in all we carried out such attacks by the direct order of the
> Commanding General Myitkyina Task Force. Usually there was no advance
> warning and we were merely ordered to 'Attack regardless'. Regardless of
> what we weren't told: Japs? Support Fire? Country? Time? Casualties?
> Anything? Such was the method of war.
>
> As a soldier it was heartbreaking to see men being killed by the avoidable
> mistakes and misdirection of higher command.
>
> Meanwhile the weather had turned the surrounding country into
> swamps, and we were wading waist- and sometimes chest-deep to keep up

the pressure on the east bank. The effect on the men's health was appalling and trenchfoot was becoming a serious factor. Malaria took a heavy toll in spite of Atebrin and we lost a large number of sick every day. It became a matter of screwing what you could out of the healthy ones and keeping the Japs worried and restless. I'm sure we did this as we retained our advantages of mobility and surprise to continually attack him from unexpected quarters. From reports of villagers escaping from the Jap-held villages, we also inflicted plenty of casualties from time to time.

Unfortunately, Lentaigne, a straightforward and personally brave soldier, was able to visit his troops, spread over hundreds of square miles of Burma, on only two occasions during the whole time they were operating in the north under Stilwell's command. He expressed his frustration at this mode of command in a letter to Tulloch:

> The biggest difficulty in this crazy warfare is that the Commander is divorced from those below him and cannot gauge the condition and tactical situation in their vicinity.

He was therefore in a weak position to argue their case with conviction when Stilwell and his staff accused the Chindits of cowardice, although he was quite prepared to stand up to him, as Alexander wrote to Tulloch on 7 July 1944:

> The gloves are off with Stilwell. It will probably be the end of the General, but I feel that he will have everyone in the Force on his side. He has borne it long enough. . . . Were it not for the political power that Stilwell sways and the repercussions that this show may have on the future of the Force, I know he would have packed up long ago.

Later in the same letter, commenting on Mountbatten:

> Anyway, Supremo has let us down and I shall place no more faith in the man.

In the face of extreme provocation, Lentaigne kept his dignity, and more importantly, his temper, doing nothing that would have imperilled the fragile Anglo-American relationships in the China–Burma–India Theatre. It is intriguing to speculate how Wingate would have handled Stilwell; very differently one concludes, and that he would have got his way, if necessary by 'pulling strings' to the very top. Indeed Tulloch tried to persuade Lentaigne to do just that in a signal, part of which read:

Consider you have every justification for demanding direct signal to be passed to PM [Prime Minister] as Wingate's successor.

The Chinese–American Task Force efforts to take Myitkyina were inept and reaped only the failure they deserved. Morrisforce War Diary:

1 July 44

Malaria taking a very heavy toll. Doctors figures of 100% debilitation and unfitness for ops were disregarded by Stilwell. We knew how badly organised the attacks on Myitkyina were. All the Task Force strength was dissipated round the large perimeter, instead of being concentrated at any point. Yet the orders were the Chinese only were to be allowed to capture Myitkyina for political reasons. This mishandling of the [Task] Force caused great disappointment – knowing that our efforts were really useless. Had we been allowed to cross the river and have a good crack with a proper L of C, much more would have been achieved.

4 July 44

Brigadier General Wessel (superseding Boatner [who had been sacked by Stilwell]) ordered another full-scale attack on Maigna.

5 July 44

Cane [Morris was sick] had a long stormy interview in Task Force HQ. Wessel imagined one squadron of Mitchell aircraft and four fighters would saturate the area and kill or render harmless all the 350 Japs. This shows how little is known of the limited capabilities of aircraft bombs. They also offered artillery support, but as this consisted of four 75 mm guns firing at extreme range from behind the enemy (across the river) [and therefore the 'overs' would hit the attacking force], this was refused. Wessel was adamant – we were cowards if we did not attack. He eventually conceded four squadrons of B-25 and eight P-40 aircraft.

On 6 July message received from SEAC [Mountbatten] limiting our operations to patrolling, but as a political gesture it was decided two platoons of 94 (Cane) and two of 40 (McCutcheon) were to attempt an entry.

6 July 44

At 13.20 hours three B-25s dropped bombs but no explosions followed. At 14.00 four more did the same. These were presumed to be dropped in the river, but it subsequently showed they had twelve-hour delayed action [fuses]. (What fun if we had managed to get into Maingna!) By 15.30 a total of six more had come. We were wondering just what had happened to the air support plan when at 16.00 hours fighters (four) bombed and strafed. We were now moving to the start line when four more fighters arrived and their bombs arrived within 150 yards of the attacking force HQ and another 50 yards from one platoon. We stopped and waited developments which came at 16.45 hours – a light plane with a personal message from Wessel: 'Do not enter town'. We left OPs and harboured back.

Meanwhile Calvert's Brigade had also been on the receiving end of Stilwell's incompetence in the battle for Mogaung, on the railway line to Myitkyina. On 2 June Calvert seized the ferry over the Mogaung river at Tapaw. This alarmed the Japanese, and they reinforced Mogaung, which until then had only administrative troops in the garrison. The Japanese III/128th Battalion and Headquarters 128th Regiment were ordered into the town.

Calvert, hoping that the Chinese would attack from the north, decided his best plan was to advance from the south-east along the road from Pinh Mi, which involved capturing the bridge across the chaung near Pinh Mi. Calvert captured the village but could not take the bridge where the enemy were dug in on the far side. He sent 1st South Staffs and 3/6th Gurkhas round to attack from the south. Lieutenant Durant, machine-gun platoon commander with the South Staffs wrote to his parents:

We pushed on slowly all day clearing villages and copses of small parties of Japs until in the late afternoon we reached the road about 400 yards from the bridge. The Gurkhas then passed through us and put in a magnificent attack through thick creeper and deep mud against well-dug Jap positions, clearing the bridge just before dark. We dug in beside the road facing Mogaung, and tried to get some sleep. Shortly after dark a party of eight Japs carrying rations came chattering happily down the road from Mogaung and one of my gunners let them come within twenty yards and made short work of them with a Vickers. Later that night a Jap patrol stumbled into our perimeter and were practically wiped out.

The following day Calvert reached the Mogaung River and the outskirts of the village of Natgyigon, which, as Durant told his parents:

was almost part of the town [of Mogaung itself]. We moved off early and took a line through thick jungle with the object of coming out well on the flank, so that progress was slow due to all the cutting that had to be done.

Durant was moving with Major Archie Wavell's company. The son of Field Marshal Sir Archibald Wavell, the Commander-in-Chief India, Major Wavell was attached to the South Staffs from his own regiment, the Black Watch. After some confused fighting the company on their right was halted, suffering heavy casualties including the company commander who had arrived as a reinforcement the day before. Durant:

> That left us in a very nasty salient. We knew it was only a matter of time before the snipers turned their attention to us. The first we knew was when Archie's second-in-command (a motherly, married and family character who should never have been in) was shot through the head and killed instantly as he fussed about getting people under cover. The sniping became heavier and still it was impossible to see where the firing was coming from. I had a Vickers mounted as if for AA, and sprayed all the large trees but it was entirely blind shooting. A platoon came up to reinforce us and was sent round to the right to clear what they could. But they hadn't gone 15 yards before four men were down and the rest pinned down. The Jap began successfully to grenade the wounded and when we tried to bring them in two more men were hit. Archie Wavell, trying a new line, set off with a section, but within a few seconds was back holding his left hand which was hanging by a thread of muscle having been hit by a sniper at 20 yards range. He was astonishingly calm and gave out orders and then walked back unassisted to the RAP. Meanwhile on the left, casualties were equally heavy and as it was getting dusk we were none of us feeling too happy, and even when the order came for us to withdraw, we knew that somehow we had to get the wounded in. They seemed to be covered by two snipers, so David Wilcox stationed himself where he might be able to get a shot, and someone began rustling the bushes nearby. The Jap moved, and, standing, David shot him at the same time, getting a graze under his chin from the second sniper's bullet. But he saw him as well, and having a beeline was able to fire quickly enough to get him. It was a very courageous action, well deserving of a decoration which I hope he will get. After that it was a matter of holding on until the wounded had got back and moving ourselves to join the rest of the Battalion.

Meanwhile Mogaung had been reinforced by II/128th Battalion and I/151st Battalion. Calvert's Brigade had now been behind enemy lines for fourteen weeks, and his three battalions totalled some 550 men fit to fight. The Chinese advanced in such a leisurely fashion that they took sixteen days to cover fourteen miles. Durant:

The next day we dug like beavers and were shelled regularly. Once again my phenomenal good luck held, for one shell burst within five yards of me, wounding my batman, killing the man next to him and leaving me unscathed. It was very wet and the trenches filled with water as soon as they were dug, but the men seemed quite happy and cursed Joe Stilwell's Chinese for not appearing, even making up a little song which they sang throughout the day with the greatest satisfaction.

I'm coming, I'm coming,
Though my pace is very slow,
I hear the Chindit voices saying,
'Jalo Joe'.*

Calvert decided he could not wait any longer. By nightfall on 23 June Natgyigon and the railway bridge over the Mogaung river had been taken with the loss of 150 casualties. The attack had been greatly assisted by bombing and newly arrived reinforcements with flame-throwers which were particularly useful when dealing with Japanese strong points dug in underneath houses. Durant:

The flame-throwers were now summoned from the rear and as they moved past where I was lying a shell burst and puncturing one of the weapons set it on fire. The wretched man who was carrying it was a mass of flame but managed to get it off and all we could do was roll him into some water in a nearby ditch. The others went forward and got to work on the position under the house, but even so it was a long time before the Japs there were finished off. One broke out, all his clothes on fire, and was shot down, the remainder preferred to stay where they were and get burnt to death, and we found that the officer had committed suicide by shooting himself in the head with his revolver. When this point was cleared, we moved on and brought all we had to bear on a red house and after half an hour had the satisfaction of seeing about 20 Japs leave it, some of whom we killed with the machine-guns as they tried to get away. The Gurkhas meanwhile meeting little opposition had reached the end of the railway bridge, and we now moved up on the line and began to dig in. By then the Brigadier was on the scene, and when he heard of our casualties, he decided to send the Lancashire Fusiliers forward with one company of Gurkhas, while the Chinese advanced from the south. Our Battalion was taken out and sent

* Hindi for hurry up.

right back to rest, but the Medium Machine-Guns were left under command of the Gurkhas so I stayed on the railway line.

Every man had fought magnificently under very unpleasant conditions, and although our casualties had been heavy, we had achieved our objective and killed a lot of Japs along the way.

The next day Calvert renewed the attack, and during the night the Japanese pulled out to the south-west. Calvert's Brigade entered Mogaung on 26 June. Durant:

> When we got to the river we found rafts made of oil-drums and planks on which the Jap had made his way out, and all that day stray bodies came drifting down on the stream and were promptly engaged by every available Chinaman in the vain hope that some at least had a breath of air in them. As I put the last gun into position on the edge of town a few half-hearted shots were fired at me from the thick reeds by the river banks, and a Gurkha patrol which was sent out found three Jap officers and six men hiding there – probably non-swimmers.

The capture of Mogaung, with a strong garrison in well-prepared positions in the built-up area and its approaches, supported by artillery, was a great feat of arms by Calvert's Brigade. His aggressive spirit and superb leadership, and the fighting qualities of his soldiers, had secured victory against the odds, but at a price. Between 17 May and 26 June, 77th Brigade suffered 950 battle casualties, and 150 men evacuated sick. Since arriving in Burma, the Brigade had lost half its strength. Only 300 of those remaining were fit to fight. During the battle two Victoria Crosses were awarded: one posthumously to Captain Allmand attached to 6th Gurkha Rifles, and the other to Rifleman Tulbahadar Pun 6th Gurkha Rifles. A total of three Victoria Crosses were awarded to officers and soldiers of 77th Brigade in the campaign.

Mike Calvert:

> When we captured Mogaung, we heard on the BBC that the Americans and Chinese had captured Mogaung. So I sent a message saying, 'The Americans and Chinese have captured Mogaung, 77th Brigade is proceeding to take Umbrage.' Stilwell's son who was his intelligence officer said, 'They've taken a village called Um-bra-gay which we can't find on the map.'

While Calvert was flying out his sick and wounded, he was ordered by Stilwell to collect together his survivors into a composite company, and move north-east to Myitkyina, at this stage still in Japanese hands. After sending a flurry of angry signals, Calvert sent a 'MOST SECRET PERSONAL AND CONFIDENTIAL' signal to Tulloch, part of which read:

I intend taking matters into my own hands. I will be glad if you see that officers and men do NOT (R) [repeat] do NOT suffer in the curtailment of awards [for gallantry] and possibly collective PUNITIVE measures. You can help by making position public. IRREPARABLE harm has been done [by Stilwell's behaviour] by all ranks never again trusting an American General.

Calvert then closed down his radios for fourteen days and marched north-west to Kamaing. Durant:

From start to finish this march was a nightmare. It took us a fortnight of marching through mud and water, or crossing deep and fast-flowing rivers, and of miserably damp nights. For the last two days of it I was sick with jaundice and had a temperature of 102.

Calvert was summoned to Stilwell's Headquarters at Shaduzup to explain his insubordination. Calvert:

He said, 'You send some very strong signals, Calvert.'
I said, 'You should see the ones my brigade-major wouldn't let me send.'
I had hit the right note, because he roared with laughter. From then on we got on very well. He didn't realise we'd done the glider-borne invasion, he didn't realise we'd blocked the railway [at White City] for almost five weeks, four of them against repeated Japanese attacks. He didn't realise my brigade had not only been decimated but had had other bits taken off to help other brigades. We had no artillery, he didn't realise all these things.
He kept on saying, 'Why wasn't I told? Is this true?'
His staff admitted it was.

The Japanese withdrawing from Kamaing and Mogaung had dug in around the towns of Taungni, Namphadaung and Sahmaw, controlling the road to the south. Lentaigne ordered 14th Brigade to take Taungni and Namphadaung, and 3rd West African Brigade was to seize Hill 60, a key position on the route to Sahmaw, and Sahmaw itself. Masters's 111th Brigade was ordered by Lentaigne to take Point 2171, a strongly held feature north of Taungni.

By now the men in 111th Brigade had been in for more than ninety days and hoped that each day would bring the order to fly out.

Publishing a 'deadline', known to every man, is usually a mistake, and it speaks volumes for the leadership and rank and file in the Chindits that they pressed doggedly on despite a growing disillusionment with the higher direction of their efforts. Lieutenant-Colonel Desmond Whyte:

> Towards the end we had some psychological cases of breakdowns, in spite of the careful selection and training. Every man has his breaking point, and we were slowly reaching it for some. You would notice a friend going down hill. At dawn stand to, you would say 'Bill, Bill', [but] Bill was dead. The flame of life had withered. I became a very firm believer in the psychological aspect of human nature, the enormous importance of the impulse; the will, the ability to make yourself live. The Gurkhas also broke down, but the Gurkha has a very hard background in Nepal and they are psychologically attuned to hardship, and starvation after a hard winter. Many Europeans are not.

From the very beginning of the campaign without the efforts of the medical officers and orderlies, and especially the American light aircraft, deaths from wounds and sickness would have been even higher, and morale would have suffered accordingly. Desmond Whyte:

> You were on your own; your own surgeon your own physician, your own dermatologist, your own eye surgeon, your own orthopaedic surgeon. Nobody to help you except your RAMC orderlies. Most very good. You could take the medical equipment that would fit in a pannier on one half side of a mule. Dressings, instruments, medicines, Mepacrine which suppressed malaria. That pannier was never large enough. So the doctor had to carry some of it in his own pack which in any case weighed 70 lb. You had your carbine as well. No antibiotics. We had sulpha drugs dropped to us in the jungle, the first I had ever seen.
>
> Those who were immobilised were dragged behind mules. The Gurkhas cut bamboos with their kukris and made a stretcher. This made a flexible stretcher bound with bamboo strips cut from the side of the bamboo. The mule towed the stretcher, with the front on his back, and the other end dragging on the ground. Four men walked alongside, with ropes, making sure that the stretcher was steered round bumps. Most of the wounded did well. But in the heat it was difficult to keep them alive. Water was a problem. We had canvas bags called chuggals for water as well as our water bottles. The water kept cool in the chuggals by evaporation, and a lot of it was lost. You passed a tube down the casualty's nose or mouth, and put water into the stomach. I mixed in brandy sometimes. We also adminis-

tered hot sweet tea, and sometimes if the medicine had to be supported by liquid we poured it in through the tube in the mouth.

The main diseases: our main enemy was malaria. Everybody, 100% got malaria. We were on Mepacrine, everybody was lined up every day and everybody had to take it under supervision. The word spread through the Gurkhas that this made them impotent. The Gurkha is a very virile man. We had to scotch that rumour. The yellow eyes worried people. But after six weeks you were so dog tired, you didn't notice what they looked like. We ran out of condition. We began to die of malaria, of sepsis, liver infections, pneumonia, meningitis.

If we could we would arrange to fly the casualties out in light planes from India. They brought these planes in in hazardous conditions, sometimes under fire. To take a man you had to remove all the splints and the stretcher, because he had to fit into a tiny cockpit. They would wrap the casualty round them and take off. Wonderful pilots – Americans. The doctor had to take the party of wounded to be evacuated away from the HQ with a small party of Gurkhas for protection. He had to be good with his map and compass. He would arrive at the fly-in area and hope and pray that the planes would find him before the enemy found him. We had some very narrow escapes as you can imagine. On one or two occasions, the planes hit the trees on take off.

Once an American light-plane pilot tried to take off with two casualties, against my wishes. He crashed. When I ran up, he prised himself out of the wreckage, saying, 'Aw shit I ought to be shot.' I said, 'You soon will be.'

I could hear the Jap mortars firing. He got the two men out. Carried them away a little and buried them. I always carried a little prayer wrapped in cellophane in my jacket. If there was time we cut down bamboo, made a little cross, said a prayer, and moved on. We always knew that the jungle was full of hungry jackals and the shallow grave would not keep them out for long.

The operations to take Point 2171, lasting from 20 June to 5 July, were as bloody as any the Chindits experienced. Exhausted, malaria-ridden British and Gurkha soldiers forced themselves time and again up the steep jungle-covered hillsides and engaged the Japanese in log-covered bunkers with bomb and bayonet. It was finally taken by Major Jim Blaker's company of 3/9th Gurkha Rifles. He was hit and went down, encouraging his men on as he lay dying, and they swept on to take the hill. Blaker was awarded the third posthumous Victoria Cross of the Chindit campaign. Harper's battalion held the feature for some days until the Japanese outflanked the position and Masters ordered him to pull out.

On 30 June 1944, Mountbatten had ordered Stilwell to fly out the remnants of 77th and 111th Brigades, accusing him of keeping them in action for far too long. Many Chindits believed, and believe, that Mountbatten should have taken charge of Stilwell far earlier. But, as Tulloch recorded in his diary after an interview with Slim on 22 July:

> He [Slim] considers that LL [Lord Louis Mountbatten] is only a playboy who tries to please everybody, and particularly the *last* person he sees. The only way to get anything done is to ensure you see him last! Agreed he [Mountbatten] had ratted on us badly.

The final objective for the 2nd York & Lancasters of 14th Brigade was Point 1497, north-west of Namphadaung, on the left flank of 36th Indian Division's drive south. Graves-Morris:

> The men were informed that this would be their final objective before evacuation. Many were very sceptical in believing this, and the general feeling was that this sort of story had been told them before – both officers and men were now physically and mentally exhausted, and there were signs that nerves were cracking.

After a ten-mile approach march by the York & Lancasters, which took a day and a morning, followed by a day of confused fighting, the Japanese withdrew on 6 August. The 2nd Black Watch passed through and after hard fighting captured Labu and Padaung. 36th Indian Division had by now taken Namphadaung on the road. Graves-Morris:

> The evacuation of sick and wounded was now made easy by access to the road. It was a sorry sight to see these columns of diseased and dying men dragging themselves along, or being helped by their less sick comrades. Most were unrecognisable, being shadows of their former selves, 12 stone men weighing 7 or 8 stone, and their sunken faces and hollow staring eyes gave signs of their condition.
>
> 84 and 65 Columns were the last to leave the hills, and they marched down to the main road through 36 Div positions in terrific heat on 23rd August. This was the first time since they had been flown into Burma in early April, twenty weeks before, that the columns were behind Allied lines. The final march to Mogaung was made during the hours of darkness on 24 August.

Of the 900 all ranks of the Battalion who had landed on 2nd and 3rd April, only 18 officers and some 380 men made the final march to Mogaung, having marched over 500 miles.

Astride the road which was 36th Indian Division's axis of advance was Hill 60, and this was the objective of 3rd West African Brigade. Shaw, the machine-gun sergeant of Number 12 Column, describes one attempt on the feature:

The Japs weren't content with slits, but dug deep enough to stand, with bamboo platforms to keep them dry, and these foxholes were then connected. Having no wire, they used bamboo stakes with needle-sharp points, then built OPs and sniper nests in trees. It became necessary to kill every fanatic – surrender was a disgrace.

I could sense the attack failing, even when the crash of in-fighting went on and on. The Nigerian sergeant firing the mobile Vickers was doing sterling work, but the weakened men had no chance. Some reached the stakes, but no further, with the Japs pouring concentrated fire upon every movement.

When the leading brigade of 36th Indian Division linked up with the West Africans, Shaw went to seek out his nephew in the 9th Royal Sussex:

I began to meet British troops who grinned widely. No haircut or shave for months, trousers rolled up to the knee, bush hat crown shoved up into a dome for coolth [sic], and every square inch of clothing plastered with rich Burmese chocolate [mud].

After favouring me with a prolonged gape, the Royal Sussex Adjutant sent for CQMS Jones. If we hadn't been on active service I would have had to stand to attention. He passed me with a puzzled stare.

'What's up Tom?' I called.

He came back and stammered, 'Why you old bleeder!'

'Uncle to you.'

'I thought you were in Nigeria.'

Hill 60 fell on 6 August to the West African Brigade's Numbers 12 and 43 Columns, and the 9th Royal Sussex, and 6th South Wales Borderers of 36th Indian Division. Shaw:

As the Royal Sussex struggled through the boggy approaches a monsoon shower broke, and directly that stopped they charged, my blood tingling at their shouts. Hill 60 was at last taken, but many Sussex men never again saw their county.

Well that was Hill 60, and here are extracts from the diary of the Japanese officer in charge:

> 'Owing to the constant mortar and artillery fire, the hilltop is bare of all foliage, giving us no concealment. Most of us are now delirious with lack of sleep and deaf with the thunderous bombings. Some are shell-shocked and in a daze.
>
> 'Our food supply is being bombed away daily. From now on we have nothing to eat. We are just existing by drinking river water. As long as there is a drop of blood we will not give up.'

The West Africans marched to Mogaung and were evacuated by rail and aircraft. So ended the Chindit campaign. Although there were plans to use the Chindits again, and Special Force was built up to strength, it was finally disbanded in February 1945 when, with 14th Army having advanced to the Irrawaddy, the strategic situation in Burma no longer lent itself to LRP operations. There was no question of using the Force any earlier. Slim later wrote to a fellow officer:

> 1. The Chindits, with the possible exception of 23rd Brigade used in Assam, were completely exhausted, terribly reduced in strength and quite incapable of further effort when they were withdrawn. They could not have been kept in the field any longer – in fact they were kept too long.
>
> 2. A considerable period of leave, rest, recovery and a great deal of reinforcement and re-training would be necessary before they could be fit for active service again – several months at least.

This is borne out by the casualty figures of all Chindit columns. Take for example Graves-Morris's report:

CASUALTIES

Nature	Officers	Other Ranks
Killed	5	24
Wounded	7 +	100
Died of sickness & exhaustion	—	58
Evacuated sick	15	315

+ Three of these officers were wounded twice during the five months.
Of the balance of the Battalion – 18 Officers and approx 380 Other Ranks – who made the final march on 23 Aug 44, all except 2 Officers and 10 Other Ranks were admitted to hospital in India within a month, and remained there off and on for the remainder of 1944 and into 1945.

Desmond Whyte, the SMO of 111th Brigade:

Over 80% were unfit for further active service.

Why were the figures of sick so horrifyingly high? Colonel Michael
Hickey in his book *Unforgettable Army* suggests that the main cause was
poor training and lack of self-discipline.[4] Bearing in mind that preventative drugs were issued and sanitation techniques were well known, his
case seems sound. He quotes the figure of nearly 10 per cent evacuated
with dysentery and chronic diarrhoea and 60 per cent with malaria. His
argument is supported by the relevant volume of the *Medical History of
the Second World War*.[5] Extracts taken from this *History* are at Appendix
B. From page 197 of this *History*, it is clear that many cerebral malaria
cases (the killer) did not take their Mepacrine. The verdict in the report
is equally damning about the lack of basic hygiene.

All very well, the reader may ask, but how can one expect men in
action and on long marches to carry out all these seemingly fanciful
hygiene and prophylactic drills? The answer is of course that they cannot
always, but with training and self-discipline the difficulties of existing in
such a hostile environment become second nature and do not detract
from operations. Out of contact with the enemy there is far less excuse
for poor hygiene. In Borneo, where British and Gurkha troops operated
from bases, some only marginally less spartan than the strongholds,
albeit not under heavy attack, and patrolled and fought small engagements in terrain and climate just as demanding as the Chindits, on
operational tours of six months, the sickness rate was a minute fraction
of that suffered by Special Force in Burma. If it had approached
anywhere near the Chindit figures, commanders would have been sacked
forthwith. The blame must be laid at the commander's, Wingate's, door;
Hickey believes that: 'Wingate, with his belief in the power of mind over
matter, placed a low value on preventative medicine.'

This is supported by the *Medical History*, and by the Deputy Director
of Medical Services of Special Force (DDMS) who took over just after
Wingate was killed, William Officer:

Wingate wouldn't take his DDMS's advice. Wingate was told he was wrong,
but he would not take this.

Lentaigne must also bear a share of the blame – see Appendix B and
the comments by the SMO of 111th Brigade.

Was it worth it? Was the huge investment in blood, aircraft and diversion of resources (not least scarce British manpower) justified by the return? The arguments still continue. What is clear is that the Chindit actions in and around Mogaung and the White City were critical in enabling Stilwell to push forward the Ledo Road. Unfortunately the Chinese offensive by Chiang Kai-shek, for which the Ledo Road was to be the artery, never came about. For reasons that have already been explained, Chiang Kai-shek had no intention of fighting the Japanese.

Less clear is the effect that Chindit operations had on the Japanese offensives in Assam, on Imphal and Kohima. The activities of 23rd Brigade were certainly a factor in hindering the offensive on Kohima, but were not decisive in ensuring a Japanese defeat. The other Chindit attacks on the Japanese supply line to the Assam front had far less effect, for the enemy had made scant provision for resupply, relying instead on capturing British stocks within ten days. Four months' savage fighting, including the masterly withdrawal up the Tiddim Road, and stubborn defence of Kohima and Imphal utterly smashed the Japanese Army, and in the process frustrated their attempts to live off captured supplies. Although Wingate and Tulloch at the time forecast a Japanese assault on the Assam lines of communication, their confident and conceited prediction of the outcome, that the enemy would withdraw in good order after about two weeks, having inflicted grave damage, was totally wrong. Instead, the emaciated survivors of the Japanese assault divisions reeled back over the Chindwin, followed up by Slim. The battles in Assam had opened the door to his great victory in Burma. It is a mark of considerable generalship to suck an enemy into a position where he contributes to his own defeat.

Wingate's supporters passionately claim that had his ideas been followed as he had intended – indeed, been expanded, as he proposed – success in Burma would have been achieved earlier than it was. One of his proposals, mooted in a note dated 11 February 1944, was to seize Hanoi and Bangkok, and maintain the forces there on air supply. Rather like a salesman he ends this note with the words: 'Details can be supplied on demand.'

Not content with this, Wingate submitted an accompanying appreciation to Mountbatten, its object:

To exploit to the maximum extent any gains, or prospect of gain, which may result from Operation Thursday.

Wingate continued by suggesting that an LRP force of 100,000 infantry be created, which would not only seize Hanoi and Bangkok, but would:

continue to carry a chain of defended airports across China to the coast where it would meet up with the seaborne forces.

This was fantasy on a staggering scale. This force would have been about ten times bigger than a normal British airborne division, and would not only have absorbed the manpower of all the infantry in 14th Army, but much of the artillery and armoured units as well. Such a vast force, as Shelford Bidwell has commented, 'If organised on Chindit lines it would also contain about 20,000 mules.' He goes on to remind us that:

In June 1944 the combined resources of the USAAF and RAF were just sufficient to transport *two and two-thirds* airborne divisions from England to Normandy [in one lift for D-Day]. (The USAAF alone assembled over 1,000 aircraft and used 882 C-47 aircraft for D-Day, and altogether some 2,500 gliders were available.)[6]

In effect Wingate was striving to turn a large part of 14th Army into long-range penetration forces, presumably on the basis that the Japanese would be so busy dashing about South-East Asia trying to eliminate them that Burma could be reoccupied while they were otherwise engaged. With much of the 14th Army so deployed, the Japanese would very likely have done no such thing, they would have advanced to seize the base in India and brought the Special Force operations to a halt for lack of supplies.

Others have suggested that if the Chindits had been used in a more concentrated way from the beginning they would have been more effective. Certainly the fly-in to areas miles from their objectives runs against all the precepts of airborne operations as they were understood at the time and have been ever since, and as has already been discussed.

Yet others argue that the break-up of the battle-tested 70th Infantry Division was a misuse of talent, and it could have been better employed in the main battle in Burma.

Whatever arguments are deployed, the fact remains that many Chindits spent a great deal of their time marching, and very little of it fighting. Tulloch commented in his diary on 13 June:

14th Brigade have had no positive effect on the campaign for over a month and are merely a wasting asset.

What Wingate lacked, through no fault of his own, were medium- and heavy-lift helicopters. He was attempting air-mobile war without the means of tactical mobility. As has already been observed, once his columns were down, they had the mobility of the boot. After the Second Chindit Expedition, Lentaigne wrote:

A column has NOT got superior mobility to the enemy in the jungle [one of the main pillars in Wingate's argument for LRP]. The rations and supplies carried by the man are heavier than that carried by the enemy, whilst the heavier weapons and W/T [radios] which make the column self-supporting entail a mule train, which inevitably slows it down and also renders it very vulnerable when attacked on the march.

But it is also important to remind ourselves that this was the biggest behind-the-lines operation of the Second World War, and also the longest involving so many men – around 20,000. By operating with forces this large, the Second Chindit Expedition was in effect a 'conventional' force, albeit lightly equipped, operating behind the lines, in jungle, or tropical Asian terrain; and at times fighting 'conventional' battles. They were at the end of a long supply line, totally reliant on air-lift for every round of ammunition, virtually every spoonful of food, and for the evacuation of every sick or wounded man. The only way out was on foot or by air.

When assessing the cost, one must also take into account the self-sacrifice, endurance and guts of the Chindit soldiers. No cold accounting of return on investment can take away what they achieved in personal terms. They truly deserve the standing and the adulation they were accorded at the time, and since.

What of Wingate? It is difficult to find a better summary of his character than that by John ('Jack') Masters, written sixteen years after Wingate's death:

Wingate was sometimes right and sometimes wrong. It really does not matter. What does matter is that he possessed one of the most unusual personalities of recent history. He had a driving will of tremendous force. His character was a blend of mysticism, anger, love, passion, and dark hatred, of overpowering confidence, and deepest depression. He could make all kinds of men believe in him, and could make all kinds of men distrust him.... It is quite unnecessary, if trying to prove Napoleon's greatness, to show that he was always right, generous, kind and humble. He wasn't, but he was a phenomenon. So was Wingate.[7]

9

Operations in the Mediterranean and Aegean: mid-1943 to mid-1944

When the campaign in North Africa finished in May 1943, the SAS and LRDG were reorganized and given new roles and tasks. 1st SAS, under Major Paddy Mayne since David Stirling's capture, was renamed the Special Raiding Squadron (SRS) and warned for operations in Sicily and Italy; as was 2nd SAS under Lieutenant-Colonel Bill Stirling, which had been operating under 1st Army in Tunisia. Both organizations functioned independently of each other. It will be remembered that the SAS had acquired the Special Boat Section (SBS) in the Middle East; a not entirely happy arrangement. The SBS was now hived off and became the Special Boat Squadron (SBS) under Major the Earl Jellicoe. Whether the retention of the acronym SBS served to confuse the enemy is not known, but it certainly makes for confusion among the readers of any history of special forces in the Second World War, since Special Boat Sections (SBS) continued to operate from Britain and eventually in the Far East as will become apparent in later chapters. For clarity from this point on the two organizations will be referred to as SB Section and SB Squadron (until 1945, that is, when the latter became the Special Boat Service).

George Jellicoe had been evacuated to England after taking part in an SAS raid in the desert in mid 1942:

> I returned to the Middle East in January 43. Mountbatten got me back by writing out, 'Captain Jellicoe is required back in the Middle East on urgent operational business.' The Special Boat Squadron absorbed what had been called the SBS under David Sutherland's command. David became one of my detachment commanders and 2ic. Fitzroy Maclean also joined me as another detachment commander. We had a winter camp by Lake Tiberias

and a summer camp on the coast [of Palestine]. I lost Fitzroy very soon to command our mission with Tito [in Yugoslavia]. In England I had met a marvellous young Dane called Andy Lassen and had persuaded Combined Ops HQ to second him to me.

The SB Squadron was organized into three detachments: L (commanded by Langton, last mentioned while escaping from Tobruk), M (under Fitzroy Maclean and later Major J. N. 'Jock' Lapraik) and S (under Sutherland). Each detachment consisted of a small headquarters and five patrols, each twelve strong including two radio operators, and commanded by an officer.

Anders Lassen was a remarkable man, already decorated with the Military Cross for his part in raids on the French coast with Captain Gus March-Phillipp's Small-Scale Raiding Force (SSRF). Lassen had spent the first eighteen months of the war in the Merchant Navy, but ended up in an SOE training school. Here his instructors decided that his talents lay in fighting rather than clandestine activities. The SSRF had been wound up in April 1943, following the realization that their raids on the French mainland endangered Secret Intelligence Service (SIS – MI6) operations in the same area. Lassen's single-minded pursuit of his aim to be where the action was hottest was to win him two more Military Crosses and a posthumous Victoria Cross. His first operation with the SB Squadron was a raid led by Sutherland on enemy airfields on Crete in June 1943. They destroyed four aircraft and two fuel dumps. At the same time a raid was mounted on Sardinia as part of the deception plan for the Allied landings on Sicily. This was unsuccessful, and the party was captured. Jellicoe was:

> not allowed to go on them [these raids], because I knew the plans for Sicily.
> I went with a submarine to pick them up [the Sardinia party], they never
> appeared.

Meanwhile the LRDG had been training in the mountains in Lebanon for their new role. When the desert war ended, they had feared that they would be disbanded, and as David Lloyd Owen put it, 'thrown on the thirsty markets at the Base Depots'. However, after attending a conference at GHQ in Cairo, the Commanding Officer, Guy Prendergast, was able to give them the good news that the LRDG was to remain in existence. David Lloyd Owen:

It was eventually decided we would operate in Europe on our feet, or in jeeps if we could infiltrate. But we would only spend about ten days behind enemy lines. Our role was recce, shipping and aircraft reporting, and communications and liaison with partisans. We had to revise our approach to the target. We had to parachute, go in by MTB, by submarine, or be air landed in places like Yugoslavia or Greece. We reorganised into two squadrons, the New Zealand Squadron, and the other squadron the rest. The Brigade of Guards withdrew their patrol because they [201st Guards Brigade] had had very heavy casualties in Tunisia and couldn't afford to reinforce them.

Squadrons were organized into patrols, each commanded by a captain or subaltern. The New Zealanders formed A Squadron, and their patrols were lettered T and R. Lloyd Owen commanded B Squadron, his patrols were lettered Y (Yeomanry), S (Rhodesians) and M (a few from the old Guards Patrol, and others from desert days). Mainly in the Cedars of Lebanon, a ski resort at six thousand feet, surrounded by peaks four thousand feet higher, but also elsewhere in Syria and Palestine, the LRDG learnt new skills: long marches over rough terrain under heavy load; the special techniques required to operate radios in mountains; boatwork on the coast; parachuting at Ramat David in Palestine; rudimentary Greek and German; and skiing. Although not destined to operate on skis, as Lloyd Owen wrote:

One of the finest methods of hardening men without destroying their interest or damping their enthusiasm was by teaching them how to ski.

The skiing taught was more akin to the cross-country version, with the majority of the time spent slogging up the mountains using skins on the bottom of skis to give a grip, rather than the kind where all the hard work is done by a ski lift. Despite the new role, the unit kept the title Long-Range Desert Group, as Lloyd Owen explains:

Firstly, it was the title by which we were known in the Middle East theatre of war and it would have caused confusion to have changed it – and anyway it was a name of which the members of the unit had become justly proud.

Secondly, there were security reasons which were valid. The Germans had suffered a good deal at our hands and were bound to be wondering where and when we might be employed again. While we were listed on the Order of Battle they would have to take precautions against our attacks.

One of the new arrivals in the LRDG was Ashley Greenwood:

I joined in a curious way. I went out from a mountain school in Scotland to the Middle East as a representative on a conference on mountain warfare. I got attached to an artillery unit in Tripoli in Syria [Lebanon]. They heard that the New Zealand Squadron of LRDG wanted a climbing instructor in the Cedars of Lebanon, a ski resort. I spent about two months there with them. I then went with them to the Dodecanese. While there we got a signal saying that a climbing instructor was required in Lebanon. Colonel Prendergast asked if I wanted to go. I said, 'No.' He sent a signal saying I was operationally vital. So I stayed in the LRDG for the rest of the war.

After the Dodecanese I was posted missing, and found I was still on the strength of Scottish Command. So I was missing in the Middle East and still officially in Scotland. My impressions of the LRDG were entrancing. I had never met New Zealanders before. They were quite different. The relationship between officers and men was different from the British Army.

On 8 September 1943, Italy concluded an Armistice with the Allies, and set in train a series of events that were to involve the SB Squadron and the LRDG. George Jellicoe:

In early September I was in Beirut having dinner with one of my officers, and a military policemen came in and said, 'Are you Major Lord Jellicoe?'

'Yes.'

'There is a message from your HQ to report straight away.'

There, I was told that a plane had been sent up from Cairo for me, and I was to be on the airfield at first light in full operational gear. On arrival at Cairo I went into a conference that had been in progress for about half an hour. I heard with some amazement that the Italian Armistice was to come into effect that evening. The plan was to send a small group to Rhodes to try to persuade the Italian C.-in-C. Admiral Campioni to come over to the Allied side. If that was successful he should be asked to hold the main airfields and the port of Rhodes.

That itself was a fairly tall order seeing that there was quite a strong German force with 70 tanks in Rhodes. But what really amazed me, and there were a lot of Generals and Brigadiers round the table, the small mission was to go up in a couple of RAF crash boats. If the weather was bad this would take some time. Furthermore, the message about their arrival would be conveyed by a Greek SOE operative in Rhodes but based on the German side of the island, and his wireless hadn't been working for the best part of a month. I couldn't contain myself and I said that it was not for me as a junior officer to comment but I would. I thought this was absolutely crazy, and the only sensible thing was to drop a party in by parachute that evening. Somewhat to my surprise this was agreed. Someone across the table called Major Dalby asked if I spoke Italian. I said, 'Not a word.'

He replied, 'You will need an interpreter, I would like to come with you.'

'Are you parachute trained,' I asked.

'Yes.'

I said, 'Fine.'

A plane was sent down, we boarded and flew around over Turkey. It was foggy, we never found Rhodes, the pilots hadn't been briefed properly, so we flew back. We found it the next night. On the way Major Dalby disclosed he had never parachuted. He asked me to push him out. We landed some way from the target as one often does. Dalby landed on the coastal road and broke his leg extremely badly. Our wireless operator fell further up the hill. I landed close to an Italian AA battery which opened up. They thought we were Germans. Already there had been some fighting between the Italians and the Germans. I heard people approaching. I had a letter from General Wilson to Admiral Campioni, and I had instructions that this letter must be destroyed if there were any danger of capture. I couldn't find anywhere to destroy it. So I ate the bloody thing. It was embossed and rather indigestible. About 45 minutes later the people I had heard came close, and I discovered they were Italian, I had thought they were German.

By the time I got into Rhodes I found Dalby talking to Admiral Campioni. How he did it I don't know. His bone was sticking out of his leg. I tried to persuade the Admiral to come over [to the Allies] and hold the port to allow the landing of a British Force. But it was beyond my powers of persuasion. He has been criticised, unfairly. He had it is true some 30,000 troops but spread all over the place, and without much transport. The last thing they wanted to do was to go on fighting. The Germans were only 7,000 strong, but held the airfields and had tanks. If I'd been Admiral Campioni I would have made the same decision. He was quite helpful. He evacuated Dalby in one of his seaplanes to Cyprus. He allowed me to use my radio to Cairo to try to speed things up to change the situation. Then he sent me off that evening in an Italian MTB, with all the plans of the Italian minefields in the Aegean to Castelrosso which a detachment of mine already occupied. I don't think he could have done more.

He was subsequently handed over by the Germans to the Italian

Government of the North and shot in Parma. He treated me absolutely fairly.

The decision was taken despite the failure to capture the airfields on Rhodes to penetrate further into the Aegean, the Prime Minister still pursuing his Aegean dream. I occupied Cos with David Sutherland in motor launches. We were welcomed by the Italian garrison in Cos. That was in the morning. Later that day I went in an Italian MTB to Leros. That was the beginning of the Dodecanese campaign and the fall of Leros.

As we saw in Chapter 3, Churchill had hoped since 1940 to entice Turkey, with its large army of forty divisions, into the war on the Allied side, and Layforce had been sent to the Middle East in 1941 to capture Rhodes as part of that strategy. The Dodecanese Islands, originally part of the Ottoman Empire, had been occupied by Italy since 1912 (the First Balkan War), but the Turks still claimed sovereignty. It was thought that if British garrisons could take over from the Italians in the Dodecanese, the Turks might be less coy about participating actively on the Allied side. Then with the Aegean in Allied control, Soviet Russia could be supplied through the Dardanelles and the Black Sea, and, as Churchill commented, 'There would be no more need for the perilous and costly Arctic convoys, or the long and wearisome supply line through the Persian Gulf.'[1]

Unfortunately, not for the first or last time in the War, these schemes did not take account of the speed and fury with which the Germans were capable of reacting. The key was Rhodes, because its airfields were essential if the Allied Air Forces were to exercise air control deep into the Aegean. However, the 7,000 German troops, who seized the island from the Italian Garrison, were too strong to be dislodged by anything other than a full-blooded amphibious assault by a division. The 8th Indian Division had actually been rehearsing for just this operation for months. But in August, the shipping earmarked for the assault was sent to the Far East for operations on the coast of Burma, and the Division was transferred to Allied Forces in the Central Mediterranean. No other formation or shipping was made available to the C.-in-C. Middle East, General Sir Henry ('Jumbo') Maitland Wilson, whose operational theatre had become a backwater since the invasion of Sicily and start of the Italian campaign, and would become more so as the Allied invasion of France loomed nearer. Wilson had to make do with his only operational reserve: the 234th Infantry Brigade, which had spent the war so far in Malta, the SB Squadron and the LRDG. Thus began the involvement of the LRDG and SB Squadron in another behind-the-lines operation together with the unfortunate 234th Infantry Brigade. The operation was behind the lines in the sense that the action took place deep in German-controlled air and sea space. Throughout the campaign, the Germans held Crete and Rhodes, as well as other islands in the Aegean, together with the Greek mainland; all of which provided bases for naval, air and ground-force operations against the British incursion into what was effectively a giant sack of which the enemy controlled the mouth as well as the sides.

When, on 10 September, two days after the Italian surrender, the call came for the LRDG to move to the Aegean, the Group was spread over Syria and Palestine. Most of B Squadron was at Ramat David on a parachute course, part of A and B Squadrons were at the Cedars with Group Headquarters, the majority of A Squadron was at Beirut about to embark on a combined operations exercise, and a large convoy of signals equipment was somewhere between Cairo and the Cedars. The LRDG were told that a (SB Squadron) base had been established on Castelrosso, and reconnaissance parties had been sent to Cos and Samos.

B Squadron, together with a detachment of SB Squadron and a company of the Durham Light Infantry (DLI), moved to Castelrosso where they 'were received with much enthusiasm by the population'. From here the Squadron was taken to Leros, where Lloyd Owen was told to form a mobile reserve in support of the Italian garrison, which by now was on the Allied side. The following day, he was told to 'send some men to Stampalia', the most westerly island in the Dodecanese not in German hands. On 20 September most of 234th Brigade arrived together with four of Lloyd Owen's jeeps. 'Three of these were promptly appropriated by 234th Brigade and LRDG were permitted the use of one,' remembered Lloyd Owen.

A Squadron arrived on Leros ten days later, by which time the Luftwaffe had started bombing the island. Two A Squadron patrols were sent to Kithnos and Giaros in the Cyclades, Greek Islands in the western Aegean, to report on enemy shipping and aircraft movements, while S1, a Rhodesian patrol, was despatched to Simi off the coast of Turkey. Meanwhile the rest of the LRDG, including Lloyd Owen's Squadron, together with the SB Squadron were concentrated on Calino, about three miles south of Leros. The only island from which Allied fighters could operate was Cos, garrisoned by a battalion of the DLI.

On 3 October the Germans landed on Cos, and by the next day the island was in their hands. The British forces in the Aegean were now left virtually without air support and fighter cover. The LRDG were ordered to counter-attack Cos, a task for which they were neither strong enough nor equipped nor trained. Fortunately this ridiculous order was rescinded. Calino was now untenable, so all the troops were ordered back to Leros. Luckily the move, in an assortment of ships and craft, was by night, and the LRDG had moved their stores away from Portolago harbour before first light and the arrival of fifty-five dive bombers in a raid lasting four hours.

Despite the lack of air cover which reduced the Royal Navy to operating mainly at night, reminiscent of the dark days off Crete two years before, the C.-in-C. Middle East decided to hold Leros and Samos for as long as possible. By 24 October, the garrison of Leros consisted of: Headquarters 234th Brigade, three battalions (King's Own, the Buffs with a company of Royal West Kents, and Royal Irish Fusiliers), about 200 men of the LRDG, 150 SB Squadron and 30 commandos. The Italians manned some 40 mm Breda flak guns, and five coastal defence batteries, each of four 6-inch guns. Destroyers, submarines and other craft brought in six 25-pounder guns, twelve 40 mm Bofors, jeeps and trailers. Mortars, machine-guns and ammunition were dropped by parachute.

The Germans had not had it all their own way. Two SB Squadron detachments under 'Jock' Lapraik, and including Anders Lassen, repulsed a German attempt to invade Simi with heavy loss to the enemy, at a cost of one of SB Squadron dead and two wounded. Enemy bombing resulted in Lapraik being ordered to withdraw, but he returned six weeks later to raid the island.

On 15 October Brigadier Turnbull was appointed Commander Raiding Forces Aegean, which comprised the LRDG, SB Squadron and commandos in the theatre. Headquarters Raiding Forces was, according to Lloyd Owen, a pretty useless organization. Almost the first decision by Turnbull was to appoint Prendergast as his deputy. Jake Easonsmith was made Commanding Officer of the LRDG, while Lloyd Owen, to his chagrin, became second-in-command, transferred from B Squadron.

Once Cos had fallen, it was thought that an immediate assault on Leros would follow. But attacks on enemy airfields in Greece, Crete and

Rhodes by the Royal Air Force, and on aircraft and shipping in the Aegean by the Royal Air Force and Royal Navy, caused the Germans to postpone their plans. The successful interdiction of the enemy owed much to LRDG patrols positioned on islands astride the air and sea routes to the Dodecanese giving early warning of the approach of hostile aircraft and shipping.

On 7 October, off Stampalia, the Royal Navy sank an enemy convoy carrying 2,500 troops following a radio message the previous day from T1 Patrol on Kithnos who had seen it pass between Kithnos and Siros. The Patrol reported the convoy's size, speed, air cover and probable route. There were only ninety survivors. T1 Patrol had been taken to Kithnos in an 18-ton caique of the Levant Schooner Flotilla manned by the Royal Navy. Although Kithnos was occupied by a small German garrison, the patrol evaded capture by hiding in sheep and goat shelters, changing location frequently, and moving only at night. The information being obtained by watchers on Kithnos was so valuable that it was decided to keep an OP in that area for as long as possible, but shift location to Seriphos when T1 was relieved by T2. Seriphos was safer, because the Germans maintained a watch on Kithnos by seaplane. T2 Patrol spent three weeks on Seriphos, which was garrisoned by about fifty Germans, without their presence being discovered. They were given considerable assistance by the Greek population, especially the postmaster and monks in the monastery. They saw only one ship, but when the Germans began a regular lift to Rhodes by four large flying boats, T2 reported by radio, and six Beaufighters shot all four down.

R1 Patrol spent seventeen days on Naxos, evading the 650-strong German garrison by frequently moving long distances at night. Again, they were given much help and warning of the enemy movements by the islanders. The patrol radioed back information of enemy shipping in Naxos harbour, which led to an attack by the Royal Air Force. Two enemy ships were sunk, but two aircraft were shot down. One crashed in the sea, and the pilot and navigator were rescued by Greek fishermen. They were taken to a local doctor, their wounds were treated, and they were hidden until R1 could take them back to Leros.

Royal Navy craft operating near Levita had been fired on by German guns, so the Navy demanded that the enemy be eliminated. As it was also thought that the island would provide a good OP site, the commander of 234th Brigade ordered the LRDG to capture it. Easonsmith's request for a reconnaissance before an assault was refused.

Captain John Olivey commanding a party known as Olforce consisting of forty-eight officers and men drawn from both squadrons was ordered 'to liquidate any enemy force that is on the island of Levita'. The plan involved a night landing by the B Squadron party, under Olivey, to the west of Port Levita and the A Squadron party, under Lieutenant Jack Sutherland, to the east. The objective for both parties was the high ground overlooking the port. The operation was a disaster. After landing, the two parties were unable to communicate with each other on the low-powered infantry sets issued specially for the operation, which were unable to cope with even a modest range or intervening high ground. The Navy motor launches, instead of shelling a house occupied by the enemy, shelled a hut near the A Squadron party, pinning them down. After a brisk battle, in which two New Zealanders were killed and one wounded, the A Squadron party captured the house on the ridge before dawn, taking thirty-five prisoners. B Squadron party under Olivey landed without incident and reached the German headquarters by first light. With the onset of daylight everything started to go wrong. Because neither party could communicate with the other, they were unable to co-ordinate the attack. German seaplanes based at Levita took off and directed JU88 and Stuka attacks on the LRDG parties all day. The LRDG had no means of hitting back, other than small-arms fire which proved ineffective. Despite repeated attempts, the enemy in prepared defensive positions were impossible to dislodge with small-arms fire. First the B Squadron party and then the A Squadron party were cut off and overrun. Olivey managed to get one message through to LRDG Headquarters on Leros, that they were up against stiff opposition.

All that day Easonsmith and Lloyd Owen stood on the highest point on Leros from where they could see the air attacks on Levita twenty miles away. There was nothing they could do in daylight. After dark, Easonsmith went by motor launch to try to find Olforce. At the agreed pick-up RV he found Olivey, the Medical Officer and five soldiers, one of them wounded. A second attempt to extract any survivors was made the following night by Major Guild, the commander of the New Zealand Squadron, and Olivey, but no one could be found.

In the conclusion to his report written afterwards, John Olivey is remarkably restrained:

4. Conclusion.

(a) The role that the force was obliged to adopt was that of a normal infantry [sub-unit] under particularly difficult conditions owing to complete air superiority of the enemy. The LRDG although highly trained in specialist work has not been trained for such work [normal infantry], and it is not considered a suitable role for the unit.
(b) It is essential that an attack under these conditions must have complete air support if the success of the operation is to be ensured. Without the interference of enemy aircraft, it is certain that the Garrison would have been overcome before dusk 24 October.

Lloyd Owen is more cutting:

We hated the whole foolish enterprise, which we felt was a wicked and misplaced attempt to regain by a spectacular success the confidence that Cairo had lost in the direction of the Aegean battle.

The Levita operation cost the LRDG two officers and thirty-nine soldiers, a bitter blow to such a highly trained unit. Easonsmith decided, after conferring with his Squadron Commanders, to recommend that the LRDG should be withdrawn, other than the patrols on the Cyclades. Major Guild was sent to Cairo to convey this view to GHQ. On his arrival he discovered that the New Zealand Government had already demanded the withdrawal of the New Zealand Squadron, because General Wilson had exceeded his authority by committing it to a new theatre, the Aegean, without first obtaining clearance from New Zealand. Wilson replied that the Squadron could not be replaced at short notice, and requested time to find and train replacements. The New Zealand Government agreed. It was too late, as the German assault on Leros began a few days later. Lloyd Owen had been sent, under protest, back to Cairo to collect recruits and train them:

I was lucky, I got out in an Italian submarine just before the battle started; one of the nastiest experiences in my life. It was putrid, stinking, they were terrified. I had to stand behind the CO because he was so frightened.

On Leros, the LRDG were deployed to bolster the Italians manning the coastal guns, and as force reserve to counter-attack enemy landings. On 12 November the Germans landed from the sea on the north of the island. Later that day, 500 parachute troops dropped on the narrow isthmus that divides the island. Having isolated the northern end of the island, the Germans concentrated on gaining key ground in the centre around the town of Leros. Although British counter-attacks made local gains, and at times it seemed that the battle might swing against the Germans, the incessant attacks by the Luftwaffe knocked out most of the 25-pounders and Bofors guns. A second parachute assault tipped the balance in favour of the enemy on 13 November. With total command of the air, the Germans could reinforce where troops were most needed to regain the initiative. The island garrison was joined by the remainder of the Royal West Kents from Samos, but no headway was made when the battalion was thrown into a hasty counter-attack.

On 16 November, the Germans attacked Mount Meraviglia where the British Headquarters, which included Prendergast, was located in some caves below the summit. The night before, Jake Easonsmith had been killed leading a patrol into Leros town. Prendergast wrote in his report after the battle:

> On hearing of Lt-Col. Easonsmith's death, I took over command of the LRDG and remained at LRDG HQ until early on the 16th, when I made a personal reconnaissance up to the top of the Meraviglia feature to see for myself what was happening above our heads. I found the top of the feature a very uncomfortable spot. It was under fire and also being mortared. There were at least six Stukas permanently overhead looking for suitable targets to attack, and periodically JU88s would come over and drop anti-personnel bombs. I lay for some time in an abandoned Italian ack ack (anti-aircraft gun) position and saw Germans ascending the feature. We exchanged a few shots and I went down to the main HQ and told the Brig that in my opinion it was essential immediately to stage a counter-attack on these troops to push them off the Meraviglia feature. He told me to return to my own HQ and he would see what could be done about collecting the necessary troops for this counter-attack.

Not long after this, the Brigadier told Prendergast that a counter-attack was impossible, and therefore he and his staff were leaving the caves to control the battle from Portolago, about two miles away on the coast. He ordered Prendergast to do likewise. Prendergast, having started off towards Portolago, realized that without the radios, which brigade headquarters had left in the caves, command and control from the new location would be impossible. He therefore returned to see if some of the sets could be salvaged. He found the sets in working order, and able to communicate with two of the infantry battalions and a set in Portolago. Prendergast spoke to the Brigadier, who told him to control the battle himself until he returned to reassume command, which he did later. Towards the end of the day, Prendergast was on his way to Portolago to drum up some troops to counter-attack the Meraviglia feature. Looking back, he saw a large number of German troops on top, and the headquarters staff lined up outside. A few minutes later the Brigadier drove up alongside Prendergast with two German officers and said that he had had to surrender. Prendergast decided to find some LRDG men, and try to escape.

While the Brigadier commanding the Leros garrison had been dithering, members of the LRDG had been busy elsewhere. Captain Olivey was in charge of a dozen LRDG, two artillery officers, several British gunners, and the Italian crews of three 6-inch naval guns situated near a fort on Mount Clidi (Point 320). Except for one officer, all the Italians deserted when the Germans started landing. For the next two days the LRDG fought with cunning and skill as successive German attacks gained a foothold on Mount Clidi. In accordance with his orders, Olivey ordered the guns destroyed when their capture appeared imminent. On 13 November, a counter-attack by a battalion of the King's Own failed, and by now the LRDG patrol were the only British troops on Mount Clidi, holding a small space behind the fort. The next day, the Buffs assisted by the LRDG, retook Clidi. Olivey then led an attack with the Buffs in an effort to clear more elbow room to the north of Clidi. The Germans had several well-sited machine-guns and mortars covering the difficult ground over which the attack was being mounted, and after suffering casualties, including the Buffs' commanding officer, the attack petered out, and Olivey and his patrol returned to Clidi. On 15 November, Olivey built himself a hide on top of the fort from where he could keep an all-round watch. Just before daybreak he visited the caves below the fort and captured four Germans and one Italian. The LRDG were bombed regularly throughout the day, and under fire from enemy machine-guns sited on a hill opposite. The next day all the infantry in the vicinity were withdrawn to a new defensive line, leaving Olivey's patrol unsupported. By now all the patrols in the north of Leros were cut off, and George Jellicoe had taken command of a composite group of LRDG and SB Squadron in that part of the island. Olivey asked Jellicoe,

> how long I had to hold the fort. He told me until our casualties were heavier than the enemy's, which seemed fair enough.

On 17 November Olivey received information that the Leros Garrison was about to surrender – or had even done so – and his patrol of three officers and twenty-one soldiers was to report to the battalion head-quarters of the Buffs. In his report:

> It had never been our plan that the patrol should surrender, and in view of our special training it was foolish to report to the enemy after the island had surrendered.

Olivey sent the two gunnery officers into the Buffs' headquarters, as he deemed that they were not sufficiently well trained to escape with the LRDG. He then decided to remain on Point 320 until he could assess the situation. By 08.00 hours it was clear from the German actions that the Leros Garrison had indeed surrendered. He ordered his corporals to withdraw their sections to the broken country to the north, and they moved out without being spotted by the enemy. Olivey remained until a German party suddenly arrived on his position. Olivey shammed dead, and the enemy passed him by. With the onset of darkness, Olivey decided to return to the fort which his men had been manning:

> with the idea of destroying one large naval gun which I felt was not sufficiently destroyed. I also considered blowing up the main magazine as a diversion to assist the Z barges which should be leaving with escapees from the north bay. My men had been informed of these barges, which were due to leave on three successive nights. I had laid the charges on the gun and in the magazine, but was without matches [special matches for lighting fuse, not the standard variety]. I returned to the fort where I knew I had concealed a box. I was surprised to find the fort occupied by two Germans who took me for one of their officers. I was forced to shoot them both, but the noise attracted others, and I had to make a hasty withdrawal.

He managed to avoid capture by hiding in some rocks, and in the early morning made his way to the RV for his patrol:

> It was daylight by the time I arrived there and I was not surprised to find no one [there]. I was tremendously tired by this time and very thirsty. I

could find no water cans in the position in which we had left them, so proceeded to the Italian barracks.

Here I found some bread, bacon, fat and water. A bed with sheets proved too great a temptation. I climbed in. As a light sleeper, I considered that I should have plenty of time to get out of the back window if anyone approached. I woke to find two German officers and some men at the foot of my bed. One spoke English fluently, and we discussed the battle at some length. I was put in a jeep and taken to a central collection point. Here were four or five officers and a number of other ranks of various regiments. A German captain informed me that the officers would be leaving by car for the docks at about 15.00 hours. I unfortunately still had my LRDG shoulder titles, badges of rank, MC ribbon, beret and identification card. When the Captain left, I went upstairs for a wash. Here I removed my shoulder title, badges of rank, MC ribbon and beret, joined the other ranks and marched with them to the docks. I contacted the men of the LRDG and informed them I had now become Private Harvey (my married sister's name) of the Sherwood Foresters (my parent unit).

Olivey managed to maintain his false identity in the days that followed. It is always best to make a break as early as possible after capture, and certainly before arriving at a purpose-built prison camp. Olivey escaped twice on Leros, but had the bad luck to be picked up on each occasion; first by German patrols looking for an escaped officer, and the second time by enemy 'on the scrounge' in a cottage in which he was hiding. Four days later with 1,500 other ranks and 20 officers, he was shipped to Piraeus on the Greek mainland, and marched through Athens, which:

was more like a victory march. The route was lined by Greeks who threw oranges, apples, cigarettes, etc. to our troops. The German guards tried to intercept these gifts. Some women were in tears, but the Tommies jested with them and cap badges etc. were thrown to the girls. Some men in the crowd spoke a word or two of English, and as we passed by we informed them we were from Leros.

By the time the POW column was through the main streets and out into the fringes of the city, it was dark:

At this stage the column had become somewhat straggly, so that the guards had become unevenly spaced. The guard beside me had dropped a little behind and taking advantage of a side street on a bend of the road, I ran down it. I believe the guard followed a little way, but he had no hope of seeing me in the dark, as I lay down under a wall.

This time Olivey's persistence was rewarded and he eventually made contact with the Greek Resistance. After four months spent in hiding in Athens, and a series of adventures in a caique taking him to Turkey, including being shipwrecked, he turned up in Cairo on 25 April 1944, five months after the fall of Leros.

Others among the resourceful and determined officers and soldiers of the LRDG also made their escape either directly from Leros or after capture. Captain Greenwood was in the combined LRDG/SB Squadron party under Jellicoe:

When the HQ surrendered, Jellicoe was at the surrender conference. He cleverly said that his chaps had been trained never to surrender unless he told them personally. The Germans let him go back. Jellicoe said to his chaps, 'I'm not going to surrender. Is anyone else?'

They all said they weren't either. So Jellicoe led us rapidly down to a harbour at the northern end of the island which hadn't been involved much in the fighting. He found a caique there. In the meantime I had been up to the various batteries to tell the LRDG patrols to go to the harbour. As I arrived at the harbour with about 11 people on my jeep, we saw the caique just leaving. We quickly pushed the jeep into the sea, the caique came back, and we jumped on board. We went to the nearest island about 2 to 3 miles away. It was very early in the morning. Jellicoe told us all to evacuate the caique. He gave us some food and water, and told us to hide ourselves for the day, because the German seaplanes would look for us and attack any troops, or the caique. Sure enough one came over, but the caique was empty, and they didn't attack.

That night we sailed to Turkey. I suppose I must have been the senior officer of the LRDG around, and when we arrived Jellicoe said to me, 'Well look here, there must be hundreds of British soldiers at large, someone must organise their escape. I myself must go off to report to Cairo.'

So I was left in a bit of a dilemma. So I said 'OK', and I returned to Leros in an RAF rescue launch with a Greek agent. We had to collect people together, and signal for the launch to come in and pick them up. After some two weeks, we went to the beach where we had been landed to be evacuated. We signalled with torches night after night. After seven or eight nights they didn't appear, although we heard a launch in the distance. So we decided they weren't going to come back. So a few of us had to organise our own escape which we did by rowing boat to a nearby island. From here the Greeks got us across to Turkey by caique.

The Germans on Leros did find out where we were assembling on Leros, but most of us managed to evade them. Most of the chaps were from the Royal Irish Fusiliers, or from the HQ. We were dressed in Greek clothes. Two signallers also dressed in Greek clothes found themselves working for the Germans in a working party, having been stopped on the road. By keeping absolutely quiet they got away with it, and at the end of the day when the working party was dismissed, they escaped and joined up with us.

The escapees ended up in Bodrum in Turkey. The Turks allowed the escapees to be repatriated to Palestine.

Lieutenant Mold was one of those who eventually met up with Greenwood, but during the long wait for the MLs, which never came, he got very bad dysentery. Not wanting to be a burden to the party, he swapped the civilian clothes he had acquired for Greenwood's battle-dress, and walked into the hospital in Alinda Bay. Here he found a British medical officer who gave him a tin of tablets and instructions. He persuaded the MO to leave him off the hospital list, before finding an unoccupied bed and sleeping, 'as well as possible with the complaint I had'.

The next morning he strolled around the former LRDG Headquarters area on Meraviglia, finding his identity discs and pack which had been looted. On returning to the hospital, he had another good night's sleep. The following morning, all the sick were taken to the hospital at Portolago, to be shipped off to Athens; still feeling very sick, and almost resigned to accept defeat:

As I looked through the broken windows at the ship in the harbour, I made up my mind that it would not be taking me. I asked several officers if they would take the chance with me and walk out, but they were not interested. So I went to a corporal medical orderly from the Royal Irish Fusiliers who I knew, and he said he was willing to keep me company. I walked out of the front entrance past a non-interested sentry, and by luck there was a water-carrying lorry standing in the drive. I indicated to the German driver and his mate that I wanted a lift back to the hospital in Alinda Bay to collect some forgotten kit. We had an enjoyable ride and jumped off the back just before arriving at the hospital.

Mold's luck was in, because he made contact with a Greek who had been looking after him during his days on the run immediately after the surrender. The Greek arranged for them to be taken to Turkey on a fishing boat. He told Mold that the boat would have no trouble passing the harbour boom:

> for he had arranged for two young ladies with some bottles of wine to pay a visit to the German machine-gun post covering the boom. He calculated that the sentries would be a little dozy by the time we wanted to pass their post. He was right, for we actually became entangled in the boom making quite a lot of noise without a sign of movement from the post. We arrived at the [Turkish] mainland without incident.

Of the 123 all ranks of the LRDG still alive on Leros at the surrender, a total of 11 officers (including Prendergast) and 58 other ranks had returned by the end of November 1943. Many more were to come in over the weeks and months ahead.

Leros was the last operation for the New Zealand Squadron. The New Zealand divisions fighting in Italy could no longer spare men for the LRDG, so the Squadron was disbanded and most of the officers and soldiers were sent to join the Divisional Cavalry (armoured cars) with the New Zealand 2nd Division in Italy. The New Zealanders were replaced with a complete squadron of Rhodesians, commanded by Major K. H. Lazarus, who had joined the LRDG in 1941. Major Moir Stormonth-Darling of the Cameronians took over B Squadron. Lloyd Owen was appointed Commanding Officer. There was a great deal to be done before the LRDG was once more ready for operations, which would be in the early summer of 1944.

The German commitment to holding the Aegean cost them about six divisions' worth of troops, as well as a considerable number of naval craft and aircraft. Because it was in the British interest to keep as many German troops as possible committed to protecting the Dodecanese and Cyclades, to prevent them being deployed to Italy or France, the SB Squadron, assisted by the Greek Sacred Regiment, naval coastal forces and the Royal Air Force, continued to maintain pressure on the German forces in the Aegean, by raiding and causing as much mayhem as possible. It is arguable that this would have been a better strategy for Churchill to have pursued in the first place rather than trying to capture and hold 'real estate'. British losses were: five battalions (totalling some

4,800 men – the majority prisoners of war), several highly trained LRDG members, six destroyers, two submarines, ten coastal craft and minesweepers and 113 aircraft, as well as four cruisers damaged. German losses were: 1,184 men, 15 small landing craft and ferries, a number of merchant ships and a few aircraft.

Throughout the Turks hunted with the hounds and ran with the hare, allowing British vessels to operate from their territorial waters, and German warships to transit the Dardanelles to and from the Black Sea. They continued to allow both sides to abuse Turkish neutrality by averting their eyes, and being deaf to any protestations.

*

In Italy neither the SRS nor 2nd SAS was used much in the deep-penetration raids for which David Stirling's SAS had become famous in the desert war. The terrain in Italy – mountains, narrow roads and the impossibility of driving across country in many places – presented considerable challenges to anyone attempting vehicle-mounted operations behind the lines, although Popski's Private Army was to try it, at first with very dubious results.

Although the SRS was used in several imaginative operations in Sicily and Italy, perhaps the most notable behind-the-lines operation in Italy in which Paddy Mayne's SRS played a part was the amphibious hook to capture the port and town of Termoli. This operation by 2nd Special Service Brigade consisting of the SRS, Number 3 Commando and Number 40 (Royal Marines) Commando aimed at countering any attempt by the Germans to establish a defensive line on the Bifurno River and delaying the British 8th Army advancing north from Foggia. The operation was a classic example of employing commandos in the role alluded to in Chapter 1: operating ahead, or on the flanks, of the main force as important players in the operational plan. To use the SRS as shock troops was an unusual role for what were in effect SAS soldiers. But they were available, and neither Mayne nor his men were averse to a bit of action.

Intelligence on the German dispositions was patchy, and although it was known that elements of the German 1st Parachute Division would be in the vicinity, the arrival of 26th Panzer Division to rest and refit after fighting at Salerno was completely unexpected. The assault on the night of 2/3 October 1943 was uneventful, except for the familiar inconvenience of a wet landing for some. After a stiff fight for the railway station, 40 (RM) Commando pressed on south, and the SRS patrolled forward to the Bifurno. Here they met the leading elements of British 11th Brigade, the advance guard of 78th Division. Both Numbers 3 and 40 (RM) Commando and the SRS laid a series of successful ambushes, inflicting damage on the enemy and taking a number of prisoners. About midday on 4 October, the British 36th Brigade, which had landed from the sea the previous night, asked for assistance in countering an increasingly strong enemy armoured threat. At the same time, 11th Brigade also asked for help. The two Commandos and the SRS had some tough fighting that night despite yet another British brigade being landed across the beaches. Finally on 6 October, the Special Service Brigade was withdrawn into reserve, having taken about 130 casualties.

2nd SAS were having a less fruitful time. They carried out some reconnaissance tasks for 8th Army, and were involved in manning RVs for Allied POWs who had escaped from Italian prison camps ahead of the Germans. But Bill Stirling did not see these as the correct use of his men, and pressed for them to be parachuted deep behind enemy lines to carry out sabotage. He was only allowed to carry out this type of operation twice. On the first occasion twenty men were dropped north of Florence to damage the railway system along which the Germans were reinforcing the front. They managed to derail fourteen trains. Unfortunately the operations was not repeated, and the lines were soon in service again.

The second target was the airfield at San Egidio, lying north of the road and railway between Perugia and Assisi, about 150 miles behind the German lines; the operation was codenamed Pomegranate. The party was commanded by Major Widdrington, with Lieutenant Quentin Hughes and four soldiers. Widdrington chose to insert by parachute rather than land by sea, which would have involved a long approach march of at least fifty miles in very rough terrain, thus limiting the load that could be carried and hence the amount of explosive taken. The DZ selected was east of Lake Trasimeno, in a valley running east near Magione. The party carried Lewes bombs to destroy the aircraft. The Lewes bombs would be detonated by lead (L) delay timers. These crude devices consisted of a metal tube containing a strong spring pulled out to its full extent. When a retaining pin was removed, the spring was held at tension by a lead wire. A combination of the thickness of the wire, and the outside temperature determined how long it took for the lead wire to snap, thus allowing the spring to drive a firing pin on to the detonator which set off the primer and the explosive. The warmer the temperature, the more malleable the lead wire, and the quicker it would break. Provided one could reasonably accurately forecast the temperature at the target, one could select the timer with the necessary thickness of lead wire to achieve the delay required; usually at least an hour to allow sufficient time to get well clear of the target area. In addition the party carried pull igniters which detonated the bomb in thirty seconds. These would be used if the enemy surprised the party during the raid, in which case the bombs would be thrown at the target. Neither type of detonator was fitted to the bomb until the last minute.

On 12 January 1944, the weather was reported as favourable, and the SAS party took off in a USAAF Dakota from Gioia del Colle, about twenty-five miles south of Bari, at 20.00 hours. On the way, the aircraft flew into cloud, but it dispersed over the DZ, and the party was dropped accurately at about 22.30 hours. After dropping the parachutists, the Dakota turned for home, but was never seen again. It was assumed that it crashed into the mountains in cloud. Icing and nine-tenths cloud was reported by a force of Wellington bombers sent to bomb Perugia to divert attention from the lone Dakota. Quentin Hughes wrote a report on the operation and a personal account in the form of a diary:

> The landing was soft and sticky but very much too near the road where some inquisitive Italians had waited only long enough to catch a glimpse of us. Four of our party closed on me quite quickly but Tony W [Widdrington] and McCormick had caught their parachutes in trees and we spent half an hour trying to find them.

After hiding their parachutes, they set off, and having marched for the rest of the night, lay up for the day in a wooded ravine. Here they were found by some Italian woodsmen who had followed their tracks. They told Widdrington that the Germans had discovered the parachutes on the DZ, and were now searching the farmhouses in the valley. The party started marching after dark. Their route was planned to take them in a wide arc well north and east of Perugia, before turning south to San Egidio. Two days' hard climbing with their heavy rucksacks took them over Mount Terzio. Here they brewed up the first hot drink since leaving

Gioia. Descending to the River Tiber, they found it in spate and unfordable. As luck would have it, they found:

> an overhead cable way, from which was suspended a cradle which could be pulled across the river, to and fro. After four crossings, which made the most indescribable noise, the whole party found itself on the far bank.

At this stage, Lance-Corporal Malloy announced that he had left his carbine on the far bank. He was winched back to retrieve it, and this fifth journey alerted the hitherto dozy German sentry, who ambled forward and challenged them. Widdrington, not wishing to draw attention to themselves by starting a firefight, ordered the party to move back through surrounding houses and into the fields. At this stage the party split, and the two officers never regained contact with the four soldiers. Apparently the party did not have a system of emergency RVs along their route to cater for just such an incident. Widdrington and Hughes pressed on, arriving at a wood about three miles north of the airfield on the night of 17/18 January. Here they cached their rucksacks and carbines. They penetrated the wire with ease. Once inside they primed their Lewes bombs, finally pulling the pins from the L delay timers. Normally, the pins were removed *after* placing bombs on the target. They had been told by Major Miller the explosives officer that the type of timer they had been given would give one hour's delay at 65 degrees F. They reasoned that the night was much colder than that, and they should have at least two and a half hours' grace in which to place their bombs and get well clear. They placed bombs on all seven aircraft, all that were on the airfield. While they were removing the fuses from the remaining bombs to make them safe, one of Widdrington's exploded, killing him and badly wounding Hughes.

Hughes, who had been blinded, was taken to hospital in Perugia. Here he was threatened with being shot under the terms of Hitler's 'Commando Order'. Eventually the sight came back to his left eye, and a German doctor operated to save his right eye from losing its sight altogether. This doctor also managed to persuade the Gestapo temporarily to rescind the order to have Hughes shot, and arranged for him to be transferred to a hospital in Florence where he would be safer from the clutches of the Gestapo.

Some weeks later, Hughes was being taken with other wounded POWs by train through Lombardy on their way to a camp in Germany. Hughes, with Bradburn, a USAAF sergeant, and Signalman Taylor, Royal Signals, who had his left arm and shoulder encased in plaster, escaped from the train as it was slowly drawing out of Modena. From his account:

> I lay flat, my heart thumping wildly as the endless train crept passed us. What an age it seemed, but at last it was gone and no shots were fired. No one had missed us. We collected ourselves and, making a large circuit of the town, crossed the railway at the far side. With the dawn we felt exhausted and timidly approaching the nearest farm, asked for assistance. They were kind, hiding us in a cold stable during daylight. By afternoon they took us and fed us and exchanged some of our clothes for scarecrow apparel.
>
> From there we wandered south by day, avoiding towns and villages, but I fear deceiving no one of our true identity in this ragged turnout, always making for the range of mountains which seemed so far away.

The Italians fed them on their route, and hid them in barns and cow stalls. When they reached the mountains:

> A succession of high ridges and deep valleys confronted us as we moved slowly southwards getting weaker all the time. Weeks in hospital had not assisted our stamina. The American had a score of wounds, many still open, and Taylor was little better.
>
> At last on 22 March we contacted a Partisan patrol, and after a good meal, were guided to their Brigade Headquarters at a little church in the tiny village of Strabetenza.

Here Hughes's party met some other escaped Allied POWs, including Brigadier Stirling (ex 13/18th Hussars and no relation of David Stirling), and a South African, Brigadier Armstrong. They had originally been held in a senior officers' camp along with Generals O'Connor and Neame. The senior officers had eventually escaped after the Italian Armistice. Many of them had already made their way to the Adriatic coast where they had been picked up by A Force, an organization tasked with rescuing POWs from central Italy. The two brigadiers were planning on following the same route arranged by an A Force agent. Hughes joined them and, with a sapper officer, set out for the coast. Taylor and Bradburn were too weak to travel, so Hughes left them in the Partisan hospital. When the Germans subsequently attacked the Partisan headquarters, these two were recaptured.

Hughes and his companions were able to make good progress thanks to money with which to pay guides and buy food:

> Using forged identity cards, and sometimes riding in pony carts, we passed through the Partisan walled stronghold of Cingoli, down through Appignano, unmolested through a police check point at Monte Giusto, and into the valley of the Tenna, at last in sight of the sea.

They reached the RV at a farmhouse at Lattanzi on 14 April, hoping to be picked up by boat the next night from a beach near Porto San Georgio. Unfortunately the boat had approached the coast at the wrong place and been fired on. The agent, Cagnezzo, known as 'Keg', had swum ashore, but his radio operator was missing. The other radio at the RV would not work, so communication with A Force HQ behind the Allied lines was reduced to sending messages by bicycle, to the Partisan radio station at Cingoli, thirty-five miles away across enemy-held country. After days of frustration, with the ever-present fear of betrayal and recapture, 'Keg' eventually managed to acquire a sailing fishing boat. Hughes's account:

> In normal circumstances I would not venture on the park lake in it, but these circumstances were not normal, so we must make do. With groans and creaks we pushed the old hulk down the shingle to the sea, stopping as cars passed along the road, hardly daring to believe that we would not be seen in the bright cold moonlight. As the bows entered the water, that cold, cold Adriatic, we all moved to the stern. The waves beat on the bows and almost immediately the boat spun round and was taking wave after wave amidships, rapidly filling. Clambering into the deep up to our chests, we eventually got her afloat, just afloat, with the water inside almost as high as that outside. Ordered to bail, we all removed our trilby hats and comically baled as the level of water slowly fell.
>
> We headed from the shore slowly standing to the south-east, all of us very wet, very cold, and some of us sick. The most dejected member of the crew was an unfortunate white rabbit the Italians had insisted on bringing for good luck, and which looked quite dead already.
>
> The old boat had not been to sea for many months, and all the boards let water in almost as quickly as our trilbys were able to discharge it over the side.

Despite their problems they made good progress during the night for by daylight the massive, snow-covered ridges of Gran Sasso d'Italia were abeam. Later they could hear the noise of gunfire as they passed the point on the coast where the eastern extremity of the Allied line confronted the Germans. They hung out a sheet with the letters POW painted on in black to avoid strafing by the numerous Allied aircraft passing overhead. At midday they turned inshore and landed at San Vito-Chietino, south of Ortona:

> A reception committee was waiting for us on the beach, a handful of Carabinieri and, behold, two British Military Policemen.

Hughes's comments in his report includes the sentence, 'I would not care to use L-Delays again.' As Captain Miller, the explosives expert, remarked in a report referring to the fact that the pins were withdrawn before placing the bombs:

> This was of course a very risky procedure, but a very brave one. I can only suggest that after they had laid the bombs, Major Widdrington carried those that he had left with the delays in his hand, or close to his body, and thus warming them up. This would reduce the timing of the delay, which, in fact, went off after one hour and twenty minutes. [Author's note: Miller is being tactful, it was an extremely foolhardy procedure with these 'Heath Robinson' contraptions. Widdrington and Hughes had no means of judging exactly what the temperature was, and even if they had, these timers were very imprecise. The bomb that killed Widdrington detonated only *twenty minutes* after it should have done if the temperature had been 65 degrees F, and not 2½ hours as Hughes and Widdrington had guessed.]

The other four members of his patrol, who had become separated at the Tiber crossing, had made their way to the airfield, but arrived after the attack so made their way back through the German lines. The final effort by 2nd SAS in Italy involved sixteen men landing from an MTB and cutting the railway line between Giulianova and Ancona; a rather fruitless operation, since railway lines are easily and quickly repaired.

The SB Squadron continued to raid in the Aegean with considerable success. For some time Lapraik had been contemplating a return trip to Simi, and in July the operation was mounted. However, two ex-Italian destroyers, now crewed by the Germans, posed a considerable threat to any force raiding Simi, and these had to be located and eliminated first. In Chapter 5 we saw that Pritchard-Gordon had brought out his section of the RMBPD to the Middle East, and come under the command of

Brigadier Turnbull's Raiding Forces Middle East. Lieutenant Richards with five men and three canoes of the RMBPD were based in a camouflaged caique just off the Turkish coast about forty miles east of Leros. On the afternoon of 16 July 1944, a Royal Navy Fairmile ML Number 360 arrived with recent air photographs of Portolago harbour on Leros, showing that not only were there two supply ships anchored there, the *Anita* and *Carola*, but also the two destroyers, a flak craft and some smaller escorts. ML 360 embarked Richards' section and their canoes, and launched them off Leros. Richards and Marine Stevens were in *Shark*, Sergeant King and Marine Ruff in *Salmon*, and Corporal Horner and Marine Fisher in *Shrimp*. Corporal Horner:

> In our canoes we had our Sten gun and fighting knife, camouflage nets, twenty-four-hour ration pack, water, and eight magnetic limpet mines. We hadn't screwed down on the delay device; a butterfly nut on top of the limpet which crushes an ampule of acid. The strength of the acid determined the time taken for it to eat through a capsule and release the firing pin. We had four and a half-hour-delay ampules, which depending on the temperature would detonate the limpet half an hour either side of the designed delay time.
>
> We followed each other underneath the shadow of the cliffs before we got to the entrance. Lt Richards told us to screw down on our limpets. I was ordered to go in first, the others to follow at fifteen-minute intervals. We used single paddle, the lowest position. We passed the boom boat, and paddled over the boom.
>
> As we got into the harbour and were approaching our target's position, we could see it looming up. The stars made the strip midstream like the beam of a searchlight. To the right and left under the cliff was quite dark, as was the naval base. Right in the centre the *Anita* [Horner's target] was lying fore and aft. We were approaching her stern, and when we were two to three hundred yards off, a motor boat came across our bow. The sailors were shouting and singing. It seemed like a liberty boat returning to their base.
>
> As we started moving towards *Anita*'s stern, we saw three or four men standing by the guard rail looking straight down on us. They shouted. There was nothing we could do. If we were caught, the raid would have to be aborted.

Horner remembered being told that a German crack unit called Brandenburgers patrolled the harbours from time to time. Whether this was true or not, he called out 'Brandenburger Patrola'.

We were now alongside, and they were still shouting at us. What seemed to be a Jacob's ladder started coming over the side and they were shining a torch. I called 'Patrola' again and proceeded to the bow [of the target] and over to the shadow of the cliffs. There we stayed silent and waited. We really thought we had opened up a hornet's nest. But nothing happened. It was very quiet, and we decided that we couldn't go up a further mile and a half to our other targets, and the best thing we could do was get away to the lie-up position at Kalymo Island two to three miles away.

We negotiated the boom successfully. We remembered to get rid of our limpet mines which were live, we set course for our lie-up position. Finally, after rejecting one sea cave because there was a net across the entrance, we got off on a rocky inlet, got our canoe out, unloaded our stores, and put the canoe in the crevasse of some rocks and covered it with the camouflage net. Taking our weapons, personal camouflage nets, rations and water bottles, we climbed the steep earth and found a large overhanging rock. From here we could see Leros and the coast of Turkey. As dawn came up we saw a canoe go by below. We knew we would have to go the same way that night to make contact.

During the day there was a lot of activity and aeroplanes flying around. We heard bangs coming from Leros. There was activity on the cliffs above us. We were told later there was a pillbox up there, and the noise could have been a patrol. But we were safe where we were.

The sea cave we had almost gone into turned out to have been a hiding place for Greek fishermen, because patrol boats fired into it to flush them out. One or two patrol boats went by our lying-up position but nothing happened.

At about 11 p.m. we made our way down to our canoe and paddled in the direction of the other canoe. I made contact using our bird call. It was Lieutenant Richards and Marine Stevens. We made contact with the ML using a walkie-talkie. As we paddled out, we heard Sergeant King on his walkie-talkie saying he was coming in. We were all picked up, and the ML proceeded to its hide-up in a bay on the Turkish coast.

Lt Richards had attacked the destroyers, and Sgt King the escort. Although badly damaged they didn't sink. However, when they were on tow to Piraeus harbour for repair, they were sunk by the RAF.

With hindsight, Horner believes that he should have approached from the ship's bow which was in darkness. However, his quick thinking, and avoiding capture, allowed the other two canoes to approach the targets and complete the mission.

Marine Stevens:

No sooner were we in [the harbour], than we heard a shout, we learned later it was Horner. We fixed about six or seven limpets, including three on the destroyer. Although a man looked down on us from one of the ships, and urinated over the side all over us, he didn't see us. We canoed out of the harbour and lay up on a little island. We arrived as dawn was breaking. We saw a canoe going by, and it was Fisher. We camouflaged our canoes using nets over chicken wire. You could make various shapes with the chicken wire, a rock for example. We heard the limpets going off that day. During that day a machine-gun opened up. You could hear the bullets ricocheting all around, and we thought they were aiming at us. But it was a fishing boat that was the target. We contacted the ML on the walkie-talkie. On the way out we met King and Ruff. We learned later that King had sunk one destroyer and we the other.

Lieutenant Richards was awarded the Distinguished Service Cross, and Sergeant King and Marine Ruff the Distinguished Service Medal for this remarkable effort. As Pritchard-Gordon remarked, 'This was one of the rare occasions when six men went out and six men came back.' This operation was perhaps the most successful ship attack by the RMBPD in their four years of life as a unit, because it had a direct relevance to a forthcoming battle. Although they were used in a raiding role subsequently in the Aegean, this was the last successful ship attack (the principal reason for their existence) they carried out.

Thanks to the RMBPD the Simi operation could now go ahead. A force 240 strong consisting of 81 from the SB Squadron and 159 from the Greek Sacred Regiment landed on 14 July. After some brisk fighting the Germans surrendered. For the loss of two Greek officers killed and six soldiers wounded, the raiders had taken 185 German prisoners, destroyed ammunition, fuel dumps and nineteen caiques, and captured two patrol boats. The raiders could not stay on Simi, but it was a good proving operation for the Greek Sacred Regiment, who from now on were to form the main part of Raiding Forces Aegean. Most of the SB Squadron were transferred to Italy, where the LRDG were already operating. Lapraik with a team from SB Squadron remained in the Aegean as part of Raiding Forces, and carried out some spectacular operations.

For months Lloyd Owen had been chafing to get away from the Aegean which he recognized was a backwater, as he felt that his men would be better employed in the Balkans and Italy. The impending return of the SAS to the United Kingdom provided the catalyst for the order which to Lloyd Owen's delight came on 28 February 1944: this was to fly to Italy and discuss future operations with the staff in General Sir Harold Alexander's Headquarters at Caserta, north of Naples. Alexander was by then C.-in-C. Allied Forces Italy. Lloyd Owen was also told to contact the SAS in order that the LRDG could take over some of their tasks for which they, the LRDG, were better trained and suited. Lloyd Owen flew in one of the LRDG's 'private air force' WACOs.

To begin with Lloyd Owen had a frustrating time, as well as discerning that 2nd SAS were not popular, as extracts from two letters to Prendergast in Cairo reveal:

> *2.3.44*
> I landed at Bari to find that no one had ever heard of me or 2nd SAS. The LG [airfield] was 7 miles from Bari and after 1½ hours I got a lift into Bari. Here I learnt that 2nd SAS were about 50 miles from Bari, but were moving at midnight en route England. I therefore got a car and went there as fast as I could. I arrived to find they had all gone to Taranto half an hour earlier, but there was one officer and about 4 chaps who knew nothing of me or anything much. . . .

After arriving at Alexander's Headquarters, Allied Command Mediterranean Forces (ACMF):

> . . . . I have got it agreed that we come under command ACMF and not of anything lower. . . .
> It appears that 2nd SAS have been thoroughly unpopular everywhere, and were always a nuisance. This must not happen with us.
> *3.3.44*
> . . . . My feelings about the future are this: if LRDG is coming here complete then it's only an additional channel and waste of time to have any part of RF [Raiding Forces] HQ with us. . . .
> Unfortunately SAS unknown to everyone have gone away with all their equipment and given the rest away. They had lots of carbines and powered dories each of which we want. From all accounts they were universally disliked and I have been trying to let people know that we are not like that. I met their detachment commander today. A tiresome bragging type. It appears too that they have achieved little as the majority of their parties have failed to return, but mainly through gross mismanagement.

To be fair to the SAS, the LRDG were to discover that operating in Italy was very different from, and in some ways more hazardous than, the desert. Not the least of their problems was that whereas in the desert the highly skilled LRDG navigators and drivers were entirely responsible for transporting themselves to the target, in Italy and the Adriatic they were sometimes in the hands of others whose navigation and professionalism were not always up to the mark. It must be said that the Special Duty squadrons, who dropped agents, were usually very accurate; as were the experienced aircrew of some RAF and USAAF transport squadrons. But for the less expert transport squadrons, British and American, inserting troops by parachute in the right place at night was difficult enough when preceded by pathfinders to set up beacons to assist navigation. Even then it was not uncommon for at least half the force to be dropped miles from the target. Jumping 'blind', without terminal guidance, was even more chancy. These problems were not peculiar to the Allied air forces in Italy, but applied to parachute operations, large or small, in every theatre in the Second World War.

The LRDG's first patrol in their new theatre set out on 16 May 1944, their target Corfu, to find out as much as possible about an enemy radar station on the island. The information brought back by Stan Eastwood's Rhodesian patrol was comprehensive and accurate; the fact that it was never used does not detract from a very professional reconnaissance. It was a good start, the LRDG had shown what it could do. There were however to be some very frustrating times in this theatre for Lloyd Owen and his men. The weather, terrain, the operational scene, and sometimes the politics, especially in Yugoslavia and elsewhere in the Balkans, often conspired to make life for LRDG patrols and their commanding officer very different from their time in the wide open spaces of the desert.

The early parachute operations were not a success. Ashley Greenwood was on one of them, his task:

> to report on the roads and German troop strength and dispositions. This was about the time that Rome was captured in June 1944. Four patrols were dropped. One patrol leader's parachute failed to open, the static line had been eaten through by battery acid. His patrol were all captured except for one man.
>
> One patrol landed intact in a fairly reasonable spot. They didn't manage to get any messages through. But the commander managed to lead his

patrol back to the British lines intact. My patrol and one led by Gordon Rowbottom were supposed to meet up. We were both dropped entirely in the wrong place. The DZ was supposed to be a secluded valley, in fact I was dropped about 20 miles away in the main Tiber valley, teeming with German troops, and I landed on the roof of a small church just before dawn. I was not injured. I had a cow bell with me to contact the rest of the patrol. But I could not use this on the roof of a church. [There are few cows on church roofs.] I got down as it was getting light. I met an Italian. He said, 'Why have you come here? It's full of Germans.'

At that moment I heard the Germans forming up. I got out of the middle of the town, and went round houses asking if they had seen any British. The inhabitants of the first house said they had two German officers staying, so I moved on. By now it was daylight. I was in uniform, so I lay down under cover. That night I went round, and was told all the chaps had been captured. This wasn't true. One had laid low, and remained in hiding until the Allies took the area later.

I was by myself thinking everybody had been captured. I walked through the hills. On the second night I was accosted by 'Qui va là, qui va là?'

Immediately a shot was fired from about five yards. This turned out to be Italian partisans, who at first thought I was a German. When I established my identity they were all over me. I spoke a bit of Italian. He had missed me at such a short range because his rifle barrel was bent. They were very helpful. I tried to meet up with Gordon Rowbottom with the help of the partisans. He had also been dropped in the wrong place, I later discovered, so I didn't find him. So I decided to walk back myself, which I succeeded in doing. The partisans passed me from one lot to another, until there were no more partisans. I met up with an Italian and we walked along the mountains near Lake Trasimeno. There was battle going on the other side of the lake between 8th Army and the Germans. We got to a farm towards evening. The Italian did a recce and said it was impossible to get through. I decided to go on alone. I descended from the mountains. I found myself among German batteries. They were just preparing their evening meal, and were fully occupied, among olive trees. I feared I might fall into a gun pit. So I decided to go to the lake and try and get a rowing boat. There were tall reeds, marsh and ditches, and I was able to use this to walk along in complete safety. There were no boats. In the middle of the night, I came across a barn, which I found was full of German equipment. I picked up a German haversack, and a helmet. I peeped into a farm, and two sentries came out. I walked on until dawn. I met an Italian woman, who told me the Germans had gone. I walked along the road until I met some South African engineers. I went on to 8th Army HQ. The haversack was full of cigarettes and cigars. I gave the cigarettes to Italian peasants, and kept the cigars.

That operation was a failure. We had not been dropped nearly far enough behind the lines; I was dropped about 10 miles behind the lines.

Rowbottom's patrol dropped together in the wrong place, but soon ran into a German patrol and had to split up. Later, after being captured by more Germans, Rowbottom escaped, and managed to rendezvous with two of his patrol. Together with two South African escaped POWs, they joined a partisan band which mined roads and caused mayhem until he reached the British lines on 26 July. Sergeant Morley of Rowbottom's patrol collected some very useful information on his way back to his own lines, which he reached on his third attempt, in a sector held by 4th Indian Division. They asked him to guide 1/9th Gurkha Rifles back to a place from which, he, Morley had just come. He did so, and was awarded a very well-earned Military Medal.

Throughout the campaign in the Adriatic, as they had in the Aegean, the LRDG maintained shipping watches on the coast; a maritime version of the road watch in the desert. Again, following the Aegean experience, they passed the details of enemy convoys to LRDG Headquarters who asked for air strikes on the convoys. Before long the reaction time to these LRDG sightings achieved by the RAF was very quick indeed. The first shipping watch in the campaign was mounted by Captain Arthur Stokes and four other Rhodesians on the Dalmatian coast. He remained behind enemy lines for five months, being supplied by air drops. He was such a thorn in the enemy's side that they put a large price on his head, and he had to keep moving to avoid detection.

Lloyd Owen also acquired the first vessel for an LRDG 'private navy', the motor fishing vessel (MFV) *La Palma*. She was stripped down, fitted with guns, accommodation for the crew, and a space was cleared so a jeep could be lashed on deck. Captain Alan Denniff, who had been Lloyd Owen's navigator in the desert, was her skipper, with 'Tich' Cave, who had been Lloyd Owen's gunner, as bosun. Possessing their own craft enabled the LRDG to go some way to regaining their independence of others less reliable than themselves.

In mid-June Captain Stan Eastwood's patrol was sent to investigate a German lookout station on a promontory south of the port of Velona (now Vlorë) on the Albanian coast. This station had been reporting the movements of Allied shipping in that part of the Adriatic. From Eastwood's reports it became clear that the position, in a concrete building protected by pillboxes, surrounded by barbed wire, and with no cover on the approaches, would be difficult to attack. Lloyd Owen discovered that the Royal Navy were keen to take a hand and offered the destroyers HMS *Terpsichore*, *Tumult* and *Tenacious* for naval gunfire support; so plans were made to attack the lookout station. Lloyd Owen sent two other patrols to reinforce Eastwood. The whole raiding force was commanded by Captain Tony Browne MC DCM, a New Zealander, a founder member of the LRDG, and one of the few who had managed to return to the LRDG from the New Zealand Division. He was now the Intelligence Officer. Lloyd Owen decided to accompany the party.

On 28 June Eastwood signalled that all was ready for their reception. Lloyd Owen's diary:

> *28th June*
> Woke up at 6.30 when Tony [Captain L. H. Browne MC DCM] went to Brindisi to tie up plans for tonight. Stan [Stan Eastwood] signalled that RAF beat up target at 07.00 this morning! What wonderful cooperation! RAF express ignorance of Stan's presence and of operation even though A.O.C.-in-C. [Air Officer Commanding-in-Chief] finally approved. At Brindisi Tony briefed S1 and S2 patrols who were doing the party. We had some food on the quay and Charles [Captain and later Major Hall from Rhodesia Adjutant and subsequently 2ic] and I went to the Officers' Club for dinner.

They crossed the Adriatic in an Italian MAS boat escorted by another. Lloyd Owen took a dislike to the Italian captain and, 'wasted some time in trying to persuade him to act with slightly less trepidation'. Eastwood was waiting for them on the beach when they arrived at 02.30 the next morning. Lloyd Owen's diary:

> Soon after dawn Stan and I moved off towards the target with a shepherd whom Cela [a partisan interpreter] had produced for us. We kept under the cover of the trees and the remainder followed us quietly. It was a long walk and we had frequent stops under the trees as the country was very rocky and very rough going. By about 9.30 we had reached a spot near a well of clear cool water and here we settled down under the trees in good cover for the day. Stan, Mike [2/Lt M Reynolds MC, Rhodesian OC T1 Patrol], Tony, the Naval FOO [Forward Observation Officer to control the

naval gunfire] and I after a while moved on up to a position where we could observe the target. We were about a 1,000 yards away and through our glasses could see the concrete pillboxes and the sentry on the roof. Other Germans were walking about around the house inside the wire perimeter.

On rejoining the others,

then had a meeting of everyone to decide on the final plans for the raid. Everyone was in very good heart and keen to get in to deal with the enemy. The plan was to move up within about 700 yards of the target after dusk and to await the blitz [*sic*] by three destroyers. After they had been successfully laid on the target by the FOO, the attacking party could move nearer and when they considered it fit would call off the fire of the destroyers and then go in and mop up the position.

The party moved towards the target:

By 11.00 [23.00] all was ready, but Stan's party had gone to within 400 yards which was closer than anticipated. In the moonlight we could see the three ships lurking in close to shore and gliding slowly along the rippled water. They were dark sinister forms. At 11.30 [23.30] a blinding flash lit up the whole mountain and a star shell floated silently down and right above our men. A frantic call to the destroyer was answered by the first ranging round from the first destroyer; a little low but right on line. After a few shots, star shells were lighting up the target, and salvoes of red tracer shells flew at the hillside, flashes lit the sky, while torrents of rocks, dust and debris flowed down the 1,000-foot cliff and came crashing into the sea below. By nearly midnight the target was obscured by dust, and we called off the HE to illuminate with star shell. Stan could see a few Germans running about in panic, but the concrete buildings still stood intact. 'Give them another dose' from Stan was translated into naval parlance and all hell was unleashed against the unhappy hillside. Then Stan asked us to call off the fire. 'I'm going in now. Will be off the air quarter of an hour. Cease fire.'

We gave him the OK and they went in. After a few minutes' silence, the patter of MGs and tommy-guns broke the quiet while a few sharp explosions made small impression [compared with] the last half-hour torrent of noise and shell.

Then suddenly 'Reinforcements arriving, have I your permission to withdraw?' from Stan.

We told him to make his own decision and we would support his withdrawal with fire. A few minutes' quiet, then a series of bright yellow explosions, three long bursts of red tracer straight into the air, and three short flashes with a torch, which was the signal for success. We informed the destroyers and sent a man down to meet our boats.

After a desperate climb down the hill over rocks and the worst going I have had to cross in ages, I arrived hot, tired, bruised and excited at about 1.45. The moon was now down, and there were only the shouts of our chaps coming down the hill and challenges from small groups as they struggled down with the enemy weapons and other kit they had removed before finally blowing the place to pieces with Gammon bombs.

Here they expected boats from the destroyers, but they were not there. Aware that the destroyers could not linger in daylight off the coast, the raiding party was making plans to lie up for the day in the hope of a pick-up the following night when the boats appeared. The force, only twenty strong, had achieved success with only one man lightly wounded. On board to congratulate them was Brigadier G. M. O. Davy, the Commander Land Forces Adriatic (LFA) under whose command the LRDG were to operate in future.

Throughout the rest of the campaign, Lloyd Owen was to find himself periodically involved in efforts to ensure that his men were employed properly, and their considerable potential was not wasted. What is also fascinating from our perspective fifty years later is the way comparatively junior and young officers (Lloyd Owen was only twenty-six) were able to shape operational-level decisions, and were not in the least shy of doing so, whereas now government ministers almost dictate the siting of machine-gun positions. By now Jellicoe had managed to cut loose from the Aegean too, although in Lloyd Owen's words, 'he (Jellicoe), had had a lot of fun'. Lloyd Owen's diary:

14th July
Davy [Commander Land Forces Adriatic] told me hopeless news that Raiding Forces come too. If that is so, I would refuse to command if we are placed under that outfit again. All the lot of them are lazy and have no idea what they are doing.

After their Aegean experience the LRDG had little time for Raiding Forces Headquarters, but much respect for the units themselves.

24th July
Got to Bari for breakfast which I had with George Jellicoe. We discussed

the whole situation and action to be taken to avoid any question of RF [Raiding Forces] HQ returning. The meeting was conducted by Mac-Namara who made no mistake about telling Turnbull [RF Commander] that he was not required. Very heated and many people fighting to keep good jobs. I said little. The result very satisfactory SBS [SB Squadron] come over here on a completely self-run affair and we continue as before. RF HQ are disintegrated and all should be well!

This was not strictly accurate, since Raiding Forces HQ remained in the Aegean until the end of the War, but at least the LRDG were spared coming under their command again. Colonel MacNamara was Brigadier Davy's chief of staff, still a Member of Parliament, and a great ally of Lloyd Owen's, until he was killed during Christmas 1944, visiting his regiment, the London Irish Rifles.

25th July
Spent whole day at useless conferences arguing about this and that. Lunch with Fitzroy Maclean, Dan Ranfurly, and George J [Jellicoe] at the Allied Officers Club. After lunch talked over the pros and cons of amalgamation with SBS [SB Squadron] and decided against it for the present. Had a meeting in the evening with Davy, MacNamara and George and decided what SBS and ourselves would do. LRDG primarily recce and SBS primarily beatup.

Lloyd Owen also decided, after some operations had been planned and then aborted, that there were no immediate suitable tasks for the LRDG in Italy. He therefore came under the command of Brigadier Davy's Army component of the Balkan Air Force, and was no longer directly responsible to Alexander's HQ. The Balkan Air Force was responsible for controlling and co-ordinating all partisan and other operations in that region. Its commander, Air Vice-Marshal Elliot, was in Lloyd Owen's words, 'not the only RAF officer in that organization to give us unqualified support in all our efforts of the future'.

While Lloyd Owen and Jellicoe had been sorting out matters in the Adriatic, not entirely, but very nearly, to their own satisfaction, great events had been afoot in Normandy.

10

The SAS and the JEDS in North-West Europe, 1944–45

By the time of the Allied landings in Normandy in June 1944, well over fifty raids, and as many if not more reconnaissance operations, had been carried out on the coast of north-west Europe and Norway. Very few of them were behind the lines. Overt, or even clandestine, operations by formed bodies of soldiers in uniform were almost impossible in German-occupied Europe, unless of very short duration or in desolate, sparsely habited areas. The difficulties encountered by Operation Frankton are proof of that. Two operations several years before the Normandy landings illustrate what could and could not be attempted.

By the end of 1941, it was apparent to Royal Air Force intelligence that one of the main causes of losses to Bomber Command over Europe was the German radar chain. A key element in the system was the *Würzburg*, which vectored night fighters on to the individual bomber. The RAF had some air photographs of the radar dish of a *Würzburg*, situated on a cliff-top just north of a small village called Bruneval, twelve miles north of Le Havre. Mountbatten, then CCO, agreed to an RAF request for a raid to bring back parts of the radar for investigation by the Telecommunications Research Establishment. Like all the *Würzburg* sites, the one at Bruneval was well protected from assault from the sea, so a parachute operation followed by a withdrawal by sea was planned. In this way it was hoped that surprise would be achieved, and the equipment could be taken before it could be destroyed. There were thought to be 170 to 200 enemy in the vicinity: 30 or so radar operators, signallers and guards at the radar station, on the cliff-top near an isolated villa; about 100 off-duty operators, signallers and coast defence troops in a group of farm buildings, Le Presbytère, approximately 300 yards north of the radar; and 40 men garrisoned in Bruneval about a third of a mile south-east of the radar station, responsible for manning the pillboxes on the cliff-tops and beach.

The raiding force, commanded by Major John Frost, consisted of 6 officers and 113 NCOs and soldiers of C Company, 2nd Parachute Battalion, including 9 sappers, 4 signallers, and an RAF radar technician. The pick-up was to be by LCAs, escorted by MTBs and MGBs, with a platoon of infantry to secure the beach. Again the drop, from twelve Whitleys, on the night of 27/28 February 1942, was reasonably accurate, only two sticks being dropped about two miles wide of the DZ. These sticks consisted of most of a party detailed to clear the beach for the withdrawal, in particular a pillbox overlooking it. One of these sticks was carried in the aircraft being flown by Wing Commander Percy Pickard, then one of the most experienced Bomber Command pilots.

The party detailed to assault the villa and the radar station, led by Frost, gained entry without any resistance, and the vital parts of the equipment were quickly dismantled by the radar technician. Fire from Le Presbytère was increasing, causing some casualties, as Frost ordered the withdrawal to the beach. However, it soon became evident that the beach was not clear, despite Frost having sent some men to clear it. At the same time the Germans had reoccupied the villa and were putting in a counter-attack. A group led by Frost quickly snuffed out this danger. Meanwhile the party dropped wide had turned up, and took the beach defence pillbox in the flank.

There was no sign of the craft. Contact by radio proved fruitless. Frost fired Very lights, still no reply. As he was making desperate plans to defend the beach, the landing craft were seen approaching. They had been delayed by having to lie 'doggo' while a German destroyer and two E-boats cruised by in the moonlight. Five hours after leaving England, Frost's company embarked in the landing craft. The casualties amounted to three killed, two missing (taken prisoner) and seven wounded. Three prisoners of war, including a German radar technician, were taken back to Portsmouth.

The raid could not have come at a better time for morale. The War had not been going well. Two capital ships, the *Prince of Wales* and *Repulse*, had been sunk two months before, Singapore had just fallen, and the Battle of the Java Sea had gone disastrously for the Allies. More important, the RAF scientists were able to work out how to defeat the

Würzburg for a time by using 'Window', strips of tinfoil which gave an echo like a target.

The other of these two operations, Freshman in November 1942, had a less happy ending. From quite early in the war it was known that the Germans were attempting to construct a nuclear bomb. Their research, which included the use of 'heavy water', was believed to be making good progress. The existing stocks of this water, which was extremely difficult to produce in quantity, were at the Norsk Hydro plant at Vermork in Norway, in a valley some two miles north-east of Rjukan, about eighty miles from the west coast and sixty miles west of Oslo. The plant was built on a shelf of rock about 1,000 feet above the valley floor, whose sides rose almost sheer for 3,000 feet. The valley, on the edge of the Hardangervidda plateau, is situated in some of the most rugged terrain in south Norway. In winter the rolling, snow-covered mountains (not high by Alpine standards – Gaustafjell, just west of Rjukan, is around 6,000 feet), the Hardangervidda plateau, and the Telemark make challenging country to cross, especially to anyone not trained in cross-country ski techniques (*langlauf*). Habitation was, and is, few and far between, although there are huts here and there, used in happier times mainly in the summer, and also in the winter by the hardier folk on ski tours. The projected area of operations in the western mountains of Norway is vividly described by Roland Huntford. As the author and thousands of Royal Marine and Army Commando soldiers who have trained there over the years could testify it is:

> ... exposed to the ocean, bearing the brunt of North Atlantic storms. Their weather is capricious.... With blizzard, burning cold, and the hiss of drift – fine grains of loose snow seized by the wind and swept over the surface from one place to another, like sand blown across the desert....[1]

Eventually it was decided by COHQ that the best method of attack would be by a party of Royal Engineers landed in gliders at a spot about five hours' march from the objective. The LZ would be marked by Norwegian agents, who would also operate the Eureka beacon. The Eureka sent signals to the Rebecca equipment in the towing aircraft, giving the crew the course to steer, enabling them to release the glider at the right moment and place from which to descend to the LZ. The agents would guide the British party to the plant. On completion of the task, the party would be guided through the mountains to Sweden.

The vast majority of Norwegians were anti-German, but the chosen route would avoid centres of population. Although the British team was trained in the use of snow boots, none were ski-trained, nor were skis included in their equipment.

At last light on 19 November, two Halifax bombers, each towing a Horsa glider, took off from Skitten, near Wick in Scotland. Only one aircraft, the first to take off, returned to base, having released its glider over the land, but nowhere near the target. A radio message was received from the second aircraft, asking for a course back to base, which by intersection using direction-finding equipment, placed it over the sea. Nothing was ever heard from either of the glider parties.

After the War, interrogation and information from agents, together with the debrief of the crew of the one surviving aircraft, enabled the British to piece together what had happened. As both aircraft approached the Norwegian coast their Rebeccas became unserviceable. They now had to rely solely on map-reading to find the LZ. About forty miles from Rjukan, the first aircraft flew into thick cloud and, dragging the heavy glider, was unable to climb out of it. Short of fuel, and with heavy icing on both tug and glider, the pilot turned for home. Eventually, the tow rope iced up so heavily it snapped. The aircraft landed back at Skitten just before its fuel ran out. The glider crash-landed on high ground east of Stavanger. Of the seventeen men in the glider, eight including the two pilots were killed, four were severely injured, and five were unharmed. The four injured were subsequently poisoned in hospital on the orders of the Gestapo, and the five uninjured were shot.

The agents on the LZ had heard this aircraft flying almost overhead, but in the cloud the pilot, unable to pick up the Eureka signals, could not establish his position sufficiently accurately to risk descending to try to find the LZ visually.

The second pair, for reasons unknown, crashed soon after crossing the Norwegian coast. The glider crash-landed in the mountains near Helleland, north-east of Egersund, and the tug crashed in the mountains to the south, killing the whole crew. Three men in the glider were killed immediately, and the remainder were captured and shot.

But for the failure of Rebecca, at least one glider might have arrived on the LZ. As the parties were duplicated, there was enough equipment in each glider to carry out the demolition task. How, without skis, the sappers would have fared on the trip to the plant in the deep snow conditions, despite agents being on hand to guide them, and subsequently make the overland journey to Sweden, (150 miles as the crow flies), is open to question.

The Bruneval raid was a 'stand alone' affair, that is without local assistance. In this case, because it was of such short duration, local support, or otherwise, was irrelevant. The intelligence about the target and the enemy was excellent. The extraction plan was good, and simple, although there were some snags with the manpack radios, which were notoriously unreliable at that stage in the War.

Freshman was planned to rely heavily on local support, but was frustrated by technical difficulties. To commit tug aircraft towing heavy gliders to the very hazardous conditions prevalent over the mountains in Norway in winter, and at night, was an extremely risky, if not foolhardy, venture. In 1942 weather forecasting was nothing like as reliable as it is today, and the weather in Norway can change in minutes. Finally, the Freshman party lacked the expertise and the mobility so necessary for survival, let alone operations, in the snow 'desert' of the Hardangervidda, the Telemark, and much of the marginally less rugged country right across to Sweden. These qualities of mobility and expertise had been so evident in the LRDG and SAS operations in North Africa and the Mediterranean, and now the latter were to put their skills to the test in France.

*

By March 1944, both the SRS and 2nd SAS had returned from Italy, and were in the United Kingdom preparing for the invasion of Europe. They became part of the SAS Brigade commanded by Brigadier R. W. McLeod, under Lieutenant-General Frederick ('Boy') Browning's British 1st Airborne Corps. The SAS, much to their irritation, were ordered by Browning to exchange their sand-coloured berets for airborne maroon berets. The SRS reverted to its original name, and expanded from a squadron to a regiment, the troops becoming squadrons. Paddy Mayne remained as commanding officer. The SAS Brigade consisted of 1st and 2nd SAS, two French parachute battalions (*2ème and 3ème Régiment de Chasseurs Parachutistes*, but called 3rd and 4th SAS), a Belgian squadron, and F Squadron GHQ Liaison Regiment (Phantom). A Royal Signals squadron provided the base communications from the British 1st Airborne Corps Headquarters at Moor Park, near Rickmansworth, to the Phantom radio operators in the field.

The GHQ Liaison Regiment had been formed early in the War to radio information back from the most forward positions in battle direct to the highest headquarters in the theatre. Bypassing all the intermediate headquarters in the chain of command, they saved an enormous amount of time, not least in unscrambling corrupt messages of the 'send three and fourpence we're going to a dance' variety.[2] A number of well-known characters served in the Regiment, including the actor David Niven. Each Phantom squadron was divided into patrols, each consisting of a corporal and four soldiers, and commanded by a captain. The patrols attached to 1st and 2nd SAS provided the radio communications from behind enemy lines back to base in the United Kingdom, without which the SAS would have soon become non-effective for lack of supplies, explosives, weapons and ammunition.

For some time after its formation, there was considerable argument about how the SAS Brigade should be employed in France. To begin with the D-Day planners proposed using the SAS just behind the enemy front line to disrupt the movement of his immediate reserves. Bill Stirling disagreed; he wanted to set up patrol bases deep behind the enemy lines, and attack his rear area installations well away from large concentrations of fighting troops. The discussion became bitter, and seeing that he was apparently getting nowhere with his argument, Stirling resigned. In the end his concepts were adopted, which was just as well, as the Germans would have made short work of anyone attempting SAS operations just behind the forward edge of the battle area.

Stirling was replaced by Lieutenant-Colonel Brian Franks, a founder member of Number 8 Commando, who had served with Layforce, commanded the Middle East Phantom Squadron, and been the Brigade Major of 2nd Special Service Brigade in Sicily and Italy. The arguments over the role for the SAS Brigade were not resolved until just before D-Day, when it was decided that they would carry out three types of operation. First, arm and train the French Resistance, to allow them to be more aggressive, and to play their part in delaying German reinforcements moving up to the main battle area. Second, aggressive operations by the SAS acting on their own in armoured jeeps dropped or flown in to them. Third, locating targets for the RAF: railway stock, tunnels and bridges. These would also be attacked by the SAS themselves.

Meanwhile 1st and 2nd SAS trained hard for the forthcoming task, and absorbed a large number of reinforcements needed to fill the expanded organization. One of them was Gordon Mitchell, who had fought with the 1st Parachute Battalion in Tunisia, and at the Primasole Bridge in Sicily. The majority of Mitchell's battalion had been dropped miles from the DZ in Sicily, although he was one of the few who landed in the right place. He came to the view that:

it didn't matter how good a soldier you were, if you were dropped in the wrong place, you couldn't do anything about it. I was looking for something where you had more control over yourself. I thought about the SAS.

After a number of vicissitudes, including contracting malaria, he:

Joined C Squadron 1 SAS. It was a totally different type of soldiering altogether. It took a little bit of getting used to. We had some extremely interesting exercises. One was dropping outside Edinburgh to attack targets near Glasgow, with all forces in Scotland alerted to find us – everyone from the Home Guard upwards, including gamekeepers. The ground was crawling with troops. Our padre, who later became the Moderator of the Church of Scotland [Fraser McCluskie] accompanied my patrol. We hadn't wanted him with us at first. But he was very fit and had no difficulty keeping up. We decided that walking into the target area was not on. McCluskie said, 'Leave it to me.'

He turned his [distinctive maroon] beret inside out, he still had his clerical collar on, and went to an Army Camp which was about half a mile away. Here he said that his vehicle had just run out of petrol. Could someone bring a vehicle out with some petrol? So an unsuspecting WO2 agreed, and, producing a small pick-up truck, said, 'OK, I'll just go and get this work ticket signed.'

Off he went leaving the keys in the vehicle. McCluskie took off in the truck and drove off to find us. We did the rest of the exercise in the truck.

Mitchell once told the author that he had been fortunate to serve under the two most highly decorated commanding officers in the British Army in the Second World War; Blair 'Paddy' Mayne and Alastair Pearson, each with four DSOs:

When I was near Alastair Pearson or Blair Mayne in action, I always felt less frightened.

Another organization was also training for operations behind the enemy lines in north-west Europe: the Jedburgh Teams, or 'Jeds' for short. These teams were the brainchild of Major Peter Wilkinson, SOE's head of Central and East European Section, and Robin Brook, SOE's Regional Director for France and the Low Countries. Their concept was to tie in the French Resistance activities to Allied operational plans in France, from the moment the invasion took place. This would be achieved by dropping small parties of officers and radio operators, who would make contact with the Resistance, arrange drops of arms, and provide the necessary communications link with SOE Headquarters in England. The name Jedburgh was allocated to the project by Major General Colin Gubbins, Executive Director of SOE, and a Scot. The story goes that travelling back from Scotland, his train passed through Jedburgh station, and he at once decided on that as the name for the teams.

The Jedburgh concept was approved by the British Chiefs of Staff as early as mid 1942. Not long afterwards Colonel William ('Wild Bill') Donovan, the Director of the United States Office of Strategic Services (OSS), the forerunner of the CIA, insisted that Americans be included in the teams. After a trial run on a large exercise six principles were agreed on for the employment of Jedburgh Teams.

1. Each team would consist of two officers, either British or American, plus one from the country in which the team was to operate. Each team would also have a radio operator.

2. The team's primary mission would be to liaise with the Resistance, and pass orders to them from Supreme Headquarters Allied Expeditionary Force (SHAEF).

3. Teams would not be dropped in the vicinity of the bridgehead, but deep behind enemy lines, and to areas where there were known to be Resistance groups. Here they would organize arms and equipment drops for the Resistance, provide communications back to England, and if required actually lead the group.

4. Special Forces liaison officers would be attached to Army and Army Group Headquarters in the field as well as SHAEF. These liaison officers would be in radio contact with SOE Headquarters, who in their turn would be in contact with the Jedburghs.

5. The teams would drop in uniform.

6. Teams would not be responsible for espionage (spying), although
   they could pass back intelligence they happened upon in the course
   of their operations, which were to be military.

Despite the above principles, many Jedburghs found themselves
commanding, not just liaising, as Major Oliver Brown, a Team Leader
found:

> The practice was totally different from the original idea of the Jeds.
> Basically once we got going, the Resistance realised we were more compe-
> tent to command than the local units, because of the factions within the
> Resistance. So we commanded, we were never supposed to but we did.

To begin with, the Jedburghs were to come exclusively under SOE
command, but Donovan soon put a stop to that, and a means of joint
Anglo-American command was established with the formation of a
Jedburgh Section working under a co-ordinating committee consisting
of representatives of the SOE and the Special Operations Wing of the
OSS. What was now needed after all this high-priced international
wrangling was settled was to recruit the 300 officers and soldiers for the
teams, and time was getting short.

It was decided to recruit the British radio operators from armoured
regiments, the theory being that they were already accustomed to
working in small groups, in a tank crew, they were trained in map
reading, small arms, radio theory and Wireless Telegraphy (W/T), which
meant they could read and send morse.[3] The volunteers were tested for
suitability and weeded out until by the end of 1943, the forty-five British
survivors were ready to be 'married up' with their officers. The
Americans followed more or less the same selection process as the British
and produced forty-six operators. Together with some twenty French
volunteers, these formed the team operators.

British and American officer volunteers were selected by a special SOE
board. Aubrey Trofimov spoke fluent French, and had spent the first
two years of the war at Manchester University studying architecture.
After call up, and basic training in the Royal Artillery, he gained a
distinction on a signals course, before being commissioned. By his own
admission, he was a loner who did not enjoy barracks and unit life. He
volunteered for Special Forces when he saw a notice asking for volunteers
for special duties, stating that a knowledge of French and signals

expertise were required. After passing the initial general test, he had a series of interviews in January 1944, including more tests in a private house outside London.

> I was locked up in a cellar and told to get out. My architectural training helped. I noticed some loose bricks in the wall near the ceiling. Removing these revealed a duct, along which I crawled. It led to a grate, and I got out. On another occasion, during dinner, someone let off a pistol immediately behind me to see what my reaction would be.

> From something like 100 volunteers we were whittled down to about 50, and later even more people were whittled out. They were looking for people with stability and who wouldn't panic in an emergency. Behind the lines is almost a permanent state of emergency.

> I loved every minute of becoming a Jed, and am proud of being one to this day. It was so exciting, the training was so varied. Most of us were loners. The course was a tremendous challenge. I liked the physical side. As a young boy I had been good at gymnastics, and enjoyed the assault course.

R. A. (Dick) Rubinstein was another who was bored with life in the Army:

> I was an Other Rank in a searchlight regiment during the blitz. After being commissioned, I was sent to another searchlight regiment. I got very bored, and it wasn't easy to get out. One had to apply to join funny things. I made up my mind that I would go for the next thing whatever happened. A letter came round asking for volunteers to serve in small groups in enemy territory. I stood there with shaking hands saying to myself, 'Rubinstein, this is the moment of truth for you.'

> I applied and went for an interview. After that there was a three-day selection board at a house in Hampshire. We were divided into teams of eight. One of the things we had to do was to put in order who of the eight we would be prepared to take into enemy territory.

> Most of the tests were like the tests in the War Office Selection Board [for officer training], like getting a wounded man across a river, using planks and barrels. For some a leader was appointed, for some no leader was made, to see who came up as a natural leader. There was an interview with a psychologist. Later I had access to my papers, illegally. They said, 'He seems to have the right motivation. Has he got the guts to stand up to operations?' As I was only 21/22 this was probably fair. They took a risk on me.

> Initial training was at Hatherop Castle near Fairford, Gloucestershire;

there we met Americans from OSS. Also there were the French, mostly ex-North Africa. Their motive for joining Jedburgh was because they were officers of Colonial Infantry caught on the wrong side of the politics in North Africa and thought they and their troops would never be trusted by the Allies, and that the only way to get into the liberation of France was to join this 'harum-scarum' outfit. Many of them didn't like it at all. It was not their idea of soldiering. My eventual partner was one of those fellows, and a splendid chap he was.

I enjoyed the training. I was fit and strong. One can get a lot of satisfaction with becoming skilled in the use of a handgun for example. I was a bit worried about the parachuting, but it went all right. I hadn't got an infantry background so it was interesting doing different things. Working with explosives was interesting. It was broadening to live with Americans and French.

We knew we would form into teams of an officer of the country in which we were operating, a British or American officer, and a wireless operator who would be British or American. We all came together at this big house outside Peterborough called Milton Hall, and for the first two weeks there was an embarrassment about speaking French. Then we all started speaking French, and the general social language was French. You'd see two Brits talking to a Yank and a Frenchman, all talking French, and the Frenchman would correct them as they went along. And after the four or five months of our training, most of us had fluent spoken French, not necessarily accurate. But fluent. It has lasted to this day. I still have to get out my grammar books to write.

When we started to do exercises around Peterborough we sometimes jumped [parachuted] in. We didn't know exactly when D-Day was going to be.

The Frenchmen were given *noms de guerre* to protect their families in France if they were captured. They also had a cover name to use if they had to operate in civilian clothes. In the accounts that follow, all three names crop up. Sometimes teams picked themselves. Aubrey Trofimov:

In my case I met André Duron [*nom de guerre* 'A. Dhomas'] in the mess. He was an experienced officer from N. Africa. Another factor that probably came into our wanting to get together was that he didn't speak English and he needed someone who spoke French fluently so we could work together. The radio operator was allocated to us. He was a young French lieutenant called Groult [*nom de guerre* 'J. Deschamps']. I never knew their real names until after the war. Our team was called Guy. From the time the 'marriage' took place, it was referred to as a marriage, you spent more time together. The exercises were done as a team to test that it was a suitable 'marriage'. The only hitch that occurred, not only with my team, was the British were essentially loners, the French came from regiments, and although they were volunteers they had a more regimental background. The idea of guerrilla warfare was in some instances alien to their background training. And there was a difference of approach. That was what I thought at the time but subsequent events proved me entirely wrong.

The purpose was to co-ord the Resistance who in many cases were working blind. They weren't working to instructions. They were attacking the Germans to the best of their ability. But in many instances this did not necessarily fall in with what was required by the advancing Allies. The Resistance might be doing things that were actually harmful to the Allied cause. So we were to go in and equip the Resistance, where necessary provide leadership, but not push that point for obvious reasons, and locate places for DZs for resupply drops, and give the requirements of the Allied forces to each of the areas. They might want bridges blown up, or they might want certain bridges left intact. They might want attacks on certain garrisons, railway lines destroyed. We were paramilitary, we were not spies.

Dick Rubinstein had his French comrade chosen for him:

I had hoped that I would go in with a particular Frenchman. In fact we weren't allowed to. Perhaps someone wiser decided who would be compatible. You had no choice over the radio operator. My French companion, whose alias name [*nom de guerre*] was 'Jean Ronglou' [actual name Roblot], was a career officer of *L'Infantrie Colonial*. He had been wounded in 1940, and joined SOE only because this was the only way he thought he could take part in the liberation. He was a proud regimental soldier, and he didn't like the work. After our second operation, he found his old division coming up from the South of France. By now the political picture had changed. The North African French troops who had been hostile to us in the earlier days were now part of the liberating forces. He said to me, 'This is where I stay. I'm not going back to London to fill in reports.'

They fought a bloody battle around Belfort. He was killed in November 1944.

Major Oliver Brown, a fluent French speaker in the Buffs, was already in the SOE which he had joined as an instructor in 1942. Brown trained

Odette Sansom and Violette Szabo, two of the leading F Section agents, and had met Gubbins several times:

> Gubbins was a terrific man, he never cut any corners. When he arrived he chucked out all the rubbish. He was a very naughty boy, he liked the ladies. Hence we had some very attractive FANYs[4] about.

When the matter of training the Jedburghs was raised, he was sent by Gubbins to Donovan and one of de Gaulle's staff to get their opinion on how it should be run:

> Donovan didn't impress me the least little bit. I thought he was just another Custer. He was an unintelligent, bombastic American. But they loved him. He said he would leave it to 'Gub'.
>
> We wanted the Jeds to do their initial training before they arrived at Milton Hall near Peterborough. Most of the Americans were serving soldiers. Bloody undisciplined soldiers too. I got to like them so much it wasn't true. We had tremendous difficulties with the Americans who wanted to start right away without any training. The French were disciplined.
>
> We didn't have anything to do with selection. I wish we had. Some of the Americans and French were unsuitable. The French were too military and rather inflexible. The Americans were too undisciplined. A lot of the British were SOE instructors who wanted to get into the war. A lot of the Americans were very educated people from places like Harvard, and influential people. In the end they impressed some discipline on their fellow countrymen.
>
> I insisted that when I took the job I would only do it if I was sent to France myself. I couldn't go on training people and sending them to their death without going myself. The response from 'Gub' was, 'Yes, but only if de Gaulle agreed.' I was older than the rest. They were in their late teens and early twenties, I was thirty. I teamed up with 'René Maître' [real name Lieutenant Karrière], and my wireless operator was old 'Smithy' [Sergeant G. N. Smith] who no one else wanted, he hardly spoke English let alone French. He was a marvellous operator.

The officers' syllabus consisted of sabotage, ambushes, guerrilla warfare, training with several types of firearm, unarmed combat, ciphers, reception of parachute drops and aircraft landings. Teams were briefed by agents specially flown out of France for the purpose. As D-Day approached, the teams due for the south of France were shipped to Algiers, to be flown in from there.

By the time the Jedburghs were ready to be inserted, the original intention of having French, British and Americans represented in each team had not been strictly followed; indeed, of the 101 teams, only 10 were formed like that: 18 teams had 2 French (one had 3), 32 had 2 Americans, and 41 had 2 British.

On 5 June 1944, two teams took off from Algiers for southern France. Neither pilot could find the DZ, both turned back to base. On the same night the first SAS patrols left for France. The SAS had pressed for permission to insert patrols in France well before D-Day. Eisenhower refused. He was understandably worried that by analysing the pattern of SAS activity, the Germans might unravel the elaborate plans for disguising the real location of the Allied landings. However, he did allow the first SAS operations to be launched on the eve of D-Day. A total of forty-three SAS operations were mounted by the SAS Brigade between 6 June and 31 October 1944 alone, and space allows for only a fraction of these to be described.

Operation Titanic consisted of two patrols, each of five men, dropped on the night of 5/6 June as part of the tactical deception plan for D-Day. Each patrol was equipped with special gramophones which played sounds of small-arms fire and soldiers' conversations, Very pistols and their personal weapons. Some 500 dummy parachutists, fitted with firecrackers that exploded on landing to simulate rifle fire, dropped with each patrol. One Titanic patrol dropped south-east of Isigny (inland from the two American D-Day beaches, Utah and Omaha), and the other just east of Le Havre on the road to Rouen. These DZs were chosen in the hope that the Germans might be deceived into moving troops away from the beachheads and actual DZs, and deploying reserves to deal with the threat, just before the real landings began starting with two US Airborne Divisions at the base of the Cotentin Peninsula, and one British Airborne Division east of the River Orne. Both patrols were successful. The Germans moved troops from the Rouen area towards Le Havre. But, far more important, the acting commander of the division behind Omaha Beach moved his reserve regiment to beat the woods south-east of Isigny for parachutists. They spent most of 6 June on this fruitless task, and were not available to counter-attack at Omaha, where the outcome of the American landings hung in the balance for most of D-Day. The SAS lost eight men out of the ten who dropped.

Operation Samwest in Brittany was also designed to help deceive the

Germans as to the planned axis of advance from the Normandy beachhead. Troops from 4th SAS (French) were selected for this task as the unit contained a large number of Bretons. On the night of 5/6 June two officers and sixteen soldiers dropped and established a base in the Forêt Duaut, west of St Brieuc. By 11 June the base had been reinforced by a further hundred men, and liaison with the Resistance had been established. Unfortunately the Resistance in the area was fragmented and persuading them to work in harmony proved impossible. Some unprofessional habits by the SAS, such as eating in local restaurants, eventually led to the Germans attacking the base in mid June. The SAS dealt the Germans a bloody nose in the process, killing at least fifty-five and wounding about a hundred. But they suffered seventeen casualties themselves, and, with the base compromised, were forced to disperse to another base, set up by Operation Dingson just north of Vannes. Here, with the assistance of a Jedburgh Team, they were able to arm and lead a well-organized Resistance group in southern Brittany.

The advance party of A Squadron, 1st SAS, landed in the Forêt du Morvan, south-west of Dijon, on the night of 5/6 June, to prepare the way for Operation Houndsworth. Eventually a force 144 strong spent three months behind enemy lines disrupting the railway network Dijon—Paris, Dijon—Châlon-sur-Saône—Lyon, and Châlons-sur-Saône—Le Creusot—Nevers. The railway lines were demolished on 22 occasions, 30 targets reported to the RAF, some 200 Germans were killed or wounded and 132 taken prisoner.

The final SAS party to drop on the eve of D-Day, also from 1st SAS, was to set up Operation Bulbasket near Poitiers. Their task: to disrupt the railway lines Limoges–Vierzon–Poitiers–Tours, which German formations stationed in southern France would use to reach the Normandy battlefront. Before the main body arrived, thanks to the Resistance, they located their first target, consisting of eleven trains of petrol wagons in a siding at Châtellerault. The radio message from the Bulbasket Team resulted in the total destruction of all eleven trains of this vital commodity by twenty-four Mosquitoes of the RAF, RNZAF and RAAF. The loss of this fuel was to impose serious delays on the move north of 2nd SS Panzer Division (Das Reich). For the next three weeks the Bulbasket Team cut the railway line in twelve places. They carried the demolition teams to widely dispersed points on the rail system, in jeeps dropped to them. At the end of these three weeks, most of the Bulbasket team were at their base in the Forêt de Verriers when they were attacked by a large force of Germans. The SAS, armed only with .45 pistols, and a few Vickers K guns on their jeeps, were no match for mortars and dozens of machine-guns which blasted and raked their camp. Only eight SAS men survived by escaping in the confusion, including Captain Tonkin, the commander of the team. Thirty-one, including four wounded, were taken prisoner by the Germans. One of the wounded, Lieutenant Stephens, was tied to a tree in Verriers, and after the villagers had been paraded past, the Germans beat him to death with their rifle butts. All the others were shot. Elsewhere in France, SAS men who were captured, despite operating in uniform, were treated similarly. Of the hundred or so recorded cases of SAS being taken prisoner, only six survived.

Although official accounts state that the Bulbasket Team was betrayed by a collaborator, the military historian Max Hastings has suggested it is just as likely that carelessness, unnecessary bravado, such as driving into Poitiers in a jeep or staying in the same place for too long, was the cause of the German attack. As he says:

> The SAS of that period were better trained and certainly men of higher abilities than British line infantry, but they were not remotely comparable in quality and expertise with the postwar SAS.[5]

Despite that, the delay imposed on 2nd SS Panzer Division by the destruction of the fuel at Châtelleraut more than compensated for the virtual elimination of the Bulbasket Team. The surviving remnants of the team were flown out from a temporary airstrip, constructed behind enemy lines, on 7 and 10 August.

What is remarkable about all the SAS operations in France at this time is the scale of support in the form of air supply that enabled such large forces to be maintained behind enemy lines. An example is given in *Airborne Forces*:

> During the night 4th/5th August, 42 aircraft of 38 Group were detailed to go to 22 different dropping zones from five departure airfields with a total load of over 150 troops, four jeeps and 700 parachute containers of arms, stores and supplies, the weight being about 100 tons. In the same 24 hours eleven gliders with 45 troops and eleven jeeps were landed in Brittany behind enemy lines. As usual, the location of many of the dropping zones

could not be finally decided until the day of take-off, owing to enemy activities, yet about 95 per cent of all these air operations were successful.[6]

This is a manifestation of the fact that after four years of special duty operations, a very high standard had been achieved by the airmen. Much of this was due to Group Captain Ron Hockey, who had been flying on special duties since November 1940. The drill on the DZ was not always carried out with strictly military precision, although it worked, as the following account by an SAS officer shows:

There was nothing either quiet or clandestine about my first what the French call 'un parachutage'.

Once the containers were released from the aircraft there was considerable drama. Albert (the local Maquis chief) began the proceedings by shouting 'Attention everyone, the bidons [literally oil-drums, which the cylindrical containers looked rather like] descend'. Everyone present repeated this, adding advice to Bobo, or Alphonse, or Pierre, or whoever was nearest to 'have a care that the sacred bidons do not crush thee'.

Once the containers had landed the parachute stakes were on. The winner was whoever could roll and hide away the most parachutes before being spotted by someone else.

The bullock carts then came up with much encouragement from the drivers such as, 'But come my old one, to the bidons advance.' Then began the preliminary discussions as to how the first container would be hoisted on to the cart and who should have the honour of commencing. I found I had to go through the actions of beginning to hoist one end myself before, with loud cries of 'But not, my Captain, permit', or, for example, 'My Captain, what an affair', my helpers would then get on with the job.

Once, however, the drill of clearing the dropping zone was understood, these helpers were of the greatest value and we succeeded one night in clearing the dropping zone in 70 minutes. This was very good as it included four containers that had fallen in trees.[7]

Gordon Mitchell describes how the jeep patrols operated:

We parachuted in, in a group of ten. We flew out in a big bomber force as part of a big bomber raid. Our aircraft peeled off and dropped us. We trained with the Resistance, and worked with them. We had armoured jeeps parachuted to us. We had twin Vickers K in front, and a twin behind. A jeep crew was three. We operated behind the lines, using side roads as much as possible. Sometimes you had to use a main road, and it wasn't unknown to meet German troops en route. But you were past so quickly and up a side road before they could take any action. Some people did get into trouble, I didn't.

Not every Frenchman belonged to the Resistance. Gordon Mitchell:

We worked with a number of Resistance groups. The most effective were the Communist. They of course had but one aim, to turn France Communist. Then there were people who were simply avoiding forced labour. Then there were a number, but sadly all too few, genuine French patriots. The majority of the French were prepared to bumble on with the Germans, after all life wasn't too hard for them, provided they didn't get involved with the Resistance.

SAS operations could sometimes have a devastating effect on the locals:

The Germans went to this village and took all the males [170] out and put them in concentration camps. Only 72 returned. This is still known as the village of the widows.

By this time the Jedburghs had been operating in France since the evening of D-Day. Altogether 101 teams were inserted in France, Holland and Belgium. What follows is only a sample of their operations. It would take a whole book to cover the Jedburghs in detail.

Before each team left Brown remembers:

You were alerted that your operation was on. You were briefed in London. Depending which section you were going to, you were either briefed by F Section or by RF Section. I went to the RF section of SOE. The briefing was good. You had the recognition signals, the signal codes, your cover story. At the end you had to repeat the brief back, except for the signal codes you had to carry the information in your head. Then you waited. I was one of the last to go because I had so much information [as an SOE instructor]. They really shouldn't have let me go. I lived with my lethal pill in my mouth for months before I went. I realised I might have to take it in France. It fitted in the gap in my upper teeth.

On 6 June the first Jedburghs consisting of Captain Duncan Guthrie's Team Harry, with two Frenchmen, Lieutenants Rousset (*nom de guerre* 'Dupont', cover name 'Gapeau') and Couture (*nom de guerre* 'Legrand', cover name Centime), dropped north of Auton to operate in the area of Saulieu and Avallon, west of Dijon. Guthrie:

> On D-Day evening we left to fly to a DZ in central France, together with two SAS officers [probably part of Operation Houndsworth] who were on the same aircraft, a Hudson. You slid out of the aircraft on a slide out of a hole. There was nothing you could do about it. As we were flying towards our destination, a message came back from the pilot that he was very sorry he couldn't find the DZ. He was going home. I sent a message, 'Do you know where you are?' He said yes but couldn't find the DZ. So I said, 'Drop us, there is no one meeting us.' I didn't want to go through all this again.
>
> We were to make contact when we arrived, but not at the DZ. He said he would drop us and tell us exactly where he was. I was the senior officer. We jumped and arrived safely on the ground. We buried our parachutes. We couldn't find 'Legrand' for some time. He turned up next day. We couldn't find some of our equipment in containers. The parachutes had candled. Two of our radio sets were useless. But 'Legrand' managed with the third. We went to the bridge which was where we were to meet our contact Maquis. We walked through the night following the jump [i.e. the following night]. I was terribly tired, and was hallucinating. I said do you see that ballet dancer over there? We discussed it and wondered what he was doing there.
>
> The chap wasn't there. We thought what shall we do. We decided to get 'Gapeau' [Lieutenant Rousset's cover name] into civilian clothes and send him into the village to see how we could contact the Maquis. The whole point of the Jeds was that they were in uniform and were to show the Resistance that the Army was there to help them.
>
> 'Gapeau' came back with a Belgian who was going to join the Maquis that afternoon. So we went with him. The Maquis were a bit surprised to see us, as we had arrived out of the blue, literally. Every night listening to the BBC one could hear '*messages personnels*', apparently pointless things like 'the cat's had kittens', which meant something to the receivers. We all had a *message personnel* which we could tell people to listen for to establish that we were genuine. I could say to the Maquis leader, 'Listen tonight on the British Radio, and you will hear them say, "The doctor's got grey hair", and then you will know I'm OK.' Fortunately they heard this on the radio, because they shot the Belgian that night suspecting him as a plant. [The Harry Team Report says he was a Gestapo agent].

Having established their credentials with the Maquis, Team Harry worked with SAS Operation Houndsworth, including laying on the reception committee for the main body of A Squadron 1st SAS, commanded by Major Frazer. They also:

trained the Maquis in weapons dropped to them. We sent signals twice a day. We only had one reply. They had underestimated their ability to receive signals. I had one signal telling me of a massive drop into my valley using about 20 planes dropping jeeps and weapons. I got very excited. Then I discovered that a whole lot of German troops were being drafted into the neighbourhood and that most of the weapons would fall into their hands. So I asked them to hold off the operation, which they did. I asked them to lay it on later, they never answered.

We had various little skirmishes. The French set up a hospital on the side of the road. I didn't think it was a very good place to put it. A few days later the Germans attacked this hospital, fortunately we got some warning. We managed to ambush the enemy and inflicted quite a few casualties, having evacuated the patients first. The next day, the Germans went to the nearest town, and took the Mayor, the Doctor, the Priest and the town Treasurer and shot them as reprisals. That made one wonder if one had done the right thing. After another of our actions, at Montsauche, the Germans burnt every house in the village of 1,500 inhabitants, except one. Everybody said, 'Now we know who has been collaborating with the Germans.'

One day a local farmer came in with a boy of about 18 years old, who was having a holiday on this farm. He was a Parisian. In his baggage he had armlets with Nazi symbols on them. He admitted that he was a member of a French Fascist organisation in Paris. The Maquis had a trial and the boy was found guilty. A chap from Marseilles came along and gave the boy a shovel. I went to the CO of the group and said 'You can't shoot this chap of 18, he's only got some armlets in his luggage.' He agreed, but asked what he could do with him. He told me to come back in one hour and tell him what should be done with the boy, or he would be shot. I couldn't think of anything. So after an hour, he dug his grave, and two shots rang out.

Our team achieved quite a bit, like involving the Germans [tying down troops] in keeping the roads open. My Maquis, called Camille after the founder, was a good Maquis.

According to the Team Harry Report:

The only bad Maquis I found was Maquis Verneuil. Verneuil himself was about 22 years old, but had managed to collect a large band around him, who began to terrorise the neighbourhood. His Maquis arrested Frenchmen and held them prisoners without any form of trial on the slackest pretext.... Later a radio operator who had been parachuted from England was kept several weeks under arrest without any attempt being made to confirm his story. Several of our liaison agents were arrested and were never asked if they were who they said they were.

In general the Maquis in Guthrie's area appear to have done well, and there seems to have been good co-operation between them and the SAS, as one incident included in the Team Harry Report indicates:

Major Frazer had by now received several jeeps (most of them had unfortunately Roman candled), and also two six-pounders [anti-tank guns], one of which he was keeping in reserve at his Chalaux base. He asked me if the Maquis Camille would like this six-pounder put into position by their Maquis, as in his valley there was no field of fire. The Maquis were delighted at the idea and Captain Tristan found a site for it covering several roads. Two days after it was put into position the Germans attacked the Maquis, and were, I am sure, more than surprised when the six-pounder opened up on them and their transport. The Maquis themselves did a lot of good work that day, and the fire discipline was a great improvement on the attack on Vermot [the hospital], Bren gunners firing in short bursts etc., and not haphazard. Major Frazer himself sent over a message congratulating the Maquis.

Although in some areas the rivalry between the Communist Resistance *Francs Tireurs et Partisans* (FTP) and the Gaullist organized *Forces Françaises de l'Intèrieur* (FFI) was pursued at the expense of attacking the Germans, this was not the experience of Team Harry:

All the time I was in the Morvan I had very little evidence of the so-called 'Communist Peril'. The FTP and FFI worked together very well, with about as much jealousy or rivalry as one would imagine would obtain under similar circumstances in England. There is little doubt that the FTP did real good work against the Germans and were notorious for their courage and 'guts'. The only times I heard of the famous rumours of the [communist] secret arms dump at Clermont-Ferrand to be used for the civil war after the war was from dyed-in-the-wool reactionaries – some of whom seemed to be in absolute terror of the communists. A good example of a more normal approach to the problem was afforded to me by the Marquis de Champean. This officer, retired Commandant of the French Air Force, was a member of one of the oldest families in France, a typical aristocrat to look at. He was approached by the FTP to be their representative, a kind of minister without portfolio, who already had of course valuable contacts. He agreed at once, put the FTP badge up, and worked hard for his group of Maquis. He would laughingly explain that he was not the slightest bit Communist, but felt that any job which helped to get rid of the Germans was a job worth doing.

As with many other Jedburgh teams, Harry's time behind the lines in France came to an end when Allied troops finally arrived. In Guthrie's case when he met the *2ème Dragons* (2nd Dragoons), the advance guard of General Jean de Lattre de Tassigny's 1st French Army coming up from the south with the United States 6th Army Group. Team Harry Report:

> I took a private soldier who had been wounded in the foot, the son of Gen Delattre [*sic*] to the Maquis hospital at Anost for treatment. Next morning Autun was liberated . . . saw Col Head [probably the liaison officer with the Allied headquarters in that area] and reported all details of enemy troops in my area, and he sent me to the G2 Air [staff officer] to give them any information they needed. I returned to Autun where I found fighting going on around the town. Ninety Germans having parleyed with the curé of a little village, surrendered to I [*sic*] on condition that I handed them over to the real army, this I managed to do to the captain commanding the squadron of *2ème Dragons*.

Aubrey Trofimov's Team Guy dropped on 11 July:

> Our briefing was ill thought out. I was surprised and later angry about the fact that they wanted us to go into Ille-et-Vilaine in Brittany [the *département* of which Rennes is the chief town], but dropped us into Mayenne [the *département* to the east of Rennes]. We were in uniform. They had lost all contact with resistance groups at Ille-et-Vilaine since March 1944. At the briefing by a French Colonel, we were told to locate suitable DZs for personnel and *matériel*, and to try and locate any groups of Resistance in the area of Ille-et-Vilaine, and await further orders. There were also some fanciful suggestions put to us that we were to capture a small airport near Rennes and the Colonel who was briefing us would fly in and take over command.
>
> We were dropped south-west of Alençon. I landed on a road some distance from the DZ, I was nearly knocked out by my carbine hitting me under the chin. Whether it was this I don't know, but I forgot the password. Suddenly I saw a shadow the other side of the hedge. I didn't know if it

was a Frenchman or a German. He challenged me with the password, and I couldn't remember the reply. Eventually I said you can check with the other two in my group. We had dropped with another group destined for another area.

My throat was parched probably with fear and excitement. I said I could do anything for a drink. The Frenchman brought out a flask, he said it was coffee. It was about fifty per cent coffee and fifty per cent Calvados.

We were put into a barn that night, up on a ledge [inside the barn]. There was a bucket for use as a lavatory. The first morning, I went down to have a pee, and was doing so when I saw through a crack in the door a vehicle covered with antennae. I thought, 'My God this is the German radio detector van.' So I signalled to the other chaps to keep quiet. We pulled up the ladder expecting to have to fight our way out. What had happened we learned was the Germans had discovered that there had been a drop that night and were going around trying to locate any radio operations. They had got to the farm, gone inside for a drink, switched off. When they came out they switched on. But it was a very quick lesson in how careful one had to be. It could have been the end of us.

We were also dropped some 70 miles from our destination, and because we were in uniform we could only travel at night. We were very heavily laden. Progress was very slow. We later found out that there had been several drops into Ille-et-Vilaine at the same time as ours so by a little bit more background research it would have been established that there were reception committees who could have met us and it would have altered the whole picture for us. We were warned that there were very few Resistance groups operating because the Gestapo had been very successful in rooting out groups in that area. The main source of help would be from clandestine groups not overt Maquis-type organisations, i.e. people that had normal jobs during the day and acted at night whenever they could, rather than semi-military groups hiding in the forests, etc. This made it difficult for us because our reception committee had jobs they had to go to by day. We had to hide up and only move at night. They could have gone into this a little more at the briefing. Clearly dropping people 70 miles away from their destination in uniform was going to raise a series of huge problems. I don't think that the briefing took that into account as much as they might have done.

From then on life became very difficult indeed. Being in uniform was a tremendous embarrassment to the Resistance. We could only move from safe house to safe house. They were not all that easy to find. The Germans, if they found that anybody had any kind of Resistance person under their roof, burned down the farm or house and took the people away and tortured them, sent them to camps, etc. We set about marching at night, carrying all this equipment. The radio equipment alone plus the generator weighed quite a bit. We didn't achieve many miles. At one stage we got to a barn and there was no contact we could go to from there. I had heard from talking to one of the guides that there was an agent operating in that area. I couldn't go in uniform, and I got some civilian clothes from our contact. I set off, on a bicycle he lent me. I went to Michel [his war codename]. He wasn't a Jed. He was part of F Section. He was a very famous agent. We bicycled back, and he was singing in English. We passed through a village where some Germans were drinking beer, and he never stopped singing.

We sorted out with him a programme to enable us to get on with our journey. He put us in contact with a member of the FTP whose codename was 'Lulu'. He organised a doctor to transport all our heavy gear in a car marked with a red cross which meant we could move much more quickly. We borrowed bicycles for some stages. We eventually got to Gorron in Mayenne [between Fougères and Bagnoles], and were staying at a farm and still making very slow progress. We needed to speed things up and decided to try and buy an old car. Eventually we bought a very old thing for 10,000 francs. We got in, we had only been going for half an hour when we ran into a German patrol. We split and ran off. We had an RV to go to. But the Germans apparently were not quite sure what happened. One of our people who spoke German was able to get back into the car and move it forward enabling the people the other side of the road to get in, and they took off. I was split from them. I went to the RV which was a farm. I had one contact in the farm. The situation was dangerous because the Germans knew something was going on. We tried to get back to the road, but the Germans were spraying the sides [of the road] with machine-gun fire.

I contacted two Gendarmes who had got us the car. They told me that the Americans were breaking through rather quickly [and were not far away]. So I thought that the best thing was to identify where the German positions were. I couldn't do this in daylight in uniform so they equipped me as a farmer. They got me an identity card and I became a student of architecture in a northern French university.

This enabled me to go into the town of Gorron at night. I had to sneak about because of the curfew. I managed to get quite close to some of the German positions, but ran slap bang into a patrol, young soldiers led by a young NCO. I pretended to be drunk, and leant against a wall and pretended to retch. They went on. I was lucky. I had a .45 colt pistol in my pocket, and had they frisked me that would have been it. I wanted to contact a Gendarme who knew the area on the side of Gorron where the Americans would come from. I set off and as I came round the bend there to my horror was a German regiment resting by the roadside. I had to walk through this. I obviously couldn't show panic. With my beret right down on my head, I limped so they wouldn't wonder why I wasn't in a labour camp. I could feel the sweat on the back of my shirt. After getting through I had to pull myself together in a convenient wood.

I spent several nights checking German positions. Word came through on the Gendarme telephone network that the Americans were approaching Gorron. I set off across the fields with the Gendarme, and eventually made contact with an American recce unit. It took some time to convince them who I was. I was in civilian clothes. When they accepted my story, they agreed to pass back my message. I gave them my codename, because every HQ [above a certain level] had special forces liaison officers. I went back, thinking that if the recce group was so close, the main body would not be far behind. I made contact with the OC of 106 Cavalry Recce Squadron whose instructions had been to attack Gorron. He invited me to join them. I told him that I could guide him on a road not strongly held by the Germans. We got into the centre of the town, to see the Germans fleeing towards Alençon.

I attached myself to an American officer as liaison for a couple of days. There were lots of people going around with armbands on saying they were members of the Resistance. Where had they been when we were there? This was a postwar Resistance set up. Some may have been genuine, a lot of them weren't. We had to take a lot of their claims with a pinch of salt. It was a question of joining the winning side.

The Americans lent me a driver and a jeep. They took me to their HQ, where I reported on what I had been up to and what the likely movements of the Germans might be.

I found where my team had got to, rejoined them, and we moved towards St Malo. The Germans were putting up a tremendous resistance on the little islands and pockets around St Malo, in concrete gun posts, etc. The Americans didn't have time to deal with these, so they handed over the task to the Resistance. We recruited quite a few people who hadn't been in the Resistance before, but suddenly now were. I moved into St Malo, I met Capitaine du Bois, head of the Gendarmerie there. There were German snipers in the ramparts of St Malo. I spent several days there with the

Resistance, and we flushed out as many of these snipers as we could. Some of the Germans fought hard. On the islands they had enough supplies to last for months.

On receiving a radio message to come in and report, Trofimov and his team went to the United States VIII Corps Headquarters near Avranches. He was able to tell them what the German activity was, including using Red Cross vans to transport ammunition. They were interested in the state of the German troops, their morale and so forth. After debriefing he was sent back to England with his team and completed formal reports at Baker Street. His Team Guy Report concludes:

> Unfortunately we were never really able to accomplish our mission as contemplated. I think we were able to render valuable service to the [United States] 6th Armoured Division and to the [United States] 83rd Infantry Division, but this was not in line with our mission.

After leave, Trofimov received a message saying he could rejoin his regiment or join Force 136 in the Far East. He chose the latter.

Dick Rubinstein's Team Douglas went in on the night of 4/5 August. They were:

> Briefed at HQ in Bryanston Square. Also in a flat in a mews nearby. We were going in with a French mission called Aloès and operate alongside the 4th French SAS, led by *Commandant* [Major] Bourgoin. He had gone in in July 1944. We flew in from Fairford in Stirlings. We didn't drop the first night, no lights or something. The second night we went in with a number of SAS going in as reinforcements. I had £30,000 inside my jump jacket which made me look very pregnant. It was all in large denomination notes. We landed at an SAS Dingson Base which had been used a lot by the SAS. It was like a fairground, full of villagers. The SAS had liberated large parts of Brittany but attracted a lot of German attention, and had lost about half their strength.
>
> We were whisked away into a wooded camp and then ended up on the Golfe du Morbihan [south of Vannes], and were involved in the reception of some gliders carrying vehicles [for the SAS] and a large quantity of arms for distribution to French recruited under Mission Aloès who would operate around Lorient. The good-grade German troops were moving east, and we were to report on their movement to bring down air strikes on them by day when they lay up. The second-grade German troops were

staying in Lorient. They were not all German, but included White Russians, etc. Because they must not be allowed freedom to roam outside Lorient, about 5,000 French were put around Lorient. We never had a very clear role. Op Aloès was already very well established. I could not see that it needed the help of a Jedburgh team. We asked if we could come out. Vannes airport had now been liberated. Three Dakotas flew in with British ammunition for the weapons issued to the locally recruited French. We were told by London we could have a ride back. We flew back with them. We had been in France for about three weeks. The only time of danger was when the Germans sallied out from Lorient. Before we came back we were established in Vannes in the old Gestapo HQ. Our radio was used to pass traffic for Op Aloès. There wasn't much threat on that mission.

Rubinstein was to go in again, as Team Douglas 2:

about ten days later. It was very difficult to be in the gentle atmosphere of one's own home in twelve hours. I found it very difficult to take. My wife and I took a rowing boat on the River Thames and camped. I had to ring up every day to see if they wanted me. After about five days they said come back. My second wireless operator was an American [Sergeant van Hart] who was still free to go, and if he was still free by September 1944 it meant he wasn't terribly good. Actually he was a good egg. Luckily the second op wasn't too significant. It was too late.

This time we went from Tempsford in a Liberator, and dropped in the hills above the Doubs valley very near Switzerland. It was part of an Allied mission, and again it wasn't a very clear role. I had a nasty feeling that a number of HQ officers were finding operational roles before it ended. If Arnhem had succeeded, and there had been a Rhine Crossing that year, our task would have been to march in a north-easterly direction towards Belfort and to send locals back towards the advancing troops with local knowledge; and to use the radio to hit military targets. It would have been difficult country in which to operate. We were told to sit tight during the time of the battle of Arnhem and remained in hiding in a little town called L'Isle-sur-le-Doubs [between Besançon and Belfort]. Once Arnhem failed there was no role for us in closely developed Western Europe. We were told to come out. We walked towards the advancing Allied troops. An American liaison officer took charge of Hart. Roblot left to become a 'proper soldier'. I was left to make my way to Paris. I had found a German motor bike so I took myself to Paris and gave myself a week's leave before reporting to the OSS/SOE office in Paris.

SOE said you've got three options: back to the Army, a job in Germany, or go to the Far East. They wouldn't tell me about the job in Germany unless I volunteered. Later I learnt it was an operation that never happened; to parachute into POW camps and encourage the German staff to cooperate in releasing or treating the inmates well, instead of slaughtering them which was thought might happen.[8]

Major Brown's Team Alastair was flown in at the end of August to the Vosges. Another Team, Jacob, commanded by a British officer, Captain V. A. Gough, had been dropped in this area earlier, but contact with them had been lost. After the war it was discovered he had been a prisoner of the Gestapo, and was shot at the end of November 1944. The landings in the South of France had taken place in mid-August:

My job was to reinforce the Resistance, and to try and take two bridges across the Moselle for the advancing forces, and to create as much havoc as I could. I went from the American airfield in East Anglia. The first night we couldn't find the DZ. We stooged around for hours. We went slap over Cherbourg and they threw everything at us. We got tagged by a German fighter, he hit us we discovered when we got back. A good job too the pilot would have dropped us over the Rhine as it turned out.

The second try was in the right place, but as the Alastair Team Report, written by Brown, says:

The dropping did not take place quite as scheduled. Captain 'Maître', who was No.1, unfortunately hesitated because he said he saw the containers going past the hole just as the despatcher said 'GO'! The despatcher then gave him three more 'GOs', which I do not think he heard as it was not until I gave him a kick that he really realized that he had to go, and jumped. This meant that it was impossible to jump more than Capt 'Maître' and Sgt Smith on the first run, and I was held back for the second run. This, unfortunately, caused me to have a very bad drop. The pilot, believing that he only had packages left in the plane, came down to what must have been about 400 ft and did not decelerate at all, the result being I got a considerable buffeting, both feet in the rigging lines, and took a number of panels out of the chute. One of the Maquis who was running to assist me, at the last moment, in order to avoid me, lay flat on his stomach, whereupon I sat rather heavily on him, saving myself a considerable amount of discomfort, but rendering him unconscious for two days.

Brown, who was 6 foot 6 inches tall and weighed about 18 stone, damaged his leg, and was unable to walk for two days. The Alastair Team Report continues:

> It turned out that we had been received by a reception committee of 500 men, which was a Maquis which had only been mobilised the night before in the expectancy of receiving sufficient arms for the whole group on the night we were dropped. All they actually received was the contents of the 12 containers in our plane which was a ridiculous load being 8 containers of sabotage equipment and 4 containers of arms. This situation was for all [of us] a pretty poor start as they had been led to expect by the BBC message that there would be two aircraft arriving on that ground which they confidently expected would be full of arms, and to receive 8 containers of sabotage equipment which, to say the least, were only a damn nuisance, and only 4 containers of arms, did not increase their confidence in the people who were coming to help them. What happened to the second plane which was supposed to drop on our ground I do not know. It left six minutes before us with a French officer on board, and 12 containers, but if it did arrive anywhere it certainly did not arrive on our ground. However, a plane did arrive which dropped ten SAS who were supposed to have been dropped on a ground 25 km away.

Team Alastair were given civilian clothes by the Resistance, but no papers, and moved into town; the Team Report continues:

> The Maquis to which we had been dropped, and who were doing liaison duties for us, were extremely careless, and as there were quite a number of collaborators in the town, including in the house next door to us and one in the house opposite, I was not at all happy about our position and on the second day I insisted that we were moved somewhere else as quite a lot of people were beginning to know of our presence even if they did not know who we were.

The second time they were moved, still without papers, they were driven through a German control post. Team Report:

> The truck behind us was stopped by the Control Post and actually we were the last vehicle in the Department to go through a Control Post unchallenged.

At a meeting with the leaders of the various Maquis in the département, Brown proposed an ambitious plan consisting of no fewer than fourteen drops of arms and equipment all on the same night. The Germans had reinforced the area, and he did not want drops night after night, alerting the enemy and allowing them to attack each Maquis in turn. This would be followed by daylight supply operations which had already been approved by SOE headquarters in London. Brown hoped to arm some 25,000 men. The Maquis leaders agreed, but eventually London vetoed the plan, telling Brown that it was impossible to send them anything by night, 'owing to unforeseen circumstances and situations beyond our control', and that the previously agreed daylight operation was now off too. Meanwhile the Team had a number of narrow escapes as their Report reveals:

> We had to use the bridge at Jarmeuil, and I was rather suspicious that this bridge would be guarded, therefore sent the guide over first. If it was guarded, to continue on his way and we would swim across ourselves later. He came back and the four of us crossed the bridge, Capt 'Maître' and Sgt Smith having the radio sets on their backs. We noticed a building on the other side of the bridge and I inquired of the guide what this was, and he told me that this was the local *estaminet*, and also that the guard was inside. Just as we got to the other side of the bridge, we heard somebody come down a path and a German officer with a girlfriend passed five yards in front of us. I quote this incident mainly for the lesson it taught us which was never to believe anything the members of the Resistance told you from the point of view of danger. They are so used to seeing Germans all over the place that they forget that whereas they themselves can pass without trouble, three odd bodies, none of whom have papers, one of whom cannot speak French, and two of whom have wireless sets on their backs, cannot pass so easily.

Later they were sleeping in what Brown describes as a hangar full of straw, about 500 yards from the nearest road. They covered themselves with straw. The Team Report continues:

> At about 1 o'clock in the morning I heard the sound of marching feet and what must have been about 15 men stopped outside the hangar. Four Germans proceeded to enter the hangar and remove the straw which they passed to others who carted it away. We were wondering all the time whether they would remove sufficient straw that they would eventually uncover us. However, after about 20 minutes they pushed off and left us in peace.

On another occasion Sergeant Smith was:

stopped by a German officer and asked for a light. Fortunately, the officer asked him in German, and he managed to make signs that he could not understand him. The German then made a sign to him showing what he wanted. He lit his cigarette with a Ronson lighter and all passed well.

Brown remembers that the Germans in the Vosges behaved appallingly:

We saw a German shoot a seven-year-old-girl just because she was nearby when he fell off his bicycle. She didn't push him off. Later we caught him. We handed him to the father of the girl he shot, and never asked any questions. If you didn't get off the pavement when a German soldier came along he knocked you off into the road.

The lack of security by the Maquis in Brown's area led to the dispersal of one group of about 400, consisting of 150 armed and 250 unarmed men, hiding in a forest north of Jarmeuil, as the Team Report says:

The Germans had a pretty fair idea of (a) where all the Maquis were, and (b) their approximate strength, and moved another division of SS troops in, with the sole task of attacking all the Resistance in the Department. They duly attacked the Maquis [north of Jarmeuil] on a Saturday morning.... The head of the Maquis was warned the night before that these troops had moved into the area and that an attack was likely in the morning. He received a further warning in the morning that the Germans were moving up towards the forest. Upon receiving this information, he took his bags, handed over the command to a lieutenant, and descended down to the village. His excuse for doing so was that he had a rendezvous with me, which was completely false. The Maquis in their battle fought with extreme bravery but very little skill. The result of the battle was 100 Germans killed and 100 wounded. The Maquis casualties were [unreadable but over 100] killed, about 15 wounded had to be left behind, and when they returned the next morning the Germans had massacred the lot. The large number of German casualties can be accounted for by the fact that Spitfires spotted them moving up the side of the mountain and attacked them causing about 50 per cent of the casualties

These exact, and suspiciously rounded, figures of German casualties need to be treated, if not with a pinch of salt, at least with reserve. It is

extremely unlikely that such precise figures of German casualties could
be established without doubt today, over fifty years later, let alone when
Brown wrote his report a few weeks after the event.

Eventually, after more frustration, Brown went to see the leaders of
two groups of Maquis; one at Éloyes being forty strong, well armed and
led, survivors from the Maquis attacked by the Germans. He agreed with
the two leaders that one group was to receive stores for 400 men, and
the other stores for 600. These were to be dropped forty-eight hours
before the Americans, who were approaching, tried the crossing of the
Moselle. The Team Report continues:

> The night before the general attack on the Moselle, the Maquis should
> divide as follows:-
>
> (a) A group of 200 to attack and take the town of Éloyes.
> (b) That 400 of the Maquis of Remiremont should take that town.
>
> The remaining 400 to be divided into one group of 200 who would take
> a bridgehead on the Moselle at its most fordable point and a further group
> of 200 should undertake general guerrilla warfare throughout the remain-
> der of the Moselle between Éloyes and Remiremont. This plan could not
> however be carried out owing to the refusal of État-Major FFI [EMFFI, the
> Headquarters of the FFI in London] to send us arms. We were therefore
> reduced to our 40 men at Éloyes with whom we first helped the Americans
> get their bridgehead with general guerrilla warfare in the mountains. Once
> the Americans made their crossing, we used their [*sic*; the?] Maquis as
> guides and *Agents de Renseignments* [intelligence agents]. This, together
> with local patrol duties, was our chief task until the time I left.

After liberation of Nancy he was returned home. He found working
underground less dangerous in some ways than he had anticipated, but
more so in other ways:

> Working to one's own timetable was easier than having to work to a strict
> schedule. One had more control of one's destiny. The unexpected was the
> most dangerous. For example having arranged to meet at a certain farm,
> 'Smithy' was on edge. We finished, the others had gone, and 'Smithy' had
> wandered into the garden. He came back and said, 'There are some bloody
> Krauts out there.' He was quite right. 'Smithy' and I set out as if to go to
> the outside loo. I said, 'Walk slowly, and when I say run, run to break the

record.' We got away. They burnt the farm down, including all my uniform. I only had one set of clothes.

My cover story was that I was Jean Ballon a wood cutter. I did a three-week course of lumbering before leaving England.

I was caught once, but was saved by my training at Beaulieu, the finishing centre. I was just wandering about. I was picked up in a random pick-up. In my pocket was a book with a coded message. I put the book on the desk as I went in. My papers passed inspection. No trouble at all. I came out, and went straight by the desk. I turned and said to the German sentry, 'I've forgotten my book', and picked it up. I would never have thought of doing that without my training. I would have automatically picked up the book on my way out, and he might have asked, 'What's in that book?'

Sergeant Frederick Bailey was the radio operator in Team Citroën, commanded by a British officer, Major Smallwood, and including a Frenchman, Captain Bloch (*nom de guerre*, Alcée), a regular French Foreign Legion officer. When the Jedburgh concept was born, the problem arose of developing radio equipment for them. Most SOE agents were equipped with radios that were powered by the mains or by acid batteries, like modern car batteries. This was fine for SOE operators who were based in houses, but totally unsuitable for soldiers living in the field and carrying their equipment on their backs. Major John Brown at the SOE special signals section near Welwyn Garden City came up with the solution. He produced a hand-cranked generator mounted on a tripod with telescopic legs, which powered the transmitter (from the B2 set) and receiver (the MCR 1). All three components, together with the telescopic antenna with guy ropes and pegs, was packed in webbing equipment, and weighed 37 lb. Freed from the need to find a power source the Jedburghs could transmit and receive their messages anywhere which was safe to do so; forest clearing or barn. All teams also carried the standard SOE mains/battery-powered B2 transceiver set. Communication was exclusively by morse.

Team Citroën went in on 13 August, just before the start of the Allied landings in the South of France; Sergeant Bailey:

From Milton Hall, we went to Algeria, and after a short period of training in the mountains, we were ready to leave for southern France. Our HQ for communications was Algiers. One set was in a suitcase and could be plugged into the mains electricity, the other in a canvas pack and a hand generator. The parachute with the suitcase set malfunctioned and mangled the set. I used the other set all the time I was in France. The drawback was that someone had to work the generator.

We were dropped away from the DZ and too high, north of Marseilles outside a town called Apt [between Avignon and Digne on the N 100]. From there we went to a town called Pertuis [just north of Aix-en-Provence]. We lived there at various addresses until we were overrun by the Americans at the end of September 1944.

We were in uniform. If picked up by the Germans, we were to hold out for at least 48 hours so the remainder could get clear. We did not have suicide pills. We had no cover story, we were to say that we were British troops dropped in the area. We expected to be treated like POW, although, with hindsight, it was highly unlikely that we would have been.

This cover story was reasonably plausible because the Allied invasion plan included the British 2nd Independent Parachute Brigade dropping some ten miles north-west of St-Raphaël early on 15 August. Team Citroën could well be mistaken for the pathfinders for this operation. In the Second World War it was by no means unusual for troops on a brigade parachute operation at night to be dropped wide, even by a margin of seventy-five miles. The USAAF, who provided the transport aircraft in the Mediterranean Theatre, and who flew without navigators except in the lead aircraft, were notorious at that period in the war for dropping their sticks in the wrong place on night operations; something that the German intelligence would know.

Bailey's impressions of French Resistance were that:

the Resistance wanted us there for the supplies and help we could give. They were extremely patriotic, but not always reliable. However important an operation might be it was difficult to get them all there on time. They were politically divided. Politics was the main subject of conversation. I mentioned this to them. They said, 'Yes, politics are important to us.' They were all concerned who would have power when the Germans left. In my opinion politics seemed to loom far too large for people who were occupied.

The most vicious people against collaborators were known as the 'September Partisans', who formed up when the Americans were about to arrive. They had done nothing to help free the country. They shaved the heads of women who had collaborated with the Germans.

Along with all the other Jedburghs, Bailey was offered the chance to return to his regiment or serve in the Far East. He chose the latter.

Oswin Craster commanded Team Stanley, with Lieutenant Cantais from the French Colonial Army, and Sergeant Jack Grinham, originally a policeman from Birmingham. The team dropped south of Langres, west of the main Langres–Dijon road, on 31 August 1944.

I and the Frenchman and radio operator and two Aspirants [young officers] went from Tempsford. It was evening, and the sun was shining on the church. I wondered if I would ever see that again. We landed in a field in the dark. We were met by a small band of Frenchwomen. We were taken off to a house in the village. Nowadays you hear that everybody was in the FFI, but they weren't you know. Some were sitting on the fence or had been compromised. We weren't allowed to put our noses outside. Next day we were taken in a van in civilian clothes and motored some ten or fifteen miles to the east across the main road. It was raining, you could see the Germans hanging about in the doorways. We weren't stopped. We were taken to a farmhouse in the woods. The farmer had a young son called Joseph aged sixteen. We recruited him to wind the generator. It was brave of them to look after us. We were visited by the Germans from time to time.

The rest of the Maquis were living in the wood. I don't know how many of them there were. At that time in France there were few men of military age about, they were either POW, in the Army [or in labour camps]. Most of the Maquis had reserved occupations, such as railway workers, or Gendarmes. We had schoolboys; they would risk their lives to get a machine pistol those boys. We also had the Vichy *Premier Règiment du France* who were busy changing sides. They never came out very much. I tried to encourage them to do ambushes, but they refused. They had had a little fight with the Germans and been mauled.

We carried out ambushes and took some prisoners, including Russians, half a dozen Indians taken prisoner earlier in the War. We took some German officers who were very annoyed to be taken by this lot. There was a lot of ill feeling about the Germans in the villages. There still is. The Germans tortured three nurses all night at Belmont to try and find out where the Maquis were hiding. They shot them the next morning. The Maquis caught the Major who did it.

Team Stanley was in for under three weeks, and the Maquis under Craster's command set about half a dozen ambushes. In Craster's opinion:

We should have been dropped sooner. On the other hand we would have been caught, if the Germans hadn't been running around in the weeks after the invasion. Once the breakout at Normandy began and the Germans were on the move, it was a bit disconcerting for them, with small groups peppering them. You had to choose places well away from villages or they would shoot everybody in the village. We sent a lot of information back on which regiments were coming through.

In the Team Stanley Report summary the assessment of the Maquis is:

The men were excellent types and after carefully placed behind cover they were excellent [sic] in small ambushes but were very rabbity if surprised by the enemy.

The Chief of our Maquis and the Officers at his headquarters were very poor, and seemed more interested in hiding themselves in the woods until the Allies arrived than inflicting the maximum damage on the enemy.

Craster recalled:

We had an old lorry which ran on charcoal gas. The Maquis were short of shoes, so they said, and couldn't walk anywhere. You parked the lorry some way from road. It took some time to start up, the charcoal takes some time to pre-heat. It was rather nerve-racking. Sometimes it didn't start, all you got was a loud bang and a cloud of smoke.

We called in an air strike on a village where the Germans were holed up. We sent the message in clear. These fighters turned up and dived on the village and destroyed 24 horse-drawn trucks loaded with ammunition. That changed the attitude of the Maquis towards us.

We set up DZs for supplies. Our transmitter was damaged on landing. Half our messages didn't get through, so we learned after we got back. We wanted PIATs and boots but we never got these. We also asked for another transmitter. We never got that either.

We dropped in our uniforms so if you broke a leg you might be able to get away with it by a good cover story [such as being dropped wide by mistake on a 'normal' parachute operation]. My cover once I was in France was that I was an engineer from Clermont-Ferrand. I had the right sort of ration card. I could pass for a Frenchman among the Germans but not with the French. I had no qualms about discarding my uniform. Thought the Germans would shoot us anyway, after pulling our fingernails out.

It all ended very suddenly; we were overrun by French troops from the south dressed in American uniform. The message came: 'return via Paris'. That was it. I wrote a report. I was asked if I wanted to go out East. My original battalion, the 5th Oxfordshire & Buckinghamshire Light Infantry, had been disbanded. I went to 2nd Battalion at Bulford [an air-landing battalion just back from Normandy]. I had a few rides in gliders. It was an unpleasant form of transport. I didn't really fit in with that lot.

It is not surprising that Craster did not fit in; the battalion, after successful glider landings in Normandy, including the imaginative *coup de main* on 'Pegasus Bridge', had spent three months hard fighting east of the River Orne. They subsequently took part in the brilliant Rhine Crossing operation. With the innate snobbery of the front-line soldier, they would probably have viewed Craster's war so far as very small beer indeed, and as he admits:

Looking back it's a lot safer behind the lines than being in front and being told to advance across a field.

Later:

I was posted to 1 Para left-behind parties at Grantham [rear details] full of cooks and bottle-washers [the battalion was at Arnhem]. They used to cause trouble in the pubs at night. I was sent in on patrol to keep order. That got tedious. I went up to London, and asked to go to the Far East because I reckoned I would be safer in the jungle than I was in Grantham. A week later I was on a ship going to Bombay.

By the end of October 1944, all the Jedburgh teams were out of France. The Americans were sent back to the United States to be given new tasks. The French were returned to their own army, and many volunteered to serve with Force 136 in Indo-China.

When the Jedburghs went to the Far East as part of Force 136, they were still regarded as, and called by, that name, although the Foreign and Commonwealth Office (FCO), which runs MI6, refused to recognize this fact in their official history. Over fifty years have elapsed since the events described in this chapter and Chapter 12, but the FCO official history of the Jedburghs is still not in the public domain. Fortunately, because the Jedburghs were under joint SOE/OSS command, the team reports, all Top Secret, were lodged in Washington as well as in London. Although the British copies of the reports of operations in France are still not available, thanks to the United States Freedom of Information

Act, the American copies of the reports are in the Imperial War Museum, so the Jedburghs can be given the credit they deserve.

The Jedburgh casualties in France were twenty killed in action, missing, or shot after capture, and twenty wounded in action; four were taken prisoner and survived captivity. The majority of the operations were successful, those that failed were in the main because there was nothing to do when the team arrived. Many Jedburghs believe that the teams were inserted too late. It is difficult to see what they could have done before the landings in Normandy, for without the activity of the Allied armies, the Germans would have crushed any overt action by partisans quite easily. However, a case can be made for dropping the teams very much sooner after 6 June 1944 than they were. Although it would probably have been difficult to judge just when the right moment occurred for a team to be inserted into its selected zone of operations; and aircraft to drop the team might not have been available at that time. It seems that the teams were at their most effective when the operational situation was fluid, which usually occurred when the Germans in the area concerned were starting to feel the effects of, or were anticipating, an attack by a main force. The Jedburghs' tying-in of the Maquis with the overall Allied activity was mainly effective; as was their task as facilitators for supply of the Resistance in a very confused situation.

SAS operations continued. The earliest operations had been aimed at attacking the communications leading to the Allied bridgehead in Normandy. This was followed by a short phase of harassment of the Germans retreating from their crushing defeat in Normandy, and operations to harass German 1st Army retreating from south of the Loire, and 19th Army from the South of France. At the same time the SAS established a series of bases from which to attack communications between Germany and France.

One of the most successful SAS operations was Operation Wallace which started on 19 August. Major Roy Farran with sixty men and twenty jeeps of 2nd SAS landed by Dakota at Rennes airfield, which was in American hands. By now the operational situation in France was sufficiently fluid to allow jeep patrols to find a way through enemy lines. Farran penetrated 200 miles behind enemy lines in four days, to join the base set up by Operation Hardy on the Plateau de Langres, near Châtillon north of Dijon. Six men of the Hardy party had dropped with one jeep to the Houndsworth base south-west of Dijon about three weeks before. More men and jeeps were dropped on subsequent nights, until the party was fifty strong. On 1 August under the command of Captain Grant-Hibbert, they left for their operating area. By the time Farran arrived the Hardy party had destroyed a number of German trucks and blown up the railway line from Langres to Dijon.

Farran covered the first fifty miles behind enemy lines without any significant encounters with the enemy. He had considerable help from the local Maquisards in finding routes round any serious potential opposition. Farran wanted to keep it that way, and not start operations until he reached the Hardy base. To begin with he tried moving at night, which was a mistake, because Allied air supremacy forced the Germans to take cover by day, and at night the roads were crawling with enemy transport.

He split his party into three groups, telling them to drive along the same road, at thirty-minute intervals between groups, and to bypass opposition. The leading group disobeyed Farran's instructions and charged through a large group of enemy in the village of Mailly-le-Château. They got through for the loss of one jeep, but Farran's group following behind came under fire. He and the group behind him detoured to the south, and managed to RV with the leading group in the Forêt de St Jean. He was now a hundred miles behind enemy lines. The next morning the leading group again ran into enemy, and all the jeeps were destroyed; although the leader escaped, the only one of his group to do so, he was unable to warn the group behind.

Farran ran straight into the same party of Germans, and in the ensuing firefight they lost a jeep and a trailer with a radio set. They stopped the first German attack, which foolishly came at them straight down the road, dead in its tracks, but had to withdraw when it became clear that the enemy were outflanking them. Farran drove in a wide sweep to the south of the enemy, and got clear. Unfortunately, the last group ran into the same enemy. The officer commanding was killed, and few of the SAS escaped. The survivors eventually drove to Paris, which had been liberated. Some were parachuted in to join Farran later. He now found himself with only seven of his original twenty jeeps. Pressing on, he was approaching a level crossing, when a goods train chugged up the line. As it passed the gates, Farran gave the order to fire, and the Vickers K guns fired a stream of incendiary, tracer and armour-piercing at point-blank range. The engine stopped with its boiler punctured about 200 yards further on. The German guards on the train were killed, but the French engine driver was unscathed.

Approaching the Forêt de Châtillon, they were fired upon by troops manning a radar station. Farran withdrew, but so did the enemy, thinking that the SAS were the advance guards of Patton's 3rd Army, as they discovered from prisoners. The SAS attacked the retreating Germans, causing thirty-five casualties. A little later Farran drove into Grant-Hibbert's Hardy base camp. The combined strength of Hardy and Wallace, now all under Farran's command as a squadron, amounted to ten jeeps, one civilian truck and sixty men. Grant-Hibbert had made the area too hot to hold him, and so Farran ordered a move to another base.

After operating as a squadron until 30 August, setting a series of successful ambushes and inflicting considerable damage on the enemy, Farran decided to split into three groups in order to cover as wide an area as possible. His squadron's operations ended on 17 September when the United States 7th Army arrived and started shelling a German battery of 88 mm guns near where Farran's group were holed up. They had spent a month behind enemy lines, and had inflicted 500 casualties on the enemy, destroyed 95 vehicles, a train and 100,000 gallons of petrol. SAS casualties were 16 men and 16 jeeps. The Vickers K machine-gun again proved itself a devastating weapon, as it had in the desert. At fifty yards it could cut a truck in two. Without the RAF the operation would not have been possible. They carried out 36 sorties, dropping 484 panniers of supplies and 12 jeeps. One SAS trooper was killed and two jeeps damaged in parachuting accidents. Farran:

> We took our time recrossing France, looking with pride at the skeletons of all the trucks we had destroyed. I allowed the squadron a week's leave in Paris, although it was supposed to be out of bounds to British troops at the time.

As the Allied armies closed up to the Rhine, and the borders of Germany, the opportunities for SAS operations tailed off. During the winter of 1944–45 there was little scope for behind the lines activity. Brigadier McLeod was sent to a staff job in India, and Brigadier Mike Calvert took his place:

> I was offered three types of jobs; to command a commando brigade, to be in charge of SOE in MacArthur's HQ in the Philippines, third to command the SAS. I thought the war in the Far East would last for two or three years, and I should get the opportunity to learn about European warfare before going out to the Far East again.

Asked why the job did not go to one of the existing SAS commanding officers, Calvert replied:

> As for the colonels of the SAS, Paddy Mayne, who got four DSOs, and Brian Franks: in action all they could do was to be just a patrol leader, so neither of them had any experience in command as a whole. When [I am] asked why Paddy Mayne was not put in command of the SAS, the answer was he had never in his distinguished career commanded anything more than about 12 men in action. He was brilliantly brave and very conscientious in planning, he could foresee an operation in his mind, so he usually brought it to a successful conclusion. The result: he had a great following among his men.
>
> Brian Franks was a different cup of tea. 2nd SAS were organised much more like the Household Cavalry. But he had vision.

Although this may sound arrogant, there is no denying that Calvert had vastly more experience in commanding a long-range penetration brigade in battle than either Mayne or Franks, who had none. He had a distinguished record of unconventional operations. His courage and coolness under fire was a byword. He was also a 'thinking soldier'. It would have been hard to have found a better man for the job.

The tasks allocated to the SAS Brigade for the last month of the War in north-west Europe were different from the long-range penetration operations in the desert and France, and more akin to the early days of the Italian campaign; operating just ahead of the advancing armies. Although the SAS had considerable success in this role in Holland and Germany, they also suffered fairly heavy casualties, not least because a jeep, even if it is armoured and fitted with Vickers K guns, does not have the protection or punch of an armoured car or light tank. In Holland especially, among dykes and canals, minefields and enemy strong points, Paddy Mayne's 1st SAS with forty jeeps, operating under the Canadian 4th Armoured Division, found conditions very difficult. Franks's 2nd SAS, operating ahead of 6th Airborne Division, 11th Armoured and 15th (Scottish) Infantry Division in turn in the advance to the Elbe, found operating easier. But even so, 2nd SAS were not being used in the way for which the SAS were raised and trained. This is a hazard which faces all 'special' troops, who by their temperament usually hanker after action. As an advance nears its objective, the amount of suitable 'real estate' available for behind the lines operations may be reduced. So the special troops in question will be tempted to take whatever roles, or targets, are on offer. Germany in particular had neither the wide open spaces of the desert nor a resistance movement with whom patrols could link up. Here any attempt at deep patrolling in jeeps would have had to cope with the hazards of a hostile population and the attendant risk of being reported to the authorities. The German Army, the *Volksturm* (Home Guard) and Hitler Youth fought almost to the end, even when they must have seen that all hope was gone. So there was little alternative to employing the SAS as divisional reconnaissance. To have left such skilled troops sitting on the sidelines in an advance, where reconnaissance is always at a premium, would have been unthinkable; nor would the SAS have wanted this. Their final operations in Italy, covered later, were a reversion to their familiar role.

What of the question of return on investment in the operations covered in this chapter? It is hard to quantify what results were achieved by the Jedburghs, and we shall probably never know exactly what their 'score' was in terms of damage and casualties inflicted on the enemy. Many of their achievements are not amenable to an objective analysis. Without doubt their activities, particularly in supplying and controlling the Resistance, where possible, bore dividends out of all proportion to their numbers, and the investment in training and resources. As we said before, by their own admission, they might have been more effective if inserted earlier. They were to play a more active role in Burma.

Statistics for SAS Brigade operations in France, Belgium and Holland from June to November 1944 only are given in *Airborne Forces*, and are contained in Appendix C. The caveat given in the paragraph preceding the statistics in this Appendix is important, and is probably too guarded. Readers will note that the figures for vehicles are rounded, and probably upwards. It is almost always impossible to find out exactly how many casualties one has inflicted on the enemy in a battle; certainly until some time, probably years, has passed. In the author's experience the initial estimates are always too high. The only true tally possible in the aftermath of battle (on land), is prisoners of war, captured guns, equipment and vehicles; i.e. anything or anyone that can be lined up and counted.

According to *Airborne Forces* the greatest value of SAS operations in north-west Europe comes under four headings:

(a) The moral support given to the resistance movements and assistance in organising and arming them.

(b) The adverse moral effect on the enemy caused by the continual harassing of his lines of communications. He had to hold considerable forces to garrison all important areas and on many occasions he had to deploy field units against the SAS and resistance units, to the detriment of his main forces. Enemy traffic and reinforcements to the front were delayed and his retreat was harried continuously.

(c) The considerable amount of information gained and transmitted both to senior headquarters such as SHAEF and 21 Army Group and to advancing Allied formations in the field.

(d) The specific pinpointing of targets for the RAF.[9]

What was also clear from all the SAS operations in north-west Europe in 1944/45 and Italy in 1943/44 is that they were most effective in two situations: first when the front was static, or not moving significantly, but the enemy was fighting hard to prevent a breakthrough; second when the breakthrough had occurred and the situation was fluid. In the first case the SAS were employed well behind the zone of fighting, in areas where communications were vulnerable and the enemy had few reserves available to round up small parties of SAS. In the second instance, the SAS were able to penetrate the line, and because the enemy was disorganized, many opportunities for harassing him were presented. In both situations, in the heavily populated terrain of north-west Europe, SAS operations would have been impossible without the Resistance, or at least the tacit support of the local population, however ineffective. Where the population was hostile, or cowed into co-operating with the occupying authorities, SAS patrols would have been quickly eliminated, or been driven into hiding and inactivity. The SAS operations in Italy in the last three months of the war in Europe, described in the next chapter, were no exception to these principles. But the rugged terrain enabled behind-the-lines operations to be conducted much closer to a static front than would have been possible in north-west Europe. In Italy, as in France, the assistance of the partisans was critical, and made movement behind the lines very different from that experienced by the parachute soldiers on the Tragino Aqueduct operation, described in the next chapter.

The SAS experience in the Western Desert produced different lessons from those in north-west Europe and Italy. The vast spaces of the inner desert presented an ever-open flank. The lack of population meant that it mattered little if they co-operated or not. The SAS, to begin with courtesy of the LRDG, were able to roam more or less at will. The overriding requirement for success was mobility: trucks or jeeps. These were lessons which were clearly forgotten by those planning some of the SAS patrols in Iraq in the Gulf War in 1991. Here some operations were mounted, albeit a minority, which failed to exploit the opportunities offered by the open desert for the use of heavily armed trucks. Instead some patrols, having been inserted by helicopter, found themselves unable to attack their targets because, once landed, they had the mobility of the 'boot', lacked firepower, and were at grave risk of compromise from the local population. In at least one case, the patrol was a disaster.

11

The Mediterranean, mid-1944 to May 1945 – Italy, the Adriatic and the Balkans

In the middle of 1944, the Mediterranean Theatre became secondary to the campaign in north-west Europe, but the Allies still devoted considerable resources to it; some say too many. For example, because of the distance from the United Kingdom, it took seven times the tonnage of shipping to maintain twenty-seven Allied divisions in Italy as it did the ninety divisions in north-west Europe.[1] Others counter by pointing out that even after six of those twenty-seven Allied divisions had been transferred to the invasion of southern France, the Germans were obliged to maintain twenty-six divisions in Italy. Furthermore, the partisans in Yugoslavia, Albania and Greece, together with Allied activity in the Aegean, tied down a further twenty or so German divisions. Opinions are divided over just what impact the campaign had on the war on other fronts. Many historians maintain that it had little or no effect on the Eastern Front. They also claim that it had far less influence on the German ability to reinforce in the west than was hoped at the time. For example, Hitler was able to find twenty-six new divisions for the Ardennes offensive in December 1944, without taking one from Italy. Others, especially those who fought in Italy, ask, quite reasonably, where would all those German divisions have gone had they not been kept busy; a question the 'anti' lobby finds hard to answer.

It was not an argument that bothered special forces, or indeed anyone who found themselves in the Mediterranean Theatre; they just got on with the business in hand. But several factors in Italy and the Balkans had a profound effect on the way the campaigns in the Mediterranean were fought, and were often to impinge on special forces operations in the Theatre, so it is important to mention them; even at the risk of presenting the reader with a surfeit of facts.

The campaign in Italy had started with the Allied invasion of Sicily in July 1943, followed by the invasion of southern Italy in September the same year. Thereafter, the United States 5th Army advanced north on the western side of the country, while the British 8th Army did likewise on the eastern side; 5th Army was substantially reinforced by a British and a French corps. By mid-May 1944 the Allied Armies had stalled for several months on a line that ran from Minturno in the west to Cassino, and across to a point on the east coast between Ortona and Pescara. The Allied beachhead at Anzio, some forty miles west of Cassino, had been in a state of stalemate since January 1944. The operational picture was about to change with the Allied offensive on the western side of the country which linked up with the Anzio beachhead, and took Rome on 5 June 1944.

Italy has been likened to the shape of a boot. But a look at a physical map shows that its boot-shape has a fish skeleton imposed on it. The rugged mountain chain of the Apennines forms the 'backbone', and numerous rivers flowing to the west and east coasts the lateral 'bones'. The 'backbone' curves so that in Tuscany and Umbria to the west of the spine there is more space between the coast and the Apennines than in the far narrower area of foothills and coastal plain on the opposite side of the country. But on both sides the going is very difficult. In northern Italy, the Apennines curve close to the coast north of Genoa, opening out the country north-east of the line Ravenna–Bologna–Piacenza, as far as the foothills of the Alps and Dolomites. The numerous rivers flowing from the Apennines to each coast offer an all-too-frequent series of obstacles to south–north movement, varying from the trivial to very challenging. The lack of east–west routes across the spine made switching troops and resources between the United States 5th Army on the western side with those of the British 8th Army on the eastern side difficult. The terrain is made for defence, and the German commander, Field Marshal Kesselring, and his soldiers proved themselves masters of the art. The German Army, as always, was tenacious, ruthless, frugal, well led; and counter-attacked whenever the opportunity presented itself. To the end, although it must have been clear that Germany would lose the war, they were an enemy with whom you took tactical liberties at your peril.

The Allies had air superiority, but the appalling weather throughout the winter, combined with the mountainous terrain, restricted air operations on many days, allowing the Germans to move by day, an activity fraught with risk in Normandy and at most other times in north-west Europe.

When Italy concluded an armistice with the Allies, and Germany took control with ruthless efficiency and lightning speed, Italian partisan bands sprang up all over the country behind the German lines, especially in the mountains. It is not clear how many partisans there were, but by the end of 1944 there were probably around 50,000. They were of mixed quality and opinions are divided on how effective they were. The rugged country offered more opportunities for overt action than France, particularly when supported, and in some cases commanded, by Allied special forces troops, and kept supplied by air drops. Italy during this period was a major area for SOE and OSS operations.

A report by a British officer, who spent five weeks with a partisan band in the massif between Florence and Arezzo, gives some indication of the state of some of the bands, which included escaped Allied POWs like him:

The Men
The only useful members of the band were four of the Italians, two Frenchmen from the Foreign Legion, two Russians and the British. The rest were so much worse than useless that it was risky to have their company in an operation.

Military Discipline and Skill
Military discipline as we know it was absent. The Leader had to contend with much 'back-chat' in making known his plans. The rudiments of tactics were neglected to the point of endangering the whole band. Thus when the band had begun its move to a new area, the four parties lost contact with one another and much calling and shouting ensued. Time was lost and the move had to be abandoned. It was later learned that the Germans in the plain had been warned by the noise and were waiting for them. Before fire was opened, to take 'cover from view' was to expose oneself to the taunt of cowardice; once fire was opened after an exploit, it was *'sauve qui peut'*.

Despite their limitations, the partisans at least enabled Allied behind-the-lines operations to have some chance of success, and at best provided considerable assistance. This was very different from the first behind-the-lines operation in Italy. To tell the story we must go back three and a half years, to February 1941 and Operation Colossus, a grandiloquent title for such a venture. To be fair, it was the first British parachute operation and an ambitious project for Airborne Forces, whose largest exercise up until then had been to drop twenty men on Salisbury Plain from two Whitley bombers. By destroying the Tragino Aqueduct, south of Calitri, the operation aimed to cut the pipeline (the *Acquedetto Pugliese*) that took water from the River Sele through the Apennines to the arid province of Apulia, and the strategically important ports of Brindisi, Taranto and Bari. A party of seven officers and thirty-one NCOs and soldiers, including Royal Engineers, volunteers from the 11th Special Air Service Battalion,[2] were picked for the task. They were dropped with commendable accuracy from six obsolescent converted Whitley bombers on the night of 10/11 February 1941. The pilots flew, in winter, in darkness, from Malta, the final approach being at 400 feet above the ground among mountains, some of which were over 4,000 feet high.

Only one stick was dropped wide; perversely the one including the senior sapper officer, five sappers and some of the containers of explosives. Some containers of explosives on other aircraft 'hung up' and would not drop thanks to faulty electrical connections. However, the other sapper officer and two sappers, from a different stick, gathered together the remaining explosives, amounting to 800 lb, impressing the Italian Railway Transport Officer at Calitri Station to help carry the load. The sapper officer placed charges on one pier of the aqueduct and its abutment, which to his dismay were made of reinforced concrete not brick as they had been briefed. However, when the charges were fired, the pier collapsed, breaking the waterway it supported in two. Water poured into the ravine below.

The Colossus party's troubles started when they began to make their way to the coast where they were due to be picked up by the submarine HMS *Triumph*, at the mouth of the River Sele, four nights later. All the parties of parachutists were arrested short of the RV, because they were seen by Italian peasants and reported to the authorities. One group which had been reported to the local carabinieri found itself surrounded by a ring of spectators consisting of children, their mothers, mongrels, some men, a few of whom were armed with shotguns, and, well to the rear, a handul of scruffy soldiers. The leader of the Colossus party could not bring himself to order his men to fight their way out among women and children, and ordered his men to lay down their arms. Captain Anthony Deane-Drummond remembered:

> I have never felt so ashamed before or since that we should have surrendered to a lot of practically unarmed Italian peasants.

Even if they had made the RV the submarine would not have been there. As a diversionary operation for the parachute drop, two Whitleys had been sent to bomb Foggia. One developed engine trouble. The pilot sent a message in code saying he was about to ditch at the mouth of the River Sele. This was pure coincidence, he knew nothing of the submarine RV. In Malta, the submarine's base, it was realized that because the code was not secure, the area round the mouth of the Sele might shortly be swarming with enemy troops looking for the crew of the Whitley. *Triumph*'s orders were cancelled. There was no alternative RV included in the plan, standard practice later in the war, and to this day.

With hindsight, it is highly unlikely that any of the Colossus team had a chance of getting to the RV. They had to cover over fifty miles as the crow flies, through mountainous country, where even in the cultivated parts the fields were interspersed with ravines, cliffs and huge rocks. The countryside was infested with small farms and villages; each house harboured at least one yapping dog, necessitating constant deviations of course. Nearer the coast, although the country was flat, the terrain was if anything worse. It was devoid of cover, and criss-crossed by irrigation canals; very difficult to transit even in daylight. As they made such slow progress across country, all the parties eventually took to the roads by night, a decision which sealed their fate. One of the two anti-Fascist Italian interpreters who had accompanied them, Picchi, the pre-war banqueting manager of the Savoy, was shot. The other, Nastri, a long-time resident of London, who spoke with a strong Cockney accent, avoided detection, and went to the prisoner of war camp with the others. The doggerel couplet:

> Big hands on little maps
> That's the way to kill the chaps

seems appropriate to describe those in Whitehall and elsewhere who selected the target and the route out. The operation had little effect on the water supply, because the aqueduct was repaired before the reservoirs ran dry.

The Tragino Aqueduct Operation is an example of much planning devoted to getting in, with rather less attention given to information about the target, which was hardly difficult to obtain. The plan for extraction of the force also left a great deal to be desired. It was designed as a 'stand alone' operation, that is without local support; rightly, since at the time Italy was one of the Axis. However, the plan failed to take account of the hazards of operating for more than a few hours behind the lines where the locals are hostile, and where there are enough of them to make moving about, without being compromised, so difficult as to be almost impossible.

Yugoslavia, Albania and Greece are also mountainous through much of the country. In the Second World War all had poor communications – even worse than they are today. All had long coastlines, with numerous bays and offshore islands. The coast of Yugoslavia and Albania was only a day's trip by fast motorboat across the Adriatic from the Allied-occupied coast of Italy. In Yugoslavia, operations by partisans, and roads that were easily ambushed, led the Germans to rely heavily on coastal shipping, The favourite route was between the island chain and the mainland.

Yugoslavia saw the development of guerrilla forces into what were recognizably 'armies', rather in the manner of Giap's Viet Minh in French Indo-China some six or so years later. However, there was more than one guerrilla organization, and the complex scene that existed in Yugaslavia between 1941 and 1945 is outside the scope of this book. Suffice it to say that in an orgy of killing, no different from the barbarity in the same region in the 1990s, the various factions, racial and religious groups massacred each other in a civil war that almost always took precedence over fighting the occupying Germans. Tito's Partisans took a hand in this fratricide, and although they undoubtedly killed Germans and Italians, they accounted for many more Yugo-slavs than Italians or Germans. Of the 1.2 million Yugoslavs who died in the Second World War, the majority were killed by their fellow countrymen.

Albania was also the setting for civil war between pro- and anti-Communist groups; and the politics were, if anything, even more convoluted than in Yugoslavia. In Albania, as in Yugoslavia, the Communists referred to themselves as the Partisans. In September 1944, the Germans began to retreat from Greece, and their route took them through Albania. British hopes of a coordinated attack on the retreating Germans were frustrated by the internecine strife in Albania.

In Greece, by August 1943, the pro-Communist National Peoples Liberation Army (ELAS), together with its political wing, the National Liberation Front (EAM) had become the most effective guerrilla force. As part of the deception plan to persuade the Axis that Greece, not Sicily, was the next objective after the Allies' victory in North Africa, the British had given ELAS a leading role in co-ordinating Greek resistance. When the Italians, who occupied most of Greece, signed the armistice with the Allies, ELAS acquired the bulk of the arms and equipment of the Italian forces in Greece. As in Yugoslavia, internal strife between ELAS and EDES (the non-Communist, anti-monarchy, National Republican Greek League) occupied more time and energy than attacks on the Axis.

It was in this turbulent and highly political arena that the SB Squadron and the LRDG in particular were to operate for the remainder of the War in Europe. As noted in Chapter 9, the LRDG mounted a shipping watch in the Adriatic throughout the period. Captain Arthur Stokes's patrol on its five-month-long stint on the Dalmatian coast radioed information back which led to the RAF accounting for more than fifty enemy vessels of all sizes. Another patrol on the Istrian coast over a period of six weeks from March to April 1945 was responsible for the RAF sinking a 5,000-ton vessel, an 800-ton ship, a 700-ton and a 500-ton coaster, two 200-ton colliers, a 100-ton tramp, five 100-ton lighters, two E-boats, an armed schooner and a midget submarine. The Royal Navy also asked for shipping watch intelligence, and as a result of sightings passed back by the LRDG were able to make several successful strikes using coastal forces at night. Once again, as in the Western Desert, small parties of LRDG, never more than an officer and eight men, with a radio, gave good 'return on investment'.

Small-scale raids were also carried out by the LRDG, despite the agreement reached between Lloyd Owen and Jellicoe at the meeting on 25 July 1944: 'LRDG primarily recce and SB Squadron primarily beat-up'; the word 'primarily' of course being the let-out. It would have been difficult to restrain the LRDG when a target presented itself, so long as aggressive action did not compromise the overall mission.

As they had in the Western Desert, the LRDG provided guides for raids and other operations in the Balkans; for example, starting in July

1944, raids by 2nd Special Service Brigade in the Adriatic were mounted from the island of Vis off the Dalmatian coast; and with Foxforce, consisting of Number 9 Commando, the SB Squadron, and other units based on the island of Kithera off the southern tip of Greece. An LRDG patrol had parachuted into Kithera ahead of Number 9 Commando's insertion by sea. Eventually Foxforce became involved in the follow-up of German forces retreating from Greece.

The LRDG and SB Squadron learned very quickly that operations in the Balkans were complicated by the politics, not least that far from all local forces were anti-German. In late August 1944, two SB Squadron parties were landed in the Dubrovnik area to join LRDG patrols M1 and X1 (Lieutenants Skipwith and Shute), who had reported possible targets on the railway. On 30 August, David Skipwith's patrol with an SB Squadron party under Captain Anders Lassen blew up a 40-foot span of a 150-foot bridge on the railway line to Dubrovnik. As the Top Secret LRDG Operational Summary for the period reports:

> This however soon brought reprisals and the combined party [both LRDG patrols and SB Squadron] was attacked by a strong force of Ustashi [sic] on the night of 2nd Sept. A fierce battle was fought and the main party withdrew without any casualties, but unfortunately Lt Skipwith and his senior NCO Sgt Leach were cut off and taken prisoner by the enemy.

Lloyd Owen commented in his diary:

> *Sept 6th*
> Very bad luck on David as it was his first patrol and Leach was missing for three weeks in the Aegean last year and also for a month in Italy this year. I hope they will get back and am very worried at the treatment they may get at the hands of the Ustachi [sic].

The LRDG also carried out liaison missions with the Partisans in the Balkans, as an LRDG report, written after the war, remarks:

> The Balkans bristled with partisans, and it was impossible for the Military Missions to allot liaison officers to every one of their units; Long-Range Desert Group patrols were frequently used to aid and reinforce them.

The LRDG soon learned that:

> In the Balkans, where political factions were ten a penny and Allied intentions were regarded with almost universal suspicion, the most success-

ful results were achieved when emphasis was laid on the purely military character of a patrol's task. Only when patrols stressed the common duty of killing Germans, but professed indifference to the political intrigues and ignorance of political motives, did they secure the cheerful, whole-hearted co-operation of the partisans. In any event a patrol was always wise to find out which were the most serious deficiencies of the ill-equipped partisans and to do everything in its power to have these deficiencies made good. In Albania and Yugoslavia, for example, where the partisans' medical equipment and services were rudimentary to a degree, large supplies of medical stores were provided, and the unit medical officer and his orderlies spent much time in attending to the Partisans' sick and wounded.

The LRDG were among the first, if not the first, to recognize the value of medical care in what we now call 'the battle for hearts and minds'. As with so many techniques pioneered by the LRDG, which have since been imitated by others, medical care for local forces has become incorporated into modern SAS and other special forces doctrine throughout the western world.

Personal example by patrols was also important; LRDG Operational Summary:

> Once the partisans had been persuaded to co-operate, their spirits rose and their fighting efficiency in the field increased perceptibly when they found themselves fighting shoulder to shoulder with British troops; whose presence seemed to incite them to yet more daring feats of arms and sometimes, perhaps, to discourage them from making an unnecessarily hasty withdrawal.

Although the LRDG were busy in the Adriatic, Lloyd Owen with an eye on the future was already planning ahead to generate new tasks for his unit. As his diary reveals he had no hesitation in going right to the top:

> *August 15th*
> Jack Aitken and Ron [Captain R. A. Tinker MC MM, a New Zealander, later second-in-command of A Squadron] came in the evening, and I discussed future employment of LRDG in the Far East. Wrote a long paper on this and I intend to send it to the War Office and Mountbatten [C.-in-C. South-East Asia Command].

He was also getting restless and keen to go on operations. He was feeling the frustration familiar to many special forces commanders who find it difficult to accept that the best place from which to control behind the lines operations is from a base in one's own territory:

August 29th

Laid on with Vivian Street that I should fly with him tomorrow night to Croatia, land on Ptzn [partisan] LG [landing ground – airstrip in modern parlance], stay next day, and return during the night. But Vivian having difficulty with AOC but he hopes it will be OK. So do I, as I am so bored with the office and conferences, and the continual struggle to get on with the war. If only everybody fought on the same side instead of amongst each other.

August 30th

My visit to Croatia was cancelled. This was a great disappointment. So I laid on to fly on the sortie to Jacko [Lieutenant Jackson MBE MM, Rhodesian OC S2 Patrol] tonight in which we were sending him a lot of stuff. Went out to the plane but was told expressly I was not to go. This made me furious.

Sept 3rd

Woke at 6.0. Five years ago today the war began.

Sept 5th

One of these days I will just go [on an operation] unbeknownst to everyone. Finally decided to send a patrol [to Kithera] by parachute on night 7/8 and I to go too, although I kept this dark. The Kithera job was cancelled! I am in despair and will work out another.

The Kithera 'job' was of course laid on again, as noted earlier, but without Lloyd Owen's participation. Eventually, he persuaded Brigadier Davy (Commander Land Forces Adriatic) to allow him to go on Operation Lochmaben in Albania. The operation was Lloyd Owen's brainchild; conceived because he realized that the Soviet advance westwards towards Austria across Hungary, Rumania and Bulgaria would force the Germans to withdraw from Greece, Albania and Yugoslavia, or risk being cut off. The plan involved infiltrating three patrols into Albania to join Captain Stan Eastwood's S1, and work in the Tirana area harrying the enemy lines of communication along their withdrawal route. The force, codename Kenforce, would be commanded by Lloyd Owen, and include Captain Ron Tinker, and a radio operator, S3 Patrol

(Lieutenant D. G. Simpson and eleven soldiers), T2 (Lieutenant R. P. Marr and eleven soldiers), and M1 Patrol, from B Squadron, under Captain K. F. ('Paddy') McLaughlan. Lloyd Owen's diary:

Sept 12th
Planning Albanian operation. This has now been agreed to and George Davy has agreed I command it. Dropping 3 parties of 12 on nights 16, 18, and 20 to where Stan is, and I go off on first one and out first of the first plane. Whoopee!

Sept 15th
Most frightful complications have arisen over the Albanian operation as I knew they would. The Ptzn [partisans] have now said that they do not want British troops in the country as they are obviously afraid of a British occupation. The Foreign Office and SAC [Supreme Allied Commander Mediterranean – at this stage General Sir Henry Maitland Wilson] have both been taking a hand. Luckily a very strong attitude is being adopted and the whole project has been postponed 24 hours to sort out this political impasse. I am simply furious.

Sept 17th
All set to drop into Albania tonight, but it was cancelled again. Goodness, I am furious.

Sept 20th
Long signal from Stan agreeing to the proposals of Lochmaben and saying how anxious they are to accept us in the country! However, still we can do nothing until we get the OK from HQ.

After several more delays it was decided that Lloyd Owen, at his suggestion, would drop in by himself and meet Eastwood in an attempt to to resolve the impasse. In a letter to his Adjutant Captain Charles Hall, a Rhodesian, he wrote that he, 'had a Yank crew and a Yugoslav despatcher'; and as his diary records:

Sept 21st
Left Brindisi at 7.45 alone in a DC-3 loaded with ammunition and mortar bombs. Felt very lonely in the dark gloominess of the plane and smoked countless cigarettes. I had a pretty vague pilot who succeeded in flying direct over the defended naval base of Durazzo [now Durrës in Albania] at only 2,000 feet. As a result I was rudely awakened by heavy AA fire. I saw beastly red and green things coming up from the ground and some were pretty near. Then they turned the searchlights on us and we were caught in

them, and I was glad there were only mortar bombs to see how very scared I was. We dived and twisted and soon we were out of it. The Yank crew were terrified and needed a lot of persuasion to continue flying over Albania. We flew around all over the place, but saw no [signal] fires on the ground. Eventually decided to fly back. I went to sleep and woke as hit the tarmac at Brindisi. An awful bore as until we hear why there was no reception, I cannot try again.

Sept 22nd

Heard that Stan at the DZ had been shelled, so probably lucky I didn't go. Had good news we were to go tomorrow, the whole lot of us in 6 aircraft.

Sept 23rd

Weather did not look too good. Was told that it was off again for the night.

Sept 26th

All well and we go tonight. I leave in the first [aircraft] at 7.45 with Sgt Saunders [radio operator] and chaps of Robin's patrol [T2 Lieutenant Marr]. After lunch I told the chaps what we were going to do, and where we were going. Delighted at the many eager faces there in front of me. A few were nervous, and perhaps many more did not show it. I felt nothing except a great excitement and a great longing to make a success of the whole operation. Spent the evening in the Club playing 'Slippery Sam' with Ron [Tinker], Robin [Marr] and Tiny [Simpson], and then had a grand dinner with Rufus [C. R. Montagu on Staff of British Minister in Bari], Ken [Lazarus OC A (Rhodesian) Squadron], and Elliot Watrous [a liaison officer in Bari] who had come to see us off. A grand evening and soon we were off.

On the night of 24 September Kenforce took off in six Dakotas from Brindisi, at intervals of an hour, starting at 10 p.m. By 4 a.m. the next morning, all troops and stores had been dropped on a DZ south-west of Tirana. The DZ was not big enough for a force of this size, and was situated between two high hills. In order to clear the high ground, the aircraft dropped from heights varying from 1,500 to 3,000 feet. Men and equipment were scattered over a wide area. To be fair to the pilots, even with today's modern navigation aids, it is very difficult to fly low over mountains at night. In 1944, it was even more dangerous, and to compound the problem, the pilots on this sortie had dropped parachutists only once before.

Lloyd Owen had a perfect landing, but on his way to the RV in the dark, fell over a thirty-foot cliff and fractured his spine. Marr and two soldiers were also injured. The next day, in response to a signal from Kenforce, the LRDG Medical Officer in Italy, Captain Michael Parsons RAMC, was warned off to parachute into Albania. In an account he wrote a few months later for his father, he says that he was told:

> The RAF were to fly me across, and with a good pilot, I might make it that night. Quite frankly by that time my stomach was turning circles inside me and I was none too happy.

In the RAF operations room the wing commander explained to Parsons:

> There were bad storms about, but I might be lucky and get down between two of them. 'Anyway,' he said, 'the best thing to do is to get over there and see how the weather is over the target.' Finally he added he himself would fly me over unescorted at sunrise if they failed that night.

After take-off in the Halifax, which had a hole in the floor for parachuting, Parsons was all alone in the dark fuselage, connected to the pilot by the intercom:

> Sitting on the little seat amidships, with all the roaring and bumping of that rather turbulent air, for some reason reminded me of sitting alone in a cathedral. No two places can be much more dissimilar, except in both one prays very fervently indeed.
> 'Hello "Doc", how are you feeling?'
> 'OK Skipper. How is the weather?'
> 'Not too good I'm afraid.'
> In view of the fact I was nearly being tossed off the seat, I knew that only too well.
> 'Stand by for the Durazzo flak, "Doc", I can see it coming.'
> 'Is there much?'
> 'No.'
> 'Thank God for that.'
> Another period of silence, and then: 'I can see the target "Doc".'
> 'How does the weather look?'
> The old heart was beating in my mouth.
> 'It looks clear to me, and ground signals it's OK. Sorry we've no despatcher, "Doc" – hook yourself up and your kit and let me know when you're ready.'
> While he flew around, ten very unsteady fingers grappled with hooks

and static lines. First the kit and then my hook, then put the kit beside the aperture, and I crawled across myself and knelt beside the kit.

'OK Skipper, I'm all set.'

'I'll give you ten seconds [after] the red light, then the green. Best of luck, "Doc", happy landings.'

'Good night, thanks a lot.'

The red light seemed a mighty long ten seconds before it turned to green. Then three quick pushes for the kit, followed by three loud bangs of the static lines [strops]. Immediately after that, my boots were in the roaring black hole, and with a small push of my wrists, I shot unhappily into the blast of four engines. It was a bad exit. I rolled over head first, and the next second was snatched feet first again by the opening 'chute.

I gave a quick look down and I could see the landing signals away below me, and observed they were drifting fast to my right. A few flashes of lightning lit up the ground, which looked rather rough to me. A loud clap of thunder frightened the life out of me, but no harm was done. A further glance down produced a mountain coming up fast on my left-hand side, and my feet wide apart. They were quickly brought together, suddenly, thump, I had landed all wrong as usual. A quick check over to see that all parts worked.

I filled my pipe and lit it slowly. As I did so, it started to rain. The 'Met' people had been correct almost to the minute. I hadn't any idea of where David [Lloyd Owen] was, my present location, or whether there were any Jerries about. Most of these doubts were solved by a little Albanian who came along a few minutes later. He seemed very excited, and pointed a gun at me. I have seldom felt more stupid, standing smoking my pipe at the wrong end of an Albanian gun. After a few minutes of dithering about we straightened out the situation to our mutual satisfaction, and he insisted on kissing me in the Albanian fashion, cheek-to-cheek. It was my first experience of that revolting ritual – onions, decayed teeth, and at least a week's growth of beard.

We set off along rocky mountain paths in the pouring rain to find David. He was a good guide I suppose, but it struck me we went through more bushes and streams than was necessary. I stumbled behind. After about twenty minutes, we came to fairly open country, and soon heard the raucous voice of Ron [Tinker] yelling for me in a broad New Zealand accent.

'Hi "Doc", you bastard, where are you?'

Parsons later learned he had been dropped from 3,500 feet above the ground, which explains the long drift and time he had to look around.

After a walk of an hour and a half he finally got to the place 'where David was lying on a stretcher under a parachute'.

Parsons put Lloyd Owen in a light plaster of Paris back splint. However, he soon realized that Lloyd Owen had a complete fracture somewhere, but as Parsons wrote:

> I had previously only seen fractured spines as a student in hospitals. There the procedure is simple – admit – X-ray within an hour – if a fracture is confirmed put up in hyperextension under a prolonged anaesthesia. The treatment for suspected ones, on your own in the field, is immediate evacuation. Behind enemy lines, you cannot do any of these, and if justification is needed for my treatment, the final result, in my opinion, supplied it.

There were other complications, but Lloyd Owen made steady progress and in under two weeks Parsons 'had him mobile'. During this time, Lloyd Owen was able to celebrate his twenty-seventh birthday with a bottle of whisky, sent by Rufus Montagu, and brought in by Captain McLaughlan, one of the New Zealanders, who had been allowed to rejoin the LRDG. Captain Tinker officially took over command of Kenforce, although, from all accounts he went off with his own patrol (T2), and Lloyd Owen seems to have remained in overall command. Eastwood had told the Kenforce party that his Patrol had been reconnoitring the coast for suitable targets, and locating a secure place from which to embark anyone who needed to be evacuated by sea. Simpson (S3) left for Arbana, where the Partisan 22nd Brigade Headquarters was located, to make final arrangements for an attack on the Elbasan–Tirana road. He was joined two days later by Eastwood (S1). Marr, who had partially recovered from his injuries, took T2 to the Elbasan–Peqin road, but returned when the partisan battalion detailed to co-operate with him was withdrawn without warning.

Meanwhile Michael Parsons found plenty of work to do among the partisans. The first was the local 'battalion' commander:

> When he came in he had ridden for about six hours on horseback with bullets in his back, upper arm and hand. He only had very dirty handkerchiefs over them. In spite of all he was smiling and seemed most cheerful. I gave him an anaesthetic and took out the bullets. When he came round, I gave him the three souvenirs. He merely grinned and shook me warmly by the hand.

A few days later Parsons, with his stores loaded on a horse, went off with an Albanian guide to see to some more partisan wounded, about four and a half hours' march away. Here he found an elderly, exhausted, Italian doctor, two grimy Italian medical orderlies, and 'a rogue who called himself a dentist':

> In two dark rooms in a dirty, heavily infected house were twenty men all in various stages of decay and suppuration. Upon my arrival dirty stuck dressings were pulled off with glorious abandon, the smell of pus being absolutely appalling. With the limited resources I had with me we set to work. We had Pentathol, as anaesthetic, some plasma, forceps, scissors and other elementary surgical instruments and antiseptics.

After several more times when Parsons, either on his own or with the Italian doctor, ministered to partisan sick and wounded, he asked for and received a sizeable drop of medical supplies. Some of this he handed over for use by the partisans, but continued to operate himself as well. One evening:

> two Albanians were brought in in an absolutely pitiable condition. They had both been involved in a grenade accident. In one there was a compound fracture of his frontal bone, with complete destruction of both eyes and most of his nose. In the other, one eye and most of one zygomatic arch had been carried away plus a severe hand wound. Using Pentathol we cleaned them up as best we could, it was a nauseating job, but the results were particularly gratifying. Within a week, both were sitting up and eating, and the one sound eye was secure.

While Lloyd Owen was still convalescing, the local partisan brigade commander visited, and tried to persuade him that Kenforce should take part in an attack on a German force which he said was about to destroy his brigade. Lloyd Owen refused; it was not the LRDG's job to take part in set-piece attacks. The partisan tried to frighten him by saying that the Germans would wipe out the LRDG patrols, but Lloyd Owen refused to budge.

Meanwhile Eastwood and S1 and S3 Patrols, with the Partisans, had mounted a very successful ambush on the Tirana–Elbasan road. They destroyed three trucks (killing all eight occupants). Another convoy of fifteen vehicles and three tanks approached, having off-loaded some 200 German infantry; the tanks attacked, supported by infantry and mortar

Johnnie Holmes (*seated in front*) and three other members of 1st SAS on Operation Bulbasket. Photographed in Le Forêt de Verrières near Châteauroux, June 1944. All in this picture, except Holmes, were captured together with twenty-eight others when the Germans attacked their camp on 3 July 1944. They were all executed four days later. (HU 66209)

Sergeant Holdham (*left*), radio operator of Jedburgh Team Jude in the Colmar area of France, with three members of the French Resistance. The two girls were only sixteen. The man with the cigarette is the brother of the girl on the right. Holdham also operated with the Jedburghs in Burma. He served with the 1st Battalion the Gloucester Regiment in the Korean War and was captured at the Battle of the Imjin River in April 1951, and spent the next two years as a prisoner of the North Koreans and Chinese. (HU 62470)

SB Squadron setting out for the raid on Santerine. (HU 71431)

Anders Lassen just before the Battle of Comacchio where he was killed winning a posthumous Victoria Cross. (HU 71361)

Three members of 2 SAS in Italy in 1945. The man on the left is carrying the tripod for the Vickers water-cooled medium machine-gun, the man in the centre carries the barrel, and the one on the right, the condenser can. (NA 25407)

S Patrol: Popski's Private Army on jeep patrol in the Apennines, Italy. (HU 1094)

A jeep crew of Popski's Private Army firing their armament: .50-inch Browning nearest the camera, .30-inch Browning on rear of jeep. (HU 1114)

Lieutenant-Colonel V. Peniakoff DSO MC ('Popski') driving his jeep in Italy at the end of the war. He has a hook on his left hand. Beside him is his gunner, Corporal R. Cokes. (HU 1122)

SB Squadron in the Aegean, Anders Lassen in shorts, jersey and beret. Canoes and craft in the background. (HU 71434)

Two LRDG soldiers, Gunner Jimmy Patch (*left*) and Trooper Ron Hill (*right*) with a bearded Macedonian Partisan named Krsto. Following capture on the Aegean Island of Levita on 26 October 1943, the two LRDG soldiers escaped by jumping from a prisoner of war train. With characteristic LRDG aplomb they attached themselves to, and operated with, Greek partisans, before meeting and continuing to operate with the British Official Mission. They eventually rejoined the LRDG in Bari on 2 February 1945. Krsto was a Partisan Band's official executioner of traitors and collaborators. Jimmy Patch remembers: 'His usual method was hanging and he was credited with 83 victims at the time we met him. He had a grim sense of humour. If you upset him, he would point to you and trace the figure 84 on the palm of his hand.' (HU 67339)

Motorized Submersible Canoe (MSC) or 'Sleeping Beauty'. (HU 56756)

MSC trimmed down underway in a test tank. (HU 56776)

Left to right: Captain Bob Page, Major Ivan Lyon, Lieutenant Donald Davidson. The three officers on the canoe raid into Singapore Harbour on Operation Jaywick. (HU 72130)

Operation Jaywick Team. *Back row:* Berryman, Marsh, Jones, Huston. *Centre:* Crilley, Cain, McDowell, Young, Falls, Morris. *Front:* Carse, Davidson, Lyon, Major Campbell (not a team member), Page. (HU 72131)

fire. They were beaten off. They tried again, and failed to dislodge the LRDG and partisans. The German losses in both attacks were assessed as eighty dead, with no prisoners taken. A mortar and bombs, four light machine-guns, thirty rifles and twenty revolvers were captured. Other German convoys, waiting to get through, turned and drove off. The two patrols attacked a German post near by, without capturing it, but inflicted more casualties. The Rhodesians and partisans remained *in situ* for the next ten days, but the Germans contented themselves with shelling and mortaring, and mounted no further attacks. When he saw enemy tanks moving in, Eastwood called down air strikes by rocket-firing Beaufighters on the post. On 13 October, without any prior consultation or warning, the partisans moved off, leaving the two patrols on their own and extremely vulnerable. Lloyd Owen, who was remarkably mobile despite his injured back, went to visit the Commissar at Partisan Headquarters (by all accounts a pompous individual), and told him in no uncertain terms that he did not intend to hold roads for partisans, while they waited outside Tirana for the place to fall, and start looting. On Lloyd Owen's instructions the two patrols were withdrawn for a rest.

The LRDG's view of the Albanian partisans is reflected in a report written to the Southern Rhodesian Government after the war, by the Rhodesian official observer with South African public relations in Italy:

> They [the partisans] were mostly an undisciplined rabble. Many of them were clothed in rags without boots, and were armed with antiquated Italian and Turkish weapons. Despite this many of them were brave and fought well, though with very little tactical organisation in any attacks they carried out. The majority of such attacks were more designed to obtain loot and weapons than to destroy the enemy and their equipment.

Parsons, while walking with Lloyd Owen on one of his visits to his patrols, passed a partisan column on the march:

> It was one of the most heterogeneous collections one could ever possibly hope to see. There were mules, donkeys and horses. There were old men, young men and girls, and every conceivable garment, from umbrellas to wooden shoes. There was singing, smoking and even saluting. It was a fantastic moving caravan of humanity, and it would have proved most interesting to know what they in their turn thought of the three scruffy British officers plodding along.

Two other successful ambushes were subsequently laid by Tinker (T2) and Eastwood with S1 and S2 Patrols. On 4 November, Eastwood arranged air strikes on King Zog's (the exiled King of Albania) palace and a barracks in Tirana at the request of the partisans to assist them to capture the city. For three days twenty-eight rocket-firing Beaufighters strafed the palace, the barracks and enemy gun positions in the vicinity. When it was learned that a large force of Germans was attempting to reinforce Tirana, Simpson (S3) was sent to blow a bridge on their route. Here he was joined by one and a half partisan brigades. Simpson blew a twenty-foot gap. A force of some 1,500 Germans with tanks, vehicles and horse-drawn transport was stalled by the blown bridge for three days, coming under partisan sniper fire. Eastwood came up to arrange air strikes, but the first response by a mere three fighter aircraft on 15 November was not sufficient to prevent the Germans from repairing the bridge and continuing the advance. Fortunately, as they started crossing, a large number of fighter-bombers appeared and strafed to such good effect that the convoy was routed. Few Germans escaped the partisans, who captured such vehicles and equipment that had survived destruction at the hands of the RAF.

Two days later Tirana fell. The partisans forbade the LRDG to enter the city. Eastwood took no notice of this order, and entered the next day to reconnoitre the landing strip. He found it prepared for demolition, but within twenty-four hours, he and two sapper NCOs had cleared the charges, and reported the strip ready to receive aircraft. Six days later, on 2 December, one DC-3 arrived and flew S1 out to Bari; they had been in Albania since early August.

Lloyd Owen had left Albania at the end of October. A signal had come from Italy saying that he and Parsons were needed there. Together with Private Jones to operate the radio, some guides and an interpreter, they walked to the coast. Before they left, Parsons paid a final visit to the partisan hospital:

> They had at last started to wake up, and there were properly constructed tents, improvised beds, good feeding arrangements, and female nursing orderlies.
> I said farewell to them with a heavy heart, and trudged back to our camp feeling very sorry indeed to be going back to normal army life in Italy.

The walk must have been a great trial to Lloyd Owen, but Parsons comments on his fortitude and good cheer, despite the difficulties:

... the major one being the crossing of the Scumbine [Shkumbin] River. The start was rather startling. Our interpreter suddenly announced he was not going any further, shook us by the hand and walked off. This rather upset our plans, because the only Albanian we knew consisted of two words which sounded like 'shoc mire', and meant 'very good'. Another peculiarity we could never get used to was their habit of shaking their heads when they meant 'yes', and nodding to mean 'no'.

The river was about 200 yards wide, waist deep and had a very strong current. We were only about 1,000 yards from the nearest Nazi-held village, and clearly visible from it. The far bank and the last 50 yards were deep in thick mud that came about half way up our calves. David got across that river with a completely fractured 4th lumbar vertebrae. It was the finest feat of will power triumphing over physical disability I ever hope to witness.

The final part of the journey was completed with Parsons in a bullock cart and Lloyd Owen on horseback. They were eventually picked up from the beach by an Italian MAS boat at night.

The activities of Kenforce proved so successful that, well before Tirana fell, three more LRDG patrols (S2, R2 and X2) were sent into northern Albania with the aim of hindering the enemy's withdrawal. It was hoped that the area around Shëgnjin at the mouth of the Drin River (the one in northern Albania, not the Drin in the south) would be a suitable place for ambushes. Although the patrols blew bridges and mined roads, they found that the partisans in this area were more of a hindrance than a help, and lacked the aggressive spirit to mount successful operations. As has been noted before, the partisans in the north had been denied British assistance hitherto for just this reason.

On 12 December 1944, the entire LRDG force in Albania was evacuated to Brindisi. The LRDG had good reason to be pleased with their efforts in Albania. Much of their success was due to their initiative and energy, and rather less to the efforts of the partisans. As the LRDG were to discover in Yugoslavia, politics, and a succession of orders followed by counter-orders from the partisan command organization, did not make for continuity and proper planning.

On the same night that Kenforce had taken off for Albania, Captain John Olivey had left Bari for Greece in an LCT escorted by two destroyers. His force consisted of eleven of his own patrol, Z1, one man from S2, and twelve jeeps. Olivey had returned to the LRDG after his escape in Athens, followed by a well-deserved leave in Rhodesia, where he recruited some men for A Squadron. His task was to carry out advanced reconnaissance jeep patrols as part of Bucketforce, under the command of Jellicoe, now a lieutenant-colonel. In addition to the LRDG, Bucketforce consisted of L Detachment SB Squadron, a half troop of Number 40 (RM) Commando, an RAF Regiment Squadron, two companies of the Highland Light Infantry, and some COPP operators. Operations started with L Detachment dropping south of Araxos in the north of the Peloponnese on 23 September. Jellicoe followed in a Dakota escorted by eight Spitfires on the 24th. When the RAF Regiment Squadron eventually arrived, they set up shop on the airfield, which became a RAF forward base. On 26 September, the LRDG landed at Katakolon, on the western coast of the Peloponnese, just north of Pirgos. After some skirmishes with the retreating Germans, they and L Detachment entered Corinth to a rapturous welcome. One of the few LRDG casualties was Corporal Tighe, MM, killed, after four years of narrow escapes, when his jeep ran over a mine south of the Corinth Canal. Tighe, a founder member of the LRDG, had survived the ambush in January 1941 at Gebel Sherif, south of Kufra, on the return from the Fezzan expedition (see Chapter 2). On 12 October the LRDG were on the DZ at Megara in time to assist when the British 4th Parachute Battalion dropped in a 25-knot wind. As the parachute soldiers were being dragged across the DZ, Olivey's men helped by charging and collapsing the parachutes with their jeeps. On 17 October, the LRDG, SB Squadron and 4th Parachute Battalion entered Athens, preceded by Jellicoe and one of his officers on commandeered German bicycles.

Olivey's patrols, as part of Jellicoe's newly formed Pompforce, took part in harassing the German withdrawal, and eventually made contact with B Squadron at Florina, just south of the border with Yugoslavia. In early October, Major Moir Stormonth-Darling, with patrols of B Squadron LRDG, had been parachuted into northern Greece to operate against the Germans in the Florina area. Stormonth-Darling's patrols mounted some successful ambushes on the retreating Germans, before being ordered to return to Italy.

Stormonth-Darling had actually left with his advance party when news came of many thousands of well-armed ELAS troops marching down from the hills and converging on Athens with the intention of taking the city by force. Olivey took the B Squadron patrols under his wing, and, with his own patrols, remained in Athens, taking part in the fighting against ELAS which lasted until early January 1945 with the total defeat of ELAS. The LRDG, under command of British 23rd Armoured Brigade, were used in patrolling, local reconnaissance and other non-LRDG-type tasks. Casualties suffered by the British force, which by now included the 4th Infantry Division, 23rd Armoured Brigade, and the whole of 2nd Independent Parachute Brigade, amounted to 237 killed and 2,101 wounded. The LRDG had one killed and five wounded, including Olivey. All the LRDG were back in Italy by mid-January, except for patrols on shipping watch.

Anders Lassen, the new commander of M Detachment, SB Squadron, had also been busy. After some frustrating excursions by caique in the Sporades (the group of islands in the Dodecanese nearest the Turkish coast), he was ordered to Salonika (modern Thessaloníki). Here ELAS, avoiding action in anticipation of the main event, the take-over of Greece, were allowing the Germans to withdraw unhindered. They forbade Lassen to attack the enemy; an order which he promptly disobeyed. In their eagerness to engage the enemy, Lassen's second-in-command, Lieutenant Henshaw, and his Naval Liaison Officer, Lieutenant Solomon, nearly overdid it when, driving up to a battery position in the Detachment's only jeep, they attempted to persuade two enemy tanks, a battery of self-propelled guns and about sixty infantry to surrender. Their bluff was called, and they had to flee. However, the next morning, Lassen commandeered four fire engines in the suburbs of Salonika and with his Detachment aboard, drove into the town centre. Here he gave the German rearguard a pasting, inflicting sixty casualties on them, for no loss to his men. He personally killed eight of the enemy, and Lieutenant Henshaw accounted for eleven. Lassen and M Detachment were not involved in the battle of Athens, being sent to Crete, where he had an uncongenial task keeping an eye on the 13,000 strong rump of the German garrison, and trying to persuade ELAS to put in an attack on them. He eventually gave up in disgust. By mid-January 1945, all detachments of SB Squadron, too, were back in Italy.

When Lloyd Owen returned to Italy he was told by the doctor that:

the X-rays showed a badly broken spine and that some deformity had set in since it happened so long ago. This shook me and I then asked how long it would be and almost wept when he said 'six months'. He said I must treat it properly, and I would have to go home and I wouldn't be fit for military service. I said I couldn't do that and must stay here, and he said that if I didn't take his advice, I would never be really fit again. This shook me terribly. I've got to be operated on, but have been promised that in a fortnight, I can go out for a week to straighten things out. All this means that I have finished with the LRDG, and I can hardly even think of it. God knows what I shall do, and what they will do. The thought of leaving them at this stage is too much for me. What an end to to such a wonderful time with the most wonderful people doing a really wonderful job. And the horror of it all is that I have failed them, failed them through my own selfish desire to do a job which others should have done. How well do I know that I should not have gone, and I should have preserved myself if only to have controlled the lives of the gallant chaps so dependent on me.

However, after an operation and much persuasion:

Nov 18th
Yesterday I had the fateful board. It lasted one and a half hours. After 10 minutes' deliberation, I was unofficially told that the board agreed with me and that they proposed to recommend me for 6 months' base duties. I couldn't have been more pleased. So anyway (when this is confirmed) I can stay with the unit.

Nov 28th
Left hospital at 11.00 with my car and lunched Foggia. Arrived at San Nicandro [new LRDG base] for tea.

Lloyd Owen bounced back with youthful enthusiasm. His injury had not dampened his determination to do his utmost to ensure his unit's future. Again his diary reveals some very interesting plotting by young and junior officers to get to the Far East, which included bypassing the complete chain of command in their theatre, right up to and including the Supreme Allied Commander:

Dec 1st
George Jellicoe and David Sutherland [second-in-command SB Squadron, and subsequently Commanding Officer] arrived and we had a long session about the future. We decided: *1* that the future of LFA [Land Forces Adriatic] and operation Fairfax [operations in Italy] were both fairly indeterminate. *2* that the sooner we extracted ourselves and made plans for the Far East the better. *3* that we would together tackle the problem of present and future operations. *4* that I would go and meet Laycock [Major General Laycock, Chief of Combined Operations in London, visiting Italy]

in Bari on the 10th and discuss with him the whole future. 5 that we would each send two officer observers to the USA and I would return to England for a short period. All this was most satisfactory, but we decided to take no further action until after we had seen Laycock and knew a bit more about the form. The evening then developed into a most alcoholic and amusing party.

A little while after this meeting, Jellicoe left the SB Squadron, after two years in command, to attend the staff college in England. Meanwhile there was good news from Laycock:

Dec 15th
Mountbatten definitely wants us, has a job for us, and we will go as a unit to work under an organisation called Special Operations Group. Laycock did not however feel that there was any hurry, and that we would be wiser to continue for a while with operations in Europe. However, he considered we must get away from Land Forces Adriatic as their war was running a tired last [*sic*], and the only place for operations was north-east Italy. This was because the Western Front and Germany held little prospect and Austria was not feasible because of the inhabitants [being pro-German]. He therefore advised coming under Allied Armies Italy again and doing a few months' really good work there. He admitted this would not be easy as Davy [Commander Land Forces Adriatic] would not of course be anxious to release us. All this was very cheering, and he also said that we would be used in the East Indies, where I suppose they will not mount major offensives but will leave us to harass and attack on the bigger islands.

In a subsequent meeting with Davy on 19 December 1944, the matter of LRDG employment was raised, and he was furious, according to Lloyd Owen, 'that we had such progressive ideas'. However, he was not put out by Davy's displeasure:

Dec 24th
Had the whole unit over to Rodi and addressed them for an hour and a quarter about the past, present and future. I told them of the possibility of the unit going to the Far East. I was delighted that almost the whole unit are apparently willing to go if they can go home first for a short leave and if they can go as a unit.

Well before the New Year, the LRDG had acquired an addition to their private navy, the MV *Palma* being joined by the aptly named

MV *Kufra* (after the Oasis in Cyrenaica which had been the base for so much LRDG activity). But for the present, there seemed to be fewer and fewer operations in sight for the future. One of the reasons for this was that major Allied offensives in Italy had closed down because the appalling conditions in winter made progress impossible; consequently many minor operations in support of them were postponed until the weather was right for a resumption of main-force activity. However, Lloyd Owen was becoming impatient, and concerned about morale:

> *Jan 12th*
> Had a long session with George Davy about the future. I have warned him of the considerable feeling of unrest that exists amongst a unit of very fit, young volunteers who want to fight. I am almost at my wits end with this hopeless attitude that one meets whenever anyone talks about getting on with the war.

In the end, it was agreed that operations in the northern Dalmatian Islands, Istria and the Croatian mainland should continue, but as the LRDG Operational Summary for the period starting 1 February 1945 says, these:

> would not afford scope for more than one Squadron of LRDG. Therefore it had been decided that A Squadron should be reserved for these operations and that B Squadron should undergo a full period of training in skiing and mountain warfare.

B Squadron was not destined to see action again.

While most of SB Squadron had been operating in Greece and the Adriatic, Lapraik had been busy in the Aegean as part of Raiding Forces. It must be said that, despite Lloyd Owen's disparaging remarks about Headquarters Raiding Forces, the units under their command carried out 381 operations on some seventy islands between October 1943 and the end of 1944, admittedly many of them in this period LRDG and SB Squadron affairs. After the departure of the LRDG and SB Squadron, the bulk of the work was carried out by the Greek Sacred Regiment. They were to continue the good work up to the end of the War in Europe, but their exploits are outside the scope of this account.

Between their formation on 15 November 1942 and June 1944, Popski's Private Army (PPA) had seen some action in North Africa and Italy, although their contribution to the war up to this point had been negligible. By the time they had been ready for action in North Africa, the advance from Alamein had overrun the Gebel Akhdar, which 'Popski' viewed as his personal stamping ground. PPA took part in the reconnaissance of the Tebega Gap with the LRDG (see Chapter 4), and also claimed the destruction in Tunisia, of 34 aircraft and 118 vehicles. These figures, plus the destruction of 450,000 gallons of petrol and the taking of 600 prisoners, are quoted in the official War Office Historical Summary, and must have been given to Headquarters 1st or 8th Army by 'Popski'.[3] As 'Popski''s biographer, Willett, says:

> In Tunisia the going was harder, the Arabs less friendly, and the front less open than 'Popski' had ever expected. He did not in his few weeks of operations in Tunisia manage to do anything very startling. . . . By his own very sketchy account he attacked one minor enemy landing ground [airstrip], and a number of transport columns. But the claims he made at the time . . . seem high for the operations described; and he does not mention them in his book.[4]

Whatever the truth of the matter, PPA's efforts in North Africa were sufficient to win it friends in 1st and 8th Armies, which ensured the continuing existence of PPA and its inclusion in the order of battle for the invasion of Italy. Here, following the Allied invasion, it spent some time engaged in what one can only describe as 'swanning about'. Although certain of these Italian operations, under the command of British 1st Airborne Division, were useful, others seem to have been self-generated entertainment. When it became apparent that infiltrating jeeps through the German lines was becoming very difficult, if not impossible, in the conditions and terrain in Italy, 'Popski' decided that a rethink was in order. Somehow he managed to persuade Major-General de Guingand, Chief of Staff 8th Army, that he should expand his private army, and this was agreed, although de Guingand makes no mention of PPA anywhere in his memoirs.[5] However, PPA expanded from twelve all ranks to eighty, including eight officers. Under the supervision of 'Popski''s second-in-command, Captain Bob Yunnie, the outstanding officer in the unit, the PPA was organized into three fighting patrols, each sixteen strong, although patrols did operate below that strength. The organization of a patrol as given in the War Office Historical Summary is one officer, three NCOs and twelve soldiers, in six jeeps. Each patrol had a formidable array of weapons:

Six .50-inch Browning heavy machine-guns	One bazooka
Six .30-inch Browning medium machine-guns	Sixteen .45 automatic pistols
Two Bren guns	Grenades
One 3-inch mortar	Explosives
Eight tommy-guns	Mines
Eight carbines	Smoke generators [fitted to the rear of each jeep to provide cover for a quick getaway]

Later one jeep per patrol was fitted with a Wasp flame-thrower

The first operation by the revamped PPA was a disaster. They were ordered to destroy a bridge opposite a position held by the Scots Guards on the Garigliano near Minturno. Trooper Ben Owen took part:

There was a bridge about half a mile behind the German lines, and 'Popski' brought us aerial photos, and we said, 'But there is another bridge there, if we blow one up they can use the other.' He said, 'We have been told the operation would have a demoralising effect on the German troops.' We set off through the Scots Guards positions. They were getting stonked every ten minutes by mortars. We went into the valley, it was dark, we were on foot. We had gone about 200 yards, the skipper in front. There was a flash about a foot in front of my foot. It was an S mine, which jumps up in the air before exploding and sprays out about 300 steel balls at about head level. Fortunately there is a blind spot with no balls. I had very little [shrapnel] in me, but my hearing went, I couldn't see out of one eye and I thought I was blinded, it was small piece of shrapnel in my eyelid, it's still there, and I had small bits in me. The man behind me was killed, the one in front, Paddy McAllister, had a bullet in his spine paralysing his legs, the chap in front of him was hit in the wrist and in the kidneys but not seriously. The skipper [Yunnie] in the front and sergeant at the back weren't touched. I was ordered back, but refused. I could see Paddy McAllister lying unable to move. So we picked Paddy up. He fainted as we carried him over our shoulders with his legs hanging down. The skipper said, 'I've got to go back', [to look for the others], he shouldn't have done, because he might have trod on another mine. After a bit I went to look for him. After another stonk, I went back to Paddy, and we got back to the Scots Guards.

After this *débâcle*, 'Popski', still casting about for a role, sent his men on a parachute course. Meanwhile he made plans to land thirty men and twelve jeeps at the mouth of the River Tenna, at that stage in the campaign about sixty miles behind the lines. He gave the operation the codename Astrolobe; a curious choice, and hardly secure, since the PPA badge was an astrolobe. After landing, he would drive inland, set up a base, and operate for up to four weeks. Yunnie was sent ahead in an ML, with two naval officers to check that the beach was suitable; these two were to return with information on the beach, while Yunnie remained. Three days later, if all was well, Yunnie was to shine a light out to sea to guide in the Landing Craft Tank (LCT) carrying the PPA party. The two naval officers returned with the news that although there was a sand bar offshore, a loaded LCT could just get over. LCT 589 sailed on the night of 14/15 June with, in addition to the PPA party, a troop of Number 9 Commando to secure the beach, while the jeeps were driving ashore. On completion of the landing the commandos would re-embark and return in the LCT.

When the LCT, escorted by an ML, arrived off the beach, Yunnie's signal was seen shining, the LCT ran in, bumped over the sand bar, and beached. The commandos landed. When 'Popski' met Yunnie on the beach, he was told that the area was thick with Germans withdrawing in front of 8th Army, and there was little chance of the PPA being able to achieve anything, let alone survive for long. The shaded headlights of masses of enemy transport, on the road a few hundred yards inland, were clearly visible from the beach. The noise of their engines presumably covered the sound of the LCT and ML approaching, and the performance that was to ensue. 'Popski' ordered the commandos back on board, and the LCT to retract. At this stage, it was found that she was aground by the stern on the sandbar. Clearly the beach reconnaissance had been less than thorough: either the beach gradient had not been correctly calculated, or the draught of the LCT with twelve jeeps and trailers, plus some hundred passengers, had been underestimated. Perhaps it was hoped that once the jeeps had driven off the LCT, its draught would be sufficiently reduced to allow it to retract over the sand bar. Certainly no proper survey had been conducted. Whatever the reason, Operation Astrolobe joined the long list of amphibious operations that have been a 'wash out' thanks to amateurs not being aware that such ventures are not a pastime for part-time participants. Apart from anything else, twelve brand new jeeps were now a write-off.

At one stage, the ML, which crossed the sand bar in a vain attempt to tow off the LCT, also grounded. 'Popski''s initial reaction was that both craft would be blown up, everybody would land and, having split up, would find their way back to their own lines. Fortunately, the ML managed to get clear. 'Popski' ordered that the LCT engines were to be destroyed, everyone would embark in the ML and return to base, except Yunnie and four men with a radio who would remain. to set up a road watch.[6] They were also able to salvage a valuable piece of equipment carelessly abandoned in the LCT; the Eureka beacon, a device used to guide aircraft in over the correct DZ in parachute operations. After some days ashore, Yunnie was sent a message telling him to retrieve it. Trooper Owen picks up the story:

> I was sent to get it. By this time the skipper had pinched a 'Jerry' staff car. We had adapted our skiing caps to look like Jerry caps. I sat in the back with a tommy-gun, we set off. There weren't many 'Jerries' about, although we met a 'Jerry' half-track. We hadn't gone far when the engine packed up. We pushed it into a wood. I sat on the bonnet reading a book so the 'Jerries' wouldn't think there was a problem. Eventually we got it going. I said if we are stopped, I would speak Italian. The Italians would think I was a German speaking bad Italian, and the Germans would think I was an Italian Fascist.
>
> We got to the place where the LCT was aground. The two engines had been blown. All the jeeps were in chaos. I sorted out the equipment. Eventually after about half an hour I found the vibrator which was the key piece of the Eureka.

They were also able to send back some information, and prevent a bridge being demolished in the path of the 8th Army. Trooper Owen again:

> We could hear a 2-pounder firing. It was an armoured car, and it was our own people coming along. We were in a farm, I was sitting on top of the staircase which went up outside the building. Stewart [ex LRDG and a member of Yunnie's team] saw a German demolition party preparing a bridge for demolition. When he drew his 'skipper''s attention to this, he said we'll have our breakfast first. But Stewart slipped down and opened fire on the demolition party who beat a hasty retreat. Soon afterwards the British armoured car came round the bend in the road. I stepped out and waved to it. I told the officer in Italian that the bridge was unblown [sic] and the Germans had scarpered. He thanked me in Italian and pushed on.

What is also not clear about Operation Astrolobe is exactly what 'Popski' hoped to achieve. In his briefing to his men on board the LCT during the voyage to the Tenna, he said:

My intention is to establish a base in the mountains, supplied from the air from which we shall operate as long as conditions remain suitable.[7]

Quite how long he hoped to survive without assistance from the partisans was problematical. Up to now there still seemed to be an element of at best improvisation, and at worst, 'suck-it-and-see, swan about, and hope something will turn up' about his planning. This was in contrast with his exploits as an agent in the desert. Why was he not challenged by his superiors and asked just what he thought he was up to? As Willett says:

Many people in Italy thought that PPA's spell of ineffectiveness was justified by legendary desert successes. For few outside the unit knew how short its African career had been, or how little it had really achieved; and most of those were not in Italy. The legend somehow balanced itself between Italy and the desert, as PPA had itself balanced itself between the 1st and 8th Armies. For 'Popski' was always looking for gaps in our own military system, just as in the enemy's, through which he and his unit could slip.[8]

It was at this stage when nothing seemed to be going right that 'Popski', in a remarkable feat of driving, managed to get his jeeps across the mountains, some up to 5,000 feet high. In places the jeeps had to be manhandled. He met up with the partisans in the area of Camerino, just north of the present-day Monti Sibilline National Park. Here he joined forces with two brothers, the Ferris, who ran an efficient partisan band. Using imaginative tactics, PPA and the partisans were able to deceive the commander of the German mountain division stationed in Camerino that he was surrounded by a superior force. Eventually, the Germans withdrew from here and four other villages. Up to the end of July 1944, PPA with the partisans had a thoroughly successful period, clearing a large area of Germans and killing several hundred, for the loss of one dead and three wounded. There were some lighter moments too, as Trooper Owen relates:

We stopped the jeep in the main street [of a village]. All of a sudden, after Yunnie and 'Popski' had gone into the *albergo* [small restaurant], there was shouting and screaming, and hundreds of people came running into the street shouting the Germans are coming. I had posted two partisans on the approaches, and they came back crying and shouting. Yunnie came out of the *albergo* and said, 'Come on "Popski"'s having a bath. We can't let the

"Jerries" spoil it.' So off we went. As we went along the lovely tarmac road, there was a farmer putting a bullock into a cart. He pointed out a big farmhouse where the 'Jerries' were. We pushed the jeep along the track so they wouldn't hear the engine. There were about thirty bicycles against the wall. Of course I had my gun ready. A 'Jerry' came out, and I fired and brassed the place up. I could hear them running. After this I was the king [of the village]. I could have been the Mayor.

When the Allies had taken Rimini, the area behind the German lines opposite 8th Army lay in the flatter country north-east of the Apennines, which, as has already been noted, curve away to the north-west. PPA's next operational area was in the area of the marshes south of Ravenna. Here the canals and rivers were formidable obstacles to jeeps. 'Popski' was not taken aback. He acquired some DUKWs. Using these, and his jeeps, he worked with a detachment of the 28th Garibaldi Brigade of Partisans. From now on PPA did not operate behind the lines, but first as part of a group consisting of 12th and 27th Lancers; and later with 27th Lancers alone. PPA worked very much as an armoured car squadron would, but in jeeps with considerable success. PPA were first into Ravenna in early December 1944. Soon after, 'Popski' was wounded, losing a hand, but was awarded a well-deserved DSO for his part in a battle in which his patrol inflicted thirty casualties on the enemy, at the cost of one wounded: himself. PPA, now under Major Jean Caneri, one of the originals, were in the thick of it until the end, their final spectacular being to capture a battery of 88 mm guns and 300 prisoners. PPA's time as part of a mixed force, fighting on the British side of the lines, was arguably the most militarily useful period of its existence. Their light, manoeuvrable jeeps, tremendous firepower, and 'Popski''s ability to achieve a rapport with the Italians gave PPA a great advantage over any other type of unit in this terrain, and particular circumstances.

By now, as Willett says:

Their general level of fighting ability, signals and administrative efficiency was not unworthy of the LRDG who had always been 'Popski''s model.[9]

But they were not operating behind the lines during this period, and as Willett observes:

PPA operated behind enemy lines for only a month in Tunisia, and for three weeks in Italy. It could only work effectively under the wing of another unit, first the LRDG, then 1st Airborne Division [the early days in Italy], finally 27th Lancers.[10]

In the end, after a number of false starts, PPA got it right. Their time of most value *behind the lines*, in the 'return on investment' calculation, was when they were working with the Partisans. This was also to be the experience of the last SAS operations in Italy.

As we saw in the previous chapter, there were few tasks for the SAS in north-west Europe during the winter of 1944/45 and early spring of 1945. But the forthcoming Allied assault on the German line (the Gothic Line), planned for early April 1945, with the rugged terrain and opportunities to work with the partisans, offered scope for behind-the-lines operations.

Accordingly, in mid-December 1944, Major Roy Farran was sent to Italy with 3 Squadron, 2nd SAS. This was a newly raised Squadron formed in early 1944, mainly from volunteers from 1st and 6th Airborne Divisions, and not the one with which Farran had operated in Sicily, Italy and France for the previous two years. It was well trained, included a number of regular soldiers, and Farran considered its discipline better than the other two squadrons in 2nd SAS. Farran came directly under the control of the Allied 15th Army Group, commanded by General Mark Clark, since Field Marshal Sir Harold Alexander took over as Supreme Allied Commander Mediterranean in November 1944.

The first operation by 3 Squadron was Operation Galia, in which Major R. Walker-Brown dropped into the mountains north of La Spezia with a troop of thirty-three men on 27 December 1944. Here they remained for two months, in appalling weather conditions. They used mules to carry the heavier weapons, including 3-inch mortars and Vickers machine-guns. They gave the Germans so much trouble that they turned out some 6,000 troops, including a ski battalion, to try to eliminate them. The party eventually walked through the German lines and met Allied troops at Leghorn (Livorno).

The next operation, Cold Comfort, starting on the night of 17/18 February, was an attempt by Captain Littlejohn and his troop to block the Brenner Pass by initiating a landslide. In grim conditions of heavy snowfalls, bitter cold and low cloud, which severely restricted air resupply, Littlejohn's men tried but failed to block the pass. Littlejohn and Corporal Crowley were captured, and later executed by the Gestapo.

Three other operations were mounted in Italy, of which the most successful was Tombola. The genesis of this operation was Farran's hopes of inserting a large, well-equipped party, behind the lines, but close enough to have an effect on the operations of the main force. His eye lit upon the province of Emilia Romagna, north of the Gothic Line, and south of the River Po. The three departments in the province, Parma, Reggio and Modena, each had its own Partisan Headquarters (*Commando Unico*), and a number of brigades of Communist or non-Communist partisans. Each 'brigade' was actually the equivalent of a weak battalion; at most about 400 men. Each *Commando Unico* had a British or American officer attached, whose job was to arrange air drops to supply them with weapons and, more difficult, try to push them into fighting. The only British liaison officer of the three in Emilia who was willing to accept SAS assistance was Michael Lees, an SOE operative attached to the Reggio *Commando Unico*. This suited Farran well, because the nearest point in the Allied line was about twelve miles away. The staff at Headquarters 15th Army Group approved Farran's plan, but said that the time to start the operation would be decided by them, in order to co-ordinate it with the forthcoming offensive. Farran wanted to command the operation, but he was forbidden to do so by the staff at Army Group Headquarters. He was, however, allowed to go on the aircraft and watch the drop. He decided to risk a court martial and drop, telling only those who needed to know, including the despatcher, whom he detailed to push his kit out of the door on its own parachute. His cover story was to be that he was standing in the door, tripped and fell out. It worked for a time, because until he sent his first radio message, Army Headquarters thought he had been killed.

On 4 March, Farran was first out over the DZ, and the rest of the stick, consisting of his advance party, followed. The drop went well, except for Captain Jock Eyston who dislocated his shoulder landing on a roof in the village. He joined Farran looking very sick and obviously in great pain. He was put to bed in the village, and a doctor was sent for, while the remainder of the party were given a meal in the village café.

Michael Lees turned up, bubbling with enthusiasm, having ridden a horse over from the village where he was based. He congratulated Farran on jumping contrary to orders, and told him he had plenty of targets, including a corps headquarters, adding:

Now we can get cracking. These farts are bloody useless. You ought to shake 'em up. Farts is our name for the Eyeties [Italians]. You know, corruption of parts, abbreviation of partisan.[11]

Lees took Farran to meet the Commander of the Reggio *Commando Unico*, which nominally controlled all the brigades in the Villa Minozzo Valley, where Farran had dropped. The River Secchia runs down this valley, one of many rivers in this sector of the province that flow north-east from the Apennine watershed into the Po. The mountains here rise up to 7,000 feet. In 1944 there were few roads or tracks, and these mainly followed the grain of the country, from south-west to north-east. Three main roads, Routes 62, 63 and 12 ran from just inland of the coast, north-east through the mountains to join the Milan–Bologna highway, then called the *Strada Nationali* (now called the *Via Emilia*, running parallel to the Milan–Rimini *Autostrada* which did not exist in 1945). The Reggio *Commando Unico* consisted of three Communist Brigades, the Garibaldini, and one Christian Democrat Brigade, with the equally flamboyant title, Green Flames.

Lees's and Farran's proposal to the Reggio *Commando Unico*, and 15th Army Group Headquarters, that a new battalion be formed, based on a British company from the SAS, was approved. It would include a company of right-wing Italian partisans, and one of Russians who had deserted from the German Army. These last had been recruited by the Wehrmacht after being taken prisoner on the Eastern Front. Farran would command this unit, named the *Battaglione Alleato*. Eyston, whose shoulder had been put back by two local doctors, was to command the British company. When Farran first met the Italian Company, he was badly shaken:

It looked like a tableau of Wat Tyler's Rebellion. The men were all young, but nearly all of them had some physical defect. Many had only one eye. . . . They all looked as though they were in the grip of some horrible disease.[12]

Farran gave them a 'pep' talk, which they greeted with a faint cheer. They were clearly worried that they might actually have to fight, rather than strut about in the mountains. Farran's next reinforcements consisted of instructors and an Italian interpreter, to start training the partisans before the main body of the SAS arrived. These instructors had been selected from volunteers among the Infantry Reinforcement Depot, and for two of them their first-ever parachute descent was to be an operational one, at night. All went well except for the interpreter who dislocated his shoulder. A great quantity of stores and weapons dropped with this party; tangible proof to the watching partisans that Farran meant business. Three days later, an advance party of twenty-four British officers and soldiers arrived on the same DZ, one officer and four soldiers to be attached to the Russian and Italian Companies. Eventually the main body dropped, and the British Company, some forty strong, was complete. Finally, 'Piper Kirkpatrick of the Highland Light Infantry, dropped by day, complete with kilt and pipes'.

> One of the greatest moments was when the British Company gave a demonstration of the 'eightsome' to the Garibaldini, who, I am sure, thought them completely mad.[13]

The Italian Company wore the SAS motto, 'Who Dares Wins', embroidered on their pockets in Italian, '*Chi Osera ci Vincera*'.

> I regret to say that the British often parodied this motto to read, 'Who cares who wins', but I am sure that nobody would believe that they meant it – much.[14]

Farran and Lees proposed that the first target for the *Battaglione Alleato* should be the German corps headquarters, about eight miles south of Reggio. Army Group Headquarters gave its approval, dropped air photographs, but then, when Farran's men were actually en route, changed its mind, and forbade him to attack. Farran decided to ignore Army Group Headquarters, on the grounds that he would lose all credibility with the partisans if the vaunted *Battaglione Alleato* was seen to opt out of its first operation. Only when he returned to Army Group Headquarters weeks later did he learn that the main attack was to come in against that corps in ten days' time, and it was thought that Farran's raid might alert the enemy. For a second time, he came within an ace of being court-martialled for disobedience.

To complicate things, at this juncture the Germans began an anti-partisan drive in the mountains. Farran decided to go ahead. His plan was to infiltrate the enemy positions by night in three columns led by himself. They would lie up in a farm the whole of the next day, about ten miles from the objective, and attack the following night. The corps headquarters consisted of the commander's villa (Villa Rossi) and the chief of staff's villa (Villa Calvi), and a number of other buildings occupied by troops; a total of around 300 men. The British, backed up by the Italians, would force an entry into the two villas, while the Russians positioned themselves as a screen to cut off the other buildings, to prevent interference by the occupants.

The approach went without incident. The attack on the Villa Calvi was initially successful. The sentries were killed silently, but the door was locked and had to be blown in with a bazooka rocket. The Germans inside fought stoutly, and the attackers could not get up the stairs to kill the chief of staff. Eventually they set fire to the villa, by piling furniture on the ground floor, adding explosives and petrol. They kept the Germans inside by bursts of fire, until the villa was blazing well. However, this alerted the enemy before the party attacking the Villa Rossi was in position. A siren wailed the alarm and lights came on. Again the attackers gained the ground floor, but could not mount the stairs against a hail of Schmeisser fire. Some Germans attempted to come down, and were killed on the half landing; one of them could have been the Corps Commander. Realizing that they were running out of time, the attackers started a fire in the kitchen, and withdrew. The Germans in the troop accommodation were very quick to react, and soon the Russian screen was under heavy machine-gun fire. Farran ordered Kirkpatrick to play 'Highland Laddie', but when some of the fire switched in their direction, Farran shoved him into an adjacent slit trench, from where he continued to play. Farran fired a red Very light signal, and the *Battaglione Alleato* withdrew to the RV.

For the rest of the night and the following day they marched, carrying their wounded. Mist and rain covered their withdrawal from the Germans combing the hills. After twenty-two hours, they paraded into a partisan-held village behind the piper, to the cheers of the 'Green Flames'. Three British were killed, and eight British and Italian wounded, including Lees, who was crippled for life. Six Russians were captured, and very likely shot on the spot. Eventually, Farran arranged for a light aircraft to pick up Lees and take him to hospital in Florence.

The German reaction was to mount a drive or *rastrallamento* to eliminate the partisans. Buttressed by the SAS, and supported by Vickers machine-guns, .50-inch Browning heavy machine-guns, a 75 mm pack howitzer and 3-inch mortars, the partisans for the first time in this region stood and fought, although there were local withdrawals.

Eventually, at a critical moment, the Russians were persuaded to put in a counter-attack, and the Germans bolted.

In early April, the United States 5th Army was about to attack along the front behind which Farran was operating. He agreed with the British liaison officer with the Modena Partisans that, subject to the approval of Army Group, he should move the *Battaglione Alleato* to the Modena *Commando Unico*'s area of operations, which was on 5th Army's main axis of advance. Army Group approved Farran's suggested move, telling him that as soon as the German withdrawal began, to attack Route 12 (then the main Florence–Modena road). Farran asked for jeeps to be dropped to him, because he foresaw that he would need to be mobile for his forthcoming role.

Knowing that he would be accused of running away by the Reggio partisans, Farran decided:

> With typical treachery, I calculated that if I did not tell Monti (Reggio *Commando Unico* commander) that I was moving until the last possible moment, I could continue to draw rations from the Reggio *Commando Unico* even after we were under way.[15]

On 5 April, Farran received the radio message that 5th Army's offensive had begun, and he set out for his new area. The ambushes on Route 12 were not successful to begin with, as Farran explains:

> The trouble lay in the fact that Route 12 [in his area of operations] ran along a ridge on which there was no cover. It is easy to ambush a road that runs along a valley, because safe cover positions exist from which it is simple to withdraw.[16]

Here the lie of the land meant that the jeeps had to drive right up to the road before they could open fire. Farran decided to switch to standing off and shelling German troops on and near the road with his 75 mm pack howitzer; then driving up, firing and withdrawing when the situation got too hot. He started with a German position in the village of Sassuolo, about ten miles south-west of Modena. The resulting confusion was so gratifying that similar attacks were carried out elsewhere on Route 12, using the 3-inch mortars as well as the 75 mm pack howitzer.

Farran also had some disciplinary problems with the partisans who complained that the British were driving them too hard. On one occasion, a lagging partisan was prodded in the bottom by a British soldier with a fighting knife (commando dagger). On another, a partisan who had been caught stealing eggs had been given a 'gentle tap with the butt of a carbine'. Farran gave the British a lecture on diplomacy:

> It was too much to expect that these willing but undernourished little Italians who had been brought up on pasta asciutta and macaroni should be able to keep up with selected parachutists who had trained to march for years.[17]

On 20 April, Farran received word that the 5th Army had broken through the German lines. Farran decided to assault the town of Reggio, astride the German withdrawal route. Driving within range, he shelled the main square. He learned later that the Fascists and local German Headquarters mistook the *Battaglione Alleato* for the advanced guard of an American armoured division, and they abandoned Reggio within two hours. News came through two days later that the Americans had broken through near Bologna, and the roads were packed with fleeing German transport. Farran moved to where a stream of transport was crossing the Sassuolo Bridge, and an enemy infantry battalion was taking a rest under some trees. Opening fire with the 75 mm howitzer, a Vickers and a 60 mm mortar, he caused pandemonium, as blazing vehicles jammed the bridge. A passing flight of Spitfires, probably attracted by the smoke, joined in to add to the carnage. The battle went on all day, and Farran withdrew at nightfall. After another day of strafing German transport, Farran's battalion moved into Modena to help mop up pockets of isolated resistance, but he soon realised that the Italians were 'best left alone' to finish the job. Orders arrived to move the British troops back to Florence. Operation Tombola was over.

> We were all covered with the grime of months in the mountains, and our shabbiness was in sharp contrast to the huge armoured columns we passed on the road. They must have wondered who on earth we could be.[18]

The Adriatic was the scene of the last behind-the-lines operations by the LRDG and Special Boat Service (having changed its name from SB Squadron). At the end of February 1945, the enemy in the coastal area of Yugoslavia and the Dalmatian Islands still held the northern quarter of the long coastline and islands. It was decided to set up a small combined operations headquarters at Zara (now Zadar) to control the forces operating in the area. These included A Squadron LRDG and L Detachment Special Boat Service, both under the command of Lieutenant-Colonel Sutherland of the Special Boat Service. The MV *Kufra* was fitted out as an advanced mobile headquarters with radio links to LRDG Headquarters in Italy and to the patrols.

The upper reaches of the Adriatic had been heavily mined by the enemy. Much of his shipping moved at night, free from interference from Allied air attack, and, because of the mines, reasonably safe from interception by the Royal Navy. During daylight, enemy shipping lay up, hugging the shoreline under camouflage nets. However, they did so under the watchful eyes of the LRDG patrols, who called in air strikes. Sometimes the camouflage was so effective that the airmen returned to base wondering exactly what they had been strafing, until a message arrived from an LRDG patrol telling them the score in damaged ships and craft. The LRDG were also able to pinpoint traffic in mine-free areas, and pass the information to the Navy, so the enemy shipping could be intercepted and sunk. Although the Germans were well aware that patrols were operating in the area, and searched for them, they were never located. Warning would be given by shepherds or partisans, in time for the patrol to lie still, or pull back into thicker cover. The first patrol to set out on this phase, Second Lieutenant Reynolds's T1, landed on the south-east coast of Istria, and was tasked to watch shipping as it cleared the island chain, and rounded the Istrian Peninsula before shaping for Trieste.

By April 1945, five A Squadron Patrols had been operating in Istria, all of whom had been received by Reynolds. Olivey's Z1 was reporting movement on the Fiume–Trieste railway. Eastwood's S1 was watching shipping moving to and from Fiume, having relieved Olivey of this task. Jackson's S2 was reporting on traffic on the Pola (Pula)–Trieste railway, and on roads in that area. Simpson's S3 was tasked to work in the Pola–Cap Premanatura area. Simpson came near to being discovered by German patrols engaged in a concentrated food drive in the Istrian Peninsula. On several occasions, the enemy came so close while beating the bushes for stray cattle that the operator could not talk on his radio. Eventually his patrol was taken off on 30 March.

The Special Boat Service, in an island attacking role, had a less happy time. The situation in the northern Adriatic was very different from the Aegean of the year before. The sea mining hampered their movement.

The restricted waters made surprise less easy to achieve. The Germans were still a formidable foe, and quite prepared to fight it out. When Captain McGonigal landed on Losinj with twenty-one men, he lost two dead and eight wounded attacking a strongly held villa for no gain whatever. On 18 March, he landed again on Losinj, this time to destroy the bridge connecting it with its neighbouring island of Cres. The landing went without incident, but on the approach march to the bridge, he ran into a German patrol, killing four. The noise of the firefight alerted the eighty-strong bridge garrison. The dug-in position behind barbed wire was far too tough a nut to crack, and McGonigal was forced to withdraw. Gallant though these efforts were, one has to ask if this was yet another example of dwindling 'real estate' and opportunities for action, leading to ill-considered attempts to use highly specialized troops in roles for which they were never intended: frontal attacks on strong positions. Commandos, supported by naval gunfire or air strikes, would have perhaps been more suitable. In fact the bridge on Cres had been blown by Number 9 Commando on Operation Gradient 1 on the night of 9/10 August 1944, but was subsequently repaired.

Elsewhere in Yugoslavia the LRDG were also busy. Lieutenant Pitt's R1 set up an observation post on the island of Rab, which they maintained for a month in the midst of a triangle of German positions from 2,000 to 5,000 yards away. They tasked some thirty-four bombing and rocket strikes, inflicting considerable casualties on the enemy and sinking a ship. R1's reports and assistance was instrumental in a successful attack on the island by the Yugoslav partisan army, landed in Royal Navy craft. Pitt reconnoitred the landing beach, and provided the radio link with the Navy. A few days later, Pitt helped with communications and advice to the Yugoslav force attacking Losinj and Cres, which fell to the partisan army with heavy casualties to the defenders.

The Yugoslav partisans had always been difficult to work with, and by early 1945 it became clear that, with the end in sight, Tito was becoming less and less enamoured of the Allies operating on Yugoslav soil, other than as a token presence. Tito was especially suspicious of Allied operations in Istria because he had designs on Trieste, which he hoped to incorporate into the postwar Yugoslavia.[19] In mid April, all the members of Jackson's, Eastwood's and Reynolds's patrols were arrested by the partisans and told to leave on the pretext that their passes were not valid.

On Friday 13 April, a large partisan group, which was being given tea in Reynolds's camp, surrounded the LRDG patrol. The partisans ordered them to hand over their arms and radio, and accompany them to the local headquarters, or be shot. The patrol, heavily outnumbered, complied. Luckily the radio operator was not having tea with the group and was able to send a short emergency signal to LRDG Headquarters.

Although Tito may have wanted to get rid of the Allied troops, he continued to rely on Allied aid in *matériel* form; Lloyd Owen's diary quotes part of a signal sent through diplomatic channels:

> *April 15th*
> Trouble with partisans who have so far imprisoned Mike [Reynolds] and Stan [Eastwood] in Istria.
>
> Extracts from signal from AOC to AFHQ – Subject is arrest of LRDG patrols in Istria. 'These patrols provide information about enemy shipping which is quite indispensable to our highly successful joint operation. Without this information our joint air and sea support for the Yugoslavs in the islands and on the coast will be seriously weakened. I think you should draw Tito's attention to this. Unless the LRDG patrol is immediately released we may well be forced to consider how much assistance we should give in the way of air support for operations and air transport for food to Allies whose reply is to put British Troops under arrest.'

The next day, the partisans returned the arms, but told the patrol not to leave the headquarters, saying that they would be transported to Zara in a partisan gunboat. The patrol refused to return to Zara. They were informed that they would be bound and put on board. The threat never materialized because the sea was too rough, and on the fourth day the Royal Navy arrived and took them off in response to a signal from Reynolds to LRDG Headquarters, recorded by Lloyd Owen in his diary. An extract reads:

> [they] would be forcibly removed on a partisan boat unless Navy could send MGB, and prefer to be picked up by Navy rather than shanghaied by garlic-eating bandits.

Sutherland was also arrested at the same time as the LRDG patrols. Lloyd Owen's diary:

> *April 18th*
> In middle night Sutherland signalled to say: 'Relations with local commander now very ugly and unless you evacuate us tomorrow night, cannot

vouch for their action. Personally do not consider that we can ever resume normal relations with these ridiculous people.' I at once decided to leave Olivey patrol in order to save face and withdraw remainder.

Sutherland had hoped to carry out one more operation, but tempers were getting high, and not only in Yugoslavia, as Lloyd Owen's diary reveals:

April 19th
At about 10.30 I received a cryptic signal from Sutherland to cancel the boat and the news later that he intended to attack some guns at dawn 21 [April] and we were to pick him up night 21/22 [April]. This I have agreed to in the hope that by then the release order will have come through. But as yet I fail to understand it. AOC has gone to Zara so I could not consult him but informed him by signal. I then received a most ridiculous and disgraceful signal from [Brigadier] Davy which said that 'being disarmed and marched off or put in a partisan schooner were inconveniences that must be accepted'. This made me boil and was the wettest and most hopeless armchair decision I have seen in ages. I replied that I thought so. AOC returned later and tore off a high-powered signal [to Davy] which included: 'cannot agree that being bundled into partisan schooners are mere inconveniences and am not prepared to accept the man-handling of our men by a gang of ghastly garlic eaters [this seems to have been a favourite expression], and have therefore told [Lloyd] Owen to act in accordance my instructions.'

After the War Lloyd Owen wrote:

I know George Davy was only passing on the broader views of Allied Force Headquarters. He never held this difference of opinion against me, nor did he ever resent my not accepting his views without argument. He was better able to appreciate that Allied Force Headquarters were in an extremely difficult position. He was in constant touch with them by telephone and, therefore, heard all the arguments.

Meanwhile the situation in Istria was becoming more tense. Lloyd Owen's diary:

April 21st
Signal from Sutherland at 10.00 saying it was essential for him to come out tonight. Now that matter is above my level. I signalled AOC, '. . . feel it is asking too much of him to continue to hold the can while the big guns are still being ranged . . . have provisionally arranged his pick up tonight

pending your approval. . . .' Reply received at 4.00 saying, 'Agree your decision. Go ahead'. So I laid on craft and then the weather was too bad for them to go! John O [Olivey] has still resisted arrest and is playing idiot boy wonderfully as only he can do.

Olivey, who had been told by signal not to offer resistance if the partisans took action, purposely left the patrol weapons lying about when a strong force of partisans visited his camp. These of course were collected. All the patrol kit was left for the partisans to carry. Crossing a road, a convoy of enemy trucks caught the party halfway across. Had the enemy been alert they could not have failed to see them. The patrol, deadpan, asked the partisans why they had not fired, after all they had all the weapons. On arrival at partisan headquarters, the weapons were offered back, but the patrol refused to converse with their captors, or to take back their weapons, which, as they saw it, would be carried for them.

Late on 21 April Sutherland sent a signal saying that he must come out, otherwise he could not vouch for what might happen. Lloyd Owen's diary:

April 22nd
Planned this pick up for today with sailors and RAF. Arranged for 2 PT boats and 4 MGBs with 12 aircraft escort to pick up at 4.00 this afternoon. Craft left Zara at 10.30 but had to return due to terrible weather. While on their way back signal from AOC cancelled the pick up and said at all costs they must stay as orders for their release had been issued and most abject apologies were on their way. All most unsatisfactory and only action seems to be a signal from Alexander to Tito expressing the astonishment of British and American governments over the whole affair. I think the whole attitude is utterly wet. However, I think also that we haven't a leg to stand on as I saw a signal today sent by AOC to Markham [British representative] at Belgrade last January saying that there was no intention of operating in central Istria. Also one from 37 Mission a few days ago saying that they foresaw the trouble but considered that the risk was a legitimate one.

April 24–25th
It was decided to bring all the chaps out of Istria as a result of Sutherland's repeated requests. Davy was here and at last has realised that something must be done. Anyhow all went well and everyone including Stan and Jacko [Jackson] were brought out in the afternoon of the 25th by PT boats and MGBs under cover of Spitfires. We had to leave John O [Olivey] as he was

too far away. But as the Ptzns [partisans] conveniently received orders for complete cooperation with British Troops only a few hours before they were forced out, all should be well with him.

This did the trick because a Political Commissar arrived where Olivey and his patrol were being held, and said they could return to their position, giving them a written order to this effect. Olivey remained in Istria until the end of the war, returning to the LRDG base at Rodi via Trieste. He was a remarkable man, of whom Lloyd Owen was to write later:

> I would not hazard a guess at John's age. He had a capacity for fun and the high spirits of a man in his early twenties. Everything he did was carried through with enthusiasm and humour. He was remarkably fit and could compete with any of us. Yet I am sure he was nearer forty than thirty. . . . At the end of it all he returned to his farm at Umtali in Rhodesia.

The last Special Boat Service action of the war took place at Lake Comacchio, north of Ravenna in early April; behind the lines, although by only a couple of miles. Lassen and Guardsman Reilly carried out much of the preliminary reconnaissance for 2nd Commando Brigade, who had to cross the lake to assault a spit of land between the lake and the coast. Four islands on the lake were captured by Special Boat Service patrols as part of preliminary operations leading up to the attack on the spit. From one of these islands Lassen led a diversion raid north of the main assault, aimed at making the enemy think that the objective was Comacchio itself. Lassen and his men landed through the reeds at the edge of the lake, and moved inland. They soon ran into stiff opposition, consisting of a series of pillboxes. Fire from the nearest killed one SB man, and wounded Reilly. Lassen charged the pillbox, clearing it with a grenade. Joined by the others, he cleared two more. They were taking prisoners, at the third, when someone shouted 'Kamerad'. Lassen moved to the entrance, and was hit by a burst of fire, dying soon after of his wounds. This gallant Dane was awarded the Victoria Cross posthumously.

When the War in Europe ended, the LRDG had high hopes of adding to their laurels in the Far East. It was not to be. On 21 June 1945 their Commanding Officer received a letter from Field Marshal Alexander:

Dear Lloyd Owen

The news of the War Office decision to disband the Long-Range Desert Group must have come to you as a great shock – as it did to me.

Long before I went to the Middle East, I had heard of the exploits of the LRDG in your original hunting grounds in Tripolitania and Cyrenaica, and it was with great pride that I first took you under my command in August 1942.

Since then you have continued your fine work with undiminished skill and enthusiasm and it is indeed with great reluctance that I say farewell and good luck to you all.

Yours sincerely

H. R. Alexander

Lloyd Owen, the fourth Commanding Officer of the LRDG, who had served in the unit for four of the five years of its existence, noted in his diary:

There is perhaps some consolation in feeling that we are going out on the crest of a wave when our star could not have been brighter.

To which one can only say 'Amen'.

12

Burma and South-East Asia: Small Operations

Although the Chindits represented the largest behind-the-lines operations conducted by the British in the Second World War – indeed in history – there were numerous, much smaller behind-the-lines operations in South-East Asia throughout the period of the war against Japan. Before the establishment of SEAC in October 1943, Burma, Malaya and Sumatra had always been part of an area of operations in which the British had taken the lead since the outbreak of war with Japan. This had been recognized as early as January 1942, when the American–British–Dutch–Australian (ABDA) command was activated under the Commander-in-Chief India, General Sir Archibald Wavell, and included the South China Sea and northern and western coasts of Australia as well. ABDA was disbanded when Wavell had to evacuate his headquarters on Java ahead of the Japanese invasion on 1 March 1942. The establishment of SEAC formalized the area as one in which the British, in modern terminology, continued to be the lead nation, with considerable assistance from the Americans.

The need for operations behind Japanese lines had been foreseen before they entered the war. In May 1941 SOE established its Singapore office. This was followed by the organization of 'stay behind' parties to work behind enemy lines, if and when the Japanese attacked. To train these parties, 101 Special Training School (STS) was set up on Singapore Island. When the GOC Malaya Command, Lieutenant-General A. E. Percival, discovered what was afoot, he objected to the scheme on the grounds that it might damage civilian morale.[1] The officer concerned had not seen fit to keep him in the picture, and it is possible that Percival's hostility to the project owed as much to pique as to anything else. The Commander-in-Chief Far East, Air Chief Marshal Sir Robert Brooke-Popham, backed Percival. In November 1941, Percival changed his mind, and instituted a 'stay-behind' policy of his own. By then it was too late. The Japanese landed less than four weeks later. Thus a great opportunity for a properly co-ordinated, well-supported operation to disrupt the Japanese line of communication when they invaded Malaya was lost. Eventually, the parties that were trained, or those few that survived, became part of Force 136. One, led by Major Freddie Spencer Chapman, accounted for the destruction of seven trains, fifteen bridges and forty vehicles, along with killing several hundred Japanese, in a period of about fourteen days during the Japanese advance down the Malay Peninsula in early 1942. From then he was out of touch with SOE, and inactive, until the end of 1943. There were others who operated behind the lines in Malaya, such as Richard Davis and John Broome. Like Spencer Chapman, they would not have survived for long had it not been for the anti-Japanese Chinese Communist guerrillas, the so-called Malayan People's Anti-Japanese Army (MPAJA), consisting exclusively of Chinese. Many Malays collaborated wholeheartedly with the Japanese. Like the Burmans, alluded to earlier, they saw the Japanese as liberators from the colonial yoke of the British, at least to begin with, although the Union of Young Malaya (Kesatuan Melayu Muda (KMM)) kept a tenuous contact with the MPAJA, just in case the Japanese lost the war. Spencer Chapman, and others, lived in the MPAJA jungle camps, were fed by them, and were escorted on their wanderings in the jungle by Chinese Communist guerrillas. Here, as elsewhere, behind-the-lines operations of any duration, by people who were not inhabitants of the country, were only possible with the active support of at least some of the indigenous population. The work of SOE, and Force 136, is outside the scope of this book, except where it touches on others, such as the Jedburghs and SAS, so their many behind-the-lines operations will not be covered further.

One of the earliest behind-the-lines operations in Malaya was the work of yet another organization, Roseforce, commanded by Major Rose of the 2nd Battalion the Argyll and Sutherland Highlanders. The 2nd Argylls, thanks to its dynamic commanding officer, was the only British or Indian unit to have done any proper jungle training in the whole of the moribund Malaya command. On Christmas Eve, a platoon of Royal Marines, survivors from HMS *Prince of Wales*'s Marine detachment, left Singapore to join Roseforce, based at Port Swettenham. From here, on 28 December, Roseforce, using boats of the Perak Flotilla, landed some 140 miles up the west coast of Malaya to attack the lines of communication of the Japanese 5th Division, fighting twenty miles to the south. They set up ambushes, and destroyed a number of trucks. The most satisfying coup was the killing of two senior Japanese staff officers in their cars. On completion, Roseforce withdrew to Port Swettenham. Two days after their return, the Japanese attacked and sank the flotilla's depot ship and most of the craft. This brought the activities of Roseforce behind enemy lines to an end, although they, with the remainder of 2nd Argylls, gave a good account of themselves during the rest of this disastrous campaign; providing one of the few bright spots in an otherwise shameful episode in British military history.

In April 1942, Wavell, by now back in India, ordered that a guerrilla organization be formed to attack the Japanese lines of communication should they invade Assam from Burma. V-Force, as it came to be called, was built around platoons loaned from the Assam Rifles, and augmented by some 1,000 hill tribesmen. The Assam Rifles were a force of five military police battalions maintained by the Assam Government, and composed of Gurkhas commanded by British officers seconded from the Indian Army. As mentioned in earlier chapters the Japanese did not follow up their conquest of Burma until 1944, with their offensives in the Arakan, Kohima and Imphal. Consequently, V-Force's role was changed to intelligence-gathering, and maintaining a line of outposts ahead of the main British units, roughly along the line of the River Chindwin as far as Kalewa, and thence across to the northern Arakan. It was a V-Force outpost that Dominic Neill encountered on the Chindwin on his return journey on Wingate's first expedition.

A remarkable young British woman played a key role in raising a similar group of Naga tribesmen. She was not the only British person to perform this service, but certainly the only woman. Ursula Graham-Bower came of an old service family, and had been educated at Roedean. She hoped to go to Oxford, but her family was too poor to afford the fees, in those pre-state-grant days. Instead she went out to Nagaland before the war, engaged on ethnographical work. She had some Red Cross training, could lance boils and apply dressings. She established a remarkable rapport with the Nagas, who had a fearsome reputation as head-hunters. She remembered:

> I had a camp which was built for me. It was on a spur outside the village. But in order to see the village ceremonies I had to live inside the village

perimeter – that is within the ritual centre of the village. And they would only agree to that if I would agree to be bound by Zemi [one of the branches of the main Naga tribe] law and not stand on my rank as a European. So I agreed to that and it worked out extremely well. And there I stayed for some years. You walked everywhere. It was walk or die.

When the war broke out she was in England, but managed to get back to Nagaland, and joined the Women's Auxiliary Corps (India) (WAC(I)) in 1942. In August 1942, she helped start a 'Watch and Ward' scheme in Nagaland:

It was set up by an ex-Assam Rifles man, a Gurkha officer called Rawdon Wright who had returned from Britain. He had a World War One wound which made him extremely lame. He should never have been allowed in. But he managed to talk me into [allowing] it. His personal courage influenced the Nagas enormously. He refused to be carried – he said he was a soldier. If he died in the road he was not going to be carried. He told me what was wanted. He went back and reported, and I got various papers and instructions. We recruited from the villages which we had decided upon as forming a screen; anything from five to ten men in selected villages which covered passes and key points – fords and main trackways. As a result of the strain he put on himself, poor old Rawdon Wright died three weeks later.

These [Watch and Ward] were intelligence scouts. At first they were very reluctant – it wasn't their war. They just wanted to be left alone. So I talked it over with Namkia [interpreter and leader] and said that I didn't think they would be able to do that [stay uninvolved]. Because if the Japanese were coming through they would come through [*sic*]. The whole area would be fought over. Eventually – and I think it was the sight of British troops [the wounded particularly] that certainly influenced Namkia and his people – they decided to come in. It took a long, long time to get their confidence and get them going. We had to be very very careful to fulfil all our promises about arming them, and giving them authority and paying them and all the rest of it. I must say the Army did fulfil its promises.

We were armed for our own protection. Twenty rifles, two tommy-guns, and my Sten. Plus 150 muzzle loaders and shot guns. I carried a kukri, a Sten gun and a pistol. My father was a very keen shot. I learned to use a rifle when I was twelve. I started on a .22, and while he was still in the Navy he gave my brother and me training on the standard service rifle, the .303. I could use a shotgun and an automatic pistol.

The Army's administration was somewhat dilatory at times:

Some time in the late autumn of 1942 they forgot to send us our usual ration money. They forgot to pay me. I wasn't at the time getting any rations. By the time I had paid the men, 150 of them, I was left with exactly 30 rupees [£2.50] to keep myself and a dog until something turned up. I did 150 miles a month in this mountain country. I lost three stone in weight. Eventually some money came through. After which I got Captain's pay.

Her job was to collect information on the Japanese. Before she was given a radio she sent messages by runner. She also decided that if the Japanese looked like coming close, she would not run away.

If I ran, I knew the Nagas would never hold. That's why I had to stay. But it had its problems. There was no hope I could conceal myself in the Naga village. First of all I am too tall, and light skinned, my hair was sun-bleached. I was blonde, obviously European. In Burma when British officers had occasionally hidden, the Japs tortured the villagers until the officer gave himself up.

I fixed it with Namkia that I wasn't going to be taken alive. So I would shoot myself, and he would take my head in if the pressure on the villagers got unendurable. But it never came to it for which I was devoutly thankful.

The Army wanted me to get out. No women were being left within range of the Japanese; after the massacre of the nurses in Hong Kong all women were evacuated [from Assam]. All the nurses were evacuated from Imphal.

From April 1944 a wireless [radio] network was laid on by 14th Army. There were four posts, each with a signaller and a man to back him up. It was called Bower Force.

When the Japanese assault on Imphal and Kohima (the administrative capital of Nagaland) began:

We were suddenly in the middle of no man's land, utterly bewildered, hardly armed. Sharing no man's land with an unknown number of Japanese. The siege of Kohima was going on. The Japs were all over the Imphal Plain. We had a very dodgy three weeks, not knowing what was going on in front of us, but trying to find out and pass intelligence back.

She was sent a personal bodyguard of a half-section of Assam Rifles, followed by Lieutenant Bill Tibbetts of V-Force. He took over the operations side, and she covered the personnel, administrative and intelligence staff work. After the siege at Kohima was broken, she got permission to throw her OP screen right forward towards the Imphal Plain to find out what was happening there. They stayed there for May and June. From here they were able to get intelligence back from within Japanese-held territory, a distance of about thirty miles; 'three days' walking', according to Ursula Graham-Bower:

> If there was any prospect of bumping the enemy, and we thought we had Japs on our immediate front, and heading towards us, we simply patrolled in military order: a Naga scout 50 yards out in front, and possibly another but not always. Then the first half of the patrol with an officer, and a 50-yard gap, and the second half of the patrol with an officer which in this case was generally me. We went very cautiously along the track or bridle roads, hoping the scout in front would see the enemy first and double back to us. We would take up ambush positions and hope to catch the Japs unawares.

Then they got orders to retreat. It was thought the position was too 'dodgy', in her words. She remembered that there were instances of collaboration with the Japanese by some tribes:

> There were two main tribal groups [in Nagaland]: the Nagas and the Kukis. In 1917, during the First World War the Kukis rose against the British, and were put down with some trouble. But by the Second World War, the British had forgotten this and recruited Kukis for the Assam Rifles because they thought they were better material than the Nagas. The Kukis who had rebelled in 1917 went over to the Japanese almost completely. Again when V-Force was recruited, more Kukis than Nagas were picked.
>
> When my husband [Lieutenant-Colonel F. N. Betts whom she married after the war] was down on the Chindwin in 1944, in V-Force, his scouts were almost exclusively Kukis. He discovered when the Jap advance began his men had been in touch with the Japanese all the time. They betrayed his whereabouts, his food dumps, everything. They led them to his camp. Fortunately he wasn't in at the time.
>
> There was one village which was friendly to the Japs. They took [accepted a bribe of] 100 rupees to bring the Japanese my head. After the 'shouting' [*sic*] was more or less over, Bill Tibbetts [Assam Rifles], and I were touring that area. We came through the village [which] clearly had a very bad conscience. We had our Assam Rifles with us. I think they were afraid we were going to take reprisals. There was no point in doing that. The headman refused to appear at all. A very nervous young man appeared with a bottle

of rice beer and a chicken, and sat looking at us with terror. I was tempted to point out that I was in possession of my head, and the Japanese weren't, and could I please have the 100 rupees which I felt was due to me.

'Watch and Ward' was wound up in November 1944, by which time the Imphal Plain had been clear for some time. To their delight, the Nagas were allowed to keep their shotguns. Ursula Graham-Bower then found that:

V-Force arranged for me [and a team of Nagas] to train RAF personnel in jungle survival. They were faintly surprised at my teaching them survival and ambush techniques. The clearing where the camp was was right on top of an elephant trail. We used to take the men out into the jungle and practise stalking and hunting techniques. One day I found a large bull elephant in the middle of my class. We tiptoed away.

At the end of the course, they [the air crew] were taken out by jeep and dropped off in the jungle about 20 miles away with a compass and emergency rations. They were taught that if you happen to meet a tiger he is probably not hostile. He wants to be left alone. If you hear a deep growl in a thicket, turn round and creep away. He won't interfere with you. One party of two walked in on a tiger, there was a growl in the thicket, and they did creep away. It worked. After that the reputation of the instruction went up a lot.

Later, Slim paid tribute to:

The gallant Nagas whose loyalty, even in the most depressing times of the invasion, had never faltered. Despite floggings, torture, execution and the burning of their villages, they refused to aid the Japanese in any way or betray our troops. Their active help to us was beyond value or praise. Under the leadership of devoted British political officers, some of the finest types of the Indian Civil Service, in whom they had complete confidence, they guided our columns, collected information, ambushed enemy patrols, carried our supplies, and brought in our wounded under the heaviest fire. ... No soldier of the 14th Army who met them will ever think of them but with admiration and affection.[2]

The long-range penetration force that Slim mentions with the most enthusiasm is the Lushai Brigade, formed in March 1944 under Brigadier P. C. Marinden DSO MC. It was an independent brigade group operating directly under 14th Army command. Its task was to hold the Lushai

Hills and harass the Japanese in the Chin Hills. The Lushai Hills were an area the size of Wales, south-west of Imphal. The Chin Hills lie to the east of the Lushai Hills, on one of the principal routes between Burma and Assam through Kalewa. The Lushai Brigade consisted of 1/9th Jats, 7/14th Punjabis, 1st Biharis, Numbers 5 and 8 V-Force groups, 1st Assam Rifles, the Western Chin Levies, and a new unit, the Lushai Scouts, for long-range patrolling. When the pressure on Imphal and the Arakan was lifted by the Japanese defeat, the Lushai Brigade was involved on the flank of 5th Indian Infantry Division in the pursuit to the Chindwin. The Brigade infiltrated on a front of a hundred miles, and by mid-October 1944, had patrols on the east bank of the Chindwin. One of the objectives for the Brigade's operations was an enemy ammunition dump at Gangaw, on the Myittha River, a tributary of the Chindwin. An account written by Captain A. I. Bowman, a V-Force officer, called 'Note on Military Operations in the Lushai Hills and North Arakan 1942–1944', takes up the story:

> This was a very remote area with no communications except crude inter-village paths, in thick jungle. Parsons [Lieutenant-Colonel W. J. Parsons] at Lightning Ridge was assigned this task. He was to move a strong fighting patrol of No 8 V Ops personnel through this rough country to Gangaw. The distance was approximately 60 miles as the crow flies, but the difficult nature of the country, with numerous rivers to cross and ranges of hills to climb, made the going slow. In the Myittha Valley there was an added hazard from scrub typhus. The party included Callaghan the medical officer, who treated several of the riflemen who came down with it, but in spite of this there were several casualties, including Callaghan himself, who died in the Valley and was buried by Parsons personally. The party reached Gangaw, managed to silence a sentry as a preliminary to a night raid, and gained access to the dump for sufficient time for Parsons to set his explosives. As a result of his efforts the whole dump was destroyed. The Japanese were taken completely by surprise. They apparently had not thought that a patrol could come so far behind their front line without being spotted. Parsons was able to withdraw his men without casualties and to bring them back to Lushai. As a result of his escapade, the Japanese were unable to continue in occupation of Haka (the Chin tribal capital) and withdrew.

Slim, possibly with Wingate in mind, was to write of the activities of the Lushai Brigade:

There is no doubt that the enterprise and dash of this improvised and lighthearted brigade were a very real contribution to the pursuit to the Chindwin. It had operated for six months on pack transport, supplemented by an unavoidably meagre air supply, across two hundred miles of jungly mountains against the enemy flank and rear. Considering the paucity of its equipment and resources, it gave one of the most effective and economical examples of long-range penetration.[3]

Parsons, an Australian explosives expert, was an extremely tough customer indeed. For a while he had been working for British intelligence in Thailand, before it became too dangerous for him to continue, and he was posted to V-Force in the Lushai Hills. His nickname in V-Force was the 'Vicar'. The year before the attack on Gangaw, as part of the reconnaissance and intelligence effort preceding operations in the Arakan, Number 8 V Operations was to move down the Kaladan Valley, to push out units of the Burma Defence Army (BDA), and set up posts from which patrolling could take place.[4] Parsons took two sections of Assam Rifles, and four other British officers, including Captains Bowman and Creech. After a reconnaissance by Bowman, Parsons decided to attack a BDA post near the village of Kaletwa on the Kaladan River. The party was to approach down a tributary river, the Sekul Lui, in canoes. Bowman takes up the story in a personal account:

> The 'Vicar' was not his usual ebullient self. I soon discovered why. He had been taken into hospital in Calcutta with a stone in his bladder. Efforts to dislodge it or crush it had been unsuccessful, and he was told that he would be in for several days, with a period of convalescence to follow. This meant that he would not be able to take command of operations in the North Arakan Section. Preparations were well advanced and it was important that it [the attack on Kaletwa] should not be held up.

Some years before, when Parsons had been serving on a remote island in the Solomons, he had taken out one of his teeth with the assistance of a Chinese servant, and a pair of forceps dropped to him by light aircraft, without anaesthetic. As Bowman remarks:

> This was the calibre of man who now refused to remain in hospital when he felt he should be with his command. He signed himself out, took a train to Chittagong, and came up [to join us]. On the [150-mile] march over the hills he produced the offending stone by natural and very painful methods,

over a period of time, working gradually out through the urinary tract. One of the first things he did when he met me was to produce a matchbox and show me the stone. Having shown me his stone, he then proceeded to tick me off for my reports on the track [which Bowman had reconnoitred earlier].

At the conference before marching to the place where they would conduct the final reconnaissance before embarking in the dugout canoes, Bowman:

> began to shiver and knew that I was starting another bout of malaria. The 'Vicar' spotted me. He was, naturally, annoyed that I should choose this juncture to have malaria. I said it wasn't very bad, and that I would manage all right. But he said he didn't want a sick man on his hands during his recce and ordered me to stay that night and come on with the main party next day, if I could. I was utterly ashamed and miserable, but the 'Vicar' would not change his mind, and set off. I got hold of some quinine, and crawled under a pile of puans (blankets) to sweat out the fever.
>
> Next morning I still had a temperature of 103°, according to my thermometer, and I was confident I could march with it. I had no intention of being left behind.

After dealing with a minor ambush on the way to the river, Bowman's party embarked in six dugouts to paddle downriver to rendezvous with Parsons. By now it was dark, with no moon. There was a fair current running, and it was difficult to see the rapids and rocks. The boatmen, two to each canoe, were reluctant to proceed, but were persuaded to do so. None of the Assam Riflemen had been in any sort of canoe before. At one of the most powerful rapids, Bowman's canoe capsized, and as he struggled in the water, was nearly hit by the bow of Creech's sweeping down on him from astern. Eventually, he and his boatmen righted their canoe, which had snagged on some rocks, and he with all his riflemen re-embarked and paddled on. At the rendezvous:

> As we pulled in beside the other canoes, I heard Bill Creech say to the 'Vicar' in a low voice, 'I'm afraid Bowman's dead. He was drowned in the rapids on the way down.'
>
> The 'Vicar' replied somewhat petulantly, 'Bugger Bowman.'
>
> Pulling my canoe up besides theirs, I said, 'Bowman reporting from the dead, sir.'

'About time too,' said the 'Vicar', whose sense of humour was never very far away, even in times of stress. He was, however, in a very worried mood, mainly because he was very ill, although he managed to conceal this from us.

The attack on the post was successful. The defenders ran away leaving a quantity of arms and ammunition, and some papers which provided information on the Thakin communications network, and a traitor among the tribesmen at Bowman's base camp. The V-Force party suffered no casualties. Another similar attack was carried out about a month later; this time the Assam Riflemen travelled on rafts, with the British officers in canoes.

From time to time throughout the war against Japan, attacks were mounted by a variety of means, on enemy shipping in harbours at points along the occupied coastline. The bulk of these attacks were carried out by American carrier- and land-based aircraft, but some by clandestine means, such as the one on Phuket harbour in Thailand by Chariots in October 1944.[5] Perhaps the most audacious attack was Operation Jaywick, in September 1943. This undoubtedly qualifies as a behind-the-lines affair since the target, Singapore harbour, lay some 1,500 miles inside Japanese-controlled waters; it was ringed with enemy occupied islands and patrolled regularly by sea and air.

The operation was the brainchild, one might say almost obsession, of Major Ivan Lyon, Gordon Highlanders. He had been involved in SOE activities in Singapore, and when the island was about to fall to the Japanese had been ordered to leave, along with a number of other SOE operatives. After an epic escape across Sumatra and the Indian Ocean to Ceylon, he managed to persuade Wavell that a raid mounted from Australia would be possible. A key ingredient in his plan was the use of a captured Japanese fishing boat, the *Kofuka Maru*, which had been taken to Bombay by escapees from Singapore. This boat, renamed the *Krait*, after a small but deadly snake, was eventually shipped to Sydney in a freighter. When Lyon arrived in Australia, he was put under command of the Services Reconnaissance Department (SRD). This was a cover name for Special Operations Australia (SOA), part of SOE, some of whose members became SOA's nucleus after escaping from Singapore. Despite considerable opposition from the Commander South-West Pacific Area, General Douglas MacArthur, Lyon managed to obtain backing for Jaywick from the Australian Army and Navy. Lyon's passion for attacking Singapore was fuelled by the knowledge that his wife and child were prisoners in Singapore; and he appears to have harboured a personal vendetta against the Japanese on that particular island on that account.

Lyon was fortunate to find an outstanding man as his second-in-command; a huge, enormously strong English RNVR lieutenant, D. M. N. Davidson. He had once been a jackeroo (cowboy) in Queensland. But more to the point, he was an expert canoeist who had once canoed the length of the River Chindwin when serving in the forestry department in Burma. On the outbreak of war, he had been commissioned in the Burma Frontier Force, but transferred to the RNVR in Singapore. He had escaped to Australia by small boat via Borneo, and joined his family in Melbourne.

Together they selected seventeen others from among forty volunteers for 'Special Service' at the Flinders Naval Depot. Six were further weeded out on a six-week selection course run by Davidson. Then began a three-month period of rigorous training in Folbots, use of limpet mines and survival. At the end of this Davidson made the final selection of five. To these were added Lyon's batman, Corporal Morris, who was a Welsh ex-miner and trained RAMC medical orderly, a leading stoker and a gunner, both from the RAN. The next problem was to get the *Krait* round from Sydney to Exmouth Gulf on the north-west coast of Western Australia. Her journey up the east coast of Australia, into the Torres Strait, and from there on the 2,400-mile leg to Exmouth Gulf was an epic in itself. She broke down four times. At Cairns in Queensland she acquired a navigator, Sub-Lieutenant H. E. Carse RANVR, a character with a somewhat chequered background, including time in the RAN, school-teaching, gold-digging, factory cleaner, running a camel team and a betting shop. He persuaded Lyon that the *Krait* needed a new engine, and after a long search, a suitable diesel (a Gardiner six cylinder, 105 horsepower) and a new propeller were found and fitted. On her arrival at the RAN Base at Exmouth Gulf, *Krait* embarked new Folbots. These had small silk sails, and their skins were of seven-ply rubber and canvas, making them difficult to hole.

No sooner had *Krait* set out from Exmouth Gulf than her propeller shaft broke. It was brazed together back at the RAN Base, and she finally motored off on 2 September 1943, with the Base engineer's warning ringing in Lyon's ears that the shaft might break at any time. Davidson kept a log, and he lists the crew as follows:

Major I. Lyon MBE The Gordon Highlanders	Captain
Lieut H. E. Carse RANVR	Navigator
Lieut D. M. N. Davidson RNVR	1st Lieut
Lieut R. C. Page AIF	Med Offr
Ldg Stoker J. P. McDowell	Ch Engr
Ldg Tel H. G. Young	W/T Operator
Cpl R. Morris BEM RAMC	Med Orderly
Cpl A. A. Crilly AIF	Cook
Able Seaman K. P. Cain	Seaman
Able Seaman A. W. Jones	Seaman
Acting A/B W. G. Falls	Seaman
Acting A/B F. W. Marsh	Seaman
Acting A/B M. Berryman	Seaman
Acting A/B A. W. G. Huston	Seaman

The morning after leaving Exmouth Gulf, Lyon assembled his men and briefed them. The *Krait* would transit the Lombok Strait into the Java Sea, and head for a suitable island off Singapore, from where three canoes would be launched to attack shipping in the Roads or in the harbour. The canoe teams would consist of Lyon and Huston, Davidson and Falls, and Page and Jones. Marsh and Berryman were reserve crew. Lyon also told them that from the following day on they would fly the Japanese flag, and there would only be two men on deck in daylight; the helmsman and one forward. They would stain themselves with a dark stain, in the hope they would be taken for local fishermen. There was to be no smoking without permission. No lavatory paper would be used; sea water would be used instead.

Davidson's log (all the following extracts in the account of Jaywick are from his log):

Sunday 5th September
06.30. Clear and calm. Light SE breeze.

Completed painting bodies. The dye is a bad one. Sweat brings it off, and oil does likewise, and clothes rub it off. It cakes black round the beard, moustache and hair, and rubs to a light brown in prominent parts. Most unconvincing near to, but perhaps effective in general from afar.

They believed from the 'pilot' (book of information for mariners) for this area that at this time of year they could expect a low haze to cover their approach to the Lombok Strait, but the information was incorrect.

Wednesday 8th September
The author of the local pilot needs his nose rubbing in it.

Krait had great difficulty transiting the Lombok Strait because of strong tide rips that exceeded her maximum speed.

Thursday 9th September
This morning the thrice-accursed Nusa Besar [island south of the entrance to the Lombok Strait] is still in sight approximately 10 miles on the port quarter. How we detest that island.

After two tries, and two days, she made it but taking thirteen hours, the first six in strong moonlight, and the last three and a half in broad daylight. The planning had been less than perfect, because they should have known that the tide flowed south for most of the night during the periods they were transiting the Straits.

Once out in the Java Sea they were safer, they could turn away from shipping, and by keeping to the shallower water, avoid the bigger vessels. They shaped course so their track took them out of sight of, but close to, the Borneo coast. In the original plan, *Krait* was to drop off the attack teams at Durian Island, in the Rhio Archipelago, about thirty-five miles south of Singapore, and go to Sumatra to lie up in a river mouth. The canoe team would paddle across to join her after the raid. However, Lyon and the other officers decided that Durian Island was too close to the busy shipping lanes, and also that it would be far better if, having dropped them off, *Krait* cruised off Borneo as if fishing, instead of lurking in a river mouth which might look suspicious. The first drop-off point they reconnoitred was Pompong Island. Here they buried emergency rations and a drum of water. Just before arriving a Japanese aircraft flew past them about a mile and a half away, followed later by a seaplane which flew low across them. Neither appeared to take any notice of *Krait*, which was good because it proved that their disguise as a Japanese fishing boat could stand up to inspection, from the air at least. The next morning, they were spotted by a Malay. So *Krait* headed north, still searching for a suitable drop-off beach. A number of Japanese aircraft passed quite close, again showing no apparent interest.

Friday 17th September
Spirits have been excellent; very high morale, which is a very satisfactory feature. It's a good bunch this.

Eventually, they decided on Pandjang Island for the drop off. But as this was too close to a Japanese OP on Galang Island, which had revealed itself by shining a searchlight, the pick-up would have to be from Pompong, to avoid visiting the same place twice. The kit was ferried ashore on Pandjang, and before dawn *Krait*, under Carse's command, was heading for the open sea.

September 18th
06.00. At dawn a family of nine otters were seen playing in the pools amongst the rocks. We named our bay the 'Bay of Otters'. A reconnaissance discovered a village abreast of Otter Bay on the other side of the island ½ a mile away, but no connecting tracks.

There was fresh water available from a small watercourse that came down to the beach. They spent the next two days getting ready, unpacking the canoes, and trying to exercise muscles, slack after nearly forty days at sea since leaving Sydney. Each night and morning, a Japanese motor launch would cruise slowly past their beach. On 20 September they dressed in black two-piece suits of waterproofed silk, closed at the wrist and ankles. They wore black sandshoes, and were armed with a .38-inch revolver and a hundred rounds. On each man's belt he carried a knife, compass and first-aid kit. Lyon had cyanide capsules, which would kill in five seconds, to issue before the attack. Each canoe carried 600 lb of equipment, including limpets, rations and survival kit.

September 20th
We loaded up and went on our way, leaving the Bay of Otters at 19.25. The first move in the 'Attack'.

After paddling about eleven miles they hauled out at Bulat Island, sore and tired. It was small and uninhabited, about 200 yards across and 30 feet high, timbered and rocky.

[we] stowed the canoes & loads as far in amongst the scrub as the darkness permitted, intending to hide them securely at dawn. Dropped on to the sand above the high water mark & slept till dawn.

September 21st

Today started badly. With the dawn came a motor sampan, flying the Japanese merchant ensign. It stopped its engine within a cable [200 yards] of us, and drifted inshore almost on top of us, while its crew held a protracted breakfast meeting. The canoes were fairly plainly visible from offshore. An hour later the motor boat [*sic*] departed without so much as having glanced at our island.

They were very lucky indeed, and they learned the lesson, never to rest until the canoes and kit were properly stowed and camouflaged. The next night, they had a hard paddle, and great difficulty finding a lying-up position. Finally they had to settle for a mangrove swamp, but only quarter of a mile from a village.

The noise we made stumbling & crashing around in those mangroves in the dark with heavy canoes & cumbersome gear was agonising. All was stowed after a fashion by 05.30, & we lay down on slimy roots and squelchy rocks and got some sort of sleep until dawn.

They had a nerve-racking day, as Malay craft and assorted motor boats came past very close all day.

September 22nd

Managed to get 1½ hours' fitful and uncomfortable sleep during the morning.

12.00 a thunderstorm broke. We caught water in canoe groundsheets, and filled our empty water containers, drank absurdly copious draughts, made tea (with Burnzo fires [smokeless fuel cookers]), soaked the dung and chaff they call M&V [meat & vegetables] in the rations, washed, did everything we could with fresh water, and immensely raised our spirits.

I can think of few situations more 'wet' than a Malayan mangrove swamp at high water in a thunderstorm, & no waterproof protection. But what a joy that rain was.

The next night they paddled to the small island of Dongas, and went ashore. The island was ideal, small, uninhabited, with water, and a good lookout position some forty feet high from where they could see Singapore eight miles away.

September 23rd

By night Singapore appears as brightly lit as of yore. Even motor car lights do not appear to be dimmed.

They planned to attack on the night of 26/27 September, from another island, as the tidal set would make the approach from Dongas Island very difficult. However, from the lookout, using a powerful telescope, Lyon spotted thirteen ships in Singapore Roads. This was too good a target to miss, and they decided to attack that night despite the tide. However, it proved too strong. After desperate paddling, being illuminated by a searchlight, with a long way to go, and only five hours of darkness left, they reluctantly turned their canoes back towards Dongas.

This was the bitterest moment yet.

The strongly running tide, and the difficulty of navigating with compasses badly affected by limpets and holdfasts (big magnets to hold on to ships' sides when placing limpets) in the canoe cockpits, instead of stowed some distance away, resulted in the canoes becoming split up. Lyon and Huston were missing all day, eventually turning up that evening, having lain up in a swamp. The previous night's disappointment convinced Davidson, who was responsible for the actual attack plan, that Dongas was unsuitable as a place from which to paddle to Singapore. That night, after another exhausting paddle, they landed on Subor Island. Daylight revealed nine ships at anchor off Singapore. Davidson decided that he and Falls would attack Keppel Harbour, and if there were no ships there, they would go on into Singapore Roads. Lyon and Huston were to attack shipping in the Examination Anchorage, and Page and Jones were to attack shipping off Pulau Bukum.

The rendezvous with *Krait* was midnight 1 October, and it was now 26 September, it was attack that night or not at all. It was decided that Davidson, who had the fastest Folbot, and was by far the strongest, would try to reach Pompong first to hold the *Krait* for the others.

From this time on Davidson's log covers only his, and his canoe partner Fall's, activity; although he clearly intended to record the actions of the others when he could debrief them, he apparently never did. Davidson and Falls paddled to where he remembered the boom at the entrance to Keppel Harbour had been:

September 26th
The boom appeared to be in exactly the same place as of old, and in excellent repair. It was open with no boom vessel in attendance.

They could not find suitable targets in Keppel Harbour, so passed through the boom again, and found plenty of ships in the Roads. They picked three medium-sized cargo vessels, the biggest they could see.

We attacked in each case on the port side as it was away from Singapore lights. Fortunately our work was dead silent without any hitches or clanging. Falls with the magnetic holdfasts was absolutely expert. We had been timing ourselves by the ¼ hourly chimes of the clock (probably on Victoria Hall) in the direction of St Andrew's Cathedral. Our time to approach, limpet & get away averaged 20 minutes per ship, a lot of this being taken up by the approach. Ships were lying 4 cables (800 yards) apart about.

01.15. Left the Roads at a moderate speed, taking our time in view of the longish run to the Rhio Straits. Limpets had been set to go off at 05.30, (switches being pulled at 23.30, with orange or 6–6½-hour ampoules). Given the maker's 15% error, one hour, the earliest expected would be 04.30. But at 03.00 a loud explosion, muffled as if under water was heard in the general direction of Keppel Harbour. We were by then only about 11 miles away from the Roads. Our speed increased to phenomenal heights, but no excitement occurred in Singapore.

They were heading for the Rhio Strait, which was the longer way back to Pompong, but avoided using much of the route used on the way north. They made Batam Island before dawn and lay up in a coconut grove.

September 27th
The second explosion was heard (time possibly ½ hour out). Between now and daylight 4 more were heard. So six limpets certainly exploded.

19.00. Got away against the tide.

Despite this they covered the first six miles in two hours. From 22.00 hours they had the tide with them, but made slow progress, because of fishing boats and other craft. After trying six landing places, before daybreak they found somewhere to lie up in a rocky inlet near a whole herd of seals.

September 28th
19.00 Punctually away against the tide. Took things easily and made reasonable headway at about 2½ knots.

Again they found considerable stealth was required when they were forced by the narrow channel to pass close to fishing boats. However, they were making good time heading for Pandjang (the drop-off island), when:

> up cropped that damned patrol boat, & we had to head for the shadows ashore. The launch passed us with sound of talking voices aboard her, but without suspecting our presence. Went round the bay to Panjang; a great waste of time. Just beached our canoe in the Bay of Otters, when a storm which had been threatening for an hour broke, bringing wind, high surf, & torrential rain. We kept a dry spot on which to lie and, with the ground-sheet over us as a blanket and waterproof slept until dawn.
>
> *September 29th*
> An idyllic day of rest and staunch eating [from cached food], including many tinned delicacies. Left a note among the 'dump' of gear for Lyon to tell him we had gone to hold the *Krait* at Pompong.
>
> 19.00 Punctually away into the lowering night.

They were heading for Abang Besar, when the storm:

> Like the wrath of God gathered from all the cardinal points and broke right above us. A screaming wind, lashing the calm sea into a maelstrom of breaking waves and thrashing spray, rapidly worked the sea into a very for-midable danger. The thunder and lightning were magnificent, the lighting left one utterly blinded for nearly a minute. Then came the rain. The only thing possible and safe was to keep the canoe head into the sea and wind. With eyes tight shut [because of the driving spray] and steering by the feel of the wind on our faces we rode out nearly two hours of this. When the wind dropped we had cause to thank heaven for the rain. In five minutes the sea was flat. The canoe behaved admirably. She rode the seas perfectly.

By the illumination of the lightning which persisted all night, they found a good lying-up position on Abang Besar.

> *September 30th*
> A restful day spent in idleness and sleep.
>
> 1900. Left on the last lap to Pulau [Island] Pompong. Our last two miles [in strong tide rips] were a sturdy fight, but we were in bed before 01.00, the shortest night yet.
>
> *October 1st*
> Another quiet and restful day. No alarms to distract us. At dark we moved to Fisherman's Bay for our rendezvous with *Krait*, who appeared at 00.15.

In this matter of fact way, Davidson described what must be one of the most remarkable canoe journeys ever made in wartime, or any other time. In four nights of paddling, these two, following several nights of equally hard work to approach the target, covered some eighty-five miles. They had had very little sleep for the previous thirteen days, and were constantly either wet and cold, or very hot and sweaty.

The other two canoe teams had also managed to place their limpets. After the war it was confirmed that in total the Jaywick teams sank seven ships. The two canoes with Lyon and Huston, and Page and Jones returned to Dongas before dawn, where they spent the day. The waters round Singapore were like a disturbed bees' nest, with patrol boats buzzing here and there, and aircraft overhead. They reached Pandjang Island using the direct route, early on 29 September and found Davidson's note. Having spent that day, and the night resting, they aimed to paddle to Pompong on the night of 30 September. A violent storm on the night of the 30th prevented them leaving. To make the 1 October RV with *Krait*, Lyon decided to risk a daylight paddle to Pompong. He wanted to avoid *Krait* having to take the risk of returning to the RV a second time; the procedure that had been arranged should they miss the first RV. The two canoes arrived eighteen hours later at what they thought was the RV on Pompong, after a shatteringly exhausting and nerve-racking thirty-mile paddle. There was no sign of the *Krait*.

The next morning, they woke to see the *Krait* about a mile offshore, heading away, having picked up Davidson and Falls during the night. They realized they were on the wrong beach. However, she was due back in forty-eight hours. After moving to the correct RV, the long, agonizing wait began. There was always a possibility that *Krait*, their only hope of getting home, would be stopped and taken by the Japanese. To their joy and relief, she appeared off the beach on the night of 3 October.

On their return they had a heart-stopping encounter with a Japanese destroyer as they were chugging at full speed through the Lombok Strait, this time with the tide rip under *Krait*'s tail. For a time the destroyer kept pace with them. They decided if called alongside to board and fight it out. If this was not possible, they would ram and detonate the explosives in *Krait*, hoping to sink, or badly damage, the destroyer, as well as annihilating themselves and their craft. For some reason, the destroyer turned away after some minutes. On 19 October *Krait* arrived back at Exmouth Gulf, after forty-seven days away from base and having been behind the lines for thirty-three, travelling some 5,000 miles. Not a single man was lost on Jaywick.

Lyon's fixation with attacking Singapore was to be the death of him and all his men, including Davidson, when exactly a year later, he attempted another operation, Rimau (Malay for tiger). The full story of this operation will probably never be told, because there were no survivors from the attack party, who either died in engagements with the Japanese in the islands south of Singapore or were executed after capture.

What about the 'return on investment' of Lyon's operations? Jaywick probably represents a good return; a handful of men travelled in a battered old fishing boat, attacked in three cheap canoes, and sank seven cargo ships. Japan relied on her cargo ships for her survival, and Lyon's men accounted for over twice as many Japanese merchant ships as were sunk by British land-based aircraft in the war (three). Perhaps more important was the morale factor. The raid struck deep into Japanese territory at a time when, after fourteen months of war, and despite their victory on Guadalcanal, the Americans were still thousands of miles from what the Japanese called 'The Southern Resources Area'.[6] The Japanese Empire was hardly dented yet. Jaywick, also, is an example of a 'stand alone' operation. Contact with the locals was avoided, the canoes and *Krait* provided the means of mobility; and the expertise of the party is self-evident.

Rimau is a different story, even had it succeeded, which was always highly problematic. Certainly the SRD regarded it as highly dangerous, but it was strongly supported by Mountbatten, possibly for propaganda reasons to demonstrate that the British and Australians were staging a come-back in the South China Sea after the shameful surrender of Singapore two and a half years earlier. The operation was much more expensive in resources than Jaywick. A submarine, HMS *Porpoise* was used to take the team to the operating area; and another, HMS *Tantalus*, was supposed to pick them up. Both submarines survived this operation. The Rimau attack party consisted of thirty-two men, some Folbots, limpet mines and fifteen motor submersible canoes (MSCs). A great deal of time and effort had been spent developing MSCs by CODC, not, it must be said, just for Lyon; but wasted nevertheless. There is no record of these craft ever being used successfully on an operation; and their performance on trials, and training with the Rimau team, showed that they were more dangerous to the operators than the target. Rimau was not quite a 'stand alone' operation. It relied for success on capturing a junk in the waters around Singapore, in itself a weak link in the plan; fatal as it turned out. After some fruitless attempts to find a suitable junk, a prahu (a rather different type of vessel) with a Malay crew was captured. It was painted white, conspicuously new, of a type rarely found in waters in the vicinity of Singapore, and, more serious, had no engine. Within twelve miles of Singapore, the junk was challenged by a Malay patrol craft, and Lyon's men, having ditched the MSCs, fled in their Folbots. Recent research indicates that Lyon and some of the party used Folbots and limpets to attack three merchant ships in the approaches to Singapore. But the Rimau party was tracked down over the ensuing days and weeks when the crew of the patrol boat reported their presence to the Japanese. Perhaps the most telling argument against attacking the Japanese merchant fleet in the way intended by Rimau was that it was rendered superfluous by the toll on Japanese shipping being exacted by submarines on the sea-lanes by late 1944, the vast majority sunk by the Americans, a few by the British. By the end of the war a total of 1,153 Japanese merchant ships had been accounted for by submarines, and a further 722 by carrier and land-based aircraft. Another 260 were sunk by mines, many of which were laid by submarine. *Porpoise* was a minelaying submarine.

In June 1944, as part of the preparations for a series of amphibious operations being planned in SEAC, the activities of all the small units in the Theatre involved in beach reconnaissance, and other amphibious advance-force operations, were brought under the command of the Small-Operations Group (SOG). The SOG was based in Ceylon with Mountbatten's SEAC Headquarters. The units involved were: the COPPs; SB Sections; the Sea Reconnaissance Unit (SRU); and, later, Detachment 385.

The SRU had been founded by Lieutenant-Commander Bruce Wright RCNVR, after visiting the RMBPD (see Chapter 5). During Mountbatten's tenure at COHQ, he had sold him the concept of reconnaissance or attack by long-distance swimmers on paddle-boards, rather like the Malibu boards used by surfers. The swimmer lay on the board, with miniature paddles, about the size of ping-pong bats, strapped on each hand, and would paddle into the coast from up to twenty miles out, having been dropped by parachute with his board. The paddler steered by compass set in the board. This unit saw little action, and perhaps the most valuable contribution made to attack and reconnaissance swimming techniques by Wright were the long fins and American pattern single-window diving mask, soon adopted by all British swimmers (see Chapter 5).

Detachment 385 was a Royal Marine unit trained in Ceylon by Lieutenant-Colonel Hasler, the founder of the RMBPD, and became operational in March 1945. The 122-strong Detachment consisted of canoeists and parachutists. This unit seems to have been dogged by misfortune. Of the eighteen operations it carried out, eight were failures. Three of the remaining ten were only partially successful. Of the seven deemed to have achieved their mission, four involved setting up dumps on the coasts of Thailand and Malaya, and at least two others involved deception operations whose effectiveness is difficult to assess. Had the war with Japan continued into 1946, or even 1947, as predicted, there might have been fruitful opportunities for Detachment 385 in the amphibious operations being planned in the SEAC Theatre.

Most of the 170 or so operations carried out under the auspices of the SOG were by the COPPs and SB Sections. The techniques they used were the same as those described already, and used in preparation for the invasions in Italy, Normandy and the south of France. However, the environment in which they worked was different; and amphibious operations in the Far East Theatre presented problems for the planners too. Not least much of the basic data did not exist: meteorological information; coastal pilots; even Michelin guides, had all been on hand when planning operations in Europe. Even the ploy of calling for private holiday snapshots would have produced a meagre harvest of information, for along the hundreds of thousands of miles of coastline in SEAC, there were few pre-war holiday resorts. The distance to the targets was also far greater than across the English Channel, or even the Mediterranean. Mangrove swamp, mud, shallow water and reefs made the approaches to many beaches difficult; as did the numerous small fishing boats, sampans and other local craft. Many of the people, Burmans, Malays, Thais, Sumatrans and Javanese, were either cowed into submission, or still collaborating openly with the Japanese.

The COPPs and SB Sections carried out some fine work in SEAC, but by their very nature their exploits do not fall within the qualification of behind the lines, and are therefore outside the scope of this book. Again this is partly explained by the fact that the war against Japan finished unexpectedly early.

On 9 September 1944, a meeting was held at Meerut in India, presided over by Brigadier D. R. Guinness, the Chief of Staff, Force 136, to examine how the Jedburghs might be used in SEAC. Here it was agreed that the British Jedburghs could be used in Burma in three ways:

(a) Teams as they now stand, to develop the potentialities of Burmese resistance, organised in the first place by Billet.[7] If Billet goes well this will be ideal ground [for the resistance], and language difficulties will not be serious as the Billet Burmans speak English.

(b) Teams, reinforced by Karen officers or English-speaking ORs used in Karenni as nuclei of Karen resistance groups.

(c) Teams reinforced by Burmese-speaking officers forming Special Groups as now constituted. It was suggested that the Special Groups should act as a bodyguard to the Jedburghs until they have raised local guerrillas.

The matter of American Jedburghs in China, Dutch Jedburghs in the Dutch East Indies and British Jedburghs in Malaya was also discussed at this meeting. As we are concerned here with only British Jedburgh teams, and the war ended before any could be dropped in Malaya, the story will be confined to their activities in Burma. It was agreed that there was a need for fourteen Jedburgh Teams for Burma to be in at any one time, a total of twenty officers and fourteen radio operators (some teams had two officers). To maintain teams on the ground throughout, it was considered that some thirty-five officers and fifty-six radio operators would need to be found. Of the British Jedburghs who served in France, seventeen officers and twelve radio operators volunteered for service in the Far East. At this time the end of the war against Japan was eleven months away, but those attending the meeting had no way of knowing this. Indeed, one of them, Lieutenant-Colonel G. R. Musgrave, said that 'the war against Japan might last another six years'. A somewhat gloomy assessment.

Force 136, with whom the Jedburghs in Burma were to work, was not, by the reckoning of many of its own officers, enjoying a high reputation at this stage of the campaign. It lacked the support of the Burmans, absolutely vital if it was to be effective. It was distrusted by

Wavell, who as we have seen usually supported such organizations. That he did not is perhaps a commentary on their lack of effectiveness to date. His views were reflected down the chain of command, especially by Slim. Without Mountbatten's backing, it is likely that Force 136 would have been thrown out of the Theatre, or sidelined as a private army of SEAC. Finally there were few officers who spoke Burmese. Force 136 had high hopes of the Jedburghs:

> Being Jacks-of-all-Trades, and having had operational experience, they would supply the technical knowledge necessary and be able to train their Groups in the elementary use of weapons and explosives. . . . Finally, having had experience of dealing with men of such varying political beliefs as Gaullists, French Communists and supporters of Giraud, and having come out with a masterly reputation and we hope with no capitalist or imperialistic intentions towards Burma, they would appear true allies . . . as in France.

As noted in Chapter 6 the Karens, Kachins and Chins, unlike the Burmans, had always been pro-British and anti-Japanese. By now the Burmans began to think that the Japanese were worse than the British and had formed an Anti-Fascist Organization (AFO). They produced a Manifesto which started:

> Drive out the Japanese Fascist barbarians.

And included statements such as:

> Our monks are most shamefully ill-treated. Our women are made to stand naked to be searched, are raped, are made prostitutes, or are left behind in a state of pregnancy.

For some time there was dissension among the British staffs and commanders over the matter of arming the AFO, and hence the wisdom of sending in the Jedburghs to people other than the Karens and Kachins. It was pointed out to Mountbatten by the commander of Force 136 that not to arm the AFO would create an embittered opposition when the British eventually reconquered Burma. This would be seized upon by the Americans with their jaundiced views on British Imperialism. One American is alleged to have said that SEAC stood for 'Save England's Asiatic Colonies'. The situation would be further aggravated because the Kachins, Karens and Arakanese were about to be armed. If the communist MPAJA learned that the British were averse to arming left-wing groups in Burma, it could have disastrous consequences when the invasion of Malaya took place.

The arguments ebbed and flowed, and as one of those against, also a senior soldier, said:

> The members of the Anti-Fascist Organisation are not patriots, such as the Maquis in France. They are disgruntled elements who have backed the wrong horse, and who are endeavouring to cover their bets.

This was perfectly true, but soldiers sometimes have to swallow the political stew, however disgusting it tastes. In the end Mountbatten agreed that the AFO be armed.

Oliver Brown had been sent out to organize the training camp in Ceylon. He was supposed to have a long leave on his return from France, but was summoned by Gubbins to start the unit in the Far East, to be operational by the end of 1944.

> When we arrived at ME 25 [training camp and HQ] we found that its [Force 136's] role was to work to Slim for Burma, and for Malaya, Indo-China, and Dutch East Indies to work to the authorities responsible for those areas. We found it different from what we had expected, with such a huge area of operations, and many races. My unit had eighteen different cookhouses, because one lot wouldn't eat what the other would eat. None of us had been to the Far East before, we hadn't got a clue what we were about. I said we would operate exactly like we would in England, and correct it as we went along. The people out there said, 'You can't do that. You can't work through the siesta.'
>
> I got on to Delhi asking for a Jemadar [Indian officer with a commission from the Viceroy not the King], a 2ic, and an Adjutant. After they arrived I asked the Adjutant if he could make out a rail warrant.
>
> He said, 'Yes.'
>
> I said, 'Can you make three out?'
>
> 'Yes.'
>
> 'Make three out, one for the 2ic, one for the Jemadar Sahib, one for yourself, destination Delhi, train the earliest one possible. You're the most useless three I've ever seen in my life.'
>
> We formed up the various teams to go into Burma, first to the Arakan, to the Shans, and then the Character Operation to the Karen Hills. We had very few casualties out there. We thought we would have many more. I didn't enjoy working in the Far East as much as in Europe, although

personally it was a more important job really. I had more responsibility. My heart wasn't really in the Far East.

Mountbatten was very difficult to work for. I admired him, but disliked him. He was far too bombastic. He thought he was God.

Some of the Jedburghs sent to Ceylon had a long period of jungle training, others clearly arrived before Oliver Brown had had a chance to reorganize the system. Aubrey Trofimov:

We had two weeks' jungle training. It was not very good or thorough training on some of the aspects of living in the jungle.

Others did no jungle training at all before their first operation, as Dick Rubinstein relates:

I went to the Far East on the trooper *Otranto*, to Bombay, and on to a camp outside Colombo called ME 25. Already one of the teams had been taken away because just at this time Aung San the Burmese who had originally sided with the Japs was about to change sides. They were dropped in and met Aung San in the Arakan.

Instead of being sent on a jungle training course, I was sent to join Hugo Hood and his wireless operator Ken Brown and as Team Cheetah we were dropped into an operation called Dilwyn in the Kachin Hills in front of Chiang Kai-shek who was advancing down the Burma Road. Dilwyn consisted of a lad who had worked in Burma before the war called Bill Howe and a Kachin commissioned officer, and they wanted to step up their ops, so we were dropped into them in January 1945. Bringing our radio meant we could operate two HQs. There were two roads we wanted to cover, a north–south road going from Hsenwi to Kutkai, and an east–west road from Hsenwi to Kunlong [south of Bhamo]. I stayed with Bill Howe. It was a matter of making a nuisance of ourselves on the fringes of the Japanese who were withdrawing on both roads. The job lasted about month. Chiang Kai-shek's troops came into the area, and were an immediate threat. They were a band of brigands demanding tribute as they went. Hugo Hood and I and Ken Brown were told to come out. We were to bring with us anyone who would be prepared to work with us in lower Burma, and be prepared to parachute. The rest of the team became a British Frontier Police. It was a good textbook operation.

On Dick Rubinstein's return to Ceylon he:

teamed up with people who had come out of Europe, some of whom had done some jungle training. I teamed up with Dick Livingstone who had come out of Greece. I had scratched myself surfing, and it started to go septic. While operating in Burma we were always sent through Calcutta [for briefing]. Here we were told we were Team Chimp and should have dropped just north of Rangoon, to make a nuisance of ourselves as the 14th Army drove down towards Mandalay. When I got to Calcutta I got blood poisoning and was sent to hospital. Within a week I was fit to go. But the situation had changed, the Army was about to burst south from Mandalay. There was a good chance of operating about 80 miles south of Mandalay. But we didn't have much time. We had teamed up with two young Burmese who had come out in 1944. They were our interpreters. So we were a team of five. We parachuted in and met a local Burma National Army leader. We took in about 100 weapons, which we distributed at once. We received more a night or two later. We laid ambushes, doing pin-prick operations on Japanese moving south, sometimes on the road, sometimes on tracks. If the parties were big we brought down an air strike on them. If they were small we dealt with them ourselves. We were quite successful. We had fantastic luck picking up a HQ party of about 17 Japs. We found a chap wearing Major-General's tabs and a lot of paper. This was handed over to the main body of the 14th Army as they came down the road.

Although the Army had passed us within about three weeks of our arrival, there were still a lot of Japs in the hills on each side of the main road. We made contact with the Army. They said they didn't want to come into the hills, and we were to continue operating and do what we could. If we met anything significant we were to tell them. For another three weeks we operated to the west of the main road. But with a line of communication to the Army at Pyinmana [about halfway between Mandalay and Rangoon].

By now Slim's 14th Army was driving hard for Rangoon, to beat the onset of the monsoon, but he also had to race the Japanese for the key town of Toungoo:

Kimura [Japanese commander in Burma] . . . had ordered all troops in the Shan Hills to get to Toungoo with 'sleepless speed'. Their roads were the fair-weather tracks that ran roughly parallel to our route, sixty or seventy miles to the east. Opposite Toungoo and about seventy miles from it this track turned abruptly west and joined the Rangoon road in the town. Led by the partly reorganized 15th Division, the Japanese, ferrying fast in any kind of vehicle left to them, made for Toungoo, and it looked as if they might beat us to it. But I still had a shot in my locker for them. As they drew south their way led them through the country of the Karens, a race which had remained staunchly loyal to us even in the blackest days of Japanese occupation, and had suffered accordingly. Over a long period, in preparation for this day, we had organized a secret force, the Karen Guerrillas, based on former soldiers of the Burma Army, for whom British officers and arms had been parachuted into the hills.[8]

Aubrey Trofimov was one of those British officers. At first it was not a happy experience as he relates:

I was sent to Calcutta for briefing. I was to go in with Major Critchley, in a force called Peacock Force. The briefing was extraordinary. We were to go in, recruit levies from the villagers, report on Jap movement, establish DZs. That was reasonable, but at the briefing, the Peacock Force started quibbling among themselves as to who was to be overall leader.

Major E. H. Peacock, who had worked in the Forestry Service in Burma and spoke Burmese fluently, was at the briefing for the operation with the overall codename Character to drop in the area north-east and south-east of Toungoo. By his account it was a far from amicable event:

The date of launching was fixed as 20 February 1945 by Dakota aircraft from Jessore. Three days was quite inadequate for briefing in such an important Operation, and I never could understand the reason for the hurry. The Briefing Officer had not been in Burma and knew very little about the conditions obtaining in Karenni.

Two of the DZs were also questionable; Peacock continues:

To add to these incompatibilities we learned that each Group was to take a Jed team (recently arrived from Europe), consisting of two officers and a wireless operator, with whom we had not been previously associated, and whose duties were defined as: (a) for obtaining intelligence, and (b) for training levies. Since these officers had never been in Burma, knew nothing of the language and were dependent entirely on the veterans of the Special Groups, the situation became confused. It was further learned that the Commander of Group 3 was to take with him an officer with whom he was strongly antipathetic, and another who was to come under his command in the first phase of the Operation, but later to take command of him and assume the title of Area Commander.

Bedlam reigned!

The staff in Calcutta at this time were largely without knowledge of military procedure. That is the kindest explanation I can give of what to the normal mind might appear rank lunacy.

Briefing was stopped while Officers discussed the situation. The Jeds, all good men, but unknown to us, naturally wanted to work in their teams of three. The Special Groups were furious at unwanted last-minute intrusions and implications against their ability to conduct jungle warfare. All agreed that the plan was unsuitable and asked me to formulate a new one.

Aubrey Trofimov:

I was the only Jed there, I didn't know these people. I didn't like them except for Major Critchley. While this was going on, I walked out of the briefing into a little courtyard, sat down, and thought, 'What am I letting myself in for?'

Suddenly Critchley appeared, he sat down, and said, 'I know what you're feeling. I saw your face. Forget about the whole set up. We'll go in, we'll team up and we'll do our own thing.'

I thought, 'I can get on with him'.

Peacock ended up by recommending that:

All 3 Groups should drop into the DZ in Hyena area, and by a show of strength, ensure the co-operation of the Karens; thereafter to settle one area and with it as a foundation to move into the others. Initially this plan worked well.

Aubrey Trofimov was originally intended to act as DZ officer for Peacock, setting up the drops for which he was trained, whereas Peacock Force were not:

On 20 February 1945, we got into a Dakota. I had never done a door jump. I asked the despatcher to show me what to do. We went in several aircraft. In mine there was myself and five Peacock Force soldiers. We came over the DZ and we seemed to be at an incredible height. Although it was dark, we could see the lights miles away. We must have been at about 2,000 feet. Then on came the light and it was go. I went. When my parachute stabilised, I looked up and saw the others, looking down I thought this is madness, we were miles from the DZ, you could see the lights. I started trying to steer the parachute towards the DZ. All that happened was I started oscillating, so I stopped in case I collapsed the parachute. I tried to spot landmarks as I came down. I landed with a crash in the trees. The parachute hung on the trees, but I landed on terra firma. I was so shaken, I took a pace forward and plunged into a ravine. When I collected myself together, I got my torch out, and dropped it. I looked for the other five. Suddenly I heard a noise, and one of the other chaps appeared. After a time, I gathered four of them. The fifth we didn't find for several days. We came to a track. After half an hour we came to the DZ. The others who had seen our drop didn't expect to see us for days. The DZ was in a paddy field in the Karen Hills.

That night had been spent collecting our equipment. From then we organised drops. As a Jed, that became my role for the next few days. I established a little camp away from the others. Critchley came to see me from time to time. There was still this atmosphere about who was going to lead. Eventually it was agreed that another major would go north. Critchley and I would go south to see if we could recruit Karen levies.

At this stage it seems that Critchley took command of two teams, one of which was commanded by Trofimov, and they no longer formed part of Peacock Force. Trofimov:

We moved to an area where there were areas of paddy we could use as DZs to take arms and equipment for the levies. We drew a blank in recruiting the Karens because they were terrified of the Japs. So we proceeded to [another area]. Here the story was quite different; we recruited about 100 levies. We took several drops and trained the levies. Several officers dropped in and we allocated levies to them. Critchley was moving around and setting up his HQ.

The worst part of being there were the insects. The first few weeks I slept on the ground and I was eaten alive by insects. I got no sleep. We often marched all night to and from DZs. I eventually had a hammock made and got off the ground and this was much better. We got orders from 14th Army to attack a Jap garrison containing about 200 troops. We trained intensively for this. I split the force into two platoons, one under Critchley and one under me. About 28th April we attacked. The air support was to attack the hill tops containing gun positions. We also had a plan of where the Japs were, provided by a district officer. We marched all night 27/28 April. By bad luck we came to a river and found myself following men who should have been behind me. Critchley had been led off on the wrong track by his men [by mistake]. We had to go through with it. I called all my NCOs in and asked if there was anyone who could lead us into the right position by [a place called] Pagoda Hill. We moved into position at dawn. The planes came over and we had not been warned that there was about a

200-yard safety margin. And we were within 50 yards of the gun position in a strong point on Pagoda Hill. It was very unnerving. I was shattered. I was worried that it would panic my men. They held. When the last plane left, we surged forward, and the plane came over again. I thought, 'My God he's going to bomb us.' He didn't. He was probably having a last look at the target. We moved in and captured Pagoda Hill. As we moved down into the village, to my eternal joy I saw Critchley coming in on the other side. We fought our way into the village. We weren't to know that the Japs had been forewarned by the Karen elders moving out of the village the night before. The machine-gun fire was intense and clearly things were getting out of hand. Many of my men and Critchley's disappeared. He blew the whistle signal to retreat. I was pinned down by a machine-gun. We had made some home-made bombs of 808 [plastic explosive].

I threw one at the machine-gun and it had the desired effect and we got away. I rallied a few of my men, and started climbing the side of Pagoda Hill when we came under intense machine-gun fire. We threw ourselves on the ground and it was each man for himself to get out. I waved them on and said, 'You go this way, you go that way.' We were fortunate we were able to get out to our RV. One of my men was badly wounded through the thigh, and was carried by one of my Jemadars [local levy officer]. We gathered [everyone together] and set out. It had been a shattering experience for the Karens, and pretty shattering for us as two officers with such an untrained force.

Trofimov was awarded an immediate Military Cross for his part in the battle. After this engagement:

I was made a sub-area commander to set up ambushes on tracks used by the Japs.

The first ambush was very successful and they killed about ninety Japanese. This was a better use of the Karen levies than attacking defensive positions. Further ambushes were laid, with the purpose of demoralizing the enemy. This must have had some effect since they noticed that the Japanese were no longer coming down the roads but deployed on each side in the jungle. He learned:

There was a price on my head.

At this stage Trofimov got orders from Critchley to meet him to discuss future moves at a place where there was an airstrip capable of

taking a Lysander. He dispersed his men and told them to take a break
of a couple of weeks, and after conferring with Critchley flew out to
Calcutta for two weeks' leave. Among other things, he wanted to sort
out the equipment, particularly the clothing being dropped to them,
which was far too big for the Karens who were rather small. On his
return he discovered that it had been decided that as the monsoon was
coming, they would come out. But every British officer refused in order
to stay with their men, otherwise they would have dispersed.

By now the situation had changed; Slim had taken Rangoon and large
numbers of cut-off Japanese were trying to escape to southern Burma
and Thailand. Dick Rubinstein was told by Force 136 to:

> go to Toungoo and help a team called Reindeer [part of Operation Nation]
> near the Sittang River. The Japs were massing between Toungoo and Pyu
> and trying to break out east. Reindeer had a big area and wanted help. On
> 30 May we left Pyinmana and on 3 June we came to Reindeer's HQ, and
> made a plan how best to use two teams. All the other team had been in
> France, already had great success fighting the Japs and done a lot of damage
> to the railway. The Team leader was Dave Britton, and included Sergeant
> Ron Brierley. The task was to keep in touch with the massing Japs and keep
> the Army informed. The day we arrived Dave Britton had gone on patrol
> in tall grass, and was killed. I took over Reindeer with Ron Brierley. We
> detached Livingstone and Ken Brown; they went south of Toungoo. Jock
> Waller went off on his own with his own radio. We were in the middle. The
> three of us [teams] were covering an area about 30 miles long. Each of us
> controlled a force of about 150 locals. Eventually the Japs broke out in July.
> The Army took up position on the road, and we manned the river line. Any
> Japs who could break across the road would come through the tall grass to
> the river. Our chaps would let them build rafts and push out into the water,
> and open fire on them. In one case they had a boat which they left on the
> banks and allowed the Japs to use it, before shooting them all, followed by
> pushing the boat back and doing it again. As the river ran, it was full of
> bodies. Our 500 chaps probably dealt with several thousand. If they had
> run past us they would have run into another guerrilla operation in the
> Karen Hills called Character. The few prisoners we took were in a pretty
> bad state, but they still fought with tenacity.

Aubrey Trofimov's Team Mongoose South on the Shwegyin was part
of Operation Character. Their action is described in Chapter 1, and this
story of British behind-the-lines soldiers in the Second World War has

thus come full circle, with the dropping of the two atomic bombs on Japan, and the rounding-up of those Japanese who did not believe their God Emperor had surrendered, until their own officers were sent in to inform them otherwise, as Aubrey Trofimov has related.

Most Jedburghs seem to consider that they were more effective in Burma than in France, and the following three views are typical:

Dick Rubinstein:

In France we were giving the French the opportunity to engage the enemy, and still feel he had taken a part in the liberation of his country. It was important that he should be allowed to do that. In Burma, in the Shan States, the chaps have a very military background; they are very akin to the Gurkha, it certainly gave them satisfaction, although it certainly wasn't strategically important. On the second operation, and the build-up to the break-out across the Sittang, we were doing a task that had to be done. We were doing it as part of the Army, probably better than the Army. They could have done it, but they had just advanced all the way to Rangoon. We had a real role.

Duncan Guthrie:

The difference between Jed ops in France and Burma: in France we were in groups of three. We went to help and build up the morale of the Resistance. In Burma we went in with our own troops and some native levies and attacked the Japs in the jungle.

Oswin Craster:

I was more use in Burma than in France. I was there longer. It is more suitable country for behind-the-lines operations. There are less roads. In France the Germans might turn up at five minutes' notice. In Burma if you had a friendly population, you knew when the Japanese were coming, and you could move as fast as them through the jungle.

The Jedburghs, with local support, their own expertise, and mobility as good as their opponents', more than fulfilled what had been expected of them by those who conceived them in 1942. The Jedburghs themselves found fulfilment in taking the war to the enemy, which, for all the reasons already rehearsed, they were able to do more effectively in Burma than they had in France.

Tailpiece

Of all the special forces that were raised by the British in the Second World War only the SAS and SBS, now once again called the Special Boat Service, survive. They perhaps come near to meeting Slim's requirement, quoted in Chapter 1, for 'one kind of special unit which should be retained – that designed to be employed in small parties, usually behind the enemy, on tasks beyond the normal scope of warfare in the field'.[1] The roles of the present-day SAS and SBS cover those carried out in the Second World War roughly as follows:

SAS	SBS
SAS all roles	SB Sections all roles
LRDG road watch and desert work	LRDG shipping watch
Popski's Private Army	SB Squadron and Special Boat Service all roles
	COPPs beach reconnaissance
	RMBPD/Jaywick/Rimau type ship attack
	Detachment 385
	SRU

Both have other tasks in counter-terrorism and counter-insurgency. Both are small organizations, and because they are expected to fulfil so many missions, avoid the characteristic Slim complained of: ' . . . formations, trained and equipped, and mentally adjusted for one kind of operation, were wasteful'.[2] He goes on to say, possibly with the Chindits in mind, that 'they [special forces] can only be employed for restricted periods'.[3] Does this always apply? What of their Second World War forebears, and indeed the other forces that appear in these pages, some of whom are also listed by Slim; commandos, airborne troops, desert groups?

Commandos and parachute soldiers were originally conceived as:

> specially trained troops of the hunter class, who can develop a reign of terror down these coasts [German-occupied Europe], first of all on the 'butcher and bolt' policy ... leaving a trail of German corpses behind them.[4]

In fact after two years, both commandos and parachute soldiers were fighting as part of, or on the flanks of, the main battle, and it was in this role that they gave their most valuable service. The feats in which 1st Parachute Brigade took most pride were the five months' hard fighting in Tunisia from November 1942 to April 1943, when they earned the nickname bestowed on them by the Germans, *Rote Teufel*, 'Red Devils'. 'Such distinctions given by the enemy are seldom won in battle except by the finest fighting troops,' wrote Browning. As the train carrying 1st and 2nd Parachute Battalions to Algiers on completion of the campaign was slowly trundling past one of the prisoner-of-war camps outside the city, the German prisoners, seeing the red berets on the men leaning out of the train windows, turned out in their thousands. They ran to the wire nearest the railway line, cheering and throwing their hats in the air. 'That', said Lieutenant-Colonel John Frost, commanding 1st Parachute Battalion, 'was the tribute I liked best.'[5] After the disastrous airborne operation in Sicily, Frost, and others in 1st Airborne Division, were to lament that the landings had not been followed by playing the same star part in the 'ordinary' fighting in Sicily and Italy as they had in North Africa. They did not want to be taken out of the fighting.

Similarly, the commandos to this day remember with pride Italy, Burma and north-west Europe. Following the Normandy landings, the 1st and 4th Special Service (Commando) Brigades, of all British formations in Normandy, held the record for continuous fighting: eighty-three consecutive days in action.[6] 6th Airborne Division had only marginally fewer days out of the line. All these formations went on to take part in protracted operations for the rest of the war in Europe, and had the atom bombs not been dropped, many of them would have taken part in fighting in Malaya, and possibly Japan itself. To this day commandos and parachute soldiers march towards the sound of the guns, if they are allowed to. Their attitude might be summed up as 'We'll do it. What is it?', or in the motto of the Parachute Regiment, *Utrinque Paratus*, 'Ready for Anything'.

The extreme view among those critical of special forces, whether of the behind-the-lines variety or not, is typified by a general who said to John Verney, who served in Jellicoe's SB Squadron, that:

> they [Special Forces] contributed nothing to Allied victory. All they did was to offer a too-easy, because romanticised, form of gallantry to a few anti-social irresponsible individualists, who sought a more personal satisfaction from the war than of standing their chance, like proper soldiers, of being bayoneted in a slit trench or burnt alive in a tank.[7]

Although this is a harsh judgement, as in many sweeping statements there is an element of truth in this one. One Jedburgh who did not go to Burma after serving in France wrote:

> While you went to Burma, I rejoined my regiment (the Royal Welch Fusiliers) and got involved in some arduous infantry fighting in the Reichswald up to Hamburg. Curiously enough I found more satisfaction in commanding a company of men up front than in my Maquis work. A different sort of courage was required – an ability to stand extreme discomfort and lack of sleep allied to a not-too-pronounced fear of enemy fire and accurate mortar and artillery. I was comparatively brave because the other poor buggers had been subjected to it since D-Day. On the other hand, one lost the fear of being taken by the Gestapo.

The strain on the infantry in particular is illustrated by Major-General H. Essame, an infantryman who fought in both world wars:

> For most of the front-line soldiers, the bleak rule was that you normally continued to fight on; either until you were killed, or so severely wounded as to be unfit for further active service in the line.[8]

But it would be grossly unfair to label all members of special forces 'anti-social irresponsible individualists'. Take the Chindits; few had any choice in the matter of belonging to Wingate's Special Force. Some of the battle-hardened and cynical, or members of proud infantry battalions, were indifferent to the so-called privilege of being Chindits. Many more, especially those wearied by the tedium of years of not too imaginative training, welcomed the opportunity to get into the fight. They certainly would not have seen long-range penetration as an escape route from danger; rather a ticket for a journey in the opposite direction. No one can deny that they suffered, and, in the case of some units, fought as hard as any in the Second World War. Certainly, although there were drawbacks to being in a line-infantry battalion, there could be benefits as well. John Masters, who found himself the GSO 1 of 19th Indian Infantry Division towards the end of the war in Burma, makes this point when describing the state of the Division the day he joined it on the bank of the Irrawaddy:

> It was on a regular supply line and the men looked fit and full of fire, very different from the gallant, ragged, deadbeat scarecrows my Chindits had become when I left Burma.[9]

The point is, was all the sacrifice by the Chindits worth it? One has to say that all the evidence is that much of it was not.

In May 1956, Slim wrote to Scoones, who had commanded IV Corps, about *Defeat into Victory*, which had just been published. After regretting that space did not allow him to do better justice to many, including Scoones, he says:

> There are others to whom you will realise that I have been kinder than strict historical fact would justify. Wingate is one of these, I think you will agree.... It was however necessary to give an idea what after all the newspaper blah [*sic*] was the effect of his operations. Compared with those of a normal corps they were painfully slight.

It is also an exaggeration to say that men joined special forces to avoid danger and death. Some might have done, but the vast majority, young and brimming with energy, joined for action, not to dodge it. One of the problems, as alluded to earlier, was satisfying the urge, one might almost say lust, for action of these people, when time after time operations were cancelled, or opportunities for fighting simply did not present themselves; sometimes for years. On the whole they were the best types, not the column dodgers, and when they saw the prospect of doing anything worthwhile in a special forces organization apparently receding, would volunteer to return to their parent units in droves. Others belonged to units whose role, a searchlight battery for example, placed them so far behind their own lines that they would volunteer for almost anything to get nearer the enemy.

The vast majority of those volunteering, or in the case of the Chindits, being volunteered, were civilians who had joined to fight in the war. There is a wealth of talent, skills, intellect and entrepreneurial spirit in the large pool of manpower in the armed forces of a nation in arms, including all manner of free-thinking spirits and individualists. This is totally different from today, at least in the United Kingdom; all special forces soldiers and marines come from within the tiny professional armed forces. This is not intended as a criticism of what are highly dedicated and accomplished people, rather to point out that in wartime there are types with much to offer, who would not sit comfortably in a peacetime army.

The contribution of special forces to the Allied victory is often hard to measure, because it cannot be calculated solely in terms of enemy hardware destroyed, but in other ways: morale, both of one's own side and the enemy's; the enemy's reactions in terms of withdrawing troops from one area to reinforce another; and assistance to an ally who might otherwise withdraw from the contest. One has to seek answers to questions such as what will be the effect of not mounting special forces operations against the enemy in a particular theatre or campaign? Will this mean that the enemy's rear areas are safe, so he does not have to provide guards at regular intervals along his line of communication, on his airfields and key points, and escorts on trains and road convoys? It is very difficult to quantify or provide subjective evidence which categorically proves that X thousand troops were removed from the main front as a result of special forces operations in the enemy rear. Even in the intelligence field, the instances when a particular piece of information is the one factor that sways the battle are rare. More usually several intelligence-gathering sources, each providing a piece, build the jigsaw puzzle to the stage where it can be used as one of the tools to stage-manage the operation. It is the synergy of all the intelligence-gathering means working together that produces the whole. Without one, others may be less effective. Montgomery's chief of intelligence, Brigadier Edgar ('Bill') Williams, once said of the time in the 8th Army in the desert:

> We used to take great satisfaction in 'beating' Ultra. But, of course, we used yesterday's Ultra to beat today's.[10]

For example, by using 'yesterday's' Ultra, he could use the LRDG road watch information in such a way as to anticipate what Ultra would tell him tomorrow or subsequently. Bearing in mind that, as Brigadier

Williams also said, 'all intelligence by its nature is always out of date', anything that sped up the process could be worth its weight in gold.

As stated before, the LRDG must rate as the most cost-effective special force in the Second World War, and its performance was the complete antithesis of a typical special force as depicted by Slim. The unit adapted to the circumstances of the theatre in which it operated. It was not expensive in resources. Its record bears repeating: during the five years of its existence, the LRDG carried out more than two hundred operations behind enemy lines, and throughout those five years there were only two periods of five months when no patrols were operating behind enemy lines. The unit was in existence, and on operations, the longest, and made a considerable contribution to Allied victory.

The SAS, especially in North Africa, were also cost-effective, barring their forays on some of the larger, abortive raids. In particular the number of aircraft destroyed personally by some SAS officers and soldiers, attacking in a few cheap vehicles, maintained by a handful of fitters, far outweighed the personal score achieved by any aircrew, whose training was both long and costly, and who attacked in expensive aircraft maintained by a large number of ground crew. That is not to say that the SAS made the RAF redundant, but that the former's efforts materially helped to tilt the balance of air power in the Mediterranean Theatre.

The contribution of the SB Squadron was particularly valuable in the Aegean, less so in the Adriatic, while much of the reconnaissance work by SB Sections, often in conjunction with or complementary to the COPPs, was absolutely indispensable to the success of the amphibious operations carried out by the Allies, of which Normandy was the supreme example.

Some special forces, like the RMBPD, the SRU and Detachment 385, saw very little action. Although the Bordeaux raid was good for morale, it is hard to see what strategic effect it had on the Allied war effort. More valuable was the attack on enemy warships at Leros, by the RMBPD, for its repercussions at the operational level in the Aegean. A great deal of time and effort was put into research by the RMBPD and SRU, some of which was valuable, some of it, for example spending years developing 'toys' like the explosive motor boats, was a complete waste of time.

There are others, including PPA, which one finds hard to see how they contributed to Allied victory in any quantifiable way.

Although Jaywick did make an impact on the enemy, by the time Rimau was mounted, this was not the most cost-effective way to attack the Japanese merchant fleet in the latter part of 1944. The preparations and training for these two operations consumed assets including manpower which, in addition to the operators, encompassed the staffs at various levels, those running the training establishments, and the back-up teams, as well as three years of work. All these were a cumulative drain on a limited pool of resources.

The Jedburghs, on the other hand, during their short life as a unit represented a good return on investment. They could be 'buttoned on' to an existing training and development organization, SOE's; they were not very costly in manpower terms for the result they produced; the ratio of time in the field to time out was as good as that experienced by many other units.

Nothing that has been said should be taken as criticism of those who served in units whose return was perhaps not as good as had been hoped, or indeed as those who were in those units yearned for. The fault lies with those who encouraged proliferation, and failed to co-ordinate their activities, thereby wasting time and precious talent. This failure manifested itself in various ways. There was sometimes duplication of effort. For example PPA's activities cut across several other types of force from the SAS to conventional armoured car reconnaissance regiments. Another example is the overlapping of roles by SB Sections, SB Squadron, RMBPD, COPPs, the SRU and Detachment 325. Some special forces units' *raison d'être* was based on their commanding officer's desire to run a special unit or feed his obsession with a particular form of warfare. Both PPA and Rimau fell into this category. Some units, such as the SRU, spent long periods conducting trials and training. There was proliferation, and at times units crowding each other, resulting in squabbles over 'real estate', such as the SAS jeopardizing LRDG road watch operations by attacking enemy positions nearby. There was sometimes self-generation of tasks and invention of roles on the part of commanders of special units. The assumption of the canoe role by the RMBPD, who had been formed originally to crew explosive motor boats, is a prime example. The personality of the commander of the force was often a deciding factor in prolonging a special unit's existence well beyond its useful operational life. This encouraged the cult of the personality, of which Wingate was perhaps the supreme example. The lesson is the need to stamp on the destructive aspects of 'private armies', and, in the vernacular, to 'grip' them. This can only be done by the senior commander.

As Slim said, in the context of his theatre:

> It was not until the activities of all clandestine bodies operating in or near our troops were co-ordinated, and where necessary controlled through a senior officer on the staff of the commander of the area, that confusion, ineffectiveness, and lost opportunities were avoided.'[11]

Co-ordination may have worked in Burma, but it certainly did not in SEAC as a whole, nor in the Mediterranean. Here we are back to personalities. Mountbatten was all too susceptible to the romantic aura of special operations, and where he commanded they proliferated. Alexander, in the Mediterranean, was not noted for an overall grasp of operational matters, and that included special forces activity.

What Slim inaugurated at what we would now call the operational level needed to be done at the strategic level. Certainly, there does not seem to have been anyone at the highest level of those responsible for directing the British war effort charged with keeping an overview on the activities of special forces in the Second World War. Apart from anything else, such an overview might have introduced some much needed pruning and rationalization. If there was such a machinery in place to prevent duplication and wasted effort, it was not very efficient.

But at the risk of repeating oneself, none of this detracts from the bravery and enthusiasm of the men, mostly very young, who served behind the lines in the Second World War. For reasons given earlier, the story of the Secret Soldiers is about people, the vast majority of whom were civilians, but who became 'super soldiers'.

Appendix A

Long-Range Desert Group

Ration Scale [for one man]

6 oz biscuits

3 oz mutton (dehydrated)

4 oz bacon

3 oz cheese

2 oz oatmeal

2½ oz tea, sugar and milk powder

2 oz chocolate

2 oz boiled sweets

½ oz Globex

½ oz Salt

½ oz lime juice powder

Horlicks tablets

Water sterilizing tablets

Ascorbic acid tablets

Breakfast Suggestions

Porridge (no milk or sugar)

Fried bacon with oatmeal fritter

Bacon and oatmeal cake

Bacon stuffed with cooked oatmeal

Bacon with oatmeal chuppatties

Tiffin

Lentil soup

Various sandwich spreads on biscuits

Cheese and oatmeal savoury

Cheese and oatmeal cake

Oatmeal and date cookies

Dinner

Stewed mutton with dumplings

Meat pudding

[RECIPES] ALL FOR FOUR MEN

When cooking the bacon a certain amount of fat should be extracted and kept to assist in preparing other food.

Porridge
For eating with salt as porridge. 4 oz oatmeal, ½ pint water, salt. Boil the water and shower in the oatmeal. Cook until tender, stirring with a wooden spoon (correct time about 40 minutes).

Chuppatties
Make porridge as above, shape into flat cakes and cook on a sheet of hot tin until browned and dry.

Oatmeal Fritter
Make porridge and drop into hot bacon fat in small spoonfuls.

Bacon with oatmeal fritter
Make porridge and chop and mix in 8 oz bacon. Fry off in bacon fat.

Oatmeal cheese savoury
Boil the porridge and add 6 oz of shredded cheese. When the cheese has dissolved allow to cool. Cut into portions.

Oatmeal and date cookies
Make the porridge as above and add 4 oz chopped dates. Bake off as for chuppatties or bake in an improvised oven.

Cheese and oatmeal cakes
4 oz oatmeal, 4 oz cheese, salt and water. Knead oatmeal and cheese together until they come to a sandy texture. Mix with water to a stiff paste. Bake off on a tin plate as for chuppatties, or bake in an improvised oven.

Dumplings
6 oz biscuit powder, 1 oz bacon fat, little water. Mix the fat with the biscuit and water and make into a stiff dough. Boil for 15 minutes in the stew.

Mutton stew
12 oz mutton (this should be soaked if possible with 1 pint water), 8 oz lentils, some Marmite and salt. The mutton, if not soaked, should be dropped into boiling water, the lentils and Marmite added, and simmered for as long as possible before eating.

Meat pudding
4 oz bacon, 6 oz dehydrated mutton (soaked), 4 oz oatmeal, ¼ pint water. Chop the bacon, add to the mutton, mix well with the oatmeal and water and cook in bacon tin for 50 minutes (in hop-on can). Pastry can be made as dumplings in bacon fat and powdered biscuits and should be baked in an improvised oven.

Spreads to be used with biscuits
Cheese 6 oz, dates 2 oz.
Cheese 6 oz, lentils 2 oz (cooked).

Lentils 4 oz (cooked), 1 oz Marmite.

Cheese 6 oz, Marmite 1 oz.

Marmite 1 oz, dates 4 oz.

In all of these, cream the indgredients to a soft paste with a fork, until they will spread on the biscuits.

Lentil soup

8 oz lentils, 1½ pints water, Marmite and salt. Bring to the boil and allow to simmer until lentils will mash.

Appendix B
Medical Statistics from Operation Thursday

Taken from *Medical History of the Second World War: Army Medical Services, Campaigns*, Volume V, by F. A. E. Crew, HMSO 1966

The material quoted in this Appendix B is Crown Copyright and is reproduced with the permission of the Controller of Her Majesty's Stationery Office.

Comments from the Report on Rations

pp. 186/187 – They [The Chindits] had a dietary deficiency of about 800 calories a day for 110 days, and the average weight loss per man was between 30 and 40 pounds.

Comments on Medical Organization

p. 188 – There was considerable discussion between Major-General Wingate and his DDMS [Deputy Director Medical Services – his senior Doctor] concerning the size and composition of the medical element of a column. The latter recommended that it should consist of one medical officer and eleven ORs, RAMC, for a British Column, or IAMC for an Indian Column. This recommendation was not accepted for the reason that in General Wingate's opinion the size of this element would increase the total size of the Column to the point where it became unwieldy. He maintained that one officer and two ORs would be quite sufficient as they would be called up to deal only with *severe illnesses or injuries*. He suggested that the chaplain should be employed as a medical orderly. Ultimately a compromise was reached and each column, it was agreed, should have a medical officer, a sergeant, and two OR, RAMC, or three OR in an Indian Column which lacked a chaplain [author's italics].

Author's comment: *minor illnesses and injuries can, for lack of treament, become severe in tropical jungle conditions and the man removed from the battle without the enemy having to lift a finger.*

Casualty Figures for 3rd Indian Division

p. 195   ### Table 4 – Casualty Figures

Brigade	Killed & died of wounds		Wounded		Missing	
	Officers	*ORs*	*Officers*	*ORs*	*Officers*	*ORs*
14th	14	227	23	191	2	32
16th	13	85	14	164	5	74
77th	46	346	84	1,156	11	168
111th	17	107	24	465	6	130
3rd WA	11	78	23	290	1	23
	101	843	168	2,266	25	427

Total Officers	294	Japanese known to have been killed,
Total ORs	3,536	wounded or captured 5,311
	3,830	

Comments on Malaria Prevention

p. 197 – Every officer and man carried his container with mepacrine tablets. But, in the conditions that existed it was well nigh impossible for the individual to observe the rules of self-care. The actual distribution of mepacrine tablets was uncertain; supplies reached brigade rear HQ but forward of this it was never quite certain that they would reach the columns. At times it was necessary for a column to restrict use of this drug to the cure of the disease, and not to employ it in routine suppressive treatment. It was often impossible, and always difficult to hold 'mepacrine parades' and thus ensure that everyone was taking his dose. It is certain that the cream, the veil, and gauntlets were not regularly used by all. There was no enforcement of anti-malaria measures; self-protection against the mosquito was not made a matter of discipline. On men who had died of cerebral malaria the containers were found to be full of untouched Mepacrine tablets.

Author's comment:

a. *One way round the problem of distribution would have been to drop Mepacrine automatically with the rations on every drop, doubling the number of tablets for the amount of rations asked for to cater for wide drops. Now, Palludrine, the modern equivalent, is included in every jungle ration pack.*

b. *The fact that 'Mepacrine parades' were considered necessary to ensure that every man had taken his pill is indicative of a lack of proper training and self-discipline. (See comments below by MO of 111th Brigade.)*

Comments on Dysentery and Diarrhoea

p. 199 – It is indeed most difficult to observe the rule that only water known to be safe must be drunk when living in such conditions as existed in the world of the Chindit. It was frequently impossible for the water to be sterilised; the sterilising tablets disintegrated, the powder that was issued in lieu of the tablets was not easy to handle in 7 lb tins and these were difficult to carry, and when they were opened frequently the free chlorine content of the powder quickly diminished. In one column the use of toilet paper was prohibited for the reason that having been used and left lying about it marked the path of the column. Far too often it was assumed that no other troops would occupy the ground that a particular column was using, so that no care was taken to keep or make it clean. There were no sanitary orderlies, as such, sanitary jobs were fatigues. In the stronghold the latrines that were constructed conformed to no known pattern, they were too shallow to be classified as deep trench latrines, and too deep to be accepted as shallow ones. Seldom did they have any kind of superstructure [*i.e. pole or plank on which to perch, so the user is poised over the centre, and does not foul the lip of the pit – author's italics*]. . . .

But granting that it must have been exceedingly difficult to follow the teaching of sanitation in these matters, it is impossible to avoid the conclusion that it was the accepted teaching in 'Special Force' concerning the relative importance of these matters that was partly, if not largely, responsible for the incidence of these intestinal diseases.

Author's note: this conclusion is borne out by Wingate's teaching, see p. 235 of the Report below.

p. 235 – In General Wingate's training pamphlet dealing with 'Comfort in Bivouac', it was taught that: 'Except when the bivouac is occupied and evacuated within the same night, strict orders must be issued regarding the use of latrines. The object of this will be to prevent flies and other annoyances. *It will, however be a waste of labour to dig latrines unless the bivouac is to be occupied for more than a week.* Men should carry out their functions at distances not less than 100 yards from the perimeter.' Such teaching is to be condemned utterly for it completely disregards the possibility that other troops will pass that way later. [*Author's italics: the amount of waste produced by 400 men in a week is considerable.*]

Comments on the results of Psychiatric Examination of Sample of Returning Chindits

p. 203 – Interrogation revealed that the factors which affected morale profoundly were:

PROMISES[1]
14th Brigade. Men of the BW and Y& L complained bitterly of broken promises. They had been led to believe that every task that was undertaken was to be the last before returning to India. Every time this promise was not kept, morale slumped. The men of the Leicesters and the Bedfs & Herts, on the other hand, had no such complaint for no such promises were given to them.

77th Brigade. The troops were told that they were to return to India before the monsoon and also after the 'White City' enterprise was completed. Their hopes, thus raised, were dashed, and their morale sank.

111th Brigade. The troops had been told that they would be returning to India before the monsoon broke. Then they were told that the 'Blackpool' enterprise was to be the very last commitment. Chaplains and column medical officers confirmed the men's assertions that when these promises were broken, the morale of the brigade was greatly and adversely affected.

Author's note: of all his Directives to Brigades, it is only in 14th Brigade's that Wingate mentions duration of operations, and here he says:

The duration of operations will be until the beginning of the monsoon, which may be taken for the sake of argument as being 15th May.

At the beginning of this period it will be decided where you are to spend the monsoon, and your role during the monsoon.

You should not lead your men to believe that they must necessarily be relieved during the monsoon, but they will as far as possible be given a rest and may be wholly relieved. [Author's italics]

Nevertheless, it is clear that all the Chindits were under the impression that they would be out before the monsoon.

Comments on medical aspects during training by MO 111th Brigade

p. 216 – up to this time [February 1944] the Brigade had been unable to obtain mepacrine. [MO 111th Brigade]

Author's comment: it is clear from the report by the MO 111th Brigade included in this volume of the Medical History *that his Brigade suffered large numbers of casualties from malaria and dysentery throughout their nine or so months of training in central India, and on the march from the railhead in Assam. One has to conclude that bad habits were allowed to go unchecked and uncorrected during training. These bad habits would have been continued, as they almost always are, on operations. This, and the fact that Mepacrine was not available, reflects adversely on Wingate's staff, ultimately on him as the Commander; and also on Lentaigne, the Brigade Commander.*

Comments on the numbers of 3rd Indian Division admitted to hospital

p. 209   Table 6 – 'Special Force' Total Admissions to Hospital on Account of sickness and wounds, by Brigade
(Ratios per 1,000 per month)

Brigade	Strength approx	Total Admissions		Total Sick		Total Battle Cas		Sick to Battle Cas
		Number	Ratio	Number	Ratio	Number	Ratio	Ratio
14th	3,600	1,433	79.61	1,271	70.61	162	9.0	7.8:1
16th	3,600	1,038	96.11	888	82.22	150	13.90	5.9:1
77th (1)	5,100	1,759	65.69	940	35.1	819	30.59	1.2:1
111th (2)	2,900	2,033	127.46	1,650	103.45	383	24.01	4.3:1
3rd WA	2,800	954	56.79	673	40.06	281	16.73	2.4:1
	18,000	7,217	100.23	5,422	75.30	1,795	24.92	3.0:1

Note:
(1) 77th Brigade had the most battle casualties and, except for 3rd West African Brigade, the lowest number of sick. The ratio of sick to battle casualties is an indication of the high standard of leadership and morale in 77th Brigade.
(2) 111th Brigade figures include Morrisforce.

Author's note: on 7 May 1944, some three months after the leading Chindit brigade deployed into Burma, Headquarters Special Force issued Training and Experimental Instruction Number 12, covering a number of matters, to all Brigades. One section read:

5. Health

Some columns have suffered seriously from the ravages of malaria. Anti-malaria precautions must be taken. It is no good distributing mepacrine at irregular intervals or hoping that men will take their mepacrine without supervision. The only solution is to have a mepacrine parade when a whole platoon is lined up and each man under the eye of his platoon commander takes his dose.

A column continually on the move may, without ill effects, get away with indiscriminate defecation in its bivouac area. Even so, it pays to dig a shallow trench latrine which can also be used as a receptacle for litter and covered over before moving off. When, however, a body of troops have to occupy a bivouac area or defended position for some days, it is courting disaster not to pay attention to elementary rules of Field Hygiene. Adequate latrines must be dug and faeces covered over.

One can only comment that it was a bit late to issue orders of this kind, and these matters should have been hammered home during training. Once again, the lack of self-discipline requiring Mepacrine parades is interesting, as is the reiteration of Wingate's instruction on there being no need for field hygiene when columns were on the move.

Appendix C

Statistical Summary of all SAS Operations in France, Belgium and Holland from June to November 1944[1]

The following figures are as reliable as possible but must be treated with reserve. The enemy casualties shown are based on claims by parties and are therefore liable to be exaggerated. They include those inflicted by 'resistance' units acting directly with the SAS. However, they serve to give a useful picture of the material results achieved during the period when most operations of the true SAS type took place, and the cost of those results.

SAS Brigade

Total approximate strength, all ranks	2,000
Casualties (a proportion of these, especially 4th French Parachute Battalion,[2] were recovered, having been captured or gone into hiding with the 'Resistance')	300

38 Group RAF

Total operational and supply-by-air sorties flown	780
Successful	600
Abortive	180
Casualties in aircraft	6
Jeeps dropped and landed by glider	86
6-pounder anti-tank guns dropped	2
Containers and panniers dropped	10,370

Enemy

(a) Personnel killed or seriously wounded   7,733

Prisoners (excluding 18,000 who surrendered at   4,784
Issoudun in France to nine US Officers partially
as a result of being cut off by SAS troops
and the French 'Resistance').

                                                 Total 12,517

(b) Motor vehicles captured   40

Motor vehicles destroyed   600

Bicycles and motor-cycles destroyed   100

                                                 Total 740

(c) Trains destroyed   7
Railway trucks destroyed   89
Railway locomotives destroyed   29
Derailments   33
Railway lines cut   164

(d) Bombing targets reported   400

Notes

For sources of quotations by people named in the text or papers in the Imperial War Museum see Index of Contributors. Where there are no notes in the text, the chapter is omitted below.

Chapter 1

1. Field Marshal the Viscount Slim, *Defeat into Victory*, pp. 463–5.
2. Andrew Roberts, *Eminent Churchillians*, p. 55

Chapter 2

1. Bagnold, *Libyan Sands*, p. 139.
2. Although inevitably a few were; one is now in the Imperial War Museum.
3. John Willett, *Popski*, p. 30.
4. Ibid., p. 30.

Chapter 3

1. Charles Messenger, *The Commandos 1940–1946*, p. 95.
2. 'Lofty' Richardson ended up in a POW camp in Italy. He escaped to Switzerland with another member of G1 Patrol, Sergeant 'Tam' Pratt, Scots Guards, but died of pneumonia a month later on 21 October 1943.

Chapter 6

1. Robin Neillands, *The Dervish Wars*, p. 32.
2. John Masters, *The Road Past Mandalay*, p. 149.

Chapter 7

1. Bernard Fergusson, *The Trumpet in the Hall*, p. 175.
2. Ibid., p. 176.

3. Ibid., p. 177.
4. Shelford Bidwell, *The Chindit War*. p. 73.
5. A plan to mount an amphibious assault on Sumatra, which was overtaken by events, as many plans are.
6. Philip Ziegler, *Mountbatten*, p. 275.
7. Ibid., p. 276.
8. Bidwell, *The Chindit War*, p. 147.
9. Slim, *Defeat into Victory*, p. 235.
10. This is not the only time that Wingate was to imply that 'true' information was not being passed on thanks to his enemies [see signal Wingate–Mountbatten for onward transmssion to PM in the Wingate papers File 10].
11. Otway, *Airborne Forces*, p. 364.
12. Slim, *Defeat into Victory*, p. 242.

Chapter 8

1. Michael Hickey, *The Unforgettable Army*, p. 189.
2. W. F. Jeffrey, *Sunbeams Like Swords*, p. 70.
3. Masters, *The Road Past Mandalay*, p. 227.
4. Hickey, *The Unforgettable Army*, pp. 138–9.
5. F. A. E. Crew, *Medical History of the Second World War: Army Medical Services, Campaigns*, Volume V, pp. 186–209.
6. Shelford Bidwell in *The Journal of Contemporay History*, Volume 15, No 2, SAGE, London and Beverly Hills, 1980, p. 254.

Wingate's notions are even more fantastic when one considers the logistical problems involved. It would have taken 5,000 Dakota sorties to fly in just the mules and their drivers (four mules and eight men per aircraft). The distances involved are: Imphal–Hanoi, 800 miles; and Imphal–Bangkok, 850. The distance from southern England to Normandy is about 100–150 miles depending on the route taken. The radius of action of a Dakota towing a WACO was 350 miles (radius of action being the distance from base to target). The Dakotas would have run out of fuel *before* they reached Hanoi or Bangkok, let alone had sufficient to return. Wingate might have had in mind setting up staging airfields in China for the lift to Hanoi. The effort to lift the necessary fuel would have been immense. Staging airfields in China would not have had any effect on the Imphal–Bangkok route. The scheme was far beyond the capacity of the Allies to implement; as some elementary checks by Wingate's staff would have revealed in a few minutes.

7. Masters, *The Road Past Mandalay*, pp. 152–3.

Chapter 9

1. Churchill, *The Second World War, Volume V*, p. 181.

Chapter 10

1. Roland Huntford, *Scott and Amundsen*, 1983, p. 46
2. A story is told of a battalion sending a verbal message back to headquarters: 'Send reinforcements, we're going to advance.' Taken by a series of runners, it arrived as, 'Send three and fourpence, we're going to a dance.'
3. In the parlance of the time Wireless Telegraphy (W/T) referred to messages transmitted by morse key, and Radio Telegraphy (R/T), messages passed by voice. Not every army signaller was trained to operate a W/T set.
4. First Aid Nursing Yeomanry, a British women's ambulance unit formed in 1907. Probably the most elite and exclusive women's service in both World Wars. Many joined SOE as radio operators and cipher clerks, and 73 were trained as agents, including Szabo and Sansom.
5. Max Hastings, *Das Reich*, p. 207. It must also be said that despite the brilliant success of many SAS operations since 1945, there have also been occasions when postwar SAS officers and soldiers have shown they were not immune to carelessness, overconfidence and unwillingness to accept advice, leading to 'cock-ups'. A good example is described in two books about an SAS patrol in the Gulf War, *Bravo Two Zero* and *The One that Got Away*. This is by no means the only instance of such failings.
6. Otway, *Airborne Forces*, p. 239.
7. Ibid., pp. 239–40.
8. This was an elite unit called the Supreme Allied Air Reconnaissance Force (SAARF). It was established at Wentworth in Surrey, and included people like Leigh-Fermor and many other behind-the-lines soldiers under Brigadier J. F. Nicholls DSO MC. Its mission was to parachute into Germany carrying anti-typhus serum, go into POW camps, administer the serum, and try to persuade the Germans not to kill the

prisoners. In the end, only six teams parachuted in, on 26 April, all bound for Stalag XI. Four teams fell into German hands, and were taken to the camp. One team fell into Russian hands. One team was never seen again.

9. Otway, *Airborne Forces*, pp. 257–8.

Chapter 11

1. Correlli Barnett, *Engage the Enemy More Closely*, p. 832.
2. The name for what soon became 1st Parachute Battalion, and not to be confused with the Special Air Service who had not been raised at this stage (see Chapter 3).
3. Popski's Private Army No 1 Demolition Squadron PPA Historical Summary. WO Document 02(41)349 [1 Demolition Sqdn]/5. MO1(R)/BM/3362, p. 4.
4. Willett, *Popski*, pp. 116–17.
5. de Guingand, *Operation Victory*.
6. Vladimir Peniakoff, *Private Army*, p. 438. In his book, 'Popski' says that Yunnie's party was 'to give 8th Army general intelligence and bombing targets'.
7. Ibid., p. 434.
8. Willett, *Popski*, p. 120.
9. Ibid., p. 120.
10. Ibid., p. 122.
11. Roy Farran, *Winged Dagger*, p. 276.
12. Ibid., p. 284.
13. Ibid., p. 290.
14. Ibid., p. 290.
15. Ibid., p. 311.
16. Ibid., p. 323.
17. Ibid., p. 327.
18. Ibid., p. 340.
19. It had been part of Slovenia until the end of the First World War, when it was ceded to Italy by the Treaty of Versailles.

Chapter 12

1. Peter Elphick, *Singapore*, pp. 91–2. The proposition that civilian morale might be damaged by preparations which implied that an invasion of

Malaya was likely was used by the civil authorities in particular to hinder realistic training, and other measures that might have been instrumental in defeating the Japanese invasion; or at least delaying it significantly.

2. Slim, *Defeat into Victory*, p. 300.

3. Ibid., p. 314.

4. The Burma Defence Army (BDA) was the successor to the Burma Independence Army (BIA) set up by the Thakin leader Aung San in December 1941, to fight alongside the Japanese against the British. The Thakin movement, or Dobama Asiayone (We Burmans) Society, was originally an alliance of nationalist and communist students from Rangoon University who before Japan entered the war, collaborated with the Japanese to gain Burma's independence from the British.

5. Julian Thompson, *The Imperial War Museum Book of the War at Sea*, pp. 245–6. Chariots were a type of human torpedo, ridden by two men.

6. The Dutch East Indies, Malaya, Borneo and Philippines; all rich in oil and minerals, and vital to Japan's survival.

7. Billet was an operation led by Nyo Tun, head of the Thakin party in Arakan to bring Burmese to India for military training. By now Aung San (see note 4 above), having seen the way the wind was blowing following the Japanese defeat at Imphal, was contemplating changing sides, which, encouraged by SOE, he finally did on 26 March 1945.

8. Slim, *Defeat into Victory*, p. 240.

Tailpiece

1. Slim, *Defeat into Victory*, p. 465.

2. Ibid., p. 463.

3. Ibid., p. 464.

4. Winston S. Churchill, *The Second World War, Volume II*, p. 217.

5. Julian Thompson, *Ready for Anything*, pp. 69–70.

6. E. Belfield and H. Essame, *The Battle for Normandy*, p. 166.

7. John Verney, *Going to the Wars*, p. 147.

8. Belfield and Essame, *The Battle for Normandy*, p. 166.

9. Masters, *The Road Past Mandalay*, p. 281.

10. Interview with author in 1994.

11. Slim, *Defeat into Victory*, p. 466.

Appendix B

1. There were other factors that affected morale, but they are not covered in this extract. Readers are referred to volume V of the *Medical History of the Second World War*, from which these extracts are taken.

Appendix C

1. Otway, *Airborne Forces*, p. 257.
2. 4th SAS.

Bibliography

R. A. **Bagnold**, *Libyan Sands: Travel in a Dead World*, Hodder & Stoughton, 1935.

Corelli **Barnett**, *Engage the Enemy More Closely: The Royal Navy in the Second World War*, Hodder & Stoughton, 1991.

E. **Belfield**, and H. **Essame**, *The Battle for Normandy*, Batsford, 1965.

Shelford **Bidwell**, *The Chindit War: the Campaign in Burma, 1944*, Hodder & Stoughton, 1979.

British Official Histories, all published by Her Majesty's Stationery Office:

F. A. E. **Crew**, *Medical History of the Second World War: Army Medical Services, Campaigns*, Volume V, 1966.

L. F. **Ellis**, *Victory in the West: The Defeat of Germany*, Volume I, 1962.

—— *Victory in the West: The Defeat of Germany*, Volume II, 1968.

I. S. O. **Playfair**, *The Mediterranean and the Middle East*, Volume I, 1954

—— *The Mediterranean and the Middle East*, Volume II, 1956

—— *The Mediterranean and the Middle East*, Volume III, 1960

I. S. O. **Playfair**, and C. J. C. **Molony**, *The Mediterranean and the Middle East*, Volume IV, 1966

C. J. C. **Molony**, *The Mediterranean and the Middle East*, Volume V, 1973

—— *The Mediterranean and the Middle East*, Volume VI part I, 1984

W. J. **Jackson**, *The Mediterranean and the Middle East*, Volume VI part II, 1987

—— **Jackson**, *The Mediterranean and the Middle East*, Volume VI part III, 1988

S. **Woodburn Kirby**, *The War Against Japan*, Volume II, 1958.

—— *The War Against Japan*, Volume III, 1961.

—— *The War Against Japan*, Volume IV, 1965

—— *The War Against Japan*, Volume V, 1969

Winston S. **Churchill**, *The Second World War, Volume II, Their Finest Hour*, Cassell & Co. Ltd, 1949.

—— *The Second World War, Volume V, Closing the Ring*, Cassell & Co. Ltd, 1952.

G. B. **Courteney**, *SBS in World War Two*, Grafton, 1986.

Peter **Elphick**, *Singapore: The Pregnable Fortress*, Hodder & Stoughton, 1995.

Bernard **Fergusson**, *The Trumpet in the Hall*, Collins, 1970.

Roy **Farran**, *Winged Dagger: Adventures on Special Service*, Fontana, 1956.

Freddie **de Guingand**, *Operation Victory*, Hodder & Stoughton, 1947.

Max **Hastings**, *Das Reich, Resistance and the March of the 2nd SS Panzer Division through France, June 1944*, Michael Joseph, 1981.

Michael **Hickey**, *The Unforgettable Army: Slim's XIVth Army in Burma*, Book Club Associates, 1992.

Roland **Huntford**, *Scott and Amundsen: The Race to the South Pole*, Pan Books, 1983.

W. F. **Jeffrey**, *Sunbeams Like Swords*, Hodder & Stoughton, 1950.

James **Ladd**, *SBS: the Invisible Raiders*, Fontana, 1984.

—— *Commandos and Rangers of World War II*, Book Club Associates, 1978.

David **Lloyd Owen**, *The Desert My Dwelling Place*, Cassell & Co. Ltd, 1957.

John **Masters**, *The Road Past Mandalay*, Four Square, 1967.

Charles **Messenger**, *The Commandos: 1940–1946*, William Kimber, 1985.

Robin **Neillands**, *The Dervish Wars, Gordon and Kitchener in the Sudan 1880–1898*, John Murray, 1996.

T. B. H. **Otway**, *The Second World War 1939–1945 Army: Airborne Forces*, reprint Imperial War Museum, 1990.

Vladimir **Peniakoff**, *Private Army*, Jonathan Cape, 1950.

Bisheshwar **Prasad**, (Gen Ed), *Official History of the Indian Armed Forces in the Second World War 1939–45. The Reconquest of Burma*, Volume I, Combined Inter-Services Section (India and Pakistan), Calcutta 1958, distributor Orient Longman.

Andrew **Roberts**, *Eminent Churchillians*, Phoenix, 1995.

Hilary **St George Saunders**, *The Green Beret, The Story of the Commandos, 1940–1945*, Michael Joseph, 1952.

Field Marshal the Viscount **Slim**, *Defeat into Victory*, Corgi, 1971.

Julian **Thompson**, *Ready For Anything: The Parachute Regiment at War, 1940–1982*, Weidenfeld & Nicolson, 1989.

—— *The Imperial War Museum Book of the War at Sea: The Royal Navy in the Second World War*, Sidgwick & Jackson, 1995.

John **Verney**, *Going to the Wars*, Collins, 1955.

John **Willett**, *Popski: A Life of Vladimir Peniakoff Commander of Popski's Private Army*, Macgibbon & Kee, 1954

Philip **Ziegler**, *Mountbatten*, Book Club Associates, 1985.

Glossary

AA – Anti-aircraft (fire) (gun)

AIF – Australian Imperial Force, the Australian Army in the First and Second World Wars.

AOC – Air Officer Commanding.

Bazooka – An American-designed, recoil-less, shoulder-fired launcher firing a 2.36-inch anti-tank rocket. The warhead had a shaped charge to defeat armour. First used by the Americans in North Africa in 1942.

BGS – Brigadier General Staff, normally the staff officer heading the General Staff at corps level, and *de facto* Chief of Staff. In the case of the Chindit force for the second expedition, although nominally a division, it was actually more like a small corps, hence Tulloch's appointment as BGS.

Bofors – A 40-mm anti-aircraft gun of Swedish design. The standard light anti-aircraft gun in the British Army in the Second World War, and for years afterwards.

Boys Rifle – A British infantry anti-tank rifle firing a .55-inch armour-piercing round. An inadequate weapon, effective only against soft-skinned vehicles or those with armour of less than 21 mm thickness at under 300 yards range. Replaced by the PIAT.

Breda – Italian machine-gun. The M30 was 6.5 mm, and the M37 was 8 mm.

Bren – The British light machine-gun of the Second World War. Fired the standard .303-inch round, from a 28-round magazine.

Camouflet – A shaped explosive charge, which punches a hole in the ground. This hole can then be filled with the main charge and detonated.

Used when demolitions are being carried out on a hard surface, tarmac or concrete.

CGM – Conspicuous Gallantry Medal, instituted 1855, and awarded to ratings of the Royal Navy (and Royal Marines NCOs and marines when under Naval command) for gallantry in action. Now discontinued. See DSC.

Chaung – Burmese for watercourse or minor river, could be as narrow as a ditch, or wide enough for small craft, particularly near the coast.

CODC – Combined Operations Development Centre.

COHQ – Combined Operations Headquarters.

C-47 – American designation for a Dakota aircraft – see below.

Dakota – A twin-engined transport aircraft of American design and construction. It carried a stick of twenty parachute troops who jumped from a door on the port side. There were several variants produced. It was the great 'work horse' aircraft of the Second World War, and for some years after.

DC-3 – British designation for a Dakota aircraft – see above.

Despatcher – In the RAF in the Second World War, on parachute operations, a job often done by the navigator, who stood by the door or hole, hooked up by a safety harness, to despatch the jumpers from the aircraft, when the pilot turned on the green 'Go' light above or beside the door. On early parachute operations, despatchers were not carried, and on many occasions throughout the war, jumps through the aperture in the floor, on some types of aircraft, were conducted without the assistance of a despatcher.

DCM – Distinguished Conduct Medal, instituted in 1854, the equivalent of the DSO for Warrant Officers, NCOs and soldiers of the Army (and Royal Marines when under Army command). Awarded for gallantry in action.

Dories – The most common type of dory used by commandos and other special and raiding forces was the wooden, 18-foot, motor-powered, whaler-shaped (pointed stern and bow) boat. It was a good sea boat, and could operate in moderate swell to land troops on rocky coasts.

DSC – Distinguished Service Cross, instituted in 1914, awarded to officers of the Royal Navy (and Royal Marines when serving under Naval command), for gallantry in action. Now all ranks are eligible.

DSM – Distinguished Service Medal, instituted 1914, the Naval equivalent of the DSO for ratings of the Royal Navy (and Royal Marines NCOs and Marines when under Naval command). Awarded for gallantry in action.

DSO – Distinguished Service Order, instituted in 1886, and until the awards system was changed in 1994, it was a dual-role decoration, recognizing gallantry at a level below that qualifying for the VC by junior officers, and generally exceptional leadership by senior officers. Officers of all three services were and are eligible. Now it is awarded for highly successful command and leadership in operational circumstances.

DZ – Dropping Zone, the area chosen for landing by parachute of troops and *matériel*.

Earth Auger – An engineer's implement, which, after being wound rather like a corkscrew into the ground, is pulled out, bringing with it a plug of earth, leaving a large, cylindrical hole into which explosives can be packed. Very useful for unsurfaced road, or airfield, demolitions. See Camouflet.

Eureka – See Rebecca.

Fifth Column – Enemy sympathizers within the population who would carry out acts of sabotage. Largely mythical and greatly exaggerated.

Flak – German slang for anti-aircraft fire from the German for anti-aircraft gun, *Fliegerabwehrkanone*.

Folbot – The Mark I was a two-man collapsible canoe built for sporting purposes by the Folbot company. It had a wooden frame and rubberized canvas cover. It was fragile, easily punctured and totally unsuitable for operations, as the cockpit was not covered, and there were no buoyancy or stability aids. Some eight marks of canoe were designed and built by the British during the Second World War. Improvements and modifications to different Marks of canoe included (the list is not exhaustive): cockpit covers; buoyancy aids; plywood decks and hulls; outriggers; a lateen sail; an engine; and a rudder. Every Mark did not incorporate every single one of these or many other features. Each Mark had characteristics suited to a particular role or roles. There was even a Motor Submersible Canoe (MSC), the 'Sleeping Beauty'. A good summary of the plethora of canoes, boats and other equipment used by the British in minor waterborne operations in the Second World War and after is given in Appendix III to James Ladd's book, *The Invisible Raiders*, Fontana, 1984.

Force 136 – The Far East branch of the SOE. It operated extensively in Burma, and also in Thailand, French Indo-China and Malaya. See SOE.

Free French – French men and women who followed de Gaulle in not recognizing the Armistice with Germany signed in 1940 and continued fighting.

Gammon Bomb – Invented by Lieutenant Gammon of 1st Parachute Battalion while serving in North Africa in 1942 to provide a ready-made explosive charge, light and easy to handle. Plastic explosive was placed in an elasticated stockinette bag, which contained a detonator in a screw cap at the neck. The explosive, being malleable, was easily squashed into a pocket or pouch, and the amount could be varied to suit the task. It could be used as a demolition, to destroy vehicles, or as a concussion anti-personnel grenade.*

GCO – Governor's Commissioned Officer. Troops (Gurkhas, Kachins and Karens) serving in the Burma Rifles commissioned by the Governor of Burma. Similar status to VCO (see VCO below).

Gliders – See Hadrian, Horsa.

GOC – General Officer Commanding.

GSO – General Staff Officer, a staff officer who dealt with General (G) Staff matters (operations, intelligence, planning and staff duties), as opposed to personnel (A, short for Adjutant General's Staff), or logistic matters (Q, short for Quartermaster General's Staff). The grades were GSO 1 (Lieutenant-Colonel), GSO 2 (Major) and GSO 3 (Captain).

Hadrian – The Hadrian or WACO (built by the Western Aircraft Corporation of Ohio), was the standard American glider. It was smaller than the British Horsa, and carried only fifteen passengers, and half the payload. Known as the WACO to the United States airborne forces, and Hadrian by the British, to keep it within the existing series of their gliders: Hotspur,

* G. G. Norton, *The Red Devils*, Leo Cooper, 1986, p. 76.

Hengist, Horsa and Hamilcar. The WACO was used by Wingate's Chindits, see Chapters 7 and 8.

Halifax – Four-engined British bomber built by Handley Page. Also used to tow gliders with a greater radius of action than a Dakota. It could drop paratroops through a hole in the floor.

Heinkel – German bomber.

Horsa – The Horsa glider, of all-wood construction, and built by furniture manufacturers all over Britain, was the principle glider used by British airborne forces. It could carry twenty-nine passengers, or a jeep and trailer, or an anti-tank gun and jeep.

Jacob's Ladder – A rope ladder, with wooden slats for rungs. Used at sea, because it is easily rolled up and stowed, and quickly unrolled over the side of a ship.

Junkers (Ju) 88 – German bomber.

Khud – British soldiers' slang. Urdu for hill.

LCA – Landing Craft Assault, maximum load an infantry platoon. Designed to be carried at a ship's lifeboat davits, and to land infantry in a beach assault. Armoured to give its passengers some protection against small-arms fire and shrapnel, but not air-burst.

LCT – Landing Craft Tank, a craft capable of taking six Churchill or nine Sherman tanks, or a mix of trucks, armoured vehicles and stores and landing them over a bow ramp on shallow beaches.

Lewis Gun – First World War vintage, air-cooled light machine-gun, firing .303-inch ammunition loaded in a circular pan on top of the gun. Superseded by the Bren before the war, but still around in some theatres for the first few years of the Second World War.

LG – Landing Ground, modern airstrip.

Luftwaffe – The German Air Force.

LZ – Landing Zone, an area chosen for glider landings. (Modern usage is for helicopter landings.)

Machan – A platform in a tree on which a hunter waits for a tiger or leopard to take the bait below before shooting it. A particularly unsporting way to behave and prevalent in India before the Second World War.

Magic – The American codeword for deciphered Japanese diplomatic communications. See Ultra.

MAS Boat(s) – *Motoscafi Anti-Sommergibli*, Italian equivalent to MTB (see below).

MC – Military Cross, instituted in 1914, and awarded to Army officers (and Royal Marines when under Army command) of the rank of Major and below, and Warrant Officers, for gallantry in action. Now all ranks are eligible.

MGB – Motor Gun Boat, a small, fast vessel mainly armed with guns.

MI6 – Also known as the Secret Intelligence Service (SIS). Responsible under the Foreign Office for the collection of foreign intelligence.

MI9 – The British escape service, a branch of the military intelligence directorate in the War Office. MI9 had several tasks: gaining intelligence about the enemy from repatriated prisoners of war and by coded correspondence with those still inside; assisting prisoners to escape by briefing beforehand; training servicemen in escape and evasion; and organizing escape lines for downed airmen and others evading the enemy.

MM – Military Medal, instituted in 1916, and awarded to Army NCOs and soldiers (and Royal Marines when under Army command) for gallantry in action. Now discontinued, see MC.

MO – Medical Officer.

MPAJA – Malayan People's Anti-Japanese Army formed by the Chinese members of the Malayan Communist Party (MCP) the nucleus of which had been trained by SOE in Singapore before the Island fell to the Japanese.

MTB – Motor Torpedo Boat, a small, fast vessel mainly armed with torpedoes.

OC – Officer Commanding.

OP – Observation Post.

Pack Howitzer – A small gun which can be taken to pieces, and the parts carried on several mules or horses, or for short distances by people. It can be quickly assembled to bring it into action. A howitzer is a short-barrelled, light gun designed to fire at a high angle in order that its shells can more easily hit targets behind cover.

Pangyi – A sharpened stake usually made out of bamboo. Sometimes the point is hardened by scorching in a fire. These are excellent for use in booby traps, or obstacle belts, and can be concealed in pits, covered with twigs and grass or leaves, or planted in undergrowth. Once impaled on a bamboo stake, it is difficult to pull oneself off, because the bamboo fibres act like a barb.

PIAT – Projector Infantry Anti-Tank. The hand-held anti-tank weapon of the British Second World War infantryman from about mid 1942 on. Consisted of a powerful spring, mounted in a tube which threw a hollow-charge projectile. Effective up to 100 yards.

PT – Physical Training.

PT Boat – American equivalent of an MTB. See MTB.

RAMC – Royal Army Medical Corps.

RAN – Royal Australian Navy.

RANVR – Royal Australian Navy Volunteer Reserve.

RAP – Regimental Aid Post, the place where the Medical Officer (MO) of a battalion, or equivalent-size unit, set up his aid post. Usually the requirement here was to administer 'sophisticated first aid' to stabilize the casualty sufficiently to enable him to survive the next stage of evacuation; in 'conventional' warfare, usually within hours. In Chindit columns casualties might spend days in the RAP before evacuation was possible, and the MO had to do far more – see Chapter 8, and Lieutenant-Colonel Whyte's remarks. The same applied to the LRDG and SAS – see Captain Pleydell's comments in Chapter 4.

RCNVR – Royal Canadian Navy Volunteer Reserve.

Rebecca – A homing device called Rebecca/Eureka was invented at the request of Airborne Forces by the RAF Telecommunications Research Establishment (TRE). The Eureka beacon was set up on the ground, set to receive on one fixed frequency and transmit on another. Rebecca in the aircraft transmitted on the Eureka receiver frequency, and received on the Eureka transmitter frequency. On receiving an impulse from the aircraft Rebecca, the Eureka on the ground automatically replied, which gave the pilot of the aircraft his bearing and distance from the beacon. The Eureka was fitted with a morse key so the operator could transmit his DZ letter number. A number of snags were discovered with the Mark I Rebecca/ Eureka, not least that when Eurekas were set up on several adjacent DZs, all aircraft approaching found their Rebeccas activated, making it impossible to distinguish the correct DZ. The only time the Rebecca/Eureka Mark I was used on operations was on Operation Freshman (see Chapter 10).

RNVR – Royal Naval Volunteer Reserve.

RV – Rendezvous.

Sapper – The equivalent of private in the Royal Engineers, or a name for all engineers.

SEAC – South-East Asia Command. The Supreme Allied Commander SEAC, Admiral Mountbatten, was responsible directly to the British Chiefs of Staff in London, and through them to the Combined British and US Chiefs of Staff for all operations by land, sea and air in Burma, Malaya and Sumatra, and for clandestine operations in Thailand and French Indo-China.

Schmeisser – German sub-machine-gun, fires a 9 mm round.

SMO – Senior Medical Officer.

SOE – Special Operations Executive, a British secret service formed to promote subversive warfare in enemy-occupied countries. It was formed in July 1940 by joining the sabotage branch of MI6, and a small branch of the War Office MI(R) and the propaganda branch of the Foreign Office (EH). After the War, all their functions reverted to MI6.

Sten Gun – A cheap, mass-produced sub-machine-gun of British design. It fired 9 mm ammunition, and had a 32-round magazine. Ineffective except at close quarters; it was inaccurate and the round had poor penetrating power. Because of its propensity to fire by mistake, it was sometimes more dangerous to its owner and those standing around than to the enemy.

Stick – An aircraft load of parachute troops due to drop on one DZ in one run over it.

Tommy – Slang name for a British soldier. From Thomas Atkins.

Ultra – Originally the British codeword for intelligence gained by decrypting German and Italian codes. When the Pacific War started, the British and Americans used the same codeword to include all Japanese military communications broken by cryptoanalysis. (Neither the Soviets, the Chinese, nor any other Allies were privy to the secret.) See Magic.

Very Pistol – A smooth-bore pistol for firing green, red or white signal cartridges.

Vickers K Guns – Originally used by the RAF in Gloster Gladiator fighters. They were twin guns firing .303-inch ammunition, but with a very high rate of fire, 1,200 rounds per minute each.

Vickers Medium Machine-Gun – First World War vintage, belt-fed, water-cooled, machine-gun; rate of fire 500 rounds per minute. Maximum range with Mark VIIIZ ammunition, 4,500 yards.

VC – Victoria Cross, the highest British award for bravery in the face of the enemy. To date, in the 142 years since its inception by Queen Victoria during the Crimean War of 1854–55, only 1,354 VCs have been awarded, including a handful of double VCs, and the one presented to the American Unknown Warrior at Arlington. This figure includes the many awarded to Imperial, Commonwealth and Dominion servicemen.

VCO – Viceroy's Commissioned Officer. Gurkhas or other Indian troops commissioned by the Viceroy of India. All VCOs were junior to the most junior King's Commissioned Officer.

WACO – Western Aircraft Corporation of Ohio. See Hadrian. The company also produced light aircraft of the type used by the LRDG.

Wehrmacht – Collective name for the German armed forces, literally defence power.

Whitley – Armstrong Whitworth Whitley twin-engined bomber. When the war broke out, for lack of anything better it was Britain's largest bomber, but because it was slow and vulnerable it soon became obsolete for this purpose. While many Whitleys remained in Bomber Command until April

1943, others were handed over to airborne forces for parachuting. Troops jumped through a hole in the fuselage. It carried a stick of ten parachute troops. Most paratroopers preferred the American Dakota C-47, from which one left through the door, 'like a gentleman'. See Dakota.

Index of Contributors

This index serves two purposes: it lists those whose writings or recordings are here quoted and gives due acknowledgement to the copyright holders who have kindly allowed the publication of material held in the Museum's collections. If the copyright owner is not the contributor, their name appears in round brackets after the contributor with whom they are associated. Where the papers quoted are not contained in a collection under the contributor's name, but form part of another collection, this is indicated in round brackets. Every effort has been made to trace copyright owners; the Museum would be grateful for any information which might help trace those whose identities or addresses are not known. The number in square brackets is the accession number in the collection.

Ranks are as they were at the time of the experiences described. Decorations are not shown.

Department of Documents

Account of the Part Played by the LRDG in the operations of 8th Army in Cyrenaica November–December 1941, Period 1 November–6 December, (Major General Lloyd Owen papers) [P219–25], 56, 58, 59.

Colonel later Brigadier H. T. **Alexander** (Major General Wingate papers) [97/20/6–12] (Lieutenant Colonel O. J. J. Wingate), 241.

Count Ladislas de **Almasy** diary (Major General Lloyd Owen papers) [P219–25], 83, 84, 85.

General Sir Claude **Auchinleck** covering letter by C.-in-C. India, (Major K. D. Gilkes papers) [66/197/1] (Mrs J. Gilkes), 167, 169, 170.

Trooper N. P. **Aylen** [80/49/1], 207, 208, 209, 218, 219, 229.

Major later Brigadier R. A. **Bagnold** (Major General Lloyd Owen papers) [P219–25] (Mr Stephen Bagnold) 16, 17, 18, 19, 20, 21, 34.

Sound Archive

Lieutenant D. F. **Neill** [133299/8], 138, 142, 146–7, 148, 149, 150, 154, 155, 158, 159, 160, 162–6.
Lieutenant Colonel W. J. **Officer** [2901/2], 253.
Corporal B. J. **Owen** [12936/5], 362, 364, 365–6.
Lieutenant Colonel Vladimir **Peniakoff**, Commander of Popski's Private Army. Account by General Sir John Hackett [12022/4], 101–02.
Captain W. H. A. **Pritchard-Gordon** [8266/4], 122.
Major R. A. **Rubinstein** [11037/4], 302–03, 304, 318–20, 407, 408, 413, 414.
Lance Corporal and later Captain James **Sherwood** [9783/8], 5, 10, 46, 47, 72, 73, 74, 75, 76, 95, 96, 97.
Marine W. **Stevens** [8269/3], 284.
Private A. L. **Stewart** [13127/2], 35, 37–8, 40, 43, 71, 101.
Captain J. D. **Stewart** [8388/4], 120, 124, 126, 127, 128.
Private James **Swanson** [11385/4], 49.
Major Aubrey **Trofimov** [11760/5], 1, 302, 303–04, 314–18, 407, 409, 410, 411, 412.
Major F. W. G. **Turner** [12260/7], 137, 150.
Lieutenant Stamford **Weatherall** [12281/5], 117, 118, 119.
Lieutenant Colonel D. **Whyte** [12570/3], 131, 232–3, 236, 237, 248, 249, 253.

Photographic Archive

The Imperial War Museum owns the copyright of the majority of the photographs reproduced in the book. The Author is grateful to the following for permission to use the photographs listed below which form part of restricted collections in the Photographic Archive, or collections in the Department of Documents:

Davidson Papers Department of Documents (Mrs N. Heath): HU 72131, HU 72130
Major General D. L. **Lloyd Owen** and LRDG Association: HU 25299, HU 25793, HU 24997, HU 25081, HU 25277, HU 69650, HU 25273, HU 25268
Colonel P. J. D. **McCraith**: HU 71713
Wingate Papers Department of Documents: HU 71286

Index

Ranks: People are given their most senior rank shown in the book even though they may subsequently have attained higher rank or title.